Te

By L

Copyright

This book is a work of fiction. Names, characters, places, and circumstances are the product of the author's overactive imagination or are used fictitiously. Any resemblance to actual places, events, or people, living or dead, is coincidental.

Copyright © 2014, 2015 LD Davis
Second edition 2015
Cover Graphics by Tina Kleuker, Focus4Media

No parts of this book may be scanned, uploaded, or shared electronically (other than for reviews) without the written consent of the author.

www.facebook.com/lddaviswrites

Prologue

I was at my best friend's wedding reception dancing dirty with her husband. I grinded, I shook, and shimmied, and dropped it like it was hot. He got into it, dancing better than most guys I have ever known, and I've known quite a few. I dared a glance at his wife. She watched us while laughing, smiling, and clapping. I loved that she knew that I didn't mean anything by it. I loved that she knew how happy I was for her and that I was not trying to screw her husband.

The song changed and he drew me in for a slower paced dance that didn't require me to shake my ass. Luke Kessler looked ridiculously happy. He was high off of his happiness. It pleased me, and it also made me sad for myself.

"You look really happy," I said to him.

"I don't think it's possible to feel any happier," he answered with a big, beautiful smile.

I don't know how Emmy has survived such panty dropping smiles.

I bit back my own smile and said, "Sweet. Cheesy and corny, but sweet. I've honestly never seen Em look so happy."

We both looked across the dancefloor. Emmy was dancing with her father Fred. I danced with Fred at my wedding too. He was the only dad I had when I got married.

"I really like you, Luke," I said, turning my eyes back to my best friend's husband. "In fact, I love you as much as a girl can love her best friend's husband without it being scandalous. But..." I trailed off.

Like Emmy, and especially like her mother Sam, I spoke my mind. Speak first, and worry about the consequences later. My words have caused a great deal of trouble over the years, but maybe it wasn't the time or place to say what I really wanted to say. Luke has been very good to Emmy, with the exception of a few months not that long ago, but that was kind of her fault. I didn't want him to think that I doubted him, because I didn't, but like the rest of us, he was only human.

"But?" Luke looked at me warily.

"If you fuck this up beyond repair, I will kill you," I promised.

I felt his body stiffen ever so slightly under my hands.

"I would rather die than to fuck this up beyond repair," he replied.

"We all say that," I said quietly. "We would rather die than to hurt the ones we love, but we do. She did it to you." Under my breath, I muttered, "Hell, I've done it."

Luke frowned and looked at me with puzzlement. I realized with horror that he heard my last few words.

He glanced curiously at my husband Jerry, who was surrounded by a few adoring baseball fans. Even if they were not Philly fans, they were drawn to the professional athlete, and he to them.

"It's my wedding day," Luke finally said with exasperation. "I don't want to talk about that, Donya."

"I just want you to always be conscious of your actions, Luke." I gave him a very hard look. "It's very easy to find yourself standing on the wrong side of the line without ever meaning to cross it."

I suddenly felt like the banquet room was too small. Ignoring the startled expression on his face, I kissed Luke's cheek and pulled out of his arms.

"Just remember what I said," I said in a rush of air.

I whirled around and raced toward the exit. It was January, in Chicago no less, but the room felt stuffy, and each new breath seemed harder to take than the one before it. I resisted the urge to wipe my sweaty palms on my maid of honor dress as I weaved my way around people and tables. I promised myself I wouldn't turn around and look. There was no reason to look.

I won't look.

With only a few steps left to the door, I turned my head and looked.

It's as if there is a magnet that pulls my eyes to his exact location every time. My eyes always find him right away, no matter the circumstances, no matter the obstacles between us.

He looked stunning in his tuxedo. By all appearances, he seemed casual and relaxed with his hands in his pockets as he stood talking to his older brother. His deep blue bowtie was hanging to one side and his shirt was unbuttoned a few buttons, revealing the beginning contours of what I knew to be a well-defined chest.

His dark hair was a little on the long side, and several strands fell across his forehead. I thought it was sexy, but his wife hated it. She must not have liked running her fingers through it.

Sadly, I looked away and escaped the crushing pressure of the room.

After retrieving my coat, I walked out of the building and into the frozen tundra. I veered away from the small group of guests that were also braving the cold, and followed a stone path around to the back side of the building. I looked around and was relieved to find myself alone.

I opened my purse and found my hidden cigarette and lighter. I put the cancer stick in my mouth and lit it up. Inhaling deeply, I closed my eyes, and let the smoke out slowly through slightly parted lips.

Smoking was the bad habit I picked up during my days as a model. I got lucky. It could have been cocaine, heroin, pills, or so many other things that strung a girl out. I quit smoking regularly when I quit modeling, but on occasion, a cigarette was necessary.

When I was about half way through my necessary cigarette, I heard light footfalls behind me. I knew who was coming without having to look. I could feel him. I have always been able to feel him. I stopped questioning it long ago.

One strong arm encircled my waist. I shivered and it had nothing to do with the chilling weather. Fingers plucked the cigarette from my lips and tossed it away. I watched as it landed in the snow a few feet off of the path. It was resilient. It burned on, despite the cold moisture under it.

Another arm closed around me, securing me in an embrace. My head naturally fell back on his shoulder and his cheek naturally pressed against my hair. I breathed him in and his scent settled my nerves better than any cigarette ever could. Feeling his body enveloping mine made me feel safe. It was only in his arms that I ever felt safe.

We stood quietly as the sun set and darkness set in. He kissed the side of my head and I closed my eyes, both relishing and cursing the kiss. His breathing changed as his arms tightened their hold on me. I felt his breath on my neck and I knew he wanted to kiss me there. I hated that I wanted him to kiss me there.

There it was. The line I spoke to Luke about. I had one foot on the right side of the line and one foot on the wrong side of it. It was the third time in a week I had found myself standing like that, with the line between my legs. The line got blurrier and blurrier every time I even poked a toe at it. If we weren't careful, the line would dissolve, and so would so many other things.

I knew that, yet I could not make myself pull away. I could not push him off of me and walk away. He would always find me again. He would always tug on the invisible tether between us, and I would always return.

Eventually, the cord needed to be severed, or we were all going to crash and burn.

I turned around and looked into those green eyes I fell in love with as a child, and spoke his name.

"Emmet."

PART ONE

Tethered

Chapter One

"My name is Emmy, and I don't like your shirt, but your hair is pretty. What is your name?"

I looked at the pretty girl with dark, long and wavy hair and then I looked down at my red and white striped shirt. What was wrong with it? My mom let me pick it out at K-Mart. I was lucky she even took me shopping because she was always so tired.

I looked at Emmy's shirt. It was blue and had a ruffle down the front with gold buttons. I frowned because I did like her shirt better than mine.

"Don't be sad," she said, touching my arm. "I just don't like the lines in shirts. They hurt my eyes. What is your name?" she repeated.

"Donya Elisabeth Stewart," I said quietly. Emmy was the first kid to talk to me since the school day started. She was sitting right next to me at our table, and we were eating a snack. Well, she was eating a snack, and a lot of the other kids were eating snacks, but my mom didn't give me money for snack time.

"Where is your snack, Donya Elisabeth Stewart?" Emmy asked as she looked at the empty space before me.

"I don't have one," I mumbled. I had looked down at my hands, feeling immensely embarrassed.

Many years later, the school began providing the snacks so that kids like me wouldn't have to endure the humiliation of not having anything to eat, but I was lucky to have Emmy. Right after I told her that I didn't have anything to eat, she wordlessly divided up her four cookies, gave me two and put her carton of chocolate milk between us.

She kissed my cheek and said, "You can share with me, Donya Elisabeth Stewart."

After that day, we were inseparable. Emmy slept on the mat next to mine at every quiet time, played with me at every playtime and shared her snack with me at every snack time. She was the first friend I ever had and meeting her changed my life forever.

My mother was late every day picking me up from school. I was always the last kid to leave. Emmy and her mother Samantha stayed with me every day until my mom or dad arrived, but one day Sam asked my mom if it was okay if she picked me up with Emmy every afternoon. She said she would take me back to their house, give me lunch with Emmy and let us play and have me home by dinner. It took my mom a couple of days to think about it, and I begged her and nagged her so much about it that she finally gave in. I didn't have anything to do at home anyway. My mom was spending more and more time sleeping or watching television and less time with me.

On that first day at Emmy's, Samantha made us a nice lunch of ham and cheese sandwiches, celery with peanut butter and we had cups of apple juice with it. It was so much better than the lunches I had at home, and I told Emmy and her mom that.

"What do you usually have at home?" Samantha asked me.

"Cereal," I answered. "But if there's no milk, I just eat it with my fingers. Sometimes there is bread, and I'll have toast."

"But you don't eat lunch every day," Emmy reminded me, and I agreed. I did not eat lunch every day.

"You need to eat more," Samantha said. "You're too skinny."

"I don't always have lunch to eat," I said very quietly.

Even at five, I knew that it was not normal for me not to have food in the house. I was on the verge of tears; I was once again embarrassed. I wasn't like other kids. I wasn't like Emmy. Her mom and my mom weren't alike either.

"Well, don't worry about that," Samantha said, tenderly caressing my wild hair. "You can eat lunch here every day, even on the weekends. If you can't be here to eat lunch, I will send something to your house, okay?"

I had nodded and smiled with relief, knowing I wouldn't have to wonder about my next meal.

After lunch, Emmy and I played in her huge back yard. We made mud pies and grass cakes and flower stew and got super dirty. There was dirt caked under our nails, all over our clothes, and I knew I had a few muddy streaks smeared across my cheek.

"Let's take a break and swing," Emmy said after we grew tired of cooking.

I followed her to the swings, but I didn't know how to swing. I had only been on a swing a couple of times, and I never learned how to swing myself. I sat down on mine and watched as Emmy began to move. Her legs kicked out and pulled back again and again until she was swinging high.

"Don't you know how to swing?" she called to me.

"No," I said dejectedly.

She tried to explain it to me, and I tried to do as she said, but I wasn't getting anywhere. I was frustrated and angry and sad because she was swinging and I wasn't.

The back door opened, and I expected to see Sam come outside, but instead a boy came out. I knew Emmy had brothers and sisters, but I had never seen them until just then.

Even from across the yard and with his brown hair falling onto his face, I could see his green eyes. I had never seen anyone with such vivid green eyes before.

He looked right at me as he walked across the yard with his hands in his pockets. He was older than us, a big kid almost. I didn't know if he was going to play with us or not, but I felt shy and nervous as I watched him approach. Butterflies swarmed in my chest, and I wanted to stop looking at him, but I couldn't.

"Emmet!" Emmy called as she swung high. "Push Donya on the swing! She doesn't know how to swing by herself!"

He never took his eyes off of me. It was almost like he couldn't look away either.

"You don't know how to swing?" he asked, stopping a foot away from me.

I shook my head, too afraid to speak.

"You have dirt on your face." He reached out and touched my cheek.

My face felt hot under his finger, and the butterflies went crazy in my chest.

He dropped his hand and sucked in a breath.

"I'll teach you how to swing," Emmet said and walked around me.

He told me how to move my legs and how fast. He reminded me to hold on to the chains no matter what.

"I'm going to push you for a little while until you get it," he said. Then his hands were on my waist, and I held my breath. "Here we go," he said gently from behind me.

He gave me a small push and then another. I started to move my legs as he told me and he continued to push me. His hands were so soft on my back even though he was pushing me higher and higher.

"You're doing it! You're doing it!" Emmy cried out as I began to fly.

Eventually, Emmet stopped pushing me and got on the swing on the other side of me. The three of us swung together for a long time. Emmy was first to stop, and Emmet stopped soon after her. I wasn't sure how to stop swinging when I was ready to get off, and before the swing could stop moving, I had let go of the chains and fallen to the ground.

"I told you not to let go of the chains," Emmet said as he helped me to my feet.

"I didn't know how to stop," I said quietly as I looked down at the ground.

"Well, that was one way of stopping," he said. He plucked me in the forehead, gave me a grin and walked back to the house.

I stood there rubbing my forehead, watching him leave. Just before he went inside, he paused and gave me a long look. Then he shook his head and went inside.

~~*

I was seven years old, and I was mad as hell. I had been riding Emmet's skateboard, even though he told me not to, and I had fallen off. My knees were scraped, and so were my elbows. I didn't just fall off of the board because I was a terrible rider. I was pretty good and getting better all of the time. I fell off because the big punk kid from a few streets over pushed me off. Benny was such a bully. He was Emmet's age, but he was always picking on kids my age.

Emmet was my best friend's older brother, but he was very much like my brother, too. We argued a lot, and he was always yelling at me not to touch his stuff, but I always did anyway, hence the skateboard. Even though I had no business being on the board in the first place, when Benny pushed me Emmet dropped the basketball he had been bouncing around in the street and took off after Benny.

"Don't ever touch my sisters!" Emmet yelled after he bloodied the other boy's lip. Benny ran away crying while I tried hard not to cry too. Boy did my skinned knees and elbows burn.

"Are you okay, Donya?" Emmy asked, bending over me. She pushed strands of loose hair off of my forehead.

"I hate that kid!" I snarled and pushed myself to my feet.

"Come on, brat," Emmet said. He picked up the skateboard in one hand and took my hand with his other. "Mom will give you a Band-Aid."

Emmy took my other hand, and we headed across the grass to the house.

"What in the lord's name happened to you?" Samantha Grayne asked with her hands on her hips. She was wearing a flowery apron that I really liked. I liked all of her aprons. She always looked like a TV mom with her perfect blonde hair and big green eyes, but she wasn't anything like a TV mom.

"Benny pushed her off of Emmet's skateboard," Emmy said, stomping a foot. "I hate him!"

"I told you to stay off of my board anyway," Emmet said, plucking me square in the forehead.

"Ow," I murmured, rubbing the spot.

"Did you kick his ass?" Samantha asked her son.

"Yes, I kicked his ass," he said, standing up straighter.

"Don't curse," she admonished and then put her hand on my shoulder. "Come on, honey. Let's get you cleaned up. You should feel blessed that you have a brother like Emmet."

Blessed? He had just plucked me in the forehead!

I stayed for dinner like I did most days after school. I had my own place at the table, between Emmy and her dad Fred, who sat at the head of the table. He talked to me like I was one of his kids. Besides Emmy and sometimes Emmet, he was my favorite. My other "brothers and sisters" were okay, but they were so much older than me. The oldest brother, Freddy was about to graduate from college already. Charlotte was only a couple of years younger than him and Lucy was about to turn sixteen, so she was a little bit closer in age to Emmy, and Emmet and I, but honestly, I didn't understand those mystifying teenage years. So, I didn't spend much time with her. I spent most of my time with Em and Em.

After dinner, Samantha packed up a bag full of food for me to take home for my parents. My dad wouldn't be home from work until it was almost my bedtime and my mom didn't cook much. She didn't clean much either. She didn't do much of anything but sleep and watch television. Sam said my mom was sick, but I never saw any tissues or anything, so I wasn't sure about that.

Sam told Emmet to walk me home. He argued. He was tired of Emmy and me. He put up with us all afternoon and even beat up Benny for me. Why couldn't Lucy walk me home, he had whined.

"Boy, if you don't pick up that bag and walk that girl home I will slap your head sideways," Samantha threatened.

Emmet huffed and he puffed and picked the bag up.

"Can I walk with them?" Emmy asked, hanging by the door.

"You need to take a bath and get ready for bed," her mother said. "You look like hell. How do you get so dirty? What happened to your hair anyway?"

Emmy rolled her eyes. "I like my hair in a side ponytail, Mom. You always put it where I don't like it. So I fixed it."

"Well, it looks stupid," Samantha spat out.

"Your shirt looks stupid," Emmy sassed. "Nobody likes stripes anyway."

"Let's go," Emmet growled, snatching up my hand. We stepped outside and the door closed behind us, silencing the typical argument between mother and daughter.

Emmet was quiet. He was probably still mad about the skateboard and then having to walk me home. He always got stuck walking me home. It made my chest feel funny to know that he was mad at me.

"I'm sorry you always have to walk me home," I said quietly.

He looked down at me with green eyes. "It's not your fault."

"I come over every day. I can maybe not come over so much and you won't have to walk me home every day."

We were quiet again until we were almost to my house.

"You have to keep coming over," he finally said.

"Why?"

We stopped at the end of the walkway to my front door. He handed me the bag. It was a little heavy, but I tried to pretend that I could handle it.

"You're special to my family," he said. Then he plucked me in the forehead. "And you're kind of special to me too."

He pointed to the house in a silent command. I walked up the sidewalk, up the two steps and pushed open my front door. My mom was sleeping on the couch with the television on. Her eyes fluttered open and she looked at me and smiled, but it wasn't a real smile. It was one of those smiles people give to kids when they really don't feel like smiling at all.

I looked back at Emmet standing on the sidewalk. He made a shooing motion, indicating I should go inside. I waved, but just before I closed the door, he shouted, "And stay off of my skateboard!"

Emmet had made my chest feel funny again when he told me I was special to him, but it was a different kind of funny. It made me feel like giggling and crying at the same time. I never forgot the day he said that and the way it made me feel and the way his green eyes looked at me. Like I was special.

Special or not, I didn't stay off of his skateboard.

Chapter Two

By the time I was ten, I knew my mom was depressed. I knew what it meant to be depressed. It wasn't one of those words that went over my head anymore.

I couldn't stand to be home alone with her. I loved her, but being in the house with her felt like being in a dead house. When my dad was home, it wasn't much different. I didn't think he was depressed, but I think he gave up on my mom and it just made him sad. He didn't know what to do with a growing young girl. It was easy for both of my parents to let the Graynes take over and do what they were incapable or unwilling to do.

The summer after my seventh birthday, I started going away with Emmy and her family. Her mother is originally from Louisiana, but her dad is originally from New Jersey. They kept Sam's family home down south and they traveled there every summer and some holidays. Sam's family was still down there, and her best friend still lived close to her childhood home. Her children were the same ages as Emmy's older brothers and sisters, and they were all good friends. The first time I went down there, I felt a little out of place, but after a few days I was just another one of the kids in the great big family.

It was my third summer in Louisiana. Emmy's cousins Tabitha and Mayson also made the trip from New Jersey. I got along with them fine, but they all wanted to do girly things. I liked girly things just as well as they did, but I liked playing football with the boys, tinkering around on cars with the older guys, and fishing. Those girls wouldn't touch a worm if their lives depended on it.

"You got your pole?" Fred asked me early one morning as we packed up to head to a nearby fishing hole. There was a great big lake right in their back yard, but Fred said he couldn't fish in peace there between Samantha and the steady stream of kids.

"Yeah, but why did you buy me pink?" I pouted, throwing the pole into the back of the big truck.

"Because you're a girl," Emmet sneered.

I took a swing at him and missed.

"I picked it out," Fred Jr. said, pulling the bill down on my hat, partially blinding me. He was twenty-five years old already and was getting married in a couple of weeks. Charlotte was twenty-three and getting married in the fall. Both of them felt more like a third set of parents rather than siblings.

"We'll buy you a new pole for next time," Fred promised, fixing my hat. "What does the princess want?"

I looked at Emmet's pole. "Green, like Emmet's."

"Copycat," Emmet said, climbing into the back seat of the truck.

I followed after him, lost my grip, and started to fall, but his hand shot out and caught my wrist. I regained my footing and my hold on the truck and let him pull me in.

"Clumsy," he teased, pushing my hat down again.

I blew a frustrated breath out and fixed my hat and turned my head to glare at him, but he was smiling at me and I couldn't be mad when Emmet smiled at me. I tried not to smile back and looked forward as Fred and Freddy climbed into the front seat.

It was very early in the morning. The sun was just beginning to rise when we reached our fishing spot. I was anxious to start. I loved fishing, ever since Fred took me when I was eight. I tried to convince Emmy many times to come with us, but the few times she did, she only scared the fish away and made her brothers mad. It didn't take me long to stop asking her to go with us.

After a couple of hours of fishing, I had to pee. I'd had too many cans of soda. There weren't any bathrooms out there in the swampy woods. When I first realized that when I was eight, I was horrified. So were the guys. They didn't know what to do about a little girl that had to pee in the middle of the woods. I quickly learned that if I wanted to keep going on fishing trips, I had to act like it wasn't a big deal, find a place away from everyone else and go pee.

"Going to the little girl's room," I announced.

"Don't go too far," Fred said over his shoulder.

"I know," I said and marched on.

I walked through the woods for a couple of minutes. Like an animal, I tended to go back to the same spot to do my business. The thought made me snicker as I dropped my pants and squatted with my back to a tree. I hated not wiping, but I thought it would feel weird to walk into the woods carrying a plastic bag and a roll of toilet paper. It was bad enough I was a girl. I didn't have to keep reminding the guys of that. I always took a shower when I got back to the house, though, which made me think of guys. They didn't wipe. They just put it back and went on with their day. It made me wonder if they smelled like pee.

"Ew," I muttered to myself as I zipped up my jeans.

I was grossed out about thinking about a potential pee smell and the thing they peed out of. I knew what it was called. I just didn't like saying it. Or thinking it.

Nasty.

I kicked dirt and leaves over the area I was just squatting in. That made me snicker again. Just like an animal. Pee and cover it up. Like a cat.

I started back towards the pond, thinking about my mom. I missed her, and my dad, even though we didn't exactly have a nice family relationship like other families. I hoped that my mom was eating and that my dad wasn't drinking too much. I was lost in such deep thought about my parents that I wasn't paying attention to where I was walking.

There was a big root sticking out of the ground. I had tripped over it several times before. I usually knew to step over it, but sometimes I forgot about it. I tripped.

I didn't put my hands out fast enough to brace myself. I hit my head on a rock that was the size of an adult human head. Why was that rock so big and why was it in the woods? Were there rocks that big all over the woods and I never took note before?

I felt the blood trickling down the side of my head as I lay on my back staring up at the canopy of trees. I didn't remember rolling over, but I had. I was tired, more sleepy than usual, even after waking up so early in the morning. My head didn't hurt, but there was a strange pressure where I had hit it.

Oh, my god, I am so tired. I can take a quick nap and they won't even know I'm gone.

I closed my eyes.

~~*

"Donya!"

Someone was shaking me. I moaned and swatted at them. My hand hit a forehead. Someone cursed. Oh, I was so telling on Emmet for saying shit, as soon as I woke up from my nap.

"Leammelone," I murmured.

"No, you brat," he growled.

I felt arms slip under me. I heard a soft grunt and then I felt him lift me off of the ground. As Emmet carried me, I tried to tell him to stop and put me down. All of the moving around was making me sick to my stomach, and I couldn't even open my eyes to throw up.

I tried really hard and after what felt like a very long time, I made my eyes open.

"Emmet," I mumbled, looking up into his face. He looked scared. Why was he so scared?

"What?" he dared a glance down at me with those green eyes.

"I'm gonna..." I couldn't finish the sentence. I puked on Emmet's chest. He was going to be so mad, but I couldn't help it.

"Great," he muttered. "Dad! Freddy!" He shouted for the Freds.

The Freds. I tried to laugh, but it came out choked. It was then that I noticed the pain in my head. It hurt. A lot.

Fear slammed into me hard. I was hurt. Emmet was carrying me, and Emmet looked scared. I tried not to cry, but my vision was blurring with tears. Emmet stopped walking and dropped to his knees. Very carefully, he put me on the ground and shouted for his dad again.

"Hey, no crying," he demanded.

"You're only thirteen," I said through my tears. "You can't tell me what to do."

"I just did. Now stop it." He wiped my face with his hand.

I heard running and then shouts of alarm. They left all of the fishing gear and rushed me to the truck. Emmet was being very nice. He had one arm wrapped around me in the back of the truck and kept talking to me and making me answer him. Fred told him to keep me talking and he did an annoyingly good job at it. I just wanted to go back to sleep, but he kept making me talk and if I didn't answer, he pinched me.

Okay. Maybe he wasn't that nice.

I had a mild concussion. My mom seemed to come out of her depression long enough to freak out over the phone. Sam fussed over me and yelled at Fred and the boys for letting me walk off on my own. Emmy ditched her cousins and curled up with me in my hospital bed.

When I was allowed to leave the hospital, Sam made me stay in bed. I argued with her, but she got her way. I was stuck in a first-floor bedroom while the other kids played outside. Emmy spent a lot of time with me, but I felt bad that she couldn't be outside and I would make her leave. Others came and went, but the best visit ever was the first night out of the hospital. Emmet came into the room with a bowl of ice-cream.

"I snuck this for you," he said quietly and threw a glance at the door. "It's mom's secret stash of mint chocolate chip."

"If she knows you found her ice-cream and took some, she's going to kick your ass," I said warily.

"Don't say ass," he said and then shrugged. "I don't care if I get in trouble. Here."

He held out the bowl. I looked at the bowl and then I looked at his face. He was smiling at me again. When he winked, I couldn't hold back my own smile, and took the bowl.

I dug in and then moaned happily when I tasted a big spoonful.

"Thank you," I said around a mouthful.

"Sure," he said, laughing a little. "It's nothing."

I ate a little bit more ice-cream and he watched me. It felt a little weird having him watch me eat it, so I offered him some. He took the spoon and ate a little bit before passing it back to me.

Sharing a bowl of ice-cream with Emmet with only one spoon between us made my chest feel all funny again like it did that time when he told me I was special. It's not like I didn't share with the Grayne kids. We were always picking at someone else's treat or taking a taste of something, but this time felt different.

"How did you find me?" I asked Emmet after a few more bites of ice-cream.

He gave me a puzzled look.

"I mean in the woods. How did you find me?"

I had a sneaky suspicion he had spied on me while I peed. The thought made me mad. I would have dumped my whole bowl of ice-cream on his head if he had admitted to doing it.

"When you didn't come right back, I went looking for you," he said and took the spoon from me. He ate some and passed it back. "I don't know how I found you. I just did. I just had a feeling and followed it."

I didn't quite understand that at that time. I can't say I ever really understood it fully later.

"Thank you for finding me," I said softly as I stared down into the ice-cream.

"You're welcome, brat."

"I hope this doesn't mean I can't go fishing anymore," I said a moment later and passed him more ice-cream.

"We'll have to sneak past mom, but I'm sure Dad won't mind."

"What if this happens again?" I worried.

Emmet smiled at me and tapped my nose. He took the empty bowl from me and stood up.

"Then I'll find you again," he said and slipped out the door.

Chapter Three

I watched my mom shuffle around the kitchen, making herself a cup of hot tea. She wasn't in a talking mood, but at least she was up and moving around.

"Mom, do you need anything before I go?" I asked her.

She looked at me briefly and shook her head.

Her hair needed a brush, badly. She had lost so much weight that her clothes were hanging off of her body. She didn't smell too good either, but what was I supposed to do? I used to try to help her with all of those things, but she was so difficult about it. I pushed and pushed and one day she snapped and slapped the shit out of me. Right across my face. The noise had been so loud, that it echoed off of the walls of her bedroom and in my ears for several minutes. I didn't push her again.

That day she had given me a hand shaped bruise on my cheek that I had to keep covered up with makeup. The only person who knew about it was Emmet, and he found out purely by accident. He just happened to show up at my door one morning to drop off the sweater I had left in his car the day before when he drove Em and me—against his will—to the mall. I hadn't had time to cover it up.

"You left this," he grunted and thrust the sweater at me without really looking at me. His gaze fell somewhere over my shoulder.

"Oh. You didn't have to bring it."

"I'm picking up the guys," he grumbled. "I don't need you and Emmy cluttering up my car."

I rolled my eyes. Tucking my hair behind my ear, I said, "Whatever. You could have thrown it in your trunk."

"Then you would have bitched about me throwing your sweater in my dirty trunk."

Sometimes Emmet was an asshole. Not all of the time. Maybe not even part of the time, but sometimes.

I was just about to tell him that it was one of those times and tell him where he could take his cranky ass, but his eyes finally scanned over my face. His hand shot out and firmly grasped my chin. I gasped softly when he made contact with my skin. It was an embarrassing, yet consistent reaction to his touch.

I started to turn away, but he tilted my head to get a better look at my cheek. His eyes narrowed and then widened and then narrowed again.

"Who hit you?" he asked with a startling amount of vehemence.

"Simmer down, big brother," I said, pulling away from him. "It's nothing."

"You have a big ass bruise shaped like a hand across your face," he growled, taking my chin again. "I'd say it's something. Is it that guy you were talking to? Joe what's-his-face?"

I peeled his fingers off of my face.

"His name is Jorge, and no. He didn't hit me. I would have kicked his ass myself."

Emmet looked at me with suspicion.

"Are you sure it wasn't him? Was it any guy?"

My eyes rolled again, and I sighed impatiently. It was a chilly morning. I wanted to close the door and crawl back into my warm bed.

"No guy hit me, okay? Pick up 'your boys' and go do whatever you nerds do on a Sunday morning while the rest of the teenage world is sleeping in or watching boring Sunday morning television."

Emmet looked away and sighed. I thought he was going to leave, so I started to close the door, but his hand smacked against the door, keeping it open.

"Someone hurt you, Donya." His voice had softened, and his eyes asked me for truth.

My stupid fourteen-year-old heart fluttered. I had to remind myself that Emmet was not only three years older than me, but he was my brother, more or less.

"She didn't mean it," I whispered and then glanced over my shoulder to make sure we were still alone. "I shouldn't have pushed her."

His eyes widened again. "Your mom? Your mom did that to you?"

I didn't like admitting that my mom hit me. People already had a low opinion of her, and I didn't want to reinforce those low opinions.

"She didn't mean it," I said again, my tone pleading.

He made a sound of disgust and turned his back on me for a moment. His hands fisted on his hips.

I looked at the back of his letterman jacket and wondered what lucky girl was going to eventually get to wear it. I was sure by the time the football season ended it would be draped across some giddy girl's shoulders. Emmet was a good looking guy, a very good looking guy. There was no shortage of hormonal teenage girls that would want to be inside his jacket and his arms.

He turned back around and looked at me very carefully.

"How many times before did she hit you?" he asked, his voice tight with tension.

I looked over my shoulder again. "Nothing like this," I answered.

"How many times?" he insisted.

"I don't know," I said after some hesitation. I leaned in the doorway with my arms crossed defensively.

Emmet stepped towards me and stopped a few inches away. We stared at each other for a long moment. He smelled good. He always smelled good. It was messing with my head while I was trying to not look intimidated by his glare.

"She's never hit me like this before," I breathed, giving in. "Ever."

"But she has hit you," he said.

"Yeah, and so has your mom. Your mom whooped my ass with a wooden spoon."

He tried not to laugh, but a smile snuck up on his face. "We all got it that day. It was all your fault."

"I threw the turkey to you," I said, smiling. "It's not my fault you didn't catch it, Mr. Football star."

He snickered and ran a hair through his semi-long dark hair, pushing some of it off his forehead.

"Yeah," he agreed. He looked at me again, and his smile faded. "You would tell me if anyone ever seriously hurt you, right? You would tell me if this happens again?"

"Yes," I said quicker than I meant to. "Now get out of here." I waved him away. "I'm cold."

"Alright," he said, backing away.

Again, I started to close the door, but he turned around and stopped me again.

"Now what?" I whined.

He looked at me like he wanted to say something but couldn't get it out. Finally, he blew out an exasperated breath and said, "Nothing. See you at dinner tonight?"

"Of course."

He smiled at me. My heart fluttered. I closed the door.

It was several weeks later, and though the bruise was gone, I could still feel the sting of her hand connecting with my face. I wasn't going to keep asking her if she needed anything. I wasn't going to suggest a shower or brush or a toothbrush or anything. I told her I would be gone for the weekend, and I left.

I pulled my jacket tight around me as I made the quick walk to Emmy's. It was late October. All of the summery days were gone. Winter was only a couple of months away, shaking its fist at us, and waiting for its turn.

I walked into the Grayne house, my real home, without knocking. I smelled something good cooking in the kitchen, and it made my stomach rumble. I didn't eat much at lunch in school because Jorge Alta had stopped me in the hallway for a chat. He was a senior, a good looking guy like Emmet, but with a bit of a bad boy flare. He seemed to have his own rules, and it seemed that those around him abided by them. It didn't hurt that he was charming as all hell when he wanted to be. At lunch, he wanted to charm me of all people. Me, the little freshman girl.

As far as looks went, I thought I was pretty enough. I was a little bit taller than most of the girls in my class and slim, maybe too slim. Every day I felt my boobs to see if they had grown any more, only to be disappointed that they had not. My hair was shoulder length and jet black, and my skin tone was as Emmy dreamily described as "yummy milk chocolate." My hazel eyes seemed to be in direct contrast to my darker features.

Did I think I was pretty? No. I thought I was fair. I didn't think badly about myself, but I didn't spend hours in front of a mirror obsessing either. I knew there were much better looking girls in the school, but I was inwardly thrilled that Jorge was talking to me. So, I missed most of lunch, and only had time to eat an apple on my way to my next class.

I walked into the kitchen at Emmy's and grabbed a banana off of the table.

"What's for dinner?" I asked as a greeting.

Sam was at the stove, stirring something in a pot, wearing one of her famous aprons. I always looked forward to her meals. She could cook the pants off of anyone I knew.

"Meatloaf, mashed potatoes and green beans," she said, fidgeting with the collar on my jacket.

I batted her hand away. "Where's Fred?"

She sighed. "You never want to just sit and talk to me, do ya? Always gotta run to him."

"I sat with you for an hour last night," I argued, heading toward the back door. "You gave me an hour long lecture on proper moisturizing and told me repeatedly how much you think I need a hairstyle change."

She gave a little shrug. "Well...I think you need to work on those things."

I sighed patiently. "I'm fourteen years old, Sam. You should be lucky that I'm not pierced and inked and pregnant."

I opened the door and went outside.

"Hey, Kiddo," Fred smiled at me when he saw me come out. He was wearing gloves and carrying around gardening equipment.

"What are you doing?" I asked him, taking a couple of rakes off his hands.

"Just finished raking the yard," he said. "And doing some other things to get ready for the winter. I have a feeling we're going to get a lot of snow this year."

"You said that last year and it rained most of the time," I pointed out.

He chuckled and said, "Right, and you complained about your hair getting wet."

"Despite the fact that I am practically your kid, I am still a black kid, and I don't want my hair wet, Fred."

He laughed again. "I'll buy you an umbrella. How's your mom?"

"You have asked me that almost every day for years. The same."

"She's still a person, Donya," he said in a lecturing tone as he took the rakes from me. "She should still be inquired after as such."

I felt a little guilty for thinking of her as any less than a person, but she kind of was in my eyes. She was just a shell really.

I followed Fred around the yard for a little while longer. We didn't talk about anything of importance. He asked about school, and I told him about my grades and about a big project I had coming up. I didn't tell him about Jorge. He wasn't the kind of parent that was okay with his teenage daughters dating, especially older boys.

Hanging out with Fred was always peaceful. He was mild tempered and kind unless given a reason to be otherwise. The fact that he was able to live with Sam for so long was a true testament of his remarkable patience.

Sam, on the other hand, was a loving and nurturing mother; however, she was loud and had no filter between her brain and her mouth. I loved her, but could only handle her in small doses.

I stayed outside with Fred until Sam called us in for dinner. Emmy and I ate quickly before rushing upstairs to get ready for a party we had no business going to. Emmet was on our heels, heading toward his room.

"What are you girls in rush for?" he asked, from his door. He looked at us with suspicion.

"None of your business," Emmy snapped. "Why are you in such a hurry, jock?"

His eyes narrowed. At me.

"What?" I asked with annoyance.

"I saw you talking to Jorge in the hallway today."

"What's it to you?"

"If he invited you to his party, you better have declined," Emmet said, sounding like a tough guy.

I mocked him, using a very proper accent. "If he invited you to his party, you better have declined."

Emmy and I laughed, and then we squealed when Emmet rushed at us. We jumped back into Em's room and tried to shut the door, but Emmet held it open with his body weight.

"Get off of the door, you freak!" Emmy yelled.

"I better not see either one of you there!" he yelled. "It's not a place for little girls!"

Emmy and I looked at each other and with unspoken knowledge of what needed to be done, we both jumped back and away from the door. It flew open, and Emmet fell on the floor. We laughed again, but then he was up, chasing us around Emmy's room. He was very mad, but I found it really funny, even as I ran away screaming. Emmy ran into her bathroom and slammed the door, leaving me to my own devices. Some friend.

I held my hands up in defeat, breathing a little hard from running and screaming. "Okay, I'm done running."

When he advanced on me anyhow, I dashed away and jumped onto Emmy's bed. I jumped off of the other side, intent on running into the hall and into one of the other bedrooms, but I was only a couple of feet into the hallway when Emmet's arms wrapped around my waist. My breath left my body too fast, and I suddenly felt light headed. I stopped struggling against him and tried to relax long enough to start breathing again. His breath was hot on my ear, and it made me feel uneasy and…well…thrilled.

"Jorge is *not* a good guy," he whispered in my ear. "I don't want to see you at that party tonight. I mean it."

Then he was gone. I heard his bedroom door close, and I was left alone in the hallway, breathless and tingling.

~~*

Like Emmet Grayne was the boss of me.

Emmy and I waited until he was gone before we lied to the parents about where we were going and casually walked out the door. Jorge's house was on the other side of town. There was no way we were going to walk there, but lucky for us Emmy was a big flirt and flirted her way into a ride from a junior guy. She sat up front with Reed, and I sat in the back with another junior guy whose name I didn't know and didn't care to learn. He was a dick. Fortunately, the ride was a short one.

"What are we going to do if Emmet sees us?" Emmy asked, biting her lip as we walked arm in arm toward the house.

"*If*, Em?" I gave her look. "Seriously? Jorge's house isn't even half the size of yours. Of course, we're going to run into

Emmet. I don't know what we're going to do. I don't think he will cause a scene."

We walked into the house, and I think we were both a little startled by the amount of people that were stuffed into the house. It must have been bursting at the seams. There were clouds of smoke, some from cigarettes, and some from not cigarettes. The music was thunderous and in every direction we looked in, people were drinking, dancing, or making out, or all three all at once.

"I guess we're done with the little princess parties," Emmy said in my ear.

"I don't know about you," I grinned. "But I'm still a princess."

She grinned back at me, and together we moved deep into the party.

Jorge found me a little while later. He was already quite buzzed, but still held a red cup full of liquid in each hand. He offered one to me, but I had seen enough talk shows to know that guys slipped things into girls' drinks. He wasn't Special K-ing me. I took the drink anyway, though, and pretended to sip it while we shouted to each other over the noise. I looked around for Emmy. We had promised to stay within eyesight of each other. After a moment, I saw the top of her head as she danced with Reed, red plastic cup in hand. I hoped she didn't drink from it.

I thought about looking around for Emmet too, just to watch my back, but then again, I didn't want to see him. He had freaked me out earlier with the heavy breathing in my ear. It did things to me I wasn't yet old enough to acknowledge. So, I told myself I wasn't going to look for him. I wouldn't look.

I turned away from Jorge once more and looked off to my right. Through the sea of people, I met Emmet's green eyes.

Shit.

How, through all of those people, did my eyes go right to his? I stared at him dubiously, but then quickly turned away when his eyes narrowed.

Thank goodness Jorge was leading me in the opposite direction. I put my cup down on a table as we went, hoping he wouldn't notice. He led me into the kitchen. It was still pretty crowded in there, but not as bad as the other rooms. Jorge looked at my empty hand and frowned.

"I thought I gave you a drink," he said, thinking about it so hard that it was rather comical.

I shrugged and grinned. He grinned back.

"That's okay," he said dismissively. "We can do some shots."

I looked through the open kitchen doorway for Emmy. I didn't see her. I was a little worried, but not that worried. What was the worst that could happen with her brother only a few feet away from her? I almost laughed out loud, because Emmet was definitely the worst thing that could happen to her.

Jorge poured four shots out of a big red, square bottle I watched him open. I knew the bottle was new, so I didn't worry about being tranquilized. He handed me a shot and clinked his glass with mine.

"What is it?" I asked, looking at the red liquid.

"Aftershock," he grinned. "It tastes like Big Red gum with a kick."

I shrugged. I liked Big Red. I took the shot.

"Holy fuck!" I yelled a moment later as I felt the stuff burning down my throat.

Jorge laughed and handed me the second shot. I had just had my very first shot, and he was already handing me another. I had sips of wine before, and Emmy and I shared a beer once over the summer, but I had never done anything hard. One shot was going to impair me. Two shots were going to knock me on my bony ass.

"You're really pretty," Jorge said in my ear as I contemplated the shot.

He took his shot and looked at me expectantly. Damn, he was really cute.

I swallowed the next shot.

Four more shots later, Emmet finally caught up with me. He had Emmy—who looked as fucked up as I felt—by the arm.

"Let's go," he said angrily. "Now."

Jorge's arm was around me. He held me a little bit closer, throwing us both off balance. We giggled as we tried to find our footing.

"She's fine where she is, Grayne," Jorge said coolly to Emmet.

"She doesn't look fine," he snapped and then beckoned me with a wave of his hand. "Let's go, Donya."

Jorge looked down at me, got nose to nose with me. I could feel his hot breath on my lips. "You don't have to go anywhere with him. He's not your daddy. He's nothing."

I laughed hysterically. Jorge laughed with me though neither of us knew what we were really laughing at.

"He's my brother," I managed through my laughter.

Jorge laughed harder. It was funny. It was freakin' hilarious.

"I'm not your brother," Emmet bit out.

My laughter died. Even in my intoxicated and numb state, that kind of hurt. Emmet had always been my brother, but he was being mean and saying he wasn't. Was he embarrassed? Was it because I was black and he was white?

I frowned and pressed myself closer to Jorge.

"You're right," I said. "You're not my brother. You're nothing."

That seemed to really please Jorge. He grabbed my face a little too roughly, pulling my eyes away from Emmet's flaming green orbs, and put his wet, alcohol stained lips against mine. But it didn't even last a full two seconds before his head was knocked sideways. I stumbled backward, watching Jorge's mouth bleed. I looked at Emmet with my mouth gaping open. He had hit Jorge!

Jorge was drunk, but he was still a badass. He stood up straight and glared at Emmet. His hands curled into fists. He drew his arm back and threw a hard punch at Emmet, but since Emmet wasn't inebriated, he was able to duck out of the way. Unfortunately, the guy behind him wasn't so lucky, and he was the one that got hit.

Emmet latched onto my arm and yanked me away just as a brawl broke out. I followed without resistance, stumbling along the way. Emmy wasn't moving any better than I was.

The louder the fight got in the kitchen, the more people pushed at us in their effort to join in the melee or watch it. Emmy fell once. I tried to help her up with my one arm, but I was just as fucked up as she was and almost went down with her.

I was alarmed. I thought she was going to get trampled there on the floor, but then big arms were around her waist, lifting her off of the floor. Tabitha's big brother Tack threw his cousin over his shoulder and before I could understand what was happening, Emmet had done the same to me. The guys didn't put us down until we were at Emmet's car.

"What part of don't go to the party didn't you understand!" he shouted at us as he unlocked the car.

"The 'don't go' part," I snickered. Adrenaline raced through my body, but I was still very much drunk. Emmet glared at me so hard, I stopped laughing.

"The 'party' part?" Emmy asked from the other side of the car. We both began to snicker.

"Your mom is going to kill you," Tack said to Emmet.

"I didn't bring them here!"

He pulled open the back door of his car and pointed angrily for me to get in. Tack was a little nicer to Emmy and helped her in. I wanted Tack on my side of the car.

"Get in the damn car, Donya," Emmet growled.

"Fu-uck you," I said, swaying, but I got into the car.

Emmet slammed the door shut. He stood outside for a moment, running his hands through his hair and trying to make the steam stop coming out of his ears. I giggled as I imagined literal steam coming out of his head.

When he got in the car, his hair was all messed up.

"Your hair is a mess, pretty boy," I teased.

He glared at me through the rearview mirror but said nothing.

"You can't take them home," Tack said to Emmet. "It's not that late. Your parents are probably still up."

Emmet looked at the time on the dashboard. It was a little after ten. He looked in the rearview mirror again, not at me but something behind me. His eyes widened with fear.

"We'll figure it out along the way," he said, quickly turning the car on and putting it in gear. "The cops are coming."

He peeled out of his parking space and took off down the road. Emmy and I looked behind us at the approaching cruisers halting in front of Jorge's house. Fortunately, none of them came after us.

We drove around for a few minutes. The guys tried to come up with some way of getting us home without Sam and Fred sniffing us out. Emmy and I giggled and laughed and shrieked about things I can't even remember. Emmet often yelled at us to shut up and we just as often ignored him. Finally, he had an idea. He parked at a 7-Eleven and got out to use the payphone.

"I'm thirsty," I said, running my finger over my dry tongue. I pulled the lock up on my door and practically fell out onto the pavement. I held onto the door laughing hysterically until I felt Tack picking me up.

"Get back in the car," he said with a little more patience than Emmet had had all night.

"I'm thirsty," I whined.

"Me too," Emmy said from the front of the car.

She had gotten out without my notice. Apparently without Tack's too, because he said, "How the fuck did you get there so fast?"

Emmy stuck out her tongue and walked into the store. Tack leaned me up against the car and looked back at Emmet, who was still on the phone talking. Emmet looked into the store at his sister with more steam pouring out of his ears.

"I'm thirsty," I whined again as I watched Emmy stumbling around inside the store. She was trying to get a Super Big Gulp and failing miserably. Emmet finally hung up the phone and rushed into the store to get her. Tack pushed me back into the car and shut the door. He leaned against it so that I couldn't get out; like I couldn't just climb to the other side.

"Hey," I said, smacking a hand against the glass. "Tack!"

He looked at me expectantly.

"Emmet stole my first kiss!"

"What?"

"Emmet stole my first kiss!"

He looked confused. I motioned for him to open the door. He opened the door and leaned over.

"Emmet stole my first kiss," I said once more.

He raised an eyebrow. "You're drunk."

"No, listen, listen, listen," I said, waving a hand and swaying in my seat. "Jorge was about to kiss me. His lips were on my lips, and Emmet punched him. Gave him a bloody mouth. I didn't want to kiss a bloody mouth, but then it didn't' matter because Emmet got all caveman on me and dragged me out of the party."

"Uh," Tack said and scratched his head. "Isn't Jorge a little old for you? I mean, you're Tabby's age."

I rolled my eyes. "We're all about the same age," I said. "You're not that much older than me. I'll be fifteen in days. We're all still in high school. It's no big deal that he's a little bit older. What I'm trying to say is you can kiss me instead and make up for my lost kiss."

Tack looked very uncomfortable. He backed away from me slowly, as if he expected me to kiss-attack him, and closed the door.

"Aww," I whined and rested my head against the cool glass.

After some more random driving around, we drove back to Emmy's house. The guys helped us get into the house and up the stairs. Emmet's hand clamped over my mouth so many times, I started to like the taste of his skin. I licked his hand just to be bratty and then giggled at the faces he made.

"I'm taking Tack home," Emmet whispered after depositing us in Emmy's room. "I'll be back in a few minutes. Don't. Leave. This. Room."

"Whatever, kiss ruiner," I yawned.

After one more warning, the guys left. Emmy and I had lain on her bed giggling and talking about nonsense for a little while.

"I feel sick," she said after we settled down.

"I think I'm going to hurl," I said and clumsily rolled out of the bed. I stumbled over my own feet and fell to the floor a few feet away from the bathroom. I crawled the rest of the way and made it to the toilet just in time. I puked Aftershock and meatloaf and mashed potatoes and string beans until I thought my head would cave in.

With much effort, I pulled myself to my feet and grabbed the toothbrush I kept at Emmy's. I brushed and rinsed and brushed and rinsed until I could only taste the mouthwash and toothpaste. My head was beginning to pound, and everything seemed off kilter. I slowly sloshed into the bedroom and found that Emmy was out cold and stretched diagonally across the bed, leaving no room for me. I tried to wake her, but she just groaned.

I felt like crap. My head felt like it was going to explode and my stomach was still churning even though there was nothing left to puke up. My face was a little sweaty, but I was shivering uncontrollably. I thought I was dying. If that was what it was like to be drunk, I vowed to never drink again.

I stumbled into the hallway and closed Emmy's door as quietly as possible behind me. It was still a slam to my sensitive head. I put my hands on my head and dropped to my knees. I was going to sleep in Lucy's old room, but I wasn't going to make it. It was all the way down the hall, and even though it was seriously only a few feet, it looked like a few miles.

I lay down in the middle of the hallway floor and waited to die.

~~*

"Hey," Emmet's voice was close to me.

I forced my eyes to flutter open and found him kneeling beside me.

"What are you doing on the floor out here?" he whispered. "I told you to stay in the bedroom."

"I puked," I murmured and rubbed a hand over my aching head. "When I came out of the bathroom, Emmy was sleeping funny on the bed. There wasn't any room for me."

"So, you were going to just sleep on the hallway floor?"

"No, dumbass," I growled. It hurt my head. "I want to go into Lucille's room."

"Unbelievable," he said under his breath. Then his arms were under me, and he was carrying me down the hall.

It was only a short trip, but I curled up close to him anyway. I was freezing, and he was warm even though he had just come out of the cold. As he pushed open the door to Lucille's room, he gazed down at me with frustration, anger, and something else I couldn't put my finger on.

Emmet carefully put me on my feet and made quick work pulling the blankets back on the bed. Then he steered me to the bed and made me sit down. I closed my eyes, trying to ignore the spinning room. I felt him pulling my shoes off of my feet, and I remember thinking how weird it was that he was taking my shoes off. When I felt his hand on my cheek, I opened my eyes and met his.

"I told you not to go to that party," he softly admonished.

His hair had fallen across his eyes. It was a little too long, but I always liked it like that, even when we were younger, I liked his longish hair.

I smiled and pushed his hair out of his eyes with my fingers. I pushed my hand through it and sighed. His hair was soft and thick. It felt wonderful in my hand.

Emmet closed his eyes, and for a very short time, we stayed just like that, his hand on my cheek, my hand in his hair, his eyes closed and mine wide open. Then the moment ended.

He opened his eyes and snatched his hand back as if it burned him to touch me. He stood up abruptly and took a wide step back, forcing my hand to fall from his silky hair to my lap. He closed his eyes again, pinched the bridge of his nose, and then opened his eyes once more.

"I need to check on Emmy," he said, making a concerted effort not to look at me. "Lie down and try to sleep."

"You stole my first kiss," I told him quietly.

The room was spinning more than before. My heart beat uselessly in my chest as if it was dying. I carefully swung my legs into the bed and lay down.

"That isn't the kind of first kiss you want, Donya."

"What kind of first kiss do I want, Mr. Know-It-All?" I challenged.

"Jorge would have kissed you, and he wouldn't have stopped there," Emmet said bitterly. "He would have convinced you to follow him upstairs, and he would have done all kinds of things to you that you don't need to know about at fourteen years old."

"You talk to me as if I am so much younger than you," I snapped. "You're not that much older than me, Emmet. Girls my age date guys your age."

"Doesn't make it right, and it doesn't mean they're…having sex."

"It's high school, Emmet. We're all still kids. It's not like I was in middle school kissing a senior. I'm a freshman."

"And you think you know so much," he said darkly.

"Maybe I don't know too much about anything, but that kiss wouldn't have been so bad."

"It's what would have come after the kiss that worries me, Donya."

I tried to focus my eyes on him.

"Why does it matter to you what I do?"

I didn't know why I was so argumentative. It's wasn't like I was really interested in following Jorge upstairs and losing my virginity where several other girls probably also lost theirs. I hated that Emmet was attempting to be so brotherly to me after denying any such connection earlier in the night, and frankly, I was angry that I didn't get that kiss. Not because it was something I necessarily wanted, but because it should have been my decision, not Emmet's.

"I care about you," Emmet answered quickly.

"Not like a sister," I bit out. "You made that clear."

He was quiet for a long moment. And then "No, not like a sister, but you're too young and too dumb to get it, which is exactly why I won't be explaining it to you."

"You don't make any sense at all," I said flatly. "Check on your sister and go away."

I rolled over, turning my back to him. My feelings really were hurt by his denying me earlier. After years of calling him my brother, he denied it when it probably could have mattered most.

I didn't hear him leave, but I assumed he did. I was mad at him, and I was mad at myself for getting drunk with a senior male scumbag like Jorge. I was mad I didn't get my first kiss. I was mad that it could have been worse than a kiss. I was mad at myself for crying.

I didn't know when I started to cry, or why I was crying.

"Your first kiss should be with someone who isn't going to try to get into your pants immediately after," I heard Emmet say.

I stiffened. My tears continued to roll down my face, but I didn't make a noise.

"I know it doesn't always happen that way, but I want it to mean more for you. And Emmy," he said more as an afterthought.

When I didn't respond, I heard him sigh, and I heard the telltale sound of the door closing as he left.

Chapter Four

Emmy and I sat on the couch in the family room like mindless zombies, wearing sunglasses, sipping on water and watching mindless television. Occasionally one of us would reach for a saltine and nibble carefully on it. Samantha and Fred left early that morning before we rolled out of bed, thankfully, because then they wouldn't have had to witness and then question our peculiar behavior. Then again, Sam was good at sniffing things out. From wherever she was, she probably could smell the alcohol and teenage debauchery in our blood.

I couldn't stop thinking about the epic mistake I had almost made with Jorge. He was cute, but that's about as far as it went. I didn't want to kiss a boy just because he was cute, and when I considered that he was probably prepared to deflower me…I sighed inwardly. I couldn't consider it.

If it were not for Emmet, I could have been in a world of pain and regret instead of just hung over. If I had listened to him in the first place, I wouldn't have been hung over either. If I would have paid attention when he was whispering to me…warm breath tickling my ear…arm banded securely around my waist…

I made a sound of disgust. Emmy looked at me curiously, but I ignored her.

I was making something out of nothing. Like, really, that whole hand in his hair and his hand on my cheek thing was nothing. I don't know what he meant about me being too young and dumb to understand. I know I wasn't the smartest person, but I wasn't dumb. He was just trying to come up with some excuse for announcing that he wasn't my brother. Like there was any excuse.

"Hmph," I said.

"What is wrong with you?" Emmy asked.

"Nothing," I said and got to my feet. "I'm going to go skateboard."

Em picked up the remote and turned off the television. "Honestly, I don't know why I even got out of bed."

Emmy went back to bed. I went out to the garage and grabbed my skateboard. Fred bought me my very own a few years back, but Emmet bought me a beautiful long board. Whenever I felt the need to shake my mind of the things that could bother someone my age, I got on my board. Once in a while Emmet joined me, but those times were few and far between as we got older. He was too cool to be caught skateboarding with his kid sister—or kid sister's friend.

I was boarding on the street for some time, letting my eyes settle on the pavement below as I tried to eradicate my brain of all of those weird memories and feelings from the night before. I heard a car coming and automatically moved over to the side of the road and out of the way. I heard a door slam and then there was a moment of silence. The pavement was all that I saw, and I concentrated on the sound my board made over it.

"Hey," I heard Emmet say to me.

I looked up. He was standing at the edge of the driveway with hands in his jacket pockets.

"Hi," I said but didn't stop.

"I haven't skated in a while. I know a pretty cool spot where we can board if you want to go."

I thought about it as I slowly rolled by him. "Why?" I asked. I was still mad.

"I don't have anything else to do," he shrugged.

"That's a lie," I said, jumping off of the board. I moved to pop it up and tucked it under my arm. I stood several feet away, studying him. "You have friends you can hang out with. I thought you jocks always did something after a football game anyway."

He shrugged again. "I didn't feel like sitting in someone's basement playing video games and eating pizza all day."

"Did you win?" I asked, pushing my hair out of my face. It was a little windy. I wished I had a hat to keep my hair out of my face.

"Yes, we won," he smiled. "I'm going to get my board, okay?"

He started to turn away, but I asked, "Why do you want to hang out with me?"

My goodness was I pissed. And hurt. And if he said something stupid I was going to hurl my board at him.

Why do I feel this way? Ugh. This is exactly why I wanted to be on my board.

"Maybe I just want to spend some time with you," Emmet said, all humor gone from his face. He looked at me hard. "Maybe I saved your ass last night, so the least you can do is just skateboard with me for a little bit."

I gripped my board in my hands. His eyes moved down to my board, and he raised an eyebrow.

"You wouldn't be thinking of throwing that longboard at me, would you, Donya?" he asked, his head tilted to one side. His hair fell into his eyes, and I wanted to run over to him and push it off of his forehead. Not because there was anything wrong with it there, but because I liked my hand in his hair.

"Fine," I said, dropping the board from one hand. "I'll go."

"Give me a couple of minutes to change and get my board," he said, walking up the driveway.

I started grumbling to myself as I hopped back on my board. I looked down the road. I was tempted to skate away.

"Don't even think about skating away," Emmet warned from the door. "I'll just find you and drag you into the car. I'll always find you."

I rolled my eyes at him, but when the door closed, I was even more tempted to skate away. Just to have Emmet put his arms around me to drag me into the car.

I thumped myself in my head with the palm of my hand.

~~*

So much for trying to push thoughts out of my head. Boarding with Emmet in an empty parking lot only made me think of Emmet. It wasn't fair. I was mad. I was hurt. I was a little thrilled, and I was crushing a little, and I guess that's what made me most angry.

I had taken pride in the fact that my best friend had two older brothers, and I had not crushed on them even once, even though they were good looking guys. Other friends drooled all over Emmy's brothers, but not me. They were my brothers too, or so I thought. Emmet apparently was not, but then again, I wasn't necessarily looking at Emmet as a brother anymore, was I?

I spared a glance in his general direction only to find his eyes already on me. It threw me. Really. It threw me. My skateboard threw me. I fell backward and tried to brace myself before my head hit the pavement, and it did, but at least it didn't bounce. That's the worst.

"Donya," Emmet called out, and I heard his footsteps running to me. I also heard my board rolling away.

I groaned and tried to sit up as Emmet reached me.

"Is my board okay?" I asked, looking around for it.

"You just busted your head on the pavement, and you want to know if your board is okay?" he asked dubiously.

He was kneeling beside me with one hand on my shoulder.

"Well, is it?"

He sighed. "Your board is fine. Come on." He stood up and helped me to my feet. "Is your head okay? Does it hurt?"

He gingerly touched the back of my head and watched my face for a reaction.

"It's fine," I murmured.

He was standing too close to me. I could feel the warmth radiating off of his body. I took a step back, and he took a step forward. It startled me, and I stepped back again and managed to mess it up. I started to fall backward, but Emmet's hands snaked around me. He roughly pulled me into his body, and we both stumbled. I grabbed his jacket to steady myself and after a moment we were still again.

I started to laugh, but it was so not funny. I was pressed up against Emmet, and his arms were around me and he was looking down at me with a weird expression that made that feeling in my chest explode inside of me. I held my breath. I should have moved away, but I felt frozen in his arms.

One arm squeezed me tighter and a hand was suddenly close to my face. I flinched, and he sucked in a breath and looked angry, but when his fingers pushed loose strands of my hair off of my face, his own face softened. My breath exploded out of my mouth, and I prayed that it smelled okay. I mean, I brushed and rinsed, but you never know about breath. Especially after a night of drinking.

"I am going to give back what I stole," he said in a soft tone that made me shiver against him.

Those green eyes burned into my eyes, and I started to whimper, but I managed to swallow it.

"Did you steal my money?" I asked stupidly.

"No," he gave me a small, amused smile.

I swallowed hard. "Did you steal my hidden stash of junk food?"

He grinned and shook his head. His grin faded back to a slight smile.

"I stole your first kiss," he said tenderly. His hand pressed lightly on the back of my head as he moved his face closer to mine. "I am going to give back what I stole."

Emmet's lips softly met mine, and I began to tremble. He smelled so good, and his lips felt…Oh, my god, nothing I could have ever imagined could have prepared me for how Emmet's lips felt against mine. Warm. Soft. Demanding.

He gave me a moment to get acclimated to his mouth on mine, and then his tongue was tasting the seam of my lips. I gasped. He could have taken advantage of my parted lips and slipped his tongue into my mouth, but he didn't, not yet.

When he gingerly pulled my bottom lip into his mouth and leisurely ran his tongue across it, I was shocked and embarrassed to hear myself moan. It was a quiet moan, but there was only the two of us in the lot. Of course, he probably heard it. I was embarrassed, but my humiliation was forgotten when Emmet's teeth gently sunk into my lip. Another sultry sound escaped my throat. That time he used my hopeless noises to his advantage. His tongue slipped gently and smoothly into my open mouth.

When his tongue touched mine, I didn't know what to do. I understood the basic mechanics of French kissing, but I didn't want to shove my tongue down his throat. I didn't want to mess it up. I didn't know what to do with my tongue, so it just sat there.

Emmet seemed not to mind that I was so stupid. He repeatedly teased my tongue, giving it small strokes with his. It started to kind of tickle. To relieve that sensation, I moved my tongue, and I gasped again. My tongue hit Emmet's and oh my god. Oh, my God. Oh, my God. I did it again, and I didn't want to stop. I didn't want to stop feeling my tongue move with his and his lips against mine. I didn't want to stop, but it was so…wrong. Wasn't it? It didn't matter. I'd worry about it later.

When Emmet finally released me, I was dazed and breathless. I stared up at him. I was shocked, embarrassed, appalled, thrilled, excited, and uncomfortable. My chest was tight with all of the emotions. My young body felt things it shouldn't have felt.

I stepped back away from Emmet. That so was not a brotherly kiss.

Emmet took a step back too. Even though he was the one that initiated the intimate moment, he looked just as shocked and appalled as I did. He pushed a hand through his hair and looked at me with big eyes.

"I shouldn't have done that," he said breathlessly.

"Probably not," I agreed weakly.

"You're too young."

"No, I'm not," I argued. I wasn't condoning what had just happened, but I was not too young for him. There was a little more than two years between us.

"You are," he said soberly.

"Fine," I snapped and turned away from him. I walked the few feet to my board, picked it up and kept on walking.

"Where are you going, Donya?" Emmet called behind me.

"I guess I'll go to the playground and play with the little kids because apparently that's how you look at me, which makes you a bit of a pervert."

I heard an exasperated growl behind me and then his hand was on my arm, spinning me around to face him. I opened my mouth to yell at him, but then he was kissing me again. My face was locked in his hands as he kissed me hard. I kissed him back, but I knew I shouldn't. It wasn't about the age. It was just an awkward situation considering my place in his family.

I pulled away with a small whimper and struggled for air as his thumbs stroked over my cheeks. I jerked back and away from him, out of his hands and out of his reach. I threw my board down on the pavement and started to skate away from him as fast as my legs could take me. I was glad he had enough sense not to follow me because I did not want him to see me cry.

Chapter Five

We didn't have cell phones back then, at least most people didn't. There was no way for anyone to call you when there was an emergency, like if your dog got sick, or your roof was leaking, or if your father died. If you weren't at home or at some known location where there was a phone, hours could be wasted searching for you, and then when you were found, they would say, "Where have you *been*?"

That's what Emmy said to me when I got back to her house just as dark was falling. I dropped my skateboard in the foyer and inspected the scrape on my elbow from when I fell.

After I had skated away from Emmet, I went to my top secret hideout so I could clear my head. I hopped a bus to Philly and spent my day at the art museum. Something about the sculptures, the various paintings and displays was soothing. My favorite spot there was European art. Sometimes I'd spend a good hour just admiring *Portal from the Abbey Church of Saint-Laurent*. I was never a religious person, but the beautiful stone work always left me mesmerized.

"Doesn't matter where I've been," I said. I was unwilling to give up my secret place. Then it wouldn't be a secret anymore. "I'm here now."

I looked up and discovered the entire family had gathered in the foyer: Fred, Sam, Emmet, and Emmy. They were all looking at me. My heart just about leaped out of my ribcage.

"Is it my mom?" I asked in a panic.

"No," Emmy said, taking my hands into hers. "It's your dad. Donya, he..." she paused and looked at me with deep sadness. "He overdosed. He didn't make it."

"Overdosed?" I snickered and shook my head. "On what? On life?" I laughed. "No, that's impossible since he was barely living one." I shook my head again. "My dad wasn't on drugs."

Sam and Fred exchanged a look but remained quiet.

"Don't have a private conversation with your eyes that I'm not privy to," I snapped, pulling out my adult words like 'privy'.

"Honey, your dad overdosed on heroin," Sam said.

"But…" I looked into all of their faces. "My dad didn't do drugs. I've never seen him do drugs."

"He hid it from you very well," Sam said sadly.

Of course, he hid it from me very well. He was never around. By the time I was thirteen, I would sometimes go days without seeing him. He would show up, pay the bills, ask me about my life and listen just long enough to get the bare minimum and when I'd wake up in the morning, he would be gone again, leaving me to deal with my mom. When I called him on it, he said he was working long hours, and it was easier to stay closer to work since it was an hour plus drive away.

I pulled my hands out of Emmy's and wiped my palms on my jeans.

"I'm going to go to my mom's house," I said, suddenly feeling as if all of the energy had been zapped from my body.

I picked up my skateboard and backed up until my hand was on the door behind me.

"I'll drive you," Emmet said.

"It's a few blocks away," I said, with an annoyance I didn't even understand. "I'll be fine."

"You shouldn't be alone," Emmy said.

I laughed and looked at her. "When I get to my mom's house, I *will* be alone. I'm always alone there. I think I can handle the few blocks alone to the house that I will be alone in."

"Then I will come with you," she insisted. "I'll stay with you."

"I wouldn't want you to get sucked into the black hole with me," I said, my voice wavering.

"You are my best friend, D. I'll go anywhere with you."

She ran upstairs to get a few things, leaving me the center of attention in the foyer. I felt like I was one of the objects I had looked at in the museum.

"I'd really appreciate if you all stop looking at me as if I'm going to fall to pieces because I'm not. My dad left me a long time ago, so this really…" I took a deep, shaky breath. "This really isn't a surprise that he found a way to leave permanently."

Without warning, without any kind of shudder or whimper, I was hit full force with grief. I hated to cry in front of anyone. I wasn't a crier, despite the tears I had shed earlier in the day after kissing Emmet. I did fall apart. Suddenly and brutally I was sobbing as I dropped my board on the floor with a loud clatter.

Emmy was halfway down the stairs when the onslaught started, but it was Emmet that wrapped his arms around me and held me. I held on to him fiercely. I was afraid if he let me go I would melt to the floor and just die myself. I cried in his arms for several minutes before I was able to pull myself together. He released me reluctantly, pushing my hair off of my face for the second time that day.

I convinced Emmy that I needed to go home alone. I didn't know how my mom was going to be, and I didn't want her there if it was bad. Emmet looked at me knowingly, but I didn't elaborate to anyone else. After some further discussion, Fred convinced me to let Emmet take me home, and I finally agreed. Sam and Fred, the parents I wish I had all along, hugged me and kissed me and promised to be a phone call away. Emmy wiped my tears and promised she would be over bright and early no matter what. She walked out to the car with us and stood in the driveway as we pulled away.

We were quiet for the three or four minutes it took Emmet to drive me home, but he drove with one hand and stroked my hair with his other hand. I was never able to find the words to explain how comforting that small gesture was.

When we pulled up in front of the house, I noticed cars of the relatives that rarely stopped over, that never helped out, and it made me angry. Emmet saw the cars too, and his eyes narrowed a bit.

"Just try to be patient," he said, picking up on how I was feeling.

"I'll try," I said without any commitment. I put my hand on the door to let myself out.

"Donya," he said my name quietly. I looked at him expectantly.

He brushed the hair off of my cheek and even in the lightly dimmed car I could see his eyes drop to my lips. Then he took a breath and pulled his hand away.

"Call me if you need me," he murmured.

"Okay," I said and then my eyes dropped to his lips.

We sat staring at each other for probably almost a full minute before I finally made myself look away. I pushed open the door and got out to face some demons.

Chapter Six

I kissed Emmet again the night of my dad's funeral. My mom had locked herself in her bedroom, and my dad's siblings and a few other random relatives were sitting in our home saying terrible things about my mom and my dad. The things they were saying were true, but they weren't trying to be helpful. They were putting themselves on pedestals, separating themselves from us as if they were somehow better people. There aren't better people. Just better circumstances. I was only nearly fifteen, and I got that. Why didn't they?

"I'm going out for a walk," I had said as I walked through the living room with my board under my arm. "And when I come back I want you all out of my house."

"Who is she talking to?" I heard my Aunt Amanda snap. "Oh, I know you're not talking to me, little girl."

I whirled around and looked at the gossipy, hypocritical bunch.

"None of you ever came over here to help before," I fired back. "Don't sit there and pretend that you give a shit when you don't. No one ever came over here to make sure I was okay or to make sure mommy was eating and none of you ever came over to check to make sure she was still breathing. Get out of our house. You don't belong here."

I slammed the door behind me. Before I could skate away, my aunt was at the door yelling at my back about how she was going to kick my ass if I ever spoke to her like that again and that I was in no position to tell her what to do, and I was just as crazy as my mom. With restraint I barely had, I skated away without looking back.

I had found myself back at that parking lot where I had kissed Emmet. It was dark at nearly eight-thirty in late October. There was a soft hum from the tall lampposts that bathed the lot in soft light. I really shouldn't have been out there by myself in the dark. It was set back away from any main roadways, and there were few houses or open businesses in the vicinity, but I wanted to clear my head.

I had been moving in slow, lazy arches for some time when I saw the headlights of a car. I started to worry that it was going to be some psychopath out for his nightly killing and violating, but when the car stopped a few yards from where I stood on my board, I realized that it wasn't a psychopath at all. It was just Emmet. I looked on with curiosity as he got out of the car, reached inside and then produced his board. Did he know I would be there, or was it coincidence?

"You shouldn't be out here by yourself in the dark," he said, stopping in front of me.

"I'm not by myself," I said pointedly.

"You were before I got here," he said, dropping his board to the pavement.

I gave him a little shrug and pushed off and away from him. We rode in a comfortable silence for a long time. It was getting very cold, and I was mad at myself that I had forgotten my gloves in my haste to get out of the house. I pushed my hands into my pockets, but it wasn't quite enough to keep them warm. Every few minutes I would take them out and rub them together and blow warm air on them before pushing them back into my pockets. I stopped for a moment to adjust my jacket and pull my knit cap over my ears. Emmet stopped in front of me just as I started to rub my hands together again.

Startling me, he grabbed my hands. He put them together as if I was about to pray, and then he rubbed his hands over mine. I sighed happily as my hands began to heat up with the friction of his hands rubbing on mine. He bent over slightly and cupped his hands around mine and blew. My hands warmed, but so did my whole body.

What the hell was that feeling? What was with the tingling that started in my fingertips and radiated throughout my entire body?

"Better?" he asked softly as he slowly rubbed my hands.

I nodded. I couldn't speak. Not with the way he was looking at me. Why did he have to have such beautiful eyes that made me feel like I was happily drowning in a green sea?

"Did you know I was out here before you got here?" I blurted out after a few moments.

Emmet nodded slowly as he again blew hot air onto my hands.

"How did you know I was here?"

He shrugged. "Just a feeling."

He had said that when I fell and hit my head years before. He had told me he'd always find me, and he had said that to me the week before, the day he first brought me to the lot and kissed me, the night my father died.

"You didn't find me after you found out about my dad," I murmured more to myself than him, but, of course, he had heard me.

"Not exactly," he said with a half of a shrug.

"What do you mean not exactly?" I had never told anyone where I had gone. It was still my secret place, and I wanted to keep it that way.

"I could...feel you," he said carefully. "I can't explain it. Sometimes I know...I just know you're close by and sometimes I know when you're not. I knew you weren't. I knew you weren't very far, but you were...out of my reach."

I stared at him with an open mouth. That was deep. Too deep for my teenage mind to understand. It was scary. Maybe it was scary because...well...I kind of always felt Emmet too. Even when we were little kids, I always knew when Emmet was near without having to look. That didn't scare me back then. I didn't think much of it then, but at almost fifteen years old, I began to understand how rare that was, and how utterly freaky it was.

We met half way. Freaky or not, his lips were so close, and we were alone. I was feeling a little miserable, and I knew Emmet could make me feel better. His lips crushed against mine and I wrapped my arms around his neck. He held me close, his hands shifting up and down my back as he kissed me. His mouth was so warm and perfect. I was getting better at using my tongue with his and I could tell he liked it. The same soft moans that I made, he was making too. I took a page from his book and pulled his bottom lip between my lips and gently sucked, then nipped, and then soothed it with my tongue.

Oh, yeah. I was learning.

Emmet pulled away suddenly and took a couple of steps back. I was left unbalanced on my skateboard. I wobbled madly for a moment on weakened knees and fell backward on my ass.

He was helping me up before I even had time to process that I had fallen. Once I was firmly on my feet, he backed away again.

"I have to stop kissing you," he said and let out a long breath.

Embarrassed, I picked up my board. "Yeah," I agreed. "I'm going to head home. I'll see you…whenever."

"Donya," Emmet said with a frustrated tone. His hand was on my arm, stopping me. I let him. "I want to kiss you, but…I'm older with…more experience, and you're making my head all cloudy. I don't want to…disrespect you."

Ohhhh, I get it.

Emmet was telling me that he wasn't a virgin and that he didn't want to do something crazy like feel me up or lure me into losing my virginity in the backseat of his car. I almost snickered at how quickly I caught on to that. Sometimes I thought I was just a naïve kid, but I got that. I understood it so fast, and I didn't want that to happen either.

"Okay," I said to him. "We probably shouldn't kiss anymore then."

"I like kissing you," he said, cupping my cheek. "I love you because you're part of my family, but I have…other feelings for you too."

Okay, now that was just too much for me. My brain was getting overloaded. I know teenage girls fall in love all of the time, but I didn't romanticize life like they did. I wasn't in any hurry to fall in love and be anyone's girlfriend and to have regular make-out sessions. I wanted to skateboard and get through school and get through life before all of that. Falling in love or lust or becoming infatuated as girls did at my age changed them. One day they were carefree and maybe a little broody because hormones do that to kids, but life wasn't…heavy. Then the next day they would be all dreamy eyed and head over heels for some guy, and then life got complicated.

I saw Emmy already headed down that path with Reed, even if she said it was just flirting. Since the party, their just flirting turned into a "just making out," and in a matter of days she had that dreamy-eyed look and started fantasizing about her future with him. I was way too young for any of that, despite how my heart seemed to beat harder for Emmet than for anyone or anything else in the world. Despite the fact that I also felt that invisible tether between us.

"I'm not ready for all of this," I said to Emmet, and gently pushed his hand off of my cheek. "You were right. I'm too young and dumb for this, and I'm okay with that. I want to be young and dumb for a while."

I stepped away from him and waited for his reaction. He looked pained, and I felt bad. I loved Emmet too, and I would never want to hurt him, but I had to do the right thing. Not many girls my age were able to think clearly like that, especially after kissing a guy.

"Okay," he breathed. He looked so disappointed. "I get it. I'll take you home."

He picked up his board and walked to his car without looking back to see if I would follow.

~~*

Several months passed by and it had felt like a lifetime had slipped past us since Emmet had given me my first kiss in that empty parking lot, the same day my father overdosed and died. Much changed since that day. My dad's death did something to my mother—like a good something.

The day after my dad's small funeral service, my mom checked herself into a hospital. She was in there for a month, and when she came out, she returned there three times a week for therapy. She began to take care of herself, and she tried to take care of me. I spent more time at home and less time at the Graynes' as I tried to get reacquainted with the mother that had been absent most of my life. I could have been a bitter teenager and rebelled against her, but I was a grateful teenager. I had a mother that did care about me underneath all of her grief and self-loathing, even if she was unable to verbalize it, and I had another family that loved me like a daughter and sister, and whatever I was to Emmet.

That tether never did go away, and though we weren't physically closer, as in we weren't kissing, I felt closer to him on other levels. I could read him very well, sense his emotions without any words or looks passing between us.

We still hung out and skated together from time to time but we talked about trivial things, or we were completely silent. Sometimes he looked at me like he wanted to kiss me, but he didn't try. At least we were friends, and for some time, we evaded the teenage angst that accompanied the relationships with the opposite sex, but we did not escape unscathed. Eventually, the angst caught up to us.

~~*

I could feel him coming down the hallway before I even looked up to see him. I told myself I wouldn't look. I pulled my locker open and then I turned my head and looked, of course. Through the crowded hallway and dozens of other students' big heads, I met Emmet's eyes.

How does he do that? How do I do that?

It took him a little while to get to me. Guys stopped him to shoot the shit. Girls stopped him to flirt and toss their stupid hair. A teacher stopped to flirt and toss her hair. Gross. Guess that's the problem with being good looking, athletic, and intelligent.

The tether slackened some as I felt him approaching me. Even though I was chatting with a couple of girls in my class, I turned around and looked in Emmet's direction expectantly. I wasn't waiting for him to come flirt with me like he did with the other girls; he was my ride home. Emmy and I had strong-armed him into driving us to and from school when the weather started to turn cold in the fall. I felt that he only said yes because I had tilted my head and batted my eyelashes and stuck out my bottom lip. His eyes had glazed over for only a second, and only I noticed it, but he did give in right after.

He was moving through the thinning crowd of students to get to me, and he was only a few feet away when Stella Cramer bounded into my perfect scene of Emmet smiling and eyes shining as he walked towards me. Stella was petite with big boobs, naturally blonde, and had big blue eyes. On top of being irresistibly adorable, she was also extremely nice and smart. Stella Cramer was the All American Girl. I would have bet cash that it was probably printed on her college applications.

Emmet seemed a little surprised to look down and see Stella in his path, but he stopped to talk to her. She smiled as she talked to him in a soft murmur, and he unconsciously leaned in close to her. I watched as he grinned and said something back to her and the pair laughed soft, secret laughs. The whole thing just seemed rather intimate. I couldn't stand to watch it, and I couldn't stand to look away.

My friend Amy snickered beside me.

"What?" I asked absently as I watched Emmet with Stella.

"Nothing," she said, though I could tell it was something.

"What?" I pressed, turning my gaze on her. She was looking at Emmet and Stella too, with a mischievous smile on her face.

I glanced at the couple and back to Amy with one arched brow.

"What?" I demanded.

"You can't tell anyone," she whispered.

"Tell anyone what?"

"They'll know I told, and my brother will kill me."

Amy's brother Aaron was a senior and pretty good friends with Emmet. He was a nice guy, but I could totally see him putting Amy in a headlock and torturing her for opening her mouth.

"Know what?" I asked, willing to risk Amy's head.

She moved closer to me and began to whisper. "Aaron had a few of his friends over last night while my parents were out. I caught Emmet and Stella screwing in the basement."

I literally felt as if she had just punched me in the chest, but I swallowed away the sudden pain and gave her a look of doubt.

"You did not," I said.

I didn't feel so doubtful, though. Why would she make it up? Was she just kidding? If she was, it wasn't funny at all.

"I did too," she said, looking at me seriously. "I went down there to do my laundry for school, and they were standing in front of our old couch trying to put their clothes back on in a hurry."

I gave her another doubtful look, but she just shrugged. "Look at them. They look like they're sharing a big secret."

I did look at them again, and they did look like they were sharing a big secret, with secret smiles and whispering. Emmet looked up from adorable Stella with a stupid smile on his face, but it faded away when he saw me watching. His eyes flicked over to Amy, and she inhaled sharply.

"Stop looking at them!" she hissed. "He probably knows I told you!"

I stopped looking. I didn't want to look anymore. I turned back around to concentrate on packing up my homework.

"If he asks you if I told you, don't rat me out," Amy whispered harshly and then she hurried away because Emmet was standing at my back. I could feel him there. The hairs on the back of my neck stood up, and my body tingled. Yeah, Emmet was there.

"Hey," he said to the back of my head.

"Hey," I threw over my shoulder. "I don't need a ride today. I have some things to do in the art room."

He was quiet for a few seconds. "How will you get home?"

"The same way I used to get home before you started driving me," I answered, forcing a smile. "I'll walk."

"It's pouring and cold," he objected.

"I have a coat and an umbrella," I said, turning around. I showed him the umbrella. "See? I'll be fine."

He studied me carefully. "What were you and Amy talking about?"

I closed my locker and looked at the wall over his shoulder. "Nothing really."

"Nothing really?" he parroted.

I nodded.

"If it was nothing then why won't you look at me?" He had spoken quietly, but I could feel his frustration and his unease.

Slowly, my eyes moved to his and I saw the truth of what Amy had said there. I exhaled and then swung my bag over my shoulder.

"I'll see you later," I said and started to move away.

"Wait, Donya." Emmet went to take my arm but remembered we were surrounded by people and stopped short.

"Hey, you don't have to explain anything to me," I forced another smile. "I'll see you later."

I hurried down the hall, ignoring his eyes burning holes into my back.

~~*

I had the art room all to myself. It was a Friday afternoon, and there weren't many kids that would want to hang out after school on a Friday if they weren't forced to, even for art.

I immersed myself in my project. It was almost Valentine's Day, and we had to do a Valentines theme. It could be anything we wanted, as long as the focus was on love, as if any fifteen-year-old kid understood anything about love.

I became lost in my project. I watched the paint appear on the canvas with the same serenity I felt when I skateboarded. The sound of the brush as it connected with the surface was soothing. I took pleasure in the careful lines and smooth curves that had to have been created with meticulous precision. The smell of paint settled my mind and feeling the colorful liquid between my fingers settled my nerves.

Hours passed. Occasionally, a rare teacher would check in on me but say nothing. Mr. Boggs, the maintenance manager, told me earlier before I got started that I could stay until nine and then he'd have to kick me out. I used every minute, every second, and put my heart into my project. Originally, I was going to do a simple, cheesy project. It was going to be your typical hearts and flowers and candy type of picture, only a few steps above what a kindergartener may create, but after I had seen the truth about Emmet and Stella in Emmet's eyes, my creative process changed. It exploded into my fingertips, and I had no control over it.

I took a step back and exhaled slowly as I looked at my work. I guess I did know something about love.

The invisible tether slackened. My back was to the door, but I knew he was there watching me just as surely as I knew my own name. I glanced up at the clock over the teacher's desk. I had roughly twenty minutes to clean up and get out, but I couldn't stop staring at my creation. I never considered myself to be talented, but even I could not deny how incredible it looked.

I heard Emmet's footsteps as he approached me. He stood behind me, looking over my shoulder at my project. I heard him exhale miserably. I didn't mean to make him miserable, but I took a little solace in knowing that he may have been a bit unhappy. Misery does love company.

"Do you forgive me?" he asked as he moved in closer to me.

"Nothing to forgive," I said, but I didn't turn around to look at him. "Why are you here?"

"It's late. I didn't want you walking home."

"I'll be fine," I said.

"You'll be fine now because I'm going to drive you home."

His arm circled my waist. I should have pulled away, but my body had different ideas. It melted back into Emmet, and my head tilted back against his chest.

"Where did you get your inspiration for this painting?" he asked in my ear.

I didn't answer him because I knew that he knew. And I knew that he knew that I knew that he knew.

The woman in the painting was bleeding from the gaping, ragged hole in her chest. In her hand was a bleeding heart. Dark blood covered her fingers and dripped down into the green grass below, staining it red. It was an offering to the man before her who had his hand extended as if to receive the heart. Their fingers touched and some of the blood dripped onto his extended fingers. The man offered in his other hand dying roses and a box of chocolates with tiny spiders crawling out of the heart shaped package.

Maybe my teacher didn't intend for us to create anything as macabre as that, but to me that was the reality of Valentine's Day. The girls I knew had big floaty ideas about February 14th. They got some stale chocolates and roses that died within hours and thought that it was true love. It's wasn't.

The painting wasn't just about the fake holiday either. Even though I knew better, I had been having silly ideas about love and relationships. I told Emmet I wasn't ready, and I probably still wasn't, but I secretly wished that he would try again. I secretly wished that he would wait for me. I fantasized about the day I would tell him I was ready and how he would kiss me and tell me he waited for me because he knew I was special. He had said so himself once, and I believed it. I fantasized that I would go away, and he would find me because he could always find me, and he would kiss me and bring me back. I dreamed up our lives through his college years, and I dreamed that when I finished high school he would propose, and we would get married before I finished college. I thought about our quaint wedding in Louisiana and the children that would follow.

I had secretly hoped that he would come to me on that stupid fake day with candy and flowers and a kiss.

My fantasies were shut down with a bang when I realized he had banged Stella. Me and my stupid childhood fantasies.

I stepped away from Emmet and started to clean up my mess. After another moment of staring at the painting Emmet helped. We cleaned up quickly and left the dark painting where it needed to be, in the dark.

After we had got into the car, Emmet started the engine but he didn't drive. He sat there staring at the cold rain pouring onto the glass. We were the only car left in the dimly lit parking lot. We were completely alone, and I hated it. I wanted to go home. I wanted to get away from him so that I would stop having the constant reminder about my stupid fantasies.

"I'm sorry, Donya," he said, his voice soft as a feather.

"I don't know why you're apologizing," I said quickly. I reached over and turned on the radio. "I'm starving. Are you going to drive or are we going to sit here?"

Emmet growled with annoyance and turned the radio off. "Stop avoiding this."

"I don't know what you're talking about, so whatever it is you think you need to apologize for obviously isn't a big deal."

"Are you going to make me say it?" he asked as his hands gripped the steering wheel.

"Say what? Do you have anything to eat in here?" I asked, popping open the glove compartment.

"Don't open that!" Emmet shouted as he reached to close it, but he was too late. The compartment door flung open, and a condom dropped onto my lap.

"That's not food," I said delicately as I picked up the foil packet. I stared at it in the palm of my hand for a few seconds, and then I put it back in the glove box and closed it. The clicking sound it made seemed to ricochet throughout the car.

The silence that followed was crushing. Emmet stared straight ahead again, but his hands gripped the steering wheel even tighter than before, turning his knuckles white.

I knew he wasn't a virgin, but I didn't want to know that he was actively screwing girls. What if that was all he wanted from me? What if that was his game all along? What if he was just priming me so he could fuck me?

I hated the way my body reacted to the thought; the way heat pooled in places there shouldn't be heat at fifteen years old. I hated the images of being under him, of him rolling on that condom I just found.

The crushing pressure in the car became too much. I needed air. I needed to be away from Emmet. I unbuckled my seatbelt and threw open the door. Rain pelted the right side of my body. It was so cold that it stung, but that didn't stop me from grabbing my bag and dashing out into the terrible weather even as Emmet yelled my name.

I only got a few yards before Emmet's arms were around me as he tried to drag me back to the car. My backpack dropped to the ground with a splash as I struggled against him and tried to pry his arms apart, but it was pointless. He carried me kicking and screaming back to the car. As he struggled to open the door with one hand and his other arm around me, I elbowed him hard in the gut. His hold on me loosened, and I managed to make it a couple of steps before he spun me around and crushed me against the car.

"I'm not letting you walk home tonight," he growled in my face. "We can fight all night if you want, but I'm not letting you go."

I stilled under him. He was too close. Pressed up against me, and I was pressed up against the car. There was no give anywhere.

We were both breathing heavily from the struggle. Our breaths were foggy against the rainy night. His hand was on my face. I shook my head to make him move his it, but he growled low in his throat and grabbed my head with both hands and held me still.

"It was a mistake," he said through gritted teeth. "I don't like her like that."

"You liked her enough to put your dick in her," I snarled and was surprised by my ferocious words.

Emmet's expression darkened. "You told me you weren't ready."

"I'm obviously still not ready because I'm definitely not ready for condoms in the glove compartment and screwing on dirty couches in damp, musky basements."

"First of all, I would never do that to you. You deserve better than getting screwed on a dirty couch in a musky basement. Secondly, I have enough self-restraint not to try to fuck you anyway. Third, you said you weren't ready, Donya. You don't want to be with me, but you don't expect me to be with anyone else."

"So, it's my fault you can't keep your dick in your pants?" I asked coolly.

"No," he snapped. "It's your fault you're hurt that I didn't keep my dick in my pants. You made your decision. I'm beginning to believe you were right. You're just a clueless kid. You wouldn't know what to do with me if you had me. You'll be better off dating someone your age, someone at your maturity level."

I cringed at his words. I felt my mouth hanging open. Damn that hurt. That hurt a lot. I felt like slapping him, but then…I am the one who told him I was too young and dumb. I all but proved it by running out of the car when the condom fell on my lap.

He stretched his right arm and pulled the door open.

"Get in the damn car."

I got in the car. He slammed my door, retrieved my backpack and then he got in. The pack was carelessly thrown on my lap. He gave me a dark look, threw the car into gear and sped out of the parking lot. His anger was apparently affecting his driving. I probably would have been safer walking, but I said nothing else.

The car was still moving when I flung open the door in front of my house. I heard Emmet's exasperation behind me as he slammed on the brakes. I slammed the car door and ran to my front my door. I had barely pushed the door open before Emmet's tires peeled on the wet ground. I turned around just in time to watch him take off like a bat out of hell.

Chapter Seven

I eased into the house as quietly as possible. I quickly punched in the code for the alarm system before it woke up the whole family. When I turned around in the dark foyer, he was standing there in a pair of sweatpants and a t-shirt that outlined is budding man muscles. I couldn't see his expression in the dark, but I could feel his mood. He was angry, he was sad, he was regretful, and he was confused. I felt another emotion radiating off of him that I could not name then at the tender age of fifteen, but I can name it now: lust.

I was soaked to the bone. My coat and knit hat did nothing to protect me from the cold rain. I shivered violently, and my teeth clattered together so hard it hurt my jaw.

Without any words, Emmet took my hand and silently led me upstairs to his bedroom. Once the door closed, he flipped on a light and moved past me while peering at me intently. He quickly rooted through his drawers and produced a pair of sweatpants, a sweatshirt, and a pair of socks. He put them on the bed and passed me the towel that hung on the back of his door. His gaze moved over my body from head to toe and back up to my eyes before he slipped out of the bedroom.

I stood there staring at the door. It was like he knew I was coming. Did he feel that slack in the tether as I hurried up the driveway? I did.

For hours after Emmet sped away from my house, I tried to ease the ache in my chest. I didn't like feeling like everything about us was ruined because I got jealous when I had no right to be. If he never put his lips on mine again, I could deal with that. What I could not deal with was losing him as I always had him, my friend, and my something-like-a-brother-but-not. I was the one that told him I wasn't ready, and I really shouldn't have expected him to hang around waiting for me. On the surface, I didn't expect it, but I guess a part of me did, and I was rather ashamed of that part of me. It was selfish.

When two a.m. rolled around, and I was still sitting in my room staring out at the dark and rainy street, I got up, got dressed, and snuck out into the night. I just wanted to apologize. I didn't want to fight with Emmet.

I took off my wet coat and hung it over the back of a chair. I put my shoes near the heater and then peeled out of my drenched clothes. I picked up his towel and pressed it to my nose. It smelled like him—clean, fresh, and his own intoxicating scent. I used the towel to dry my hair and body and hung it back up before I began to pull on the clothes he'd left for me. I was just pulling the sweatshirt down over my stomach when Emmet quietly re-entered the room. He handed me the hairbrush I kept in Emmy's room. I knew he had to sneak in there to get it. I don't think either of us wanted to wake her or anyone else in the house.

"Thank you," I whispered, taking it from him.

I walked over to his mirror and brushed my wet hair back and used the emergency scrunchy that I kept on the brush handle to pull my hair into a ponytail. I was going to hate my hair later in the day when it became a ball of frizz.

I put the brush down on his bureau and turned around to face him. He had pulled back the covers on his bed while I brushed my hair. I looked at him with fear that threatened to choke me. He stood on the other side of the bed watching me.

"Just sleep," he said, speaking for the first time since I arrived.

"I didn't come here to sleep," I said and swallowed hard. "I just…I don't want to fight with you, Emmet."

"So, stop fighting with me, Donya, and get into the bed."

Without waiting for a response, he locked the door and turned the light off. The room was dark, but I heard the bedclothes rustling as he got into his queen size bed. I hesitated in the dark.

I knew I should have demanded him to turn the light back on. I should have put my wet shoes and coat back on and left. I should have gone and slept in Emmy's room.

I ignored my objecting thoughts, and I stepped forward and slipped into Emmet's bed, and into Emmet's waiting, open arms.

His body was firm against mine. His arms caged me securely as I rested my head on his chest. His skin was hot, but I was cold. I snuggled closer to him to warm my own skin with his. His scent soothed, and the sound of his heart beat was like a lullaby. The tether between us felt comfortable, not stretched or twisted.

I slept more peacefully than I ever had before.

~~*

I felt all kinds of wrong when I woke up, cocooned in Emmet's arms. I felt all kinds of right, too—warm and snuggly—but mostly wrong. I was only fifteen years old. I shouldn't have been sleeping in any guy's bed regardless of the innocent circumstances behind it. I wasn't even sure just how innocent it really was. I was fifteen, not stupid. I knew what that thing was pressing against my leg.

Why is it so big? How is it so big?

Wow, when I heard the term "hard" before, I didn't know it was so literal.

I tried to shake my head of those thoughts and carefully attempted to extract myself from Emmet's arms. He groaned and held me tighter and then rubbed that thing against my thigh. It made me anxious. I couldn't fathom how girls at my age took the leap and lost their virginity when faced with the possibility of something that size and that hard going inside of them.

Goosebumps rose up and down my arms and my pulse was erratic. I squeezed my thighs together in an attempt to release some of the pressure I felt.

Oh, my god! I have to get out of this bed, I thought.

Feeling a bit panicky, I tried harder to get out of his impossibly tight embrace. Emmet shifted, yawned, and opened his eyes.

"What are you doing?" he questioned me and looked at me through droopy, sleepy eyes.

"Trying to get up," I said with frustration.

"Why would you want to do that?" His smile was like a warm blanket clinging to my skin. Why would I want to leave the comfort of a warm, skin clinging blanket? That would be stupid. It was cold out there.

I shook my head. I needed to get away from Emmet so I could think clearly.

"So I can pee?" I asked instead of telling.

"You have to pay the toll if you want the gates to open."

"Are you a troll?"

He laughed softly. "Do I look like a troll?"

My eyes traced over his face. No, he did not look like a troll. Definitely not.

"What's the toll?" I asked instead of answering his question. "I'm sure I have some spare change in my jeans."

"I don't want your money," he said. He was looking at my mouth.

My voice faltered as I looked at his mouth. "I don't think I have any gold...or whatever trolls collect."

"You know what the toll is," he whispered, as his head dipped closer to mine. "So pay it."

"But I thought we were just sleeping!" I blurted it out before his lips could touch mine.

"We slept. New agenda."

I had no further opportunity to object because Emmet's tongue was in my mouth and his lips were massaging my lips and I was kissing him back. I knew I shouldn't have been kissing him in his bed, but I couldn't make myself stop. Kissing Emmet was exactly how I always thought it should be like to kiss a boy, sweet and full of emotion. I felt connected to him on levels my young mind was yet to comprehend. The tether hummed with pleasure between us, as if it had a mind of its own and we made it happy when we connected like that.

When we first started kissing, Emmet was beside me. We shifted without me paying it any mind until I felt him on me. There.

I tried to gasp, but my mouth was getting consumed by Emmet's mouth. I opened my eyes and saw my arms wrapped around his neck. When did that happen? He was on top of me. When did that happen? And he was hard against me, where no one had ever touched me before.

I started to pull away from the kiss. My hands were on his shoulders to push him away, but then he shifted again. My eyes closed reflexively and stars burst into light behind my eyelids. I moaned into Emmet's mouth at the same time he moaned into mine. My arms were wrapped around him again, and I kissed him harder, or maybe he kissed me harder.

He rocked against me again, and I couldn't help myself. I pushed my hips up against him. I needed to get rid of the pressure between my legs. He pushed back, and I shamelessly groaned and pulled his hair. I wrapped my legs around his waist and raised my hips off of the bed again to meet his next thrust. We moved against each other fluidly, in perfect synchronization.

I need to…I need to…I have to…

I clung to Emmet and tightened my legs around him. He pressed harder against me, and the pressure built and built and I felt like I was going to explode. I wondered if that was what it was like. Explosions? Would I explode into a thousand pieces and scatter into the universe? I didn't care how many pieces I was in. I needed it. I needed him.

Someone banged on the door. Our lips separated with a soft, wet sound and our movements froze. We both looked towards the door.

"Emmet," Sam's voice said from the other side of the door.

Fear gripped my heart. If Sam caught me in Emmet's bed especially with Emmet on top of me, she would have flipped out. It could have been a very scary situation.

"Yeah, Mom?" he said as he struggled to catch his breath.

I unraveled my legs from his waist and let my arms fall away from him, but he didn't pull away. He was still pressed against me and caging me with his arms.

"Are you going to make me talk through the damn door?" Sam snapped.

Emmet hung his head and growled in frustration. He pecked me on the lips and got up, pulling me up with him. He opened the closet door, and I stepped inside. I almost laughed at the absurdity of it. I grew up in that house. Sam was just as much a mother to me as my real mother, maybe more so, but I had to hide in the closet.

I covered my mouth to keep from laughing.

"What do you want?" Emmet asked Sam as I heard the door opening. He didn't bother trying to hide his aggravation.

"Your daddy and I are going to Newport for an anniversary party. Did you forget?"

"No, I didn't forget, Mom."

"We'll be back Monday morning. We're dropping your sister off at Mayson's on our way but you have to pick her up tomorrow night. Don't forget."

"Okay," he said impatiently. "Anything else?"

"Why are you trying to get rid of me? Do you have a girl in here again?"

Again?

"Mom! There's no one in here. What else do you want? I want to go back to bed."

"No parties and no sex."

I blushed and covered my mouth again, biting back nervous giggles.

"Can I party and have sex somewhere else?" Emmet asked dryly.

I heard Sam's slap to his head. "Don't be cheeky."

"Anything else?" Emmet asked with little patience.

"Don't forget to take care of the garage like your daddy told you."

"Okay."

"Hug your mama, child."

I heard slight movement from the door, and I heard Emmy talking in the hallway.

"If Donya comes over tell her I took her boots."

I put a hand on my hip. I saved up long and hard for those boots. My mom couldn't afford things like Emmy's parents, and though Fred and Sam treated me like their own, I tried not to take advantage. I would have never asked them for two hundred dollar boots. I was tempted to go out there and steal my boots back from Emmy and hit her with them.

The commotion in the hallway faded as Emmy and Sam went down the stairs. I heard Emmet out in the hall, probably standing at the top of the stairs as he spoke to them. A couple of minutes later the front door slammed and a few seconds after that Emmet's door closed. I pushed out of the closet, tripped over the length of Emmet's sweat pants, and nearly fell on my face. I pulled at the pants to uncover my feet.

"I can't believe she took my boots," I murmured.

I stood on one side of the rumpled bed and Emmet on the other. We looked at one another. I tried not to show how horrified I was by what almost happened in that rumpled bed. It scared me how far I let myself go. How much farther would I have gone? Would we have been joined in the most intimate way? The thought scared the crap out of me.

I tore my gaze away from Emmet and looked at my wet clothes hanging on the chair. I was lucky Sam didn't venture further into the room and see them there. I was glad I kept a whole wardrobe in Em's room.

I walked over to the chair and gathered up my wet clothes. I knelt down and picked up my wet sneakers. Emmet watched me with apprehension.

"What are you doing?" he asked hesitantly.

"I'm going to change into my own clothes and go home."

He stepped in front of the door. I stopped a couple of feet away.

"You are home," he said.

"My other home."

"I don't want you to leave. Stay here. Spend the day with me, just the two of us."

He looked so hopeful that it made my heart ache.

"I can't," I whispered.

"Why can't you, Donya?"

I gestured to the bed. "That scares the shit out of me," I admitted forcefully. I wasn't sure if I should admit the next part, but I didn't think Emmet would take advantage of my confession. "If your mom hadn't come to the door, I'm not sure where I would have stopped—*if* I would have stopped."

"I know you're not ready to go all the way. I wouldn't have—"

"Emmet!" I shouted his name in frustration. "You were no more in control than I was. You probably didn't think you'd grind with me like that either."

He let out an exasperated growl, put his hands on his hips and looked down at the floor for a moment. When he looked back up at me, I knew that I had been right. He hadn't expected to kiss me, let alone push me towards my first ever orgasm.

"We'll stay away from the bedroom," he suggested.

"Well we both know that you have nothing against sofas," I said and instantly regretted it. He looked hurt by my words. I didn't mean to hurt him. "I'm sorry."

He took in a breath. Some of the pain cleared from his face and once again he looked hopeful.

"I just want to spend the day with you," he said softly.

I shook my head slowly. "I don't trust myself, Emmet. Move away from the door so I can leave."

He stared at me for a few long moments before he finally stepped aside and opened the door for me. I rushed past him and into Emmy's room and locked the door behind me.

Even after I stripped out of Emmet's clothes, I still smelled like him. I held my hair to my nose, inhaling deeply. It was driving me crazy. I had half the mind to run across the hall and get wrapped up in him again. Instead, I marched into Emmy's bathroom and showered. I stayed in there a long time washing traces of Emmet off of my body.

When I got dressed, I carried my coat and wet clothes downstairs to the dryer. Emmet was in the kitchen cooking something as I passed through on my way to the laundry room.

"Can you at least stay for brunch?" Emmet asked when I returned to the kitchen.

My stomach rumbled.

"Okay," I conceded.

"Have a seat."

I sat down at the table. Emmet made an effort to talk about anything but us. While he cooked, he talked about college and possible law schools, and I talked about the colleges I was considering, even though I still had a few years yet.

"Breakfast is served," he said dramatically, putting a plate before me. It was loaded with pancakes, eggs, fried potatoes, and toast. I laughed and clapped. He smiled fondly at me and winked. "Orange juice? Coffee?"

"Orange juice, please."

He poured me a tall glass of OJ and got himself a cup of coffee before sitting down at the head of the table beside me. We dug into our food and ate in a comfortable silence for a few minutes, but the silence didn't last. Neither did the comfort.

"What happens now?" Emmet asked me as he stabbed at his pancakes, but didn't pick any up.

I looked at him cautiously. "What do you mean?"

"With us."

I took a sip of my juice as I considered a response. He waited patiently. He had put his fork down and given up on eating, but he looked patient.

"I think…" I looked at him, and I felt his body on mine and felt his lips on mine. "I'm still not ready," I whispered.

"You seemed ready a little while ago." He didn't say it with any menace. It was an observation.

"I lost control a little while ago, and I don't want to be out of control," I said apologetically. "I just want to be friends."

I wanted more than friends, but that didn't mean it was the right thing. The right thing was to move on and let him do the same.

"Donya, I lo—" I cut him off with my fingers on his lips before he could finish that thought.

"Don't say it," I begged. "Please don't say it. I'm not ready for all of that, Emmet. Please."

His eyes closed slowly, and I knew I had hurt him. I pulled my fingers away from his mouth and folded them in my lap.

"Be my friend," I whispered.

His eyes opened. "I'll always be your friend."

We sat at the table in a pained silence until our food was cold and unappetizing.

Chapter Eight

I was on the boardwalk beside my best friend, eating cotton candy and being rebellious by riding my skateboard. Skateboard riding wasn't permitted on the boardwalk, which just baffled me because people were allowed to ride bikes and roller skate. I pushed myself alongside Emmy slowly, enjoying the leisurely pace as we talked.

It was mid-June. School had ended only days before. We would be leaving for Louisiana in another week, but we were spending a few days at the shore first. Since my mother was beginning to find some level of normalcy, I was reluctant to leave her. With my dad gone, there wouldn't be anyone at all to watch over her, but she insisted that I go. She got a job waitressing and said she would be working all summer, and that would keep her busy enough. It took her a whole week to convince me to go. Once my mind was made up, I looked forward to the summer down south, fishing with Fred and maybe Emmet and hanging out with Emmy's myriads of relatives.

"I don't want to live in Louisiana," Emmy was saying to me. "I love going down there for visits, but I don't want to set up shop and get all cozy like my brother and sisters. Besides, Mom will be moving back when I get out of college, and I don't want to be near mom."

"Don't blame you there," I said.

"Emmet thinks he's definitely going to go back after college. I don't understand how they all could just give up their lifelong friends up here and move down there."

"Maybe you will change your mind when you're older," I said.

"No way. Besides, I need to be near you. Like always. My other half." She grinned at me, and I grinned back. I loved that girl to death.

"I definitely will not be living in Louisiana when I am an adult," I assured her. My dream of living there with a certain husband faded away months ago.

I had finished my cotton candy, and as we were passing a man operating an ice-cream cart, I stopped and got an ice-cream cone. I loved getting ice-cream at the beach. It seemed like the two went hand in hand at the Jersey Shore. You couldn't walk on the boardwalk and not get ice-cream, or cotton candy, or fries, or pizza, or funnel cake. I knew I was going to be so fat by the time we got to Louisiana that I wouldn't feel like doing anything. Emmy would have to roll me everywhere.

The ice-cream man had just rolled away when a man, a very nice looking man with dark hair stood in our path. He wore a Rolex around his tanned wrist. He was preppy in his khaki shorts, button up Ralph Lauren shirt, and expensive loafers. His hair looked like every other guy's hair in the mid-nineties, like he had the same hair stylist as the guys from *Beverly Hills, 90210*.

He tipped his Cartier sunglasses so he could peer at us with his piercing brown eyes. Emmy and I stood there for a moment, looking at him, waiting for him to move.

"Hello. My name is Max," he said in a fading Italian accent.

"So?" Emmy said.

He flashed a smile at her but brought his eyes back to me. I momentarily looked away from Max to my ice-cream cone and my hand. I watched vanilla ice-cream drip onto my wrist, already melting quickly in the early summer heat. I didn't bother cleaning it up because more would drip and I'd spend more time cleaning myself than eating it.

"I promise you this is not a pickup line," he said to me.

"What's not a pickup line?" Emmy demanded fisting one hand on her hip. "That already sounds like a pickup line."

More ice-cream dripped down my wrist. I felt it sliding slowly down my arm. I ignored it and put the cold treat to my lips as I eyed Max. What did he want? Why was he looking at me like that? He was cute, but he had to have a good fifteen or twenty years on me. I was a little grossed out thinking that maybe he was trying to pick me up with a non-pickup-pickup-line.

"I work for a New York agency that represents models," Max said to me. "Forgive me for saying so, but you are exquisite. Do you work as a model?"

"Exquisite?" Emmy and I said together and laughed.

"Donya," Emmy said in a fake Italian accent. She took my free hand and looked up at me with well-overdone adoration. "My darling, you are exquisite. May I kiss your exquisite lips and touch your exquisite behind?"

I laughed at my friend's stupidity. We cracked up while Max patiently waited for us to stop.

"Dude, that's a great pickup line," Emmy said, patting Max's arm.

Max passed me a business card. It said Maximus Sobreno, Talent Representative. The address and phone number were out of New York. I wasn't very impressed. Anyone could make business cards, and I told him as much as I tried to pass the card back to him.

"You are right to question my validity," he said. "But before you disregard me entirely, do some research and find out for yourself whether or not I am as I say. I can change your life, beautiful girl. You may have potential."

"Right, because ice-cream dripping down my arm is one of those modeling qualities," I said.

He shrugged. "You look like a model posing as a carefree woman on the boardwalk eating ice-cream. It would have made a perfect shot, right down to your mode of transportation, but what caught my eye was when I saw you further back eating cotton candy. Something about it struck me."

His eyes traveled leisurely over my body before he spoke again. "Don't lose my card."

He pushed his sunglasses back into place and walked away.

"That was weird," Emmy said.

I nodded in agreement. I looked at the card for a little while longer and then pushed it into my back pocket. There was slight pressure in my chest that I instantly recognized. I looked up and met Emmet's eyes as he walked over to us.

"Who was that?" he asked, looking in the direction Max had walked.

"Modeling scout," Emmy said.

Emmet looked doubtful. I only shrugged.

Emmy announced her need to pee and walked off towards the public bathrooms.

"You're wearing more than you're eating," Emmet said. His eyes were hidden behind sunglasses, but I knew he was looking at the ice-cream dripping down my arm.

"It's melting faster than I can eat it," I giggled and took a lick.

"You got too much. You always get too much." He closed a hand over my sticky wrist. I watched without breathing as he slowly sucked some of the vanilla goodness into his mouth. He licked his lips as he moved my hand so that the dessert was pressed against my lips. I parted my lips and sucked-slurped. He brought it back to his lips and ate some exactly where my mouth had been. I shivered in the ninety plus degree heat.

"Thank you," he murmured and released my hand. He sucked a few drops of ice-cream off of his fingers. "I'll see you later."

I watched him walk away, pulling on my tether, as the ice-cream melted in my hand.

~~*

Wildwood was the go-to beach location for most teens and families in the South Jersey and Philadelphia area. During the summer, no matter what day you are there, you are guaranteed to run into no less than five people that you know. They may be a neighbor, a teacher, the clerk at the grocery store, or just people you recognize but don't know by name.

By nightfall, there was a huge group of us from our town and nearby towns strolling down the boardwalk. We started out small, just me and Emmy, but then her cousins Mayson and Tabitha arrived. A little while later Tabitha's best friend Leslie and her boyfriend Leo joined us. A few kids a year ahead of us at our school adhered to the group and soon after that Emmet and his friends were there. The group grew and grew, even kids we only knew from the shore joined in until we were at least twenty-five strong. Laughter and constant talking and shouts to one another filled the air. Whenever anyone bought any food, it was instantly shared with the people around them. It wasn't unusual to see someone's hand in my bucket of fries or to share a soda with three other people. Many years later I would look back on times like this and wonder how I made it through my teenage years without getting mono or some other highly communicable sickness from all of the sharing we did.

I had so much fun. I felt so alive. I felt happy. It was one of few times in my life where I can say I was one hundred percent happy. One of the other times was sleeping in the arms of a certain guy.

The crowd started to disperse a little after midnight. Many kids had a two-hour drive ahead of them and even more had curfews. The few kids that were staying at the shore headed back towards their respective shore houses, hotels and motels, including us. Sam was up waiting for us when we got in, but she went to bed soon after that. Emmy managed to make it another hour, before she dragged herself into our shared bedroom, leaving me alone in the living room with Emmet.

All night, I was always aware that he was near, even if he wasn't in my immediate vicinity, but I was distracted enough to not let my thoughts stray to the ice-cream incident from earlier in the day. Later, sitting only a foot away from him on the couch, it was all I could think about. I considered going to bed so that I could stop feeling awkward about it.

Emmet hadn't tried to kiss me again since that February morning. He had seemingly moved on. He started dating Stella "The Mistake" Cramer and I had done my best to pretend like I didn't care. I was nice to her and even helped her pick out Emmet's birthday present. He treated me like he used to, like an annoying kid sister and he stopped showing up at the empty lot to board with me. He was never cruel to me, but sometimes there was a coolness between us that stung.

That tether, however, was very much intact. I could feel him wherever I went. I knew when he was close, and I knew when he wasn't. I didn't know if he still felt it, too. I wasn't going to ask.

As his presence on the couch became enormous and seemed to surround me, I got up. I wasn't tired, but I sure couldn't sit there with Emmet as if everything was normal. I almost laughed. There wasn't anything normal between us. I started towards the bedroom I shared with Emmy but then abruptly I took a detour. I grabbed a room key off of the counter and started for the door.

"Where are you going?" Emmet asked. It was an accusation.

"For a walk," I said over my shoulder without looking at him. "I'm not tired."

"You shouldn't go out there by yourself," he warned, and I felt him closer than before. I looked back, and he was walking toward me.

"I'm going for a walk," I said it with irritation and with a note of finality.

I went out the door and hurried down the hall to the bank of elevators. When I felt the tether contracting, I got irritated. I crossed my arms as I waited for the elevator to arrive.

"I don't need you to take me for a walk," I said dryly. I knew he was standing behind me.

"Maybe I want to go for a walk too."

"Isn't it almost time for you to call your girlfriend?" I asked, referring to his nightly phone calls to Stella.

"She's not my girlfriend," he said as the elevator doors slid open. He waited for me to step on before him.

I gave him a disbelieving look. It was only a few days before that I last saw his tongue massaging her tonsils.

"We broke up on last night's phone call," Emmet said as he punched the button for the lobby.

Baffled, I asked, "Why?" I was genuinely curious.

"She's going to Oklahoma. I'm going to Harvard. Long distance relationships aren't my thing."

"How did she take it?"

"She thinks we can make it work." He shrugged. "I don't."

"You won't even try. That's stupid."

"Donya, don't preach to me about trying," he snapped.

The doors slid open, and I stormed out.

"What is that supposed to mean?" I asked though I knew what it meant.

"You didn't try either," he said sourly as he held the door open for me.

We stepped outside and started to walk the few yards to the boardwalk.

"The difference is that I wasn't ready. She clearly is."

"Why are you so concerned about my relationship with Stella?" Emmet asked angrily.

I looked over at him. "Why are you so mad? I'm just saying that you could be throwing something good away because you won't try."

"Maybe *you* threw something good away because you didn't try."

I sighed in exasperation. We stepped onto the boardwalk, and I immediately felt the chill from the water. Emmet looked at me with fury, but he pulled his jacket off and handed it to me. I took it and slipped my arms inside.

"I thought we were passed that," I said to him when we started walking again.

"I'm not past it, Donya. I just put it aside."

"Well put it aside again!"

He stopped walking and got so close to me I felt the need to take a step back, but he didn't let me. He grabbed my arms and kept me there.

"Did you kiss Andrew?" he demanded.

My mouth dropped open. Sam, Fred, and even my mom were still strict about Emmy and me dating, but they finally broke down and said that if we double dated somewhere public, we were allowed to date. I was in no hurry to date anyone, but after listening to Emmy beg me for a week I agreed to go on a double date with her and Corey Newland. She set me up with Corey's twin brother Andrew. The brothers were fun, hilarious and kind of sweet. Most importantly, they were our age. So when more double dates were proposed, I went. Andrew was a good guy, and I had fun with him. When he kissed me, I kissed him back. It was nice, but it wasn't great. It wasn't like Emmet's kisses, and he wasn't Emmet. The bar was set high and poor Andrew didn't make it. I didn't go on any more double dates and Andrew moved on.

"That's none of your business," I whispered.

"You dated him. You kissed him!" Emmet yelled, drawing a few looks from the few people left on the boardwalk. "But you won't date me and you won't kiss me anymore. Was it good, Donya? Did he get to touch you? Maybe make it to third base? Were you ready for a homerun?"

I slapped him. Hard. My hand stung, but I wanted to slap him again, so I did.

"Fuck you, Emmet Grayne." I took off his jacket and threw it in his arms. "Stay away from me."

His face changed immediately, and I knew that he regretted his words, but it was too late.

"I'm sorry," he said and reached for me, but I backed away from him.

"Stay away," I said once more and then I turned away from him and ran.

Chapter Nine

At the last minute, Emmet pulled out of the annual family trek to Louisiana. He told Sam and Fred that he wanted to spend his last few weeks before college with his friends. Fred asked him to reconsider but didn't push. Sam, on the other hand, put up a huge fight.

"What about spending time with your family?" she had demanded over dinner two nights before our departure.

"I've spent the last eighteen years with my family," Emmet snapped. "And I'll spend the rest of my life with my family."

"I ain't gonna let ya stay up here," Sam said in a tone that implied that she didn't care what he wanted.

"It's his decision, Sam," Fred said patiently. "He's not a little boy anymore."

"He's my little boy, Frederick Grayne!"

Emmy snickered beside me. I elbowed her. She wouldn't be laughing in a few years when she was put in a similar position.

"I'll join you guys during the last week," Emmet said, trying to sound reassuring.

"That's not good enough. You have cousins and aunts and uncles and friends down there that are looking forward to seeing you before you go away to school."

"It's not like he's going to school on the moon," I muttered.

"I heard that Donya Elisabeth Stewart," Sam snapped.

"Whoa," Emmy said with amusement. "Full name."

"Ya'll think this is funny and it's not," Sam whined.

Emmet put his pizza down and rested his chin on his folded hands and listened as Sam continued to rant. I felt sorry for him. It was his last summer before he was forced to behave somewhat like an adult, and Harvard was no joke. There wouldn't be too much time for fooling around.

Part of me felt he wasn't going with the family because I would be there, but I told myself how conceited that sounded and shut the thought down.

I cleared my throat and cut Sam off.

"He should stay," I said. I felt Emmet's eyes fall on me. "If you force him to go, he'll be miserable the entire time. Do you really want his last summer as a kid to be miserable?"

Sam sputtered for a moment. "But what about Lucy's wedding?"

"I won't miss the wedding," Emmet promised.

"You're not going to get your way on this one," Fred told his wife gently. "Let it go."

"Can I stay home, too?" Emmy asked with hope.

"No," Sam, Fred, and Emmet said at the same time.

Sam stopped bugging, but she frowned her way through dinner and barely spoke, which appeased all.

After dinner, I left to spend the rest of my time with my mom. I made it around the block before I felt the familiar tug and Emmet pulled to the curb. I stopped walking and hesitated before approaching the car. We had barely spoken more than a handful of words since that night on the boardwalk. He had written me a simple apologetic note that said, "I'm sorry." I didn't acknowledge it and he didn't push.

I stopped a foot away from the car.

"Thank you," he said.

"For what?"

"Speaking up for me at dinner."

I gave a half shrug. "I would have done the same for anyone. No big deal."

He flinched a little. He thought I had done it because I cared. I did, but he didn't need to know that.

"You haven't forgiven me," he said, frowning.

I shrugged again. "I forgive you. You won't be the last guy to call me a slut."

His eyes darkened. "I didn't call you a slut, Donya."

"You implied it. Same difference."

"I would never call you that."

"Maybe not directly, but accusing me of getting felt up by Andrew isn't any better."

"I was jealous," he grudgingly admitted.

"Well, I get jealous, too," I snapped. "But you don't see me making remarks about Stella."

He raised an eyebrow. "You've made a couple of references to couches."

I bit my lip and crossed my arms defensively. Emmet sighed.

"I didn't come here to fight with you. I just wanted to thank you."

"You're welcome," I said curtly.

"Okay."

"Okay."

He gave me a final look of regret and drove off.

~~*

The tether was stretched to the point of pain. I thought it would get better with each passing day, but it didn't. It got worse. I tried to keep myself busy while I was in Louisiana, even going as far as spending a day cooking and baking with Sam and arguing with her, but the ache was still there. I wondered if he ached, too. Or if he was just having so much fun with his friends and various girls that he didn't notice?

"What's on your mind, Kiddo?" Fred asked me one morning at our fishing spot.

I looked over at him. "Who said there's anything on my mind?"

"A father knows these things," he grinned. His words warmed me and I smiled. "Now tell me what's going on in that teenage head of yours.'

I couldn't tell him the truth, that I was in way over my head, meaning that I was in love, with his youngest son who is supposed to be like a brother to me.

That was the first time I really admitted it to myself. I was pretty sure I was in love with Emmet. I couldn't feed myself any BS about my tender age. Absence really did make the heart grow fond.

"I like a guy," I said slowly, deciding to give Fred some of the truth.

He groaned. "Go on."

"You have to promise not to hold anything I say against me. It wouldn't be fair."

He looked at me with amused suspicion. "Am I going to have to crack some guy's skull?"

The image of him cracking Emmet's skull made me shudder. "No skull cracking," I said, shaking a finger at him.

"I will not make that promise, Kiddo. Continue."

I inhaled slowly and let it out in a rush. "He's…incredible," I said softly with a faint smile. "He makes me feel incredible. I have this really strong connection with him. I can feel him when he's near and when he's not, I feel…like a part of me isn't with me at all, but gone with him."

Fred looked grim. It must have been hard for him to sit there and listen to this from a kid who wasn't even supposed to be dating seriously.

"I keep pushing him away," I admitted. "I told him I'm not ready for all of the things I'm feeling. I don't want to be like so many girls my age. Their worlds revolve around these guys, and when it falls apart it gets gruesome and they lose all focus on the things that matter. I lost enough of my childhood to my parents' issues. I don't want to lose any more of it to all of the drama that comes with relationships. I want to be a teenage, carefree kid as long as I can, because once these years are gone, they're gone."

Fred looked at me with a sympathetic smile. "For someone who wants to be young forever, you sure have a grown up way of thinking."

"I just think it's a responsible way of thinking."

"Since when are teenage, carefree kids responsible?" He chuckled.

"You know what I mean," I smiled. "Besides, I'm not even supposed to be dating."

Fred straightened up in his chair. I could tell that he was thinking before speaking, something Sam never learned to do.

"How old is this kid?" Fred asked casually.

"A couple of years older than me," I said carefully.

He looked at me thoughtfully for a long time. I felt like he saw right through me, that he knew I was talking about Emmet.

"Donya," he said and then his shoulders dropped a little. "I'm not condoning a serious relationship at your age, but…" He looked like he may not finish, but took a breath and went forward. "You are a sensible kid. You are older than your years because of the things you have gone through. You can't compare yourself to people in your age group because you've already lived a little longer than they have, at least mentally and emotionally. I don't think that what you're experiencing is trivial or something that will just pass as things do with kids your age. Because it's you we're talking about, and not say, Emmy or Lucy, I know this guy is probably as incredible as you say. You are young, and you should enjoy these years, but…" he struggled for words and I hung onto every one. "Maybe this guy is supposed to be a part of these years. Maybe you will only experience happiness and not all of the…drama as you kids say."

He leaned toward me, and it looked like he was going to confess something to me. I leaned forward too, completely caught up in everything he had to say.

"I married Sam when she was only nineteen, but I fell in love with her when she was only fifteen. She was your age, Donya, and I was a little bit older than Emmet. Things were different back then. Kids were raised differently. Society as a whole was different. If I were raising you girls in those times, you would be free to date—under my watchful eye, of course. Things were different, and it was a long time ago, but it doesn't mean that you can't experience what Sam and I experienced. Maybe this guy is your forever, Donya, and maybe he came at an unexpected time, but maybe you shouldn't be so quick to push him away."

He got to his feet, as his line had a bite. He looked back at me and said all parental-like "But I'm not condoning a serious relationship."

"But…how will I know what the right thing is?" I called after him.

"When you're doing it," he called back to me.

I sat back in my seat and considered my options.

Chapter Ten

Lucy's wedding was the third weekend of July. Emmet was due to arrive three days before the event, but five days away from the wedding night, I woke up in the middle of the night because I felt the band between us retracting. I sat there in the dark in disbelief for a few minutes. I could have just been imagining it. The whole idea that there was an invisible tether between us sometimes seemed ridiculous in my head anyway. Maybe I dreamed of Emmet and that's why I was feeling that way.

I got out of bed. My mouth was dry, and it was a hot and sticky night. I needed some water and maybe a slice of the lemon cake Sam had made earlier. When I stepped into the hallway, I stopped and listened. I thought I heard some movement, but then it could have been coming from behind any one of the closed doors. All but one of Emmy's siblings was in the house, plus spouses and children, and a few other relatives and friends. I shrugged it off and quietly made my way down the stairs.

In the kitchen, I poured myself a cup of iced tea instead of water and started to slice myself a piece of cake. The feeling that Emmet was near did not subside, but it grew more intense. I rubbed my chest with one hand, trying to figure out what was wrong with me. He obviously wasn't there. I was one of the last ones to go to bed, and he had not been there and whenever he was mentioned no one said, "Hey, Emmet is coming tonight."

"I'll just eat my cake and go to bed," I whispered harshly to myself. "I'm imagining things."

When a hand closed over my shoulder, I spun around with the butter knife poised to…well…butter…and with a scream in my throat, but a hand clamped over my mouth to muffle the scream. It took me a few seconds to understand what I was seeing, but then my eyes narrowed on the form of the quietly laughing man in front of me.

"I couldn't resist," Emmet whispered as he quietly laughed. "You walked right past me in the living room and then you were in here talking to yourself."

I pushed his hand off my mouth. "I could have stabbed you to death!"

He looked at the butter knife in my hand. "With that?" He looked at it with amusement.

"Shut up," I said and quickly lowered the knife. "What are you doing here? I didn't see you on the couch. Why were you sitting on the couch in the dark?"

"I decided to come down a little early," he said, reaching behind me for my slice of cake. "I thought mom would appreciate that." He pinched off a piece of cake between his fingers and offered it to me. Not in my hand. He put it at my lips.

I opened and allowed him to gently push the cake into my mouth. It was like the ice-cream all over again. He took the next bite.

"I was sitting on the couch because I was exhausted and I just wanted to stretch out for a little while before I came in here to look for food."

He offered me another piece of cake, and I accepted. I felt relief I hadn't felt in weeks with him standing so close to me. That invisible line between us wasn't fooling with me. He really was there. I would never doubt the tether again.

I had considered Fred's words hard. I felt better after talking to him, but I had come to no definitive conclusions. I had no idea what to do with my feelings for Emmet. I felt like my indecision was further proof that I shouldn't get involved with him. Besides, I didn't know if in my absence he had picked up another girlfriend or not. My pondering could have been for nothing.

"Do you want me to heat up some leftovers for you?" I asked him after another bite of cake.

He smiled. It made me sigh inside. "Please and thank you."

I moved away from him and went to the refrigerator. I started pulling out the leftover fried chicken, fried okra, smashed potatoes and corn on the cob.

"I heard about your modeling opportunity," he said as I worked.

"Oh," I laughed lightly. "Yeah. Turns out Max was the real deal and not some pervert picking up teenage girls on the boardwalk."

"You think you'll do it?"

"I don't know," I said glancing at him as I put the plate loaded with food into the microwave. "I'm still not sure that I'm modeling material."

"I think you're modeling material," he said sincerely.

"Thanks," I said as I pulled open the fridge to put the food back inside. "Your parents set me up with a photographer. We'll see how the photos turn out. How's Jersey? Are you having fun without your parents around?"

"It's okay. I had a couple of parties. The cops weren't as nice the second time as they were the first time."

I looked at him. "Emmet!" I laughed. "Better hope Sam doesn't find out."

"I just hope she won't notice that I had her antique couch professionally cleaned after someone puked all over it. That would be far worse than knowing the cops showed up and took our kegs."

"Someone threw up on the antique couch?" I had to try not to shout as I stared at him with wide eyes.

We couldn't even look at the couch sideways without Sam going on about how we'd better not get anything on it.

Grinning ear to ear, Emmet nodded and offered me the final bite of cake. I took it. His grin faded some as he used his thumb to wipe a crumb off of the corner of my mouth.

"You owe me another slice of cake," I said as I turned to the microwave.

"We'll share another slice when I'm done eating," he said.

I bit back a smile and told him to sit.

He complied just before I put the hot plate on the table. I got him some silverware and poured him a glass of iced tea. I took my drink and sat down near him. I loved that the tension that had been between us weeks before was gone. I was glad to be near him again.

"Tell me what you've been up to," he said and began to eat.

I talked to him about the usual things I did during my Louisiana summers. I told him about swimming in the lake, fishing with Fred, napping in the hammock and playing football with whatever kids showed up for the day. I told him about the time the bathroom doorknob broke, and I was locked in the bathroom and about my failed attempt at baking bread with his mom. By the time I ran out of stuff to talk about, he had been long finished with his plate and had cut a huge slice of cake.

"Sounds like you're having a good summer," he said, offering me a piece of the cake.

I opened my mouth and let him feed me. I chewed slowly and thoughtfully as I looked at him.

"I'm not," I said after I swallowed.

"You're not what?" he asked, confused.

"I'm not having a good summer."

He looked at me with concern. "Why not? What's wrong?"

"You're not here," I said softly.

He looked at me for a silent moment and then looked away. "You wanted me to stay away. So, I did."

"I was wrong."

His eyes met mine. He looked hopeful. He also looked doubtful. He fed me cake.

The silence that hung between us made it difficult to breathe. We didn't speak. We shared the cake until the slice was gone. When the plate was empty between us and he still hadn't spoken, I put my hand on the table and stretched my fingers to touch his. I just barely stopped myself from gasping when he withdrew his hand a few inches to escape my touch. I snatched my hand away, picked up the empty plate and took it to the sink.

I quickly washed the dishes we had used with trembling hands. I felt so disappointed, angry at myself, humiliated, and sad. I couldn't even blame Emmet for not wanting to be bothered with me.

I blinked back tears as I washed the last dish. I turned the water off, dried my hands on a dishtowel and moved away from the sink.

"Goodnight," I managed to say to Emmet as I made a wide berth around him. "I'm glad you got here safely."

"Thank you," he said, watching me.

I left him sitting at the kitchen table and hurried to my room where I could cry alone in the dark. I hated that I was crying at all. I hated that Emmet had the power to make me cry. I kind of hated Emmet for having that power over me.

I wiped at my stupid tears and lay in bed staring at the ceiling fan. It was fairly dark in my room, but I could hear the hum of the fan above me. I wondered if I should talk to Emmy about Emmet. She had no clue that there had been anything between us. I hid it well. Emmet hid it well.

I wasn't sure why I had not told her when we told each other everything. I knew about every boy she kissed and how far she went with them in great detail. She told me about the hidden bottle of tequila in her closet and the bag of weed at the back of her underwear drawer. She shared her thoughts and feelings with me on everything from her mother to her cousins and even told me her biggest insecurities. She trusted me implicitly, yet I withheld much from her. Emmy should have been the first person I told after Emmet kissed me, and really, it would have been good to have someone to talk to after he had insulted me on the boardwalk. I didn't tell her that I felt brokenhearted when I created my Valentine's Day painting. I had shrugged as if I hadn't had a clue when she asked me where my inspiration had come from.

Emmy didn't have a big mouth. I didn't for a second believe that she would blab about Emmet and me to anyone, but I guess I didn't want to be hassled about the fact that I experienced all of those things with Emmet. He's her brother, and he was supposed to be like a brother to me. I didn't want to hear her disgusted remarks, her jokes, or her objections. The whole situation already felt weird, and I really thought that with Emmy involved, it would feel extra weird, but I was beginning to reconsider it. I felt like I was going to vomit out my heart, because I sure as hell wasn't going to need it anymore. I couldn't possibly deal with the pain on my own.

"Exactly why teenagers don't need to be in love," I whispered harshly to the darkness, angry at my melodramatics.

I felt warm air rush into my bedroom as the door was quietly pushed open.

"Emmy, it's like, three in the morning," I said quietly. I didn't even look at her. It was just as well that she was coming in for a late night visit. Maybe it was time for me to tell her what had really been going on in my life.

My chest fluttered as it did when Emmet was near. Maybe he was just going to bed, and that's why I felt him nearby. Then again, he had fooled me in the kitchen, but he had made it pretty clear how he felt. It may as well had been spelled out in cake crumbs on the table.

Emmy's footsteps were a little on the heavy side as she walked across the room…

I slapped my forehead. I should have really trusted my instincts.

"Take your sneakers off before everyone in the house knows you're in here," I snapped as much as one can snap in whisper mode.

There was a long pause and then some soft noises as Emmet, not Emmy, took his sneakers off. I heard the shoes gently touch the floor as he put them down and then a moment later he was climbing into my bed. I looked over at him, just barely making out his face in the dark.

"I don't even know why you're in here," I said with irritation. I was suddenly angry with him. I wanted to shove him out of the bed and beat him with his own shoes.

"You're hurt," he said with a sigh. He slid an arm across my waist.

"A little bit," I answered stiffly and pushed his arm off of me.

"If anyone should be hurt and angry, it's me," Emmet said sourly. "You aren't the one who has been repeatedly rejected."

"I tried to make up for it!"

He put a hand over my mouth. "Keep it down," he snapped. "And for the record, you can't think that telling me your summer sucks without me makes up for anything. What does that mean anyway? Like, do I amuse you? Am I a fun summertime toy that you just drop when autumn comes?"

I shoved him hard. "It means that my life isn't the same without you in it."

"My life isn't the same without a variety of people in it. That doesn't mean anything except that maybe you have a hard time dealing with change. It doesn't necessarily have anything to do with me."

I held my fists to my eyes, clenched my jaw, and kicked my feet in the quietest temper tantrum I had ever thrown. I was so angry and confused. I was going to punch him square in the face if I didn't calm down.

Stupid teenage hormones.

"Why are you in here, Emmet? If you think I'm so shallow, why are you in my bed? Get out if that's how you really feel."

"I want you to tell me how you really feel, Donya."

"I've told you before," I argued.

"Not really," he said flatly.

I had to think back to all of our conversations. I'd expressed my anger, my disappointment, and told him when I was hurt, but I had never outright told Emmet how I felt about him. I had alluded to it and maybe it even translated in my kisses, but was that enough? Actions only speak louder than words when the words have already been spoken.

I deflated in my bed. My back lost its rigidness and my tensed muscles melted. My anger sunk away, too. Emmet needed to hear it, or he wouldn't believe it. I had not said nearly enough to convince him of my feelings. I had said more to his father than him about how I felt about him. I took a deep breath and let it out slowly before rolling onto my side to face him.

"I love you," I said so softly, I was barely able to hear it even in my own ears. "It scares me. A lot. I don't know how to handle the range of emotions I feel for you, and I still think I'm too young, but I want to figure it out. Not by myself, but with you."

I put my hand over his heart and whispered, "We're connected. Don't you feel it?"

He gently placed his hand on my chest. "I've always felt it," he whispered back.

We stayed there like that for a long time. I felt his racing heart beneath my hand, and he felt my racing heart beneath his hand. My chest felt hot where his hand was. Heat spread lazily from that point and up my neck and throughout my head and down my spine. I welcomed the heat and wanted more. I began to move closer to him to receive his body heat even though the night was warm and humid.

"Say it again," he said. His hand slid across my chest, over my shoulder, and down to the small of my back.

"Say what again?" I asked as I moved my hand to his hair.

"The sentence that began with 'I' and ended with 'you,'" he said and gently pulled me closer.

"I love you," I said again.

"Once more." His lips were so close to mine. I tried to kiss him, but he pulled back. "Say it."

"Why don't you say it?" I pouted.

"I love you. Now say it."

"Can you say it with a little less rushing? Like you weren't just trying to appease me?"

"I love you," he said in a tone that made my nearly sixteen-year-old toes curl entirely too much.

"I love you," I said in a tone that wasn't nearly as sexy but was effective enough because he leaned in and kissed me hard.

I moaned softly as he nipped at my tongue and then sucked it gently to soothe it. I tugged at his hair and squirmed against his body as his hand moved off of my back and down to my ass. He gave it a firm squeeze and moaned into my mouth with approval. He was hard against my thigh, and it made me nervous, but I couldn't stop kissing him. Part of me wanted to be under him as I had been in his bedroom that one morning when I almost reached a level of pleasure I had never even imagined. I moved closer to him and swung my leg over him.

Suddenly Emmet pulled away. I looked at him with some concern, but I was ready to get back to what we were doing. I pulled on the back of his head, trying to bring his lips back to mine even though I was breathless.

"What is it?" I asked in exasperation.

"We have to stop," he said, sounding defeated.

"No, we don't," I said and tried to kiss him again.

He chuckled as he gently pushed me back. "Yes, sweetie, we do. You said yourself you're not sure if you'll be able to stop yourself. I know I won't be able to stop myself if we keep going right now."

I growled and rolled over onto my back. Emmet laughed again and kissed my nose.

"How about we just sleep?" he suggested.

"We can't do that without getting caught this time," I said. "You drove here. Whoever gets up first will see your car and go looking for you."

He sighed. "So, this is goodnight?"

"Yes," I said unhappily.

"I'll make it up to you tomorrow," he said and nuzzled my cheek. "I'll kiss you all day tomorrow."

"How are you supposed to accomplish that?" I asked sarcastically. "Make out over your mom's pancakes?"

He shrugged. "Works for me."

I slapped his shoulder.

"How do you think they'll all react when they see us together?" Emmet asked me.

I looked at him with confusion. "We're not telling them. They won't see us together."

He looked at me with a small smile, but it dropped away when he realized I was serious.

"You don't want to tell anyone we're together?" he asked incredulously.

"No," I said with just as much incredulousness. "We have to keep this on the DL."

"Why?" I could see and feel that he was starting to get perturbed.

"First of all, your parents and my mom don't think I should have any serious boyfriends at fifteen."

"Almost sixteen," he amended.

"Whatever. It's all the same. You know that."

"I think they'll overlook that since it's me."

"Well, I don't want them to know it's you," I said and then rushed to finish before he got the wrong idea. "This is still new to us—super new—like an hour new. I don't want to share us with your family, or anyone just yet. Everyone is going to have something to say, and I don't want to hear it. I don't want anyone to screw us up before we even really get started."

I could tell by Emmet's heavy sigh that he reluctantly agreed with what I said.

"So, are we just supposed to sneak around like we're doing something wrong?" he asked.

"It isn't forever, Emmet," I said as soothingly as I could. "Even if no one says anything bad, you know your mom and your older sisters will put a lot of pressure on us. I don't want our relationship under everyone else's watchful eye, with their butting in and unwanted comments."

"Okay," he said with a sigh. "You're right, but how long are we supposed to keep our relationship hidden?"

"I don't know," I said honestly. "Depends on a lot of things."

"Okay," he said again.

"Are you still going back to Jersey after the wedding?" I asked.

"Only if you're coming back with me," he said firmly.

"Yeah, that would be all kinds of trouble," I laughed and gave him a quick kiss. "You better get out of here."

Emmet kissed me tenderly until it started to get a little wild. Then he pried himself off of me and hurried from the room before our teenage hormonal lust got the best of us.

Chapter Eleven

If anyone was asleep or dead, Sam woke them up with her shrieks of joy fairly early in the morning when she realized her baby boy had arrived early. Soon other voices joined her in the hallway, half of them asking her to shut up. I rolled onto my side and covered my head with a pillow and then inhaled deeply. It was the pillow Emmet had lain on, and it smelled just like him. I smiled and kicked my feet excitedly. I had a boyfriend! And it was Emmet!

After the excitement had died down in the hallway, my door opened and slammed shut. I peeked out from under my pillow at Emmy's disgruntled face. She got into my bed, forcing me to move over to make room for her.

"Didn't you hear all of that damn noise?" she grumbled. "It's only Emmet. She acts like the fucking Pope paid us a visit."

I giggled and draped an arm over my best friend. "She's excited to have her baby boy home."

"She never gets excited like that for me. Like ever."

I sighed and let my smile slip away. I felt bad for Em. She took a lot of crap from Sam. My second mother loved her family and took very good care of everyone, but she was also hard on everyone and brutally honest. Unfortunately, it seemed like she picked on Emmy a little more than anyone else. Maybe it was because Emmy fought so hard against her while the rest of the kids seemed to do whatever it was Sam wanted, or…maybe they were a little too much alike…

Emmy closed her eyes, and I followed suit. We managed to sleep for another hour before the smell of bacon and pancakes had us slowly stretching and working towards getting out of bed. I wondered if I should tell her about Emmet. How long was I going to carry on a secret relationship with her brother before I told her what was going on?

It's only for a little while, I thought. The idea of anyone dissuading me from being with Emmet made my chest burn with worry. I just needed a little bit of time alone with him before anyone else nudged their noses in to our business.

I looked at Emmy and felt guilty. She wasn't like her sisters and mother. She wouldn't express outrage or tell me not to do it, but I wasn't sure how she would feel about me dating her brother who was supposed to be very much my own brother.

We went downstairs together and joined everyone for breakfast at the huge dining room table. Lucky for me, there was a seat open between Emmet and Charlotte. Emmy was irritated with Emmet for showing up early and getting Sam excited enough to wake the entire household, so she sat away from him and away from her mom.

"Didja say hello to your brother," Sam asked, looking from me to Emmy.

"Hi, Fred," Emmy said crisply to her older brother without looking at Emmet.

Sam frowned. She looked like she was about to start in on Emmy and Emmy didn't seem to be in the mood for any crap. A big fight would erupt in the middle of breakfast if someone didn't intervene. The fights weren't unusual between the mother and daughter, but they sure were annoying.

"Hi, Emmet," I said to Emmet. I had felt his body heat the moment I had sat down.

"Hey," he said casually, but I could see the desire in his eyes for a split second before he looked away.

Breakfast was noisy. Everyone tried to talk at the same time. Several conversations were going on at once around the table. It was chaos, but it was the normal chaos that was part of the Grayne family. It was warming to have everyone together, talking, debating, arguing, laughing, and eating and drinking.

Under the table, fingers trailed over my knee. I casually dropped my hand into my lap and even as I spoke across the table to Freddy's wife Yasmine, I hooked my fingers with Emmet's. He squeezed my hand softly and stroked the back of my hand with his thumb. Goosebumps rose up and down my arm. I had to tone down my sunshiny smile that was probably blinding half of the table. I wasn't a miserable kid, but I wasn't All Smiles All of the Time either. Emmy, Fred, and maybe even Sam would pick up on my unusually high mood quicker than a police dog could sniff out drugs. I didn't have an excuse readily available, so I forced my smile away and continued to hold Emmet's hand under the table.

After breakfast, everyone scattered in various directions. Everyone seemed to have an agenda except for me. I decided to go upstairs and lounge in bed with a few *Vogue* magazines. When I got upstairs, I found Emmet standing in the hallway with his arms crossed, leaning against the wall. He looked so good, with his muscular arms, sparkling green eyes and bed hair.

"Are you waiting for someone?" I asked softly so no one else could hear.

"Not anymore," he answered.

His kiss was hard and hungry as he put his hands on my hips and guided me to the wall he had just been leaning on. He pinned me there with his body as he kissed me. His hands were in my hair, and my hands were in his. We were all arms and fingers and mouths.

Kissing Emmet was exhilarating. My brain kind of floated away and thoughts about anything else but the moment we were in vanished. My skin was ultra-sensitive to his touch. His hands drifted slowly down my sides and then slipped under the hem of my shirt. I was nervous about where his hands would go next, but I wasn't nervous enough to stop kissing him.

His hands were hot on my skin. His thumbs stroked the soft flesh of my belly, sending tingling sensations to places that made me feel light-headed, made my heart race, and my body temperature rise. Did he have any idea what he was doing to me? I knew what I was doing to him. The evidence was rock solid against my lower belly.

That would have scared the crap out of me months ago, not excited me. I suddenly felt raw with need. I remembered how he felt on top of me that day in his room, and I wanted to repeat it, and finish it.

I pushed against him and let his mouth swallow my soft moan. He pushed back against me but then moved his body away from mine so that he was no longer poking me with the proof of his excitement. I protested with a mew and tried to move against him again, but he held me against the wall with his hands and pulled away from my lips.

"Don't tease me like that," he warned in a whisper.

"Who said I was teasing?" I pushed against his hands and peered up at him.

He groaned lightly and then shook his head. "I don't want you to go too fast. I don't want to screw this up."

My horny haze lifted and I felt the blood rush to my cheeks. Wasn't I always preaching to Emmet about being too young for so many things? Yet, there I was, trying to grind against him in the hallway with members of our family only steps away.

"Ugh," I said and dropped my head to his chest. "You're right. I don't know what's wrong with me."

"I'm hot, and I turn you on."

I slapped his arm as his body shook with laughter.

"Is it always going to be like this?" I asked. "Because I may succeed in grossing myself out. There has to be more to us than making out."

"Of course there is more to us," he said with a gentle smile. He put his hand on my heart and lifted my hand to his. "We're connected. Remember?"

My heart melted. I smiled and nodded. "Yes."

His other hand cupped my face. He made no move to kiss me, and I was more than okay with that. Staring into Emmet's eyes with our hands on each other's hearts made me feel more exhilarated than any kiss.

The door to the bathroom began to open. Emmet backed away from me and threw me a quick smile as he headed towards his room and I stepped across the hall to mine. Emmy came out of the bathroom wrapped in a towel, steam billowing out behind her.

"What are you doing just standing there?" she asked me.

"I can stand here if I want to," I shot back and then went into my room.

~~*

Emmy and I swung lazily in a hammock later that afternoon, reading magazines and talking about boys. Well, mostly Emmy talked about boys. I listened and commented. There was only one boy for me, and I wasn't ready to talk about him.

"Is there anyone back home you like?" she asked me.

"No," I answered honestly. I wasn't lying. Emmet was nearby.

"Are you a lesbian?" She looked at me with a serious expression. "If you are, it's okay. I don't want you to munch my rug or anything, but I'll love you anyway."

I raised an eyebrow. "No. Why would you ask me that?"

"Because you're weird," she shrugged.

"So...lesbians are weird?"

"That's not what I meant!" She bristled, and I laughed. "You don't talk about any guys, and you only ever go out with a guy if I make you go out on a double date. Since you almost kissed Jorge last year, I haven't seen you try to kiss anyone else. You're so...good. Like, you don't care about boys the way the rest of the girls our age do."

I tried to hide my guilt with a smile. I wasn't that good. I attempted to jump her brother only a couple of hours ago. I wanted to tell her about Emmet. I wanted to tell her I wasn't so good and that I had indeed kissed another boy since Jorge— two if I included Andrew Newland.

"I wish I were like you," Emmy said quietly before I could decide whether or not to tell her about her brother.

I looked at her with some amusement and a lot of confusion. "Why would you want to be like me?"

"You're comfortable in your own skin," she murmured and looked up at the canopy the two trees holding our resting place made together. "You're not a horny teenager. You don't do drugs. You don't drink."

"I'm just as horny as any other teenager," I argued. "And I smoked with you once or twice and hello! I was just as drunk as you at Jorge's party last year!"

"D," Emmy said my abbreviated name with exasperation. She looked at me carefully. "You may be a horny teenager, but you have that shit in check. You're not like me, sneaking out to make out with the boy of the hour. You have everything in check. Nothing rules you. You rule yourself. You don't have weed hidden in your underwear drawer and tequila hidden in your closet. I'm all kinds of fucked up, Donya. You ground me. You had a rough life with your parents, and I had everything, but you're the one with her head screwed on straight."

"Girl, you'll be alright," I nudged her with my shoulder. "And my head isn't screwed on as straight as you think."

"Whatever," she said, unconvinced.

I needed to tell her about Emmet. She had the wrong idea about me. Yeah, I wasn't into the drugs and drinking and screwing around like she was, but I wasn't entirely innocent. It wasn't fair that she shared her whole life with me, and I couldn't share this one thing.

"Emmy, I have a confession," I said quietly.

"You are a lesbian?" she asked, her eyes wide.

"No," I sighed, shaking my head. "What's with you thinking I'm a lesbian?"

She shrugged and then a mischievous smile appeared on her face. "Bethanne Wendzel is a lesbian. I know she's a year older than us, but she's kinda hot."

I rolled my eyes and laughed. "So, you want to set me up with another lesbian?"

"Another hot lesbian, bay-bay," she said rubbing her shoulder with mine.

I laughed again. Emmy always made me laugh, even when we were little kids, and I was struggling at home, she would make me laugh. I loved her for it.

"Well, I'm sorry to disappoint you, Em, but I'm not a lesbian. Bethanne will have to find some other hot girl."

"She is hot, though," Emmy said and looked at me for a response.

"Yes, she is hot," I admitted of the blonde bombshell.

"Emmet totally nailed her. Male slut," she said with disdain.

I gave her a look. "You just said that the girl is a lesbian. Why would a lesbian screw your brother?"

"Okay, so maybe she's bi, but I know she likes girls, too."

Just like that my laughter was sucked into the humid Louisiana air.

"You seem to know an awful lot about Emmet's sex life," I said as lightly as I could manage.

"Not on purpose," she said, making a disgusted sound. "Ew. I called Mayson last night, remember?"

I nodded and waited for her to continue.

"She told me that Emmet had a couple of parties over the summer. Of course, he would have the parties when we can't get to them," she complained. "May said that Emmet and Bethanne were slurping all over each other, but then they disappeared.

Mayson overheard a couple of Emmet's friends talking about Emmet hitting it—Bethanne's 'it'."

I waited a moment before speaking. I wanted to be sure that my voice wasn't trembling.

"So, there is no absolute proof…" I said carefully.

"Donya, where have you been?" Emmy looked at me like she didn't know who I was. "If you paid any attention, you would know that Emmet can't keep it in his pants. Bethanne, Stella, Sheila, Jane—they're all a few names on a pretty long list of hoe thangs."

I fought against the urge to close my eyes in disbelief. I looked at my hands and realized I was rolling up the magazine into a tight cylinder that could be used to maybe beat Bethanne, Stella, Sheila, Jane and of course, Emmet.

I let the magazine fall into my lap and forced a small laugh.

"How do you know these things?"

"I'm in the know," Emmy said proudly.

"Are you sure you're just not in the rumor mill?" I offered.

"I am positive that these aren't just rumors, D."

I searched wildly for a ray of hope.

"Well, at least they weren't all in one summer," I said.

"The summer is only half over, baby cakes," my friend pointed out. "Bethanne was only last week. I know he did Stella again before she took off for California, and that was just before we left to come down here. See? Male slut." She shook her head. "I'm ashamed to be his sister sometimes. Then again, I'm no prize either I guess." She frowned for a moment before looking at me earnestly. "Thank god he looks at you like a sister, or he'd probably try to screw you, too." She made a disgusted face and then made the international Gag Me sign. "Gross. So glad you're not one of those girls that go for the best friend's brothers. Then again, you're not like other girls. I love you for it."

She kissed my cheek and beamed at me. I reached deep, deep down and found a smile for her.

"I'm starving. I'm going to make a sandwich," she said, carefully rolling off of the hammock. "Want one?"

"No, thanks," I said with my plastered smile. "I think I'll go for a walk in a few."

"Yeah, I'm not walking in this heat. Have fun with that, sister."

She grabbed her magazine, threw me one last carefree smile and headed off to the house, her ponytail bouncing perkily as she went.

My fake smile fell away. While I was alone and there was no one to witness it, I let my real feelings come through for a few moments.

I knew Emmet had been with a few girls, but I didn't know that it had been so many and so recently. Even though we weren't together and I had pushed him away, I felt rather betrayed that he had slept with Stella again. I had no idea when he had slept with most of the other girls.

Why couldn't he seriously just keep his dick in his pants? If he loved me as much as he said he did, why was he sleeping with half of the female population of our school?

Even if I could get past his sexual adventures, things wouldn't be easy for us. I had been right about keeping our relationship from the family. Emmy had made it abundantly clear how she felt about her brother being in a relationship with her best friend. My hopes that she would eventually come around fizzled out when I heard the contempt in her voice for such an idea.

I got out of the hammock and put on my shoes. Emmet and Fred had gone out after breakfast, but they would be back anytime. I didn't want to look at him and imagine his face attached to the faces of those other girls. I didn't even want to look at Emmy at that moment.

As I began to walk down the long dirt driveway, Fred's truck turned onto it off of the main road. I thought about going off of the road and cutting through the woods to avoid them, but it was already too late. The truck came to a stop beside me.

Emmet smiled at me, but I didn't return it.

"Where you off to, Kiddo?" Fred asked.

"I'm just going for a walk," I said, trying to sound casual.

"You okay?" he asked. Fred always knew when something was bothering me. I was thankful for it, but it was unwelcome at that moment.

"I'm good," I lied. "I'll be better after a walk."

"Don't go too far," he warned.

"You're going to let her go?" Emmet asked his dad incredulously.

Fred looked at Emmet as if he had sprouted another head. "Emmet, she'll be fine."

"She's a young...pretty girl...walking alone," Emmet stammered.

"And she's a young, pretty girl that's walked through this town more times than she can probably count." Fred looked at me and smiled. "Have a safe walk, Kiddo. Don't stay out too long."

"Thanks, Fred."

I gave Emmet a short look, and he gazed at me with his eyes full of questions. I again wondered if he could feel my emotions like I could feel his.

"I'll walk with you," he said, pushing open his door, but his father put his hand on his son's shoulder.

"Son, it is obvious that she wants to be alone for a little while," he said quietly.

Emmet looked like he wanted to argue, but he sighed and shut the door, not wishing to cause a scene in front of his dad.

"See ya later, Kiddo," Fred said and stepped on the gas.

The truck continued down the driveway with Emmet's head hanging out of the window, watching me.

The tether stretched. It pulled. It twisted. It hurt.

I took a few more steps toward the main road and then halted.

I was doing it again. I was running away from Emmet instead of talking to him. I did it after he first kissed me. I did it when I found about Stella and tried again after I found the condom in his car. I ran again on the boardwalk after I slapped him in the face and once more a couple of days before my departure from New Jersey.

Emmet was the only person I figuratively and physically ran from. The emotions he made me feel were overwhelming, and they were no less overwhelming when I had to face them head on. The discomfort I felt whenever we had a serious discussion was crushing, but as I stood there on the side of the road, I realized that I couldn't keep running away from him when I was angry or hurt. My mother turned inward instead of dealing with her emotions. My father turned to drugs and distanced himself from us rather than face my mom and me. I didn't want to be like either one of them in that regard. I knew there would be times in my life when I would have to walk away from a fight or avoid adverse situations, but this wasn't one of those times.

I turned around and went back to the house. Emmet was outside, sitting on the porch, but my attention was drawn to Samantha and Fred walking hand in hand to the deck by the lake. As I neared the house, my eyes stayed on them for some time. They had been married for thirty-one years, and though it was a fact that Sam drove Fred crazy, they were still very much in love. Fred adored Sam and Sam still looked at Fred as the young, charming marine that she fell in love with when she was apparently only a little younger than me.

I didn't think Emmy and her siblings really appreciated the love that was between their parents. They had no idea how lucky they were as a whole to witness true love. I wanted that someday. I wanted to marry a guy that I would be with forever and not have any regrets.

I turned away from the happy couple and looked at Emmet. I didn't know where Emmy was, and I didn't want to alert her. I silently gestured for Emmet to follow me and walked away.

I didn't turn around to see if he would follow. I felt his hesitation, but a moment later, I sensed him following me around the house in the opposite direction of the lake. In silence, we walked towards the line of trees at the front of the house. There were several acres of woods there, but years of kids venturing into it have cut out easy to navigate paths, though they weren't as well used as they used to be. I waited until we were well beyond the sight of anyone that may be looking from the house before reaching out for Emmet's hand. His fingers closed over mine without hesitation.

We were in the trees and out of sight before I broke the silence.

"Did you sleep with Bethanne?" I asked him as we continued to walk.

"Shit," was his reply. He stopped walking and stared at me anxiously as he pushed his hand through his hair. "I'm sorry, baby," he whispered.

I looked down at the ground with a sigh and released his hand. I crossed my arms over my chest as if to protect myself.

"I know this is probably the wrong thing to say," Emmet said softly. "But you and I weren't together. I would never cheat on you. I know you're angry nonetheless."

"A little bit," I admitted. "And a little jealous. A little worried."

"You don't have anything to be jealous of."

I looked up into his eyes. "You did sleep with her, didn't you?"

He looked away from me. "I did."

"Then don't tell me I don't have anything to be jealous of," I said softly. "She's been with you like that, and I haven't."

"But you said yourself you aren't ready for that, and I don't think you're ready either."

"I know," I agreed, looking down at the ground again. "But I'm still jealous. Other girls know you in ways I don't yet."

"No," Emmet said the word firmly and moved closer to me. "Donya, look at me." He put his fingers under my chin and lifted my head. "Whatever I had with any of those other girls will never be able to touch what I know I will have with you. I didn't love any of those girls. Okay?"

I nodded, unable to speak as I looked into his green eyes. His thumb gently moved over my lips and then he dropped his hand from my face.

We resumed walking, carrying silence between us for a few minutes.

"Why are you worried?" he finally asked.

"How many girls have you been with?" I asked instead of immediately answering his question.

"Does it matter?"

"It matters to me."

He sighed and glanced down at me. "Not as many as you think."

"How many?" I insisted.

"Three," he said hesitantly.

"The rumor is that you've been with more."

"Are you going to believe the rumors, or are you going to believe me?" he asked with irritation.

I was quiet for a moment. Emmy was sure that Emmet had been with more girls, but then how could she know for sure unless she asked him directly or witnessed him in the act?

"Is that all forms of sex?" I asked reluctantly.

"Yes," he said impatiently. "Why do you want to know?"

"Did you like it?" I asked, again avoiding another question.

"It's sex. Yes, I liked it," he snapped. "I don't want to talk about other girls when I'm with you."

I was quiet again. I had never felt insecure like girls my age tended to do. Despite my hardships with my parents, I didn't think any less of myself. I was self-confident without being conceited. I didn't obsess over my body. I didn't struggle to fit in anywhere. I didn't care too much what people thought about me, and I didn't kiss anyone's ass. I did well in school, and I was satisfied with my life in spite of my mom and dad, butt with Emmet, I was second guessing myself.

"What if I'm not ready for a long time?" I quietly inquired. "You're going to be in college with beautiful girls your age that are ready."

We stopped walking again. Emmet wrapped both of his arms around my waist.

"Donya, is that what you're worried about? You're worried that I am going to lose interest in you? That I'm going to become impatient and go somewhere else?"

"Yes," I whispered.

"I love you," he said seriously. "I promise you I will never betray you. I promise you that I will wait for you, patiently, for as long as you need me to wait." He cupped one side of my face. "I don't want you to worry. You have me, okay? No one else."

"Okay," I said, managing a smile.

I met him halfway, my lips burning to connect with his. We kissed slowly and softly until parts of my body began to tingle. I pulled away from him then. He smiled knowingly at me but didn't push. He took my hand into his, and we walked back the way we had come. Just before we reached the clearing, he gave me one last quick kiss and then we stepped onto the lawn with several feet of our invisible tether between us.

Chapter Twelve

Lucy's wedding and reception took place outside on the expansive property that the big house sat on, right in front of the lake. The yard was transformed, with small lanterns and soft white lights strung overhead for the reception. There were even candles floating in the lake. A dance floor had been erected and there was an endless amount of food. Lucy and her husband Eric must have invited no less than three hundred and fifty people. It was very easy for a teenage girl to slip away with her secret boyfriend during the celebration.

Emmet led me into his bedroom, which was risky, but we had been trying to find some alone time for days. He closed and locked the door and led me to his bed where he put a firm and possessive hand on the back of my neck.

"I hate the way that guy is following you around," he said of the son of one of the wedding guests.

Taylor was the son of one of the people that worked for the Grayne's, and he was a couple of years older than me. I met him a few summers back, but it was the first summer that he realized I was an actual girl with boobs—finally—and all of the other primary female parts. He actually was following me around, but he was interesting enough for me not to be annoyed.

"Don't worry about him," I said to Emmet. "I'm all yours."

He kissed me, hard and greedily. I grabbed onto his shirt and allowed him to dominate me with his powerful kiss. He continued to hold me by my neck, but his other hand wandered up and down my bare leg. His fingers brushed under the hem of my skirt with each pass, reaching farther up my leg each time until his hand was completely under my dress on my upper thigh. It was hot on my skin and sent tingly waves across my flesh. He took his hand off of my neck and gently pushed me back on the bed, never taking his mouth off of mine or his hand off of my thigh. He stretched out over me, leaning to one side so not to crush me under his weight.

Emmet's fingers moved in slow circles over my thigh. When the tips of his fingers brushed over my panty line, I gasped against his lips. He continued the slow circles, moving away from my panties, but only for a short time before making his way back again. Next time his fingers stretched a little farther, but still missed the mark that my body had become desperate for him to hit. He circled outward again but returned quickly. When his fingers finally trailed over my virginal sex, I moaned into his mouth and tugged on his hair.

Boldly, he put his thumb flat against the swollen nub and pressed. I writhed beneath his touch and moaned wildly in his mouth as his thumb began to circle. It felt even better than that morning in his bed. I was so much closer this time than I was then. Only a few more seconds and I would—

Emmet pulled away from me. Entirely. Lips. Hands. Body.

He sat up, breathing heavily and looking at me as if I had somehow just offended him.

"What?" I asked, pushing myself up on my elbows.

He sighed and closed his eyes for a moment. When he opened them, he carefully pulled my dress back down over my thighs and offered me his hand. Confused, I took it and he pulled me into a sitting position, but he stood up the moment I was up. He took a few steps away from me, running his hands through his hair.

I realized then that Emmet had been on the verge of losing control, and I *had* been out of control. I knew I wasn't ready for sex, but my body had been so receptive to his touch. Was it like that for everyone else? I wished that I could have asked Emmy without bringing suspicion upon myself. She had been to third base more times than some baseball players.

I snickered out loud at my joke. Emmet looked at me with one eyebrow raised.

"Nothing," I said waving it off.

I got to my feet only to realize my knees were too weak to hold me. I started to fall forward, but Emmet was there, with his arm around my waist, holding me up. I held onto his arms and looked up into his face with a stupid smile.

"You literally made me weak in the knees."

He smiled down at me and placed a soft kiss on my lips.

I regained my footing after a few more seconds.

"There isn't any rule against us dancing together," Emmet said with his hand on the doorknob.

I grinned. "No, there isn't."

"Miss Stewart, will you honor me with a dance?" he asked eloquently, bowing deep.

"Why, Mr. Grayne, the honor is all mine," I answered primly with a curtsey.

I kissed him once more, and after we made sure the coast was clear, we left his bedroom together and rejoined the festivities outside.

~~*

The original cotton farm on the land where the big house was located, and where we spent our summers, originally belonged to Samantha's family, but it was mismanaged. By the time Sam got it in her early twenties, it was failing. Fred took it and made it flourish and then bought several more like it in the south. He then became a silent partner in a textile company that later expanded and became a big textile supplier. In addition to that, Fred still had a pretty decent stake in oil and owned several pieces of prime real estate.

He was semi-retired, but it was impossible for him to get away with not working at all. A few days after Lucy's wedding he announced that he needed to head back up the coast to take care of a few things. He needed to go back to New Jersey and I wanted to go back with him. I still felt bad for leaving my mom behind, and Max had requested an appointment with me in New York.

Emmy wasn't a big fan of Louisiana, but Mayson had gone down for the wedding and the pair had reconnected with some friends and wanted to stay. In a couple of weeks, they would return and a couple of days after that we would be helping Emmet move into his apartment in Cambridge.

The reality of that was sinking in. In a few short weeks I would be back in school and Emmet would be hours away. We never discussed how we were going to work through that and it was making me a little nervous as we inched closer to the day he would move away. Since I wasn't even old enough to get into a car and drive to him, we would only be able to see each other on holidays and during the summer.

Realistically speaking, I had no idea how we were going to pull it off. On the other hand, it made hiding our relationship that much easier, at least until I was ready to tell Emmy and old enough to date seriously.

Emmet was also returning to New Jersey, though he would be driving his car back and not flying with Fred and me. He didn't really give any explanation to his inquisitive mother other than telling her he hadn't planned on staying too long in the first place. I didn't ask him to leave Louisiana, but as soon as he heard that I was going back north, he made plans to leave too. It made me rather giddy, because I would be able to spend a little more time with him without too many obstacles.

I still didn't want to tell Emmy about Emmet. I had poked at the idea with her casually when we were talking about guys and she wasn't at all receptive.

"I should hook up with Emmet," I had said jokingly. "You seem to think he's so easy."

Emmy made a disgusted face and said, "I love my brother and I love you, but no! Besides, it's like…incest. Emmet is just as much your brother as mine, and ew. No."

"You seem to feel very strongly about this," I said, forcing a smile.

"I do, and Emmet isn't a bad guy, but you deserve better. You deserve the best." She made a funny face and added, "I don't even want to joke about it. It's gross."

She changed the subject and I pretended that I wasn't hurt.

I really shouldn't have let her opinions bother me, but she was my best friend. It really mattered to me what she thought, and I wanted her support, not for her to oppose me. I didn't want to deal with the stress that her opposition could possibly bring to my relationship with Emmet. Maybe later she would feel differently, and maybe not. I couldn't keep our relationship a secret forever, however; so eventually she would either have to accept it or deal with it.

I was rather excited to see my mom. I was hoping that we would be able to spend some time together and get to know each other again—if I ever really knew her. She knew I was coming home, so it was no surprise when I fell through the door with several bags and a large suitcase.

"I'm home," I said happily as I dropped my stuff by the door.

"Hi," she said from the kitchen doorway. She was in her waitressing uniform.

"You're going to work?" I asked, trying to hide my disappointment. "I thought we could have dinner together. I have a few dollars. I can treat us to Nifty Fifties."

"I couldn't get any time off," she said, but didn't sound at all apologetic.

In my mind I had imagined a pleasant homecoming. I pictured my mom hugging me when I walked through the door and telling me how glad she was to see me, not standing in the doorway looking at me casually as if it hadn't been weeks since she last saw me. I thought she would have taken the night off and would like the idea of spending some one on one time with her only child. I did not expect her to be so indifferent. I guess I thought that her medications would have improved her cool disposition towards me, but maybe I hadn't given it enough time to work.

"It's okay," I said as if she had apologized. "I'm tired anyway."

I walked across the small living room and opened my arms for a hug. I ignored the ache I felt in my heart when my mom hesitated before accepting the embrace. It was short and lifeless on her end.

"Did you make my appointment with Max?" I asked her after I stepped away from her.

She shook her head. Speaking carefully, she said, "No. I'm not sure it is something I want you to do."

Up until that point, I didn't have any feelings on the subject either way. I was willing to try because the opportunity was there, but if it didn't pan out, that was okay; however, when my mother attempted to take away my right to choose, I suddenly realized how much I really wanted to try it.

"What do you mean?" I asked her.

"You have this naïve idea that it will be easy." She shrugged and went into the kitchen.

"I never said that," I argued as I followed her.

"I don't think you know how much work it will be to find work *and* get paid. Who is supposed to traipse around New York with you and wherever else while you try to get a job? You know sometimes you won't even get paid money? Just clothes? Clothes don't pay the bills, Donya."

Like she knew about paying bills? She was employed for the first time since I was a little kid!

I bit my tongue on that remark and said instead, "I understand that, but I would like to try."

"I can't just quit my job and run all over the world with you. We don't even have the money to do that. Did you think about that?"

I deflated. I had not thought about that. I had not thought much about the details at all. It wasn't as if my dad was around to pay the bills while I pursued a modeling career. It was just my mom and the money she made and a little bit of social security. It wasn't very much. We had enough to live with electricity, heat, and to not starve and that was about it. I had become accustomed to the Graynes making up where my parents fell short over the years, but that wasn't something I wanted to continue to do. I had no expectations or illusions of them supporting me and my mother while I 'traipsed' around trying to find work.

But still...

"I understand," I said slowly. "But can we at least meet Max? I would like to at least hear what he has to say. Maybe I can try on my own in a couple of years."

Mom shrugged. She was spreading butter on toast, but she looked over her shoulder at me.

"You're pretty, Donya, but there isn't anything extraordinary about you. I don't even know what that Max was talking about. What if he's just a pervert?"

I pushed away the self-conscious feelings she had just evoked within me. "You and Sam both found out he was the real deal," I reminded her patiently.

She shrugged again. "I don't really have time or money to go to New York anyway. You may as well have stayed down south."

That was probably one of the longest, sanest conversations I had ever had with my mom. Sadly, it was just that...sad. She had not said one single kind word to me since I walked through the door.

"I have to go," she said after wrapping her toast in a paper towel. "There's some food in the fridge."

She moved past me into the living room, grabbed her keys off of the coffee table, stepped through my obstacle course of bags and walked out of the door without even a glance back in my direction.

~~*

Emmet got back to New Jersey a couple of days after me. He had driven straight through and was exhausted, but he insisted on seeing me before he slept. It was mid-morning when I walked the few blocks to my other home. Fred wasn't home. He had flown to Chicago the night before for some early morning meetings. He had called me to let me know he would be gone a couple of days, and it was that small act that made me smile for the first time since I returned to New Jersey. I wasn't even his real kid but he treated me like I was his more than my biological mother did.

As I let myself into the house, my heart fluttered madly in anticipation of being reunited with Emmet. I followed that invisible line between us and found him in the kitchen, dressed in shorts and a t-shirt, yawning and scratching his chest tiredly. I couldn't help thinking how cute he looked.

"Hey," I said, stopping a few feet away from him.

"Hi," he said with a grin. He closed the distance between us and wrapped his arms around me. He planted a kiss on my neck that made me shiver before releasing me. He affectionately tugged on a piece of hair that had fallen from my ponytail.

"How was your drive?"

"Too slow," he said, putting a hand on my hip. "Mom tried to sabotage me and flattened two of my tires."

"She did not," I said disbelieving, but at the same time totally believing it.

He nodded and laughed. "Yes, she did. She didn't like me driving home by myself."

"She didn't have any arguments when you showed up five days early," I pointed out.

"That's what I said." He yawned loudly.

"I'm not going to stay long. You need some sleep."

"Stay," he said quietly as he looked down at me. He put his other hand on the back of my neck and dragged his thumb across the nape. I shivered.

"I don't know if I should," I whispered as his thumb made another pass across my skin.

Instead of answering me with his words, Emmet leaned over and gently placed his mouth on mine. The tip of his tongue slid across my lips. I granted his request and parted them. He kissed me slowly and softly. I melted against his body and he wrapped his arms around me. After a couple of minutes, he pulled away and rested his chin on my head as he held me. I held onto him tightly. I didn't realize how much I needed his embrace until that moment.

My days at my mother's house had been long, lonely and rather sad. She never made any further effort to be near me. If we ended up in the same space together, it was purely by accident on her part. We hardly spoke more than a few sentences to each other since my return. It saddened me deeply. I always believed that if my mother was well, she would be different. It hurt a lot less when I thought it was her mental illness keeping her emotionally detached.

"You okay?" Emmet asked worriedly.

"I'm just glad you're here," I said and then cursed in my head when my voice broke on the last word.

His green eyes burned into mine with concern.

"What's wrong?"

"I'm fine," I murmured.

"I can *feel* that there is something wrong," he said, frowning. "We're connected, remember?"

It was impossible to forget, but at least I knew for sure that he could sense my emotions.

"I remember." I gave him a small smile.

"So, talk to me, sweetheart," Emmet said softly.

"My mom hates me," I blurted out. My teenage hormones raged and I burst into tears and became bitterly angry at the same time.

Emmet looked alarmed as he attempted to wipe away my tears, but they came faster than he could keep up with.

"Come on," he said, taking my hand.

I let him lead me through the first floor and up the stairs. He pulled me into his bedroom and made me sit on the bed. He walked out of the room and returned a few seconds later with a box of tissues. He took a couple out and kneeled before me and blotted my tears.

I was so embarrassed. I wasn't a crier. I hated sissy crying girls. I was tougher than that. I tried to stop, but couldn't.

"Donya, what happened?" Emmet asked desperately with his hands on either side of me.

"Nothing," I laughed and sobbed.

Humiliated by my weakness, I turned my face away from him. I gently pushed him away until he stood up and stepped back. I crawled onto his bed and lay down with my back to him. I covered my face with my arm in an attempt to hide from him. I felt him move onto the bed behind me, however, and he gently pulled my arm from my face and wiped away my tears. He didn't ask me anymore questions. He simply wrapped his arms around me and held me close and let me cry like the baby I felt like.

I don't know how much time passed before I stopped crying. My body still shook involuntarily with small shudders and Emmet continued to hold me while stroking my hair. The sob session had taken a lot out of me. My eyes began to droop. I struggled to stay awake, but tucked in Emmet's hold, I lost the battle and slept.

~~*

It was late afternoon when I opened my eyes again. Emmet's digital clock next to his bed glowed 4:45p.m. I felt his chest rising and falling gently against my back. I carefully rolled over to face him. I tried not wake him, but completely failed. He was smiling even though his eyes were still closed as he pulled me closer.

"I like waking up to you," he murmured.

"Even though I cry like a little girl?" I asked, feeling the mortification in my warm cheeks.

Emmet's smile faded and his eyes blinked open. He looked at me with worry again.

"Why were you crying?"

I sighed and picked at an imaginary piece of lint on his shirt.

"My mom doesn't like me," I said in a small voice. I told him about my arrival back home and how she had behaved. I told him everything she had said about Max and how she made no real effort to be near me.

"I usually don't care if someone likes me or not," I said at the end. "I was able to deal with it before because she was sick, but she's better now and she still doesn't want anything to do with me. I'm trying not to care, but I do. I wish I didn't."

"I don't really know what to say about your mom," Emmet said. He seemed to be dumbfounded by what I told him. "But I do know that my parents love you as much as they love us." He chuckled and said "Sometimes I'm sure my dad loves you more than Emmy. Don't tell her I said that."

"Your parents are great and you know they've been the only parents I've really had most of my life, but it's not the same thing. You expect your real parents to love you, too."

Emmet kissed my forehead. "I know. I'm sorry. I don't know what to say. I feel really bad for you."

"I'll get over it," I sighed, though I wasn't sure if I could ever get over it. How does a kid get over being disliked by her own mother?

"I don't want you to give up on the modeling thing. It pisses me off that she said you weren't good enough."

"There's nothing I can do about it," I said resolutely. "It costs money we don't have."

"Yeah," he said distractedly as he absently rubbed my back.

We lay there in silence for a little while, just holding each other. With Emmet rubbing my back, the constant movement gradually pushed my shirt up. Instead of pulling it back down, his warm hand slid across my bare skin, sending small shivers up and down my spine.

"Remember the last time we were in this bed together?" he asked in a murmur.

How could I forget it? I squirmed slightly just thinking about how his body had pressed against mine.

"Yes, and I should get up so we don't have a repeat session," I said, but made no effort to move away from him.

"I'm not letting you get up," he warned, looking at me with mischief in those sparkling eyes.

"I don't need your permission."

"Yes, you do, but even if you asked, I wouldn't grant your request."

He pulled on my ponytail, forcing my head to tilt up towards his face. He smiled like a villain and then kissed me.

Though I knew I should have probably got out of his bed, I fisted my hand in his hair instead and wriggled closer to him as his tongue stroked mine. His hand roamed over my bare back and down to my butt where he squeezed and kneaded. I moaned softly against his lips. When I felt him erect against my thigh, I pulled away from his lips and gently pushed at his chest.

"We should stop," I said. I didn't really want to stop kissing him. I loved kissing him, but we were completely alone. Sam and Fred were both hundreds of miles away. There was no chance of anyone banging on the door to interrupt us, no chance of getting caught.

Emmet squeezed my butt again and ground against me. He groaned and then suddenly released me and rolled onto his back. Relieved and disappointed, I fell onto my back too.

"I should go home," I said.

"You should stay," he said and hooked his pinky with mine.

I snorted. "Yeah, right."

"Seriously," he said. "Sleep in Luce's room like you normally do, or Emmy's. Or…" Quickly, before I could register what he was doing, he rolled on top of me. He straddled my legs and leaned over me, trapping me beneath his body. "You can stay here. In my bed."

His words sent warmth between my legs and my breath hitched ever so slightly.

"You know I can't do that," I whispered.

"Yes, you can," he whispered back and left a soft kiss on my lips. "Please, stay." He kissed me again, taking his sweet time.

"Emmet," I sighed. I wanted to tell him no, but I had a romantic image in my head of falling asleep in his arms as the stars came out and waking up in his arms as the sun rose in the sky.

"How many opportunities will we have like this?" he asked.

None, I knew. Fred would be back the next day, and we didn't know for sure if he would be out of town again, and soon Emmy and Sam would be back. Then Emmet would be gone.

Emmet will be gone.

"Okay," I said. "I'll stay."

His smile melted me and I completely forgot the anguish I had felt earlier in the day. I reached up and put my hands on his face and pulled him down for a kiss. The kiss was light and flirty at first. We chuckled and giggled as we teased each other with our lips and tried to nip each other. I tried to tickle his side and he succeeded in finding a ticklish spot right under my arm. When I tried to fight him as I laughed, he wrapped his hands around my wrists and pressed my arms down above my head.

"Oh, now what will you do?" he teased and managed to hold my wrists in one hand while he tickled me with his other hand. "You should have never started this tickle fight, Donya."

I laughed and squirmed as he tortured me. He took great satisfaction in my helplessness. I begged him to stop and after another minute he finally did. I felt my shirt hiked up over my belly button and he must have noticed it at the same time. He looked down and saw my bare stomach and his playful grin turned into a heated smile. He dragged his hand down my side and over my bare skin. Caressing my belly, Emmet leaned down and kissed me. There was nothing playful or soft in the kiss. It was hard and demanding.

As he kissed me, his hand moved under my shirt. His fingertips came in contact with my bra and then stopped. He breathed a little heavier as he kissed me, as if not touching me any further was taking a tremendous amount of energy. I tried to release my wrists from his hands, but he growled low in his throat and his grip tightened as he simultaneously cupped my breast. When his thumb moved over a hard peak I groaned loudly and absent mindedly lifted my hips off of the bed.

Emmet stretched out over me and settled his body on mine. He released my wrists and kissed me along my jaw as his free hand joined his other hand under my shirt. I stared up at the ceiling as his kisses continued to my neck. His tongue tasted my skin as his hands rubbed the aching tips of my breasts. I didn't recognize the mewling sounds coming out of my mouth.

I put my hands on his shoulders with the intent of making him stop, but when I felt his hair between my fingers, I realized how powerless I was to stop him. My hands pressed gently on his head as he suckled on my neck and I arched my back slightly, pushing my breasts into his hands. Even as I wrapped one leg around one of his, I knew I needed to push him away. When Emmet suddenly pulled away from me and sat up on his knees, I should have taken that opportunity to make him stop.

His hands tugged at the hem of my shirt. I sat up, fully intending to end it, but quickly complied in taking off my shirt by lifting my arms. He moved his body over mine and kissed me hard while he continued to touch me in ways I should have objected to. His lips left mine as my eyes stared up at the ceiling again. I should have spoken up, but when my lips parted, I only groaned as he again suckled on my skin.

When one of his hands drifted away from my chest and began to migrate south, I didn't stop him. He angled his body so that he was not directly on top of me, giving his hand the space it needed to explore. His fingers edged just under the waistband of my shorts, moving slowly back and forth, from hip bone to hip bone. I soon felt the button release on my jean shorts and heard the zipper as he pulled it down. When my shorts were open, Emmet looked me in the eyes and pushed his hand into my shorts and under my underwear and pressed his palm down on the swollen button that had been waiting for his touch.

He stared at me heatedly as he palmed me. I pushed my hips up, increasing the friction as my mouth made more noises I was unfamiliar with. I stared into Emmet's eyes as I began to feel pressure building inside of me. I squirmed and mumbled incoherent words as the pressure increased at an alarming rate. Emmet rubbed me faster and harder and moaned, which I couldn't understand because I was the one being touched, but he seemed to be enjoying it just as much as me.

"Emmet," I gasped, gripping his shoulders. I was suddenly afraid of what I was feeling. I wasn't stupid. I knew I was on the verge of my first orgasm—again—but I had no idea how I would look or how my body would react, or if it would please him.

"It's okay," he said in a surprisingly soothing tone. "Don't fight it."

So, I didn't.

"Emmet!" I cried out his name as the most incredible sensations attacked the sensitive flesh beneath Emmet's hand. I dug my nails into his shoulders and bucked my hips into his firm hand. My toes pointed to the end of the bed and then curled and pointed again and curled again. I tried unsuccessfully to close my legs around his hand even as he continued to rub me.

I screamed, shuddered, and fell back against the pillows. Emmet pulled his hand out of my underwear and softly kissed the corner of my heavily breathing mouth. Though I felt him hard against my leg, he didn't try to get back on top of me. He simply wrapped his arms around me, kissed my forehead, and then we both slept.

Chapter Thirteen

It was a little after seven that night when I woke up ravenous and amazingly relaxed. Though my stomach growled, my muscles and limbs felt ridiculously pliable. After kissing Emmet for a few minutes longer than my hungry belly could take, I escaped from his bed and ran from his grasp and jogged downstairs to the kitchen in search of food. Emmet wanted to make me dinner. Like his mother, he was capable of cooking great food, but since the family was gone all summer, there wasn't much in the refrigerator to work with.

"We can order take-out," he suggested.

"I'm starving," I said, shaking my head. "I can't wait for take-out. Can you drive us somewhere?"

"Sure," he said and grinned when he looked at my hair and my clothes.

I put a hand in my hair and knew that it was probably wild from being in bed all day, but I didn't care. Emmet had seen me first thing in the morning on countless occasions, but when I looked down, I realized I was still shirtless, and my shorts were still unbuttoned. Memories of why I was wearing less clothing made my cheeks warm with embarrassment. I avoided his eyes and crossed my arms self-consciously across my breasts.

"Come on, beautiful," he said holding out his hand to me. "Let's get some clothes on you."

I took his hand and allowed him to lead me back upstairs. When I started searching the floor and bed for my shirt, Emmet gave me one of his instead. It was a button down blue short-sleeved shirt. It was long on me, giving the illusion that I didn't have anything on under it.

"I like that," he said with a wink as he slipped his feet into a pair of sneakers.

I slipped on my flip flops, put my hand in his and we went to his car. I was glad it was parked in the garage. Though the neighbors weren't very close in his neighborhood, if any of them spotted us coming out of the house together looking like we had spent all day in bed—which we had, but they didn't need to know that—I was sure someone would say something to Fred or Sam.

We made a quick trip to a Burger King and bought entirely too much food for two people. We sat down side by side in the kitchen, but I had turned my chair to the side and put my legs up on his lap, just because I could. Emmet ate with one hand and caressed my bare skin with his other. Mostly he stayed below the knee, but sometimes he would venture further up my leg and under the long shirt. Sometimes when he looked at me, I knew he was thinking about what he had done to me earlier in the day.

"I really like you in my shirt," he said, tracing small circles just above my knee. "I want you to keep it."

I pulled the shirt up to my nose and inhaled. "It smells like you."

"Good. My pillows smell like you."

His eyes fell to my legs as his hand smoothed over my thigh. I unconsciously pressed my thighs together as shocking sensations traveled up my leg and settled between my legs. Emmet's green eyes looked into my eyes knowingly as a small, sexy smile appeared on his lips.

"I can't stop touching you," he murmured as his hands drifted ever higher. His fingertips eased under my shorts.

"So, don't stop," I heard myself say in a breathy voice and could hardly believe it.

He gave me a look that should have scared me, but it thrilled me. He threw his fries down and took my milkshake from my hand and put it on the table. He pushed my legs off of him and stood up. Without asking, he took my hand, pulled me out of the chair and lead me through the house and back upstairs to his bedroom.

I had to question my sanity as he positioned me in front of the bed and kissed me. I knew it was going to lead to more third base action, but I didn't want to stop him, though I knew I should. Even as his hands reached under the shirt to undo my shorts again, I knew I should have pulled away, but instead, a moment later my shorts were falling to the floor at my feet and I was stepping out of them.

Nervous, with a hard beating heart, by Emmet's guidance I got on the bed and reclined back on the pillows. I watched, biting my bottom lip as he pulled off his shirt, revealing a nicely toned chest and abs that would only become more defined as he got older. He kicked his sneakers off and got into bed on his side beside me. He rested his hand on my rapidly rising and falling chest.

"Don't worry," he said softly. "If you want me to stop at any time I will, okay?"

I nodded, unable to find my voice.

"I can stop now if you want," he offered. "I love you, but we don't have to do anything but lay here and watch television. Do you want me to stop?"

Did I want him to stop? The sensible part of me definitely thought that we should. What if we went too far? Was I ready to lose my virginity? Was I even ready for more third base action? My sensible side said no, but my body ached for his touch. Though his hand on my chest was nonsexual, my breasts swelled in need, and I couldn't escape the thought of his hand in my panties earlier in the day and how I had felt.

I shook my head no.

Emmet smiled and brought his lips to mine. His hand slid down and answered the needs of my nipples, and I gasped. As he manipulated my nipples through the shirt, my legs crossed and squeezed as that pressure built. With a light groan, he sat up and began to slowly unbutton the shirt.

"I feel like I'm unwrapping a present," he said with a sexy smile.

When the shirt fell open, revealing me clad in my bra and panties, he groaned again as his eyes traveled over my body.

"You are and always have been the most beautiful girl I know," he said as his fingers trailed between my breasts, over my tummy and stopped at the top of my panties before retracing their path.

"Yeah, right," I said, rolling my eyes. I knew I was a good looking girl, but I'd seen the other girls Emmet had been with. They were all well-endowed. I wasn't flat chested, but my boobs weren't big and bouncy either.

"Hey," he said, putting fingers under my chin and making me look at him. "You are the most beautiful girl I know or have ever seen."

I looked at him with doubt before looking down at my chest. He looked, too. He cupped a breast in his hand and kneaded.

"You fit perfectly in my hand," he said with a groan. With one-handed skill, he unhooked my bra.

I tried to cover my face, embarrassed by my nakedness in front of him, but he took my hand away.

"You're perfect, Donya," he said sincerely. "Don't ever doubt it."

He put his hand on my bare breast, and I gasped and moaned as he pulled the nipple between his fingers. I couldn't believe I was lying mostly naked on Emmet's bed with him fondling me, turning me on and making me moan. When he looked me in the eyes as his head moved towards my breasts, I began to believe that the real Donya had exited the building, and I was an imposter because I didn't stop him. I watched with fascination and licked my lips as his tongue flattened against my nipple. I groaned as I watched him repeat the action twice more before pulling the bud between his teeth.

"Oh, God!" I cried and threw my head back.

Once again I stared up at the ceiling as Emmet suckled me and tugged at the other nipple to give it proper attention. My fingers wound in his hair, and I held him to me. I didn't want him to stop—or Imposter Donya didn't want him to stop. She wanted him to suck harder, so she said it.

"Suck harder," I—she, the imposter—panted.

Emmet growled with pleasure and granted my request and sucked with such force that I cried out in pain. He looked at me with questioning eyes but did not stop, because I had not told him to. When I still did not stop him, his teeth sank into the sensitive peak, and I screamed as an unexpected, sudden orgasm slammed into me. My back arched, my hips rose off of the bed, and I squeezed my thighs together trying to drawl the orgasm out, as it was already beginning to die. Then Emmet's hand was on my thighs, forcing them apart. Sensing time was of the essence; he cupped me through my shorts and rubbed, hard.

I shuddered and writhed and once again made sounds that I did not recognize. My whole body was over sensitized, and my orgasm seemed to go on and on. I couldn't take any more, but he seemed to sense that too and stopped. I shuddered violently as my breaths came out uneven and ragged. I was completely caught up in my orgasmic haze and didn't immediately register Emmet pulling off my panties.

The fog lifted a little and for a moment I was able to think clearly and again ask myself if this was something I wanted. Imposter Donya was all for it, but Sensible Donya told me to think hard about it because there was no returning once it was done. The moment I felt Emmet's fingers sliding through my vaginal lips, the haze returned in full force, and I was once again arching off of the bed.

"Oh my god," Emmet said in wonder. "You're wet. I've never seen anyone so wet before."

My cheeks blazed with embarrassment. Was I abnormally wet? Was that gross? Being wet to begin with sounded gross, but was I extra gross? The fact that he alluded to the other girls he slept with had not missed my notice, but I started to wonder if they had set expectations that I could not meet.

Emmet looked at my face and saw the concern there under the lust.

"I like it," he whispered to me and planted a small kiss on my lips. "I like that you're so wet. I know it's for me."

He groaned softly as he swiped his fingers between my lips again. He held them up to the light where they glistened. I looked away embarrassed.

"I fucking love it. Look at it, Donya," he quietly commanded.

Reluctantly, I looked at his fingers.

"This is just on the outside," he murmured and then looked me in the eyes. "I wonder how wet you are inside."

I was looking at him when he said that. Even though I saw his hand go back down out of my peripheral vision, I did not know what he was doing until he was doing it.

"Oh my god," I whimpered as I felt one of Emmet's fingers slide inside of me.

Emmet groaned again as he continued to hold my gaze and swirled his finger in a slow circle. It was just one finger, but I felt invaded. My walls involuntarily squeezed his finger.

"You are so snug," Emmet whispered. "So warm and wet and perfect."

He pulled his finger out of me and held it up for re-inspection. I was definitely wetter on the inside as he had suspected. I was surprised when Emmet looked down at me with a bashful expression. What did he have to be embarrassed about? It wasn't his body fluids on his fingers.

"I've never wanted to taste anyone before," he said shyly and then whispered. "I want to taste you."

My eyes exploded out of my skull as I looked at him. My mouth had fallen open so wide; I was sure he could see every tooth in my mouth.

That one statement brought Sensible Donya back. I don't know why. Maybe it was how intensely erotic his words were, and because it was only a brief glimpse of what the rest of the night entailed. Imposter Donya tried to hang on to the lust and even licked her lips as Emmet licked his finger and smiled down at her like maybe she was thinking of tasting herself on his lips!

Nuh-uh, Sensible Donya said. Sensible Donya asked me why, after all of my fighting about not being ready for sex, I was on my back with my shirt and bra hanging open and no bottoms on. She wanted to know why my so-called boyfriend agreed not that long ago that I wasn't ready for sex, but he just licked my essence off of his finger. Sensible Donya reminded me that Emmet wasn't a virgin and questioned whether or not he had any real intentions of waiting to begin with. She wondered if Emmet was going to get what he wanted and then walk away. It didn't matter how well or how long we had known each other. Sensible Donya wasn't sure if Emmet's actions were acts of love or acts of pure teenage-boy horniness.

I agreed with Sensible Donya and my lust filled haze lifted.

I shot up in the bed so quickly that I narrowly missed bumping heads with Emmet. I got on my knees and scrambled to hold the shirt closed over my body as Emmet sat up and watched me with alarm.

"What's wrong?" he asked, reaching out to touch me, but I backed away. I backed away and almost fell off of the bed. I stumbled to my feet and backed away from the bed and out of Emmet's reach.

"Donya," he said my name with exasperation. "What's wrong?"

"We agreed that I wasn't ready," I said, trying to keep my voice from shaking as much as my body shook.

Emmet's eyes opened wide for just a few seconds before they grew dark and stormy. "Downstairs, you practically invited this to happen."

"Up here you told me I could stop at any time," I snapped.

He held his hands up to placate me, but his expression was still angry.

"And I stopped," he said. "But you were really into it."

"We're moving too fast," I said, searching for my panties. I spotted them a few feet away and moved to pick them up. "It seems that every time we're alone, we go too far."

"We go far together," Emmet pointed out defensively. "It's not just me."

"I know that," I said, pulling my panties and shorts on together. "But I don't want to be that girl. I don't want to be that girl that sleeps with her new boyfriend this early in the relationship. Then our relationship will be based on sex more than our feelings. It happens to our friends all of the time, and it blows up in their faces all of the time, and when they move on to the next boyfriend or girlfriend, they make the same stupid mistake and it happens all over again."

If Emmet looked angry before, he was infuriated now. He got off of the bed and stalked towards me. My heart twisted with anxiety as he backed me up against a wall and caged me in with his arms.

"There will be no other boyfriends for you, Donya," he said, his tone harsh and possessive. "I am your boyfriend now and someday I will be your husband."

I couldn't help the humorless laugh that burst from my mouth, in his face.

"You're leaving for college in a few weeks. How do you think we're going to stay together then? You'll be hours away, and I can't drive for at least another year."

"We'll make it work," he said through gritted teeth. "There are holidays and the summer and—"

"And what?" I demanded. "Are you kidding me, Emmet? Did you forget that no one can know about us, so even if you're home from school, we still have to find time to sneak off together? That seriously reduces how much time we will get to spend together, and I'm betting it won't be very much at all in the end."

"So, we'll tell everyone."

"We can't tell anyone! Your parents will still say I'm too young, they'll question our relationship, and your sister has already made it more than clear that she would not approve."

"I don't give a shit what anyone else thinks, Donya!" I shrunk back as he yelled, but then I straightened up and yelled back.

"I care, Emmet! Your family is the only family I have. Excuse me if I don't want to do anything that would make me lose them even a little bit."

My words seemed to hit him hard. His mouth had fallen open, and he had stared at me intensely, with shock and then sadness, but he pushed it away. Anger returned to his features, but not as hard as it was moments before.

"So, when you agreed to be with me, were you going to dump me at the end of the summer?" he asked bitterly.

"I didn't know what I was going to do," I answered honestly.

"But now you do?" His voice rose again. "Now you know you want to break up with me?"

"I don't see where we'll have much of a choice." Pain weaved through my words. "I don't know how we can pull it off."

My shoulders slumped, and my head dropped. I felt a sob begging to escape free in my chest, but I managed to keep it there when I spoke again. "I wanted to be with you, and I didn't think that far ahead."

Strong fingers were on my chin, tilting my head up.

"Do you still want to be with me, Donya?" Emmet asked softly. His eyes still looked stormy, but the muscles in his face had softened.

"Yes," I said weakly.

"Then we need to find a way to work it out in the fall," he said. "Because I want to be with you too."

He kissed me sweetly, but briefly. He took a small step back and pulled the shirt together to hide my nakedness.

"I won't do anything more than kiss you until you are absolutely sure you are ready for more," he said gently, but then in a firmer voice, he added, "But you will have to convince me that you are actually ready."

I nodded once.

"And I still want you to stay here with me when you can this summer," he went on. "Tell me you'll stay."

Hesitantly, I nodded again. "I'll stay."

Emmet looked relieved. He kissed me once more and then moved away from me.

"I'm going back downstairs to finish dinner. You can fix your clothes and join me."

He gave me a small smile, but there was sadness in his eyes before he walked out of the door.

Chapter Fourteen

Fred returned late the next morning. I thought it would be a good idea to be absent when he got back so that he wouldn't have any wild ideas about his son and his almost-daughter shacking up in his son's room. Sometimes wild ideas are truths, but Fred didn't need to know that.

Even though I was pretty sure that my mom didn't want to be bothered, I still tried to connect with her before she left for work. I talked about my time in Louisiana and considered what colleges I may want to attend in a couple of years. She listened, asked questions, and said the appropriate things, but part of me sensed that she wasn't really into it. I felt like she was only communicating with me to appease me since I had the nerve to sit down directly across from her at her kitchen table.

When she finally left for work, I felt more relieved than anything. I didn't have to put on the charade of chatty, loving daughter while the tension in the air between us hung heavy and pregnant, threatening to engulf me.

In the early afternoon, I called Emmy. I never went more than a couple of days without talking to her. It was second nature to include her in my daily life—except where her brother was concerned. I did tell her about my mom's indifference to me, but I didn't break down and cry like a baby like I had with Emmet.

"I can't believe it," Em said when I told her. "Your mom was never a social butterfly, but she was never mean like that. That's just mean, and hurtful. Did she forget that you used to take care of her when she was 'sick'?"

I also never told Emmy about the time my mom slapped me in the face. Only Emmet was privy to that information. So, she had no idea of my mom's mean streak.

"Em, it's been so long since I've really known my real mom," I said. "Maybe she's normally this way. Maybe I need thicker skin."

"You're in a lose-lose situation. Your real mom is a nut job, and your fake mom is a whack job."

I laughed. What else could I do? I did enough crying for a lifetime already. It was laugh or cry or walk around with a chip on my shoulder. It was easier to laugh.

"I think you should still try for the modeling thing," Emmy said after we laughed.

"I don't have that kind of money," I reminded her.

"Ask Mom and Dad." She had said it in a tone that implied that I was an idiot for not asking in the first place. Emmet had suggested the same thing. I gave her the same answer that I had given to him.

"Your mom and dad have been great to me, Emmy, but they're not my mom and dad and I've never asked them for anything—well except a green fishing pole," I said, smiling at the memory.

"But they've always taken care of you like you're one of us," Emmy objected.

"I won't ask," I said firmly. "And I don't want you to ask either."

"Fine," she huffed. After a pouty moment of silence, she asked, "So, have you come across any guys from school?"

I shook my head and laughed. "You're so boy crazy."

"I am, aren't I?" She asked it with pride. Only my friend would take that as a compliment.

We talked about boys for a little while and then clothes and hair, and then she needed to go. She and Mayson were going to meet some kids in town. I felt a little jealous when I hung up the phone. That was the first summer that we were apart since we were seven.

Around three, I thought it would be a good time to go back to the Grayne's. When I got there, Emmet was cutting the grass in a pair of shorts and no shirt. He was hot and sweaty and dirty. I loved it.

Control your hormones, Sensible Donya told me. I listened to her, gave Emmet a quick wave and went inside the house.

"Hey, Kiddo," Fred said when I found him in his office behind his big mahogany desk.

"How was your business trip?" I asked, sitting on a leather couch against the wall.

"Boring," he chuckled. "How are you? How is your mother?"

"Good," I lied. I told Emmy, and I told Emmet, but I didn't want to tell Fred and Sam about my mom. It just didn't feel right.

"Did you meet that modeling agent?" There was a small hint of disapproval in his voice. It was so tiny; I almost missed it.

Fred didn't think that young girls my age should be modeling. He said that the modeling world was seedy, that some of the pictures he'd seen were nearly pornographic and that someone my age shouldn't be viewed that way, but he didn't want to stand in my way. As long as I had proper supervision, he would go along with it.

"I didn't, but I have time," I said, choosing to avoid any talk about money.

"Good, good," he said absently as he looked at something on his computer.

He was obviously busy, and I didn't want to keep bugging him. I stood up and started for the door.

"Do you want me to make dinner for you guys?" I asked.

"You don't have to do that, Kiddo," Fred said, but he looked at me with hope, like he was hoping I would overrule him and insist upon it.

I shook my head at his expression and smiled.

"I'll make dinner. If I don't come over here and cook for you guys once in a while, you'll live off of moldy cheese and take-out."

"Thanks, Kiddo," he said with a thankful grin.

I nodded and started out of the door, but Fred spoke again, and his question caught me off guard.

"Donya, whatever happened with that young man you told me about?"

I stood there just over the threshold looking into the office at him with a dumb expression on my face. It had been quite some time since we had that discussion. When he didn't follow up a week or so later, I didn't expect him to follow up at all.

"What?" I asked to buy some time.

"That boy you spoke about when we were fishing," he said, leaning back in his chair as he studied me. "What happened?"

"Well," I started slowly. "You don't condone dating, so…"

I didn't want to have to tell him the big lie, and boy was it a doozy.

Fred looked at me silently for what felt like forever. I had a crazy feeling that he not only saw right through me and knew who the mystery boy was, but he knew the wicked, dirty things we had done in said boy's room.

"Is it Emmet?" he asked bluntly.

I don't know where the strength came from, or the ability to mask my emotions, but they were both there at full power. My knees did not give out on me, and the mask slid perfectly into place with a surprised smile.

"Now you're just talking crazy," I said in a joking tone, though I don't even know how I found my voice.

I laced my fingers together tightly in front of me to hide how much my hands shook.

"I was just curious. You know it wouldn't be so unusual for you to have formed an attachment to him. The two of you grew up very close."

"You wouldn't disapprove of such a match?" I asked suspiciously.

"Of course I would disapprove of such a match," he said, sitting up in his chair and leaning on his desk.

My heart sank as I waited for his explanation.

"Emmet should be looking after you as a little sister," Fred explained, taking his glasses off. "If he looked at you as anything more than that, I would feel that he didn't respect you as you should be respected. I would feel that he took advantage of his place in your life as a brotherly figure. It would be inappropriate and a little twisted for any of my boys to think of you as anything but a sister. Besides, he's a little too old for you and you're a little too young to be dating."

I was shocked. Usually, Fred was not so judgmental. Fred was the parent kids went to when they needed an open mind and to make sense of something. I expected him to mention the age difference, but I did not expect the rest of it.

With a suddenly dry mouth, I smiled wide and said, "Thank God you have nothing to worry about then, huh? I'm not even sure why you asked about Emmet." I laughed to imply that his idea had been ludicrous, even though I felt like bawling.

"The night of the wedding, you were talking to the Sampson boy, Taylor?" I nodded but remained quiet. "I watched Emmet watch you, and then I watched you and Emmet talking. I watched his face as you walked away. Not too long after you went in, he went in, too."

We hadn't been as careful as we thought. Fred had noticed. Who else had noticed?

"Emmet was just being a big brother," I said dismissively. "I promise you that is all it was."

Lie. Broken promise.

Fred smiled at me and nodded. "Of course." He relaxed and then asked, "So, who is this prince charming?"

"No one anymore," I said with a shrug.

"Well, you're young. You have many years ahead of you to fall in love. Take your time."

I bobbed my head in agreement and continued the façade of casualness. "I'm going to make dinner now."

"Thanks, Kiddo," he said. He gave me a wink and turned his attention back to his computer.

I went into the kitchen and tried not to cry.

Emmet and I were doomed.

Chapter Fifteen

The next two weeks flew by. Fred went out of town once more for four days. I stayed with Emmet in the house most of the time. It was strange to be in the family house without the family. We didn't have any more serious discussions about our past, present, and future, though Fred's words haunted every moment I spent with Emmet.

I didn't want to tell him about the conversation because soon he would be going away to college. I had once looked at that as a negative point, but I began to welcome it. Maybe we would see what we were really made of with the separation. My hope was that it would give me some time to consider how to later break it to his family.

We didn't have any more pornographic make-out sessions. We slept in the same bed, holding each other. We kissed, and we caressed. With great restraint, Emmet always pulled away from me first. I knew he wanted more, and Imposter Donya wanted more. Imposter Donya wanted to jump on top of him, pin him down, kiss him and make him do bad things to her. However, I kept Imposter Donya chained up in the basement and let Sensible Donya prevail—though there was nothing sensible about a near-sixteen-year-old girl spending the night in the house alone with her older boyfriend. Sensible Donya was not without her flaws.

During the days that Fred was home, so not to bring any suspicion upon Emmet and me, I chose to hang out with my other friends during the day. Emmet would come over later in the evening while my mom was at work and he would leave before she got home. I cooked for him and Fred a couple more times, giving me an excuse to be there in the house. I didn't really need an excuse, it was practically my home too, but I didn't want to give Fred any more reasons to suspect that anything was happening between Emmet and me.

Sam and Emmy returned one week before Emmet was supposed to leave for Harvard. Though I knew my time with Emmet was going to be severely impeded, I was glad that everyone was back in New Jersey. None of my other friends could ever replace Emmy, and though Sam was nosey and too opinionated, sadly, she was still a decent replacement for my own mother who barely knew I existed.

Two days before we were to escort Emmet to his off-campus apartment, Sam and Fred asked to speak with me in Fred's office. The request made me want to throw up. Were they going to ask me about Emmet again? Were they going to admonish me for my behavior? They never asked to speak to me alone before, not even when my dad died. Was there something wrong with my mom? Were they about to break more bad news to me?

When I looked at Emmet and Emmy for clarification, they gave me twin, suspiciously innocent shrugs. I couldn't read Emmy's emotions if she chose to keep them from me, but Emmet was a different tale. I was getting better and better at sensing what he was feeling, and I sensed that he was being elusive. I narrowed my eyes with distrust but followed Sam to the office.

Nervously, I sat on the edge of the couch, looking from Fred to Sam.

"What's going on?" I asked, trying not to sound as frazzled as I felt.

I braced my hands on my knees and waited while Sam sat down on the other end of the couch.

"Now don't get upset," she said, putting her hand up to calm me even though I had no idea why I was there. "But Emmy told me about what your mama said about the modeling."

"Emmet told me," Fred said from behind his desk.

"Traitors," I muttered. Even though I did not want Sam and Fred to know about the modeling thing, I was extremely relieved when neither of them brought up my relationship with Emmet.

"Why didn't you tell me?" Fred asked, sounding genuinely hurt. I talked to Fred about everything—well most everything.

I wasn't sure how much my traitorous boyfriend and his traitorous sister had told them about my mom. I had to tread carefully.

"It isn't your problem," I said without malice. I said it simply because it was simple. It wasn't their problem.

"Haven't we always treated you like one of our own?" he asked.

"Yes, but I'm not."

He winced and Sam shook her head. "That really hurts, Donya," she said sadly. "You're just as much our child as Emmy and Emmet are."

Before I could respond to that, Fred said, "You should have come to us."

"For what?" I asked defensively. "You want me to come to you and ask for money so I could possibly model? No matter how close we all are, you're not my parents. My father is dead, and my mother is poor. That's my reality, and I'm dealing with it."

"Bullshit," Fred snapped. Sam and I looked at him in surprise. Fred was not the cursing kind of guy. Maybe in his Marine days, but he wasn't as a father and husband. "You forgot that you have another family that wants to see you happy and successful. You forgot that this family in this house is part of your reality. This isn't about being close, Donya. We are a family, and you are a part of this family and always will be. It is a goddamn slap in the face when you sit there and try to pick at the threads that bind us together."

I sat there in a stunned silence. I greatly underestimated how the Graynes felt about me and what I meant to them. I felt as if everything they had ever done for me was invalidated by my careless words.

"You're our daughter," Sam said quietly after a long minute of silence. "And we want to help you."

"Maybe I'm not good enough to be a model," I said in a shaky, low voice, echoing my mother.

"Emmet told me what your mom said," Fred said. "I don't think she meant to hurt your feelings. When we called her earlier today to discuss our plans for you, she was supportive."

I looked at him with doubt. I had no support in that household.

"We are going to financially support you while you pursue a modeling career," Sam said softly, but with a big smile. "Even if that Max won't take ya, we are convinced that you are cut out for it. You didn't see your portfolio yet."

I had nearly forgotten about the photo shoot I'd had in Louisiana. The photographer, Tori, had worked in the modeling industry before, and she thought I did really well, but she was getting paid, and she wasn't even in the industry anymore. I couldn't take her words at face value.

Sam got up and walked over to her husband's desk. He handed her a flat looking black book and she gave it to me before sitting back down on the couch. I put it on my lap and ran my fingers over the leather cover. I took a deep breath and opened it to the first page.

The very first picture was just a simple headshot. My hair was hanging loose on my bare shoulders and I was void of any makeup or moisturizer or anything on my face. My smile was pure and genuine. The second photo was another headshot without the smile and my hair was pulled up in a ponytail. The next photo was one of the ones taken during the photo shoot. I was modeling the Gucci dress that Sam had bought me the previous summer for a formal party. My hair was professionally done, my makeup was professionally applied and I was several inches taller in a pair of Manalo Blahnik sandals. My body was bent and twisted into awkward angles. I remembered posing and trying to find a good angle and feeling like an idiot, but apparently it worked. I looked like one of the women in the fashion magazines.

In the next photo I was in a classic looking white and red polka dot bikini and a black pair of heels. I had on an enormous pair of Dior sunglasses and my hair was pinned up. I was standing at the end of the pier with the lake at my back. I hardly recognized myself, and I barely recognized myself in the next three photos.

When I turned to the sixth picture, I had to swallow back a gasp. It was a picture of me standing with Emmet at Lucy's wedding reception. There was a whole party going on around us, but in the photo, it was as if he and I had completely forgotten we weren't alone. He was smiling affectionately at me and I was looking up at him with a raw, passionate, adoring expression. He had just told me how beautiful I was and how he wished he could wrap his arms around my waist and dance with me until the sun came up.

"It's a beautiful picture," Sam said. "Maybe Emmet should be a model, too. You two posed well together. Very convincing."

I didn't tell her it was very convincing because it was real and we had not even been aware of the camera. I looked at Fred and couldn't read his expression. So, I turned back to the book and finished looking at all of the photos. I was beyond impressed by both Tori's skills with the camera and my own skills that I had not been aware of until I looked through my portfolio.

"You're stunning," Sam said with another smile when I finished with the book. "I believe with a little makeover to fix your hair and maybe a push-up bra you can do this."

I rolled my eyes and groaned as Fred snapped at her.

"No one said anything about a makeover or a damn bra," he spat out.

"Just making a suggestion."

"I like my hair," I objected. "And believe it or not, I like my boobs!"

I liked that Emmet liked my boobs too.

Fred groaned as Sam and I bickered back and forth about my boobs and my hair.

"Enough!" Fred bellowed making us stop immediately.

Emmy was right. I had a nut job and a whack job for mothers, though for some reason, I didn't take Sam's words to heart like I did my mother's.

"Now," Fred said after we were quiet. "We are going to support you while you take a shot at a modeling career." When I started to shake my head and speak, he raised his hand to silence me. "It isn't a free ride, Kiddo. You will have a tutor, and you will keep up with your school work. You will be supervised around the clock wherever you go, and you will stay out of trouble, and you have to really try. You have to put everything you have into this. We will make sure you have everything you need. We already spoke to your mother, and she will do her part as far as your legal concerns."

It really began to sink in what he was saying to me. "So…I won't be going to school in September?" I asked.

"Doesn't look like it," he answered and didn't seem too happy about it. "It all depends on this Max fella and other resources we are gathering for you."

Just like that, my life was going to change.

"We still have many kinks to work out," Sam warned. "But for now you'll stay here or at your mama's, but if you'll need to be in New York or wherever for an extended period of time, we may have to consider other options."

I looked from Sam to Fred and back and forth so many times I thought my head would tilt off of my neck and roll to the floor.

"You guys believe in me that much?" I asked in a small voice.

"We all do," Sam smiled.

"Even with my little boobs and ugly hair?" I asked her dryly.

She gave a noncommittal shrug but then winked at me.

"My mother doesn't believe in me," I murmured. "She always goes with what you guys say because she doesn't want to do the actual work of raising me. She's just a…formality. She will probably be glad to be rid of me."

I couldn't stop myself from saying that out loud. I didn't want them to know about my relationship with her, but any fool could see that my mom had stood on the sidelines all of those years, watching someone else raise her daughter, and she hadn't cared. I thought under all of her depression and sadness and weakness she cared, but she didn't, and it was time for me to come to terms with that.

"Things are not always what they seem," Sam said carefully.

"Your mother does care about you," Fred said just as delicately.

I had a feeling they were hiding something from me, but it wasn't the time to squeeze it out of them. I needed to push aside how I felt about my mom and focus on the fact that I was going to actually pursue a career in the modeling industry. I never thought I would hear those words even in my own head, but there they were.

I smiled again at Sam and Fred, my parents.

"I'm going to pursue a career in the modeling industry," I said with amazement.

"Yes, you are," Sam said and then held my chin between her soft, delicate fingers. "And you're going to kick ass at it."

The door flung open and Emmy came in with Emmet on her heels.

"What the hell is going on in here?" she asked in exasperation. She beckoned me to get up with her hands. "Up! We have a party to get to!"

I was pretty sure that she and Emmet had been listening outside of the door. It was confirmed when I saw sister and brother exchange a quick smile with each other before looking at me.

"Let's go," Em commanded, trying hard to hide her smile.

Sam looked at the three of his disapprovingly. "Will there be parental supervision at this party?"

"Probably not, Mom," Emmy said. I could tell she said it just to rile the woman up. "There will probably be drugs all over the tables, beer kegs in every corner, and hot and sweaty sex on every piece of furniture."

Emmet skillfully cut in between Emmy and Sam before the two started fighting. He looked at both of his parents and said, "I'll take care of both of them, I promise. No one will be high (lie), drunk (another lie) or having sex (possible lie)."

Fred and Sam didn't look appeased, but after a few warnings and rules, we were allowed to escape from the office. I was last out of the room, but I stopped before closing the door and looked at both of them.

"Thank you," I said softly from the bottom of my heart. "Thank you."

"Let's go!" Emmy shouted from the living room.

I threw them one last smile and hurried after my impatient friend.

~~*

Perry Hinson was having the biggest party of the summer. Kids were coming from all over the area. Perry lived out in the middle of nowhere in a big farmhouse. The closest neighbor was a half mile away. While life was probably very boring growing up in the middle of rural New Jersey, the kids that lived out in those areas always threw the best parties because the cops were less likely to stumble upon them.

The party was already in full swing when we got there at eight-thirty. There were kids everywhere. I swear the house looked like it was vibrating as we walked from Emmet's car. When we got inside, I saw a lot of kids I knew from school. I realized then that I probably wouldn't see a lot of them for some time, depending on how my career went. Being there was bittersweet.

"Stick with me all night," Emmet said in my ear while Emmy was distracted.

He was pressed up against me because there were so many people surrounding us. I could smell his cologne and the shampoo he used for his hair. I wanted to wrap myself in him, but that wasn't an option.

"Emmy will probably want me with her," I said after I pulled his head down close to me so he could hear me without anyone else hearing me. Honestly, I could barely hear me over the music and noise in the house.

"Tabitha and Mayson will be here, too. She'll be distracted."

I nodded, letting him know I understood. His fingers quickly, but affectionately had squeezed mine before he dropped his hand away.

True to Emmet's word, Emmy ended up very distracted and wasn't worried about having me attached to her side. I didn't feel the jealousy I had felt when she was in Louisiana. I had other friends to talk to and new faces to get acquainted with.

Despite Emmet's insistence that we stick together all night, we ended up separated repeatedly. Eventually, I gave up and just tried to enjoy the party. I would have him all to myself the following night.

After two hours in the house, I was feeling hot and stuffy. The three beers I'd had probably didn't help either. I pushed my way through the sweaty partiers and stumbled onto the back deck where more people were hanging about. The air quality outside wasn't much better than it had been inside.

"It's hot, right?" Stella asked me from my left. She was holding a cold beer to her face and smiling at me.

"Summertime in New Jersey is usually pretty warm," I informed her in case she didn't know it.

She laughed pleasantly as if I hadn't just insulted her intelligence.

"I'm complaining about the heat now, but in a couple of months, I'll be freezing my ass off in harsh New England winter."

I tilted my head, but thought better of that move when it felt like my brain sloshed in my head.

"What are you talking about?" I asked, confused. "I thought you're going to school in Oklahoma or some other landlocked, tornado state?"

That sweet laugh again. She really was a nice girl. It wasn't her fault that I disliked her just a little bit. If it was anyone's fault, it was Emmet's. So, I tried to smile back at her.

"I was going to go to Oklahoma," she said and then took a sip of her beer. "But I changed my mind. I like the idea of being a train ride away from home. So, I'm going to go to Brown."

I wasn't positive about the timing and mileage, but Brown was uncomfortably close to Cambridge by my estimate.

I didn't bother forcing any more smiles for Stella's benefit. Even though she didn't say it, I felt like she was impeding on my territory, stepping on my toes. Damn it, she was going for my man.

"Emmet and I figured it out," she said casually lacing her arm with mine. I allowed her to lead me to a far corner of the large deck as she spoke. "It is only forty minutes or so for each of us if we meet halfway."

"Meet halfway for what?" I asked.

She shrugged her shoulder. "For whatever. Lunch, dinner, or a night out."

Okay, I told myself. *At least she didn't say for sex.*

She leaned in conspiringly and said, "Maybe more." She sighed as I felt my shoulders slump a little. "Emmet can be wild sometimes, but he has a good heart. You're lucky to have him as a brother."

"Yes, he's a good brother," I said absently.

I wanted to get away from Stella. I didn't want to have distrustful thoughts of Emmet in my head, and she was pounding them in there with a giant mallet.

I started to move away, mumbling something about finding Emmy, but Stella didn't hear me because she continued to speak as if we were best buds.

"We're forever bonded," Stella said, looking off into empty space.

I raised an eyebrow. No one could be bonded with Emmet the way I was. We shared a link, a tether, an invisible line that kept us together even when we were apart. I took some satisfaction in that, until Stella pushed a small pin into my bubble. Only one little pin prick is all it takes to deflate a bubble.

"I know I don't really know you, Donya, but I never hear you gossiping with the other girls, and Emmet always said good things about you. I can't even trust my own friends with this," she said with a sad laugh. Then she leaned in close to me so that she wouldn't be overheard. "We got pregnant. I lost the baby after a few weeks, but we both said that the experience would keep us tied together, even if we weren't *together*. But now that we'll be older and living kind of close, maybe we *can* be together, you know?"

I couldn't process her words or the hopeful gleam in her teary eyes. I spun around, held onto the railing and hurled into the grass below.

~~*

"We were looking all over for you!" Emmy cried when she found me sitting on the hood of Emmet's cherry red Audi.

Mayson, Tabitha, and Leo trailed behind her.

"I'll tell Emmet we found her," Tabitha said and started walking back the way she had come.

Without a word, Leo turned around and caught up to Tabitha.

"What are you doing out here?" Emmy asked and it was then I noticed how much she struggled to stand still. She was pretty drunk, and her eyes looked dilated. She had most likely been smoking something.

Mayson didn't look any better. In fact, she looked like she was flying in space, not even in the same galaxy. She gave up on standing and dropped slowly to the ground and stretched out on her back.

"You guys really need to lay off the weed," I said.

"She didn't smoke," Emmy said, leaning against the car for support.

I wondered what she had inhaled or injected. Long before Emmy and I ever had our first drink, Mayson had been doing a variety of drugs. She seemed to have a grip on it; I had only seen her really messed up only a couple of times and it was always at a party. Otherwise, she seemed to be okay with weed like Emmy.

"Hey, I totally kissed Leo," Emmy snickered.

"Leo has a girlfriend," I said in Leslie's defense. I didn't really know her well at all, but when I thought of Stella trying to pursue *my* boyfriend, I felt like I had a secret camaraderie with Leslie.

"No, no, they broke up."

My relief was small. In our age group, relationships broke apart and reformed quicker than others could realize there had been a change. My relationship with Emmet, apparently, was no different, because I didn't know how we were going to last the night, let alone nine months apart.

Earlier, after I puked, Stella didn't try to stop me from leaving. I went inside to find Emmet, but I didn't see him. I mentally pulled on the tether, searching for him, but it was stretched and tangled around the horny, high, and hot and sweaty teenage bodies between us.

Stella found him first, or maybe he found her. I don't know. I only saw their backs as they descended the deck steps into the large yard. He was so wrapped up in conversation with her that he did not feel me. They continued to walk towards the edge of the yard where it was darker and more private. I stopped doubting Stella's claim of a bond.

Dejected, I had turned around, pushed my way through the bodies to the front door and left the party behind.

By the time Tabitha and Leo returned with Emmet and Tack, Emmy had joined her cousin in the grass. Tack didn't look too much better than they did.

"He's not driving is he?" I asked no one in particular as I watched Tack swaying and stumbling.

Leo held up a set of keys. "I'm driving."

"Do you have a license?"

"Practically," he said with a wink.

I remained quiet as he and Tabitha helped Mayson off of the ground. Practically having a license while sober was better than having a license being drunk and high.

Emmet unlocked the car with his key fob before picking Emmy up off of the ground. I jumped off of the car and opened the back passenger's side door and stepped aside so he could help her get in.

"See ya," Tabitha said with a sigh as she helped Mayson walk.

"Are you going to be okay?" I asked.

"Yeah," she said. "I think we're just going to all go to my house and crash."

"Okay. Be careful."

When I turned around, Emmet was holding my door open for me. I got into the car without looking at him or saying a word. Before he closed the door, he dragged his knuckles over my bare arm, making goose bumps race to the surface on my skin. I gently, but obviously, pulled my arm away from his hand and looked straight ahead. He stood there silently for a moment.

"What?" he finally said with a trace of frustration in his tone.

I didn't answer. I reached for my seatbelt and pulled it across my chest and lap and clicked it into place while Emmet stood there in the open door watching me.

Finally, he slammed the door. When he got into the car, I could feel his aggravation. He put his seatbelt on, turned the engine and then slammed on the gas. We went unnecessarily fast down the long driveway. He barely paused to check for cars before racing onto the pavement and rocketing down the road.

I ignored his careless driving and looked into the backseat to check on Emmy. Her head was resting against the window as she slept with her mouth wide open. Very attractive, especially with the drool pooled at one corner of her mouth.

"Unless you need help getting Emmy into the house, you can drop me off at my mom's," I said quietly.

"No," Emmet said. He sounded appalled that I even said it.

"It wasn't really an option or a question," I said evenly.

"I'm driving and I'm not giving you the option."

"Fine. I'll walk."

"That also is not an option," he said, gripping the gear shift harder than necessary as he made the car go even faster.

"You're going too fast," I snapped.

"Yeah, I hear that a lot from you, but when I go slowly, it's not fast enough for you."

I looked at him with murder in my eyes. There was plenty I wanted to say, but I didn't know how much Emmy could really hear. If she had been listening at all, our conversation would seem innocent enough. I decided to keep my mouth shut for the rest of the ride home, choosing to ignore the ridiculous speed we were going and Emmet's eyes often burning a hole into the side of my face.

When we got to the Grayne's, Emmet got out and slammed his door before walking around to help Emmy. She couldn't walk on her own. Hell, she could barely walk at all. Emmet picked her up and threw her over his shoulder, making her laugh.

"I love my brother," she said, her voice echoing into the night.

"Quiet," Emmet commanded as he kicked the car door closed.

I knew he could take care of her, that he would be able to get her into the house and to her room, hopefully without getting caught. I turned away from them and hurried across the grass, towards the sidewalk.

"Donya!" Emmet's harsh whisper carried across the yard.

Knowing he wouldn't just leave Emmy, I walked faster, ignoring his commands to return. I figured I had only about five minutes before he would come after me.

I knew I was doing it again. I was running away instead of facing the problem, but I really needed some time to think. I wasn't going to ignore the problem. I just wanted to ponder on the problem. Sitting on the hood of Emmet's car for an hour watching other drunken people walk by and listening to the music blasting from the house party wasn't really a great environment for thinking. I was only able to replay my conversation with Stella over and over in my mind.

Emmet had knocked Stella up and never said anything to me. I would think that would be information I needed to know. I started to wonder if he still had feelings for her. I wondered what they were talking so intently about when he didn't even know I was standing behind him. I wondered if there was a chance they were going to get back together while they were away at school. They were 'bonded' after all.

I groaned in misery. They were bonded alright. He had put his bare dick in her. No condom. No sense. What had he been thinking? What if she had some kind of disease and he could have potentially given it to me?

"Careless, selfish, horny son of a bitch," I muttered as I neared my street.

I didn't make it home. I heard the powerful engine and the squeal of his tires as he flew around the corner. Before he even screeched to a stop beside me, I knew it was him. I felt it was him. I kept walking, but Emmet was on the sidewalk before I could even get past his front bumper. He roughly grabbed my upper arm.

"Get in the car, Donya," he said with a clenched jaw.

"I need to go home and think," I said, irritably as I tried to wrench free of his hand.

Emmet's eyes glowed a serious, stormy green as he engulfed my personal space. His grip on my arm increased to the point of pain. As an automatic reflex, I tried to step back, but he held me firmly and I couldn't move anywhere he didn't want me to move. Emmet had never scared me before, but I felt danger from him on that sidewalk. The tether between us twisted painfully, twisting my insides with it.

"I said to get in the fucking car," Emmet said so close to my face that I could almost see the words in the air as they came out of his mouth and landed softly, yet threatening on my face.

He pushed and pulled me to the car. He opened the door and pushed me inside and slammed the door so hard the car rattled. When he walked around the front of the car, the headlights illuminated his face. I didn't recognize him and that scared me.

"Put your seatbelt on," he commanded, but I just stared blankly at him. Angrily, he reached across me and put it on for me. After he was latched in, he worked the gears and clutch and we sped off into the dark night.

Chapter Sixteen

The parking lot where Emmet first kissed me hadn't changed. He parked in the furthest corner where very little light reached. He got out of the car, slammed the door, and walked around to my side. He opened my door and waved for me to get out of the car. He was still terribly angry, and I didn't him grabbing my arm again. I could already feel it bruising.

I got out and quickly tried to step away from him, but he put his hand on the car, blocking me with his arm. He shut my door and then used his other arm to trap me against the car.

"Talk."

"I don't want to yet," I mumbled.

"Not an option. Talk."

I scowled. "You can't make me talk."

"If I have to put a hand up your ass and make your mouth move like a fucking dummy I will. Talk!"

"I need some time and space to think!"

"I leave in less than two days!" he yelled in my face. "There is no time! Why do you keep doing this to me?"

He slammed a hand on the hood of the car behind me, startling me and making me jump. I had never, ever seen that level of anger from Emmet. I was sure that if I reached out and touched him my hand would burn in his fury.

"I talked to Stella tonight," I started in a whisper. "She told me she's going to Brown."

"Is that what you're mad about?" he asked incredulously. "Like I have some control over where she goes to school?"

"She said you guys plan to get together, and often."

Emmet rolled his eyes. "Seriously, Donya? That's what you're fucking mad about? Did she tell you that we would also be meeting up with a few other people who will be in school in the area?"

"No, but she did tell me that she thinks there is a chance for you two to get back together," I murmured. "And a part of me believes her; especially since you guys are 'bonded' by an unborn baby."

I dropped my eyes and cursed myself for my voice breaking on the last part of my sentence. Emmet became extremely quiet and still. I wasn't even sure if he was breathing. I felt tears sliding down my cheeks. I wiped at them with a surprising amount of anger. It rose without warning inside of me and Emmet's silence only added fuel to the fire.

As if I had suddenly gained super powers, I looked up into Emmet's face and shoved him away from me so hard that he stumbled back and almost fell on his ass. I moved forward and shoved him again. Next time he was prepared and had time to steel himself. I was still much smaller than him and didn't move him much, but that didn't stop me from shoving him again.

"You fucked her without a condom!" I yelled. "Thank god I found out, or I would have made the mistake of letting you take my virginity and possibly give me some STD!"

I shoved at him again, but he just stood there. His anger had evaporated, and he just looked sad, scared, and full of regrets.

"I was looking for you at the party, and when I found you, you didn't even know I was there. You were too busy walking off into the dark with the mother of your dead baby."

Even I knew how cruel and utterly wrong that was as I said it. The words were ugly and bad tasting on my tongue even as I spat them out at him.

Emmet's anger returned.

I had no recourse, nowhere to go before he reached me. I was shoved into the side of the car so hard that it rocked, and all of the air left my lungs. He crushed my body to the Audi with his and put his face so close to mine that our noses touched.

"That baby was a mistake," he said in the scariest hushed tone I had ever heard. "But that doesn't change the fact that it was a life lost. It wasn't what I wanted, especially with Stella, but it was mine, and it mattered even if it never had a chance. Every life matters, Donya. I thought even you would see that when *I* was ready to tell you, but clearly I was wrong about you."

He stepped away from me and walked around to the other side of the car. I bent over, with my hands on my knees, gasping for air and trying to push down the astonishing panic I felt bubbling in my throat.

Emmet was not only angry with me for my terrible words, but his opinion of me as a person changed for the absolute worse.

It was more than I could take. Why did I have to say that? Why couldn't I just ask him to tell me about Stella and the baby and be supportive? Why did I do that?

"Get in the car," he commanded.

I couldn't be in the car with him. I just couldn't do it. I staggered a few steps away and without warning I started to heave. I dropped to my knees and dry heaved repeatedly until I thought my stomach was going to turn inside out to get out of my body. When it finally stopped, I was crying. It was disgusting, snotty, hiccupping crying. I wiped my mouth with the back of my hand and bent over with my head in my hands, sobbing.

I thought Emmet had given up on me. I thought he was probably standing by the car, impatiently waiting for me to get my shit together so he could drive me home. But then his arms were around my waist, carefully lifting me until I was standing. He made no effort to comfort me, but he half carried, half walked me to the car and helped me inside. He closed the door, and when he got in behind the wheel, he didn't make me put my seatbelt on or do it for me. He didn't even look at me. He drove the few minutes to my house without saying a word as I sat there doing that ugly crying.

When he stopped in front of my house, I looked at him with all kinds of apologies stuck to my tongue, but he gently shook his head, shutting me down. His eyes were shimmering with unshed tears, but his jaw clenched with anger and resolution. Feeling clumsy and stupid, I turned away from him and stumbled out of the car. He sat there at the curb as I staggered up the sidewalk to the door. I don't even know how I managed to use my key to unlock the door, but the moment the door was open, Emmet drove away. He didn't peel away like a bat out of hell like he did that one night we had fought. He drove away at a normal, decent pace.

Somehow, that seemed that much worse.

The tether stretched and threatened to break. With all of the frayed pieces that were now in it, I knew it was only a matter of time before it pulled apart.

Chapter Seventeen

My bedroom door opened, and my mom stepped in holding a laundry basket. She looked startled to see me there.

"Oh, I didn't know you were home. I thought you were at your other house," she said, setting the basket down. "These are clothes you left in the dryer. I folded them up for you."

"Thanks," I said. My one word sounded as dead as I felt.

She looked at me for a long moment. She started to leave the room but halted. Slowly she turned back to me.

"Are you okay?" she asked carefully.

"Since when does it matter to you if I'm okay," I said and chose to stare at the ceiling. It was barely a question. It was more like a statement.

"Well, I'm asking," she said tightly. "Obviously it matters to me."

"Well, this is new. My mother gives a damn for a change."

"Donya Elisabeth," she said my name in warning, but I didn't care about her warning. What could she possibly do to me that I hadn't already done to myself?

"Get out of my room. Go back to your lonely existence of only caring about yourself."

She gasped, but my words didn't immediately chase her away.

"I care about you very much," she said. Though her voice shook slightly and there was evident emotion behind it, I didn't care.

"And I care about cotton candy and shoes very much. So what? Get out of my room."

She stood there a moment longer before quietly slipping out. Later I would feel sorry about the way I treated her, but at the moment, I didn't care that I hurt her.

It was the middle of the afternoon. I had only gotten out of bed once to use the bathroom when I first woke up. If I was hungry, I didn't feel it. If I was thirsty, I didn't notice. The only thing I was aware of was the gaping, ragged hole in my chest. A bullet to the chest would have probably felt significantly better.

I lay in bed, in the silence of my room, staring at the walls, staring at the ceiling, or with my eyes closed. I was continually assaulted by the smell of Emmet's body and cologne. I had slipped into his blue shirt before stumbling into bed in the wee hours of the morning. I had cried myself into a fitful sleep, full of nightmares I couldn't recall. I only slept a couple of hours before I woke up and stayed up.

I didn't try to call him, and as far as I knew, he didn't try to call me either. Part of me had hoped that he would have come to me at some point in the night, or in the morning, but he never came. I didn't deserve it anyway.

I stopped crying in the middle of the morning, but the pain only became more and more magnified as the hours ticked by. Soon Emmet would be gone, and I had ruined our last bit of time together. I hated myself so much for my careless words. Even though he had also done something careless, I should have at least given him the opportunity to explain himself.

Around four-thirty, my mom ventured back into my room.

"I'm going into work early," she said. "They're short-handed, and it's busy. I won't get off until eight and then I have some errands to run."

When I didn't answer her, she asked, "Are you going to be okay? Is there something I can do for you?"

"No."

"To which question?"

"Both."

She hesitated. She sucked in a breath like she was going to speak, but she changed her mind and left the room without another word.

~~*

I had fallen asleep at some point. It was dark when I heard someone calling my name from the front of the house. A few seconds later, Emmy threw open my bedroom door and flipped on the overhead light. I blinked up at the brightness and then gave up and covered my eyes.

"What are you doing in bed?" she asked, alarmed. "I called you like thirty times! You have to get up and get dressed!"

I heard my closet door open and hangers moving as Emmy started searching for something.

"Mom and Dad are going to be here to get us in a few minutes," she said. I felt something land on the bed. I forced my eyes open, uncovered them and blinked down at a little black dress.

I had not forgotten about Emmet's going away dinner. It was at a nice restaurant in Philly. I had been excited about going. I even had a going away present for him.

"I'm not going," I said to Emmy and kicked the dress to the floor.

She watched it fall and stared blankly at it for a few seconds. Then her eyes narrowed.

"What's wrong?" she asked suspiciously. "Did your mom say something to you?"

"No. I don't feel good. I don't want to go."

"But..." She floundered for something to say.

"I'm not going," I said firmly. "Wish Emmet well."

"But why?" She was genuinely confused. I was always included with any Grayne family function. Also, it was unfathomable to her that I would miss an opportunity to dress up.

"I just told you I don't feel good," I snapped at her.

"I guess I believe you," she retorted, snatching the dress up off of the floor. "You look like shit."

After hanging it back up, she lingered by the closet watching me with her arms folded. I knew she was trying to figure out what was going on with me.

"Well, then I guess you'll be over later tonight?" she asked with a trace of doubt.

Fred had rented a trailer to attach to the back of his truck for Emmet's move. Emmy and I were supposed to ride with Emmet to New England while Sam and Fred followed behind us with Emmet's belongings. Obviously, riding in the same car for an entire day with the guy who couldn't even stand to look at me was not going to happen.

"I don't think I'm going to Cambridge either," I told Emmy.

She frowned. "Emmet's going to be disappointed."

"I highly doubt it."

Her frown deepened, and she again studied me for a few moments, biting her bottom lip.

"You're my best friend, Donya," she finally said, shaking her head. "I know you. I know you aren't sick. Something has happened. What is it?"

I almost laughed. If she knew me so damn well then she should have been able to see how much I loved her brother, but she didn't. Even if she did, she wouldn't have approved.

"Maybe I have what my mom has," I whispered.

Her eyes widened. "Depression?"

"Maybe." I was depressed, so I wasn't exactly lying, but I wasn't diseased with it like my mother.

"Oh, D." Emmy rushed over to the bed. I didn't want to be touched, but I let her hug me. "Maybe I should stay with you."

"No," I said quickly. "I'll be okay. Just let me take a couple of days to get myself together. I'll be okay."

"Did you tell your mom?"

"No. No need to tell her. She was about to work almost a double shift. She didn't need to know."

Emmy sighed and then pushed loose strands of hair off my forehead.

"Is there anything I can do?"

I forced a dead looking smile. "Go. Eat a lot of food and annoy your mom."

"I can manage that." She hugged me once more. "I love you, D."

"I love you too."

"I'll call to check on you later, okay? Make sure you answer or I'm going to worry."

"I'll answer," I promised.

She got up, offered a few more kind words and left me alone.

"Finally," I breathed and rolled over to fall back into darkness.

~~*

Emmy called me after dinner later that night. She offered to come over and stay with me, but I insisted that I wanted to be left alone. I asked her about dinner; though I wasn't sure I wanted to know the details. She said it was fine, but Emmet seemed a little on the quiet side.

"Probably some floozy got to him," she had joked, not knowing that I was the floozy.

She asked me to reconsider the ride to Cambridge because there was bound to be plenty of hot college guys to cheer me up. I declined again, but at least gave her the impression that I was a little regretful that I'd miss the hot college guys. What about saying goodbye to Emmet? Was I going to say goodbye to Emmet?

"I'm pretty sure Emmet's world won't end if I don't say goodbye," I said, trying to sound light about it, even though I was dying inside. *My* world was going to come to an end because I wasn't going to say goodbye.

I listened patiently while she talked about Leo and his kissing skills. Leo was a good looking guy, but hearing about kissing made me think of kissing Emmet. It didn't look like I'd be kissing him again.

My sadness began to consume me, and I couldn't stand to stay on the phone a minute longer with Emmy and all of her cluelessness. I told her I was going to watch television and go to bed and that she should consider going to bed too since they were leaving bright and early in the morning. She offered once more to stay the night with me, but I convinced her that I was fine though I was anything but. I loved her and appreciated her, but she needed to go.

I kneeled down and opened the cabinet door next to the fridge. Inside were several bottles of various sizes, shapes, and colors. There was wine, vodka, tequila, whiskey, brandy, and more. My mom wasn't much of a drinker, but my dad had been. For whatever reason, she never got rid of the booze.

Emmy drank when she was mad, sad, happy, horny, melancholy and just for the hell of it. It was rather disturbing how much a sixteen-year-old girl could drink, but I wasn't a drinker. I drank at some parties, but for the most part, since that one night at Jorge's, I didn't drink much at all.

I reached into the cabinet and pulled out a bottle of red wine. I liked the taste of wine, much more than I liked the taste of beer or anything else. I found a corkscrew, pulled the cork out and grabbed a wine glass. If I was going to do something I shouldn't do, I figured I may as well do it with style.

I filled the glass and then held it close to my nose as I inhaled the scent. Then I put the glass to my lips and sipped. My shoulders relaxed as the sweet liquid drifted over my taste buds. Grateful for the smooth, delicious taste, I tipped the glass again and drank with more enthusiasm.

When I finally began to feel drunk, I welcomed it and the dreamless bliss it brought to me later in the night.

~~*

I woke up before dawn, wondering if Emmet had discovered the gifts I had buried in his suitcase. I had done it before the party. His suitcases were already mostly packed at the time because he didn't want to have to do anything last minute.

Chances were he wouldn't discover the two jars until he was already at Cambridge. Yesterday when I knew that no one was home at the Grayne's, I had been tempted to walk over there and take back the gifts, but after I'd thought about it, I knew that I wanted him to have them.

I had filled one large Mason jar with Hershey Kisses. Under the lid, I had written lines from "Endymion" by John Keats that spoke about a kiss and endless bliss. That's how I thought of Emmet's kisses, blissful.

The second jar was the same size, but contained only one item. It was a single candy heart. It was one of those candies with the cute little sayings on them that are hard to find outside of Valentine's Day, but I found some in a specialty candy store in the mall. The single heart in the jar said one word: Mine. Under the lid of that jar, I wrote, "I only have one heart to give to you. Handle it with care."

I wanted Emmet to keep the jars. He was the only person I wanted to have my kisses and despite our sad circumstances, he still possessed my heart.

I stood at the living room window as the sun began to rise. I stood stock still for a long time until I felt the familiar tug. I put my palms flat against the glass as the line stretched, twisted, and resisted. It stretched and stretched and pulled and yanked on me until I was sure my heart would burst from my body and splatter, bloody and dead on the window. He was gone, and when I really understood that and felt his loss, I collapsed to the floor in mourning.

Chapter Eighteen

Oh, how naïve I had been.

I truly believed that after my meeting with Max, he would just start sending me to various clients for work. I didn't imagine that I'd find work quickly, but I at least expected that by the time the end of October rolled around that I would have at least been on a freaking casting call or go-see. I was so wrong!

Max first gave me hell for taking too long to get back to him. By his estimate, I should have been clamoring to get into his office the week after he first met me. Then the jerk flipped through my portfolio with disgust and tossed the book back to me.

"I look good in those photographs," I snapped at him as I caught the book.

My mother put a gentle hand on my arm, implying that I be patient. I had been pretty snappy with people since the end of August.

"Yeah, you look very pretty," Max said dismissively. "But pretty doesn't sell, unless you want to advertise twenty dollar dresses for K-Mart."

I frowned.

"I don't want to do commercial modeling," I said. "I want to do high fashion."

He sighed and leaned back in his seat. "Stand up."

"What?"

"Stand up. Up!" He raised his hands impatiently.

I passed my mom the portfolio and stood up.

"Stand over there," he waved with his hand. I walked to the general place he waved to. "Spin around—slowly!"

Sucking in a breath so that I wouldn't snap at him again, I spun in a slow circle.

"You've aged since I last saw you," he said bitterly.

"What? That was only the beginning of summer!"

"You're a *child*," he said. "Children *grow*."

Well, duh, I thought, but remained silent and waited for him to speak again.

"Okay, sit down," he said with another sigh.

"So, can you work with her, or not?" my mom asked as I took my seat beside her.

"She got old, but yeah. I can work with her."

So, my old butt sat there, expecting him to give me clients to see and what I got was an appointment with a test photographer. The test photographer basically did the same things Tori did, but I didn't argue. I guess I passed the 'test' because Max was really happy with my new portfolio.

Again, I thought the phone would be ringing off of the hook, but after weeks of getting tutored at home for nothing and missing everything going on in school with my friends, I got pissed off enough to venture into New York by myself. I told Emmy where I was going, but I didn't tell my mom or my other parents. I stormed into Max's office—well…I tried to storm into Max's office, but I was stopped first by security that had to call up to the agency to let them know I was there. Then I got stopped by the main receptionist, and again by Max's secretary. Finally, when I was able to storm into his office, I was exhausted.

"You told me I was exquisite!" I said, slamming my palms onto his desk. "You said I had potential!"

He looked up at me, not at all fazed by my tantrum.

"Yeah, you are, and you do," he said casually and looked back to his computer.

"Then why am I still sitting in Jersey staring at the walls?" I demanded.

He looked me up and down. He actually stood up, leaned in close to me and dropped his eyes to my feet on the floor. I was confused, but said nothing, nor did I back away from him.

"It looks like you're standing in my office in New York City, Donya, not sitting in New Jersey."

I wanted to punch him, but I kept my cool and met his eyes, only inches from mine.

"Max," I said his name sweetly. "If you're waiting for me to kiss your ass to get me some work, you will be waiting a very long time."

"You have balls to come into my office and talk to me like that. I am the man who can make or break you."

A corner of my mouth pulled up into a soft smirk. "Max, I am *shattered* inside. If you think you can break me any more than that, I welcome you to try."

His eyes narrowed and discriminated. Then he sighed and sat back down in his chair.

"I think I have the perfect client to send you to."

~~*

"Did you brush your hair?" my mom asked me, as she got into her bed.

"One hundred strokes," I murmured as I flipped through an issue of *Vogue*.

"Did you moisturize?"

"All greased up," I replied automatically.

"How do your nails look?"

I dropped the magazine on my lap and sighed as I looked over at her. I was glad she was with me. I was glad she wasn't only with me, but truly trying to be a loving mother, but she was driving me bat-shit crazy.

"Mom, my nails look as good as they're going to get. I'm going to sleep in a few minutes so I won't wake up with red eyes, okay? Everything will be fine."

She nodded. "Okay." She sighed and nodded again. "Okay."

She pulled back the blanket and bedspread and got into bed. I went back to reading my magazine even though I could feel her eyes on me.

"What?" I finally said, dropping the magazine again.

"I'm really proud of you," she said softly.

I snorted. "Mom, I haven't done anything yet," I said bitterly.

I had been on several casting calls and had actually had a few call backs and landed some decent gigs. We had been at it for months. My mother quit her job as a waitress to travel with me. It made way more sense than the Grayne's hiring some stranger to chaperone me or having someone from Max's company glued to my hip. I didn't think my mom wanted the task, especially after the cruel things she had said to me the day I returned from Louisiana, but she surprised me. She surprised all of us.

She drove me to Emmy's one day, and we all sat around the table discussing and planning. She didn't want the Grayne's to have to pay for everything, but they came to some kind of agreement I wasn't privy to because I was sent out of the room. That made no sense to me since it was about me.

"You're trying really hard," she said to me in the hotel room, months after we started on this venture. "When someone tells you you're too skinny, too fat, too short, too tall, too old or too young, or too dark, you shrug it off and move on to the next one."

What I didn't tell her, was that when someone called me too fat, I surreptitiously skipped meals. When someone said I was too skinny, I ate a candy bar. When I was looked at with disgust or boredom, I waited until I was in the shower that night to cry about it. I didn't tell her any of that. I simply shrugged and said, "Someone will eventually think I'm just right."

~~*

Work was trickling in. Some of it was behind the scenes stuff, like being a human mannequin for designers. I had several photo shoots for various publications, and a couple of them were with influential designers for ads that ran in *Vogue* and *Vanity Fair*.

I wasn't what I'd call a model in demand, but I didn't complain. I was gaining experience and learning about the business. I was also learning patience and restraint because many of the girls I encountered in the industry were straight up bitches. I didn't get into any physical altercations, but I quickly had to let a few of them know that this Jersey girl wasn't really down for any catty shit.

"I will beat your ass and ground my Blahnik into your skull as I step on you to continue to the next gig," I had told Inga, one of the girls I repeatedly had to work with.

Between working, looking for work, and my schooling, my contact with Emmy and the family began to slip. For the most part, it couldn't be helped, but admittedly I avoided the holidays. I didn't want to have to face Emmet, not yet. In the late winter, however, I wanted to spend some time with the family. Though I had been home several times over the months, I had never stayed more than a couple of days because I was sucking up every little bit of work I could get. I was ready for some comforts of home. I needed Emmy and her undying friendship. I needed Sam and her craziness. I needed Fred and his warm fatherly ways. I needed to sleep in my room at the Grayne's that used to be Lucy's.

The other things that I needed were sadly unattainable and several hours north of home.

I also thought my mom needed a rest. She had been traipsing all over New York with me, and we had taken two trips to L.A. She was looking more and more worn down and tired. All of the activity was apparently draining her more than I would have expected. My mom wasn't old, she was only in her late thirties, but she laughed about her aches and pains more than any older person I knew. She tried to joke about it and claim it was her old age kicking in, along with years of inactivity, but I suspected there was more. I could not for the life of me figure out what that may have been.

She kept chugging along without much complaint, though, and she was so different from the person she was a year before, I didn't complain either.

Another reason I needed to be home was because Emmy needed me. A lot was going on in her life. She admitted to me one night in the late fall that she had been getting high with Tack and Mayson on a regular basis. I chastised her, and she promised it wasn't a problem. By the time New Year's had passed by, the three of them were doing heavier stuff than weed though Emmy never clarified what. She was, in essence, their supplier, because she had significantly more funds than her cousins, but Emmy started to hate the way the drugs made her feel.

"I hate *needing* it," she had cried on the phone. "Mayson and Tack are getting really bad. Tack's failing all of his college courses and Mayson is making really, really bad decisions. She's dating this guy…my god, he's *awful*, Donya. He keeps her high and I think when she's bothering to eat, she's doing the finger throat thing because he likes her thinner. He's called her a fat pig in front of everyone and instead of punching him in the face as she should, she promises to do better. What the hell!" she screamed in frustration.

I wanted to ask so many questions, but I had to let her finish with her tearful rant and confessions.

"She's getting violent. She hit her mom a few times recently, and she slapped Tabby when she called her a junkie. Oh, my god, everyone is unraveling. I don't want to unravel. I don't want to be a junkie. I did this shit because it was fun, but it's not fun anymore."

I turned down a few jobs to go home to my friend the following week. The modeling world would still be there when I returned.

As I made the usual walk from my mother's house to my other home, I considered how brave Emmy had been to go to her parents and tell them about her problem. I didn't agree with her keeping Mayson's and Tack's problems a secret, but it took a lot of strength for her to go to her parents. Fred and Sam being the awesome parents they are immediately put her in an outpatient program. They didn't yell at her, they didn't tell her how disappointed they were, they just did what needed to be done.

I walked through the door at the Grayne's and gave myself a moment to feel the rush of memories soar through my mind. I had so many, from jumping on the antique couch as a child and getting my ass handed to me by Sam, to the chaos of a house full of kids when all of the older siblings were still home. I thought about the scraped knees and elbows that were bandaged under that roof, the excellent meals Sam provided, and Fred's kindness. I also thought about how the whole family stood in the foyer waiting for me when my dad died, Emmet's arms around me comforting me, and Emmet's arms around me in his bed, and the days that we spent without parental supervision.

Without meaning to, my eyes drifted to the top of the stairs in the direction of his bedroom. I hadn't been in there since the previous summer. I hadn't seen him since the night I uttered those cruel words to him about his unborn baby. There had been no phone calls, no letters, no postcards, smoke signals, courier pigeons or telegrams. There had been nothing; yet...I still felt him, moving on in the world, going on without me. I still felt that tug though it wasn't as strong. I wondered if he felt it, too.

"You're here!" Emmy squealed, appearing at the top of the stairs. She skipped down and crushed me in a hug.

"You're going to suffocate me," I laughed as I hugged her back.

"I'm so glad you found time to come home," she said, pulling back from me.

I didn't tell her that I turned down work to be there. I smiled and looked her over. My heart broke looking at her. There were dark circles under her eyes, and her usually vibrant brown and green eyes were dull. She was at least twenty pounds lighter than she should have been. I know I had only been around a few times, but how could I have missed the signs? How did I not hear it in her voice before she broke down to me?

We were both getting too good at keeping secrets from each other, except it had become one-sided again. I knew all of hers, and she still had no clue about one very big one of mine.

Sam and Fred joined us on the foyer, hugging me and telling me how glad they were to see me. Sam hated my outfit and told me how pretty I was regardless of my eyebrows.

Fred wanted to hear all about work and city life. The conversations were never-ending as we sat down for dinner. For a little while, we were able to take the focus off of Emmy and her issues and Mayson and Tack. I wowed them with my stories of work and misadventures in the city. Some stories they'd heard before, but they seemed to like hearing them, and I was glad to oblige. I was indebted to that family. If I had to talk until my mouth was dry to make them content, it was the least I could do.

Later that night I climbed the stairs to meet Emmy in her room. We were going to lounge on her bed and eat junk food and drink too much Pepsi while we chatted with the radio on in the background. I knew I would later pay the price for the junk food and cola, but Emmy needed what used to be our normal, and so did I.

I stopped in the middle of the hallway and looked at Emmet's door. There had been a time, not too far back in my past when I had been happy behind that door. Happy, aroused, smiley, and loved. I wondered if I opened the door if I would feel all of those emotions again or if I would only feel the empty space that it was. An even more alarming thought occurred. What if I found the jars I gifted him sitting on the bed or bureau, left behind and unwanted?

I didn't remember crossing the hallway, but suddenly my hand was on the doorknob, and I was turning it slowly. I shrunk back as if the door had burned me. I didn't know if I was strong enough to push it open. What if the jars were really there? It would gut me.

But I had to know.

I pushed open the door.

~~*

"I'm so glad you're here," Emmy told me for the hundredth time that day.

"Me, too," I said, smiling at her.

"I'm going to be a better person, Donya," she said earnestly. "I want to be like you. You're always so damn strong, and you don't take any shit."

I looked away from her. If only Emmy knew what kind of a person I really was. I was tempted to tell her, but she was looking at me as if I was her rock, and the last thing she needed was for me to roll on her.

"It's so lonely here without you and Emmet," she said sadly. "I guess that's why I was hanging around Mayson and Tack so much."

"They're your cousins and friends," I said gently. "There wasn't anything wrong with hanging out with them."

"Yeah," she said unconvinced. She sighed and changed gears. "Meet any cute guys?"

I laughed. With Emmy, it always came back to the cute guys.

"You are so boy crazy!"

"A little bit," she grinned and then looked at me sheepishly as her fingers twisted the Pop Rocks package in her hands. "I really like Leo."

I raised an eyebrow. "Is he on again or off again with Leslie?"

"They're on again I think," she frowned. Then she shrugged her shoulders. "Not like it matters either way. I really like him, but it's no secret that he's a slut. I want someone who wants me and me only. I want to be the first thing he thinks of when he wakes up and the last thing he thinks about when he goes to sleep."

"You sure have some romantic notions," I said.

"There isn't anything wrong with that. Hell, if I were in Leslie's shoes, I wouldn't keep getting back with Leo. I will never be so wrapped up in a guy that I'd let him repeatedly hurt me like that. That's bullshit. She's a nice girl. She should be with a guy who respects her and wants her and her only."

I nodded in agreement as I considered that. I had a guy that wanted me and me only. I blew it.

"She must really love him though," I said thoughtfully. "If she keeps taking him back."

"That's not an excuse. She should love herself more. That'll never be me, sister."

I had no idea that many years later I would recall that conversation and remind Emmy of her words.

"Have you spoken to Emmet?" she asked me. "He didn't make the trip to Louisiana for Thanksgiving, and he skipped out of Christmas the day after instead of hanging around. I was hoping we would be able to spend some time together. I kind of miss him. Don't tell him I said that," she followed up quickly.

"He didn't go to Louisiana?" I asked, surprised. I had no idea that he had not been there. No one had mentioned it.

Emmy shook her head. "He said he was spending the time with friends in Boston. Mom gave birth to a full grown cow."

"No doubt," I murmured, lost in my thoughts. I wondered if Emmet was with Stella for Thanksgiving and if she was the reason he skipped out of Christmas early.

"Oh, shit," Emmy said, jumping off of the bed. "I forgot!"

I watched her hurry to her closet.

"Forgot what?" I asked, shoving a handful of chips in my mouth. I knew I was a pig and the crumbs falling on my lap and the bed wasn't cool, but it wasn't often that I got to indulge in the salty snack.

"Emmet left your gift here," she said, shuffling back to the bed.

I blinked at her. "Emmet got me a gift?"

She presented me with a small rectangle box wrapped neatly in silver gift wrap. A red ribbon was tied around it and formed a perfect bow on top. There was a small tag attached to the ribbon with my name written in Emmet's handwriting. I held the box in my hands, staring at it with a hard beating heart and large, surprised eyes.

"I told him to just drop it off in New York on his way back to Cambridge, but he gave me an excuse so lame I can't even remember what it was," Emmy said, waving her hand. "Then mom thought it would be nice if you had a gift to come home to."

"I've been home since Christmas," I said pointedly, looking at my friend.

"Yeah, I was kind of screwed up on drugs," she said defensively. "Cut me some slack."

I wasn't going to give her a speech about the drugs. She didn't need a speech, and frankly, I wasn't in the mood to give her one.

"Are you going to open it?" she asked, reaching for the bag of Doritos.

I wanted to open it alone. I had no idea what to expect in the package, but I had a feeling it would be something very personal.

"What did he get you?" I asked, looking steadily at the box.

She fell silent, and I sensed the change in her. I looked up, but Emmy was looking down at the bedspread.

"What?" I asked. Did he not give her anything?

"A bracelet," she said quietly. "But I lost it while I was fucked up one night. It's gone."

I frowned too and reached over to rub her arm. There was nothing I could say. I couldn't tell her it was okay because really it wasn't. She had fucked up and losing the bracelet her brother had given her was only one of the consequences.

"Open your present," she said, trying to rally. "I'm thinking you got the same as me."

"Maybe," I shrugged.

I pulled at one end of the ribbon until it unraveled and fell away from the box. Carefully I peeled away the wrapping paper. I was going to save every bit of it and the ribbon too. When the paper was gone, I held a velvet black box in my hands.

"For the love of all that's good in this world," Emmy sighed in exasperation. "Can you just open it already?"

"My gift, my speed," I said curtly.

"Slow speed," she muttered.

"Says the girl who gave me the gift *months* later!"

"Open the damn box, Donya!"

I scowled at her but flipped the box open anyway. Immediately my scowl disappeared. My mouth fell open, and my eyes widened once again.

"Oh, it's…gorgeous," I whispered.

"Yeah," Emmy said sadly. "Mine was similar."

Lying on the satin lining inside the box was a charm bracelet made of white gold. There were two charms already linked to it, and I touched them gingerly. I fought really hard to not show Emmy how deeply affected I was.

"My charms were an E and a little girl with 'sister' printed across her dress," she said quietly. I glanced up at her and knew that she was struggling not to cry.

"Maybe we'll find it someday, Em," I said, though I seriously doubted it.

"Yeah, and maybe pigs will fly," she snorted and shook her head. "Don't mind me. Let me put your bracelet on you."

I allowed her to take the bracelet from the box, and I extended my right arm. Emmy carefully put the bracelet on my wrist and smiled, but she looked at the jewelry with obvious confusion.

"I don't get it," she said, fingering the charms.

I shrugged like I didn't know either, but I did know, and the knowledge made my heart both joyful and sorrowful at the same time. I had the strong urge to run into Emmet's room and cocoon myself in his bed or his closet of clothes and wrap myself in his scent.

When I went in there earlier and found a single Hershey Kiss on his bureau, I knew it was left there for me. I felt it deep inside. Emmet had not only found my jars but taken them with him. There was a chance he had since trashed them, but maybe not.

I smiled at the charms on my wrist and lied to Emmy once again. "I have no idea what they mean."

"Oh, who cares," she said. "It's a nice bracelet."

"Yes, it is," I said.

The white gold Hershey Kiss and diamond heart glittered in the light of the room, and for the first time in months, my heart sighed.

Chapter Nineteen

Felix Hunter was the man of the hour. He was young, sexy, talented, and a bit of a bad boy. He even looked like a bad boy with his wild, dark hair, deep gray eyes, and his crooked smile that drove women across the world wild with desire. Felix often found himself in situations that made him look like the bad boy too: caught in bed with the wife of a senator, bar fights, and driving recklessly on his Harley or in one of his fast, fast cars.

Felix first broke onto the acting scene as a preteen, doing bit parts in various television shows before landing a major role in a teenage prime-time soap opera that ran for five seasons. Critics didn't think Felix's career would go much farther, that he would bounce around from one failed show to another until he eventually disappeared into obscurity, but he surprised everyone. He was cast in one of the hottest action movies of the decade and proved his kickboxing skills and his acting skills. If that wasn't enough to quell the critics, he next starred in a blockbuster drama that won him an Academy Award. The critics shut up after that.

I, along with fifteen other girls, was chosen to be in a photo shoot with Felix for the cover of *Rolling Stone*. The other girls were giddy at the prospect of meeting Felix, but I was more worried about standing out amongst them. I didn't care about getting Felix's attention as they all had seemed desperate to do. My goal was to make sure that the photographer didn't forget my face. I didn't want to blend in. I needed to make an impression, but I wasn't sure how I was going to do that.

The girls went into a tizzy when Felix came out for the shoot, dressed in an open button down shirt and white linen pants that hung low on his hips. He had a well-defined chest with a smattering of hair, ripped abs, and a trail of hair that disappeared into the pants that barely covered his genital area. I couldn't deny that he was good looking, but I wasn't going to trip over myself trying to get his attention.

He smiled tightly at the other girls and allowed himself to be positioned for the shoot. I was the only girl who hadn't run up to him squealing like a stuck pig. I stood off to the side, listening for direction, watching everything very carefully until I was told to find my place. Felix was supposed to sit on a stool, looking relaxed and unbothered by us, his adoring, horny fans. The vision was that we were expected to reach for him, pulling at his clothing, touching his chest, his arms, and make him look like a wanted man. Most of the girls positioned themselves at his feet or beside him. The photographer insisted I stand beside him too. I did as I was told and we began.

The shoot was boring. Felix yawned boringly a few times, and the photographer was frustrated. He kicked a couple of the girls out of the shoot because, in his words, "You suck at life. Go suck somewhere else."

I didn't want to suck at life, and I surely didn't want to do it anywhere else. While those girls were moping away and the rest of the girls vied for the perfect position, I decided to go against the grain. I stood directly behind Felix while lights were readjusted and the crew geared up to restart the shoot. Like the other girls, I was wearing a white tank top, hip-hugging blue jeans, and no shoes. I took a deep, fortifying breath, just as the photographer started yelling out instructions again.

"What the hell is the black girl doing behind Felix? I can't see you, black girl!"

Moving at lightning speed, I pulled off my tank top, tossed it offset, and stepped onto the back rungs of the stool, elevating myself both above Felix and the other girls. Before Felix could look back to figure out what the hell I was doing, I wrapped one arm around his waist and positioned my hand on his hard stomach with my fingertips just touching the waistband of his pants. I dug my knees into his sides for leverage, splayed my fingers across his strong jaw and gently bit down on his ear as I stared ferociously at the photographer who, fortunately, stopped asking questions and started taking pictures.

Felix wasted no time resting his arms on my legs and following *my* lead with poses as the other girls continued to reach for him. There were pictures with my hands twisted in his hair, my lips on his jawline, his head turned towards me as if we were about to kiss—and then he *did* slip me the tongue— and pictures of my hands all over his body. When I say all over, I mean *all over*. No matter what the pose was, I made sure my face was seen.

At the end of the shoot, I crossed my arms over my chest, suddenly embarrassed about my nakedness. I hadn't felt any embarrassment while working; I only felt the adrenaline as I did what I felt I needed to do—and exhilaration. I wasn't Donya, Sixteen Year Old Model Wanna-Be. I was Donya, Super Model at Work. The sounds of the camera whirring as the photographer took shot after shot was like music to my ears, and his exclamations about how "fucking wonderful this black girl is," made me feel bolder and empowered. I knew my mother, Fred and Sam would probably all have coronaries together once they found out what I had done, but my life changed that day.

"Here," Felix Hunter said, literally handing me the shirt off of his back. He grinned at me and ignored the other whiny girls as they were ushered away from the star.

I managed to ignore their glares and mutterings of "bitch" and "whore" and racist words I don't care to repeat. When Inga glared at me, I smirked at her. She would have given her left arm to be where I was at that moment.

"Thank you," I said, taking the shirt from Felix.

Even though I had my boobs pressed to his back for forty minutes, I wasn't really up for giving him a full show. I turned my back and slipped the shirt on. After I had buttoned enough buttons to hide my bare breasts, I turned back around.

"What did you say your name was?" he asked, offering me his hand.

"I didn't," I said, and placed my hand in his. "Donya Stewart."

"Felix Hunter," he said proudly as he shook my hand.

"Yeah, what're you an actor or something?" I asked innocently.

He laughed and said, "Yeah, or something."

"Thanks for the shirt, Felix," I said as I looked around the set for my tank. "As soon as I figure out where mine went to, I'll return it."

"Keep it," he said, though I knew it wasn't necessarily his to give. He had been dressed by a stylist moments before coming on set.

"Thanks," I said with a small smile. "Have a good day."

I started to walk away in the footsteps of the whiny girls that had exited the space, but the photographer stopped me. He bitched about me not following directions and then raved about my creativity. I smiled gently the entire time, listening carefully to everything he said, even if some of it sounded like nonsense. I must have behaved appropriately because he was already discussing my next gig with him.

By the time I left the room, I could barely contain my excitement. As soon as I saw my mom I grinned. I was about to tell her everything that happened, when a strong hand closed on my shoulder. I turned around, startled, and found myself face to face with Felix.

"You're the only girl in there that wasn't fawning over me," he said, his cute face curled into confusion. "I put my tongue in your mouth, and you walked away from me afterward like it was nothing."

"What do you want?" I asked, crossing my arms. "An apology or something?"

"Do you not like my work?"

"I like your work," I shrugged.

"But you don't like me," he said, frowning.

"I don't know you."

"Huh," he said and looked at me thoughtfully. "You may not have an opinion about me, Donya, but I think I like you."

"I'm flattered."

"Are you?"

"Kinda," I said with another shrug.

To my surprise he grinned. "I like you."

He motioned to a man I didn't immediately see and then I wondered, as the man approached, how I had missed him. He was huge. Muscles were bulging out of every part of his nice suit. Felix asked the man for paper and a pen. He reached into his suit and produced both pen and paper.

"I'm giving you my phone number," Felix said and motioned for me to turn around. When I didn't comply, he insisted that I turn around. I turned. Seconds later I felt pressure on my back and realized he was using my back as a writing surface.

"You call me whenever you want. This is my mobile number, so I can be reached almost anywhere."

"I'm not going to call you," I said, shaking my head.

"Sure, you will," he said. "What's your number?"

"You're not going to call me either," I laughed, despite myself.

"Sure, I will. Number."

Laughing at the absurdity of Felix freaking Hunter writing down our phone numbers on *my* back, I told him both my hotel number and the number to the mobile phone I recently acquired.

"I'll be in touch," he said a minute later as he handed me his phone number. "Don't lose that."

"I won't."

Felix and his beefy bodyguard went back through the door. My mother rushed over to me, grinning as she grasped my hands.

"That was *Felix Hunter*!" she said excitedly.

"Yeah, I know," I said, rolling my eyes.

"What did you do to impress Felix Hunter?"

I shrugged, pulled my hands from hers and started for the exit. I looked over my shoulder at my hesitant mother and said, "Took off my shirt."

Even with my back turned, I knew her mouth had dropped to the floor.

~~*

An hour later, after I had dropped my tired mother off at the hotel, I decided to take my school work to a coffee shop not far from the hotel to get some work done. As I was on my way there, the mobile phone rang in my bag. I wrestled it out without stopping and answered without looking. Very few people had the number. I expected my mom or one of the Grayne's, or even Max. I did not expect to hear Felix Hunter's voice so soon. Honestly, I didn't expect to hear his voice at all.

"Donya, Felix Hunter."

"Who?" I asked, biting back a grin.

"The guy who had his tongue down your throat not that long ago."

"Which guy?"

I held back my laughter as he groaned and said, "You're killing me here."

"I just saw you, Felix. Do you miss me already?"

"In fact, I do," he said playfully. "That's why I'm calling to see if you want to come out and play with me tonight."

I almost stumbled over my own two feet. I stopped in the middle of the busy New York sidewalk.

"You're asking me out?" I asked, not hiding my surprise.

"I'm pretty sure that is what I am doing."

"What if I decline?"

"I'd insist upon it. It is the least you can do considering how you violated me today."

My anger flashed, and I almost stomped my foot. "Violated you!" I cried indignantly. "You're the one that shoved your tongue in *my* mouth."

"Babe, you had your hands *all over* me. Then you put your sweet lips near mine as you manhandled me. What was I supposed to do?"

I blushed when I considered where my hands had been on his body. I had only touched Emmet's body like that in the past, and no other. I didn't get all heated and slick touching Felix but standing on the city street thinking about how brazen I had been sent a warm tingle crawling up my spine.

"Donya," Felix said my name softly, sensually.

"Yes?" I managed.

"Come out with me tonight."

I wanted to say yes, because getting seen with Felix could be an asset to my career, but as I looked at the bracelet on my wrist, my mind began to fill up with Emmet. Plus, there was the obvious issue.

"I'm only sixteen," I blurted.

"And I'm only twenty. Do you have a point?"

It was the lifestyle I wanted, right? I wanted to be seen and to rub elbows with the big guys, and from what I rubbed on Felix, he *was* a big guy.

I covered my face, mortified, even though he couldn't see me.

"Donya," he prodded less patiently than before.

"Okay, sure," I said quickly, releasing a long breath. "What did you have in mind?"

"How about dinner and a movie?"

"Seriously?" I questioned with suspicion. Felix Hunter couldn't just go out like a normal guy to dinner and a movie.

"Seriously. Wear something spicy."

"Spicy?"

"Hot," he said the word with emphasis on the H.

"Hot?"

"Sexy."

"Sexy," I said resolutely. "Okay."

"I'll send a car for you at six-thirty," he said cheerfully.

"You don't know where I'm staying."

"Yes, I do. I asked your agent. I have to go. See you at six-thirty. Remember, wear something spicy."

"Hot," I added.

"Sexy," he added in a voice that maybe made me melt just a little bit.

~~*

"Does this suffice?" I asked Felix after I climbed into his limo later that evening.

His driver had just walked me out of the hotel to the waiting car. Felix didn't get out, and I didn't blame him. As a star, he virtually had no privacy. If he got out of the car chances were he'd be bothered by some undying fan.

"It wasn't what I was expecting," he said to me, gazing at me from head to toe. "But this definitely, definitely suffices."

There were so many different directions I could have gone in to be 'spicy'. I could have been spicy-slutty, spicy-scary, spicy-bad girl, and so on and so forth. I chose a little bit of everything and squeezed into a pair of skin-tight dark blue jeans, a red halter top that made me appear to have more boobs than I actually had, and a pair of fire engine red stilettos. My hair was pulled back in a ponytail with a bit of a poof up front, and while I went easy on the red lipstick, I applied a more than generous amount of eyeliner, mascara, and eyeshadow. My hazel eyes looked so awesome with the make-up, it took me a good ten minutes to stop admiring myself in the mirror.

"So, what movie will we be seeing?" I asked, crossing one leg over the other.

"First thing is first," he said. He moved from his seat to the space immediately next to me. His arm slipped over my shoulders. "That's better," he said with a sigh.

I looked at him with raised eyebrows, but he ignored it.

"We are going to see the new Bruce Willis movie."

I nodded appreciatively. "I like Bruce Willis. He's a native of New Jersey, like me."

"That's all very entertaining," Felix said dismissively. "But what I'd really like to talk about is that kiss today."

My eyebrows shot up impossibly higher. Beads of sweat formed on the back of my neck and I shifted beside him, accidentally rubbing my thigh with his. No other guy besides Emmet ever had that effect on me before.

"Puh-lease," I said, trying to sound cool. "You've kissed a girl on set before. I have seen a couple of your movies. It was just work." I shrugged and looked at him like I didn't care, and I hadn't really, until he brought it up earlier in the day when he called me.

Felix's fingers lightly trailed over my bare shoulder and down my arm.

"All of those kisses I was prepared for," he said, pushing my hair back off of my neck with his other hand. His knuckles grazed my skin, and I had to fight back a gasp. "First I read them in the script and then we read them together. Then we discussed what the kiss would look like and how it would be approached. It was all very technical. Kissing you, however, was entirely unexpected. If it was just work, it had to be one of the hottest days at the office ever."

I cleared my throat and shifted away from him. I had a "What the hell am I doing alone in a limo with a twenty-year-old bad boy actor" moment, but if I was going to enter into the world of high fashion and celebrities, I was going to have to get over some of my reservations. Hell, I did it so easily earlier in the day when I took off my shirt in a room full of people.

"That's all very entertaining," I said, using his tone from earlier. "But what is for dinner, Felix? I'm starving."

He tilted his head back and laughed. I liked it. It was loud and obnoxious but genuine.

"Most women in your position don't eat."

"I'm going out to dinner with Felix Hunter," I said. "I better get his money's worth."

Felix laughed again and said, "I knew I liked you."

"I like me too," I said loftily.

"Yes, very entertaining, Miss Stewart, but back to that kiss…"

"Well, damn, Felix," I said with amusement. "You keep coming back to that kiss. You must not get too much action if you keep coming back to the moment you violated my mouth with your sticky tongue."

His eyebrows rose and the look of surprise on his face had me biting my tongue to keep from laughing.

"*Violate?*" he cried. "*Sticky!*"

"Mmm hmm," I said with a nod. "Tacky. Like glue."

"For the record, Donya, you're the one that smashed your cute little tits up against *my* back. You're the one that put your smooth, little hands all over my bare chest and in my pubes." I blushed furiously but didn't change my expression as he continued. "You're the one that bit my neck like a vamp and went all cannibal on my ear. You can't blame me for wanting to repeat that kiss. You should feel lucky that's all I want—for now."

"Is that all?" I asked, rolling my eyes. "You just want a little kiss?"

"For now," he said huskily, drawing nearer.

"Then you should ask your driver to stop at the store so I can go buy you some," I said with a big smile. "A big bag of chocolate Hershey Kisses."

His eyes narrowed even as they heated. "I want chocolate, and I want a kiss, and you sure do taste like candy."

"I don't remember what you taste like," I said nonchalantly. "I've already forgotten."

Felix's hand gently cupped my face. His thumb slid over my lips, and I tried really hard not to gasp, but I let a little one slip through anyway.

"Are you always so hard to get?" he asked softly.

"Always," I confirmed in a whisper.

"Good. I like it."

Felix Hunter pressed his mouth to mine and I damn near melted. I moaned softly, giving him an opening to dip his tongue into my mouth. His hand continued to hold my face possessively, and his arm around my shoulders squeezed, pulling me in close to him. I held onto his nice button down shirt, held on for dear life because his kiss was sweeping me away.

When he finally pulled away from me, my lips ached, and my mouth felt hot.

"There is something very unscrupulous about a twenty-year-old man kissing a sixteen-year-old girl in the back of his limousine," I said, gasping softly for air.

"That's a mighty big word for a sixteen year old," he teased, tracing my moist lips with his fingers.

"We're not all clueless," I said.

"Clearly not."

He kissed me again, and I didn't mention his lack of scruples again.

Chapter Twenty

"I can't come up there," Emmy mumbled on the phone. "I caught some kind of bug. I'm hurling and shitting and shitting and hurling. Sometimes at the same time."

"Ewww," I said, scrunching up my face. "I did not need all of the details."

I collapsed onto the bed. I had just returned from a photo shoot, expecting to find Emmy already at our suite. A few weeks after my shoot and the subsequent make-out session with Felix, Emmy was supposed to make the trip to New York to accompany me to a party Felix was throwing. I wasn't going as his date because we weren't dating.

After we saw the Bruce Willis movie, we made out in the car again on the way to dinner. As if we were in some comedy, my bracelet got caught in his hair. After the initial laughter, I looked at the charm bracelet and felt a crushing guilt on my chest. I loved Emmet, and though we weren't together and had not spoken in months and months, I still felt connected to him, especially while wearing the gift he had given to me. How could I just kiss someone new as if Emmet had never been?

Felix had noticed my change immediately and had the decency to pull back.

"Hey, what's wrong?" he asked, gently lifting my chin with a finger.

I fingered the bracelet.

"Someone very important gave me this," I said softly. Then I sighed with exasperation and looked away from him.

Why shouldn't I have moved on? Emmet left without saying goodbye. Emmet made no effort to call me or contact me at all. Emmet didn't send me a note and congratulate me on my first photo shoot or call me during the holidays.

But he gave you this bracelet, and that means a lot of somethings.

"Ex-boyfriend?" Felix asked, touching the bracelet.

"Something like that," I said with a humorless chuckle. "Whatever he was to me…" I put a hand on my chest, feeling my heart beat wildly under my palm. I looked at Felix. "I love him. I'm not over him."

The words hurt to say out loud. I balled my hands into fists and tried hard not to cry. For all I knew, Emmet was lying in bed beside Stella or some other girl and not thinking about me at all. Until I could not think of him, I couldn't be with anyone else. Especially someone like Felix with far more experience in the world than me. I would do nothing but slow him down, and I had to face the fact that he may have only been trying to seduce me. Felix Hunter wasn't known for monogamy or keeping his dick in his pants.

Felix put his fingers in my hair and twirled. His voice was soft and gentle when he spoke.

"I want you to know that I really, really, really like you," he said.

"Are you trying to make me feel bad?" I asked and bit down on my lip.

"No, not at all," he said soothingly. "But I really like you and even though I want to keep kissing you until the sun comes up, I respect you and what you're feeling. You've been real to me since the moment I stepped on set, and you barely paid me any mind." He smiled at the memory. "It's rare to find someone who is real when you're a guy in my position. If you promise to always be real with me, Donya, we can be friends. I would love to have a friend like you."

I looked at him suspiciously. "You're not 'acting' are you?"

He laughed and shook his head. "Nope. Just being as real as you are."

I looked away and then looked back at him bashfully. "Do you still want to take the stick in the mud to dinner?"

"I like mud," he shrugged and grinned. "And I like a girl with a good appetite. Of course I want to take you to dinner. I'd be honored if you'd go to dinner with me."

"You know that you're tarnishing your bad boy image, right?" I asked with a small smile.

He shrugged and grinned. Smugly he said, "Adding a little sweet to the badness makes me all that more appealing to the ladies."

I had rolled my eyes and laughed. Moments later I followed my new friend out of the limo to show him how real women ate.

Weeks later, with Emmy sick, there was no one to go to the party with me. I had made a few acquaintances while in New York, but none that I wanted to take with me to Felix's party. It was a private party, and I didn't trust anyone enough to bring along with me. I had been stabbed in the back more than once in my months in New York, and I wasn't looking for anyone to stab Felix in the back too.

I sure as hell couldn't go to the party alone. Well, I *could*, but my mom wouldn't let me, and most likely she wouldn't have approved of any of my acquaintances either. She barely approved of Felix.

"I guess I'm not going," I sighed miserably. I had met a few more celebrities through work and hanging with Felix, but his party would put me elbow to elbow with people that could really elevate my career. I didn't want to use him for my own personal gain; however, that was exactly what Felix intended for me to do.

"You're going," Emmy said groggily. "I sent someone in my place. They're probably almost there now."

"How can they almost be here if you're just now calling me to tell me you're sick?" I questioned. Anyone she could send—and I couldn't think of anyone—lived well outside of the city. She couldn't have called anyone moments before me and had them almost to my doorstep.

"I've been sick all day, Donya," Emmy sighed. "When I knew I wasn't getting any better earlier today, I made the arrangements. I waited until now to tell you so that you wouldn't freak out, but you're still freaking out."

"Who did you send?" I demanded, not denying that I was freaking out.

"Why don't you get ready?" she suggested, remaining aggravatingly obtuse. "By the time you're all dolled up, your plus one will be there."

"Why won't you tell me who it is?"

"It's a surprise, damn it!" She made an awful sound that made *my* stomach churn momentarily. "Gotta go," she said quickly. "Go get ready."

The line went dead. I slammed the phone down and growled in frustration as I got to my feet to get ready.

I had no idea who Emmy could send. Did she send Tabitha? No, Tabitha wasn't really talking to her. Mayson? No, Mayson was going through some unpleasant things. Leo?

I groaned, hoping she didn't send Leo. I liked his off again on again girlfriend Leslie and I did not want to get tangled in that web.

Feeling extremely frustrated and worried, I quickly got ready for the party. I dressed in a flirty yet classic black, strapless, asymmetrical dress by Coco Chanel. Felix had been kind enough to buy it for me, and I had been appreciative enough to accept it. It fit my body as if it had been made specifically for me.

I paired the dress with a pair of gold Manolo Blahnik stiletto sandals that wrapped sensually around my feet and ankles. I had my hair pulled back in a tight ponytail at the base of my skull secured by a gold barrette.

I had liked looking through *Vogue*, *Elle* and *Cosmo* and other fashion magazines when I was thinking about becoming a model, but in my everyday life, I had dressed like an average person. I had a few designer items, thanks to the Graynes, but I otherwise dressed pretty basic in jeans and a t-shirt. However, since my arrival in New York, I pushed myself to learn about the various designers, and whenever I could get my hands on any of their clothes and shoes, I did. I never went to a casting call without being draped in designer clothing, and since Felix's party was my first big party, I splurged on the Blahniks.

"I still think that you're too young for what you're wearing," Mom had said from the doorway.

I stood in front of the floor length mirror smoothing my dress and adjusting it needlessly. Like I said, it fit perfectly.

"What do you want me to wear, Mom?" I asked, not really expecting an answer.

"I think you're moving too fast with everything," she repeated. She had been saying it since the day I took my shirt off for *Rolling Stone*.

"I'm working, and more work is coming in all of the time," I reminded her. "I can't drag my feet in this business. I'll be too old by the time I'm old enough to legally drink."

She sighed in response. She knew what I said was true. Max and his partners had told her repeatedly whenever she tried to stop me from doing something. I really appreciated that she was being a mom, but under the circumstances, I needed her to take a step back.

"I am really nervous about you going to this party," she said. She had been repeating that statement since she found out I was going to the party.

"Mom, I've been to parties before," I said, turning around and grabbing my black clutch off of the bed. "I've been to parties that would give you a heart attack. I really don't think that I can get into that much trouble tonight."

"You're so naïve," she said, turning away from me.

I rolled my eyes and bit my tongue so that I wouldn't argue with her. Maybe I was naïve, but how many more opportunities like the one I had would I get?

I took a breath and marched into the living area of the suite, a nice upgrade from the one room we had when we first arrived months before.

"Do you know who Emmy sent to go with me?" I asked my mom, knowing she had to know because she had to approve the person as good enough to accompany me.

She nodded with a small smile. "They are the only reason I'm letting you go without me."

I didn't know who it was that my mom trusted so much to escort me to the party without her, but I was grateful because the one thing I was dreading was showing up at my first VIP party with my mommy.

"Who is it?" I asked.

"Emmy asked me to surprise you," she shrugged.

I frowned. I still had no clue. Emmy had some cousins that lived in the area, maybe it was one of them, but I hardly knew them. It definitely couldn't be Emmet because that would just be bizarre. Why would Emmet show up to take me to the party after we had gone three-quarters of a year without speaking? That option just seemed highly unlikely, which left me wondering once again.

I adjusted the charm bracelet on my wrist, wishing for the unlikely. I snorted.

What would I even say to him? What would he say to me?

"Is something funny?" Mom asked me from the couch.

"Nope," I said, deciding to go look in the mirror once more.

Then I felt it.

That tug.

That pull.

I hadn't felt it so strongly in nearly a year. It made my gut clench and twist and lurch. My heart raced so fast that it made me light headed. The bracelet seemed to burn into my skin.

Abruptly, I turned away from the bedroom and just barely kept myself from stumbling to the door of our suite. With a trembling hand, I touched the door handle but didn't immediately open it. What if I was wrong? What if I just ate something that disagreed with me and I confused the feelings? What if I was right? Could I handle it? Could I handle it if I was wrong?

"Damn it!" I bit out in a harsh whisper.

I pulled the door open. There was no one on the other side. I stepped into the hallway and found it empty.

The invisible tether strummed and vibrated and hummed.

The elevators at the end of the hall made that pleasant *ding* indicating that a cab had arrived on my floor. I stood there waiting for someone to appear around the corner, but all I heard were carpeted footsteps going in the other direction towards the other wing of the hotel.

I stepped back into the suite, confused. I rubbed my sternum, trying to ease the pressure and pulling I felt there. I began to believe that I had conjured the feelings by subconsciously wanting the person coming for me to be Emmet. I had somehow, in the deeper parts of my mind, convinced myself that Emmet was coming for me.

Disappointment washed over me and weakened my knees. I held onto the wall to keep myself from falling over.

"Are you okay?" Mom asked, getting to her feet.

"Fine," I whispered. "Who is coming for me, Mom?"

"I told you Emmy wanted me to keep it a secret."

"That's stupid!" I snapped. "Don't I deserve to know? Is it one of my friends from New Jersey?"

"Yes," she said simply.

Andrew? Would Emmy send Andrew Newland?

I had run into Andrew on my last trip to New Jersey. Emmy thought there was a spark between us. If there had been a spark, it was all on Andrew's side.

I was angry that I seemed to have no control over my current circumstances. Bitterly, I stood on one foot and reached for my shoe. I was going to take the damn shoes off, take the damn dress off and close myself into my room for the night with my hidden stash of junk food and watch reruns of *My So-Called Life* because the whole situation was a bunch of bullshit.

My hand had just touched the strap around my ankle when someone knocked on the door. Even though my chest was almost exploding with emotion and it felt like that damn binding was on fire, I told myself that I had conjured it. Whoever was at the door I was going to send away and carry on with my plan of junk food and television.

I opened the door, with curses on my lips, but the only one that made it through was, "Shit."

Emmet stood in front of me, gazing at me with those green eyes through that too-long hair in said eyes, and smiling with lips that I knew could knock Felix's kisses out of any park, out of any universe.

"Emmet."

Chapter Twenty-One

"One more picture," my mom said, grinning like it was her birthday.

"No," I sighed.

"Just one more, one more," she said. "Emmet put your arm around your sister."

I glowered at her. "This isn't prom!" I said and then thought how pathetic it would be if my prom date were a sibling.

"You're never going to get to go to a prom, so humor me," she said with a note of sourness. "Emmet. Arm."

I liked her better when she was a near-dead blob on the couch.

Emmet's arm slinked around my waist. I gasped lightly as he pulled me close to his body. I wanted to pull away. I wanted to move closer.

I didn't smile for the pictures. I was trying to focus on breathing while in close proximity to Emmet.

He hadn't said much since he arrived. He said hello, and I said hi. Then my mom jumped in, rambling on about how it had been a surprise because she knew I hadn't seen Emmet since he left for college and wasn't it nice to see him again. Then she started in on the pictures.

My mother's behavior was…perplexing. She was never the giddy type, but while taking the pictures she didn't stop smiling. She took picture after picture and even dabbed at her eyes a few times. I didn't understand it. I wanted her to simmer down and go back to being her quiet mildly pessimistic self.

When her excitement got the best of her, and she started looking tired and drained, she finally let us go. Though I had just thought some unkind things about her, her seemingly constant state of tiredness was nagging me a little. As Emmet and I walked out of the door, I kept throwing glances at her. Before the door closed, I saw her sag with exhaustion.

"She must be on some really good drugs," Emmet said, leading me by the elbow towards the bank of elevators.

My attention shifted from my mother, and I looked at the man beside me. He was wearing a dark Armani suit without a tie.

Several buttons of his white shirt remained undone, and the jacket was open. He looked good, really good. I couldn't drag my eyes away from him for several moments. Only because I had to step onto the elevator did I finally tear my eyes away.

"You look amazing," Emmet murmured.

"Thank you," I managed in a soft voice.

We were quiet for the rest of the ride to the lobby. Emmet put his hand on the small of my back to guide me outside where a limo waited for us.

"Where did this come from?" I asked as the driver opened the door for us.

I carefully got in first and moved over as far as I could go. Emmet slid in after me and left very little space between us.

"I thought since we were going to a VIP party, we should at least ride in style," Emmet said.

"You did this?" I asked, turning my head like a puppy.

He nodded as his eyes raked over me. I suppressed a shiver and folded my hands in my lap. I looked down when I felt his fingers on my wrist. He was slowly turning the bracelet.

"How have you been?" he asked softly.

I looked up and met his green eyes.

"Surviving," I whispered. I turned away from him and looked at the bustling city life outside of my window. My chest hurt. My skin burned where he was touching me. The invisible tether vibrated softly between us. I wanted to cry. I wanted to cry so badly. Emmet was finally right next to me, but I almost couldn't handle it.

After he had left for college, it took me a few days to get myself together. The experience left me gutted and weak. I couldn't erase the memory of Emmet's face when I uttered those terrible words. I couldn't forget the shake of his head when I turned to him in the car to apologize. I couldn't forget how it felt to feel him leave me without a goodbye. It took me a couple of months to accept the fact that he wasn't going to call, and he wasn't going to reappear in my life.

By the time New Year's had rolled around, I had to accept the fact that he was gone from my life entirely. Those weren't easy circumstances to accept. I had to let some coldness seep into me. I had to let it settle in and harden. Only when Emmy gave me the bracelet did the bitter cold wall begin to crack a little. Sitting within inches of him, I felt like it was going to shatter altogether, and that wasn't necessarily a good thing.

Emmet must have sensed the tension and emotions within me. He pulled his hand back and put it on his knee with a sigh.

"So, you met Felix at a photo shoot for *Rolling Stone*?" he asked.

"Yes," I nodded.

"That's incredible. You must have impressed the right people to get that gig."

The impression came during the shoot, but I didn't tell him that. Instead, I said, "Just got lucky I guess."

"Donya," Emmet said my name softly, but it sounded like he was pleading.

I turned my head and looked at him. His eyes were so damn sorrowful that it made my breath hitch.

"Do you want me to take you to the party and leave you there on your own? I can come back for you later."

I was startled by his question. "Why?"

He sighed. "You're so stiff," he said inaudibly. "I have the feeling that you really don't want me here."

I stared at him. I wasn't entirely sure what I wanted, and I told him so.

"What will make it easier for you?" he asked with sincerity. "I'll do whatever you need to feel comfortable."

My eyes closed slowly, and I took a long, deep breath. As I let the air out slowly between my lips, I opened my eyes and looked at Emmet again with a little more clarity.

"I want you here," I said honestly.

Some of the tension eased on his face. "Can we just try to have a good night?" he asked. "Can we just for tonight put the past out of our minds?"

"I don't know," I said softly, but then continued bitterly. "What happens at the end of the night? If you're just going to go back to hating me, I don't think I want to continue. I'll go back to the suite and go to bed."

"I don't hate you. I've never hated you. I promise you that," he said quickly.

"Don't promise me anything, Emmet," I snapped. "You promised that I would always have your friendship, but you broke that promise. You didn't even give me that much before you ran away to Cambridge."

"I didn't run away, Donya," he said defensively. "I went away to school."

"You cut me off!" I yelled.

Emmet opened his mouth to argue but quickly shut it. He sighed heavily and rubbed a few fingers across his forehead. After a moment, he was able to look at me again.

"Coffee," he said.

I tilted my head. "What?"

"Coffee," he said the word slowly.

"What the hell are you talking about?"

"You asked what happens at the end of the night, and I'm answering your question. Coffee. At the end of the night, we will have coffee."

I crossed my arms and faced the front of the car. It was eerily quiet inside the vehicle.

"I want a donut," I said stubbornly after a minute.

"What?"

"I want a donut with my coffee," I snapped, glaring at him.

His lips twitched as he tried not to smile. "You drive a hard bargain."

"Shut up," I said, as my anger began to slip through my fingers.

"I hope you don't ask for a special donut, like one with sprinkles or something," Emmet said, unable to hide his smile. "I'm not sure if that would be a deal I could close on."

I bit my lip to stop myself from laughing. It wasn't even that funny, but I couldn't help the little bit of laughter that bubbled through my lips.

We fell into a light conversation for the last few minutes of the trip. I was still off-kilter being so close to Emmet again, and I was still shocked that he came at all, but I tried to push that to the back of my mind and just enjoy the conversation.

When he got out of the car in front of Felix's building, he held out his hand to help me out of the car. I looked at it blankly for a moment before placing my hand in his. His thumb glided gently over my knuckles, sending tiny shockwaves of electricity racing up my arm. I smiled shyly at him on the sidewalk before security escorted us through some paparazzi and bystanders.

The Paps asked questions that I didn't hear. I heard my name, but I had heard it more than a few times since hanging around Felix. I didn't pay them any mind.

"What are they talking about?" Emmet asked me after security cleared us to go up to the penthouse.

"Who?"

"I couldn't hear everyone all at once," he said, his brow creasing with concentration. "But I heard the word 'nude' more than once."

My eyebrows arched. It was possible they were talking about the *Rolling Stone* cover, but that wasn't supposed to be released for another few days, not to mention I wasn't really nude. Just partially…

"Maybe they have me mixed up with someone else," I said, waving my free hand dismissively as we stepped into the elevator.

"Hmm," Emmet said. I thought he would harp on it, but he didn't. He looked me over again and ran a knuckle up my bare arm, making me shiver. "Did I tell you how awesome you look?"

"No," I said, biting back my smile. "You said that I looked amazing, but you may tell me how awesome I look."

He chuckled and said, "You look awesome, Donya."

"Thank you, Emmet." I gave him a full blown smile.

His smile not only touched his eyes but filled them. If the elevator doors didn't open just then, it was possible that I could have stared into his eyes all night in that small box.

"Hello, Miss Stewart," Rocco, the big beefy man in the suit that followed Felix everywhere greeted me with a smile outside the double doors that lead into Felix's penthouse.

I smiled at him and introduced him to Emmet before stepping towards the doors. Already we could hear the loud music, laughter, shouts, and what was probably a jolly good time on the other side.

"You complimented Felix well," Rocco said, pulling open one of the doors.

I looked at him curiously, but then the door was open and the noise filtered out and I was distracted. Emmet and I stepped inside and took a good look around. There were no less than two hundred people inside. Though the penthouse was very spacious, it felt cramped having so many bodies in the space. Instantly I recognized half a dozen celebrities, from local celebs on up to the powerhouse couple whose faces were splashed on some tabloid almost daily.

"Are you okay?" Emmet asked in my ear.

"Sure," I said absently. "Why?"

"You're squeezing the hell out of my hand."

I hadn't even realized it. I apologized and tried to pull my hand from his, but he held me firmly.

"It's okay," he said soothingly.

I sighed and smiled a little. "I don't know why I'm so nervous. I've been hanging around Felix for weeks, and he's never made me feel nervous."

"Too much power in one room, maybe," Emmet suggested.

"You have an incredible pair of eyes," a woman I recognized from a soap opera said to me and then turned to the other woman at her side. "Doesn't she have incredible eyes? You take one hell of a picture."

Emmet and I looked at one another and then back to the women, but they had already moved on. An uneasy feeling began to grow in my gut, and I unconsciously gripped Emmet's hand in a vice hold again. I only realized it because my hand started to go numb.

We moved through the crowd. I knew a few people from working and through Felix. A very recognizable runway model I had met months ago rolled her eyes at me but couldn't keep her hands off of Emmet. I felt some satisfaction when he blew her off and wrapped his arm around my waist, drawing me close. The more people we met, the more we heard things like, "Good job" and, "Great photos." Many of them handed me business cards and asked me to keep in touch or to give them a call.

I was growing increasingly nervous as we slowly moved towards the other side of the room. I felt like everyone was looking at me, though I couldn't imagine why. I wasn't a celebrity. I was just Donya and in the grand scheme of things, I ranked about where the servers were.

"Do you know what any of them are talking about?" Emmet asked in my ear.

"No," I said, but that wasn't quite true. I had a very strong feeling what it was about, and it was only a matter of moments before we would find out.

"Donya!" Felix shouted my name from a few feet ahead.

He pushed his way through people and ripped me from Emmet's hold by lifting me off of my feet for an embrace. When he put me back down, I stumbled slightly in my heels, but Felix steadied me even though he was clearly unsteady himself. I couldn't miss the heavy scent of alcohol on his breath just before he kissed the corner of my mouth.

I glanced quickly at Emmet and nervously forced a smile as I tried to pull away from Felix, but he wasn't finished with me yet. He went in for another kiss, except next time his lips crushed mine, and he tried to slip his tongue into my mouth.

"Felix!" I forced a laugh and shoved him away. "Stop kidding around."

I went back to Emmet, ignoring the murderous gaze in his eyes as he looked at my friend. I nudged his hand with mine. Stiffly, he took my hand again.

"Felix Hunter, this is my…this is Emmet Grayne," I said and cleared my throat nervously.

Felix regarded Emmet coolly and nodded in his direction. He turned his attention back to me and openly ogled my body.

"Spicy," he said and winked at me.

I smiled and said, "Thank you for the dress. It's perfect."

He grinned. "Anything for you. I was expecting you to bring your girlfriend. I was going to push her off onto Dave and sweep you away somewhere private."

Emmet's hand gripped mine as if he expected Felix to pick me up and take me away.

Dave Cowell was a year older than Felix and just as successful an actor. The two became good friends while filming the movie that changed Felix's career.

I peered behind Felix and saw Dave talking to a beautiful blonde.

"I think Dave will be okay," I said teasingly.

"Come on. You need to see something."

He took a hold of my wrist and pulled. I held tight to Emmet's hand as the three of us, linked together, walked through the party goers. When Felix finally stopped and released my wrist, I moved around him to see what he wanted me to see.

I gasped and threw my clutch over my mouth. Emmet cursed beside me. We finally got to see what everyone had been talking about.

"Fucking awesome," Felix said excitedly.

Displayed as a focal point of the room were three large photographs from the shoot. The first one was the cover. The shot was that first one I had posed for with my fingers on Felix's hard stomach and his ear between my teeth. It was blatantly obvious that I was topless. Even as my face warmed with embarrassment, I couldn't deny that the photograph was incredible. Felix and I looked like a great fit in the picture as his arms rested on my legs, and though the other girls' faces weren't visible, their many hands all over him somehow gave the photo an erotic feel.

In the second photograph, I was standing high on the back of the stool with my hands twisted in Felix's hair. I had carefully hidden my breasts behind his head and my arms, but the curves of each breast was visible, as well as the curve of my bare torso down to my hip hugging jeans.

The third picture had been taken without my knowledge. I was facing a shirtless Felix and buttoning the shirt he had given me with one hand, but my other hand was in his. We were just officially meeting at that time, but the captured moment appeared more intimate than it was. We looked like a love-struck, lustful couple that just fucked and were in the process of getting dressed. Even the way my knee bent towards him seemed intimate, as if I was about to walk into his arms.

"Oh, shit," I spat out. I looked at Felix with wide eyes. "How did you get these?"

He pinched my chin between his thumb and forefinger. "Sometimes you're too damn cute." He grinned arrogantly. "I'm me. I can get stuff like this. I have smaller proofs in my bedroom for your portfolio too. Glen told me to give them to you."

Glen was the photographer, and I had just shot with him earlier in the day. Why didn't *he* give them to me?

"You want to get your friend a drink and come with me to get them?" Felix asked suggestively.

Emmet began to move, and I was afraid of what he would do. I put my hand on his chest, trying to appear casual. I grinned at Felix as I felt Emmet halt.

"You're such a flirty bastard. Find a girl who cares. You can give me the proofs over that lunch you owe me next week."

I nudged him playfully and pulled Emmet away into the crowd.

~~*

I sat quietly without objection as Emmet told the limo driver where to take us. Despite the thick tension in the car between us, he still wanted to take me out for coffee and a donut, and honestly, I was relieved that he still wanted to go.

After we had walked away from Felix and my partial nude photographs, Emmet had banded his arm around my waist possessively. I felt the tension in his body and saw the fury in his eyes, but despite that, his social skills never wavered. Samantha had pounded social skills into us at a young age. We had a lot of practice before Fred was retired and he would have business associates over for dinner. As we got older, we were allowed to go to the occasional function that required fine dressing and impeccable social skills. I supposed that being at his fancy elite school only reinforced those skills in Emmet.

We mingled and chatted. He made a couple of new friends with a couple of guys who were also studying prelaw. I networked, reacquainting myself with the few people I already knew and established new friendships and business contacts. I received many compliments on my photographs.

We sipped on non-alcoholic beverages and tried some hor 'd oeuvres. We danced a little and observed a lot. Through all of it, Emmet kept his arm around my waist. If that arm got tired, he would smoothly glide behind me, placing both hands on my waist and move to my other side, always leaving at least one hand on me through the night. If it appeared that I was going to move away from him or if Felix came near, he would hold me closer and tighter. He didn't have to say it, but it was clear that leaving his side was not permitted.

We left the party a little after two in the morning. I didn't get to tell Felix I was leaving because once we decided to go,

Emmet held me tightly and led me out of the penthouse. In the car, he settled into the seat beside me, but he didn't make any effort to touch me or my bracelet. There was only silence inside the car. The only noise came from the traffic outside and the soft hum of the engine.

Emmet was first to speak.

"Did you sleep with him?" he asked tightly.

I looked over at him, startled. "No!"

"That one picture…"

He didn't have to say which picture, because I already knew which picture. It was the last one, the one that made Felix and I look like lovers.

"I know how it looked," I said, a little alarmed at the desperation in my voice. "But that's not how it was. He gave me his shirt after the shoot and introduced himself."

"Everyone said that you took your shirt off yourself, no one told you to do it," he said, watching me carefully.

I nodded slowly.

Emmet let out a low curse and pushed his hair back.

"Why, Donya? That's not like you."

"You're right," I said with a small shrug. "It's not. I was someone else. That's my job."

He sighed. "I'm sorry," he said meaningfully. "It was a shock to see you topless and pressed up against another guy for the entire world to see."

"You would have found out in a few days," I sighed.

"You did look…like a model," he said reluctantly.

Hesitantly, I smiled. "Thank you."

There was another moment of quiet. I looked out the window, and Emmet looked straight ahead.

"Are you sure you didn't sleep with him?" he asked in a harsh whisper.

"I am still very much a virgin, Emmet," I said, patting his hand.

He flipped his hand and laced his fingers with mine.

"He likes you," he said softly. "He's attracted to you."

"Felix Hunter is attracted to anyone with a vagina," I snickered but stopped when Emmet didn't laugh.

"He bought you this dress," he said, touching my knee with his other hand.

I shifted uncomfortably. "He was just being nice."

"What would have happened if I had not come with you? Would you have gone with him to his bedroom?"

"Emmet," I sighed. "Give me some credit. Is that what you really think of me?"

"No," he said, shaking his head. He closed his eyes and let his head fall back on the seat. "I'm sorry. I'm just…jealous, and I have no right to be. I hated watching him touch you…and kiss you."

I sucked in a breath and let it out in a rush. I didn't want to have to admit to him that I had made out with Felix in a limo much like the one we were in.

"If it's any consolation, I'm here in the limo with you. I'm not in the penthouse with Felix Hunter."

He opened his eyes and smiled a little. "I suppose that is true."

We arrived at the little coffee shop a few minutes later. We each ordered coffee and a slice of pie. We talked about the people we met at the party, laughing at things we couldn't laugh at while in attendance, and we discussed scandals that happened right before us. I teased Emmet about the super model that kept trying to pull him away from me, and he teased me about the older gray-haired man that looked a lot like Hugh Hefner that invited me to his mansion in Newport, Rhode Island.

When all of the pie was gone, and we were on our third cups of coffee, the polite conversation ended.

"I miss you, Donya," Emmet said frankly, looking me in the eyes. "There isn't a day that goes by that I don't miss you."

I couldn't hold his gaze. I looked at my coffee cup and stirred the spoon slowly.

I had managed to keep that pain at bay for a long time. Though I had been hurting from our break, I needed to be able to focus on my career, but with Emmet before me, it was all pushing up towards the surface.

"What happened with us?" he whispered.

"You hid something very important from me," I answered weakly. "I should have never found out the way I did, but that was no excuse for the cruel things I said to you. I hurt you, but hey, you got me back really good, right?"

"Donya," he said my name desperately and reached across the table to hold my hand, but I pulled it out of his reach. I knew without looking that I had hurt him in that small action.

"Whatever you are feeling right now is not even a fraction of how I felt when you left," I said and finally met his eyes.

"I know." He fisted his hands on the table. "I know. I didn't do the right thing, but I thought maybe we needed some time apart."

"You don't walk away from a relationship every time it gets hard," I snapped, surprised by the vehemence in my voice.

He closed his eyes for a moment. When they opened, I saw his emotions like I was peering through a window.

"I know," he said again. "I wanted to come back to you, but by the time I stopped being an ass about it, you were already in New York. I didn't want to be a distraction to you."

That revelation hurt me instead of soothing me. "You should have come to me," I said bitterly. "Damn it, Emmet, I thought you hated me!"

There were about twenty other people in the shop. I didn't care if anyone heard me.

"When you got the bracelet at Christmas, why didn't you call me?" Emmet asked accusingly.

"I didn't get the bracelet at Christmas!"

He looked confused and then patiently said, "I left it with Emmy to give to you."

"I didn't get it until a couple of months ago."

He cursed and slammed a hand on the table. He looked away from me for a moment. When he turned back to me, he still seemed accusatory, but only a little less than before.

"Why didn't you call me when you got it then?"

"Because I thought that if you wanted me to call you, you would have attached a note or something. Giving me the gift didn't necessarily mean that you wanted to talk to me. Maybe you were feeling reminiscent when you bought it. Maybe you were saying, 'to hell with your kisses, Donya, and your stupid candy heart. I can't give them back to you because I got hungry and ate them, but I'll put them on this bracelet instead so no one will ask questions about why I didn't get you a present.' Maybe that's what you were saying." I crossed my arms, completely vexed.

Emmet stared at me for a long time with his mouth slightly ajar. Suddenly, he burst into laughter. I tried not to react. I didn't think it was funny. I was serious, but watching his green eyes twinkling with laughter made my smile come anyhow. Then I was laughing with him. Then I was mad at him for making me laugh.

"Stop making me laugh," I said trying to suppress my giggles. "I'm mad at you."

"What are you doing tomorrow?" he asked, ignoring my remark.

"You mean today? Nothing. Why? You want to laugh at me some more?"

"I want to spend the day with you. I know we can't go backward, but can we move forward?"

I pretended to think about it, but I didn't have to really think about it. Of course, I wanted to spend time with Emmet. It's what I had wanted for months and months.

"Listen," I said with a long sigh. "I really want to, Emmet. I really do, but you've already screwed up."

His eyes widened in surprise. "I'm sorry I was jealous at the party. I think I handled it pretty well."

"You mean other than holding me like a piece of property?" I countered.

"Well…" He looked for the right words, but I cut in.

"But that's not where you screwed up."

"Tell me then so I can fix it," he said anxiously.

I leaned forward and looked at him hard.

"You promised me a donut, but I got pie."

He smiled warmly at me. "I promise to give you a donut later."

He slid out of the booth and stood up and offered me his hand. I put my hand in his.

"With sprinkles," I added.

"Hard bargain, Miss Stewart."

Chapter Twenty-Two

"Emmet!" I clapped my hands and jumped up and down.

It was ten in the morning, and I had just answered Emmet's knock on our suite door. He stood on the other side holding two longboards under his arms. I hadn't been on a skateboard in about a year, and I probably wouldn't have thought about it if he didn't come to my door with one.

"Let's get back to our roots," he said with a grin that made my heart beat a little faster.

I said goodbye to my mom and joined him in the hallway. I threw my arms around his neck and hugged him, knocking him back a few unsteady steps.

"Whoa," he laughed. "Had I known you would get this excited, I would have showed up with your board months ago."

We left the hotel, hand in hand, carrying our boards. Emmet was taking me to a skateboarding park. We walked down the sidewalk, chatting about nothing of importance. I barely paid attention to the people around us. I was happy to be holding his hand and on our way to do something we used to love doing together.

"What the hell are you doing with that board?" I heard a familiar voice demand right in front of me.

"Hey, Max," I said to my agent. "This is my friend Emmet."

"I don't care who he is," Max said sharply and jabbed a finger at my board. "What the hell are you about to do with that?"

"New York is a big town. How did I get so lucky to run into you on the street?"

"No skateboarding," he growled.

"Relax," Emmet said, stepping in front of me a little. "She knows what she's doing."

"I know what she's going to be doing if she falls and gets hurt—nothing. Not in this town or anywhere else. Clients don't want pretty girls with banged up knees and elbows."

"Peace out, Max," I said, tugging Emmet along.

"You better have some knee pads hidden somewhere in those short shorts of yours," he yelled after us.

"Those are some very nice short shorts," Emmet remarked, looking at my legs.

Getting to ride on a board again was exhilarating. I had forgotten how much I loved it, how much it eased my mind and quieted my nerves. I had especially forgotten how much I loved to board with Emmet. I looked away from the beautiful sky above us and settled my eyes on him as he boarded wide circles around me. When my board stopped, I just stood there watching him until he was standing on his board in front of me.

"Hi," he said, smiling down at me.

"Hi."

He reached over and tugged on my ponytail, and I smiled like an idiot.

"I'm glad you came, Emmet," I said sincerely. "I didn't think that you would, and then I wasn't sure if I wanted you to, but I'm so glad you did."

"I couldn't stay away," he whispered, taking my hand into his.

We were standing in the middle of a noisy skateboard park. People were zooming past us. Boards were falling, riders were falling. The sounds of wheels on the ground and landing on the pavement after jumps surrounded us, but we didn't notice. I was looking into those emerald eyes and wondering how I had gone so long without them.

My mind drifted back to a long ago evening at the vacant lot in New Jersey. Emmet and I had skated for a long time that night before ending in the same positions. He had kissed me, and I had fallen off of my board.

I wanted to go back to that day. I would do a lot of things differently. I wouldn't have pushed him away. I would have admitted to myself how I felt about him and embraced it. Maybe we would have still been together.

But as Emmet had said over coffee, we couldn't go backward, but we could try to move forward. Where would we end up, though?

"Let's get some lunch," Emmet said, frowning slightly. He had apparently been in deep thought too.

"Okay," I said. I got off of my board and tucked it under my arm.

We walked wordlessly side by side. When Emmet's fingers nudged mine in question, I answered by curling my hand around his.

We decided to stop back at the hotel and ask my mom if she wanted to go to lunch with us. I told Emmet about all of the progress she had made, but her life had become all about me. I wasn't even sure if she had any friends.

"And she's always tired," I said as we walked across the lobby to the elevators. "I think I'm wearing her out."

"She does look drained," Emmet agreed, frowning.

"Maybe she just needs to get out a little bit more. We're in New York City. She should be out enjoying it just as much as me."

"It's probably not easy for her to return to the real world after so many years of being out of it."

"Probably not."

When I stepped through the door of the suite, I was surprised to find that we had a guest. I was so surprised that I had halted, and Emmet had run into the back of me.

"What's..." he started to say but then saw what I saw. His hand shot to my waist in a possessive hold.

"It's about time you got back," Felix Hunter said. "Your mom is kicking my ass in poker."

"What are you doing here?" I asked, stepping farther into the room and out of Emmet's hold.

I opened the small closet behind the door and stashed the skateboard in there. Emmet followed suit. He stood very close to me and again I could feel the tension in his body.

"I brought your pictures," Felix answered, holding up a manila envelope. He smiled, but it was a tight smile. His eyes flickered to Emmet and back to me. "I'm afraid I can't have lunch with you this week. I have to fly to L.A. to start filming. We're starting a couple of weeks early."

How strange my life has become, I thought as Felix handed me the envelope. I had my...Emmet, my semi-sane mother and a megastar standing in the middle of my New York City hotel suite.

"Thank you," I said, smiling at my friend.

"Can I talk to you?" he asked and nodded towards the hallway. "Alone?"

I didn't need Emmet's permission, but I found my head swiveling towards him anyway. His eyes darkened, but he stepped around me and started talking to my mom about our afternoon plans. I took that as a yes, put the envelope down on the table and followed Felix into the hallway. He gently took my arm and led me down the hall and into the stairwell.

"I guess this is as much privacy as we're going to get," he said.

I watched, stunned, as Felix Hunter nervously ran a hand through his hair and looked at me almost as if he was afraid to speak. Felix Hunter didn't get nervous. Felix Hunter always said exactly what was on his mind. Those were two of the many staples that made Felix Hunter wanted and idolized by millions of females and some males across the globe.

"What's up?" I asked, leaning back against the wall.

He looked at me for a long moment before speaking. There was something in his eyes that made feel a little uncomfortable, and a little excited, which immediately made me feel guilty with Emmet only a few yards away waiting for me.

"Is that the guy?" he asked. He glanced at my bracelet. "Is that the guy that hurt you?"

I shifted from foot to foot. I didn't like the way he worded that. Emmet and I hurt each other, and yeah, I was probably hurt more than Emmet when he left, but I didn't like Felix making him into a villain. I had told Felix a shortened version of our story, but I had never expected the men to meet.

"Yes," I finally answered.

"Are you two back together now?" Felix asked. He put a palm on the wall beside my head, partially caging me in.

"No." I shook my head.

"I have to admit, I was very surprised and very disappointed when you brought him to my party."

I defensively crossed my arms and couldn't help how my brow creased with irritation. "I didn't know I had to check with you first, Felix."

He made a small sound of exasperation and rolled his eyes. "Don't go getting your feathers all ruffled up, Miss Stewart. Of course you didn't have to check with me first, but I had expectations that were thwarted."

"My friend was sick, so she sent her brother in her stead," I said, speaking quickly. "I had no idea that she was going to do that. He was the last person I expected."

"He looked like he wanted to *try* to kick my ass," Felix snorted.

"Probably because he *did* want to kick your ass."

"It's a good thing he doesn't know what I wanted to do to you last night," Felix said in a low voice and put his hand on my hip.

"Felix," I said his name in warning. "On our first day together you told me that you'll be my friend."

"I also told you that I really, really like you. I've tried to just let it go, but I still really, really like you, Donya. In fact, I like you more than ever."

He took a step closer to me. Our bodies were almost touching. My chest rose and fell too quickly.

"I was going to ask you to reconsider last night," he said softly. "I was going to ask you to come with me to L.A. and try with me."

"Try what?" I asked just above a whisper.

"Try us," Felix said even softer. "So, I'm asking you now. Come to L.A with me."

"That wasn't a question," I said dumbly.

He was so close. His forehead was touching mine. My breathing was so erratic; I began to feel dizzy.

He smiled and asked in a very low tone, "Will you come with me to L.A., Donya Stewart?"

My chest twisted in pain. The truth was, I wanted to. I wanted to go with him. I wanted to fight my mom and other parents and take off with Felix to L.A. I remembered what it felt like to kiss him and thought about how nice it would be to kiss him every morning and every night. I imagined holding his hand while walking down the famous streets of L.A. and swimming in the Pacific with him outside of his Malibu beach home. I shamefully imagined losing my virginity to him on an enormous bed inside an insanely expensive hotel suite.

If Emmet had not showed up at my door the night before, I might have seriously considered it. The truth was, I really liked

Felix. I probably could have been quite content with him in L.A. for a little while, but Felix played hard. He would get bored with me, and he would want more. His drinking and partying would eventually become an issue between us. And my career? What would have happened to it if I moved out of New York?

"I can't," I said with a sigh.

I felt Felix's body sag a little, but he didn't back away.

"Is it because of him?" he asked, and I could hear the disappointment in his voice.

"Somewhat," I admitted. "But there's more. I don't think I will live up to your expectations, Felix. I like parties and excitement, but only in small increments." I put my hand in his hair and ruffled it. "You're a wild one, and you don't need anyone holding you down or holding you back."

He threw his head back and groaned with frustration. When he looked at me again, he was smiling, though his eyes were rather sad.

"You're sixteen years old," he said incredulously. "Why are you so damn responsible?"

I smiled too. "Trust me. I think it's more a curse than a gift."

"I'm definitely feeling cursed," he groaned again.

I put a hand on his chest as I looked into his gray eyes. "Are we still friends, Felix?" He was the one true New York friend I had, and though he was about to leave for a few months, I didn't want to end our friendship.

"You can't get rid of me that easily," he said with a grin. He kissed my cheek, sweetly and slowly before stepping away from me. "I better take you back to your suite before your boyfriend comes after us."

"He's not my boyfriend," I said as I stepped through the door he held open for me, but I did suspect that Emmet would come looking for us soon.

"Whatever," Felix said flippantly. He pulled a pair of sunglasses out of his back pocket and slipped them on. "Is this a good disguise? I don't want the press claiming that your suite is our personal love shack again."

"Your disguise stinks, Hunter," I laughed. "And the press can claim anything it wants. I'll get free PR."

Felix wrapped his arms around my waist and lifted me off of the floor in a big hug. I wrapped my arms around his neck and hugged him back and planted a kiss on his jaw.

"Don't forget about me," I said.

"Impossible," he said in my ear. "Besides, you're flying out to visit me."

"I can do that," I grinned.

He put me down on my feet and kissed my cheek once more. "I'll call you soon."

"Okay," I said and watched him walk down the hallway.

"By the way," he said, walking backward. "Those shorts are spicy."

"Hot," I added with a laugh.

"Sexy," he grinned and then disappeared around the corner.

I turned around and reached into my pocket for my key, but the door swung open, and Emmet stood on the other side.

"I was just coming to find you," he said rather stiffly.

"Now you don't have to." I smiled and stepped past him into the room. I expected to find my mom sitting on the couch waiting to go to lunch. "Where's my mom?"

"She said she was tired," Emmet said, leaning against a wall and crossing his arms. He appeared to be a little beefier than he was before he went off to college.

"She went to bed?" I asked, surprised.

"Yes."

I frowned. I looked towards her bedroom door and half considered going in there. I couldn't shake that nagging feeling that something was wrong with her.

"Do you still want to go to lunch?" Emmet asked quietly. "Or are you going to do something with Felix?"

I looked at him. His body was rigid, and his jaw was clenched.

"Felix is going to L.A.," I said carefully. "He came by to say goodbye."

He seemed to relax a little, but only a little.

"I'm surprised he didn't ask you to go with him."

I picked up the envelope of pictures. I didn't open it, but I played with the flap that kept them enclosed.

"He did ask me."

Emmet sucked in a breath, and his body stiffened once again. The muscles in his arms rippled as his hands fisted.

"I said no," I continued. I put the envelope down and took the few steps to Emmet. I put a hand on his arm and said, "Let's go to lunch."

He looked down at my hand and then my face. After a moment, he let out that breath he had sucked in and took my hand in his. We were just stepping out of the door when Emmet asked me, "Did you want to go?"

I glanced up at him and quickly looked away. "Part of me wanted to go," I admitted.

"Which part would that be?" he asked stiffly as we walked down the hallway.

"Does it matter?" I shot back. "I'm not going, and for the record, you're not allowed to be angry about this."

I punched the button for the elevator. We got on in silence and silence followed us all the way downstairs and through the lobby.

Chapter Twenty-Three

When the *Rolling Stone* issue hit the magazine shelves, my life changed. People recognized me on the street. Men asked me out. Women questioned me about Felix and about breaking into the modeling business, and shockingly, more than a few people requested my autograph.

My workload quadrupled. I went from working a few days a week to working sometimes seven days a week, and sometimes with some very long hours. I landed a small part on a sitcom filmed in the city and a commercial for a hair care product that would run nationwide.

Fred had a conniption about the *Rolling Stone* cover. He went as far as calling it child pornography, which was very unfair. I was barely a child, my lady bits weren't showing, and no one was exploiting me. Sam surprisingly took my side and regarded the cover as artful and tasteful, and even though she had seen my hair have better days, that I looked beautiful. Emmet said he had to struggle not to punch any guy that either ogled the cover of the magazine or talked about it.

Secretly, that brought me a little satisfaction.

Emmet had returned to Cambridge the same night Felix had asked me to go with him to Los Angeles. He had considered staying another few days, but I had convinced him it was best to stick with his regular schedule. Since mine was all over the place, I couldn't guarantee that we'd be able to hang out anyway.

We stayed in touch through phone calls and emails. The conversations were light and friendly, but every night when it was time to hang up the phone, we each hesitated and dragged the call out another few minutes. When the semester ended not long after his visit, instead of hitting up some warm beach with scantily clad women in bikinis with his friends, Emmet came to see me in New York.

When working in the modeling business, life tends to be unpredictable. You may have your whole day planned out ahead of you. You may have plans of getting some breakfast with an old friend, going to the American Museum of Natural History, eating fattening pizza for dinner and then seeing where the rest of the night takes you. However, when your agent calls you while your pancakes are still hot on your plate and tells you to get your ass to a casting call, nothing else matters. You drop everything, including that piece of pancake you were shamefully about to put into your mouth.

As you apologize profusely to your visiting friend and scoot out of the booth, you pray that the other twenty bites of pancakes and four slices of bacon and coffee with extra cream and extra sugar don't ruin your chance to get the job. You pray that you don't look as fat as you feel, and if you have to squeeze your ass into any clothes, you know you better be able to button or zip whatever it is. That was the case on Emmet's first day back in the city.

"Don't worry about it," he had said and smiled at me as we rushed back to my hotel suite so I could get ready. "This is why you're here. Now I get to see you in action."

"Or inaction," I sighed. "Depending on which way this goes."

"Whatever way it goes, I think you're great," he said and squeezed my hand.

"Careful, you're going to give me an enormous head. I'm going to start believing I'm better than every other girl there."

"You should because you are."

Usually, I didn't care for someone overindulging me in compliments. I needed constructive criticism, not to hear things said to make me feel better, but Emmet's words made me smile. I had a feeling that he really believed what he said about me.

We went back to the suite. I rushed around, changed my clothes and grabbed my bag of fun that consisted of makeup, hair products and more. My mom was still in bed, but I checked in with her and let her know what was happening before we left.

I was going to have to leave Emmet to his own devices for a while. I had no idea what kind of situation I was walking into. I didn't know if I would be one of a few girls under consideration, or one of a hundred. If chosen, I didn't know if I would get a callback or if I was expected to hang around for another round of eliminations or get to work right away.

Before I went inside, Emmet pulled me into an embrace. His breath was hot on my neck as he wished me luck and gave me words of encouragement. When his lips gently touched my neck, my skin burned and sizzled, and I gasped. His hands caressed my back, and though they didn't go any lower, it felt sensual and sent warmth rushing up my spine. When we finally separated from each other, he gave me his winning smile that sent my heart into wild fluttering.

I wanted to kiss him. I wanted to put my hands in his hair and pull his head to mine and get back what I had been missing for so long, but I didn't. I took another step back and bit my lip. While Emmet and I had been rather cozy, holding hands and whatnot, I wasn't sure if it was a good idea to go any farther than that. We were both still hurt from our breakup and we were living in two different universes. It made me sad to think I may never get to kiss him again, but I was relieved to have his friendship, and his hand to hold. For the time being.

"I'll call you when I'm finished," I told him.

He pushed his hands into his pockets and also took a step back, as if he had been thinking the same things as me.

"You're going to be great," he said and smiled sadly.

I couldn't help the frown that formed on my face before I turned away from him and went inside.

The casting call lasted all day. The good news was that I was one of a few girls chosen. The bad news was that I was one of few girls chosen. A good portion of the next day was going to be spent working, which meant that I would not be spending that time with Emmet.

I didn't complain about it or whine about it, because like Emmet had said earlier in the day, I was doing what I went to New York to do, and honestly, I was beginning to get very excited about my future prospects. I was able to get some work on my own, but after several weeks in Felix's presence, many more doors opened for me. Sometimes it really was about who you knew.

Later that night as we were walking aimlessly after our pizza dinner, the sky opened up to give us a healthy dose of a spring thunderstorm. Since Emmet's hotel was nearby, we went there.

"There is something I want to show you," Emmet said, once we were in the elevator.

I lifted an eyebrow. He smiled and tapped me on the forehead with two fingers.

"Pervert."

I blushed and said, "I didn't say anything."

I was standing in a corner. Emmet closed me in by placing his hands on the railings on each side of me. We were both wet from the storm. Emmet's t-shirt clung to his chest, and his wet hair was mussed. The rain did something to amplify his scent because the smell of his cologne and his skin was a deluge on my senses, and I felt myself squeezing my thighs together.

"You were thinking something," he admonished quietly, gazing at me with those sparkling eyes.

My eyes roved over his wet, muscled body. I licked my lips. "You're not a mind reader."

"I don't have to be a mind reader," he chuckled softly. "It's written all over your lovely face."

The elevator came to a stop and made a soft chiming noise. He stepped away from me and held out his hand. I took it without hesitation and followed him out. When we walked into his room, the first thing I noticed was the enormous bed that dominated the room. Images of Emmet's body pressed to mine drifted lazily into my brain, and I was just as lazy about sending them away.

"Written all over your face," Emmet said, grinning at me.

"I don't know what you're talking about," I said lightly and turned away from the bed.

I walked over to the large window and pulled back the curtain. My hotel room view was of a busy street and other buildings, but Emmet had a beautiful view of Central Park.

"I guess you're getting good use out of your newly acquired trust fund," I teased lightly.

All of the Grayne kids were trust fund babies. They start getting quarterly payments at the age of eighteen, but it wasn't free money, not exactly. As a stipulation of the trust, they were required to go to college or join the military. There was no toleration for failure; a minimum GPA had to be maintained, or they were cut off. Once out of school, they had to be employed full-time, unless they were a married female with a working husband, which was rather sexist. The payments decreased over the years too. There were more stipulations, but since they never applied to me, I didn't care to remember them.

Emmet stood very close behind me. His wet chest was against my wet back.

"Is this what you wanted to show me?" I teased, trying to hide how nervous I suddenly felt.

"It's not, but do you like it?"

"I do," I said. "It's a beautiful view, even in the rain." I sighed contently as I looked at dusk settling over the city. "I love New York."

The air seemed to vacuum out of my lungs when Emmet wrapped his arms around my waist.

"You appear to have adapted well to the city," he said, and I could feel his voice vibrating against my back.

"I had to adapt quickly," I responded with a shrug. "The city moves pretty fast, and the modeling business moves even faster. I had to leave my preconceptions and emotions at the state line."

"Your emotions?"

I shifted slightly in his arms. I had not meant to bring up my emotional state before moving to New York. I had been nervous about the life I was about to begin and sad for the one I was leaving behind. I didn't want to leave my best friend and my other friends and family, and I was still very much heartbroken. My mind had still been full of Emmet and my regrets. I had to harden myself, and it was a good thing I did, because rejection didn't come easily. It wasn't always just a, "no" or, "we'll call you" and you receive no such phone call. It was sometimes a, "you're too fat" or, "you're too dark" or, "you're too plain" or, my favorite one was, "whoever told you that you could be a model lied." Yes, I had to grow some hard skin, and that had to come from the inside out. I had no room inside for tears, remorse, and heartbreak.

"What about your emotions?" Emmet pressed when I didn't answer.

"You already know," I said dismissively with a smile as I moved out of his arms and took several steps away. I was careful to avoid the big bed as much as possible. "Do you have a dry shirt I can borrow?"

Emmet sighed. He looked frustrated and angry, but he also looked sad and regretful. I understood the mix of emotions because I felt the same way. His suitcase was open on the floor on the other side of the bed. He went over there and produced a t-shirt and a pair of cotton shorts.

I thanked him and went into the bathroom to change. I looked at my watch while I was in there. It wasn't late yet, but I would have to get plenty of sleep before reporting to work in the morning. I was going to have to cut my night short with Emmet and take a cab back to my hotel within the hour. I was feeling a little let down that I wouldn't get to spend too much time with him before he headed back to Cambridge to begin an internship, but maybe it was for the best. I would get accustomed to him being around, and the fact was that it wasn't a reality for us.

I walked out of the bathroom holding my wet clothes with one hand and the hem of the shorts with the other. The shorts were just too baggy for me, and the draw string really didn't help. I had it cinched tightly, and the shorts still managed to slide down as I moved. Several steps into the room I gave up and with an exasperated growl, I let the shorts fall to the floor. I scooped them up and tossed them to an amused Emmet.

"I like you better bottomless anyway," he said with a teasing smile.

I ignored the crazy thoughts his words put in my head.

"Amusing," I said, rolling my eyes. "Are there laundry facilities here? Maybe I can throw my stuff in the dryer."

"Sure, I'll take them down for you in a few minutes, but first..." He pulled open the drawer of one of the bedside tables and produced a camera. "I'm not leaving New York without a few pictures of you, and us together. What kind of a guy would I be if I know a super model and don't have any pictures of her or with her?"

I laughed. "Emmet, you'll have few days to take pictures. Can you wait until I'm not half naked? Seems pretty suspect to me." I crossed my arms and looked at him with raised eyebrows.

He laughed too. "I swear to you that I was going to ask for pictures regardless of what you had on. I had no idea that you would end up in my room half naked."

I rolled my eyes and sighed in defeat. "Can I at least brush my hair first?" I asked, reaching for my bag.

"No," he said, holding the camera up to his eye. "I like you just the way you are."

"My hair is a mess," I cried, trying to cover my head and face with my hands.

Emmet closed the distance between us and batted my hands away.

"You're perfect. Put your hands down."

"I'm perfectly disgusting you mean!"

Emmet captured one of my hands in his and held it firmly while he looked me in the eyes.

"Donya." he said my name with authority. He gave me a look of warning before taking several steps back.

I had no qualms about taking my shirt off in a room full of people the day I met Felix, and I had done it once more during another shoot. On more than one occasion, I had modeled underwear and bras, and I still did not feel as nervous as I did standing before Emmet in his t-shirt and my messy, wet hair. I felt more self-conscious than I ever remembered feeling.

Emmet grinned at what he saw through the viewfinder. I didn't understand why, because I couldn't even make myself smile at first. I just stood there, fidgeting with my hands in front of me, biting my lip and trying to fade into the background.

"Photographers must love photographing you," he murmured. He was taking shot after shot.

After a couple of minutes, Emmet paused and walked over to me. He smiled softly and without warning he used his free hand to tilt my head aside and kissed my neck. I shuddered and closed my eyes as his tongue made lazy circles on my skin.

He pulled away from me, and though my eyes were still closed, I heard the clicking of the camera. When I opened my eyes again, I was a little more relaxed and slightly giddy. I found myself smiling and not so fidgety.

"Thanks for showing up," Emmet teased behind the camera.

I grinned and rolled my eyes.

"Oh, I love that attitude! Give me more sass."

I stuck my tongue out at him.

Behaving like an over the top photographer, Emmet started shouting out various expressions and poses he wanted me to make and saying ridiculous things when I did it. I was laughing and having a good time doing stupid poses and making faces that no real photographer would ever want to see on my face.

"Alright, you're totally hogging all of the camera time," he said after putting in a new roll of film. "Time for some pictures with me."

He stood beside me and turned the camera around.

"Even though I will outshine you in these pictures, don't doubt that you're kinda pretty," Emmet said with such a serious expression that I burst into laughter.

We had no way of knowing how the pictures would turn out without anyone manning the viewfinder, but we took picture after picture anyway. We made faces; we said stupid words other than, "cheese" and did poses that I was sure would not turn out well on film since we were taking the pictures ourselves.

Sitting on opposite sides of the bed, we took turns taking photos of each other. I made Emmet flex his biceps and make intimidating faces that only cracked me up, and he made me put on sunglasses and a hat that made me look like a total fool.

"Come over here," Emmet said after he lay down on his back across the bed.

He pulled on my arm until I was beside him, looking up at the camera. I threatened to punch him if he dropped the camera on my face, and then I smiled for a few pictures. He slipped his free arm under me, drawing me closer. He planted a kiss on my cheek, making me smile, and took the picture. We had done several more similar poses before Emmet insisted on a lip to lip kiss.

"I am a professional, ma'am," he had said in a very deep voice that had me giggling. "This pose is for professional purposes only. Please do not take advantage of the situation and slip me your tongue."

I laughed and laughed even harder when he loudly puckered up.

"Come on," he said, trying not to laugh as he kept puckering his lips. "My arm is getting tired holding this damn camera."

Finally, I stopped laughing long enough to also pucker my lips. I tried not to snicker as his duck lips touched my duck lips. When I heard the camera click, I giggled.

"One more, one more," Emmet insisted, chuckling. "Come on, stop laughing. We're professionals here."

I laughed for a few more seconds and then puckered my lips once again. Emmet brought his lips to mine and held the camera above us once again. My lips touched his and even though it felt weird and silly with our lips puckered, it also felt very familiar, and I couldn't help but to gently touch his face as we posed for the picture. Once the camera clicked, however, neither of us immediately pulled away. Our lips relaxed, and the silly duck-like kiss became much less silly.

Emmet's lips moved slowly and gently against mine. Even as I heard the clicking of the camera, I pressed my mouth a little harder to his. Another click as Emmet gently nipped at my bottom lip and soothed it with his lips. Another click as I dragged my tongue along his top lip. Finally, the camera was set aside and then he held the back of my head as his tongue slipped between my slightly parted lips.

He kissed me sweetly, softly, and slowly, as if he was relishing every curve and corner of my mouth, and tasting every taste bud on my tongue. His hand moved over the curve of my neck, between my shoulder blades, down my spine, over the curve of my butt and onto my bare thigh. It was only then that I remembered I was only wearing the tee and panties, but I didn't let that stop me from kissing Emmet, but when he pulled away from me, I gasped in protest.

"I still have to show you something," he said.

"Now?" I asked in disbelief. "Your timing is really, really bad."

He laughed softly and kissed my nose. "Stay put."

He got off of the bed, leaving me feeling cold and a little frustrated. I sat up and sat with my legs crossed and his shirt pulled down over my knees as he dug around in his suitcase.

"Close your eyes."

I gave him a look of exasperation.

"Close your eyes," he repeated more firmly.

I growled, but I closed my eyes as Emmet laughed at me. A few seconds later I felt him put something on the bed, but since I didn't hear any telltale sounds, I had no idea what it could be.

"Okay. Open."

I opened my eyes and looked down. A few inches from my folded legs was a jar full of Hershey Kisses and a jar with a single candy heart in it. The jars I had given to Emmet.

I stared at the jars with my mouth hanging open. I didn't know what to think or how to feel. It didn't appear as if any of the kisses was missing. Was he giving them back to me? Did he not want my kisses? Did he not want my heart? I frowned and looked up into his face.

"Every damn day since the day I dug these out of my suitcase, I've wanted a kiss," Emmet murmured. "And I wanted to hold the person who so kindly bestowed upon me her heart. I put these jars on the table next to my bed. They were the last thing I saw every night before I crashed and the first thing I saw every morning when I woke up. When things got to be too much, I would hold this heart jar and think about your face and your smile and try to remember how your voice sounded in my head. I bought you the bracelet as an even exchange."

He smiled and touched the bracelet on my wrist. I was surprised to see big drops of water falling on his hand. I realized that I was crying and hurriedly turned my head away and tried to wipe away my tears. Emmet put his fingers under my chin and gently turned my head back so that I was looking up at him.

"Thank you for these jars, Donya," he said hoarsely. "I will always have them with me when I don't have you, but I wanted you to know that whenever it is possible, I want the real thing."

His thumb dragged across my lips and then he used both hands to wipe away my fallen tears.

"I love you," he told me. "I've never stopped loving you and I never will."

I looked down at the jars and carefully picked them up. I leaned over the bed and as carefully as I could I put them in his suitcase. Then I got on my knees, grabbed Emmet by the collar of his shirt and yanked him forward. I kissed him hard and deep, making him groan. He reached out to touch me, but lost his footing and stumbled forward. Our lips didn't part as I fell backward and as he fell on top of me. He stretched over me and kissed me greedily. Our mouths fought for domination, but Emmet battered my mouth with his and I gladly submitted.

Chapter Twenty-Four

Hot. Slick.

Beads of perspiration formed on my neck and between my breasts. My fingers twisted in Emmet's hair as his lips kissed away the beaded moisture. My back arched as he fondled a taut nipple between his fingers. My lips fell open with a moan. His other fingers caught the moan as it escaped me and, as if it had substance, he spread it across my mouth, over my jawline, and down my body. His mouth closed over my other nipple, and I cried out his name.

My shirt was gone. Right after Emmet pulled my shirt off of me, I pulled his off of him. To be fair, I had also insisted that he lose his shorts. When he settled back over me and pressed his bare skin to mine, I wrapped my arms tightly around him and held him close. His skin was scorching against mine. It didn't matter how hot it was outside; I wanted to envelop myself completely in Emmet's heat.

His teeth grazed my nipple and nearly sent me over the edge. He grinned up at me as he switched to the other nipple. He pulled the hard bud into his mouth and flicked his tongue across it, making me moan and writhe. Grasping my breast in his hand, he opened his mouth wide and filled his mouth with my flesh. He moaned as he suckled and I moaned with him. Every lick and nibble and pinch to my nipples sent ribbons of electricity shooting down between my legs where pressure slowly built. I tried to close my legs and press my thighs together to relieve some of that pressure, but Emmet's body on mine made it frustratingly difficult.

He released my breast and began to kiss his way down my body. He nibbled at my hipbone before kissing a line across my panty line to my other hipbone where he also took a tiny bite. He looked up at me with questioning eyes as he hooked a finger into my panties. I bit my lip and nodded eagerly.

Emmet began to pull my panties down. Even as I lifted my hips off of the bed so that he could get them down, I knew that I was about to pass the point of no return. I not only wanted to go past that point, but I wanted to forget where it was on the map. I wanted to go forward and never look back. I wanted Emmet to explore my body inside and out, and I wanted to roam every inch of his well-maintained body. I wanted him to do things to me that my virginal mind couldn't even dream of, and I wanted to feel him moving inside of me until we both collapsed in exhaustion.

"Fair is fair, Emmet," I said silkily as he tossed my panties to the floor.

"Fair is fair," he agreed, but with reluctance.

"What?" I asked, pushing myself up on my elbows.

Emmet sat up on his knees and ran a hand through his hair.

"Are you ready for this, Donya?" he asked, looking very unsure.

"Yes," I said without any explanation. I didn't need any explanation. My nipples were hard, my sex was slick, and I was ready to wrap my legs around his neck to make him do what he was about to do. Screw Sensible Donya and Imposter Donya. Donya, Sex Goddess, and Lover had entered the building.

"We can stop right here," Emmet said and then seemed to battle within himself as he looked down at my naked body. He cursed under his breath. "I'm sorry. We shouldn't have come this far."

He started to move away from me, looking miserable, as if he had just done something terrible.

"Emmet!" I said his name as a command.

He looked at me as if he was afraid of what I would say to him. He seemed fearful of both my invitation and my rebuke.

"I am ready," I told him. "I want this with you."

"If you're not really ready and we do this, you'll hate me."

"I'll never hate you," I promised. "I want you, Emmet."

He looked at me for a long moment. "Do you promise to tell me to stop if you change your mind?"

"I promise, but I won't change my mind."

"I might do something that makes you uncomfortable," he whispered and caressed the inside of my thigh with his fingers.

"I might feel uncomfortable at first," I admitted. "But I'll get over it."

"Did you feel uncomfortable when I sucked you here?" he asked heatedly as his fingers trailed over a nipple.

I groaned. "Only for about three seconds."

"Did you feel uncomfortable when I kissed your body?" His fingers moved over my abdomen and across my pelvic bone.

"Not much," I breathed.

His fingers moved slowly to my inner thigh, only inches from where I was slickly waiting for him.

"If I pushed my fingers inside of you…" he said, and slid two fingers inside of me. I drew in a breath and bit my lip as I looked at him. "Would you feel uncomfortable?"

I shook my head as he slowly eased his digits in and out of me. Emmet groaned when he looked down and watched his fingers getting wet from my excitement.

"If I pulled those fingers out and slipped them into my mouth…" He pulled the fingers out of me, and I gasped as he pushed them into his mouth and closed his eyes with delight. "Does that make you uncomfortable?" he asked in a whisper.

"No," I groaned.

"So," he said as he lay down between my open legs. He nipped at my inner thigh and then nipped at the other. "If I tell you I want to taste you until you come, you're okay with that?"

I gasped as his tongue darted out and quickly licked me. The way he was talking to me was driving me crazy.

Emmet smiled lazily at me as he slowly opened my legs farther.

"I just want you to know that I've never done this before," he said with a serious undertone. "So, if you don't like it, tell me what will make it better. Okay?"

I nodded and waited with anticipation.

Emmet pushed his tongue into my virginal opening, and we both groaned at the same time. He looked up at me with hooded eyes as he moved his tongue.

"You taste so good, baby," he murmured. He licked a trail through my sensitive center to my swollen bud. The second his tongue made contact I shrieked and lifted my hips off of the bed.

Emmet savored that part of me as if it was a tiny piece of candy in his favorite flavor. He moaned against me as I pulled on his hair and ground myself against his face and called out his name. The pressure was so bad; I pushed at the back of his head as I sought relief.

"Emmet, oh god," I cried out as his tongue moved faster.

When he pulled the swollen little knot between his lips and sucked hard on it, the pressure gave way, and I exploded. I held onto his head with both hands as I screamed his name and cursed. I tried to clamp my thighs shut, but Emmet held me open and licked and sucked me until I was climaxing once again. When he finally stopped and again lay down on top of me, I fell limply onto the bed.

"I wish I could kiss you right now," he groaned, rubbing his erection on my leg.

"So, kiss me," I panted. "Kiss me."

"Really?" he asked, looking unsure.

I considered that as one of the things that I couldn't have dreamed up on my own.

"Kiss me," I repeated.

He hesitated only for another few seconds and then kissed me. I moaned into his mouth as I smelled and tasted myself on his lips and tongue. While we kissed, I tugged on his boxers, pulling them down over his hard ass, springing his erection free. I felt it, warm, silky, and hard against me. I squirmed to feel it against my clit. Emmet repositioned his body over mine so that his erection was right where I needed it at that moment. I gasped into his mouth and moaned as he moved against me. Within moments, I was climaxing again, but my cries of ecstasy were trapped in Emmet's mouth. He finally pulled away from my mouth and smiled with satisfaction.

"I'm going to get a condom," he said and moved off of me.

I watched as he rooted through his suitcase.

"Did you know we were going to do this?" I asked curiously.

"No, but I thought I'd be prepared anyway."

"You weren't preparing for other girls, were you?" I asked and instantly regretted it.

Emmet gave me a hard look. "I promise you, baby. You were the only one on my mind when I put these in my suitcase."

"These?" I asked with amusement as he climbed back on the bed with a foil packet in his hand. "As in more than one?"

"Yes," he grinned as he opened it.

"So, you think you'll get lucky more than once?"

"A guy can hope," he shrugged.

I sat up on my elbows again. "Before you put the condom on....can I...touch you?"

Emmet froze for a moment and then smiled. He nodded and lay down beside me. I rolled onto my side and smiled shyly at him as my hand moved slowly over his tight abs. My fingertips glided along the line of hair that started at his navel and ended in a neat patch of hair. I looked at the large erection and very carefully put my hand on the shaft. He hissed, and I snatched my hand back in surprise.

"No, it's okay," he said quickly. "It didn't hurt. Touch me."

Reluctantly, I reached for him once again, and I didn't pull back when he hissed.

I wasn't completely naïve about sex. I knew how it was done. I knew that guys jerked off, but it wasn't something that I had ever seen done. I had never even caught a glimpse of a porno. So, when I started to slowly, yet awkwardly stroke him, it was with complete inexperience. I was so nervous that I wasn't doing it right until Emmet groaned softly and gently thrust his hips so that his cock slid through my hand.

"Donya," he moaned my name as he thrust again. "Stroke the whole thing, baby," he directed and then threw his head back. "Yes, just like that. Stroke a little harder. Oh, yeah," he moaned. "Good. Just like that."

I watched with fascination as little droplets of moisture began to seep out of the slit of the bulbous head. Curiously, I ran my thumb over it, and Emmet cursed. I rubbed the moisture over the head and then stroked him a few more times until there were more drops. I used the palm of my hand to gather it and then used it to lubricate my strokes.

"I need you," he said roughly and sat up quickly. He reached for the foil packet on the bed next to us and tore it open. It wasn't until the condom was securely on Emmet did I get nervous.

"Is it going to hurt?" I asked, trying to remember what other girls had said about their first time. Emmy had said the pain was barely noticeable, but Mayson had said it burned like a bitch.

"I don't know," Emmet said honestly as he positioned his body over mine. He held himself up on his forearms as he looked down at me, waiting for me to either invite him or deny him. "But I'm pretty sure if it hurts it will only hurt for a moment."

"You're so...big," I said nervously biting my lip.

"Donya, we can stop. Right now. It's okay," he said, sincerely trying to reassure me.

"I'm just nervous," I admitted.

"Me, too," he said with a small smile.

I touched his face and looked into his eyes.

"Okay," I said, letting out a breath. "Let's do it."

Emmet positioned the tip of his cock at my entrance.

"Are you sure?" he whispered.

I nodded though my heart was pounding in my chest.

"I love you," he said and dropped his head to kiss me.

As Emmet's mouth devoured mine, he very slowly pushed himself inside of me until he hit resistance. My eyes flew open. He pulled out, and then slammed into me.

I pulled my lips from him as I cried out in agony as my hymen tore. Emmet held very still inside of me, stroked my hair, and apologized repeatedly in a barely audible whisper in my ear.

After a few moments, the pain began to fade, and I started to really feel him inside of me. My nipples hardened painfully. I felt so full of him, and so very connected with him. I became hyper aware of the tether between us, softly vibrating, humming with anticipation.

"Emmet," I whispered his name. "Make love to me."

He looked into my eyes and began to move slowly inside of me. Drawing out slowly and then slowly pushing back inside. He took my hands and put them above my head. He linked his fingers with mine and thrust deeply inside of me.

"Tell me how you want it, baby," he said. "Faster? Slower? Harder? Softer?"

"Harder," I whispered.

Emmet pulled out and slammed back inside of me. He grunted, and his eyes rolled back in his head. He repeated the move, squeezing my hands as he rammed into me. My nipples rubbed against his chest. I needed to feel his fingers or mouth or something on them.

"Touch my nipples, please," I nearly begged and then licked my lips as Emmet ducked his head and pulled a hard nipple into his mouth. "Oh, god! Bite it!"

If my hands were free, I probably would have covered my mouth in disbelief. Not only had I asked him to touch my nipples, but I demanded that he bite the one he had in his mouth. Donya the Sex Goddess and Lover was shocking!

Emmet complied and sunk his teeth into the sensitive flesh. I groaned deeply and arched my back, giving him better access to my breasts. Moaning loudly, Emmet released that nipple and sucked in the other one as his thrusts became faster and harder. Without having to be told, he bit down on that nipple too. I cried out and pushed against his hands, but he held me down securely.

"Emmet," I groaned, pushing my hips up to meet his thrusts. "Emmet, please…"

"Please what?" he asked as his teeth grazed my jawline. "What do you want, Donya?"

"Harder, please," I whined. He pounded into me so hard; I was sure I was bruising, but I didn't care. It felt so damn good. Donya SGL was screaming with delight, and it still wasn't enough. "Deeper!" I pleaded.

"I don't want to hurt you any more than I already am," Emmet said, panting.

"Please, please, please," I said, whipping my head back and forth.

Emmet released my hands and got up on his knees. He slipped his arms under my knees, and I immediately felt the change. When he repositioned himself back over me with my legs over his shoulders, I screamed at the exquisite, painfully, delicious sensation of his cock buried dangerously inside of me. I knew that couldn't be right. I knew that he should not feel as if he was in my womb, but I wanted it.

"Do you want me to stop?" Emmet asked, alarmed.

"No," I said quickly. "Please keep going."

Emmet seemed reluctant at first, but when I pushed my hips up and took him in deeper, he growled ferociously and slammed into me. I screamed as he thrust in and out of me, and begged him not to stop.

My orgasm came out of nowhere, blindsiding me and figuratively knocking me on my ass. My body stiffened and then jerked and shook uncontrollably as I sobbed. Emmet dropped my legs and wrapped his arms around me as his own orgasm hit. He growled and groaned as he pumped his spurting manhood inside of me. I clung to him, my legs wrapped around him and my arms pulled him as close to me as we could get. I cried as the powerful orgasm continued to wash over me.

When the last of the intense tendrils of pleasure left me, I lay under Emmet a limp and teary mess.

"Are you okay?" he asked, looking at me with concern. He wiped at my tears with his fingers.

I nodded and smiled happily at him.

"Why are you crying?" he asked softly.

It was by far the most powerful experience of my life and even though I was able to think it, I didn't think the words could properly verbalize it. So, instead of answering him with my words, I smiled happily and pulled his face to mine for a long, appreciative kiss.

Chapter Twenty-Five

We sat on the bed, watching television and eating chocolate cake and ice-cream that we ordered from room service. I was wearing another one of Emmet's shirts with nothing else underneath and he had on a pair of boxers. I was comfortable sitting beside him. The whole scene felt perfect and right. I kept glancing at him as I imagined us sitting in a similar fashion years down the road in marital bliss.

"Why do you keep looking at me?" he asked with a smile without taking his eyes off of the television. "If you want me again, all you have to do is ask, or demand, or just take."

"I will always want you," I said. "But that isn't why I'm looking at you. I'm just trying to imagine us ten years from now. Will it be like this you think?"

"Maybe with a kid sitting in bed with us?" Emmet said, looking at me with gleaming green eyes.

"Maybe two kids?" I smiled.

"I'll have a promising position in a law firm."

"I'll be a retired supermodel working as a fashion consultant on some cable network."

"Where will we live?" Emmet asked as he gave me a spoonful of his ice cream. I already had my own, but it was sweet and romantic and made my smile widen.

"We will have to live in New York or L.A., depending on where I will be working, but I guess it also depends on where you will be working too."

"I'll go wherever you go, baby," he said and kissed me.

"Mmm," I said and licked my lips. "You taste delicious."

"Not as good as you," he said and judged by the way he was looking at me, I knew he wasn't talking about my ice-cream and cake flavored lips.

Emmet put his dishes down on the table on his side of the bed. Then he took my plates away from me and put them aside too. He held the back of my head and kissed me deeply. I wrapped my arms around his neck and maneuvered myself onto his lap and straddled him. His hands moved over my back and then under the shirt. I felt him growing hard beneath me and couldn't help but to rock myself against him.

"Do you think we'll be this hot for each other ten years from now?" I panted as Emmet kissed my neck.

"I'll always be hot for you," he said against my skin. "You'll always set my blood on fire. I'll always be hard for you."

We groaned together as I reached down between us and pulled his erection out of the top of his boxers. I wanted to feel it against me, bare and unsheathed. I rocked my hips forward and slid along the length of it, shuddering and moaning.

"Donya," Emmet growled my name and then crushed my mouth with his.

I wrapped my arms around him again and rubbed my bare pussy on his bare cock. I was slick and ready for him, but before I let him get another condom, I wanted to come like that.

He put his hands on my hips, moving me harder and faster against him. I was getting so hot. I was going to combust soon. I moved wildly against him, seeking my release. Moaning in his mouth, Emmet pulled hard on my hips at the same time I had lifted myself to adjust my position for more pleasure. When I came back down, Emmet's hard length sunk into me. It was an accident on both of our parts, but my orgasm was instant and mind numbing. We looked at each other with surprised eyes as my walls gripped and squeezed his cock.

"You feel so good," Emmet whispered and thrust gently inside of me. I gasped and moaned. "Tell me you'll always be mine."

He thrust into me again and squeezed my nipple through the shirt. I couldn't answer him because I was falling apart again, coming hard on the heels of my last orgasm.

"Tell me," Emmet said, gazing into my eyes as he continued to roll the nipple between his fingers.

"I'll always be yours," I panted.

He gripped the hem of the shirt and pulled it over my head. He held me close and moved slowly inside of me as he gently kissed my neck, my shoulders, and chest.

"I'll always be yours, too," he said, and then he was done being gentle.

Emmet grabbed my hips and began to thrust hard inside of me. I bounced up and down on his hard shaft as it stretched me and filled me and pressed too deeply inside of me.

"I want you to come," Emmet growled. "Come for me, Donya."

"Emmet!" I shouted his name as my orgasm took hold.

"Donya," he groaned and lifted me a little and pulled out of me. A second later I felt his seed, hot and sticky, spurting on my belly. He held me tightly as he came with his cock nestled tightly between us.

I liked watching his face as he climaxed. His eyelids were heavy as he looked at me with lust and love, and his jaw set as he groaned and grunted.

"I love you," he said, breathlessly and put his hand in my hair.

"I love you," I echoed and kissed him.

"I'm afraid I got us a bit sticky," Emmet said tiredly a few moments later.

I pulled back a little so that I could look at the mess. I reached out and touched some of it on Emmet's stomach. It wasn't exactly how I pictured it would look, and I wondered how girls actually swallowed it, but seeing the sticky white liquid on both of our bodies was a bit of a turn on.

"Oh, my god, I'm a freak," I whispered, horrified with myself as I rubbed the stuff into his stomach.

"Yeah, but you're my freak," Emmet said and kissed my forehead. "Come on, Freak. Let's have a shower."

"Together?" I asked as I moved off of him.

"Of course," he smiled and took my hand.

"Okay, but no more hanky panky," I said. "I'm sore."

"I promise," he said, holding up two crossed fingers.

"That's really not a good sign," I said doubtfully.

He totally broke his promise.

~~*

Several days later, I stood by the window with the beautiful view of central park. Emmet stood by the bed shirtless and angry. I understood his anger, but he didn't understand my viewpoint at all.

"I don't understand why you need to go out there when there is plenty of work for you here," he said again.

"My work isn't in just one place, Emmet," I said, sighing.

I had gone over it with him half a dozen times since Felix called earlier in the day and told me that he thought he could get me a part in his movie. It wasn't a huge part. I would really only be on screen for a total of seven minutes altogether, but the opportunities that could result from a job well done in a movie were endless. I was fortunate that the part even opened up thanks to some last minute rewrites.

"What are you going to do if I get work overseas?" I asked him. "Are you going to want me to turn it down and possibly ruin my career before it even gets a good chance to start?"

He groaned in exasperation and spun in a full circle with his hand in his hair.

"You don't even know for sure if you got the part," he pointed out.

"You're right. I have no idea, but I'd rather go out there and find out than to wonder about it for the rest of my life. I know what you're worried about, and you don't need to worry about it."

"The media thinks that you and Felix are screwing around," he stated the obvious.

"I am well aware of that."

"And you're okay with it because even bad PR is good PR," he said dryly.

"It's not bad PR."

"It's a lie!"

"Yeah, it is," I snapped. "It's a lie, but I didn't make up that lie, and that lie is not killing my career. In fact, it is helping my career."

"I don't want you to go," he said through gritted teeth.

"I appreciate your opinion, but it isn't your choice," I said coolly and turned my attention back to the approaching night outside.

"Then I'm going with you."

"I don't need a babysitter, Emmet," I sighed and then muttered under my breath "I already have my mommy for that."

"You need someone to look out for you because your mom sure isn't doing it."

While that was true, it was still a low blow. I turned away from the pretty view and looked at Emmet with a murderous gaze.

"You're right. If my mother had been doing her job, I wouldn't have lost my virginity on your hotel bed and been here every day and night since screwing you like a fucking bunny." I stormed past him and the bed and grabbed my bag off of the floor on my way without missing a step.

"Where are you going?" Emmet said behind me.

"I'm going back to *my* hotel suite so that my *mother* can attempt to do her job better and keep me out of trouble, and your bed."

I put my hand on the door handle, but Emmet put his hand on my hand.

"You're being dramatic," he snapped.

"Good. Maybe I can use it in the movie," I snapped back and elbowed him in the gut to make him move away from me so I could get out of the door.

I got the door open, but Emmet slammed it shut.

"Stop fucking running away every time things get hard," he growled.

I opened my mouth to make a comment, but Emmet cut me off with, "And don't make any smartass comments about your virginity."

I closed my mouth.

"Come on, Donya," he said with a little less aggression. "You can't blame me for being worried."

I looked over my shoulder at him. "I don't blame you for being worried, Emmet," I said, trying to keep my temper under wraps. "I blame you for asking me to stay. I blame you for asking me to possibly thwart my entire career because of your jealousy."

He sighed and rested his forehead on the back of my head. When he spoke, I felt his breath on my neck.

"I'm sorry. I don't want to hold you back, but..."

"Of course there's a but," I muttered.

"There must be some other way to help your career."

"Emmet!" I yelled, frustrated and angry and damn tired. I had been up since four in the morning because I had to be at a shoot by five.

I shoved backward, making him move away from me. I turned around to face him, with my hand on the door behind me.

"I am getting on a plane tomorrow morning, and I am going to California. Either support me or shut the hell up!"

He sighed and pushed his hand into his hair again. "I support you," he said in such a low voice I wasn't even sure I really heard him.

"You what?" I prodded and put a finger to my ear.

"I support you," he said louder and with a scowl.

"That's what I thought you said," I nodded.

"Come over here," he demanded, pointing to the spot in front of him.

"No," I said. "I'm going 'home' to prepare for my trip."

"Prepare for your trip later. Come here."

"No," I said incredulously.

Emmet quickly closed the distance between us and kissed me hungrily as he pushed me back against the door. When his hands began to slide up the inside of my shirt, I pushed him away. He was undeterred, however, and pressed his body against mine.

"I think we should slow down," I said to him, even though I wanted to try sex against the door. We did it missionary, with me on top, and tried doggy style more recently. Why not try standing up against the door?

Oh, my God. I'm becoming a little slut!

"I don't want to slow down," he said, pressing his erection against me. "You're addicting."

"Emmet," I sighed his name as his tongue flicked at my earlobe. "Stop."

I didn't have to repeat myself. He froze for a moment and then looked at how serious my face was. He stepped away from me, and I honestly missed his body that quickly and despite the fact that I was the one that pushed him away.

"This isn't what I wanted," I said, running a hand through my hair with frustration. "I didn't want us to be all about sex."

"We're more than sex," he said, crossing his arms.

"I hope so," I whispered.

He put both hands in his hair and took another step back.

"You're beautiful, and your body feels incredible," he said. His hands were still in his hair, holding it back off of his forehead. "I love you, and I feel like I can't stop touching you or I'll die."

I understood that. I really did. I wanted to reach out and put my hands on his strong chest and nibble on his juicy biceps and make love to him on the floor, but sex clouds the brain, and my brain had been pretty damn cloudy lately. I didn't necessarily like the fog that I was in. I didn't think it was a safe place for either of us.

"After I'm all packed and ready to go, I'll call you," I promised. "We can meet half way and say goodbye. I'll see you when I get back."

"I have to go back to Cambridge this weekend," he reminded me in not the kindest of tones.

"Oh," I frowned. "I forgot. I got so used to seeing you every day."

Emmet smiled and took a few steps towards me. My hand closed on the doorknob.

"I don't mind missing a few classes if it means I can be with you on the west coast," he said.

"No," I said firmly. "You need to do what you need to do, and I need to do what I need to do. You're just going to have to get used to the idea that what we need to do for ourselves may not always bring us together."

He frowned and rolled his eyes. "Fuck, Donya," he growled. "You make it seem like we're doomed."

I hadn't thought about us being doomed. I had only thought about how our roads were going in different directions with the occasional crossing, but since he put it like that…

"Don't say that," I admonished.

He rolled his eyes again and sighed loudly. "Yeah, okay."

I didn't want to argue, and I didn't want to be exposed to his worsening attitude.

"I'm going to go." I opened the door and quickly stepped into the hallway. "I'll call you soon," I promised.

Emmet simply nodded, acknowledging that he had heard me, but he didn't seem to be in the mood to talk. I walked away, letting the door close behind me.

Chapter Twenty-Six

My mother looked sick, I decided. She looked sick, and she acted sick. Though she had the skin tone of dark caramel normally, she was looking a little pale. She had lost weight, she was overly fatigued, and she couldn't do much without wearing herself out, and it was very, very obvious that she was in a great deal of pain.

I stood in the doorway to my bedroom watching her move around the suite, packing for our trip to California. She walked as if every inch of her body hurt. She looked twice, if not three times, her age of thirty-seven. She wasn't wrinkled or gray, but she looked old, nonetheless.

Whatever was wrong with her was making her deteriorate fast. Every day she was a little worse than she was the day before. Admittedly, I tried not to notice. I went on with my life, pretending everything was fine. She didn't have to accompany me to work, so almost daily I left her in the hotel in the mornings. I had refused to actually look at her and see what was happening. I told myself she was just under the weather and maybe a little depressed, and she would get better eventually, but the truth was staring me in the face, and I couldn't ignore it any longer.

"Mom," I said her name in a way that demanded attention. I wanted her to look at me, to see me and hear me.

She turned around and looked at me. She folded her hands in front of her and tried to stand up a little taller. Andrea Stewart did not know her daughter well at all, after years of living only inside of her own head, but she knew me well enough to guess at what I was about to say.

"What is it?" Again I spoke in a way that demanded an answer. My voice was hard, and my words crisp.

She took a breath and said, "You have a lot on your plate already for a child," she tried to beg off. I noted that she did not deny that there was an *It* to speak of.

"We both know I am not much of a child," I said rigidly. "I took care of you for years, like the adult."

That hit her hard. She swallowed and blinked rapidly for a moment. "Well, now I'm taking care of you," she said gently.

"But you're not," I pointed out. "I appreciate you being here with me, but you've been more like a companion and legal advisor than a mother."

I remembered how she insisted on taking pictures of Emmet and me before Felix's party. That was as close to a mom as she got. It had annoyed me then, but as I stood before her weeks later, my heart expanded in my chest, and I felt touched by that one sentiment. Facts were facts, however, and the fact was that we didn't have many moments like that like other mothers and daughters.

"I don't know how to be your mom," she said softly in a quavering voice.

I was stunned. I expected her to feed me bullshit, or to cop an attitude and try to turn it around on me, but she didn't. She spoke truthfully, and obviously from her heart.

"You're more Sam's daughter than mine," she continued. "I don't even know you."

"I'm here," I said patiently. "If you want to know me, I'm here, Mom, but you can't bullshit me. If we're going to try to be a mother and daughter, you can't withhold things from me. Tell me what is wrong."

She started muttering more shit about me having enough on my plate, but I cut her off.

"Andrea!" I shouted her name and slammed my hand on the door.

She looked at me with a hardness in her eyes that had not been there moments before.

"Last year before you left for the summer I found out I had breast cancer. Stage four and it had metastasized. I declined chemo because it will only kill me faster, and I wanted to see if I could at least see my daughter graduate from high school before I died, but I'm pretty sure I won't make it that far. I'm pretty sure that I will be dead before the year is out. I've accepted the dying part, but the not seeing you graduate from high school part, I haven't accepted. I haven't accepted all of the years I lost with you. I haven't accepted all of the years I will lose with you in the future. I haven't accepted what a terrible mother I have been and how much you suffered because of me. I've accepted that I'm going to die, Donya. I just haven't accepted all of the shit I'm leaving behind."

Speechless. Dumbfounded. Confused. Hurt. Angry. Mind blown.

I pushed it all aside because it wasn't about me.

I moved across the room and embraced my mother—gently so that I wouldn't hurt her.

"You should have told me," I whispered.

"I didn't want you distracted," she said, echoing Emmet's words. "I'm very proud of you."

"I haven't done anything," I chuckled to hide the pain I felt.

"You've done more than I have ever done," she said, petting my hair. "Your dad and I didn't do right by you, but you're still so strong and good, and responsible."

I didn't feel strong, though, or good, or responsible.

I pulled away but kept my hands on her frail shoulders. I dug deep into that place I've had to dig into many times over the years and produced a smile for my mother.

"Have you ever been to California?" I asked her lightly.

She smiled too as she wiped at a few tears. "When I was about your age, me and your Aunt Candy hitchhiked our way to San Francisco. I felt bad and called my mom to let her know we were okay. Don't you know she came all the way to California and beat our asses all the way back to Philly?"

She laughed softly at the memory, and I forced myself to laugh with her. I had never known my grandmother. She died when I was a toddler, and my mom rarely spoke about her. I had no idea what she was like, but strangely the story reminded me of Sam.

"I want to hear more about her," I said. "You can tell me some stories on our way to L.A." I walked back towards my room. "And if I get this part, we'll celebrate with a shopping trip on Rodeo Drive and have dinner in the nicest restaurant."

"We can't afford that," she said behind me. "But thanks anyway."

"Oh, I'm sure we can find the money," I said over my shoulder. "I'm almost finished packing. As soon as I'm done I'll help you. Sit down and relax."

"I can do it."

I turned around, just inside my room. "Mom, please," I said in a soft, but pleading voice. "Let me help you."

She looked like she was going to cry, but she nodded silently. I forced another smile and went to finish my packing.

When I met Emmet later, I didn't bother telling him about my mom. I didn't feel like discussing it, and I didn't want any pity or for him to ask me if I was okay every five minutes. We ate dinner at what was becoming our favorite pizza place, and I tried to keep the focus on his upcoming internship at a law firm near his apartment. I tried to keep the conversation light and comfortable and hoped that when it was time to say goodbye, he wouldn't give me a hard time again about Felix and the trip.

"What's wrong?" Emmet asked as we left the pizza joint.

"What are you talking about?" I asked, putting my hand in his.

"You're really good at hiding your true feelings, but we're connected, remember?" He stopped walking and put his hand over my heart and softly said, "I know when you're hurting, angry, happy, or sad."

I put my hand on his and squeezed it gently. "I don't want to talk about it right now."

He sighed and looked away from me as if the sight of me vexed him.

"Emmet," I said, touching his face. I waited until he was looking at me again. "It's not about you or us, okay? But I don't want to talk about it. Just show me a good time for the next…" I looked at my watch. "…half hour."

A devious smile that made him look like a naughty little boy appeared on his face. I couldn't help but to smile, too. He hadn't even said anything really, and he had the ability to make me feel better.

"Is that enough time to get back to my hotel room?" he asked, wiggling his eyebrows.

"No," I laughed. "But it is plenty of time for you to buy your girlfriend an ice-cream."

"As long as it makes you smile," he said and kissed my smiling mouth.

I left my worries there on the sidewalk for the rest of the evening. There would be plenty of time to pick them up later.

~~*

The plane ride out had been enlightening. I heard a lot about my grandparents and my mom's childhood. Her father worked at the DuPont plant in Delaware, and her mother cleaned offices and houses a few days a week from time to time to supplement their income when things got a little rough, but, for the most part, she was a stay at home mom for my mother and her three siblings. The kids never knew they were poor because my grandparents always made sure that they had plenty of food to eat and nice, clean clothes.

Mom had been close to her siblings when they were growing up, but her oldest brother died in a car accident when mom was around my age. My other Uncle Roger met and married a Brazilian beauty and moved to Brazil. I had only met him maybe twice in my life. Then there was my Aunt Candy. She and my mom had been very close growing up, but Candy had a superiority complex after marrying a well-off Texan. She judged everything my mom did. They went from being inseparable to speaking maybe once a year.

"Do you want to see your brother and sister again before you go?" I had asked her. I couldn't bring myself to say the D word out loud.

Mom had shrugged like it didn't matter, but the frown lines around her mouth said differently.

"I'm used to being without them," she had said.

I didn't understand that. I wasn't very close to Charlotte and Lucille and Fred Jr., but I looked forward to seeing them on special occasions. I would not get used to being without them. I knew I would never get used to being without Fred, Sam, Emmy and Emmet. I couldn't even get used to not seeing my dad. Some days I still thought about him like he was alive.

I had looked at my mom and knew instantly that I would never get used to being without her. We weren't close, that was true, and as she had admitted, she had not exactly been a model parent, but I knew I would have a difficult time once she was gone. I wouldn't be able to just get used to being without her.

My mom was exhausted and in pain by the time we made it to our hotel. She tried hard to pretend that things weren't as bad as they undoubtedly were, but I knew better. I found her stash of painkillers and other drugs, loaded her up with what she needed and left her tucked in the giant bed.

I showered, redid my hair and changed my clothes. I took the script Felix had left at the front desk for me and sat in the living room reading it over. It wasn't very extensive, as I said. I would only be on screen for a short time, but I couldn't get the words to stick in my head. My brain was overflowing with thoughts about my mom. How much longer would she live? How much pain would she be in until her last breath? When she died, where would that leave me? Would I be allowed to live on my own? Would I get sent to a relative I barely knew or would I have to go back to Sam and Fred?

Wait a minute...

I put the script down on the couch and went to the phone on the desk. The phone call would probably end up costing more than a few dollars, but I'd worry about that later.

"Thank you for calling the Grayne residence. This is Emmy Grayne, sexy, foxy, hot—"

"How did you know it was me?" I interrupted her ridiculous greeting.

"Caller ID, bay-bee," Emmy said. "I can't believe you're going to be in a movie! I can't believe you're screwing Felix Hunter! I want your life."

"First of all, I didn't get the part yet. Secondly, I am not screwing Felix Hunter. Now you're starting to sound like the tabloids."

"Well, if I believed the tabloids, I'd believe you were screwing my brother too."

I didn't think it was possible to choke on air, but there I was, choking on air and then gasping for it.

"What are you talking about?" I managed.

"You know I stalk you via the tabloids," she laughed. "It's such a thrill seeing *my* best friend holding hands with Felix Fucking Hunter and kissing Felix Fucking Hunter."

"Someone totally blew that out of context," I said the same words I had said to her two days after Felix's party. Someone had snapped a picture of Felix kissing me right before I pushed him away. Even though I had shown up at the party with and stayed with Emmet, he had not been mentioned at all. At least not then. My life had become so surreal.

"What are you talking about—with Emmet?" I asked her.

"There's just a small section in *Gossipers* with a few pictures of you and Emmet holding hands. They are speculating that you are now involved with our dear brother—gross—and because of that Felix ran away to California, broken hearted of course."

I rested my head in the palm of my hand. "That's not so bad I guess," I said weakly.

"Yeah, except it's *Emmet*," Emmy snorted. "Just the idea of you screwing our brother makes me almost throw up in my mouth."

I closed my eyes and tried not to sigh too loudly. "Emmet isn't a dog or anything, you know."

"Oh, I know our brother is a hottie. That's not the issue. The issue is he's our brother, and he's an okay guy, but he's essentially your brother, Donya. It just seems all kinds of wrong. Wait." She paused for a moment. "Are you calling me to tell me you're screwing my brother? Please don't tell me you're screwing my brother."

Not this time, I thought.

"Our conversation took like three left turns," I sighed wearily.

"Right. We were talking about you screwing Felix Hunter, and you said you're not…even though you totally made out with him once…and he flew you and Andrea out there first class, and he's paying for your hotel accommodations in one of the most prestigious hotels out there. I'll bet his suite is close to yours, isn't it?"

"So what if it is?" I snapped, not mentioning that his suite was apparently right across the hall. "Look, I'm not screwing him, and I didn't call you to discuss who I'm screwing."

"Who *are* you screwing?" she asked with a super secretive tone.

"Emmy, my mom is dying," I said, ending her who's screwing who line of questioning. "I know you didn't know, or you would have told me, but Sam and Fred…"

"What?"

I told her about the conversation I had with my mom in New York and my observations before that. I also told her that I believed that Sam and Fred knew and withheld the information from me, and she agreed. Before I even asked to speak to them, she shouted for both of her parents to pick up a phone. It took a minute for them to get on the phone. They tried to begin the conversation with the usual pleasantries and inquiries. Sam even asked about the tabloid Emmy had mentioned, but I didn't want to talk about all of that.

"Why didn't you tell me about my mom?" I asked, cutting Sam off as she began a tirade about the tabloid pictures.

There was a moment of hushed silence and then all three of them started talking at once. I cut in too, trying to voice my anger and feelings of betrayal, but we were all only getting snippets of what was said. It was telephonic chaos until I got sick of trying to shut everyone up and just hung up the phone.

I paced the large room for a couple of minutes, trying to calm myself down. When the phone rang I almost didn't answer it, but I wanted some answers, and I had a few things to say.

"What?" I replied crossly.

"Your tone needs a slight adjustment," Fred said carefully.

I took a deep breath and let it out slowly. I realized that he was the only one on the phone. I knew that was the case because Sam and Emmy had the inability to control their big mouths.

"I'm very angry, and I'm very hurt," I said to him, but with a little less 'tude.

"I understand."

"I don't think that you do," I said and then dug my nails into my palm to once again reel in my anger. "You held back very pertinent information. Don't you think that I would need to know that my mother was sick and dying?"

Fred sighed deeply. "You're growing up so damn fast," he said, sounding both proud and sad.

"Why? Because I used a big word?" I asked, irritated. "I've been using big words since I was a kid."

"You're still a kid."

"I'm not a kid, Fred. I haven't been an actual kid in a very long time, and we both know it. Don't tell me one moment that I am growing up so damn fast and then in the next moment call me a kid. I'm not a damn kid. I know chronologically—yes, I used another big word—I am almost seventeen, but we both know that I am older than that. So, please, stop treating me like I'm five and be straight with me. Even little kids have the right to know that their closest blood relative is about to die."

There was another deep sigh and then Fred said, "Donya, when your mom found out, she wanted to get a second and third opinion before telling you. By the time she got all of that, you were very much interested in pursuing a modeling career. No one wanted to—"

"Distract me?" I cut in bitterly.

"Your mother didn't want you to hold back. She wanted you to have a chance without her illness on your shoulders."

"Do you understand how fucking selfish that makes me look? Do you have any idea how much guilt I feel now? You guys made a piss poor decision about *my* life, and you didn't give me a chance to choose!"

"We believed we were doing the right thing for you," Fred argued.

"Do you know who has been making the 'right' decisions for me for the last few years? Me! Not you. Not my mom. Not Sam. Me. You were all *wrong*!"

There was a long silence on the other end. I was breathing heavily as I paced back and forth as far as the cord would let me. I had never felt such anger in my entire life, and I had never felt so cheated. Maybe I wouldn't have given up my career, but I would have spent my time with my mom more wisely.

"Did you talk to your mom about this?" Fred finally asked.

"No," I said. "I can't. I won't stress her out like that."

"So, you're taking your anger and distress out on us," he concluded.

I dropped into the chair and closed my eyes. Tears squeezed through anyway.

"Yes," I admitted. "And I apologize, but…" There wasn't a but, not really. It was exactly as he said. The one person responsible for telling me was lying in bed, probably in excruciating pain even while she slept. It wasn't Fred's duty to tell me, nor Sam's. As much like real parents that they were to me, my mom was still my actual mom, and they had to abide by her wishes.

"Now that you know, what are you going to do?" Fred asked after a minute of quiet.

"I'm going to try to give her as much time as I can," I said, sniffing. I wiped my nose with the back of my hand and simply allowed my tears to fall into my lap. "But I'm going to keep working. She seems to really want that, and frankly, I really want that."

"That sounds like a very sensible plan, Kiddo," Fred said gently.

My cell phone began to ring in the other room. I put Fred on hold and ran to answer it.

"Hey, beautiful," Felix said cheerfully.

"Hi," I said, walking back to the living room. "What's up?"

"I know you're probably tired from flying, but you'll have to get over it. They want to see you. Now."

"Now?" I asked, running a hand through my hair.

"Now. They're doing me a huge favor by even entertaining the idea of 'some unknown model wannabe' taking this part, regardless of how small it is. They have other people that can easily take the spot, so you need to get your hot ass down here and prove me right."

I had barely looked at the script, but I didn't have a choice. I had to prove that I could do it not only after a day of travel but also on short notice.

"Okay," I relented. "How do I get there?"

"I've already sent a car over to get you. You should be downstairs in fifteen minutes or so."

"Okay."

"Did you learn your lines?"

"Kind of," I said hurriedly. "Look, if you want me downstairs in fifteen minutes, I have to go. I have to get ready."

"Right. I'll see you soon, okay?"

"Yeah, bye." I said and hung up before he could respond. I picked up the phone on the desk. "Fred?"

"I'm here," Fred answered.

"And me," Emmy said. "And mom," she said with a little less enthusiasm.

"How quaint," I muttered. "I have to go. Felix just called, and they want to see me now."

"Good luck!" Emmy said. "Kiss Felix for me. Like, really kiss him. Put your tongue in his mouth and—"

"Emmy," Fred growled in warning.

"Make sure you fix your hair before you go," Sam said quickly. "I wouldn't wear it in a headband like you sometimes do. Makes you look homely and unattractive."

"Thanks?" I said, shaking my head. "I gotta go."

"We love you!" Emmy rushed before I could hang up.

I sighed and gave a silent prayer of thanks that I had this insane adopted family.

"I love you guys too. Thank you. For everything."

"You're welcome, Kiddo," Fred said and then hastily added. "We'll continue our conversation at another time."

I hung up the phone and then rushed into the bedroom to get ready. I recited the lines out loud and carried the script with me. I was going to nail those lines or go back to New York a loser.

~~*

"Hey, can you hang around a couple of hours?" Felix asked me after my audition. "When I'm done we can go back to the hotel together."

He was standing very close to me, and I had the urge to hug him so that I could be hugged in return. I pushed my hands into my pockets instead.

"Is there somewhere quiet I can wait for you?" I asked, looking around us. "I need to make a couple of phone calls."

"Yeah, sure," he said, looking at me with concern. "I'll take you to my trailer."

I waited while he let the necessary people know where he was going and that he would be back shortly, and then I let him take my hand to lead me to his trailer.

"You did very well in the audition," Felix said as we stepped out into the bright sunshine. "You got the part—I knew you would, but you don't look too happy."

"I'm tired," I said, forcing a smile.

"It's more than that," he said quietly and then said hello to a group of people as we passed. He glanced down at me over the rim of his sunglasses. "Something is bothering you. You're all deflated."

"I'm fine," I lied. I didn't feel fine at all. I felt crazy. I felt like laughing, crying, screaming, and fighting. It had hit me suddenly while I was reading my lines during the second part of the audition. My character, Destiny, was a hopeless young girl derived from hopeless circumstances. Her hopelessness felt very real.

"Donya," Felix said my name and then halted. I stopped and looked up at him. "You can't bullshit me. Besides, I'm your friend if nothing else. What is wrong with you?"

I sighed and considered. I couldn't talk to him before talking to Emmet. It just didn't seem right even if he was a very good friend.

"I got some very bad news yesterday," I said honestly. "But I can't talk about it with you right now. I haven't even told Emmet."

He knew Emmet and I had renewed our relationship. He even knew that our relationship was pretty much a secret and why it had to be that way. I probably told Felix almost as much as I told Emmy. Then again, I hadn't told Emmy about me and her brother and hadn't planned on it. I realized how screwed up it was, that Felix knew about Emmet and Emmy didn't.

A smile slowly appeared on Felix's face. It was playful, yet sad at the same time. It broke my heart just a little.

"I'm still jealous about that," he said and tapped my chin with his finger.

"With the millions of women pining for you, I'm sure you can find one almost as exceptional as me," I gently poked at him.

He chuckled and shook his head. "Maybe, but probably not."

We resumed walking. Felix didn't ask me about my troubles, thankfully. He pointed stuff out, told me what other stars were in the vicinity and who I'd be working with. Before leaving me alone in his trailer, he gave me a hug that almost brought me to tears.

As soon as the door closed, I sat down on the couch in the posh trailer and picked up the phone that left in there for his personal use. Emmet answered on the third ring. It sounded like he was out on the streets of New York. I had expected him to be back in Cambridge already.

"Hey," he said.

"Hi. Where are you?" I asked curiously as I fidgeted with my charm bracelet.

"Times Square. Some of my friends were already headed here for the weekend, so I decided to hang out. Are you okay?"

"What friends?" I asked, my brain automatically fixing on Stella. "And why are you asking me that? Have you talked to Emmy or your parents?"

It took him a moment to answer. At first I thought it was because he didn't want to tell me who he was with, but then if he didn't wish to do that, he wouldn't have answered.

"I haven't spoken to them. Why? What's wrong?" he asked and sounded a bit alarmed.

"Who are you with? I asked questions first," I said and then couldn't believe I had said it, just like a jealous girlfriend. I wanted to slap my own mouth for letting the words escape.

I heard Emmet let out a small sound of exasperation. "A few people from school that you haven't met yet." He had answered the question, but not fully. I knew Emmet, and he knew I knew him, so I remained silent until he told me the whole truth. "And Stella and a few of her friends."

"Oh wow," I said and forced a chuckle even though my head dropped into my hand. "I would think the Cambridge crowd would find themselves too good for the Brown crowd."

"They got over it," he said tightly and quickly. "Donya, we're just hanging out."

"You don't have to explain it to me," I said.

Even if you didn't want to tell me.

"Anyway, that isn't why I called, really," I said before he could speak again.

"Why did you call? What's happening?" That hint of alarm had returned to his voice.

I suddenly regretted calling him and wondered if I should even tell him about my mom. He was busy with his friends, and I didn't want to take him away from them, but to be honest, I was feeling a little perturbed by Stella's presence.

"Hey, what's going on?" Emmet asked in a softer tone.

I took a breath and got on with it.

"I told you I didn't want you to come with me, but I was wrong. Is it too late for you to come out here?"

I put my palm on my chest as I waited for him to answer. That link between us strummed, anxious to have its two ends brought together.

"If you can't come, I understand," I said quickly. I already felt bad for asking him to walk away from his internship for me.

"Baby," Emmet said with a sigh that made my toes curl. "Of course I'll come out there. I'll follow you anywhere in the universe."

I sighed a deep sigh of relief. "Thank you," I said shakily.

"Now tell me what's going on," he gently urged.

I stood up and began to pace Felix's trailer. I put my hand on my stomach where the adrenaline seemed to be gathering. I felt like if I didn't hold myself tight enough, the adrenaline would tear a hole in my stomach and leave me gutted on the pretty, blue carpet.

"My mom is dying," I managed to say though it felt like my throat was closing up. "I know she hasn't been much of a mom over the years, but she's still my mom and this is still very, very hard."

"Shit," Emmet whispered sharply. "Is that what you didn't want to talk about before you left?"

"Yeah."

"Donya," he said with both reproof and sadness. "You should have told me, baby."

"I know," I said, nodding to no one. "I was scared and trying to handle it on my own."

"You never have to handle anything on your own again, do you hear me? I will always be there for you. Don't push me out again. Do you understand?"

"Yes," I whispered.

"Good. I'll go back to my hotel and start packing and see when I can get out there."

"It's a good thing you have that trust fund to lean on," I teased.

"One day, when we're married with our two kids in bed with us, you'll happily lean on it, too," he said, and I could tell he was smiling.

My heart warmed, and the adrenaline racing in my stomach eased.

"What about your friends?" I asked.

"They'll be fine," he said dismissively. "But I need to tell them I'm leaving. They're half a block ahead of me."

"I hate to take you away from them," I said meaningfully.

"I hate anything that keeps me away from *you*," he responded. "How long will we be out there?"

"Well, that's the kicker," I said. "They liked me more than I expected. They're rewriting the script a little to give me more screen time. I have to start filming tomorrow, but I don't know how long it will all take in the end."

"I am *so* proud of you," Emmet said. I smiled. It made me glad to know that he was proud of me. "I'm going to go. I have to email the law firm, but I'll call you when I know when I'm leaving, okay?"

"Are you sure it will be okay?" I asked, biting my lip.

"You are all that matters right now," he said, but then added, "But I'm sure it will be fine."

"Okay," I smiled again. "I'll talk to you soon."

"I'll see you soon."

"Good. I love you."

"I love you, too, Donya."

When we hung up, wave after wave of relief washed over me, settling my nerves and making me feel lighter. I sat down on Felix's ultra-comfy couch and grinned.

Emmet was coming.

Chapter Twenty-Seven

I stared at the new script in my hands that I received early the following morning. The director, Trip Brigs—what a Hollywood name—yammered on and on with high energy. I tried hard to keep up with what he was saying and what he needed, but my eyes kept falling back to the script.

I had to kiss Felix. I knew that going in, but before it was just a few seconds of kissing. The new script, however, was more than a kiss. It was a full on make out session, in a bed. He would be shirtless, and I would be in a tiny camisole and tiny shorts. The director and writers were sorely disappointed that I wasn't yet eighteen and couldn't be nude.

We ran through the written lines a couple of times. We were all going to have to learn on the run. Soon we were sent to hair and makeup and wardrobe and my first day as a movie actress was underway.

Besides being nervous about the obvious, I was excited to be there. The previous summer when Max approached me on the boardwalk and Emmy, and I had made fun of him, I never, ever would have foreseen how far that little conversation would have carried me. My modeling career had picked up faster than so many girls' I had met along the way. I befriended a superstar and was about to act in a movie side by side with him and several other talented people. I was damn lucky. My success was already more than I could have ever hoped for when I first started and I couldn't wait to see what else waited for me in my career.

"Oh, look at you," Felix said a little while later as we met on set. He had a hand on my hip as he looked me over.

"I need a pair of these jeans," I said, turning my head to look at my ass. "Did you see my ass in these jeans?" I asked Felix, pointing to my rear.

"Sweetheart, I always see your ass, no matter what's on it."

I rolled my eyes and gave him a shove. He chuckled and then reached out and grabbed my hand.

"Let's go, hot ass," he said, with a wink. "Did you learn your lines?"

"As much as I could," I said nervously.

"Don't worry, you'll be great," he said and squeezed my hand.

The rest of the morning was a learning experience, and not always a fun one. I didn't know how movies were filmed, but I honestly didn't think it was as hard as it was proving to be. It was similar to modeling in that you had to be well aware of the lighting, the camera, and your own body, but on a much bigger scale. I had to pay attention to every movement and be aware of every camera, light, microphone, and person while reciting lines. At one point, I got so frustrated I threw my script at Kent Decker, the hot older actor in front of me because he didn't like how I was saying my lines.

"Then you say them the way you want me to say them if you know so much," I had snapped. It probably wasn't a good idea to snap at the seasoned actor who probably really did know so much.

"You're unprofessional," he snarled.

"You're dressed in a Hawaiian shirt, ugly plaid shorts and flip flops," I argued. "Don't tell me about professional."

Felix came on set, even though the director was yelling at him and me and Kent. He picked up my script and put a hand on my shoulder to quiet me. He looked at Kent patiently.

"How do you think she should say it, Kent?" he asked quietly.

I understood in his quiet tone that he was showing the older actor some respect, and I realized I should have been doing the same. He was in his mid-thirties, but he had been acting since he was very young and he had more than a few good titles under his belt.

I glanced over at the writers, producers and at Trip, who had come to stand with us. I was suddenly fearful of getting a bad Hollywood rap and never getting work, not just there, but even as a model in New York.

"I apologize," I said quickly before Kent could begin speaking. "When we went over these specific lines yesterday, everyone was fine with it."

"The script has changed," Kent said, frustrated. He was a little high on his horse, all of the tabloids said so, but I kept quiet and listened anyway. "You have to adapt. If you can't adapt, you shouldn't be here."

I nodded in agreement. "You are right. The dynamic has changed and I must adapt. Let's try again."

"You're inexperienced," he growled, crossing his arms.

"At some point in your career, you were too," Felix reminded him, rubbing my back.

"Let's do it again," I said louder, hoping everyone would get back into their places.

"Maybe this isn't a good first role for you," Kent said. "Just because you're a pretty model doesn't mean you can act."

I managed a smile and started speaking before Felix could snap at him.

"I am determined to prove you and your hideous Hawaiian shirt wrong."

"I didn't pick this disgusting shirt out," he argued.

"Doesn't make it any less hideous," I muttered. I shook out my hands and rolled my shoulders. "Let's do this."

"You okay?" Felix asked me quietly as Trip and Kent moved away to talk quietly.

"Yes," I said and smiled at him.

"No one ever talks to him like that—at least no one as new as you or me."

"You're not so new."

"I'm still a rookie in his eyes. You handled him well in the end, though. Good job." He kissed the side of my head and walked off set with Trip.

Kent and I got into our places while the crew got ready. When Trip yelled action, I threw out the lines differently. We had one good, long take, and at the end of it, Kent actually smiled at me, kind of.

I had a few more scenes to film for the day before I was released from my acting subjugation in the late afternoon. There were some technical issues and rewrites to be done, so I would have to return to finish the next day. Usually, for only a few minutes of screen time, I would have been finished already.

I walked to Felix's trailer to grab a few of my things. I was in a hurry to get back to the hotel. Emmet's flight had landed in the late morning, but other than a few brief words, I hadn't spoken to him since he got in.

My heart knew he was close by again. It sung in harmony with the line that binds us together. I could always feel him near, but I couldn't always pinpoint exactly where he was if he wasn't within sight. So, sometimes he had the ability to surprise me. When I opened the door to Felix's trailer, Emmet was standing there with his hands in his khaki shorts, smiling at me.

"Emmet!" I squealed and ran into his arms.

"Surprise," he murmured into my hair as he held me tightly.

"How did you get in here?" I asked, pulling away far enough to look up at him.

His lips twitched and then he rolled his eyes. "Felix arranged it."

"See? He's a good guy," I said, nodding.

"I guess," he said with a shrug, but he was smiling. "I missed you."

"You went months without seeing me," I pointed out. "Surely, you were able to go a couple of days without missing me."

"I didn't see you for those months, but I sure as hell missed you, and I missed you the minute you left my arms in New York."

"Mr. Grayne, you are making me swoon," I grinned.

"Miss Stewart, I am only speaking the truth," Emmet said softly and then he was kissing me.

It felt like it had been months since I last kissed Emmet, not mere hours. I wrapped my arms around his neck and kissed him back with hunger. I needed to so badly. I needed to feel his hands rubbing my back as he kissed me. I needed to feel his tongue in my mouth and his lips on mine, making me submit to his love. I needed to feel my hands in his hair and his body pressed against mine. I needed his comfort and he was giving it away freely.

"I'm so glad you're here," I whispered tearfully when we stopped kissing.

I hugged him tightly, resting my face on his shoulder.

"Hey," he said gently, pulling back. He held my face in one hand and wiped a tear with his thumb. "Don't cry. You break my heart when you cry."

Somehow his words had the opposite effect and I broke down into full sobs. I had not sobbed so hard since Emmet had left for college. Sad Pathetic Donya was on the scene, and she was relentless, wringing tears from my eyes when I thought no more could come. She made my body shake and shudder and I think she secretly loved the snot running out of my nose.

Emmet reached behind him to a table and grabbed a few napkins. He wiped my face and then kissed my forehead. He pulled me into his arms and despite how much I was hurting, I felt safe and protected and strength I really didn't have.

"I want to tell her about us," I said weakly.

"Whatever you want, baby," Emmet said soothingly and kissed my head.

I wanted Sad Pathetic Donya to take a hike. I wanted to stop crying and find my own inner strength. I knew it was there somewhere, but SPD kept hiding it from me. She liked me weak and blubbering. She was a drama whore.

"Are you done for the day?" Emmet asked me.

I nodded. "Can we go back to the hotel now? Have you been there yet?"

"Felix had someone take my bags over, but I haven't been there yet."

"Are you staying with me?" I asked, feeling hopeful. I picked up the sunglasses and bag I had come for. Emmet took the bag from me and threw it over his shoulder even though it was pink.

"That's up to your mom," he said, taking my hand and leading me out of the trailer. "But if she isn't comfortable with it, Felix has an extra room in his suite."

"You two are getting downright cozy," I teased, still shuddering from my crying.

Emmet rolled his eyes. "I suffer him for you."

"Thank you," I said, squeezing his hand.

"You owe me so big." He looked down at me with lust in his eyes.

"Oh, I will pay you more than what you are owed, sir," I promised.

~~*

Felix insisted that we utilize room service anytime while we were staying in California. My mom and I both argued with him about it, but he was insistent. He even had the hotel staff call us around four thirty to ask if we would be dining in and to please take a look at the menus and order when we were ready. I gave up on saying no. Room service was a treat and if he wanted to foot the bill, I didn't have the energy to argue anymore.

So, we ordered dinner and dessert when we got back to the suite. While we waited for our meals to arrive, I left Emmet with my mom at the dining table and went into my room for a shower. Emmet and I had decided that we would tell my mom about us over dinner. He had asked me why not tell everyone, but then I told him about Emmy's reaction to the tabloid photos and how his mom had started to comment on it also.

"Eventually, they will all have to deal with it," he had muttered but didn't push the subject.

By the time I got out of the shower, dinner had arrived. I sat across from Emmet at the table, with my mom between us.

"I'm starving," I sighed, lifting the lid off of my plate.

"Don't they feed you there?" Mom asked.

"Yeah," I said. "And it was delicious, but that was hours ago."

"It always amazed me how much you can eat and not gain any weight," she said, shaking her head.

"One day my ass will pay for it, I'm sure," I said distractedly as I sprinkled pepper on my mashed potatoes.

"When did you start cursing like that?" she asked giving me a look that promised soap in my mouth.

"When she was seven," Emmet mused. "But she was wise enough not to do it in front of adults, or often."

I looked across the table at him. "Thanks a lot."

"No problem," he winked.

My mom looked at him and back to me before lightly clearing her throat. She looked back down at her pasta dish and pushed it around on the plate. I knew she probably didn't eat earlier in the day. I had a feeling she wasn't eating much at all.

"So, Emmet," she said. "Where are you staying?"

"I was hoping Emmet could stay here," I said optimistically.

Her eyes rolled onto me in a way in which only a mother can roll her eyes onto her child. It would have been heartwarming if it wasn't rather scary.

"But I can stay with Felix or even get my own room if you're not comfortable with it," Emmet said quickly.

Now her eyes rolled onto Emmet, but it wasn't like a mom looking at her son. It was like a mom looking at the man that was dating her daughter. I knew at that moment that she knew. Some of my breath escaped my mouth with a light sound as it hung open while I gawked at her and Emmet.

She put her fork down, pushed her plate away and folded her arms on the table. She looked back and forth between us. For something better to do with my gaping mouth, I sipped on my glass of water.

"Please, Lord, please…" she muttered under her breath as she looked up at the lord, I assumed. "Please tell me that you two didn't sit me down at this table to tell me that you're pregnant."

Water sprayed across the table, all over mom's food, Emmet's steak and on his shirt and in his face. As if that wasn't enough, I started choking again for the second time in two days. I fumbled for my glass of water again and swallowed big gulps, nearly choking it up.

"No one is pregnant," Emmet finally said quietly as I caught my breath.

Mom slumped with relief and then picked up a few napkins and started wiping the table. "Thank God. She's entirely too young. You're too young too, Emmet."

"You were near his age when you had me," I pointed out. "And Sam was nineteen when she had Freddy."

"Those were different times," she said, reminding me of Fred's words. "And Sam was a married woman before she got pregnant, and so was I."

I picked up napkins and started to wipe up, too. I looked at Emmet and apologized.

"A little bit of spit and water isn't going to deter me from my steak," he shrugged and dug in again.

"Mom," I started, but unsure of how to proceed. She had shaken up my whole game plan.

"I have cancer," she said to me. "I didn't get a Stupid-Dumb-Blind-Mom disease. You think I didn't see your face when Emmet came to take you to Felix's party?" She looked at Emmet. "I saw your face when Felix showed up to bring D those pictures. When Emmet would bring you back to the suite at night when you thought I was sleeping, I couldn't always hear what you were saying, but I could hear the emotion in the words." She smiled sadly. "Reminded me a lot of your dad and me when we were dating."

"Why didn't you ever say anything?" I asked quietly.

"I wasn't sure how I felt about it," she shrugged, but her forehead was creased. "I'm still not sure. I always looked at you two as a brother and sister."

"That's how everyone else sees us too," Emmet said slowly, looking at her. "I don't think they'll take it as well as you're taking it."

Mom snorted. "Every one of Samantha Grayne's hairs will fall out of place as she loses her damn mind—more than it's already lost."

I laughed though there was more truth to that statement than not. Emmet smiled with amusement and nodded in agreement.

Mom looked at me seriously. "Fred loves you like a daughter, Donya," she said gravely. "More than Sam probably loves you like a daughter. He's not going to approve of this."

"I'm well aware," I said softly, resting my hands in my lap.

"And honestly, I'm worried about how your careers are going to affect your relationship. You'll be in New York and possibly all over the place." She looked at Emmet. "You have years of hard schooling in front of you. Neither of you can afford the distraction."

"She's not a distraction," Emmet said carefully. "Donya is my whole world."

I smiled at him, but my smile was cut off by my mom's next words. "That is a beautiful thing to say," she said dryly. "And naïve. You're very young, so I'm sure it really feels that way for both of you, but the paths you will follow separately will slowly take you apart, piece by piece."

"Oh, great," I said with mocked exuberance. "The mother I have been in search of for nearly seventeen years has made another appearance."

"You underestimate our connection and love for each other," Emmet said.

"I'm not trying to make you break up," she said quickly, looking back and forth between us. "I'm trying to prepare you for the obstacles and people that may."

"We'll be fine," Emmet said, pushing his plate away and crossing his arms.

"I hope so," Mom said, looking at him hard. "I hope you two are stronger than I think. I hope you never have to break her heart—again, and I hope she doesn't break yours."

"You know about that?" I asked quietly, looking at the table. It still hurt to think about those long, sad days when Sad Pathetic Donya first made an appearance.

"I had a feeling it was a boy, but I didn't know it was Emmet at the time. I figured it out later."

I finally looked up into Emmet's eyes but spoke to my mom. "That was just as much my fault as his."

"And look at us now," he said shifting his gaze to my mom. "We're together now."

She nodded, but she didn't look agreeable.

"Mom," I said her name quietly and pleadingly as I looked at her. "Please have some faith in us. Please don't make this difficult."

She sucked in a breath and looked down at the dishes on the table as she spoke just above a whisper. "Donya, I'm not going to be here much longer. I'm not trying to make anything more difficult on anyone, but I've neglected to give you advice that you've needed for so long. I'm sorry if I'm dumping it all onto you all at once, but I might not be here if something terrible happens between you and Emmet."

I swallowed back tears and blinked rapidly to make sure none slipped by.

"Mom," I said again. "I understand that, but part of being a mom is making me believe everything will be okay. I know I'm not four, but as much as I need your honest advice, I need you to paint me a fairytale picture of princesses, knights in shining armor, castles in the sky and happy endings."

She looked at me with tears in her eyes. We looked at each other for a long time and I was only vaguely aware of Emmet sitting across the table from me. Finally, she nodded in agreement.

"I'm sorry to break up this depressing conversation," Emmet said, standing up and taking his near-empty plate. "But I am in need of some dessert. I ordered the most expensive one on the menu since Felix is paying for it."

Mom and I laughed. She went back to pushing her food around on her plate, taking very few bites. I went back to eating my dinner and Emmet dug into a decadent slice of chocolate fudge cake with large scoops of ice-cream on the side. We let the serious conversations go for the night, and simply enjoyed each other's company.

~~*

My mom wanted me to be happy, so I was allowed to keep Emmet. She didn't want to add to our possible hardships later down the road, so she agreed not to tell anyone about us, but my mom was being a mom and there was no way in hell Emmet was allowed to sleep in our suite. I pointed out that we slept under the same roof most of our lives, but she didn't care. When she dragged herself off to bed later that night, she reminded Emmet that before it got too late, he was to take his butt across the hall to Felix's suite.

I sat on the couch curled up at Emmet's side, listening to the sound of his heart beating. His fingers trailed over my arm and his other hand rubbed my bare leg. I was glad I was wearing shorts again so I could feel his hand on my skin. It felt delicious and so did his skin under the palm of my hand that was under his shirt touching his chest and abs.

Emmet reached around me and tilted my chin up so that my lips met his. He kissed me slowly at first, but when his fingers curled in the hair at the back of my head, the kiss became harder and more passionate. His hand on my leg rubbed harder and higher until his fingers were reaching under my shorts and grazing my upper thigh right near my panty line. My fingernails grazed his skin right at the hem of his shorts. I moaned softly as his fingers lightly moved across my dampening panties.

With as much effort as I could muster, I pushed his hand away and pulled away from his awesome mouth.

"She's probably not even tucked into bed yet," I whispered, breathing heavily.

"Tell her we're going for a walk on the beach," he said, getting to his feet and pulling me with him.

I looked at him dubiously, but he waved me on. "Go on," he urged.

I watched with surprise and longing as he adjusted his erection in his shorts. Without another word, I moved across the room and tapped on my mother's door. With as straight a face as I could manage, I told her Emmet and I were going for a walk on the beach, that we wanted to take advantage of what little time we had together in L.A. especially since I never knew what my schedule was going to be like. She told us to be careful and to have fun. When I returned to the living room, Emmet took my hand and walked quickly towards the door.

"Are we really going to the beach?" I whispered as he opened the door.

"Not tonight," he whispered back as the door closed behind us. He reached into his pocket and pulled out a keycard I didn't know he had and put it in Felix's door.

"Definitely cozy," I smirked.

"Watch your pretty mouth," Emmet snarled and then kissed me as he pushed me into the suite.

Felix's suite was three times the size of ours. The room he slept in was on one side by itself. He had given Emmet a room in the far corner, affording each of them some privacy.

"What time will Felix be in?" Emmet asked, as he kissed my neck and walked us towards his room.

"Huh?" I asked, in a lust induced daze.

"Felix, babe. What time will he be in?"

"Oh. He thinks he'll be done around midnight tonight."

Emmet looked at his watch. "We have plenty of time for you to pay me back for putting up with that bastard."

I laughed and pushed him away. I bit my lip and took a few steps away, looking at him with sparkling eyes.

"Maybe I'd rather be at the beach," I said nonchalantly.

"Don't make me chase you," Emmet warned, taking a step toward me.

"You can chase me all you want, but there's no guarantee you'll catch me, Yale Boy."

His eyes darkened.

"Oh, I'm sorry," I said, grinning. "Did I mix that up? It's what…the extra snooty one you go to, right? Do you walk around with a cardigan tied around your polo shirt and wear loafers without socks?"

Emmet lunged for me, but I shrieked and jumped out of the way.

"You're walking a fine line," he warned.

"When you go to parties, does everyone stand around congratulating each other on being filthy rich while you all smoke cigars and drink high-end brandy from crystal snifters?" I moved around the couch and then faked back the other way when he started to come after me. "Do the girls have silly names like Muffy and Coco and Trixie? Actually, I take back the Coco, because I love Miss Chanel. Does everyone play tennis and go golfing for fun?"

I squealed when he almost reached me, but I got away again. I was standing on the other side of the large, shining dining table.

"Do all of you models stand around together talking about how fat you are in your size zero dresses?" Emmet asked mockingly.

"I'm actually a size four this week," I said, stroking my ass. Emmet groaned.

"Isn't that fat for the modeling industry?" he teased.

"For some," I admitted with a shrug. "But you know some people, men especially, like a little junk in the trunk."

"I like your junk in your trunk," he said, slowly pursuing me.

"How rude," I gasped.

"Oh, you have no idea how rude I can be."

"Is that some kind of threat?"

"No, baby, it's a little insight to how the rest of your night is going to go," he said, looking at me like he was going to eat me.

"Oh, you think?" I asked, raising an eyebrow.

"Oh, I know. Why don't you unbutton that pretty shirt you have on." It wasn't really a question. It was a demand, and it turned me on.

"Like this?" I asked, walking backward as I unbuttoned a couple of buttons.

"More." Emmet pulled his shirt off and tossed it aside.

I licked my lips when I saw his chest and unbuttoned two more buttons.

"More?" I asked with my hands on my shirt.

"All the way," he said.

"What if I refuse?"

"I'll tear it off of you."

I swallowed hard. I kind of wanted him to tear it off of me. Well, not me. It was all Donya the Sex Goddess and Lover. I quickly unbuttoned the last few buttons before Donya SGL took over completely and I was left picking buttons up off of the floor.

I tossed the shirt onto the couch and hoarsely asked "Now what?"

Emmet was unbuttoning his shorts, revealing Calvin Klein boxer briefs. He could have easily fit in with the male models that advertised the underwear.

"Pull your shorts off," Emmet commanded softly, nodding at my bottoms.

"Let me guess, if I don't, you'll tear them off?" I asked dubiously.

"Do you doubt that I can tear them off of you?" he asked menacingly as his shorts dropped to the floor. He stepped right out of them without losing his stride.

I swallowed again. SGL wanted me to keep the shorts on and let Emmet tear them off, but I thought about going back to my suite without shorts on. If I ran into my mom before I made it to my room, I wouldn't have a reasonable lie to feed her.

I pulled the shorts off, but with a lot less gracefulness than Emmet. I lost my stride and before I could find it again, Emmet had caught up to me.

"Damn it!" I laughed as his arms circled my waist. His erection pressed against my ass and his lips moved over my neck.

"Now, what were you saying about Yale and cardigans and loafers?" he murmured into my skin.

"I don't remember," I breathed and moaned softly as the palm of his hand moved over my breast.

"Maybe we should recount the conversation in the bedroom," he suggested. Before I could respond, he lifted me into his arms.

"I don't suppose I can talk you out of that," I said.

"No, baby, you started this. I'm just going to finish it."

He kicked open the bedroom door and a moment later tossed me onto the large bed. He closed and locked the door and then climbed onto the bed over top of me. He plucked at a bra strap and shook his head with disapproval.

"This has to go," he said and began to pull it down my arm. His lips followed, but between kisses he said, "Now, about Yale?"

"What about it?" I snorted.

His teeth nipped at my skin in warning.

"I mean…Harvard, right?" I asked as the strap slipped off of my arm completely.

"Mmm hmm," he said and licked a path across my cleavage. Then his fingers were lifting the other strap. "What did you say about cardigans and loafers?"

"That it's preppy and ridiculous looking?"

His teeth sunk into the upper curve of my breast, making me groan.

"I mean, you don't dress like that. You dress like a real college boy."

"Boy?" he growled, looking up at me.

"College man?"

"Better." The other strap was off.

"I guess you want me to say that you don't stand around patting each other's backs for being rich?" I asked as his fingers began to release the front clasps of my bra.

He nodded.

"Fine," I said, rolling my eyes. "I recant, but we both know it's true. I won't take back the tennis and golfing, though."

"Well," he grinned. "That much is true."

He released the last clasp of my bra and my breasts spilled free. Emmet groaned and dragged his tongue slowly over a nipple.

"Emmet," I gasped.

He pulled the nipple into his mouth and sucked hard on it and the flesh surrounding it. I moaned and put my fingers in his hair. Each suction sent signals to the junction between my legs.

"Touch me," I whispered earnestly as I moved his hand down. His fingers grazed over the cotton panties and I moaned loudly. He gripped the side of the underwear on my upper thigh and yanked. The tearing sound both shocked me and turned me on.

He released my breast with a wet sound and moved to the other one, shifting his body slightly over me. After he had sucked that breast into his mouth, he tore away the other side of my panties. I groaned and pushed my hips up to meet his fingers.

"Did you like that?" he asked, releasing my breast.

I nodded but couldn't find my voice as his fingers moved through my folds.

"One day, I want to tear every inch of clothing off of you," he groaned and licked my nipple. "Will you like that, Donya?"

I nodded again, eagerly.

"There's so much I want to try with you," he whispered, pushing a finger inside of me. I groaned and lifted my hips slightly to take him in deeper. He added a finger and pushed in deeply.

"Emmet," I whispered. SGL needed more. That vixen reached up and squeezed her own nipples. Emmet groaned when he saw it.

"You surprise me every time we do this," he said, sliding his fingers in and out of me. "You *are* a freak."

"Only for you," I panted.

"Maybe you'll think I'm the freak after I tell you all of the things I want to do to you," Emmet said.

"Tell me."

"Someday soon, I want to come inside here." His fingers swirled inside of me and I bit my lip and groaned. "I want to feel you come on my cock as I come inside of you. I want you to have that part of me. Do you want that, too?"

"Yes," I cried. I had never thought about it before, but I really wanted it and thinking about it was making me impossibly slicker. "What else do you want to do to me?"

"I want to tie you to the bed and make you come until you can't take it anymore. Then I'll keep making you come anyway."

His thumb pressed down on my clit and his teeth closed on my nipple. I screamed his name and shuddered as I came hard on his fingers. He pulled his fingers out of me, kissed me and then rolled out of bed.

"I'm not finished with you yet," he said as he walked over to his suitcase.

"I hope not," I said breathlessly.

I watched as he opened his suitcase and moved a few things around. I saw my jars in there and smiled. A moment later, he produced a condom. He tossed it onto the bed and pulled his underwear off before getting back onto the bed between my legs.

"Do you know what else I want to do to you?" he asked as he opened the condom.

"Talk me to death?" I asked.

He lightly slapped my thigh.

"Ow," I laughed.

"I want to try every sexual position we can think of. I want to slide my cock into every hole you have."

My thighs tried to close automatically as I frowned at that one.

"I think I have my limitations," I said.

"I think we can explore them," he said, lowering himself over me.

"Maybe," I said doubtfully. "What else do you want to do to me?"

He slid into me. My head tilted back as I cried out. He was so large and filling inside of me.

Emmet laced his fingers in mine and put our arms above my head. He moved his hips back and forth, stretching me in every direction. He kissed me passionately for a moment. Then he slid out slowly and then rammed himself back inside of me.

"I want to marry you and give you a baby," he whispered.

"Is this a proposal?" I asked, jokingly, but Emmet didn't laugh. He stared into my eyes with such intensity that I stopped laughing.

"Let's prove to everyone that we can be happy together, Donya," he whispered. "Let's do it for us. I can't live without you. Marry me."

"When?" I croaked as I looked up at him in shock.

"Next year. We'll do the responsible thing and at least wait until you're eighteen with a high school diploma. I never wanted anything more in my life. Will you marry me?"

Donya SGL got bored and sat down in the corner. She wanted raunchiness and hard sex, but she was shit out of luck this night.

"Yes," I said, smiling up at the love of my life. "I'll marry you, Emmet."

His smile was so big it made my heart flip over in my chest. I had just agreed to marry Emmet Grayne. I knew in my heart he was the only man on earth that I wanted to share my life with.

"I love you," Emmet said and kissed me before I could return the sentiment.

His fingers closed tightly around mine as he moved inside of me. It was painfully and wonderfully slow. With every deep thrust, his hips pinned mine to the bed and he rubbed against my clit. My breasts rubbed against his bare chest. The sensations were overwhelming and I wanted some control, but I was helpless with my hands pinned above my head.

"Donya," Emmet gasped my name as his lips tore away from mine.

His hands squeezed mine as he thrust harder and deeper.

"I'm going to…" He groaned loud and long as his orgasm took over. He held himself deeply inside of me, sending me over the edge screaming his name and nearly sobbing.

When he released my hands and collapsed partially on top of me, I put my hands in his hair and kissed him.

"I love you," I said, when I released him. "You make me happy even when things are dark around me. You bring me your light, Emmet."

"Whatever is inside of me is also inside of you, baby," he said, touching my heart. "Because…"

"We're connected," I finished for him and put my hand on his heart.

"Even if I'm not near you, I know you can look inside of yourself and light those dark places. As long as you know I love you and I am yours, and you are mine."

I kissed him again and didn't mind the few tears that trickled out of my eyes.

Chapter Twenty-Eight

Felix finished filming earlier than expected that night. When he walked into his suite, I had just buttoned the last button on my shirt that I had only moments before plucked off of the floor along with my shorts. The only thing I was missing was my panties, but they were destroyed and tangled in Emmet's bedding.

"Hey," Felix said when he saw me. His tired eyes lit up a little bit, and he managed a sleepy smile. Then with a less than thrilled tone, he asked, "Where's your boyfriend?"

"Sleeping," I said, trying to act casual. I didn't want Felix to know what I was doing with Emmet before he crashed.

"Well, it helps that I'm not here most of the time," he said with a shrug. He dropped onto the couch and threw an arm over his eyes. "Sit down and talk to me for a little while."

I felt naked without my underwear on, but the least I could do was sit down for a few minutes with Felix. I joined him on the couch, keeping a safe distance between us.

"Did you have a good day with Emmet?" he asked quietly.

"Yes," I said. "Thank you for bringing him to me today."

His only response to that was a halfhearted shrug. I knew it must have taken an enormous amount of Felix's pride to do what he did for me.

"And thank you for listening last night," I added.

When he finished filming the night before, we went to dinner, and I told him about my mom's illness and gave him a history lesson about my relationship with her and my dad. He had mostly listened, which was fine. I wasn't expecting him to produce any miracles.

"I'm your friend," he said, peeping at me from under his arm. "I'll do my best to always be there for you."

"Thanks, Felix," I smiled warmly at him. I relaxed and pulled my legs up on the couch and rested my head on the back of it. "Isn't it funny how close we are in such a short time?"

"Yes," he said, dropping his arm from his face altogether. "I trust you, and I don't trust many people. Trusting anyone is hard.

I never know who is just out to use me for my fame or money or who wants to stab me in the back and break my kneecaps."

"I only want to break your kneecaps on occasion," I said.

He grinned. "I don't know about breaking them, sweetheart, but you bring me to my knees almost daily."

I rolled my eyes but continued to smile at him. I'd gotten used to Felix's blatant flirting. Though I knew he had some more than friendly feelings for me, I also knew that he was just a big flirt in general, and I didn't have to worry about him going over the line. Well, at least not too far over the line.

"I was thinking about your situation," he said after a comfortable moment of silence.

"Which situation would that be?"

"Your homeless situation."

"I'm not homeless," I said, looking at him with a perplexed expression.

"You may as well be. You guys are living in a hotel."

"I was thinking about getting an apartment."

"I have a better idea," he said. He sat up straight and looked at me conspiringly. "Why not move into the apartment that's attached to the penthouse? You will have full access to the loft of course, but the apartment will give you the privacy you need when you want it. It will take some of the stress off while dealing with your mom too."

"So…" I looked at him with my head tilted slightly. "You want me to move in with you?"

Felix chuckled and rubbed the back of his head. "I didn't quite put it like that, but yeah, I guess. When I'm in New York, we'll be roommates, more or less."

I thought about the empty apartment adjoined to Felix's penthouse. I had been in it once before when he took me on a tour. It had three bedrooms, two and a half full bathrooms, and an open floor plan with an eat-in kitchen, a small dining area, and a large living room area. One whole wall in the living room was all glass, with an awesome view of Times Square. The apartment had a separate entrance so that I wouldn't have to walk through Felix's penthouse to get to it.

It would have been great to have an actual home to go to at the end of a long work day or after returning from a trip. No matter how cozy the hotel suites I had stayed in were, they never quite felt like a home, but I imagined that I could make Felix's place feel like home. Emmy could visit and have her own space. Most importantly, it would be good for my mom to have a more permanent residence while we were in the city. I had been seriously considering getting an apartment anyway, though I knew I'd never be able to afford the location and size of the apartment Felix was offering.

"How much would my rent be?" I asked.

Felix bristled as he gave me a look of disdain. "I don't want your money, sweet cakes."

"In the real world, I'd have to pay rent, Felix," I said with disapproval in my tone.

"Donya, I understand that, but I'm not charging you rent. You'll still be on your own for everything else, but I'm not going to make you pay to stay in the apartment."

"You can't just give it to me for nothing," I objected.

"I can do whatever the hell I want," Felix snapped. "Look, I own real-estate all over the place. I have the house in Malibu and another house in Napa Valley, a flat in London and a penthouse in Paris. I'm about to buy a villa in Italy. Not only do I not want or need your rent money, but as your career carries you around the world, mi casa es tu casa. You can stay in any of the places that I own, *rent free*. It's not open for negotiation."

I looked at Felix for a long moment. My heart swelled for him and his generosity.

"Why are you being so generous to me?"

He looked me directly in the eyes as his expression sobered. When he spoke, his voice was low and soft.

"Because you are a humble, honest, hard-working woman that doesn't like to take advantage of anyone, not even those of us who willingly put ourselves out there for you to do just that." His eyes drifted away from mine before he continued. "And because I'm pretty sure I love you."

Suddenly, he was on his feet and stretching his limbs as he did an excellent job of avoiding eye contact with me after his confession that left me feeling surprised, flattered, sad, and unworthy.

"I will have someone go in and clean up the apartment for you," Felix said. "Now all you have to do is tell your boyfriend that you're moving in with a real man."

He looked at me with his acting skills up to par. All signs of his confession were gone.

"That's exactly the kind of thing to say if you want to make my life more difficult," I said, getting to my feet. I started towards the door, but I turned around and looked at him again. "Thank you, Felix."

"You're welcome, gorgeous," he said sincerely. "Now I'm going to bed, and you should, too," he said around another yawn. "We have to be up early." A mischievous smile appeared on his handsome face. "You can sleep in my bed if you don't think you'll make it across the hall."

I rolled my eyes at him, grabbed my water and headed to the door.

"See you in the morning, Casanova," I said and went back to my own suite.

~~*

My big scene with Felix was up, but the only way Emmet would allow me to go through with it was if he got to be there to watch it happen. I wasn't too keen on the idea. I didn't want to have to worry about the things that would be going through his head while I was working. I was nervous enough about all of the crew that would be watching.

"Are you nervous?" Trip asked me as Felix and I stood by the ominous looking bed.

I had a robe on until it was time to film the scene, but Felix was just as happy to walk around in his boxer briefs, showing off to the ladies on set and flirting.

"I'm nervous about doing this in front of a whole bunch of people," I answered honestly.

"Sweetheart, I'll make you forget about anyone else within miles of us," Felix purred at my side.

I slapped his arm as I threw a quick glance at Emmet, who was staying out of the way but was still within hearing range. His arms were folded across his chest, and he was glaring at us. Glaring and scowling.

"I've kept only the essential people for this scene. Okay?" Trip tried to reassure me.

I nodded.

"Okay, I want to see passion here," Trip said, back to business. "I know you're nervous, but pretend you're not. You're an actress now."

He gave us more directions as someone messed with my hair and another person arranged the bed sheets to look like they had been slept in. Before I knew it, it was time for me to slip off the robe and get into the bed. As I climbed into it, I looked at Emmet's hard face. I offered him a small smile, and he forced one back.

Felix got into the bed beside me, looking more than a little giddy. We had several lines before the hot scene began. Trip wanted us to try hard to get it all in one take. Felix and I got into position, with me lying on my back and him lying on his side beside me. I knew I couldn't just lay there like a lump, so I put my arms above my head, forcing my camisole to slide up my stomach. Felix put his hand on the exposed flesh. I tried to turn off the burning sensation I felt under his touch.

"Good, good," Trip said.

I threw Emmet one last glance. It was hard to see his face with all of the lighting, but we were connected. I could feel his seething jealousy in my gut. I was forced to look away and concentrate on the task at hand.

Trip called out action. Felix became Drew, and I became Nina. We had a serious conversation as Felix's hand roamed over my belly. There was a tightness there that nearly left me breathless. My nerves were a mess. It was incredible how I managed to say my lines and move and behave appropriately.

As he leaned down to kiss me, he whispered one word to me in a barely audible tone. "Relax."

I had not kissed Felix since that first night in his limo, but my lips remembered his and burned with yearning as he kissed me slowly. I cupped his face in my hand as I pressed my lips to his. He groaned softly and slipped his tongue past my lips. His hand slid under my camisole and smoothed across my skin just under my breasts. I moaned softly and moved my hand from his face to his hair. Felix carefully moved until his body covered mine without breaking our kiss. There was no ignoring the erection that was pressed firmly against my thigh. Though I almost expected it, I was still surprised to feel it.

His hand moved over my hip and down my thigh. When he reached my knee, he gently lifted it. I took his hint and hooked my ankle over the back of his leg. His hand moved back up my thigh and then to my ass. Our kiss was losing its sweetness and becoming more wild and aggressive. I had both hands in his hair as I arched my whole body up towards his. He groaned and pushed against me. I moaned into his mouth and ran one hand down his strong back. We kissed and moved gently against each other for a long time while our hands explored one another's bodies.

The volume of our moaning, grunting, and groaning had been increasing, but when Felix peeled away from my lips to kiss my neck, my moan was as loud as thunder in my ears. Before I could feel embarrassed about it, Felix's teeth were nipping at my shoulder where he had pushed the strap of the camisole down. My fingers dug into his shoulders as he kissed across my cleavage.

Suddenly, we were rolling over in the bed. I didn't hear cut, so I kept going, allowing Felix to pull me on top of him. We both gasped loudly. I stared down at him with my lips slightly parted and my hair hanging down one side of my face. He stared back with his mouth slightly open and his eyes hooded. He had rolled me directly onto his erection.

We were both shocked, but the film was still running. Felix gripped my hips and moved me slowly. Shamefully, I bit back a startled, yet salacious and carnal cry. Though the only sound Felix made was another gasp, his head had tilted back, and his eyes had closed as pleasure made his body tremor beneath me.

When he opened his eyes again and looked up at me, we stared at each other for a moment before I leaned down to kiss him.

"Cut!" Trip yelled.

Felix, surprisingly, looked just as thrown by the whole experience as I felt. With his guidance, I carefully and quickly moved off of him. He hastily covered himself in the bedding and I looked away with my face burning.

"That was fucking perfect!" Trip exclaimed.

"Good, because I'm not doing it again," Felix growled. "I have to piss and damn it, can someone get me a sandwich? A guy's gotta eat!"

I was relieved that he didn't openly make a big deal about the uncomfortable situation. As I climbed out of the other side of the bed, a hand held out my robe. I looked up the hand and arm and met Emmet's eyes.

"Thank you," I said, as he helped me put it on.

When I turned back around, I looked up at him again, searching his face for his thoughts and feelings. With adrenaline rushing through my veins and all of the activity around us, I couldn't get a good read on him. He put his hand gently on my face, and I closed my eyes with relief as I pressed my cheek into his palm. Emmet put his other hand on my hip and leaned over and put his lips close to my ear.

"As soon as it is possible I am going to erase all of his kissing and touching," he whispered as his thumb stroked over my hip. The stroking sent heated waves of pleasure right to my core.

His lips softly touched my neck and then he pulled away. He looked down at me with a loving smile that made me fall in love with him a little more.

I didn't care that I had just been in bed with Felix, that we were surrounded by people, that Trip was trying to talk to me or Felix was in the background being loud and obnoxious. I linked my fingers behind Emmet's head, pressed my body into his, stood on my toes and pulled him down for a kiss.

When we pulled apart a moment later, I said, "Sorry. I just thought we should get a head start."

Emmet chuckled and kissed my nose before releasing me so I could get back to work.

Chapter Twenty-Nine

Though my last day of filming had been the same day I had my big scene with Felix, we had hung around L.A. for a few extra days. Emmet and I spent a lot of time at the beach, kissing and touching in the water and holding hands as we walked the shoreline. The chances of some paparazzi taking candid shots of us didn't elude me, but I assumed since we were in L.A. there were many more important folks to harass, and that one spot in the tabloid the week before had been a fluke.

The day before our departure, Emmet and I went for an evening walk along the beach. I walked along in the surf, enjoying the spray on my ankles and calves while Emmet walked a few feet away in dryer sand. Now and then I'd crouch to pick up a colorful or unusual looking stone or pebble and drop it in a small bag I had slung over my shoulder. I was going to give them to Emmy to go along with the shells that we had collected over the years as kids.

Though I knew I should have been heading back to New York as soon as possible, we were going to fly to Philly and go back to New Jersey for a little bit. My mom had doctors' appointments and personal business to tend to. Emmet wanted to spend a little time at home before he got wrapped up in his internship, and I wanted to spend some time with Fred and Emmy. I even missed Sam and her cuckoo ways.

"So, I have something to tell you," I said carefully to Emmet as I brushed sand off of a pink, smooth stone.

"Sounds like the beginning of an interesting conversation," Emmet said warily.

I glanced over at him and put the stone in my bag. I didn't see any point in beating around the bush. I had withheld the information from him long enough.

"Felix offered me his New York apartment. It's attached to the penthouse, and I can live there rent free."

Emmet didn't say anything for a while, but his brow was creased with concentration as he was no doubt in deep thought. We walked along quietly for a few minutes. Earlier the beach had been crowded with sunbathers, frolicking children, and swimmers, but the crowds had thinned. There was still many people on the beach, but they were disappearing little by little. Several surfers were out in the waves, and I imagined they'd be there even after nightfall.

"When Felix finishes filming, he'll be back in New York full time," Emmet said, seeking confirmation.

"I suppose so."

"So, you will be, in essence, living with Felix."

I felt him looking at me as I picked up a purple stone and rolled it around in my hand.

"Yes," I said and finally looked at him. "But I will have my own space. I even have my own private entrance in addition to the access through the penthouse."

"I don't think I like the idea of you living with him," Emmet said, frowning.

"Don't think of it as me living with him. We'll be more like neighbors than roommates, and mom will be there with me too."

He pushed a hand through his hair as he looked at a group of surfers ahead of us.

"Why is he going out of his way to help you so much?" he asked after a moment. "He gave you the dress; he paid for your flight and accommodations out here. He got you into the movie and now he wants to give you an apartment. What does he want out of it?"

"Emmet," I sighed. "Just because he's being kind doesn't mean that he wants something out of it."

"No man is going to give a woman all of that without expecting something in return, Donya. Don't be naïve."

I stopped walking again and spun to face him.

"I am getting really tired of people thinking I'm some stupid little girl!"

"I didn't say that," he argued. "But you have to admit that you are being stupid about this."

"I'm not being stupid about this," I snapped. "I didn't ask for everything he's done, but he's not going to come asking for his recompense later, Emmet. I know he's a pig, but he's not that kind of pig."

"Right," he said with a humorless laugh. "You two are such great friends. You know him so well in so little time. You trust him one hundred percent."

"We are, I do, and I do," I said, nodding stubbornly. "You should take some notes on trust and maybe then you'll be able to trust me."

I walked away, but I was no longer walking at a leisurely pace. I walked to put some distance between Emmet and me before I swung my bag of rocks at his face.

A hand closed around my wrist and yanked. I splashed in the water as I was pulled into Emmet's body. I pushed at him, but he grabbed my other wrist and forced my arms down to my sides.

"Stop," he grunted. "Damn it, Donya, stop fighting me!"

I stood still, but wouldn't look at him. I looked at the Pacific on my left, scowling.

"Hey, look at me," he said, trying to meet my eyes. "*Look at me*," he demanded.

Reluctantly, I looked up at him.

"I hate that Felix is helping you and not me," he admitted angrily. "Maybe it is selfish and conceited, but I wanted to be your hero. I want to be the one that takes care of you and finds solutions for your problems. You belong to me, and I haven't been able to do shit for you. Not because I can't, because I can. I have the means to help you, but Felix keeps swooping in and saving the damn day."

I tried to check my attitude and pissy mood before I spoke. I was still irritated, but I attempted to speak gently.

"I don't need saving, and I don't need you to save the day, Emmet. I *need* you there at the end of the day. I need to know that whether the day was saved or not that you are there in the end."

He sighed heavily and rested his forehead on mine. He released my wrists and put his hands on my waist.

"He keeps kicking me in the ego," he said, pouting.

I couldn't help but to smile at his poked out lip. I tapped his boo-boo lip with my finger and put my hands on his chest.

"Here's an ego booster," I said. "You have me, heart and soul, and he doesn't. You and I are connected in ways that no one else will ever be able to touch or understand. How's your ego now?"

One corner of his mouth pulled up a little bit.

"You might want to say something about my body and my looks. I'm no superstar," he said as his thumbs stroked my stomach.

"You're *my* superstar," I whispered. "And for the record, you're the hottest guy that matters."

"You didn't say I was the hottest guy you know," he pointed out.

"I don't like to lie to you," I teased.

He slapped my ass hard enough to make it sting, but I laughed nevertheless and wrapped my arms around his neck.

"I need to be kissed," I said, looking at his perfect lips.

"I better hurry up and do that before Felix sweeps in to save the day," he said.

"Shut up and do it already."

Emmet complied. The sun set as we kissed. It was a movie moment for the books.

Chapter Thirty

Emmy waved herself with a magazine.

"You had movie sex with Felix Hunter," she said breathlessly.

I laughed and nudged her. "Stop saying that. It wasn't sex. There wasn't any penetration or oral activity."

"But you were pelvis to pelvis in a bed half naked with his hands on you and his tongue in your mouth. That's pretty damn close if you ask me. Just let me have the illusion in my head."

"The fact that you want to imagine me banging Felix is a little disturbing."

"I don't care," she said dreamily. "I can't wait for you to move in with him."

"I'm not moving *in with* him," I said. "We'll be like neighbors."

"Whatever. The chances of 'accidentally' finding him naked are high."

I laughed. "Please, when you visit me, don't stalk my landlord."

"I make you no promises," she grinned.

We had been laying on her bed, reading magazines, eating junk food, and chatting for hours. I was going to have to work my ass off to lose all of the calories I was ingesting with Emmy, but it would be worth it. She was worth the calories and the days of starvation that would most likely follow.

"How did Emmet end up in California?" she asked a little while later.

"I asked him to join us," I said with disinterest. I pretended an article in *Elle* was beyond interesting, but truly I had no idea what I was reading.

"Why? When you could have asked me? The better, hotter sibling."

"You had school, and he didn't," I told her, though that wasn't an explanation at all.

Emmet had said that eventually Emmy and the rest of the family would have to deal with our relationship, but I honestly didn't want to have to deal with them trying to deal with our relationship with everything I had lying before me. In addition to moving forward with my career, my mother's death was inevitable, and I wasn't sure where my life would go after that, if I would have to fight for my independence or if I would be allowed to stand on my own.

As if to solidify my decision to remain quiet about it, Emmy followed up with, "Whatever. As long as you're not screwing our brother like the tabloids think." She shuddered in disgust.

"Wouldn't be the worst choice," I heard myself mutter and then bit the inside of my cheek to shut myself up.

"No," she said and then paused thoughtfully. "It wouldn't be the worst choice, but ew."

"How are Mayson and Tack?" I asked, ready to shut that subject down.

Emmy sat up, and I sat up with her. I crossed my legs and dropped the magazine on the bed between us and looked at Em. The topic clearly pained her, but she was trying to play it cool.

"Mayson walked out of rehab. She's dodging her parents and the police, on the run with that stupid asshole," she said, staring down at her hands.

"What about Tack?"

"On a steady downward spiral. I tried talking to Tabitha about him, but she doesn't seem to want to talk about it—or to me for that matter."

"Well, it must be hard on her," I said, trying to comfort her.

She shrugged and then nodded. "I guess I would feel the same way if it was Emmet." She looked at me with a guilty expression. "Is it terrible that I'm more worried about Mayson than Tack?" she whispered.

I shook my head gently. "You were always much closer to Mayson than Tabitha and Tack," I told her, and it was true. Mayson and Emmy were probably just as close as Emmy and me. Tack and Emmet had been close, but they had started to drift apart before the drugs, and Tabitha was always a little standoffish.

"I feel awful for Tack, I do," Emmy said as if she had to convince me. "But what Mayson is going through is *killing* me. She's one of the few people that I need to exist in this world."

"I understand," I said, rubbing her back. I had people I needed to exist in the world too. My mom…Emmy. Emmet.

I smiled at Emmy to hide the guilt I felt. Guilt, and then sadness, because as close as we were, she was unable to see past whatever face I gave her. While I could read her like a Dr. Seuss book, she only saw in me what I wanted her to see. I liked having that control, to be able to hide behind my face, but at the same time, I sometimes wished that she could figure me out and just as easily as I could figure her out. Sometimes I wished that I was wide the hell open for her and that there were no secrets between us.

"Anyway," Emmy sighed and wiped at a few stray tears. "How are you handling things with your mom?"

"Okay, I guess," I said with a small shrug. "I'm sad about it, but…I've accepted it. Is that bad?"

Emmy shrugged too. "I don't know the right way to feel in your situation."

"Maybe there is no right or wrong way."

"Maybe not," she agreed. "Are you going to take more time off of work to be with her?"

"I want to, but you know time is of the essence in this business."

"Very true," Emmy agreed. "You're considered 'old' in your mid-twenties."

"And between you and me, I think I want to go to Europe soon," I said. "I met a designer at Felix's party. Alberi Durand," I said regally in a French accent.

"Ohhhh," Emmy breathed. "I've seen his designs. You didn't tell me about him!"

"You didn't care about designers," I laughed, dodging a playful punch. "You only wanted to know about movie stars and rock stars."

"God, I want your life," she said wistfully. "So, what about Alberi Durand?" She asked in her own French accent.

"He likes me. He said if I was interested in coming to work in Europe to let him know. He emailed me recently and told me he hadn't forgotten about me. Isn't that cool?"

"Cool," Emmy agreed, and then, "But creepy. The old weird guy is still thinking about you."

"He's like thirty."

"Yeah, like I said, old weird guy. I can't even imagine thirty," she said, getting out of the bed. "Let's do something instead of laying here getting fat."

We left the magazines and junk food on her bed and left her room. I followed her downstairs and into the family room. That was exactly where my body would have lead me anyway. Emmet was sitting on the couch with a soda flipping through channels on the television.

"You poor loser," Emmy teased, moving to the other side of the room where all of the music and movies were shelved. "No friends, brother?"

"I'm going to a party later tonight," he said, ignoring her jibe.

"Can I go with you two?" Emmy asked in a tone laced with jealousy.

"Who two?" I asked her back. She was rooting through the CDs.

"*You two*," she said over her shoulder. "Please. You two are like two damn peas in a pod lately." She spun around and glared at Emmet. "You're stealing my best friend! Go find your own best friend."

Emmet looked amused. "I can't help if I'm more fun than you."

"You wish. She probably only keeps you around because you're nice to look at."

Emmet looked at me with that amused grin. "Is that why you keep me around, Donya?"

"Is there any other reason?" I asked with a blank expression on my face.

"Ha!" Emmy said triumphantly. She turned back to looking through the CDs.

Emmet raised an eyebrow at me, and I gave him a little shrug, trying to hide the smirk on my face before joining Emmy at the bookshelf.

An hour later, the three of us were bouncing around the living room to Rob Base's "It Takes Two." Emmet had on a backward baseball cap as he rapped into a wooden spoon. Emmy and I did back up singing as we danced around him. We were all laughing and smiling and carefree and utterly stupid. We listened to early nineties music for the rest of the afternoon, acted goofy and ridiculous and earned several shouts from Sam to shut the hell up.

It was an afternoon that will always stand out in my head, because it was the last time I remember feeling my age. The road before me was going to be a rough one, but dancing, singing, and laughing with the two people I loved most in the world, I thought that I could handle anything as long as I always had them. I knew I would be okay.

~~*

When I walked into the party and promptly spotted Stella, I almost turned and left, but Emmet was directly behind me. His hand was firm on the small of my back. I glared at him over my shoulder, but he simply raised an eyebrow as if to say, "Seriously, Donya? Like you weren't just humping Felix in front of a hundred people a couple of days ago?"

He didn't say it out loud, but I knew Emmet, and I knew that's what he was saying in his head. I could practically hear the words echoing down the cord that bound us together.

"Hey, look, Emmet has a piece of ass for the night," Emmy said cheerfully in my ear.

I scowled as she laced her fingers with mine. "Come on, let's go find some tequila."

I shook my head as I let her lead me away from where Stella stood, waving to my boyfriend. I felt Emmet's fingers on my shirt, but Emmy didn't know that her brother was trying to stop me and pulled me through the crowd, making Emmet lose his grasp.

"You really need to lay off the tequila," I told Emmy twenty minutes later as she downed her fourth shot.

"But I love it!" she said gleefully and then offered me a shot. I put my hand up and shook my head.

"That shit is disgusting," I said. "And it's not good for you. Seriously, you're turning into a real alcoholic."

"Better than being high as a kite," she muttered and then took another shot.

"Hey," someone said close to me.

I turned my head to see who it was. It was Benny, the same kid who used to enjoy knocking me off of Emmet's skateboard when I was little. I had not seen him in years. His parents divorced, and he had moved away with his father. He was just about to hit puberty the last time I saw him, but puberty had come and gone. He was tall, well-built instead of just brawny, and well...kind of cute.

"Are you here to push me around?" I asked him, smiling a little bit.

He laughed and put a hand to his heart and looked at me with sincerity. "I'm sorry for all of those times I bullied you, but to be honest, I liked getting a rise out of you."

"Well, don't expect to get a rise out of me now," I said loftily.

"I wouldn't want to antagonize the superstar," he teased.

"What superstar where?" I asked.

He grinned. "The one standing right in front of me. The same one who is always traipsing through New York with Felix Hunter for fuck's sake."

"It's just Felix." I waved a dismissive hand. The last thing I needed was for more people to believe that I was doing more with Felix than traipsing anywhere. "What have you been doing with yourself, Benny?" I asked, taking the attention off of me.

"I just moved back to my mom's from Maryland. I'm going to go to U-Penn in the fall."

"Impressive."

"Hard to believe the neighborhood bully could make something out of his life, huh?"

"I had my doubts," I teased. I did a visual check on Emmy and sighed when I saw her taking another shot. "So, what is your major, Benny?"

We talked for a long time as I stood watch over Emmy. We talked about his plans of becoming a doctor and about his time in Maryland. He was funny and easy to talk to, so unlike the brat he was many years ago. I told him how I got discovered by Max on the boardwalk and gave him some vague details about my life to keep the conversation light.

When Emmy could no longer stand up without stumbling, I had to end the conversation with Benny and go help her. I knew she had been to some parties in my absence, and I wondered if she always got so drunk or worse and if anyone helped her. The idea that someone could have possibly taken advantage of her while she was like that and she not even remember it terrified me. I was going to give her an earful when she was sober.

"Can you stay with her while I go find Emmet?" I asked Benny as he supported the blabbering, drunken idiot around her waist. It probably wasn't a good idea to leave her with someone I hardly knew, but I would find Emmet faster than Benny.

"Sure, go ahead," he said, pushing Emmy's hand off of his face.

I rolled my eyes at her and went to find Emmet.

It wasn't a big party. There were clusters of people here and there. The music was loud, and the alcohol was flowing, but it was otherwise a toned down party in comparison to some I had been to over the years.

I followed that internal mapping system that seemed to always lead me to Emmet and found him in a game room with another cluster of people. He and Stella were standing close together, heads bent close, talking. He was holding a pool stick in one hand and a beer in the other hand. Her hand was on his arm, and he seemed okay with it. Suddenly, he looked away from her and right at me.

I didn't want to be the jealous girlfriend, but I had a sore spot for Stella. If it were any other girl, I wouldn't have put much thought into it, but it wasn't any other girl. It was Stella.

Still, I tried to quell the resentment that was inside of me, especially considering how close I was with Felix and the feelings he had for me. I also couldn't forget the heat between us while we were filming. Though it wasn't at all on purpose, I still felt guilty for it. Felix's penis had been right against my vagina. Stella simply had her hand on Emmet's arm.

And she also was the mother of his baby...

I sighed, shook the baby thought from my head and discretely beckoned Emmet with a wave of my hand. I didn't wait to see if he would follow before leaving the game room. I went back into the dining room where I had left Benny and Emmy, but they weren't there. I asked an acquaintance that had been there all night if she had seen where they went. She didn't know; she only saw them leave the room.

I started to panic a little. What if Benny was still a bully, but just a different kind of bully? What if he took her into a bathroom or some closet and was violating her? I hadn't been gone that long. I didn't think they could have gone far, but as I looked through the kitchen and the living room and checked the closets and bathroom, I began to panic. I didn't have an internal mapping system for Emmy, which pissed me off. It was like some cosmic joke that I could be connected with Emmet and not Emmy.

I was going to go upstairs and look for them, but as I passed the open front door, I spotted them outside at the end of the sidewalk. I rushed outside, prepared to kick Benny's ass, but as I got closer, I saw that Emmy was doubled over puking into the street while Benny held her hair back. I moved to the other side of her to help support her.

"What are you doing out here?" I questioned him over Emmy's retching. I looked away from the tequila vomit and looked at Benny for an answer.

"She turned green, and someone was in the bathroom," he said. "I carried her outside before she could puke all over the floor in there. She first puked back there," he said pointing towards the house. "I didn't want anyone stepping in the shit, so I brought her down here."

"Thank you," I said with sincerity. I felt bad for mentally accusing him of wrongdoing.

"I must really like you if I'm willing to babysit Pukey here," he teased.

"I appreciate it. Emmet should be out here any second," I said, looking towards the house. I was surprised he hadn't come out yet. Granted I didn't give him any indication of where I would be, but I knew he had that same mapping system inside of him for me. The only explanation was that he was still inside talking to Stella.

"Maybe this isn't a good time to ask," Benny said as Emmy retched especially loud.

"Ask what?" I said, frowning at Emmy. She had begun to dry heave, but she was doing it so hard, I was afraid she was going to hurl up a kidney or something.

"For your phone number."

"My what?" I asked stupidly.

"Your phone number? You know that thing that rings? Alexander Graham Bell invented it in 1876."

I smiled at his humor, but I didn't know what to say. I had a boyfriend, but I couldn't tell him that, because Emmy was right there. Even though she was royally fucked up, I didn't know what she would remember later.

"I'm going back to New York the day after tomorrow," I said carefully. "And my schedule is…unpredictable."

There. At least I wasn't lying. My schedule was entirely unpredictable.

Benny was persistent though.

"I just want to keep in touch," he said. "I'm not asking you to go steady."

I laughed. "Who says that anymore? You sound like Emmy's mom."

He laughed, too, but persisted. "I like talking to you, Donya. I swear I have no ulterior motives."

I bit my lip as I thought about it. "When I tell you that my schedule is unpredictable, I really mean it," I warned. "You might not catch me on the phone."

"Then I'll take your email too." He smiled encouragingly.

I gave in. He seemed genuine, and I had liked chatting with him too. "Well, what are you going to write it with? Vomit?" I asked.

"I have a pen and paper in my purse," Emmy slurred, standing upright. I was glad for her sake that only Benny and I could see her. Her hair was messed up and even by the little bit of light where we were standing, I could see her face was all blotchy.

"I hope you have gum and a brush in here," I said, taking her purse from her and letting Benny support her.

I was only a little surprised to find a drunk's arsenal in the purse: gum, travel sizes of toothpaste, mouthwash, and a toothbrush, and sure enough there was a hairbrush in there, too. I handed her the mouthwash and then dug around for a pen and paper. While Emmy leaned against a car rinsing her mouth, Benny and I exchanged phone numbers and emails. I had just pushed his info into my pocket when Emmet stepped up beside us. I knew he was coming, I had seen him come out of the house and, of course, I sensed him coming.

"Hey, what's up," Benny said, acknowledging Emmet with a nod of his head.

Emmet looked him over, frowning. "Hey."

"Thank you for your help," I told Benny with a smile.

"No problem. Take care of yourself up there. I'll email you or call you soon," he said, holding up the piece of paper.

"Okay. It might take me a little bit of time to get back to you, but I will."

"That's cool." He reached for me, for a hug no doubt, but Emmet rudely stepped between us to get Emmy.

Benny looked at Emmet with amused confusion, but when Emmet seemed to be taking his time to get out of the way, I waved a hand of dismissal and forced a smile.

"Next time," I said. "We have to care for the drunk."

He nodded his understanding and started to back away. "See ya, Donya."

"Bye, Benny," I smiled at him as I helped Emmet support Emmy.

He threw me one last grin and walked back toward the house.

"Seriously?" Emmet grumbled as we started walking down the sidewalk toward his car. "Benny?"

"What about Benny?" I asked.

"Benny got all cute," Emmy said. "Holy hell did you see those abs, Donya? Do me a favor and totally lick those abs for me."

"I'm not licking his abs." I sighed. I could feel Emmet's anger without even meeting his angry gaze.

"But you gave him your phone number and you guys talked all night," she said. "I'll bet he won't mind licking you." She snickered at her dumb joke. She had no idea that she was stirring up trouble for me and Emmet.

"No one is licking anyone else," Emmet said irritably.

"Donya licked Felix's lickable mouth," Emmy said dreamily.

Though Emmet had mostly gotten over the scene I had with Felix, I knew he wasn't in much of an accepting mood, which really wasn't fair. I had done nothing wrong. If anyone was wrong, it was him, but I wasn't about to start pointing fingers.

We reached the car and helped Emmy into the backseat. I sat up front and pulled on my seatbelt. Emmet jerked the car out of the parking spot and sped down the road.

"You need to slow down," I told him.

I watched his hands grip the steering wheel, but he did not slow down. Despite the fact that Emmy was in the backseat, I reached out and put the palm of my hand against his cheek.

"Emmet," I said softly. "Slow down."

I felt his jaw clench, and then suddenly he sighed, and his jaw relaxed, and his foot eased off of the accelerator. I dropped my hand to his leg and glanced back at Emmy. She was already asleep, her forehead pressed against the glass.

Emmet dropped his right hand from the steering wheel and held my hand.

"Neither of us should make any assumptions," I said softly, hoping Emmy couldn't hear me.

"But I watched you put his number in your pocket," he argued softly. "You talked about it right in front of me."

"Right," I agreed. "Which should more than prove that there was nothing nefarious happening between us."

Emmet sighed again and glanced over at me. "Funny how I overreact about this, but I was okay watching you make out with another guy."

"Very funny, and very silly," I said, squeezing his hand.

His thumb dragged across my skin and whatever tension that was in my body went away.

"We were just talking," he said after a few quiet minutes. He glanced over at me for a reaction. "We're still friends, but if you want me to stop being her friend, I will."

"No," I said, shaking my head. "You don't have to do that, and I would never make you do anything like that. I wouldn't want you to tell me I couldn't be friends with Felix anymore, or that I couldn't talk to Benny."

"I don't want you to feel uncomfortable or to worry," Emmet said.

"I'm not and I won't," I promised. "Much," I added.

I smiled at him. He looked over at me as if he was hesitant to believe that it could be so easy. I wanted to make it as easy as possible for both of us, but selfishly, for myself as well. I needed the path of least resistance over the next few months or more. So, I squeezed his hand again to reassure him that it *was* that easy. I loved him, and that was all that really mattered.

Finally, Emmet smiled, and it made me feel warm all over. I glanced back at Emmy. She was drooling, a sure sign that she was out cold.

"I love you," I spoke softly to Emmet.

"I love you, too," he answered. He brought our hands up to his lips and kissed my knuckles.

It was nearly two in the morning when we pulled into the driveway. There was a light shining deep in the house, and I had a feeling it was Sam in the kitchen.

"How are we going to get her inside without getting busted?" I asked Emmet, staring at the house.

"Maybe she needs to get busted," he said, shaking his head as he peered back at her.

"Ain't that the truth?" I muttered, getting out of the car.

I opened the back door, and if it weren't for the seatbelt holding Emmy in, she would have fallen out of the car. As it was, she hung grotesquely against the binds.

"Em," I said, shaking her.

She groaned in response but didn't move.

"Emmy, wake up," I said harshly and shook her harder.

"Stop fucking shaking me, you bitch," she snarled and slurred.

"Oh, you want to call me a bitch?"

I reached across her, unbuckled her seatbelt and stepped back. She fell out of the car, face first onto the driveway.

"Was that really necessary?" Emmet asked, standing beside me. He watched as Emmy cursed and struggled to get up, but he made no move to help her.

"That and so much more," I said without a trace of regret.

Emmy got to her feet, but she was very unsteady. Her face was scraped a little, but I didn't feel bad about that either.

"You are a bitch!" Emmy yelled at me.

Emmet sighed heavily and then, eliciting a shriek from Emmy, he lifted her and threw her over his shoulder. She bitched and moaned, smacking his back with her hands. I picked up her purse and followed them into the house.

Sam was up, and Sam had a cow, several in fact. She had a whole herd of cows. If Emmet hadn't been there to protect his sister, Sam would have beaten her ass with an enormous wooden spoon that I hadn't seen in years.

"Were you drinking too, Donya Elisabeth Stewart?" She pointed the spoon at me with vehemence. "God help me, if you've been drinking I will turn your dreams of moving into that apartment in the city into *smoke!*"

That was harsh, but...reasonable...

"No, I haven't been drinking," I said. "You wanna smell my breath?"

"This ain't funny!"

"I'm not trying to be funny," I argued. "I haven't been drinking. Do I look like I've been drinking?"

She pointed the spoon at Emmet next. "How much drinking did you do before you put yourself and your sisters in harm's way and got behind the wheel? How much?"

Emmet's face reddened, and he actually looked guilty. "Two or three," he answered sheepishly.

Sam stepped towards him with the spoon, but I stepped between them with my hands up. I don't know how I would have felt watching my guy get a spanking from his mommy.

"Psycho child abuser," Emmy muttered.

"Oh, honey, you ain't seen child abuse just yet," Sam said, trying to go after her.

"Can we just go to bed?" I asked with a long sigh. "Can we deal with this in the morning?"

Sam sighed heavily and then pointed her spoon at Emmet.

"I am very disappointed in you, Emmet Grayne," she said. "It's one thing for you to have a couple of beers, but you got in a car and drove."

"I'm sorry, Mom," Emmet said with sincerity. "You're right, and it won't happen again."

"What the hell is going on down there?" Fred called from upstairs.

We all looked at each other. Fred was usually pretty level headed, but if he knew about Emmet and had seen Emmy, it would have been like an atomic bomb going off inside the house.

"Everything is fine, honey," Sam called, lightening her tone deceptively. "I'll be up there in just a minute."

"Why are you yelling?"

"You know how Emmy and I get" She forced a laugh. "Go back to bed, Frederick. I'll be right there."

I heard a grumble, and a moment later the bedroom door closed. Sam turned her eyes back on Emmet and Emmy.

"Emmy, you're punished until you're twenty-one years old," she hissed. "Emmet, you get your shit together, or I will yank you out of that school so fast your head will spin."

"Yes, ma'am," he said respectfully.

She looked at me but said nothing before she finally put the spoon down on the counter and walked out of the room. There was a collective sigh of relief.

"Come on, Emmy," I said, taking her arm. "Let's go to bed."

"I can walk by myself," she snapped and snatched her arm away.

She walked unsteadily down the hallway and began to stumble up the stairs.

Emmet leaned against the counter with his arms crossed, looking angry. I walked up to him and wrapped my arms around his waist, but he didn't reciprocate.

"What's wrong?" I asked him.

It took him a few moments to answer me.

"My mom was right for a change," he said tightly, just above a whisper. "I was drinking, and I shouldn't have driven you guys. What if we got into an accident? What if I hurt you or Emmy, or something worse? I'd never forgive myself. I was so stupid."

"If you were twenty-one, this wouldn't even be an issue," I said to him.

"If you hadn't come to get me, I would have kept drinking," he said roughly. "And I would have still driven. It's not about my age; it's about my limitations. Clearly, Emmy doesn't have any, and I'm not sure that I do either."

"You can't change the past, Emmet," I said, taking his face into my hands. "We didn't get hurt; no one died. Let's move past it. Learn from it, don't do it again, know your limitations."

"I keep trying to take care of you and failing," he said, looking at me miserably.

"I'm standing here in one piece, touching you," I smiled at him. "You took care of me, okay?"

He rolled his eyes. "You took care of yourself, like you always do."

Finally, he opened his arms and pulled me into them.

"I love you," I whispered, my lips close to his. "I know when I really need you, you'll be there to take care of me, and I'll be there to take care of you when you really need me."

"Okay," he said. "I can handle that."

"Now quit whining and kiss me."

Emmet grinned. "Oh, this is certainly a way I can take care of you."

And take care of me he did.

Chapter Thirty-One

As the months slipped by, my career picked up to an insane pace. I was working sometimes six or seven days a week, from early morning until late at night. I took my first overseas trip to Milan, but couldn't stay to play because I had to immediately fly back to New York for another job. I picked up more acting gigs, more commercials, and landed the cover of a widely viewed teen magazine.

I became friendly with certain designers and other big names in the modeling world. I met various celebrities and was often invited to parties in mansions, on yachts, and in exclusive clubs. Despite all of that, I tended to fly under the radar, mostly graciously declining. I loved seeing my photographs on magazines or seeing my face on television or previews for the movie I did with Felix, but I didn't really feel like I had to constantly be seen hanging with the cool kids.

The work was very often arduous and frustrating. There were many nights when I returned to the apartment and crashed in whatever I had been wearing at the time. Some of the designers and photographers were not the nicest people. Working with them took an enormous amount of patience. I had learned to not take every terrible thing they said to heart, but sometimes it was hard to ignore the insults about my skin color or my 'black' hair, or some other feature of my body, especially when I was hungry, tired, and sore. The glamorous part of the industry only appeared in pictures. In reality, it wasn't that glamorous, but I loved it anyway, and I wouldn't have been happy doing anything else.

I got to see Emmet every other weekend. Between his internship and my unpredictable schedule, we struggled to find time to spend together, even when he was in New York. My career especially put a strain on us, but we were determined to prove my mom wrong. More than that, we were determined to prove to ourselves that we could withstand anything. We still hadn't told Emmy, Fred and Sam about us, but then with the distance between us and the few times that either of us was able to be home in New Jersey, it was easy to hide.

My mom hadn't relaxed on her rules about Emmet staying the night in our apartment, so he stayed in one of Felix's penthouse rooms when he visited, whether Felix was around or not, and Felix wasn't around often. He was very busy filming and promoting. *One Chance*, the movie I had a part in, came out at the end of summer. Emmy came to New York to attend the premiere with me and finally got a chance to meet Felix. I was amazed that she was well behaved and didn't once throw her underwear or bra at him.

My mom's health deteriorated so quickly, if I sat and watched her long enough, I would have literally seen her withering away. She grew weaker as cancer ravaged her body, and she could no longer hide her pain like she used to. Before Felix went back to California, he hired a housekeeper and a nurse to help out while I was working, but my mom always managed to chase them away, saying she didn't need anyone to take care of her.

When there were more days spent in bed than not, I fought with her until I convinced her to go back home to New Jersey, to the comfort of her own home. She was less than thrilled about leaving me to my own devices, so just for show, to ease her dying mind, I asked my cousin Kera to stay with me in New York and to travel with me if I had to go somewhere. She was only a few years older than me and had just graduated from college. She hadn't found a job yet, so she was more than willing to spend some time in Felix Hunter's apartment and follow around her somewhat famous cousin.

I had Kera's mother, one of my dad's sisters, track down and call my mom's siblings. She had been so stubborn about calling them just because she was dying, and I thought that was stupid. To my surprise, her sister Candy that she had been estranged from all of those years dropped everything and flew to New Jersey to be with her. My uncle Roger was a little bit slower at getting to the states, but when he arrived, he came with his wife and their three children. I forced the issue and made time to be there with them all for a few days. Even my dad's sisters who hadn't been helpful or very kind at all the years before had a change of heart and everyone came together.

I managed to make it to Louisiana for a few days at the very end of the summer. One of Emmet's southern cousins was getting married. I had been working nearly nonstop, and it was never a good idea to turn down work in this industry for something as unimportant as a wedding, but I hadn't been down south in over a year, and that big home in the hot swamps of Louisiana was my comfort place.

Emmet and I flew down together out of New York. On the plane, we shared entirely too much time with public displays of affection, but we knew that the opportunities for alone time would be very few while we were with the family. We still weren't ready to tell them about us—well mainly *I* wasn't ready. Emmy was still making well-placed statements about how gross it would be, and on more than one occasion Fred reiterated Emmet's place as my big brother. Point taken.

I sat between Emmet and Emmy at the wedding. Very discreetly, Emmet held my hand between the seats and stroked my ring finger throughout the ceremony. You might wonder why, after his proposal in California, he had not made it official and given me a ring, but I didn't wonder at all. I had Emmet's word that he wanted to marry me, and I had no doubts. I never even considered getting an engagement ring. I wore my charm bracelet every day, and any time I could get away with wearing it in a shoot, I did. That was confirmation enough for me, but the day after the wedding, hours before we were supposed to board a plane back to New York, Emmet surprised me.

In the dark hours of the morning, I met him outside by Fred's truck. I was excited because we were going to squeeze in a couple of hours of fishing at our old fishing spot. Though I was disappointed Fred was sleeping in instead of coming with us, I was happy that I'd have some time alone with Emmet in one of our favorite spots. Often when I daydreamed about Emmet and me sharing a romantic moment, the fantasy took place there at the water's edge, surrounded by the swampy woods.

"Try not to fall and hit your head, baby," Emmet teased as we walked from the truck to our spot.

"Hardy har," I said dryly. Visions of Emmet finding me and pushing my hair off of my forehead while he held my hand swarmed my mind and made me smile. "Did you love me back then?" I asked him.

"I think that's when I began to understand what was wrong with my brothers when they were around certain girls," he said with a chuckle. "I was too young to really formulate into words what I felt for you, but I know now that it was love. You made me feel weird, and it pissed me off."

"Clearly. You teased me mercilessly," I reminded him. "What about when we were younger?"

I remembered one of many incidents when Benny had pushed me down. Later that day Emmet had walked me home, and he had told me I was special to him and I remembered how good that made me feel to hear that from him of all people.

"Again, I was too young to understand what I was feeling, but I guess you could say that it was love," he said as we reached the fishing spot.

He put everything down carefully and took a few steps to close the distance between us. He pushed my hair off of my cheek and dragged his knuckles over my skin.

"Donya," he said my name with such intensity that my breath hitched. I stared up into his eyes, mesmerized. "I've always loved you. I think I loved you the moment you were born into this world even though I didn't know who you were yet. The moment you were born, our bond formed. We were meant to be together. The force holding us together is bigger than us; it's bigger than the entire universe. No matter what, baby, I was meant to be yours, and you were meant to be mine."

He reached into his pocket and produced a small black velvet box. My eyes grew so wide that it hurt. When my beautiful Emmet dropped to one knee, my breathing went haywire. My lungs forgot how to function. My heart pumped and stopped and pumped and stopped and stopped and stopped. I was lightheaded, and I was crying. I had said that Emmet's word had been enough, but as he opened the black box and presented me with a beautiful cushion cut diamond set on a white gold band, I was moved beyond words. It was the perfect proposal in the most perfect place by the most perfect man.

"Donya Elisabeth Stewart, will you marry me?"

I managed a half laugh, half sob and a bit of a snort as I nodded frantically, totally unable to find my words. Emmet smiled warmly and pushed the ring onto my finger. It fit perfectly, like Emmet. He fit me perfectly too.

Before he could stand up, I dropped to my knees, threw my arms around his neck and kissed him hard. He chuckled against my mouth as his arms snaked around me and he held me close.

"I love you," I whispered to him when our kiss finally broke.

He pushed my hair off of my forehead again and kissed it. "I love you," he said tenderly.

He grabbed the back of my head and dipped his tongue into my mouth. He tasted sweet and fresh and like…Emmet. I met his strokes with my own, tasting him as my tongue slid over his.

"I'm going to make love to you, right here," Emmet said hoarsely as he kissed across my jawline. "Right now."

I groaned when he nipped at the sensitive skin just below my ear.

"You always smell so good," he whispered. "Like wildflowers after a rain storm." His nose ran over my clavicle. "And vanilla."

Gently, he pushed me backward until I was lying in the soft grass a few feet away from the shoreline. His knee pushed between my legs as he leaned over me. He held himself up on one forearm so he wouldn't crush me as his other hand began to slip the straps of my tank top and bra off of my arm. He kissed me across my sternum until he reached my other arm and pulled the straps down that arm.

"You're everything I want," he said, pulling my shirt and bra down, freeing my breasts.

As if he couldn't wait another second, he dropped his head and pulled a perk nipple between his lips. My hips automatically lifted off of the ground as I moaned his name. When his tongue flicked over the hard peak, fire ignited there and raced through my veins and ended in a near explosion between my thighs.

"You're so beautiful," Emmet said and flattened his tongue between my breasts. "So, sexy."

He moved slowly down my body, trailing his fingers down my sides until he reached the waistband of my shorts. He hooked his fingers inside and slowly began to pull my shorts and panties down over my hips. His wet tongue slid from hip bone to hip bone, making me squirm and bite my lip.

Donya SGL was creeping onto the scene, whispering in my ear to grab Emmet's head and make that tongue lick me lower. Sensible Donya blushed and dug her nails into the grass and dirt.

Donya SGL scared me sometimes. She made me feel like a slut even though the only person I was with was Emmet, but she made me want to do things I'd only read about in romance novels and caught glimpses of on the internet. She made me want to behave in a way that made me want to cover my face with shame, but hell, Donya SGL's ideas turned me on. Imagining Emmet doing any of DSGL's suggestions increased the moisture between my legs and made my nipples swell.

As Emmet pulled my bottoms off and tossed them aside, I came out of my haze long enough to remember that we were outside in the open. Though the area was secluded and rarely did we see another soul, I felt vulnerable lying on the ground with only my shirt and bra bunched up around my ribcage and nothing else on my skin.

"What's wrong, baby?" Emmet asked, trailing a finger over my pubic bone.

"I never thought I'd be one for public sex," I said nervously.

He chuckled softly. "What public, babe? It's just you and me."

"What if someone is in the woods watching?" I asked, suddenly frantic and searched the trees. The sunrise was nearly complete, but the woods were still rather dark.

"No one is watching us, I promise," he said soothingly, rubbing the inside of my thigh.

I gave him a look of doubt.

"I guess I'll have to take your mind off of people in the trees spying on us," he said dramatically.

I looked towards the trees again. "I don't think that's possible."

I pushed myself up on my elbows and let my eyes scan the circumference of our fishing hole. The only movement I saw was the swaying of leaves in the light breeze. I started to sit up so I could pull my shirt and bra back on, but suddenly Emmet was hovering over me, nearly nose to nose with me. My eyes jerked down to his tanned, bare chest and followed his tasty abs down to his naked lower half. My eyebrows raised and my mouth formed an O.

"Lay back, Donya," he quietly demanded.

Yes! DSGL shouted and did a fist pump.

I dropped back onto the grass. My head had barely touched the ground when Emmet was on me, kissing me deeply as his erection ground against my crease. Groaning into his hot mouth, I thrust my hands into his hair.

"Emmet," I whispered harshly after he broke the kiss to suck and nibble on my earlobe.

He adjusted his erection with one hand until the head was pressed against my slit. He looked me in the eyes and used one hand to stroke my cheek.

"Tell me you love me," he commanded in a whisper.

"I love you," I breathed.

Emmet slammed into me, to the hilt. I cried out, but it was cut off by Emmet's mouth taking mine. As his mouth ravaged my own, his cock slid out until just the very tip was barely inside of me, and then he slammed into me again. He was so hard, long, and thick. It felt like he was trying to stretch me, to break me, but my inner walls clung to him, wrapped tightly around him like a suctioning sheath.

As Emmet's thrusts became more forceful, I felt myself sliding across the dewy grass. I tried to find purchase, digging my heels into the ground, but I only succeeded in taking his rigid member impossibly deeper. My hands slid out of his hair, down his neck, and across his strong, muscular back. He put a hand under my knee and lifted my leg over his shoulder. I tore my mouth away from his and screamed into the humid air.

The new position had Donya Sex Goddess and Lover screaming with joy. The pain was exquisite as his hard shaft rubbed against sensitive areas inside my body that I didn't know were there. Before I could even understand what was happening, I was sobbing through a hard orgasm that made my entire body shudder and shake.

"You're so damp," Emmet growled, pounding into me. "Fuck, Donya. You feel so good."

He moaned loudly as his pace increased and he seemed to lose all control. Sensible Donya was in pain and had the urge to put her hands on Emmet and make him stop, but DSGL cheered him on. The pain made her wetter, made her nipples more sensitive and made her curse dirty things into the air.

"Oh god," Emmet groaned through a clenched jaw.

I fell over the edge again, crying out his name, and my body bucked violently.

"Donya," he moaned long and low and then suddenly pulled out of me. He shouted curses as he came onto the grass between my legs. DSGL wanted me to sit up and help him stroke out the rest of his orgasm, but I really felt that DSGL had taken me far enough for the day. She made me blush and feel a bit ashamed as I lay there breathlessly watching until he finished, groaning and trembling.

Exhausted, he collapsed beside me and pulled me into his arms and kissed me gently on my temple.

"Are you still worried about people watching us?" Emmet murmured in my hair.

I laughed lightly, but the Sex Goddess piped in with an answer. "If they were watching, they sure got one hell of a show."

Chapter Thirty-Two

Death didn't come easily for my mom. She didn't just stop breathing in her sleep or go out in a drug induced coma. It was nothing like I saw on television and in the movies. She struggled, gasping and choking for air on her final breaths. I knew she was ready to go, but she couldn't help her body's automatic response to try to get oxygen into her lungs. Her eyes were wide with fear and they stayed that way until my Uncle Roger closed them for her.

Her hand in mine was still and already cooling. I gave her cold, dead hand one last stroke of my fingers and then gently placed it on the bed at her side. I stood up and moved away from my sobbing aunt and teary uncle and my dead mother. I left the bedroom only to come face to face with the rest of my family that had been mostly absent up until recent months.

"Is it over?" Kera asked, already clutching a tissue.

I nodded and then held up my hands to fend off any form of physical contact as my cousins and aunts tried to hug me. I didn't answer their sympathetic commentary. I quickly left the house of death and hurried down the sidewalk.

It was late in the fall. The warm summer weather was gone. Cool breezes and lower temperatures moved in seemingly overnight. It was cool enough to wear a jacket, but I had forgotten it and didn't want to go back for it.

A few minutes later I let myself into the Grayne house and headed into the dining room where the family was gathered for dinner. They all looked up at me with surprised expressions.

"What are you doing here?" Emmy asked in a high pitched voice.

"Why aren't you with your mama?" Sam questioned, even as she got up to no doubt get me a plate.

"She's not going to notice that I'm not there," I said flatly, taking a seat beside Emmy and across from Emmet, who had a school book and notebook open on the table next to him.

He looked at me knowingly. He felt what I felt, and I felt his need to take me into his arms, but instead he sat there and stared at me.

"Is she..." Emmy started, but couldn't finish.

Sam put an empty plate in front of me and sat back down, but stared at me also, waiting for an answer.

"Yeah, she is," I said, scooping a tiny bit of potatoes onto my plate. "Pass the pepper."

"Pass the pepper?" Emmy asked. "Pass the damn pepper, Donya? Your mom just died!"

"Which doesn't change the fact that my fucking potatoes need fucking pepper, Emmy," I snapped at her and held out my hand expectantly.

Under normal circumstances, Sam would have chased me around the house trying to slap the taste out of my mouth for dropping the F-bomb, but the circumstances weren't normal. She sucked in a breath and looked at me with pity. Fred and Emmy also looked at me with pity. The only one who wasn't giving me a piteous stare was Emmet.

I took a piece of chicken, a big scoop of peas, and poured myself a glass of iced tea. I was about to reach for a biscuit when I remembered that I hadn't washed my hands after touching my mother's dead hand.

"Gotta wash my hands," I muttered and pushed away from the table.

I went into the powder room near Fred's office and thoroughly washed the dead off of my hands. When I returned to the dining room, it was obvious a hushed conversation halted at my appearance.

"Please, don't stop talking about me just because I'm back," I said dryly, putting a napkin on my lap and reaching for that biscuit.

No one spoke. Everyone but Emmet ate in silence but eyed me carefully. Emmet picked at his food with his fork as he watched me.

"How is school?" I asked him. He only came home for the weekend because he knew my mother was about to die. I told him I didn't want him to disrupt his schooling for me, but he insisted.

"Donya," he sighed. "Stop."

I was chewing chicken that I was sure tasted delicious since Sam had made it, but it was like cardboard in my mouth. I had to chew an extra few times and force it down with half a glass of tea.

"Stop what?" I asked after I was sure the food wouldn't get lodged in my throat. There wasn't much room for swallowing with the big knot in there that had been there since my mother's last breath.

"Stop," he said in a tone that would normally have had me halting whatever action I was doing.

"You have to be more specific, Emmet," I forced a chuckle. I took a glance around the table and found that the other three were watching our exchange with curiosity and foreboding.

"Stop trying to force yourself to feel fine when you're not," he said gently.

I gave him a look that suggested that what he was saying was ridiculous. Sam tried to cut in and said Emmet's name in warning.

"No," I said, holding a hand up to Sam as I glared at Emmet. "I'm sorry, am I not behaving how you think I should behave? Because I didn't know there was any precedence for this."

"Your mother just died," he said, his voice low.

"And?" I shrugged. "I hardly knew her. Your crazy mother is the only mother I really ever knew."

"Trying to harden your emotions isn't going to help you," Emmet said firmly. "You're going to bottle it up, and it's going to explode when you least expect it."

"When did you become the authority on her emotions?" Emmy demanded. "Maybe she's handling it the best way she can."

Emmet didn't take his eyes away from me when he spoke to Emmy. "No, she's not."

"Again," Emmy said, irritated. "When did you become an authority on her emotions?"

"You're way off base, buddy," I lied, forcing down another bite of food. "I guess you expect me to be falling into your arms, emotionally wrecked." I was mean to him, and I knew it, but I couldn't help myself.

"Stop," he said again.

"You know what?" I threw my napkin on my plate and pushed away from the table. "I came here for a good meal and to escape the herd of sobbing people in my mom's house, but you won't shut the hell up and just let me be."

Four voices called my name as I marched out of the dining room and towards the front of the house.

"Donya, come back here right now," Emmet demanded from behind me.

"Fuck you," I said harshly over my shoulder.

As my fingers closed over the door handle for the front door, strong hands gripped my shoulders, almost painfully. I was yanked away from the door and spun around to face Emmet. I slapped him hard across the face. I heard Sam shout my name in horror, but I ignored her and punched him in the chest. As I continued to beat on Emmet, he took it with an occasional grunt, but he didn't release me.

"It doesn't matter!" I shouted at him as I slapped at his arms. "She didn't matter to me, and I didn't matter to her, so it doesn't matter that she's dead!"

The last few breaths my mother took replayed in my mind and I could feel her hand go limp in my hand all over again. I stood there staring at Emmet with wild, wide eyes.

"Your mom loved you," he said firmly. "She knew she fucked up before, and she tried really hard to make it up to you. You were the only reason she was afraid to die, Donya. She never thought she'd be able to make up for what she failed to give you all of those years, okay? She told me you were the only thing that mattered. You did matter."

It was right there in that foyer that I broke down when I found out my dad died. It was Emmet's arms that held me then, and as an onslaught of grief slammed into me, it was Emmet's arms that kept me from crumbling to the ground in that same foyer again.

I clung to him as I sobbed, and he held me securely, rubbing my back and smoothing a hand over my hair.

"It's okay to cry," he whispered in my ear. "I'll take care of you. Always."

I don't know how long we stood there like that before Emmet pulled away a little. Emmy was beside us, offering up a box of tissues as she cried for me. Emmet took a few tissues and began to gently wipe away the moisture off of my face. I was so thankful for him. I was so glad that he didn't listen to me and came down to be there for me despite my objections.

"Thank you," I said softly to him. I was still crying. I was pretty sure I couldn't stop, but I had to tell him how much it meant to me that he was there with me.

"You don't have to thank me," he said, holding my face in his hands. "I promised to always be there for you when you need me. It doesn't matter where in the world you are or what other obligations I have, Donya. You supersede anything and anyone. Okay?"

I nodded, and I didn't pull away or push him away when he leaned down to press his lips gently against mine. It didn't matter that everyone we had been trying to hide from was there watching with rapt attention. The gasps and the curses didn't matter. The only thing that mattered was that I was in Emmet's arms, and he was going to take care of me. Always.

~~*

I didn't cry again after that initial breakdown. I was sad, but I was functional. Emmet and Emmy drove me back to my mom's house after I had calmed down. I helped my aunts and uncle plan my mom's funeral and write the obituary. Emmet stayed by my side, and Emmy helped out by making tea and coffee and chatted up my cousins. Sam and Fred came by later that day with food.

My family showed me old pictures and videos of my parents, and I almost cried again, because they had been happy at one time. Extremely happy. I requested to keep all of the pictures of us all together when I was very young. I needed to know that at some point in my life, I had a happy, functional family.

Emmet and Emmy rarely left my side in the days following my mother's death. Sometimes I felt like one of them would come into the bathroom while I was peeing, and I suspect they would have if I didn't lock the door. They bickered a lot about who was going to do what for me, as if I was an invalid. I had had enough after a full day of it. I reminded them that my mom had died, but I was alive and well and perfectly capable of going into the kitchen to get a cup of water for myself. I didn't need help going up the stairs, and I didn't need anyone to hold my hand all day.

The funeral was at the burial site. It was small with only my family—biological and adopted—and a few people that my mom became acquainted with when she came out of her depression. Even Felix showed up. He couldn't stay afterward, but he wanted to be able to pay his respects to my mother who he had liked and to give me his support. Lucille, Charlotte, and Fred Jr. didn't come up, but they each called me, and I appreciated it.

At my insistence and the insistence of Fred and Sam, Emmet agreed that he would return to Harvard the day after the funeral. He had wanted to stick around for me and then escort me back to New York, but he had already missed almost an entire week of school for me, and that didn't sit well with me at all. I would never want to be in a position where I held Emmet back. I still felt badly for making him start his internship late earlier in the year.

No one spoke about what had transpired in the foyer the day my mom died, but that was simply a courtesy. Even Emmy managed to keep her mouth shut for a while, though I could see it all over her face that she was not only shocked but hurt because I didn't tell her. Sam and Fred watched us carefully, making sure that we weren't left alone too long and checked up on us to be sure we slept in separate rooms at night. It was almost laughable considering how much alone time Emmet and I had shared in the past.

The courtesy that had been extended to us, however, did not last once the funeral was over and done. Later that evening, we were summoned onto the back patio where Fred and Sam were sitting and drinking hot beverages. It was a little chilly outside, but not unbearable with a jacket on.

Emmet pulled out my chair for me. I smiled graciously at him even though I was nervous about what was coming. Before he could even put his butt down in the chair beside me, he started talking.

"I don't know what you're going to say, though I have some idea," he said. "But I'm letting you know right now that I'm not giving her up, and you can't make me give her up and you can't make her give me up, either. You're just going to have to get over it."

I was looking at Emmet with awe, because he sounded so damn powerful as he spoke to his parents and stood up for us. He met my eyes and changed his tone for me before speaking.

"Put your ring on, baby," he said gently. "And don't ever take it off again."

"Except for work," I said with a nervous smile as I dug the engagement ring out of my pocket.

"Except for work," he said with a soothing smile as he took the ring from me. It was as if his parents weren't sitting there glaring at us as he slowly slipped it back onto my ring finger and then placed a soft kiss on it.

"Oh, for crying out loud!" Fred...well...cried out loud as Sam let out a string of curses.

Reluctantly, I looked away from Emmet's green eyes and faced the parents.

"I'm about to put my foot right into your ass, Emmet Grayne!" Sam yelled. She went to stand up, as if she really was going to put her dainty foot in her son's ass, but Fred pushed her back into her chair and gave her a stern look. She stayed seated, but she threw violent threats across the table at both of us until Fred told her to zip it.

"How long?" Fred demanded. "How long has it been going on? For once the damn tabloids were telling the truth a few months ago, weren't they?"

"It doesn't matter how long it's been going on," Emmet said firmly to his father. "What matters is from here forward."

"Oh give me a break with the romance," Sam snapped. She pointed in our general direction. "You two have been lying to us, and I'll bet my sweet Louisiana ass that it's been for a long damn time. You've been sneaking around up there in New York, doing God only knows what while we were down here believing that Emmet was just being a good friend and a good brother. You led us to believe things were different than what they really were. You lied, you sneaked, and you betrayed our trust."

Both Emmet and I began to object, but Fred cut us off. They weren't finished lecturing us yet.

"Donya is barely seventeen and her career path is unpredictable. You have several years left of school. What made you think that getting engaged was a good idea?"

"You married Mom when she was nineteen," Emmet objected.

"Times were different then," Fred snapped.

"I don't care if you don't approve—" Emmet started, but Fred cut him off again.

"You're damn right I don't approve!" he roared.

Though I shouldn't have taken it personally, I did. I felt like it was me specifically he didn't approve of, and that thought hurt me deeply.

"You don't have to approve," Emmet argued. "I'm old enough to make my own damn decisions, and you have no legal claim over Donya, so you don't get to make her decisions either."

"Your relationship is entirely inappropriate," Fred said, slamming a hand down on the table. "You were supposed to look after her like a younger sister, Emmet, not seduce her."

"I wasn't seduced," I piped in, insulted, but I was ignored.

"She is *not* my sister," Emmet spat out. "My mother did not give birth to her. Your sperm had no part in her creation, and she's not adopted. She's part of this family, yes, but she's not my damn sister, dad."

"You stepped over a line that should have never been approached!" Fred yelled.

"The only line between Donya and I is the one that tethers us together," Emmet, said, getting to his feet. Holding my hand, he pulled me up, too. "I'm disappointed in both of you," he said angrily. "I didn't expect you to be happy about being lied to, but you should be relieved that we have each other."

Emmet led me inside. Sam followed us.

"Emmet," she said his name firmly. "Come back outside."

"I don't want to go back outside," he snapped. "I don't need to hear any more bullshit about how you don't approve and how inappropriate our relationship is."

"We're upset," Sam said with a frustrated sigh. "We are all saying things we don't mean."

I thought Sam met every word of what she said, but I remained silent.

"What do you think I'm saying that I don't mean?" Emmet demanded. "Do you think that I don't mean it when I say I love Donya? Do you think I don't mean it when I say that I won't give her up? Which part, Mom? Because I happen to mean every last word of it!"

I put my hand on Emmet's arm to calm him. He glanced down at me and took a deep breath. He looked back at Sam, but there was a little less tension on his face and his body.

"You're making a mistake," Sam said gently with a gentle nod as she looked at us. "It was easy to fall for each other because you're close, and you've spent so much time with each other, but once this initial…infatuation or whatever it is passes, you're going to realize that you've made a mistake, and I don't want it to be after you're already married."

I stared at Sam with my mouth hanging open. Her words were like ice cold water pouring over me. I didn't believe we had made a mistake at all, but it chilled me and hurt me that she and Fred believed that we did. I had always been rather sensible, but they didn't believe I was being sensible at all. They thought that Emmet and I were just lusting after each other.

Before Emmet could open his mouth and verbally rip his mother's head off, I spoke first, just as gently as Sam had.

"I love Emmet, Sam. He loves me, and maybe you will never understand the connection we have, but this is more than lust. This isn't a wild, short affair, and it's not some childish puppy love. This is *real*. I *feel* him here," I said, putting a fist to my heart. "No matter where we are, how far we are from each other, I *feel* him, and he feels me. We had no immediate plans of getting hitched soon, but Emmet wanted to claim me, and I wanted to be claimed." I looked at Emmet lovingly for a moment before turning back to Samantha. "Maybe life will be unpredictable. Maybe there will be something strong enough out there to tear us apart, but we are eternally joined. In the end, we'll always find each other. So, you don't have to approve. You don't have to like it, but even if we wanted to, we can't break the bond that holds us together. It will always be there, regardless of what you or anyone else has to say about it."

Sam stood there gaping at me for a long time. When she finally closed her mouth, she looked dazed. To my surprise, she dabbed at her eyes, but no tears fell.

"I'm going to go talk to your father," she whispered, and without another word or glance, she went back outside.

Emmet looked down at me and cupped my face in one hand.

"You are so perfect," he whispered before kissing me gently. He pulled me into his arms and kissed the top of my head.

"I better go talk to Emmy," I said after a moment.

"Do you want me to come with you?" he asked, releasing me.

"No. I have to do this one on my own."

I left him in the kitchen and went upstairs to face my best friend.

~~*

"I am trying to be understanding here, I really am," Emmy said a little while later in her room. "Your mom just died, and the dirt hasn't even settled on her grave yet, so I really am trying to be sensitive to your emotions and all of that shit, but you're sitting there with that big ass rock on your finger that I didn't know about until now and you what? Want me to be excited? You want to start discussing bridesmaid's dresses and color schemes? Because I'm so not there yet, D."

I sat in the chair near her bed, nervously pulling on my ponytail. Emmy sat on her bed with her legs crossed facing me.

"I'm just trying to make you understand why I didn't tell you," I said to her.

"I don't think there is a reason in the world for you not to tell me if I was really your best friend," she said. "Unless imminent death was one of those reasons. Was there a chance that someone would die if you didn't tell me, Donya?"

"No," I said quietly.

"Then I see no reason for you to withhold such pertinent information from me. I tell you everything. You know me right down to the deepest, darkest corners of my life, Donya, and you give me nothing. Like ever. I got used to not knowing what you're thinking or feeling, I actually kind of admired that, but this wasn't one of those things that you do not tell me. All of the times I brought it up—"

"You mean all of the times that you told me how much the idea disgusts you?" I interrupted, releasing my ponytail. I folded my hands in my lap and stared at her.

"Emmet is my brother, Donya," she said, looking at me as if I was stupid. "I would be grossed out by him kissing *anyone*. It's a sibling thing, and you should have known that because you've been a part of this family almost all of your life."

"In the beginning I was just afraid of how I was feeling," I said to her. "I didn't want to talk about it with anyone because I couldn't even wrap my own mind around it. And everything was so touch and go in the beginning. Everything was so complicated."

"What about when you got your mind wrapped around it, Donya?" Emmy asked. Her tone was harsh, but I didn't blame her. "It doesn't seem so complicated now." Her eyes flicked to my engagement ring.

"I was going to tell you a couple of times, but you always had perfect fucking timing, and you would tell me how gross you thought it was."

"So what?" she retorted.

"I didn't want to hear your shit about it, and then we weren't together for a long time, so it just didn't seem to matter."

"How long has this been going on?" she cried. "You make it sound like it's been years and years."

I looked down at my jeans and started picking at imaginary strands of fabric.

"It was years?" Emmy nearly yelled.

"Not exactly," I answered.

Emmy groaned in exasperation and looked away from me for a moment while thoughts raced through her head. When she finally looked back at me, her face was harder than it was before.

"Whenever it started, you should have told me long before now," she said. "I want to know details, every detail, but before that happens, I'm going to tell you that you shouldn't have held back, Donya. I am your best friend, at least I thought I was," she said bitterly. "Your true friend may give you some shit about who you love, but in the end, if he is good for you and to you, your true friend would have been supportive. I would have been a little grossed out at first, but I would have gotten over it. You didn't even give me a chance to experience any of this with you, or to be there for you, and I know you needed me. I finally figured out that when Emmet left for college, and you got all depressed that it was because of something that happened between the two of you. You didn't have to do that alone,

Donya, but you chose to shut me out. You've shut me out for a long time, and I'm not sure if I can get over it."

I bit my lip and willed myself not to cry. There were a lot of people I could live without in the world, but Emmy was not one of them. If she couldn't get past it, I didn't know where our friendship would be, if we'd even have one. The thought of not having her hurt so badly, I had to put a hand on my chest to try to relieve the ache. That ache combined with other aches, like the loss of my mother and the conversation I had with Fred and Sam were almost too much to take, but admittedly, the possibility of losing Emmy caused the most pain.

She took pity on me. Her face softened some, and when she spoke again, her tone was gentler.

"We are best friends, Donya," she said. "And sisters. I would have never done anything to make you unhappy, and you should have known that."

"You had grandiose thoughts about who I was and I...I didn't want to let you down," I said just above a whisper.

"I wouldn't have felt let down because you were screwing my brother," she objected. "*Now* I feel let down."

She got off of the bed and went to her closet. She came out carrying a bottle of tequila, of course, and two shot glasses. She stood between me and the bed and put the shot glasses on the nightstand and filled them up with the amber liquid. She handed one to me and took one for herself. I wasn't much of a drinker, but I was thankful for the shot. We took them together. I made a face, but Emmy may as well had been drinking air because she didn't even blink after swallowing the shit.

"Pussy," she muttered and bumped me with her leg. "One more and then you're going to tell me everything, from the beginning. You won't leave anything out, unless it's specifics on sex because I don't want to know anything about my brother's junk."

After a second shot that I swear took a year or two off of my life, Emmy settled back on the bed, and I propped my feet up on the bed and rested my head on the back of the chair.

"It started when I was seven," I said, feeling less tense than I had minutes before.

"You're kidding me."

"Do you want to hear the story, or not?" I eyed her.

"I have a feeling by the time I'm done listening to this I'm going to need at least a half dozen more shots."

Chapter Thirty-Three

Emmet and I stood on opposite sides of the small island in his modest kitchen inside his apartment in Cambridge. It was rare that I got to visit him because my schedule was so bizarre. In fact, I had just flown in from Paris earlier that day. Instead of flying to New York and hitting the ground running, I flew into Boston, shut my cell phone off and surprised Emmet as he was coming home from a class.

Emmet, Emmy, and Sam had gone to Paris to watch me walk the runway in ten shows during Fashion Week. It was a fabulous cluster of shows from the audience's perspective, but in reality, behind the scenes it was stressful and exhausting. The weeks leading up to the event made me wonder how there weren't mass model suicides.

It had been more than a year since my mother's death and the Graynes' discovery of my relationship with Emmet. It took some time for my relationship with Fred, Sam, and Emmy to improve, but I never felt that they loved me any less, and their support never wavered. In fact, days after my eighteenth birthday, Fred and Sam met me in New York for dinner and presented me with my very own trust fund.

"You are as much our child as Emmy," Fred had said. It took everything in me not to start bawling with love and appreciation there in the restaurant. Since the fund was set up by Fred and Sam, I didn't have the same stipulations that the other kids had. Obviously, I couldn't lounge on my couch and watch soap operas all day every day and expect to collect, but I definitely was not as bound as Emmet, Emmy, and the rest.

My career had become a behemoth. I was a young fashion and commercial model in demand. My face was in all of the top notch magazines, on a few billboards, and I had been on television and had small parts in two more movies. I had a fantastic contract with a major cosmetics brand and was favored by a couple of the best designers on the planet.

I was a very busy woman, and for a long time, Emmet had been a very patient man. There were many missed holidays, missed weekends together, and sometimes weeks without seeing each other. I even missed several family events. I promised Emmet that I would be all his for his spring break, but Alberi Durand, the designer that had been so kind to me when I first got started in the industry, had offered me a major campaign after I walked in his show. His brand had rapidly grown in popularity. His designs were loved by models, celebrities and even other designers. I had two days before I had to be back in Paris, and by the time it was all over, spring break would be all over, too.

"You've been in Paris for weeks," Emmet argued after I delivered the news. "And you promised that you would take this time off."

"I know I promised," I said solemnly. "But it's a major campaign with Alberi Durand," I added imploringly.

"I don't care if it was the fucking French president, Donya," he snapped at me. "I've been patient and supportive all of this time, and all I have asked for is one week."

"I know," I said again. I knew I was beginning to sound like a broken record already. "But that's why I'm here now. I can give you two days before I have to fly back."

"Two days?" he asked incredulously, with his eyes opened wide. "You're going to sleep at least one whole day, as you always do when you have a moment to catch your damn breath. It's really just one day, Donya."

He was so disgusted with me. It was all over his face, in the tone of his voice, and I could feel it radiating off of him. I opened my mouth to apologize again, but he talked over me.

"You promised me, and I believed you," he said, jabbing a finger in my direction. "You swore that you would take the time off. When I last talked to you less than two days ago, you gave me your word that you would not work for a week and that you would be here tomorrow. I believed you," he said again, glaring at me. "I had plans for us, and you just blew them all to hell."

"What plans?" I asked quietly. I felt like a douche rag, but it wasn't like I was breaking our plans to go be with someone else. I was breaking our plans so that I could work.

Emmet stormed out of the kitchen without saying a word. Hesitantly, I turned and followed him. In the living room, he opened a drawer in his desk and produced a long, thick envelope.

"What is that?" I asked when he only stood there holding it.

"Airline tickets for Mexico!" he shouted. "And confirmation for the all-inclusive beachside resort we were going to stay at. This was supposed to be our little getaway—away from school, away from your work, and away from the family. This was supposed to be our time to get our relationship realigned before you went traipsing off across the globe again, and you just fucked it all up!"

I stood there, stunned, as he slammed the envelope into my hands. I blinked down at it. It felt like a hundred-pound weight sitting in my hands. I felt really bad about canceling last minute on him, but he had to have known it was a possibility. He knew how unpredictable my schedule could be.

Something he said dawned on me. I looked up into his seething eyes.

"Realign our relationship?" I asked. "Our relationship needs realigning?"

"Are you *kidding* me?" He gaped at me.

"What's wrong with us? I didn't think there was anything wrong with us," I said in a bit of a panic.

Emmet snatched the envelope out of my hands and put it back in the drawer.

"I can't believe you even have to ask that," he snapped. "You have your designer head so far up your own designer ass right now."

I gasped, and it was my turn to gape at him. Emmet had not said anything as cruel as that to me since he told me I was too young and dumb, and even then that had not hurt as much.

"You're never here," he said. He was trying to control his anger, but he was barely holding back. "You show up late, if at all when we're supposed to meet somewhere. You begged me to meet you in Milan for New Years and you 'got stuck' in Berlin for two days. There have been countless cancelations when we're supposed to meet in New York or here, and even when you're supposed to be taking time off to be with me or the family, you end up working. If you're not working, you're exhausted from working, and you sleep our time away. You don't know anything about my life anymore because it's all about you. You don't know shit about my classes, my GPA, or my applications to law schools. You don't know who my friends are or what I do with my time. We've been slipping apart for months, Donya, and you don't even fucking *feel* it!"

I felt as if he had slammed a sledgehammer into my chest. There was so much pressure, and it hurt like hell. I couldn't breathe. I couldn't move; I was rooted to the floor in front of him. I wanted to look away from his hurt and angry expression, but I couldn't make myself turn my head or avert my eyes. Everything he said was true, but I felt like I had to justify my actions.

Softly, with a quavering voice, I said, "My career is so short. Soon, I'll be too old for the work I'm doing. My time in this aspect of the industry is so very limited. In a few years, I'll shift gears and slow down."

"In a few years," Emmet said with distaste. "What are you willing to lose before then, Donya? What are you willing to give up?"

The way he said it implied that maybe he thought I was willing to lose him; that I was willing to give him up, and that wasn't the case. I had always thought as Emmet as the constant in my life, that no matter where I went or what I did, in the end I would always be able to rely on him to be there for me, waiting for me. Just considering the possibility of not having Emmet as that constant in my life terrified me.

"Do you want me to quit?" I asked weakly. As soon as the question was out of my mouth, I began to feel resentment. Not necessarily at Emmet, but in general. I didn't want to quit my job. It was a job that only a very small percentage of the population could do, and I was fortunate and talented enough to do it and do it well.

Emmet dragged a hand through his hair, looking exasperated, angry, sad, and hurt all at once. He stared at me with his hand still in his hair, pushing his hair off of his forehead.

"If I ask you to quit, you will resent me," he bit out. I didn't know if he said it because he believed it or if he could feel me feeling it, but I didn't deny it. I didn't object or argue. I just stood there, waiting for a direct answer to my direct question.

"I want you to quit because *you* want to," he finally said. "Not because I want you to."

I bristled. "That really puts me in an awkward position."

Emmet released his hair and put his hands on his hips as he went back to glaring at me.

"Because you can't decide whether or not you want your job or me?" he shot out.

"That's not fair!" I cried. "Why can't I have both you and my job? I love my job, Emmet, and I love you, and I shouldn't have to choose!"

"You love your job more!" he shouted. "It's not even a fucking contest between me and the conceited thrill you get out of seeing your ass in a pair of jeans on a billboard!"

More hurtful words. I was confident in my abilities to model, which was a necessary component, but I wasn't conceited about it. I didn't think I was better than anyone else, and I didn't feel self-important.

"What am I supposed to do if I quit now?" I challenged. "Get married, stay at home and pop out five kids like your mom?"

"You could get married, pop out one kid and stay at home like *your* mom," he snapped.

"Wow," I smiled cynically as I backed away from him. "If your goal was to hurt me with your words, you're doing one hell of a job. Is insulting your fiancé an elective course you can take at Harvard? They give you lessons on how to treat your future wife?"

"My future wife?" Emmet laughed without humor. "You're married to your work, Donya. You don't need me," he said tauntingly. "You have Coco and Prada and Coach to keep you warm at night, and I'm sure if you get hot and bothered any one of your male modeling buddies can help you out. Hell, in your industry, I'm sure one of your female counterparts would help you out."

If I had been standing closer to him, I would have slapped him in the face, but I was standing several feet away. All I could do was stand there and stare at him as I let more of his hurtful words sink in. When I finally found that I could move again, I turned away from Emmet and walked to the foyer where I had dropped my luggage. I yanked my jacket off of the coat rack that hung on the wall behind the door and pulled it on. Emmet was standing a few feet away watching me as I zipped up and draped my scarf around my neck. I grabbed my hat off of the rack and pushed it on my head before bending over to pick up my bags.

"Don't you dare walk out that door," Emmet said ominously. "If you leave, there is no going back from here, Donya. I'm done waiting around for you if you go."

I hesitated but didn't look back at him. I could feel his anger. I could feel his apprehension too, but mostly his anger. It overpowered everything else at that moment. I was willing to work on our relationship, but I didn't think that I needed to hang around and continue getting verbally punched in the gut. I never purposely hurt Emmet, but he was going out of his way to hurt me.

After a strained moment, I pulled the door open and dragged my bags outside into the cold winter air. It was almost spring, but there was a lot of snow on the ground from a recent snowstorm, and it was very cold. I didn't have a car—I didn't even have a license to drive a car—and the nearest mode of public transportation wouldn't be easy to get to with all of my bags. I could go back inside and try to get Emmet to calm down and carry on with our weekend, but I wasn't sure if I could calm him down. I felt like my only option was to close the door between us and sit on the curb and call and wait for a cab.

Without glancing back at him, I closed the door and walked to the curb. A large part of me hoped that Emmet would come out and convince me to go back inside, but I gave up hope by the time the cab pulled up, and the driver put my luggage in the trunk. I looked back at his apartment before getting inside, wondering if I was making a mistake. The tether between us ached painfully. We were both hurt, but Emmet's anger was still strongly felt, and I didn't think I could deal with it.

I got into the cab and asked to be driven to the train station. I managed to keep it together for hours while I waited for a train and then rode to New York. I waited until I had let myself into the apartment attached to Felix's penthouse before I checked my phone to see if Emmet had called. He had not.

That was when I fell to pieces.

Chapter Thirty-Four

"Bonjour!" the woman said and eagerly kissed both of my cheeks. "Je suis Helene. Etes-vous Donya?"

I nodded. "Oui."

She started to speak rapidly in French, but I only caught a few words. I held up a hand to politely stop her.

"I'm sorry, I'm still learning the language," I said apologetically.

"I'm sorry," she laughed. "They told me you were fluent."

"I basically know how to ask for food and shoes and that's about it." I couldn't bring myself to laugh. I had to save all of my energy for the long ass day I was about to have. We were not only creating several ads for magazines, but we were also doing a commercial for a new fragrance Alberi was releasing.

"That is a beautiful ring," Helene said in awe as she gently held my hand close to her face. "You are engaged? You are very young."

"Actually," I said, carefully pulling my hand back. "I'm not sure if I'm still engaged."

I had no reason to tell this complete stranger that information, especially a complete stranger that would be, in moments, taking pictures of me all day.

"I'm sorry," I whispered. "I didn't really mean to volunteer that information."

"You look very sad, mademoiselle," Helene said with her heavy French accent. She looked at me with kind eyes.

"I'll be okay to work," I promised her.

"I hope so," she said and touched my arm before walking away.

I immediately liked her. Most other photographers would not have been cool with my mopey attitude, and they would have had serious doubts about whether or not I would have been able to turn it off for the cameras. I'm sure Helene had her doubts, but she didn't verbalize them, which made me more determined to prove that I could go from Pathetic Stupid Donya to Super Model Donya in a blink of an eye.

I had not heard from Emmet by the time I boarded my flight to Paris. I was not such a prideful person that I waited for him to call me. I did try to call him a few times, but he never answered. I cried for almost the entire trip across the Atlantic as I felt that tether stretching painfully.

"Donya," one of the assistants called and waved me on.

It was time to get to work. As finishing touches were made to my hair and makeup on the set, I reminded myself that it was a huge privilege that I had before me. Millions of women would give almost anything to be in my position. Hell, apparently I had given up something to be in my position…

When Helena picked up her camera and asked me if I was ready, Pathetic Donya took a seat, and the Super Model in me took over.

~~*

It was nearly two in the morning when I took a cab back to Felix's penthouse. I was exhausted and achy, but more than anything, my heart hurt. The moment all work was finished, my modeling façade fell away, and I was back to looking miserable. Helene had been ecstatic about my shots and the production team that filmed the commercial was pleased. I should have felt pleased and ecstatic too, but I felt lonely and I wanted Emmet.

I wanted him so badly that I felt like he was with me all day. I imagined that he wasn't thousands of miles away and that he was close to me, and by the feeling in my chest, I had seriously convinced my body and soul that Emmet was near. I tried to hold on to that in the back of a cab as we raced through the Parisian streets.

Before going into the building, I turned and looked at the Eiffel Tower in the distance. I had never gotten used to looking at it in all of its splendor. It was a beautiful sight against the sky; tall, solid, and sure. I decided that I would keep my curtains wide open so that I could look at the tower out of my window as I fell asleep and it could be the first thing I saw when I woke up. I needed something solid and sure to look at because my solid and sure was MIA.

The doorman let me inside of the building, and I was greeted by the overnight concierge as I walked across the marble lobby to the elevators. I used my key fob to get to the top floor—of course Felix would have it no other way.

I wished that he was around, but he was filming. Occasionally our paths crossed, but I didn't see him much anymore. We were both very busy. He had quickly become one of the few people I couldn't live without. He was a good and loyal friend. He was still a terrible flirt, but he made me laugh, and he was reliable.

With a weary sigh, I unlocked the door to the enormous apartment, walked inside and swallowed back a scream. Emmet stood in the foyer, just like the fucking Eiffel Tower, beautiful, tall, solid, and sure. His hair was sexily disheveled, and he was barefoot like he had been there for some time. His eyes burned into me with undeniable love. I blinked once, twice, three and four times.

I burst into tears when I realized that it was actually him and that my mind was not playing tricks on me.

He closed the distance between us in two long strides and then his strong arms were around me, pulling me against his body. I let my bag slip off of my shoulder and onto the floor before I wrapped my arms around his neck and buried my face in his shirt.

"It's okay," he whispered as he kissed my head and smoothed my hair and back. "I love you."

The deluge of tears that had burst forth soaked his shirt, but he didn't seem to notice. He continued to hold me and murmur his love for me. Soon the soul-killing emotions and my long day working and my days of travel began to take their toll. I felt weak and dizzy as my legs began to turn to gelatin.

Emmet swept me off of my feet into his strong arms and kicked the door shut. He carried me easily through the apartment to the bedroom that was reserved for me. He sat me carefully on the bed and used the bottom of his shirt to wipe my face. The shirt quickly became soaked with my tears. He gave up on it and pulled it off, revealing his gorgeous body.

Kneeling before me, he untied my sneakers and pulled them and my socks off of my feet. Next, he pulled off my jacket and my shirt. He had me stand so he could remove my pants and then I sat back down on the bed in my bra and underwear. When he unbuckled his belt, I pushed his hands out of the way and started to unbutton his jeans. I put my fingers under the elastic of his boxer briefs and pulled his pants and boxers down together.

I knew that he had only planned on getting me into bed to hold me and sleep, but I needed him. I needed to touch him, to taste him, and to physically connect with him.

Breathless with anticipation, I reached out and grasped his erection in my hand. Moisture glistened on the tip. I looked up into his green eyes as I dragged my tongue over the wide tip, licking away the liquid proof of his excitement. Emmet moaned deep in his throat and cupped my face in his hands as he looked down at me lovingly.

I sighed with pleasure and relief as I took him deep into my mouth. He groaned and whispered my name. Stroking the base of his rock hard cock with my one hand, I sucked hard as I dragged my mouth up his shaft until just the bulbous head was left between my lips. I swirled my tongue over it before taking him deep again. Emmet gasped and grunted. I knew he wanted to close his eyes and let his head fall back, but he didn't take his eyes off of me.

Feeling encouraged by the glazed look in his eyes, I put both of my hands on his ass for leverage and took him so deeply that I started to choke on his length and girth. He cursed and groaned loudly and twisted his fingers in my hair. He thrust once in my mouth, and because I was no longer Pathetic Donya or Super Model Donya, I moaned and looked at him encouragingly. Donya SGL wanted her lover to thrust his appendage into her mouth. Emmet took his cue and began to gently thrust in and out of my mouth. The look of pleasure on his face made me feel empowered. I was the one making him feel that way. I dug my fingers into his ass cheeks, making him thrust deeper into my mouth.

I knew he was getting close because he began to move faster and harder. My throat would be sore in the morning, but I didn't care. When he tried to pull away so that he wouldn't finish in my mouth, I held onto him and made my mouth as tight as I could. Emmet gave me one questioning look, and when I only moaned in response, he gave in completely.

Groaning loudly and calling my name like a mantra, his cock began to spasm in my mouth and then warm, sticky liquid was shooting onto the back of my tongue. He pulled out of my mouth slowly and once his cock slipped from my lips, I took a few swallows. It was the first time he had ever finished in my mouth. He more than earned it.

I fell back onto the bed, exhausted. Since I had not made my bed that morning, Emmet easily pulled the blankets up over me after he repositioned me more comfortably. He turned off the light and then climbed in beside me and pulled me into his arms. He kissed me slowly, lazily, but passionately. My toes curled at the way his tongue moved in my mouth, and I could feel him still hard against me. His hand traveled over my bare belly and up my ribcage until he was cupping my breast. He squeezed it gently as his thumb moved over my hard nipple. I squirmed and moaned softly.

Emmet pulled his lips from mine and kissed my chin, down my neck and across my collarbone. He expertly unhooked my bra, releasing my breasts to the mercy of his hands and fingers. Whatever exhaustion I had felt was disappearing as he sucked a nipple into his mouth and his other hand rolled my other nipple between his fingers. I slipped my hands into his hair. I still couldn't believe that he was there, that he had come to Paris for me. Part of me felt like I was dreaming and I worried that I would wake up, and it would have never had happened.

He left my aching breasts glistening from the moisture from his mouth as he kissed a path down my belly and over my panty line. He gently pushed my legs open and to my surprise and excitement, he licked my sex through my underwear. I groaned and lifted my hips off of the bed. He linked his fingers in my panties and pulled them off, but I was suddenly self-conscious.

I had showered at five in the morning, but I had been working all day. I didn't feel very...fresh, and I told him as much, but he shut down my worries when his tongue dipped inside of me. I wriggled against him as his tongue eased in and out of me. When he licked between my swollen lips up to my sensitive clit, DSGL grabbed the back of Emmet's head and ground against her lover's face.

He moaned as if he enjoyed my aggressiveness. He flicked his tongue over my clit repeatedly. I squirmed and moaned and bit down on my lip. When he put his lips over it and sucked, my hips shot off of the bed, and I cried out. I pulled on his hair and cried out his name as I ground on his face. He slipped two fingers inside of me, and I came undone.

I tried to push him away as my orgasm punched through my body. It was too much to take, but Emmet didn't allow me to push him away. He sucked my clit harder and added a third finger. I felt like I was spinning out of control, ready to crash into the earth in a heap, but another orgasm rocked through my body, and I found myself hurtling through space once again. Emmet licked me lazily as I began to come back to Earth, and his fingers moved slowly.

My orgasm subsided, but my body still trembled even as Emmet positioned himself over me. In one smooth move, he sank his cock deep inside of me. My head tipped back and my eyes closed as I moaned loudly. My back bowed away from the bed in a natural reflex that only buried Emmet's erection deeper inside of me. He groaned my name and crushed his body against mine, pinning me to the bed beneath him, and he kissed me with unbridled salacity. My lips felt as if they were bruising and my tongue and mouth felt battered, but I not only wanted his violent passion, but I craved it and loved it.

My nails dug into his flesh as pleasure and pain mingled together. When his lips left mine and began to move down my cheek, I turned my head to give him full access to my neck. The curtains were open after all, giving me the perfect view of the Eiffel Tower. It struck me how perfect the moment was. I was making love with my soul mate in Paris with one of the most romantic structures in the world within view. Not only did I have Emmet in my arms and inside of me, but he had also traveled thousands of miles to make the moment happen. My love for him was already at depths I'd never be able to quantify, but it suddenly blossomed further, and my chest felt like it was going to explode with passion, appreciation, and love.

My tears started again, just as Emmet's teeth sunk into the curvy flesh of my breast. I cried out in pain and delight that was cut short by Emmet's mouth quickly finding mine again. His rhythm increased, as did the power behind his thrusts. With his elbows on the bed, his hands held my face and his thumbs wiped away my tears as he continued to kiss me and make love to me with unchecked fervor. My screams were met by his increasing moans and grunts. His chest rubbed against my sensitive nipples and his body pressed against my clit with his movements.

My whole body felt like it was on fire. I was burning with passion and pleasure. Emmet's body was hot against mine. Together we would erupt into flames and set the entire bed on fire, maybe the entire city. That's how hot I felt with him. His body was touching mine in all of the right places, and I began to see white spots behind my eyelids. There was a keening coming from within me, but it was caught by Emmet's warm, silky mouth.

Suddenly, I pulled my mouth away from his and screamed his name as a scorching, explosive orgasm tore through my body. It sparked hot delight over every inch of my skin. I clung to him as the orgasm continued to sear me through and through. Emmet followed, holding me tightly to his body and calling out my name as his seed spilled inside of me. Before I could stop violently trembling from the last orgasm, I was desolated by another.

"Don't let me go," I whimpered breathlessly, wrapping my limbs around him. "Please don't let me go."

Emmet continued to hold me and gently kiss my moist face as he made a solemn promise to me.

"I'll never let you go," he said.

And I believed him.

~~*

Of course, Felix couldn't just have a normal guest bathroom with a toilet, shower, and tub. The on-suite bathroom in my room had a large oval shaped, glass enclosed shower stall. There were shower heads from above and shower heads built into the wall so that you were sprayed from all directions. The tub wasn't just a tub, but the size of a small pool with a Jacuzzi setting. Even the toilet was elaborate.

I sat in the tub with my knees drawn up to my chest and my arms wrapped around my legs. I rested my cheek on my knees as Emmet sat beside me gently running a sudsy pouf over my body. I was exhausted and sore by the time he pulled out of my body, but I felt a shower or bath was necessary. While I lay in bed staring out at the Eiffel Tower, Emmet had gone into the bathroom and drawn a bath for us.

"How did you get in here?" I asked him sleepily.

"I called Felix and told him I screwed up, and he made things happen for me," he said. He sounded just as tired as I felt.

"You and Felix are mighty cozy," I teased softly.

Emmet smiled and gave a nonchalant shrug. "He's not so bad."

I raised my eyebrows. "Not so bad? You hung out with him all weekend last month. You guys are like, dare I say it, friends now."

He flicked his fingers at me, sending drops of waters and suds flying onto my face.

"Don't push it," he said.

I wanted to laugh and to tease him about Felix, but despite our intense lovemaking, there was still some tension between us. We still had some unresolved issues.

"If I had known about the trip to Mexico, I would have never accepted the campaign with Alberi," I said. We had been quiet for a few minutes, each of us lost in our own thoughts.

"Whether you knew or not doesn't change the fact that you made a promise to me," Emmet quickly responded with a soft, but hostile tone that made me cringe.

I hugged my legs closer to my body and turned my head away before again resting my cheek on my knees. I heard Emmet's soft expulsion of air. The water lapped gently at the sides of the tub as he moved closer to me.

"Donya," he said my name softly. "Baby, look at me."

Reluctantly, I turned my head back to look at him. The features in his face that had been hard a moment before had softened. His fingers stroked down the ponytail hanging down my back.

"I didn't fly over thirty-five hundred miles to fight with you and make you feel bad," he said. "I came here to be with you. I don't care if I only get a half hour with you a day while I'm here; it's better than nothing. I'll take what I can get."

"I'm really sorry," I whispered.

"I know you are," he said solemnly.

"What are we going to do, Emmet?" I asked weakly.

"Don't worry about it right now, baby. We'll work it out. I promise."

He kissed me. It was very brief, but it warmed me in the cool water.

Chapter Thirty-Five

I loved mornings with Emmet. I loved watching him stretch and scratch at his chest and sometimes his beard if he had one growing in. His hair was messy; his t-shirt had ridden up to just below his belly button and his lounge pants hung low on his hips revealing the top of that contoured-V shaped part of his pelvis that I wanted to lick. I was in the bathroom brushing my teeth when he shuffled in, yawning, scratching, and looking hot.

"Good morning, beautiful," he said and kissed my temple.

"Hello," I smiled. I watched his ass as he walked away towards the toilet, but turned away when he started to pee.

I finished brushing my teeth and filled a cup with water so that I could take my vitamins and birth control pill. Emmet washed his hands and found a new toothbrush in a drawer on his side of the double sink vanity. He brushed his teeth while I took my pills and began to brush my hair.

"I can get used to this," I said as I pulled the brush through my hair.

"Get used to what, baby?"

"*This*," I said, gesturing between us. "Us, moving about in the mornings together and getting ready to face the day. What makes it even more alluring is that we're in one of the most romantic cities in the world."

Emmet moved behind me, wrapped his arms around my waist and looked at our reflections in the mirror.

"It doesn't matter what city it is," he said in my ear. "As long as we're together, it will be the most romantic place in the world."

I turned my head and met his lips. The kiss was minty and warm and made me happy.

"Yeah, I can definitely get used to this," I said as Emmet released me.

He grinned at me and said "Anytime and anyplace you want to get official with me, beautiful, I'm there. Now get a move on before you're late." He smacked my ass, making me yelp and left the bathroom chuckling.

The week had started out rocky, but it turned out better than expected. I finished shooting for the campaign the day after Emmet arrived. Though I received phone calls for other work, I turned it all down so that I could be with Emmet like I was supposed to in the first place.

We fell into a comfortable routine during our days together. Whenever we would finally make it out of bed, whether groggy from sleep or electrified from sex, we would take a shower together. We'd floss and brush our teeth while music played from the bedroom. I'd wash my face while he shaved, and while I moisturized my skin and brushed my hair, Emmet would go into the kitchen and make coffee for himself, tea for me, and breakfast for us. I'd join him at the breakfast table that had an incredible view of the tower and the city, and we would attempt to read the newspaper that was delivered to the door every morning. I had a better understanding of the French language than Emmet did, but it was always a fun time to try to pronounce and decipher the articles.

After breakfast, we would hit the streets of Paris for sightseeing or shopping and then we had lunch at a different café each day. We always returned back to the penthouse by early evening. Sometimes we'd grab food on the way home, or sometimes we'd eat out, but my favorite times were when we cooked together in the top of the line kitchen. Emmet did most of the cooking, though. I wasn't much of a cook, but Emmet showed off with his slicing and dicing, sautéing and flipping. He plated the food like a five-star chef and placed it in front of me with a loud, obnoxious, "voila!"

We also talked all day, every day. I asked Emmet question after question to prove that the life he lived in Cambridge was important to me.

Helene, the photographer that had been so kind to me, joined us for lunch one day. We had exchanged numbers on the last day of working together. She brought her husband Marcus with her. The pair bickered back and forth over trivial things. They would start to argue in English, but they effortlessly continued to argue in French and Marcus's native Italian. Emmet and I looked at each other in amusement before turning back to our new friends to try to get them back on topic, but it was clear they loved each other. In the middle of an argument, Marcus would kiss her all over her face, and they never stopped touching one another.

"Your fiancé is brilliant," Helene said to Emmet towards the end of our meal.

I looked at her with amusement and confusion. "What are you talking about?"

"I know she is, but why do you think so?" Emmet asked after glancing at me with a soft smile.

"I do not know what happened between you two—it's none of my business," she said, waving her hand. "But Donya was devastated. It was written all over her face. It was in her body language. She looked stiff and lifeless, but..." She shook a finger at me and smiled. "Once she stepped in front of the camera, she transformed. It was like that hurting girl had gone away. She became who she needed to become, and there are very few girls in this business that can do that effectively. I usually have to yell at them all day to take their heads out of their asses."

Emmet looked at me with adoration. It made me feel embarrassed, though I didn't know why.

"She is incredible," he murmured.

"She is," Helene nodded and looked at me. "The sky is the limit for you, Donya. If you want something, you will be able to take it." She made a snatching motion with her hand.

Emmet looked at Helene with a thoughtful expression. The conversation changed after a moment, but Emmet had grown quiet. I don't think Helene and Marcus noticed because he still participated in the conversation, but I knew he was preoccupied. Later as we walked back home, Emmet was still clearly lost in his thoughts. I chatted on anyway, carrying the weight of the conversation until we were inside the penthouse, coats closeted and shoes kicked off.

"What's on your mind?" I asked him as we settled on the couch.

He looked at me quietly and thoughtfully for a moment before speaking.

"Do you really love what you're doing?" he asked.

"Yes," I answered without hesitation. "It's hard work, and sometimes I'm treated like shit," I admitted. "But...I really do love it. I love the clothes, the hair, the makeup, and becoming someone else in front of the camera. I love the chaos before and during a shoot and the satisfactory feeling I have afterward."

I pulled my legs up onto the couch and rested my head on Emmet's shoulder.

"Emmy and I used to look at *Vogue*, *Cosmo*, and *Vanity Fair* for hours at a time when we were younger. I didn't necessarily want to be a model then, but I envied them sometimes. They got to wear incredible clothes, shoes, and jewelry created by some of the most talented minds in the world. I loved their poses and the expressions on their faces. When I realized that I could be like those models, I really wanted it. When I realized that I was good at it, I wanted it even more. I didn't understand what it meant to have a passion for a hobby or an occupation until I got to New York and got my first real modeling gig."

I looked up at him with narrowed eyes. He looked back at me questioningly.

"For the record, I do love the final result of a shoot, but I actually get embarrassed when I see myself in a magazine or a commercial. I damn near had a heart attack when I saw that billboard advertisement for those jeans. If you noticed, I get uncomfortable when people approach me as if I was someone important or famous."

Emmet smiled, but he sounded sincere when he apologized for his comment about me being conceited. "I know you're not like that," he said gently and put his arm around me.

"Why did you ask me if I love what I do?" I asked him.

He ran a hand over his jaw and sighed. "I knew you were good at what you did, but Helene has been in the business for a long time, right? It takes things to another level when someone like her says that you're good."

"I believe she said brilliant," I said with a smirk.

Emmet grinned and poked me in the side, making me giggle. "Oh, no, you're not conceited or anything," he teased.

"Just stating the facts."

"Okay, so she said you're *brilliant*," Emmet amended, but then his face grew serious. I sat up straight and looked at him, waiting for him to spit out whatever it was he had to say. "Donya, I don't want to hold you back—ever. I tried to hold you back when we were arguing in my apartment. I told you that I wanted you to quit because you wanted to, not because I wanted you to, but I really did want you to want to quit. I tried to make you feel that quitting was your only option, and I feel like such an asshole for that."

"It's okay," I said, touching his face. "I understand, I do. You missed me, and I *have* been inconsiderate over the past several months."

Emmet captured my fingers in his hand and looked at me with a troubled expression.

"Donya, I don't want to hold you back," he said again. "I want you to go as far as you can go with this, and I know that there will have to be some sacrifices made, but I'm unwilling to sacrifice any more unnecessary time away from you. As soon as the semester is over, I'm going to join you in whatever corner of the world you're in."

I stared at him stupidly for a moment. "What…what do you mean? You're going to skip the internship and travel with me for the summer?"

"That and more," he said, watching me for a reaction.

"I don't think that's wise," I said. "But what 'more' are you talking about?"

I had an uncomfortable pressure building in my chest. I didn't want Emmet to skip the internship at the law office. He was lucky to have the position in the first place, and he was learning a wealth of information that would aid him when taking the bar and in his subsequent career.

"I'm going to take a year or two off from school," he said quietly.

I felt my eyes widen, and my mouth fall open. I shook my head slowly, indicating that I didn't think that it was a good idea at all, and it wasn't. Emmet had one more year to go before he got his bachelor's degree and then he had at least three years of law school ahead after that. The years were going to be long enough without putting one or two empty ones before them.

"Why?" I choked out. "Why would you want to do that?"

Emmet turned his body towards mine and cradled my face in his hands.

"Donya, I don't want to live without you anymore. I can't stand being away from you. I want to be able to kiss you every morning, every night, and as much as I damn can in between. I can't go through another year like this, and if what Helene said is any indication of what's to come, it will only be worse, or better for you, but worse for us as a couple."

I held onto his wrists and carefully pulled his hands away from my face.

"Emmet, you only have one year left of college," I made a sound of exasperation. "And that internship is important. You were incredibly lucky to get it in the first place."

He frowned and sat back away from me. "That wasn't the response I expected."

"I know, and I'm sorry, but I don't really think you thought this through."

"I thought it through enough," he said defensively.

"Emmet, you can't..." I said, shaking my head. "Your parents will have a fit for one, and you'll lose your trust fund money if you drop out."

"I don't care what my parents say," he frowned. "And money isn't everything."

"No, but it sure is nice to have when you want to go to a prestigious law school," I said. "And if you take a year or more off, you may ruin your chances of getting into the law program. I can't let you do that."

Emmet scowled. "You're not *letting* me do anything, Donya. It isn't your decision, and I can get into some other law school later."

I wanted to smack him in the head and wake him up. He was on track to graduate with honors and was almost guaranteed a place in Harvard's law program. He was willing to throw away all of the hard work and money spent on his education and go to some community law school so that he could be with me. In theory, it was a romantic gesture, but in reality, it wasn't a great move.

"I think you should think about this a while longer before you make any permanent changes," I said.

"You don't want me to be with you?" he asked with a disbelieving and hurt look on his face.

"Of course I want you to be with me," I snapped though I didn't mean to. I had taken a breath before I spoke again. "It's just that I really want you to live your life, too, Emmet. Law school is important to you."

"Donya, you are my life," he said. "And you are the most important thing to me in the world. My mind is made up."

He got off of the couch and went into the kitchen. I sat there staring out of the window at the Eiffel Tower in the distance, with a feeling of dread.

Chapter Thirty-Six

Weeks later, Emmy and I sat in a busy New York café sipping cappuccinos after a small salad with no dressing for me and an enormous cheeseburger and fries for her. I had put on a couple of pounds, absently eating all of the wrong things over the weeks. I wasn't anywhere near fat, but one designer disagreed. He told me to come back Monday with a smaller ass. I was lucky that he didn't replace me instead, so I took the hint and got to work on minimizing my ass.

Emmy was telling me about the colleges she had applied to and the responses she got. She was excited about getting accepted to Penn State. She and Fred had visited the campus last spring, and she had liked the atmosphere and the course selection, but she wanted to get her bachelor's degree in business administration as soon as possible and was already considering ways to cut some time off of her four years. She seemed very motivated, and I wondered if she would ever give up her education to be with someone she loved. Fred and Sam would probably blow gaskets if she did.

That was another thing to worry about. I worried that Fred and Sam would blame me for Emmet dropping out of college and subsequently derailing his future. They were the only family I had and I worried that his decision would put an enormous rift between us. Fred and Sam didn't put a lot of demands on their kids, but a college education was a must, and though none of the other kids ever attempted it, I was pretty sure that dropping out to follow your girlfriend or boyfriend around the world wasn't an acceptable reason not to go to school.

My biggest concern, however, was Emmet. He took his education seriously, and he put in three hard years already. I worried that later, when it was too late, he would regret his decision. I understood what he was trying to do, but he needed to live his own life. He needed to finish school and get his career on track. His life couldn't be just about me. For the first time since Sam and Fred discovered our relationship, I started to consider

Sam's words. I began to believe that maybe…what we were doing was a mistake.

Emmet would eventually get tired of following me around. The romanticism would fade, and he would start to rethink his decision to drop out of college. He would get tired of sitting in whatever hotel or temporary home we were in for the week and waiting for me to come home.

The Graynes were loaded, but they were hard workers. They liked to have a purpose. Fred still kept a close eye on his businesses even though Fred Jr. was running things. Sam worked hard to take care of her home and family and was putting more and more of her time into charitable organizations.

Though Charlotte was pregnant with her second child, married to a man with deep pockets and she still got a piece of that Grayne pie, she had a successful consultant business that she ran out of her home. Lucille's husband was in medical school and didn't have deep pockets, but even though they had enough money between them for her to lounge at home and do nothing, she worked hard for a large marketing firm.

Emmy was in her last year of high school, but she had a part time after school job and I knew she would work her butt off in college and work hard after that.

I was one hundred percent positive that Emmet would not be okay with sitting at home doing nothing while I was out working. It maybe would have been okay at first, but eventually it would have gotten to him. Eventually, the regrets and resentment would have come.

"Hello?" Emmy said, waving a hand in my face.

I blinked a few times and focused in on her face. "I'm sorry. I'm listening," I promised.

"You are not," she argued. "You haven't heard a word I said for five minutes."

"It took you five minutes to realize I wasn't listening to you?" I asked dubiously.

"See, you just admitted you weren't listening to me. What's going on with you? You're completely preoccupied, and you've been quiet since I got here."

After hurting Emmy with the secret of my relationship with Emmet, I stopped withholding anything major about me. I was still more or less a private person that kept a lot to myself, but nothing major, and what Emmet was about to do for me was pretty major.

"Emmet wants to take a year or two off of school so he can be with me," I said, getting straight to the point.

Emmy's face went from curiosity to dismay. "He can't do that," she said, shaking her head adamantly.

"I have been trying to talk him out of it for weeks, Emmy. He won't listen to reason."

"Mom and Dad will flip out," she said, staring at me incredulously. "He'll lose his scholarship. He'll stop getting money from his trust fund. He may not get into law school."

"I know, and I've told him all of that, and he doesn't care. So, now I'm worried about it all of the time. I'm terrified that he's going to give it all up to be with me and then resent me for it later."

Emmy sighed deeply. She looked at me as if there was something she wanted to say, but she was reluctant to say it. She bit her bottom lip to keep herself from blurting it out.

"What?" I asked tiredly. "Just say what you have to say."

"It's just…" she started but stopped to release what sounded like a sigh of defeat. "I didn't want to say this, but this is one of the reasons why they didn't want you and Emmet dating. They thought he would eventually do something like this."

I thought back to the conversation Emmet and I had with my mom what felt like half a lifetime ago at the dinner table in L.A.

The paths you will follow separately will slowly take you apart, piece by piece.

I was so sure that she had been wrong. I didn't think we were naïve and I didn't think there could be anything to pull us apart, but the very thing my mother said would ruin us was ruining us. Though she was gone, I had the sudden urge to yell at her for bringing this upon us with her negative words. Sam's words to us the night after my mom's funeral weren't any more warming, but also hit their mark.

"Sam and Fred will hate me," I said, staring down at my cappuccino.

"They won't hate you," Emmy said soothingly.

"They will blame me, Emmy," I quietly snapped, turning my gaze upon her. "Maybe not out loud and maybe not directly, but they will know that I am the reason and no one else."

She wanted to argue, but she didn't have an argument. Every word she started to say in objection never made it past her lips because she knew I was right. Finally, she gave up on arguing and asked me what I was going to do.

"Maybe I should quit," I said so quietly, I wasn't sure if she heard me over the other diners in the café.

"Quit what?"

"Modeling."

"So you can be with Emmet?" She asked incredulously. "You would give it all up for him?"

"You say that like it's a terrible thing," I snapped.

"Well, for someone your age, it is," she snapped back. "You're eighteen years old. Even though you're more mature than me, you're still very young, and you're still growing as a person. You're going to hand yourself over completely to a man who is barely a man, who is still between being a boy and being a man, and lose yourself completely? You won't even know who you were supposed to be or who you wanted to be in ten years because you will only be what Emmet wanted you to be."

Those were the most serious words I had ever heard come out of my friend's mouth, serious and true, but I wasn't ready to concede just yet.

"People give up their careers for the person they love all of the time," I pointed out. "In a way I understand where Emmet is coming from."

"Sure, people give up their careers to be with someone they love," Emmy nodded. "But how many of those people are eighteen years old? How many of those people are in the unique situation that you are in? You are an in-demand high fashion super model, Donya. You aren't a twenty-seven-year-old system's analyst or a thirty-year-old school teacher."

Emmy leaned forward and grabbed my hand in a death grip as she looked at me with earnest.

"When we were younger, I had all kinds of dreams and aspirations. I wanted to be a singer. I wanted to be an actress. I wanted to be a news reporter, and I wanted to be a whole list of other things before I finally settled on going into business administration. You never joined in with my schemes to become Miss America or a princess or any of that. Instead, you just played a supportive role. Not too long before we first met Max at the beach, I asked you what you wanted to be when you grew up. Do you remember what you said to me?"

I closed my eyes for a moment. I remembered the conversation. When I had answered Emmy's question back then, she didn't even know what to say to me for a minute. She finally had just hugged me because there was nothing to say.

I opened my eyes and looked at her across the table. I let out a shaky breath and nodded that I remembered. Recalling that conversation changed everything and we both knew it, but Emmy still felt it necessary to say it out loud.

"You told me that you didn't have any desire to be anything," she said quietly with tears in her eyes. "You just said that what you did not want to be was your mother."

Emmy released my hand and dropped her hands in her lap. The realization of what I had to do slammed into me hard. My hands balled into tight fists, and I swallowed hard repeatedly to keep my emotions from overtaking me right there in the restaurant.

"Can we cut his weekend short?" I asked her in a haggard whisper.

She nodded solemnly as she looked at me with sad eyes.

"I know I said a lot of things in the past to discourage you about Emmet," she said quietly. "But I know you love him, and I know he loves you. I don't want to see either one of you hurt. I didn't say the things I just said to hurt either of you."

I nodded once. "I know," I managed.

I took money out of my purse and left it on the table even though the bill had not come yet. I put down more than enough to cover it and a very generous tip. Following my lead, Emmy stood up, and together we walked out onto the busy city street.

~~*

Emmet knew there was something wrong when I called him and told him I was driving up to see him. He asked me what was wrong repeatedly in the short conversation, but I gave nothing away and told him I'd be there as soon as I could.

Since getting my license a couple of weeks after the spring break fiasco, I rarely drove anywhere. I didn't feel the need to drive in the city, and I always took the train to Emmet's, but I didn't want to have to rely on a long wait for a train later. I borrowed one of Felix's cars and started the drive to Cambridge.

Emmet opened the door to his apartment before I could even get out of the car. I saw him standing in the doorway waiting for me, and I had to take several deep breaths before getting out.

"Is that Felix's?" he asked, eyeing the flashy car as I approached him.

"Yes," I answered and hit the key fob to engage the alarm.

Emmet's eyes met mine, and I knew that he knew that something bad was coming.

"Why did you drive and not take the train?" he asked. He hadn't moved out of the doorway yet.

"I didn't want to deal with the train today," I answered quickly.

He looked at me with unease for another moment before stepping aside to let me in.

Usually, we met with embraces and sweet kisses, but I walked into the apartment and stood on one side of the living room, and Emmet took his stance on the other side.

"What are you about to do, Donya?" he asked quietly.

I held a hand to my stomach as I tried to calm myself, but I couldn't. My breaths were short and labored as my heart hammered in my chest.

"What are you doing?" Emmet asked, but his voice cracked on the last word.

"I'm ending this," I managed to say, and then to clarify, I added, "I'm ending us, Emmet."

And then I burst into tears.

Emmet rushed over to me and tried to hold me, and I wanted him to hold me. I wanted to melt into his arms and never leave, but as much as it hurt, I had to stick to my guns. I pushed him away from me and took a step back. My whole body shook with sobs and tears gushed out of my eyes, nearly blinding me.

"Why?" he asked pleadingly. "Why are you doing this?"

"Because we're going to two different places," I said through my tears. "We're on two different paths in life. They don't parallel, and they don't converge, they go on and on in opposite directions."

"That's why I'm leaving school, Donya," he nearly yelled. "So that I can be with you."

"I don't want you to leave school," I snapped. "That is not an acceptable option, Emmet."

"Then quit modeling, or slow down or take some time off, but don't quit us. We love each other, Donya, we were made for each other."

I was only mildly surprised that he made that suggestion. A few minutes before he was willing to follow me across the earth, but in desperation he asked me to give up my job.

"When I was younger, I never had any hopes of becoming anything," I started, wiping at my tears with my hands. "I thought I'd end up married, waiting for my husband to take care of me and then become my mother. She got married young and gave up all of her own hopes and dreams and lost herself along the way. I didn't want that for myself, but I didn't think there could be anything else for me. Then Max found me on the boardwalk and for the first time in my life I had a dream, I had a desire, and I quickly realized all of the things I could have. I had a sense of purpose, but with independence and with independence I won't become my mother. I can't give it up, not now. If I did, I know that no matter how perfect you are, that I will become my mother. I'll regret, and I'll resent and sink into despair and I will ruin both of us. We would be so unhappy together, and I know that I will be unhappy without you, but I'd rather be alone and sad and heartbroken than to find myself in a failed, loveless marriage fifteen years from now."

Emmet's eyes glistened with tears. When I watched a few slip through, it almost brought me to my knees.

"Then don't quit," he said desperately. "Let me be the one to make the sacrifice like I wanted to in the first place."

"The result will be the same, Emmet. I can't be happy with you knowing what you threw away, and it would only be a matter of time before you regret and resent me. You can't tell me that you would be happy doing nothing with your life and following me around."

"I will be happy with you!" he shouted.

"Maybe at first, but after some time, you'll keep telling yourself that even though you're not, and you'll stay because you are the kind of man that would stay forever in an unhappy situation out of loyalty if nothing else."

My beautiful green eyed Emmet cried openly, letting his tears flow freely down his cheeks.

"There has to be some other way," he pleaded. "Don't do this. I can't live without you."

"There is no other way," I whispered and closed my eyes so I wouldn't have to watch him crying. It was destroying me inside.

"You can't do this," Emmet suddenly yelled, making my eyes snap open. He suddenly looked so angry, but I could still detect the pain under the anger. I felt it shooting through that tether right into my heart. "You can't make this decision for the both of us!"

"It's the right decision," I said softly.

"We can find another way," he said pathetically. "Give me some time to figure something else out."

I took a couple of weary steps towards him and put a hand on his chest. He stared down at it, and his tears splashed on my skin.

"We're eternally joined, Emmet," I sobbed softly. "That will never change. I will always love you, but this is not our time. Our time is not now."

He put his hands over my hand and cried hard, making his whole body shake. I pulled my hand from his and wrapped my arms around him. I sobbed on his chest as he cried into my neck. I wanted to change my mind and try to find another way, but there was no other way, and I think Emmet knew it too.

He grabbed a hold of my head and tilted it up to his face. His lips crushed mine in a kiss clouded with grief and desperation. Our tears slid to our connected lips and converged and seeped into our mouths, adding a salty taste to our bittersweet kiss.

I wrenched my mouth away from his, pulled out of his arms and stepped away from him. Before I chickened out, I pulled the beautiful engagement ring off of my finger and carefully put it on the glass coffee table in front of the couch. I ran then, because I couldn't take another moment of that utter destruction of our hearts. I ran out of his apartment and to the waiting car. I cranked the engine without looking back to see if Emmet had followed and sped away from the man who held my heart and the other half of my soul.

PART TWO

Frayed

Chapter Thirty-Seven

"Pancakes! Bacon! And Eggs!" Felix cheered, putting a plate loaded with the breakfast trio in front of me. He stood on the other side of the bar grinning at me. "I ordered it all by myself," he said proudly.

"Thank you, but I'm not hungry," I said, pushing the plate away. "I'll just have coffee."

He frowned, but poured me a mug of coffee and mixed in the right amount of cream and sugar for me and put it next to the plate.

"You should eat something," he said.

Opening the latest issue of *Vogue*, I shook my head without looking at him.

"Not hungry," I repeated.

"You're ridiculously thin, Donya."

"I am a supermodel," I said, picking up my coffee. "I am supposed to be thin."

"Sure, that explains your eating disorder," Felix said dryly.

I looked up at him as I sipped my coffee. I put the mug down and said, "I don't have an eating disorder. I am not hungry. I will eat later."

"Well, that's bullshit, and we both know it," he said. "I've been home for an entire month, and I haven't seen you eat more than four meals the entire time, and they weren't even meals. A handful of carrots or a few bites of a sandwich hardly qualifies as a meal."

"You only see me for a few minutes a day," I said, climbing off of the stool. "You don't know what I eat or don't eat."

"You're so fucking skinny that you look sick," he snapped. "Just appease me and eat a fucking bacon strip."

I sighed with impatience. I snatched a strip of bacon off of the plate and took a bite. Chewing felt like a chore that took way too much energy and the piece of meat tasted like paper, as did everything else I ate.

"Happy?" I asked Felix after I ate the bacon.

"It's bacon," he grumbled, snatching the plate of food off of the bar. "I expect a little more enthusiasm."

He threw the entire plate in the trash. I looked at him blankly before taking my coffee and magazine and heading back to my apartment.

"Thanks for the coffee," I said over my shoulder.

"Yeah, whatever," he mumbled.

I went into the apartment and started packing. I was going to do a photo shoot in Hawaii. Emmy was on her way up to New York so that she could fly out with me. We weren't going to have a lot of leisure time after the shoot, only a day, maybe two, but Emmy was all for it. She had been traveling with me more and more since she graduated high school. She said she wanted to suck up as much time with me as she could get because she would be away at Penn State starting in September and we wouldn't get to see much of each other.

I absently packed for the trip. I wasn't thinking of anything really; I just rather zoned out, but when I went to push my hair out of my face, I was startled to find my wrist naked. I stared at it, dumbfounded for a moment before I started to turn in a frantic circle, searching for my bracelet. When I didn't find it on my bureau or in the bathroom, I started tearing the clothes out of my suitcase. I found it about half way through, just lying there on a pair of shorts. I released a deep breath as I picked it up.

I inspected it to see if it was broken, but found nothing to indicate that it was. I slid it over my hand and back onto my wrist. I shook my wrist a little to see if it would come off. It didn't come off, but it slid dangerously low on my hand, so I knew it had probably fallen off with some help from a little friction from my clothes.

I sighed. Felix was right, of course, I had lost weight, and because of that, my wrist and hand were smaller, making it easy for the bracelet to slide off. I hadn't meant to lose the weight, but my appetite had been gone for nearly three months. I felt dead inside and dead people don't eat.

I hadn't spoken to or seen Emmet since the day we broke up. I had driven back to New York that night, crying until I was dehydrated. I had lain in bed completely devastated and half hoping that Emmet would come after me again. If he came after me again, I'd drop everything to be with him, even though I would risk becoming my mother. But he didn't come, and though it killed me that he didn't come, I was glad he didn't come. It was for the best for each of us.

I gave myself one more day to grieve, to feel bad for myself and Emmet. When I woke up the following morning, it was with a hardened heart and erected walls. Whatever that was soft in me dissolved. I became a machine, smiling at the right moments and speaking the appropriate things, but the smiles were empty and meaningless, and my words didn't ring sincere. I had emotionally cut myself off from most of the world, only leaving just enough heart for Emmy and Felix, but not much.

"I'm here," Emmy called from my living room.

"Hey, Jersey," I heard Felix say, entering from the penthouse.

"Hi," I heard Emmy say and could practically hear her grinning. She was always well behaved around Felix, which was hard considering how ill-behaved he could be, but I don't think she ever quite got over being in his presence.

I stepped out of the bedroom, holding the bracelet to my wrist.

"Hi, Em," I said to her.

She turned away from Felix and looked me over with a surprised look on her face, but she quickly covered it with a smile.

"Hey, D," she said. "Almost ready? Our flight leaves soon."

"Yeah," I nodded. "I'll be out in a minute."

I went back into my room, leaving the door open a crack. I heard Emmy whisper, "Why is she so skinny?"

"You know why," Felix answered back in a low murmur.

"You think it's because she's not over what happened between her and Emmet? Are you sure she doesn't have an eating disorder?"

"I think she does have an eating disorder, but it's because of what's going on inside of her."

"Which is?" Emmy implored, still whispering.

"Nothing," Felix said with a sigh. "There's nothing there."

I zipped up my suitcase and dug a pack of cigarettes out of my purse. It was a habit I picked up only a week after I lost—or gave up Emmet. It helped me keep my emotions buried. Maybe it was all psychological, but I did what I had to do.

I sat down on the edge of my bed, smoking a cigarette and listening to my friends talk about me as if I wasn't even there. I guess that would be right, though. Inside my shell of a body, I wasn't really there at all.

~~*

"Why can't I have an apartment like Emmet?" Emmy whined.

"Because you're *you*," Sam said with a hand on her hip.

"What is that supposed to mean?" Emmy demanded.

As mother and daughter began to bicker, Fred and I shook our heads and headed back to his SUV with the attached U-Haul trailer. It was the weekend before the start of Emmy's classes at Penn State. She and her parents had driven in from Jersey, but I flew in from New York, preferring to travel alone than to be stuck in a car with Sam for the drive to State College and the return trip.

"How are you doing, Kiddo?" Fred asked me as we walked to the car.

"Great," I lied. "I should be asking you that. All of the kids are gone now. How do you think that's going to feel when you get back?"

"I'm going to be stuck alone with Sam," he said, giving me a knowing look with gleaming eyes. "How do you think I'm going to feel?"

I managed a smile, because it seemed like the right moment to smile. Super Model Donya always knew when it was time to smile.

"I'm sure you will be fine," I said reassuringly.

We had a brief discussion about what to take in next, but before I could lift anything, Fred put his strong hand on my arm, making me look up at him, a bit surprised.

"Now, how are you really, Donya?" he asked.

I stared up at the man who was more of a father than my real father had ever been. Fred may have been slow catching on to my relationship with Emmet, but overall, he was always really good at knowing when something was wrong with me.

"Breathing," I finally answered and looked away.

"Just barely," he sighed. "I didn't want to ask you this because I didn't think it was possible, not with you anyway, but I'd be a bad parent if I didn't ask."

"Ask me what?" I looked back him with curiosity.

"Are you on drugs?" Fred asked, with a stern expression.

I almost laughed, like a real sincere laugh, but it died in my throat.

"No, I'm not on drugs, Fred," I answered.

"Because I heard that drugs run rampant in your business. A lot of girls are on something because they're stressed out or need to stay awake or stay thin."

"You're right," I said. "A lot of girls are on drugs for those reasons. I know a lot of them, but I'm not one of them. I promise."

I started to pick up a box, but he stopped me again.

"You are withdrawn and extremely thin," he said. "Those are signs of drug usage. Donya, if you are on something, I don't want to lecture you, Kiddo. I want you to get help."

Frustrated, I turned my body fully to look up at him.

"Fred, I am not on drugs," I said irritably. "I will gladly piss in a cup or give you a hair or blood sample to be analyzed, and you will find that I am telling the truth. But if that's what you want…"

I turned away again. Frustration and anger were the only two emotions I let out of the cage. They were necessary, especially in my business.

"Okay," Fred said with a sigh. "I believe you. You're not on drugs. I'll ask you one more question, and then I'll let it go."

"Fine," I answered.

"Does this personality change have to do with Emmet?"

I looked up at Fred. I gave him one quick nod, grabbed a box, and walked back towards the dorms.

After we helped Emmy get some of her things unpacked and met her roommate, we all went out to dinner. I ordered a small meal to appease the stares of my family, but since I had no desire to eat the food and it still tasted like paper to me, I mostly nibbled at it.

Sam and Fred were going to stay in a hotel nearby and leave in a couple of days, but I was flying back out that night. After dinner, they drove me to the airport. Emmy got out of the car with me at the curb and hugged me fiercely.

"Donya, please take care of yourself," she said in a soft voice before pulling away. "And for the love of god, eat a damn sandwich!"

I rolled my eyes and gave her a genuine smile, one of few that were only reserved for her and Felix.

"And quit smoking," she admonished, shaking a finger at me.

"Who are you? My mother?"

Em bit her lip and looked as if she wanted to say something more.

"Spit it out," I sighed. "What is it now?"

"I just thought you would like to know that Emmet goes back to class on Monday."

No one ever talked about Emmet around me. It was like they understood that discussing Emmet wasn't an option. Even Sam managed to keep her big mouth shut, but I was glad to hear that Emmet did go back to school. I felt a small stir of emotion. It was bittersweet.

"Good," I said with a small nod. "Then he's doing exactly what he should be doing. Thank you for telling me."

She gave a small shrug. "I wouldn't have known if Dad hadn't told me. Emmet doesn't talk to me that much anymore."

I felt like that was my fault, but before I could say anything about it, Emmy said, "Which is fine, because I don't really talk to any of my siblings."

Fred blew the horn then, and we took our cue. I gave her one last hug and went inside.

As soon I got back to New York I had to pack for a shoot in Milan. By Monday morning, I would be on my rightful path in life, and Emmet would be back on his.

Chapter Thirty-Eight

Every Thanksgiving Sam and Fred throw a party. They invite every single person they know and their relatives to the big house in Louisiana. There is always enough food to feed a small country and people stay late into the night, hanging around the bonfire, milling around the inside of the house and hanging out on the porch.

I had not planned on going. I didn't want to see Emmet, and I didn't want him to stay away because they were more his family than mine, but Emmy said that Emmet was staying in Cambridge and having dinner with friends and was not expected to be in Louisiana. I didn't necessarily want to be around all of those people, but Felix had taken to calling me Cat Lady, and since he was having his family over for the holiday, I decided to leave. That way his family could use my apartment as it was originally intended and I wouldn't have to listen to his commentary about my lack of a social life or my thin frame.

I arrived at the house two days before the holiday. I was exhausted since I had just returned from L.A. only a few hours before I began the long drive from New York. I drove straight through and arrived in the wee hours of the morning. As I climbed the steps to the silent, dark house, I was reminded of the night Emmet surprised me in the kitchen after making almost the same drive. I could almost smell his cologne, and hell, I could almost taste the lemon cake we ate that night.

I used my old key to let myself into the house. I locked the door behind me and started through the living room to take the stairs to the second floor. I looked at the couch, half expecting to find Emmet's form lying there, but I was disappointed to find it empty.

I climbed the stairs and quietly slipped into the room I had to share with Emmy. She was sound asleep, curled up on one side of the bed. Tired beyond reason, I kicked my shoes off, stripped out of my clothes and quickly changed into comfortable sleeping clothes and got into the bed.

I was so tired, but I couldn't sleep. The house held too many memories. Every time I closed my eyes, I saw Emmet's face, heard Emmet's voice, and felt Emmet's touch. He haunted me every night when I tried to sleep, but being in that house made it so much worse. I hadn't even spent the night in the house in New Jersey since we broke up.

I still felt Emmet moving around in the world. That tether never dissolved, it never severed, and it was strong. Sometimes when my chest ached, and I felt a painful pressure, I had to wonder if it was Emmet. Was Emmet upset? Was Emmet hurting? Could Emmet feel me too?

When I finally drifted off to sleep, Emmet came to me in my dreams, and everything was perfect between us. He had finished school and my career had shifted to something that allowed me to stay in one place most of the time. We were happy, and we were in love. It was as if our broken hearts had never happened, but then I woke up and realized it was just a dream. The reality of my life set in, I allowed that hard cold hardness to take over, and I found a way to breathe.

~~*

By mid-afternoon on Thanksgiving Day, the party was in full swing. The yard was crowded with people, from the very young to the very old. There were a couple dozens of tables full of food, and even more food roasted on spits and sizzled on grills.

I did my best to be social and speak to people I hadn't spoken to in a long time, and to introduce myself to those I had never met. I spent some time with Fred Jr.'s children and Charlotte's kids, too, and I rubbed Lucy's pregnant belly. I appeased Sam by eating a hotdog, but it felt like a rock sitting in my stomach, so soon after I ate it, I escaped into the house and into the upstairs bathroom and puked it up. I brushed my teeth and started back downstairs, rubbing at the discomfort in my chest.

I wanted a cigarette, badly. I felt like I was about to puke up my heart next by the way it was slamming around in my chest like it wanted to get out. Whatever emotions that were trying to climb their way into my chest needed to be suppressed. I walked over to a group of smokers standing away from the bulk of the people. I pulled my clove flavored cigarettes out of the front pocket of the lightweight hoodie I had on, lit up, and fell into conversation with a girl I used to occasionally hang out with during the summers as a kid.

While I feigned to be interested in her life, my hand busily rubbed at my chest. The pressure and aching were intensifying, so I took deeper drags of the cigarette. For no reason that was clear to me at the time, I looked back towards the busy area where all of the food was, and even with the dozens of other bodies moving about, I was immediately met by a pair of green eyes. I looked away quickly and tried not to panic.

"Hey, are you okay?" the girl asked me.

"Fine," I said quickly. "I'm sorry. I just…have to…" I didn't even finish the sentence before I walked away from her.

I hurried in the opposite direction, away from the party, and away from those damn green eyes. I puffed on my cigarette until it was down to the filter. I stopped to snub it out against a tree. I didn't want to flick it into the grass, so I put it back into my pack, and while I was at it, I took another cigarette out and lit it up.

I headed into the woods, hoping that none of the kids had ventured out there. I just needed to get away from everyone and put some distance between me and Emmet, because my chest was burning with pain and it wasn't from the cigarettes.

I leaned against a tree and tried to get myself together. I didn't understand why Emmet was there when he had told the family he wasn't coming. I had to wonder if he did that on purpose, so that he could run into me there, but then he knew where I lived in New York. I had no doubt in my mind that Felix would help Emmet out and lock me in a room with him.

"What the fuck," I muttered to the tree across from me.

I let the cigarette sit in a corner of my mouth as I closed my eyes. I was trying to think of what my next move should be. I couldn't hide in the woods all day.

I rubbed at my chest again and felt tears forming behind my eyes. I had worked hard to keep those horrible emotions away, but they were bursting from their chains, and I didn't know how to stop it.

My cigarette was plucked from my mouth, and I opened my eyes and whirled around, prepared to yell at Emmy for sneaking up on me, but I found myself face to face with Emmet. He snuffed out the cigarette and then tossed it away. In his other hand was a plate loaded with food. He picked up a can of soda he had put down on the ground and then he met my eyes and thrust the plate in my face.

I took a step back and looked at the plate like it was poisonous.

Emmet took a menacing step towards me and thrust the plate at me again.

"You look like a fucking skeleton," he growled between gritted teeth.

With a shaky hand, I reached out and took the plate from him. I expected him to go away after that, but he stood there, staring at me.

"Eat something," he snapped after a moment of mutual staring.

"I'm not hungry," I whispered.

Another menacing step from Emmet had me backed into my tree.

"Eat something or I'll start shoving food down your throat," he promised.

I looked at the plate and chose the least offending item, a small buttered roll, and took a nibble. I started to put it back, but a glare from Emmet stopped me. I took the roll a little more seriously and took bigger bites. It was tasteless, as was the piece of turkey he made me eat next.

Every few bites, Emmet silently handed me the can of soda to help wash down the food. When he tried to make me eat some kind of potato salad next, my stomach finally revolted. I turned away from him and retched violently. I felt my hair being pulled back away from my face as I released all of the contents of my stomach.

I was in tears by the time I finished. My emotions had burst free and were running amok. I wiped my mouth with one sleeve and my tears and nose with my other sleeve. I felt humiliated. I felt angry. I felt overwhelming sadness, and the shards of my broken heart poked at me without mercy.

Emmet put his hands on my shoulders and pushed me up against a tree. He stood close to me, but not close enough for our bodies to touch. He looked at me with anger and pain.

"You wanted to live your own life, Donya, and I fully expected to find you satisfied with your decision. Instead, I find you smoking cigarettes and practically emaciated. You said you didn't want to be your mother, but you are. You're just another version of her. Get your shit together, Donya, and prove to me that breaking our hearts was worth it."

He looked at me with great sadness for a moment and then left me alone sobbing softly in the woods.

Chapter Thirty-Nine

My flight landed in New York a little after nine p.m. on New Year's Eve. Getting to the penthouse near Times Square so close to midnight was going to be tricky, but I was going to try very hard to get there so that I could ring in the New Year with Emmy and Felix.

During one of Emmy's visits to New York over the summer, she and Felix kind of started dating. I say kind of because both of them claimed that it wasn't that serious, but she was spending time at the penthouse whether I was there or not, and a few times Felix met her out by Penn State, out of the public eye, of course. To make me farther question the seriousness of their relationship, the pair was throwing a New Year's Eve party together.

I had told them that I wouldn't be able to make it home for the celebration. I thought for sure that I wouldn't be able to wrap up the television appearance I made in London and hopped across the pond in time. I had accepted the fact that I was going to be spending the holiday in the U.K., but my portion of the show had been taped earlier in the day to be played later that evening, and I was lucky enough to get one of the last tickets for a flight to New York. I kept the information to myself, choosing to surprise Emmy and Felix upon my arrival.

It had been a long and eventful year. I had worked hard, and it had paid off. I made the *Sports Illustrated Swimsuit Edition*, I was an angel in the Victoria's Secret runway show, and I had several reoccurring roles in a British prime time reality television show.

After Emmet damn near force fed me in the woods a little more than a year before, I had snuck away from the party and headed back to New York to get my head together. After a few days of deep thinking, I realized how true his words had been. I was just a different version of my mom, and that was exactly something I didn't want. It took some time, but I got myself together and made the necessary changes. I was still a little hard on the inside, but I had to be to survive.

A lot had changed in that year. Fred and Sam were spending more and more time in Louisiana with Emmy gone away to college. I handed my finances over to Emmy because I didn't have time to keep track of what was going in and what was coming out. Some may question why I would put my financial livelihood in the hands of a young, tequila drinking college student, but I trusted her, and she was one of the most organized people I knew. She kept me and my money in check, and amazingly, she somehow made it grow.

Felix had taken a break from making movies and took a leading role in a new Broadway show, leaving him in New York full time. Though he could be rather obnoxious at times, I liked coming home from a trip and finding him there. We had settled into comfortable routines with each other. Whatever feelings he may have had for me at one time had passed, but we were still very close, and he was still a big flirt.

I had not seen or spoken to Emmet since that day in Louisiana, but I had sent him a card when he graduated from college. He started law school, and he was actually working for a paycheck at the attorney's office a few days a week. I still missed him, and I still felt tethered to him, but I went on with my life and was glad that he was moving on with his.

Sometimes I could feel him close by, and I never knew if I imagined things or if he was somewhere in the city. Once, I swore I caught a glimpse of the back of his head in the crowds of Manhattan. By the time I made myself move to go after him he was gone, but the bind between us had felt alive and excited, so I had every reason to believe it was really him.

I was desperate for the day when it wouldn't hurt either of us for me to pick up the phone and call him. I was eager to find some kind of common ground between us so that I could have him in my life again, even if on a small level. I had been tolerating living without him, but I wasn't sure how much longer I could do it. There were some things in the world that are simply intolerable and living without your soul mate is one of them.

Earlier in the year when I was concentrating on fixing myself, out of want of something to do with my hands besides smoking a cigarette, I picked up a pencil and a notepad and started doodling; except the more my doodle took shape, I realized it wasn't a doodle at all. It was a dress, one that I had created in my own mind. Soon, I was sketching clothing designs for women, men, and children.

I wasn't much of an artist, and I wasn't even sure if my designs were any good. I hadn't planned on showing anyone, but I had found that the hobby was soothing and relaxing. Between my busy schedule, my internal struggles, and my broken heart, I needed something soothing and relaxing.

I started carrying sketching pencils and a sketch pad with me when I traveled. On an airplane ride, for example, while everyone else was sleeping or trying to read a book, I would have my pad on my lap, and my ideas would float from my mind right onto the paper via my fingers.

Even as I rode in the back of the cab on the way to the penthouse, I was sketching in the dim light. As we got closer to Times Square and traffic became thicker, I put the pad and pencils away and had the driver let me out, even though I was still several blocks away. My bags were heavy, and chances were that any good pickpocket would relieve me of half of my belongings before I got to the penthouse, but I didn't have much of a choice. The cab wasn't going to get any closer. I pulled my hat down over my ears and forged ahead.

As I took the elevator to the top floor a grueling forty-five minutes later, I wondered where Emmet was and who he was with. I wondered if he was out in the streets of New York waiting for the ball to drop with some of his friends from school. I even wondered if Stella was with him, but the idea didn't bother me as it would have in the past.

I felt a pressure in my chest that indicated that Emmet was near, but neither Felix nor Emmy had mentioned anything about having him at their party. Besides, Emmy and Emmet rarely spoke anymore, and whatever friendship he had been forming with Felix when Emmet and I were together dissolved along with our relationship.

I bypassed the entrance to the penthouse and headed down the hall toward my apartment. There was no denying there was a major party happening behind the penthouse doors. The music was blaring, people were loudly chattering, laughing, and yelling, and there was a distinct sound of glasses and beer bottles clinking.

After my long flight, I wanted to take a quick shower and change into something festive before joining the party. I still had about an hour before the ball began its descent and it wasn't like I had far to go. Pushing away the discomfort in my chest, I took a quick shower and slipped on a blue sequin baby doll mini dress I had been dying to put on. I made quick work of putting my hair into a messy, but fashionable bun, hastily put on a subtle amount of makeup, and then pushed my feet into my favorite designer black pumps. I gave myself a quick spin in the mirror and headed next door.

As I moved through the crowd in search of either Felix or Emmy, anxiety fluttered through my chest. People I knew stopped me to talk, but I could barely hold a conversation over the loud music and the loud thudding of my heart. By the time I spied Felix and Emmy on the other side of the room I was having trouble breathing. It was as if I was on the verge of a panic attack, but with no trigger. There was no less than a hundred and fifty people jammed into the penthouse, but I was used to big and crazy parties; I'd been to enough of them since my career began. The proximity to all of the other bodies shouldn't have bothered me at all.

Maybe you're just tired, I told myself. *You've been up for thirty hours.*

I didn't care how tired I was; I was going to push through whatever psychological thing I was going through and watch that damn ball drop with my friends. I had given them so little of my time over the years; I wasn't about to give up.

I was only about six feet from Emmy and Felix. They had both spotted me and looked excited to see me. Emmy waved me over to where they were standing and I started to take a step, but something stopped me. It was as if someone had physically prevented me from taking another step towards my friends. I put a hand to my chest to battle the evil butterflies flipping out in there and then slowly turned my head to look over my shoulder.

"Emmet," I whispered to myself when I saw him staring at me from the other side of the room.

I couldn't figure out how he did that, how he always managed to draw me right to his gaze no matter how many bodies were between us. Hell, I could have probably found his gaze across a sold-out football stadium.

Emmet gave me a small nod. I nodded back and then somehow found my feet and made them move towards Emmy and Felix. I allowed hugs and kisses and questions about my trip and work, but I wanted to ask them what the hell Emmet was doing there. However, it wasn't my place. He and Felix were on good terms despite their lack of friendship, and he was still Emmy's brother despite the rift between them, so I didn't ask.

I pretended that it didn't bother me. I tried to pretend he wasn't there at all, but that was impossible. Every time he moved, I felt a tug on the line, and I was forced to look up and meet his eyes. There was not one time that I looked for him and did not find him already watching me, oblivious to the people talking and laughing around him. With every glance, my eyes stayed fixed on his a little longer than the time before, until I was no longer glancing, but openly staring. His green eyes burrowed into me and sent waves of warmth spreading beneath my skin.

When I was forced to look away to acknowledge someone's attempt at conversation, my eyes constantly moved back to Emmet's. It seemed that he didn't turn away from me even when someone was trying to get his attention. He was ever watchful, like if he stopped staring at me I would disappear. I could relate because every time I looked away I felt a small panic that when I looked back he would not be there and that I had imagined the whole thing.

When there were only a few short minutes left of the twentieth century, Emmet called to me. Not with his lips, and not with a wag of his finger. His eyes implored, but more than that, I felt as if he was tugging on the tether. His heart was calling mine, and at that moment I knew I would always answer, I would always obey.

As the bulk of the party turned towards the wall of glass for a view of the ball, I started to push through the small sea of bodies, following the tangled soul-infused rope to the man it was attached to. I lost sight of Emmet when a few drunk, large men moved in front of me. They were cast members in Felix's play. I couldn't remember their names and I didn't care to, even as they blocked my path to make small talk. They couldn't understand why I would want to move away from the focal point of the party.

In a bit of a panic, I looked around to find an easier route to Emmet, but there were people everywhere. It seemed as if the party had grown exponentially since I first arrived less than an hour before. Having that many people in one room had to be some kind of fire and safety violation, but I would have happily burned alive at midnight if I was burning in Emmet's arms.

With only a minute left, the excitement grew as the ball began to drop outside. I turned my head to see the enormous glittering globe beginning its descent with sadness, because I didn't think I'd make it to Emmet in time. I had started to second guess whether or not he had summoned me or if it was something I had wanted so badly that I imagined it. Why hadn't he met me halfway if he really called to me?

My body went lax as I gave up, believing that I had definitely conjured the entire thing. I was beginning to wish that there were a pair of sheers large and sharp enough to cut through that invisible thread when a hand closed over my arm. Before I could even turn to see who had grabbed me, I was being pulled through the crowd at top speed. When we broke through the throngs of people, Emmet took my hand into his, and together we hurried down the corridor that led to my apartment.

With only fifteen seconds left to spare, we burst into my apartment and rushed over to the glass. We looked out at the ball hanging over thousands and thousands of people counting in one loud voice. When the ball stopped, a tremendously loud chorus of Happy New Year was heard from the streets below and the party next door. Emmet looked into my eyes, and I knew in that instant that I had not imagined what I felt.

"Happy New Year, Donya," he whispered on my lips.

"Happy New Year, Emmet," I whispered back.

His mouth sweetly took mine as one hand pressed against the small of my back, and the other gently held my face. My arms wrapped around his waist as my tongue lovingly met his.

"Auld Lang Syne" was being sung by thousands as horns blew, noisemakers clanged loudly, ticket tape floated through the air, and fireworks were going off above the jumbo Tron. So much was happening around us, but I only knew it because I saw the news footage the following day. The only thing I heard was our low moans. The only thing I saw was blissful darkness because my eyes were closed as I held onto Emmet for dear life.

The only thing I could feel was him, his soft lips, his tongue dancing in and out of my mouth, his arm around my body and his hand on my skin. For several minutes, the only thing I cared about in the world was being in Emmet's arms and feeling Emmet's kiss as my lips grew delightfully sore from our growing eagerness.

   I knew it wouldn't last forever. I knew in the end he would have to walk away, but I was going to taste every corner of his mouth until then and enjoy how my skin warmed under his touch for as long as I could. When it was all over, the cord that bound us together would stretch painfully, and I would be bereft, but I was willing to suffer the pain and sorrow for that one moment of undeniable, eternal love.

Chapter Forty

The party raged on next door and outside. My body was pressed up against the cool glass; my legs wrapped securely around Emmet's waist as he kissed and nibbled the skin on my shoulder. The strap of my dress hung limply after Emmet had slipped it off moments before. My fingers curled in his hair and with a small tug I brought his lips back to mine.

My body tingled with need as Emmet pressed his erection against me. My dress had long ago been hiked up to my waist. The windows were tinted on the outside for privacy and to reduce some of the heat from the sun's rays, but at that moment, I didn't care if my entire ass was on display. The sun could burn a hole in my back, and I wouldn't notice. I tightened my legs around his waist and moaned softly as I deepened our kiss.

One of his hands was splayed across my thigh, caressing and kneading. The fingers of his other hand trailed softly over my cheek as we kissed. His thumb pulled gently on my chin to force my mouth to open more. His hand grazed back across my cheek, over my ear and into my hair where he worked to release my hair from the bun. It fell across my bare shoulders, and Emmet growled appreciatively as his fingers combed through my tresses.

My fingers moved over his broad shoulders to the front of his shirt. As I began to unbutton it, he gave me the space I needed to work, but his lips didn't leave mine until I had finished with the last button. He gazed into my eyes as I pushed the shirt over his shoulders and down his arms until it fell away to the floor.

It was the dead of winter, and he had not worn an undershirt under his dress shirt, but I was thankful for the immediate access to his smooth skin that covered muscles that had been worked into perfection since the last time I had the pleasure of being so intimate with him. I dipped my head and kissed his throat, eliciting a low groan from his chest. I kissed my way down his skin until I got to his appreciative pecks. I sunk my teeth into the flesh, making him hiss and tangle his hand in my hair. He yanked my head up and devoured my mouth as my hands moved down his body. I placed my hand over his jeans, and his erection twitched in my palm.

Emmet pulled his mouth away from mine and eagerly tugged my dress down over my breasts until they were naked and available for his touch. He took a hard peak and rolled it in his fingers, making me moan and squeeze his cock in response. He bent to take the other nipple into his mouth. I cried out as his tongue flicked over the sensitive point. Emmet moaned as he sucked as much flesh into his mouth as he could while twirling and pinching my other nipple. I threw my head back and moaned loudly as I stroked him through his jeans.

Suddenly, he released my breasts and gently smacked my thigh, indicating that he wanted me to stand. Carefully, I disentangled myself from him and put my high heeled feet on the floor. He kissed me briefly on the lips before yanking my dress down from my waist. I stepped out of it, and he threw it aside. I knew what he intended to do as his fingers stroked through my moist heat, but there was something I wanted too. Before he could lower himself to his knees to drag his tongue through my center, I dropped to mine and got to work opening his belt.

"Donya," he objected, but I ignored him and released the button on his jeans.

He tried to object again and tried to step back, but I had just pulled down his zipper and even as he went to move away, I reached into his boxers and grabbed a hold of his hard cock. He groaned and looked down at me with molten emerald eyes as I pulled it out and flicked my tongue across the bulbous head.

"Donya," he said my name in a groan as I took him into my mouth.

Holding the base of his cock in one hand, I gently squeezed his balls in my other hand and started to suck him feverishly. He put one hand in my hair and the other hand slapped against the glass to brace himself. I kept my eyes on his as his slightly salty, but clean tasting cock slid in and out of my mouth. I pulled my head back until the tip of his manhood was on my lips. I licked away the clear fluid that had seeped out and then closed my lips over the head and sucked hard. Emmet cursed and grunted and thrust his cock deeper into my mouth. I moaned and nearly gagged as he thrust harder the next time.

"Stand up," Emmet commanded hoarsely as he stepped back. His cock left my mouth, and I actually pouted. He chuckled softly and helped me to my feet.

I watched as he kicked off his shoes and quickly removed his pants. He pulled me against his body and my own body reacted hotly at being skin to skin with him. My hard nipples pressed against his hard chest and his erection pressed against my belly. He kissed me, hard, nipping at my tongue and lips, teeth crashing with mine.

When he broke the kiss, I put my hand on his shoulder, fully expecting him to lift me into his arms and enter me that way, but to my surprise, he took my hand and spun me around and pressed me against the cool glass. With a hard nudge of his hand, I parted my legs. Emmet put one hand on my waist and guided his cock to my entrance with the other hand. He paused before entering me. He kissed my shoulder and then my neck before I felt his tongue on the curve of my ear.

"I love you, do you understand?" he asked hoarsely.

The words squeezed at my heart and made me gasp. I was painfully reminded that Emmet would be gone in a matter of hours, and we would have to continue on our own, separate paths.

Finally, I nodded. I understood. It was going to hurt both of us when it was all over, but I didn't think either of us could stop if we wanted to.

I nodded again and bit back the despair that started to climb up my throat from my chest. Emmet must have felt it too, because he rested his forehead on my shoulder and breathed heavily for a moment. Then he straightened up and with one swift thrust, he had buried himself inside of me. I cried out and braced myself against the glass.

The streets below was still filled with people celebrating. I felt like if anyone of them looked hard enough they would see me, naked, wet, and happy and shattered, pressed against the glass as Emmet thrust his beautiful engorged cock in and out of my wanting body.

Breathing heavily and groaning, Emmet turned my head at an angle so that I could kiss him. I was losing my mind with pleasure. It had been so long since he had been inside of me. My sex gripped at his cock to keep him there. I hadn't been with anyone else since Emmet. My body only wanted his. Our bodies were made for each other.

He released me from the hot kiss and banded his arm across my neck in a possessive hold. He held onto my hip tightly, digging his fingers into my flesh as he slammed into me from behind.

"No matter what," he breathed and then groaned. "You will always belong to me."

His words sent me over the edge suddenly, screaming his name as my pussy clenched and squeezed at his cock. Emmet covered my mound with the palm of his hand and pressed hard, prolonging my orgasm until my knees were barely holding me up.

"No one else will ever completely own you," Emmet growled in my ear. "I am the only one who will ever completely own you, and you are the only one that will ever completely own me. Do you understand?"

"Yes!" I screamed as he punched his cock into me violently. "Always yours. Always yours," I repeated over and over as he continued to slam into me so hard I thought for sure we'd go flying through the glass.

"Donya," he groaned my name. His arm around my neck tightened and the fingers of his other hand made hard circles on my clit. "Come with me, baby," he commanded.

His cock throbbed and seemed to swell impossibly thicker inside of me before I felt the first stream of semen shoot inside of me. Emmet began to curse and yell as my orgasm slammed into me so hard that it was painful. Tears fell from my eyes as I sobbed through an intense, heartbreaking orgasm as Emmet filled me with his seed.

He was still hard a minute later when he slid out of me. My legs gave out on me, and I started to fall to the floor in a tearful mess, but Emmet caught me and effortlessly lifted me into his arms. He carried me into my bedroom and gently lay me down on the bed. He pulled my shoes off and then climbed in behind me. He pulled me into his arms and held me as I cried. He didn't say anything, because what could he say that would make any difference? But he kissed my shoulder, my hair, my cheek and anything else he could reach. I turned my face toward him, and he kissed me slowly and lovingly as his thumb caressed my cheek.

We made love again, slowly, stretching every minute as much as we possibly could. Even though my heart was breaking all over again, I felt loved and secure in his arms. Every touch, every kiss, and every gaze was memorized and filed away for me to reminisce upon later.

I fell asleep with my legs tangled in Emmet's and my face pressed against his chest, my head tucked under his chin. He rubbed my back and my hair as I inhaled his inebriating scent. When I woke up in bed alone, the sun was out and lighting up my entire room. I didn't have to look around my apartment or the penthouse to know that Emmet was gone. The tether was stretching painfully, and the overwhelming sense of loss hung around me in a dark cloud. I picked up the pillow that Emmet had lain on and held it to my nose. It smelled just like him, and I found some relief that he had at least left his scent behind.

I hugged the pillow to my chest and stared out at the cloudless, sunny day as I tried to mentally and emotionally put myself back together.

Chapter Forty-One

A year and a half later, Sam was demanding that Emmy, Emmet, and I make some time to visit Louisiana for a few days. None of us had really been down there much over the years.

The guilt trip Sam put on us was thick, and since I really had not spent much time with the family at all since that fateful Thanksgiving when Emmet turned me in the right direction, I gave in. Emmy gave in grudgingly, and I wasn't sure how easily Emmet gave in, but he did.

I had to turn down an offer to make it work, but I was ready for a bit of a break anyway. I was beginning to feel a little burned out from all of the traveling and working. I wasn't even close to the top of the modeling totem pole, but my life was still chaotic and hectic, but then, that's what I had wanted.

So the Wednesday before the long Memorial Day weekend, I met Emmy at the house in New Jersey where we would fly out of Philly later that evening.

"I think we should have a drink, don't you think so?" Emmy asked cheerfully soon after I arrived. She busied herself getting out glasses and bottles of alcohol while I sat at the kitchen table.

"A drink will knock me on my ass," I said tiredly.

"Right, but you'll need a drink for what I have to tell you," Emmy said, glancing at me over her shoulder.

"God, are you pregnant?"

She scowled. "No, I'm not pregnant. I'm not even having sex," she scoffed.

"Well, that's just completely unbelievable since you're the biggest ho' I know," I teased...kind of.

"I think I screwed around enough as a teenager," she said soberly. "I date, but I don't give the booty up."

"You always make me laugh when you talk about having a booty," I chuckled.

She looked at me accusingly and then tried to get a look at her own ass before looking back to me. That made me laugh more.

"What are you trying to say? You don't think I have a booty?"

"It just sounds funny coming out of your mouth," I said with a shrug.

She placed a tall, purple drink in front of me. I eyed it with some amount of fear. I still didn't drink much. Emmy could drink the whole glass and be ready for seconds before I even had three sips. She would be able to function perfectly fine, and I'd be knocked out.

"Is that some kind of comment about me being a white girl?" Emmy asked, taking the seat across from me.

"I didn't say anything about you being a white girl," I said, but looked at her like that was totally what I meant. "Anyway, what do you want to tell me?" I gasped and leaned forward. "Are you getting back together with Felix?"

The pair had stopped seeing each other soon after the New Year's Eve party. There didn't seem to be any animosity between them. They just went their separate ways, confirming their claims that their relationship had not been serious.

"Why would you even ask me that?" Emmy asked, looking at me with mild irritation. "That's not what I have to tell you, and FYI we were never really 'together'. Take a sip of your drink. Take a few sips."

I raised an eyebrow at her as she waited for me to do as she instructed. Whatever she had to tell me must have been deep if she wanted me drunk for it.

"I prefer to remain lucid," I said, pushing the glass aside. "Just tell me whatever it is you have to tell me."

Emmy sighed heavily. "Okay, but first I need a drink."

I waited while she took a long sip from the glass.

"Please, the suspense is killing me," I said in a bored tone and rested my cheek in my hand.

"Okay, I won't beat around the bush," she said.

"Em, you have beaten the fuck out of the bush already. Just say it."

She took a breath and then blurted out her next words. "Emmet is bringing a girl with him to Louisiana. I think they're serious. I mean, they would have to be for him to expose the girl to our mother."

I raised an eyebrow. "Is that it? Is that what you needed me to drink for?"

Her forehead wrinkled. "Not that I would want to hurt you or anything, but why are you not surprised and why don't you look heartbroken?"

"Because we have been broken up for three years, Emmy."

"But I thought that maybe you guys were just going to wait a few years and get back together when your career slows down, and Emmet is out of school."

"So, what…did you think he was supposed to save himself for me? What a romantic notion."

Emmy frowned. "I thought…I don't know…I thought…"

"Would that have been fair to either of us?" I asked her. "To be alone for years and years? We were both so young at the time; so much could change in a few years, Emmy."

"You still love each other. That hasn't changed," she pointed out.

She knew that Emmet and I had left the party together on New Year's Eve; she and Felix had seen us make our escape, but she thought that we just kissed and talked. I didn't bother correcting her, because the night had been sacred and somehow speaking of it to her would have tarnished that.

"No, that will never change," I admitted. "But it doesn't change the fact that we are not together."

Emmy was quiet for a minute, sipping her drink and staring at the fake fruit basket in the middle of the table.

"Do you think you will want him later? When your career has shifted into something more manageable?" Emmy finally asked.

I would always want Emmet, but I didn't want to tell Emmy that. It would lead off into a whole other conversation that would leave me feeling more sad and sorry, and I was sad and sorry enough.

"There isn't any point in me thinking that far ahead, because I have no idea when that time will be or what I will be doing or where he will be or what he will be doing," I said to her.

"Are you going to be okay with him and *her*?" Emmy questioned worriedly.

"I'll be fine," I promised as I got up from the table. I made a show of checking my watch. "Don't get too drunk or they won't let you on the plane," I warned her. "Benny will be here to pick us up in an hour."

"What's up with that anyway?" she asked with a snort.

"Nothing is up with that," I called over my shoulder as I exited the room.

"Benny and Donya sitting in a tree," she began to sing, but I ignored her as I went up the stairs.

On New Year's Day, I got an email from Benny. He wished me a happy new year and asked the obligatory questions one asks when you're contacting a friend you only speak to once or twice a year. It took me a day or two to answer him, but I did, as I always did. Usually the emails came to a halt after a couple of days, usually on my end, but this time I kept it up for a few weeks, even when I was working away from home. The emails turned into phone calls, and the phone calls turned into sporadic platonic dates. My schedule was still insane, so I didn't see him much, but he didn't seem to mind.

I had no doubt that I initially latched onto Benny because I wanted to shake Emmet from my system, but then I realized I really liked him, as a friend, of course. Whether or not Benny liked me more than that, I never considered it, even when Emmy made stupid remarks about it.

Even though I just wanted Benny as a friend, I kind of wished he was going with me to Louisiana, just so that I wouldn't look like the loser ex-girlfriend when Emmet showed up with his new girl. Despite how strong and sure I appeared to be to Emmy, it hurt me deeply to know that Emmet was with someone else. Em was right, it had to be pretty serious if he was willing to expose the woman to Sam.

Did he love her? Was he *in love* with her? Did he mean it when he said that I would always own him completely no matter what? If that was the case, did he see my face when he kissed her? Was it my body he envisioned when he was intimate with her?

My chest hurt just thinking about the long weekend ahead, but I had to remind myself, as I had been doing since our breakup, that my pain was my own doing. I chose my career and forced Emmet to choose his, and that was where it left us, him with a new girlfriend, and me still alone.

~~*

Emmy was going to be staying in Louisiana for a couple of weeks, so she had more luggage than I did. Benny helped us lug it all into the airport and get it checked in. He walked us to the gate, insisting that he'd hang around until we boarded.

"Well, isn't that sweet," Emmy drawled and then looked at me, batting her eyelashes. "Donya, isn't Benny sweet?"

I narrowed my eyes at her for a fraction of a second before agreeing with her.

"Yes, he is indeed very sweet," I answered and smiled at him.

"Well, I am going to call Mayson and see how she's doing in her new program," Emmy said, walking backward and grinning entirely too much for a phone call to a struggling Mayson. "I'll be back in a little while. Why don't you two sit down and chit chat?"

If I had something to throw at her at that moment, I would have. I glared daggers at her until she winked and turned her back on me.

"She's a nut job," Benny joked, gesturing to a pair of chairs.

"Like mother like daughter," I said, sitting down.

Benny sat down beside me. He leaned over with his elbows on his knees and his hands clasped together. I surreptitiously checked him out as I always did. He was a good looking guy. I would have had to have been blind to miss that. His body was in fantastic shape, all lean muscle, and tanned skin. He had dark hair, cut short on the sides and a little longer on the top. His brown eyes were warm and open and, okay, a little sexy. He also had a nice pair of lips that he occasionally bit down on. I really liked when he bit his lower lip.

I nearly smacked myself in the head. I had been looking at him for too long, and he noticed.

"Do I have something on my face or something?" he asked, but I had a feeling he knew I was simply checking him out.

"No," I said and looked away.

"You know while you were locking up the house, Emmy invited me down for the weekend?"

My head snapped back to him.

"She did not," I said, but I knew she probably most likely did.

Benny nodded with a small chuckle. "I told her I appreciated the invitation, but unless I got it from you, I would have to decline."

"You wouldn't decline if I invited you?"

His eyes moved down to my lips before meeting my eyes again. "No, I wouldn't decline, but I figured if you wanted to ask me, you would have already."

"Oh," I said and suddenly felt like an asshole. I didn't even consider seriously bringing anyone, not even Felix, who had an open invitation. I especially didn't consider Benny, even though he was already familiar with the family.

"No big deal," he said, waving it off.

"Well, no, it's not that I wouldn't enjoy having you there," I said hastily. "It's just that Sam and Emmy and possibly even Emmet would make a big deal out of it, you know?"

"Yeah, I get it." He nodded, but he wasn't smiling anymore. I didn't blame him. Even to my ears, what I'd just said sounded like an insult.

"It's not that I wouldn't want…to…you know…" I gestured wildly with my hands between us. "But my schedule is insane, and I never stay in one place for very long."

Benny looked at me intently.

"Donya, I understand your schedule. I get it, but if I were ever lucky enough to be the guy you came to when you had a minute to breathe, I would count myself lucky and take what I could get."

I looked down at my lap. Emmet had said something very similar once.

"What if I don't have much to give?" I asked when I looked back at him. "I don't know if I can ever…love you, and certainly I can't guarantee my time."

"I didn't ask for your love," he said quickly. "If that comes later, we'll worry about it then. But I enjoy spending time with you—when I can get it, and I will be fine if we stayed just friends from here on out, but I'm not going to lie. I wouldn't mind holding your hand…" He took my hand into his. "I wouldn't mind holding you in my arms while we watched a movie or being able to kiss you before you board a plane." He inclined his head toward the window and the planes outside. "And I certainly wouldn't mind finding out how you'd react to my hands on your naked skin."

I sucked in a breath and stared at him.

"You wouldn't have to love me for any of that, Donya, just like me...a lot," he grinned. "We can have monogamy without the commitment if you aren't ready for one. I wouldn't want you sharing all of that with another guy. I'd want all of that for myself only, but there wouldn't be any of the other rules that govern a committed couple."

Part of me was elated. The other part of me only wanted Emmet and no one else, but Emmet had moved on, and Benny was offering me a relationship without all of the added drama.

"But you see how busy I am," I said. "You wouldn't demand more of my time?"

"No," he said shaking his head. "Don't get me wrong, I would love more of your time on any given day, but if I don't see you for a few weeks, I won't cry about it."

That seemed too easy, and I told him as much.

"Look, there is no pressure now and there will be no pressure later if you decide to do this with me. It really is as easy as that. Think of it as a friends with some really nice benefits kind of thing."

I thought about Emmy's relationship with Felix. They had both said that it wasn't a serious relationship. They enjoyed spending time together and sleeping together, but their hearts weren't in it. When they split ways, I barely noticed because they were each fine with it and remained friends.

Could I do that with Benny? In a way, I felt like I would be betraying Emmet, especially since I was the one that ended our relationship. I felt like it would make me a hypocrite. Was the situation different enough to justify doing what Benny was proposing? I wanted to discuss it with Emmy and see what she thought.

"I can't give you an answer right now," I said quietly.

"No pressure," he reminded me. "But can I give you something to think about?"

I raised an eyebrow in question. Benny leaned forward and with his free hand he took my chin between his thumb and forefinger. His lips touched mine firmly, with purpose. Without much thought, I opened up for him, and his tongue slipped inside my mouth. I audibly sighed, because the kiss was really good, and when he pulled away a short time later, I almost chased his lips with mine.

"So, think about that while you're gone," he said quietly.

Before I could answer, our flight was announced, and then Emmy cleared her throat behind me. I stood up suddenly, tearing my hand from his, and began to gather my things. We thanked Benny again for the ride and Emmy again extended an invitation to him. I pinched her hard on the arm and steered her towards the gate and waved goodbye to Benny.

Chapter Forty-Two

Silence had fallen across the entire dinner table, except for the sounds made by forks clinking against plates, glasses being set down on the table, and the occasional clearing of a throat. Even Sam was markedly quiet as she looked Emmet's girlfriend over, but Laura was looking me over, trying to figure out from where she knew me.

"You look so familiar," she had said after introductions had been made, but no one volunteered the two pieces of obvious information.

Somehow, while Emmet and I laid eyes on each other for the first time in over a year, and during the introduction to my replacement, I had managed to smile and pretend it was nice to meet her. Since it was obvious she had no idea that Emmet and I had been together, I had to be sure not to look as hurt as I felt when he held her hand or touched her. I had no idea how I was going to make it to Monday without breaking into a million pieces.

"You know who you look like?" Laura said, breaking the silence at the late evening dinner and pointing her fork at me. "You look like this girl who was in my favorite Felix Hunter movie. I think she's with Felix, I mean, I don't really pay attention to the gossip shows and magazines, but you know sometimes you hear things or see things and don't mean to? I'm pretty sure I've seen pictures of them together. Damn…what is her name? She's been in a few other things, but she's not an actress, clearly. She wasn't that good. I can't even remember her name." She giggled and blundered on. "She's a model, or was. I don't know. I don't really follow those things. You look a lot like her. She's really pretty, but I'm guessing a lot of those models are all looks and no brain. What the heck is her name?"

The silence at the table turned into one of stunned disbelief. I stared blankly at her. After all, I was all looks and no brain, wasn't I?

"Her name is Donya Stewart," Emmy said coldly, glaring at Laura.

Laura began to laugh but then took a good look around the table at everyone staring at her. Her eyes landed on me and grew wide.

"That's *you*?" she exclaimed.

"I didn't know Harvard had a special program for the daft," Emmy muttered, pouring herself a glass of wine.

"Emmy," Fred warned.

"Explains how Emmet got in," she added in a murmur.

"Are there any more insults you want to throw at me?" Emmet asked, throwing his fork down.

"Oh, please, may I?" Emmy asked sarcastically.

"Esmeralda, don't blame your brother for his girlfriend's lack of wits," Sam admonished.

"If everyone is just going to insult Laura, we can leave," Emmet snapped.

"Oh, I'm sorry, honey," Sam said, patting Laura's hand. "But you have to admit that you kind of dug yourself into a bit of a hole there."

"I really am sorry," Laura said to me with sincerity. "That really was careless of me."

"Are you apologizing for calling her a bad actress or for calling her stupid?" Emmy asked her.

"That's enough," Fred said to her. "It was an honest mistake. Leave her alone."

"Laura, I say things to upset people all of the time in this family," Sam said, almost proudly. "You'll fit in just fine."

"Yeah, because you fit in," Emmy scoffed.

Sam glared at Emmy. "You know, I can't think why I asked you to come here, you miserable twit."

"I don't know why you asked me either. You don't even like me."

"Sometimes I wonder," Sam said.

"Don't you two start," Fred growled.

"You're really pretty, and I'm sure you're very smart," Laura said desperately to me from across the table.

"But you still think she's a bad actress," Emmy concluded.

"Leave her alone," Emmet demanded. He looked at Laura apologetically. "I'm sorry about my mom and sister," he said softly.

I had a hard time looking at the way he looked at her.

"What did I do?" Sam wailed.

I had enough of the stupid fighting. Any other time it would have been entertaining, but I was anything but entertained. Watching Emmet jump to Laura's defense and put a protective arm around her was killing me.

I put my napkin on my plate and stood up. I started to walk away from the table, but thought better of it and snatched the bottle of wine and exited the room, ignoring Sam and Emmy calling my name.

~~*

I was sitting out at the dock, smoking my second much-needed cigarette and sipping the much-needed wine when I felt Emmet's approach. Moments later my cigarette was snatched from my mouth and tossed into the water before he sat down in the chair across from me. Then he thought better of it, got up and took the bottle of wine from me, too.

"You don't drink," he said.

"I'm thinking I should start," I answered wearily and tilted my head back to look at the night sky. Stars that I could never see in New York glittered in the darkness.

"I'm sorry about Laura," he said on a sigh. "She's really a nice person."

"Don't worry about it," I said meaningfully. "It's not even close to the worse thing I've heard about myself. Emmy took it hard, though."

"I guess I don't blame her. She's kind of pissed that I brought Laura with me."

"Yeah, she is," I admitted.

"What about you?" he asked quietly. "How do you feel about me bringing her?"

I turned my head to look at him in the semidarkness. "You're free to bring home whoever you want."

"That's not what I asked you."

"You don't need to ask to know how it feels," I said quietly. "You already know, but it shouldn't matter how I feel. I could have chosen not to come when I found out, but honestly, I'm tired of playing the 'avoid Emmet' game. Why can't we just coexist?"

He was quiet for a long time. Only the water lapping at the shore and the dock and the occasional nocturnal animal could be heard in the night.

"She's pretty," I said when he didn't answer me. "Is she in law school too?"

"She's not you," Emmet said simply.

I swallowed hard and looked back up at the stars. They were starting to blur with unexpected tears.

"Why is this still so hard all of this time later?" I whispered.

Emmet stood up and took my hand and tugged me to my feet. He wrapped his arms around me, but I tried to push him away. I looked back at the house worriedly, expecting Laura to come bounding out at any second.

"She's taking a shower and then calling her sister," he said soothingly, pulling me back to him. "She won't come out, and she can't see us."

"Doesn't make it right," I said, brushing at my tears.

"We're not doing anything wrong," he murmured into my hair. "Put your arms around me."

I complied and a rush of air blew out of my lungs. Everything about Emmet felt perfect for me, the way his arms held me and the way my arms molded around him. My head fit perfectly between his shoulder and jawline, and when he held me like that, I could always feel his heart beating.

"I'll give it all up," I heard myself say to him.

Emmet inhaled sharply and remained quiet for a moment. When he spoke again, his voice was heavy with regret.

"No," he said. "I follow your career very closely, and it is bigger than anything I ever expected. Helene was right about you, and you're not even close to being done yet, Donya. I am so damn proud of you, and I want to see you reach your full potential just as much as you want to see me finish law school. I love you, more than anything and anyone, and I meant what I said last time we were together. No one will ever own me completely but you, but you have to see this through."

I wiped away at my tears, but I refused to give in and sob in his arms. If I started to sob, I would start to beg—with his girlfriend within a stone's throw. I pulled away from Emmet and even in the dim light I could see the moisture in his eyes.

"You never answered my question," I said, hugging myself. "Can we coexist?"

Slowly, Emmet nodded. "I'll try."

"Me too," I said.

We walked back to the house together in silence.

The rest of the weekend was uneventful, with the exception of Emmy's and Sam's typical bickering. I spent as much time as I could alone, sketching new designs on the dock or in the hammock. Laura didn't make any more stupid comments and actually proved to be rather funny and intelligent. Even Emmy softened for her a little. I didn't spend any more alone time with Emmet, but that tether was ever present.

I flew back to Philly on Monday afternoon. Benny picked me up from the airport, and because Emmet had denied me and I felt more alone than ever, I gave Benny what he wanted and what I needed.

Chapter Forty-Three

The agreement I had with Benny had been comfortable and satisfying for what it was. True to his word, he made no demands and didn't put any pressure on me. He was good company and had a way of making me feel cherished even though we weren't committed, and admittedly, he was a good lover. He was patient with me as I got acclimated to him since I had only been with Emmet before him.

Our non-relationship relationship had lasted for about eight months before Benny said he had met someone. Even though we weren't supposed to be emotionally vested, it still hurt both of us to end it, but there were no hard feelings. He married that woman a year and a half later.

Emmet and Laura broke up about six months after the trip to Louisiana. He later told me that she had become too needy and demanding, especially after she found out that Emmet and I were once engaged. She had become insecure and distrustful, and Emmet didn't have the time or patience for any of it.

The world suddenly and significantly changed, not just for me, but for everyone on a September morning in 2001. I cried for weeks afterward. Our carefree existence had gone away, but not only did the country and city pull together in unity like I had never seen before, but on a more personal level, I found new appreciation for all of the people I loved.

I spent more time with family and friends, and Emmet and I learned for sure that we could coexist. We spent a couple of comforting days together and found some solace in knowing that we had not lost one another in ways that others had lost on that dark day. Being friends wasn't always easy, and, in fact, it was sometimes painful, but the alternative was living without one another entirely. Neither of us found that very appealing, and quickly threw that option out.

The family had pretty much dismissed our past relationship as a childhood thing, and no one talked about it anymore. They assumed that because we were on friendly terms, that we also had chocked it up to childhood infatuation, but that wasn't true.

That tether was still connecting us down to the molecular level, and it seemed that there wasn't enough time in the world to cure us of that. Sometimes I really wished there was a cure because then it wouldn't hurt so much when that bond was tested, and it would be put to the test again, sooner than I could have imagined.

Two months before he was supposed to graduate, Emmet told me that he was moving to Florida. Freddy was having some trouble with business and asked Emmet for his help. Since he had mostly escaped having to do anything in the family business, he felt the least he could do to show his appreciation to his parents for supporting him through college was to help out his brother. While he was there, he was going to study for and sit for the Florida bar.

Any hope of our lives realigning and of us getting back together for good shattered at that news. I was glad that he had told me over the phone while I was out of the country, so he couldn't quite pick up on my emotions. Again, I didn't want to hold him back, so I had swallowed back my pain and gave him my support. He promised that he would be back, but it felt like a hollow promise in a shell of good intentions.

When Emmet finally did graduate from Harvard Law, I was there. I would have moved heaven and earth to be there, and damn near had to. Tears had threatened to spill out of my eyes when they called his name. Seeing him holding his law degree in his cap and gown was bittersweet. I was so proud of him, so happy for his success, but he would be leaving, and I would be without him again. Maybe forever.

Later that night after a celebratory dinner, Sam and Fred retired to their hotel room, and I met Emmet at his apartment so that I could give him his gift.

"You know you didn't have to get me anything," he said when I handed him the beautifully wrapped box. "Having you here for the graduation was enough of a gift."

"Oh, you always say such sweet words with your adorable mouth," I teased even though his words had warmed me inside. "Just open the damn gift."

Emmet shook his head and tried to hide his amused smile as he set the box down on the kitchen island. His couch and most of his other furniture were already gone and on the way to his new place in Florida. I didn't like to think too much about how far away he was going, and how far we would be stretched again.

He looked up at me suddenly, most likely sensing my roller coaster emotional state, but I gave him my best Donya Super Model smile and gestured for him to get on with the unwrapping. Reluctantly, he turned back to the task at hand. Once the paper was removed, there was a simple brown box, taped shut.

"Is there going to be a box inside this box?" he asked skeptically. "And another box inside that box and so on?"

"Would I do that to you?" I asked innocently.

"Valentine's Day," he said, narrowing his eyes at me.

For Valentine's Day, I had given Emmet a simple Hershey Kiss, not because I could afford nothing else, but because it had significant meaning for us. I had put it in a tiny box, within a box, within a box, within a box, and…within a box.

By the time he reached it, he was frustrated and demanded the real thing, but I denied him until I opened my gift. It was a new charm for my bracelet. Like the others, it was white gold and encrusted with diamonds. Although it was a bit smaller than the other two, it had an enormous impact that had me blinking back tears. It was a key. Just a key, but I knew what the key was for.

Even though we weren't a couple, and we were just friends, I kissed him that night, for a solid ten minutes before I was able to step away. The days that followed were awkward, but whenever I thought about it, I smiled.

I was smiling about it as Emmet stood there watching me instead of opening his graduation gift.

"Open it," I said. "I promise you it is not a box inside of a box."

He gave me a look that promised retribution if I was lying and then cut the tape away with his car key. He pulled the flaps apart and stopped. He stared down at the box for a long moment before glancing at me as he carefully lifted his gift out of the box.

It was a Ghurka chestnut brown briefcase. It was custom made with his initials engraved on the front flap. Emmet ran his hands over the leather appreciatively.

"This is…this is great," he managed, glancing up at me.

"Open it," I quietly commanded.

He looked at me with a bit of skepticism but unlatched it and carefully lifted the flap. His eyes narrowed in on the underside of the flap, and I watched his lips move as he silently read the quote stitched there. It said, "Great achievement is usually born of great sacrifice, and is never the result of selfishness. – Napoleon Hill."

"Donya," Emmet said, his voice full of emotion as he looked at me.

"There's more," I said softly. "Look inside."

He looked into the bag and produced a nameplate, engraved in gold and set on a block of chestnut wood to match his bag.

"Emmet Grayne, Esq.," he read aloud and then looked at me. "You know I haven't passed the bar yet."

"But you will," I said confidently. "One more thing." I reached into the bag for him and produced a pen in the same color as the bag and nameplate. Emmet Grayne, Esq. was engraved on the pen too. "It's refillable, so you'll never have it sitting around being useless."

Emmet held the pen and nameplate in his hands as he stared admiringly at the bag. I felt the shift in him before I saw it, a deep, emotional change that made my heart beat off rhythm. He met my eyes.

"I can change my plans," he said quickly. "I can move to New York and take the bar there."

I inhaled deeply as my fingers curled around the edge of the counter.

He was offering me something I really wanted. I could have him back and for good. My heart would be where it belonged and...

"I'm leaving for Paris in two days," I whispered. "And you have to take your prep course for the bar and help your brother."

"I'll take the bar later. Freddy can find someone else to help him out. He'll figure it out," he said, putting the pen and name plate down carefully on the countertop. He came to me, snaked his arms around my waist and drew me flush with his body. "Say yes."

"You have to keep going," I said, putting my hands on his chest. "You have to reach your full potential too, and you can't do that following me around."

"I can study for the bar anywhere," he argued.

"You said yourself that your dad seemed happy about you going down to help your brother. I don't want you to disappoint him, and you do need to take that prep course you signed up for and you need to stay focused and you will be able to do that if you stay in one place." It was killing me to deny him. I blinked back tears and bit my bottom lip.

"What I need is you," he said hoarsely.

I stroked his cheek slowly with the back of my hand. He closed his eyes and leaned into my touch.

"I'll quit," I said hurriedly. "I'll finish out my contracts and meet you in Florida."

His eyes flew open, and he shook his head. "No. You can't," he said firmly. "You have to keep going until you are absolutely ready to stop, and I know you're not. Stopping for me isn't the same as stopping for yourself."

I sighed heavily and closed my eyes for a moment. When I opened them, I did so with resolve. I pulled out of his arms, blinked back any tears that wanted to come, and stood out of his reach with my arms crossed in front of me.

"Anyway," I said, pretending that what had just transpired never happened. "I'm glad you like your gifts. You deserve them."

"Thank you," he said, looking at me with sad eyes.

Emmet left later that week, and I went back to my life, and it was never the same again.

~~*

I opened my eyes and squinted at the bright sunlight pouring in through the window. I stretched, starting with my toes and fingers and reached and reached until my fingers were at the top of the headboard and my toes were close to the end of the bed. Stretching finished, I rolled into a sitting position with my feet flat on the floor. I stared at the alarm clock and sighed.

Another day, another dollar.

As I showered and got dressed, the 4 Non Blondes' song "What's Up" was on a loop in my head. It had been on a loop since my twenty-fifth birthday. Nearly two years later I was still asking, "What's going on?" I totally felt like I didn't have a clue sometimes.

In the modeling world, I was over the hill, but even as most of my counterparts in my age group started to fall away, I had managed to hang on, though I didn't know what for. The job was becoming more like...well a job, a chore even, rather than something rewarding, but there I was, on my way to another shoot.

One of the reasons I believed I was still somewhat in demand was because I kept myself fresh. I changed my hair up from time to time, kept myself dressed in the newest styles before they even hit the general public, and I changed with the changing times. Also, over the years I had been a sponge, soaking up every bit of information about the business that I could, and I used it to my advantage when booking a job or while on a job.

So many of the girls just showed up to look pretty and didn't care about what was happening behind the scenes, but not me. I learned from the designers who were willing to teach me about the design process from beginning to end. I learned about fabrics and textiles, and I even learned how to sew and tailor my own clothes.

Helene and whoever else had the patience taught me about photography, including how to develop film and how to digitally manipulate the photographs. I also learned the processes of putting the fashion magazines together and other avenues of advertising.

I kept up with all of the big designers and paid close attention to the newer ones who had high potential. I was all business when working, but I knew how to stroke an ego without being obvious and shameful about it. It also helped a lot that I aged gracefully and did not look as old as I was.

I was happy to still be working, but I was exhausted. I had reached a point in my career where I could graciously turn down work and not get chastised for it, but there was still some that I just couldn't say no to.

I could have easily shifted into another aspect of the business. I could even continue modeling but do more commercial modeling rather than high fashion modeling, but I wasn't really sure if that was what I wanted to do.

One thing was for sure, I didn't expect to model forever, and I didn't want to find myself jobless without any other skills to fall back on. So, right before my twenty-fifth birthday, I started taking online college courses. The online courses were easier to manage with my schedule. I still had to struggle to meet deadlines, but I was making it happen.

I was still living in the apartment connected to Felix's penthouse. His career was bigger than ever, and though he was still a big flirty wiseass, he had settled down significantly and was engaged to marry a make-up artist he met on the set of a movie. They had been friends until two years ago when their relationship escalated, and he fell head over heels for Ginny. She was pretty, smart, talented, and took absolutely no bullshit whatsoever from her man. I loved it.

I checked my watch and decided it was time to light a fire under my ass and get moving. I wasn't necessarily looking forward to this shoot. My coworkers for the day were going to be a few other female models, but also several MBL players. I didn't know much about baseball. All I really knew was that Derek Jeter was a fox... and a good kisser.

I didn't really pay much attention to the baseball players when I walked into the building. They were milling around looking big and sporty and arrogant. Jeter inclined his head to me, and I simply responded with a slight raise of my eyebrow.

When I got into the makeshift dressing room behind a curtain and saw what I would be wearing, I rolled my eyes. It was a tiny baseball uniform. Instead of the longer pants the guys wore, I had to put on short shorts and a tight jersey.

I slipped my feet into a pair of red heels to match my Phillies' 'uniform' and a hat was placed on my head over my just done hair, which seemed stupid to me. Finally, I was given a bat as a prop.

"What the hell am I supposed to do with this?" my friend Kerry asked, holding up a glove and a ball.

"The only thing a bat is good for is breaking knee caps," Rochelle said with her thick Boston accent.

I concurred, and even smiled at their reactions, but I didn't speak my thoughts out loud. The powers that be don't like to hear their models complain. I learned that when I was just a rookie.

A little while later I was introduced to my 'partner', the man I would be modeling with. Most of the shots were going to be group shots, but since this Jerry guy was the Philadelphia player and I was in Phillies' gear, he was going to be my new and very temporary buddy.

I guess I didn't mind Jerry. He was good looking enough, with a dark caramel skin tone, short dark, wavy hair, and gorgeous gray eyes. He had a very nice, sturdy build. His Armani suit fit him perfectly. He wasn't as bulky as some athletes I had met over the years, but he looked like he could take down a lion nonetheless. What really wrapped up the package, nice and sweet like was those gray eyes. I had to force myself not to stare at them.

"I'm not really much of a model," Jerry said close to my ear before the shoot started. He had a vague accent I couldn't place, maybe somewhere from the Caribbean. "You may have to lead me on."

My forehead furrowed as I looked at him. He realized his choice of words and covered his mouth with an, "Oh shit" and big eyes.

"That's not what I meant," he held up a defensive hand. "What I meant was that you may have to show me how you do it. Wait. That doesn't sound right either."

I couldn't help myself. I started to smile. He wasn't faking the underlying nervousness, and he looked genuinely sorry and a little embarrassed for saying all of the wrong things.

"I'm sorry," he said, putting a hand on the back of his neck. The suit looked ready to tear at the seams where his muscles bulged out of his arm.

"It's cool," I said. "I get it. You're a baseball player, not a model. Is that right?"

"Right," he smiled softly, showing off straight, pearly white teeth. Dimples appeared on his cheeks, and I think I may have sighed. "Unlike Jeter over there. He loves the cameras."

"You'll be fine," I assured him. "If I think that you're not, I'll correct you. We'll have fun with it, okay?"

"Fun I can do," he said, nodding.

"Hey," I said getting an idea. "Do you have any gum?" I patted his jacket pocket in search for gum.

He looked at me in confusion for a second before reaching into his pants pocket. He produced a whole pack of strawberry Bubbalicious.

"I haven't had this gum since I was like twelve." I grinned as I tore it open. I jammed piece after piece into my mouth until I had a pretty nice size wad against my cheek. Jerry looked at me as if I was crazy, and I worried that he actually believed it.

I turned my back on him and looked over my shoulder. "Stand behind me, Jerry. Hurry."

He did what he was told, though he still looked very confused and maybe a little bit more nervous than before.

"Put your hands on my hips. Hmmm, no lower. Great," I said.

Just as the producers and photographers started giving direction, I held the bat low and at an angle. I grabbed my crotch and put a nonchalant look on my face. When they caught sight of us, they back peddled and demanded gum for more of the girls.

"Wow," I heard Jerry whisper behind me, and I grinned around my large wad of gum.

~~*

"You set the pace for the whole shoot," Jerry said in awe later in the day after I was back in my street clothes.

"That photographer likes to shoot edgy stuff," I said with a shrug. "If he was another photographer, I might have taken a different approach, but then there are some who want you to pose a certain way and look a certain way without trying anything crazy."

"Sounds like you really know your stuff."

"I would hope so after ten years." I adjusted my bag on my arm. "Well, it was nice meeting you."

"Wait," he said, stopping me as I turned to go. I looked at him expectantly. "You robbed me of my gum, and you're just going to walk away from me?"

"You want a dollar to cover the cost?" I asked, reaching into my jeans pocket.

"No," he scoffed. "I want dinner."

"You want me to buy you dinner?" I asked, cocking my head to one side.

"You're really good at modeling and being obtuse," he said with a grin, showing me those dimples again.

"What are you good at?" I challenged.

"Home runs," he said, puffing out his chest.

I stared at him blankly. "I don't follow football."

"Damn, you're adorable."

"I know," I said, batting my eyelashes dramatically. "Anyway, thanks for the gum, Jerry. Have a good one."

"Oh, no you don't." He gently grabbed my arm again and pulled me back. "You owe me dinner for stealing my gum and grabbing your crotch in front of me. Usually, I at least get a dinner before any of that happens."

"You really do want me to buy you dinner?" I asked incredulously.

"No, I'll buy you dinner, but you have to eat it."

"I'm a model, Jerry. I don't eat."

"You know you're breaking my poor heart, right?" he asked, putting a hand to his chest.

"Do you just want to take me out to dinner because you want to fuck me?" I asked with a sigh. "It's best just to get your intentions out in the open right away. That way you won't waste my time or yours."

His eyes widened, and he looked surprised by what I said, but he didn't back down, and he didn't wipe that smirk off of his face.

"Look, I know I'm an attractive guy, and maybe you would like to get some of this, but I just want to take you out to dinner. But if all you want to do is fuck me because I'm a baseball player, I'm afraid I must decline."

I looked up at him thoughtfully. "You really only want to take me to dinner?"

"Just dinner," he said with that soft smile.

"Okay," I conceded after a moment. "Can I at least go home first and wash all of this hairspray out of my hair?"

He turned halfway and reached for a hat off of a table behind him. He put the Phillies cap on my head and pulled the bill down low over my eyes.

"Nope."

I giggled and pushed it up some.

"Okay, hot shot. Let's go."

He offered me his arm. I looked at it stupidly before I realized what I was supposed to do. I so used to the men in my life just taking me by the hand and leading me around.

I slipped my hand into his arm, and we walked out of the building.

Chapter Forty-Four

"So, what's your story?" Jerry asked me over a table full of food.

"What story is that?" I asked, picking up a French fry slathered in cheese.

"The story about why you are single."

"Does there have to be a story?" I asked after I swallowed my fry. "Maybe I just like being single."

"Maybe that's a load of BS. Come on, give it to me."

"Why are you still single?" I asked defensively.

"Because I'm not sure if I'm the settling down type," he answered, looking me square in the eye.

"So, you like sleeping around?"

"I don't sleep around. I find a girl who I can share my time with, but I don't commit."

"Sounds a lot like sleeping around to me," I said.

"I don't commit, but I don't cheat. Does that make sense?"

It did, because I had that same relationship with Benny once. "Yes, I understand," I nodded. "So, why don't you commit?"

"You know I asked the question first."

I waved a hand dismissively. "Whatever. Why don't you commit?"

"I have a very busy schedule when I'm in a season," he explained. "I travel a lot for games, and if I'm not traveling, I'm practicing. If I'm not practicing, I'm sleeping. The women who stick with men with a schedule like that are rare, and I haven't found one yet who understands. She may say she understands, but you know I'll give it a trial run and usually after a few weeks I start to hear the whining and badgering about not being home."

"I can relate to that," I said after a moment.

He raised an eyebrow at me as he prepared to take a bite of his mammoth cheeseburger.

"Really," I said. "My career has been slowing down some lately, but in the past I was never in one place for very long."

"So, is that your story then?" he asked after chewing and then thankfully swallowing.

"Basically," I answered. I didn't want to go into details about Emmet.

"So, if you dated a guy with a similar schedule, you could deal with it?"

"I think I could *understand* it. I can't sit here and say that it would be easy because I don't know. I've only been on this side of the equation. For all I know, I could find myself in that situation and be a total lunatic about it."

Jerry wiped his mouth with a napkin and stared at me for a long time. I wasn't one to feel self-conscious about myself or my body, but his direct gaze made me shift a little in my seat.

"That's the most honest answer I've ever heard," he said. He looked at me with admiration.

"Well, don't get all mushy about it," I said, sitting up straight. "It's just a conversation. I'm not going to marry you and bear your offspring or anything."

"Until you can predict the future, don't count me out," he said with a wink.

Our conversation was lighter after that. We talked through our meal and dessert and coffee afterward. We must have spent a good three hours in that diner, but Jerry tipped the waitress well for taking up her table time. When we stepped out into the cool night air, I fumbled with the scarf around my neck, trying to tuck it in just right to help keep me warm.

"Oh, you're hopeless," Jerry said with a smile and gently knocked my hands away.

He rewrapped my scarf and tucked it into my coat and then pulled the bill of the cap down over my eyes again. Giggling, I pushed it back up so I could see him.

"Can I hold your hand?" he asked, like he was asking me what the temperature was.

"What?" I asked dumbly.

"Did I not speak clearly?" he asked.

"Yes," I said and then shook my head. "I mean no. I mean, sure. You can hold my hand."

When did I become a bumbling fool?

"Have you never had your hand held?" Jerry teased as he took my hand in his.

"No one usually asks," I explained as we walked down the sidewalk. "They just do it."

"The first time, a man should always ask. He should ask for the first kiss too, not just take it."

I gave him a teasing smile. "What a gentleman."

"Not really," he said, looking at me with those gorgeous eyes. "I just know how to please a woman."

Heat rose in my face and in other places I wasn't ready to think about.

"But after today," Jerry continued. "I won't ask before I take your hand or kiss you."

"You're assuming that there will be an 'after today,'" I said.

"What I like about your statement is that you did not say that I am assuming that you will kiss me. Now I know I have a very good chance of getting the green light on that."

"Because you are so damn sure of yourself, I am going to give you a red light just to be spiteful."

"No, you won't," he said, caressing my knuckles with his thumb. "You may pretend you don't want me to kiss you, but the truth is that you do want me to kiss you."

"I hardly know you," I pointed out. "Maybe I don't like to kiss strangers on the first date."

"I'm hardly a stranger," he scoffed. "Thanks to the media, people seem to know me better than I know myself."

"I wouldn't know since I don't follow soccer."

"Damn adorable," he grinned at me. "Where the hell are we going? Where do you live?"

"Why should I tell you?"

"Because you want to invite me in so I can kiss you properly," he said casually.

"I don't even know your last name or where you're from. What the hell kind of accent is that and how do you know that when you try to kiss me I won't knock that accent right out of your mouth?"

"My last name is Vasquez. I was born in the Dominican Republic but moved to New Jersey when I was fourteen. Now tell me where you live."

"How old are you?" I asked, refusing to answer his question even though we were heading in the wrong direction.

"Twenty-seven."

How many siblings do you have?"

He chuckled. "You really need all of this information before a kiss?"

"I didn't say you were getting a kiss, Vasquez. How many?"

"Two sisters and a brother. Sofia and Martina are twenty-two-year-old twins, and Diego is a year older than me. Now about that kiss…"

"And you get stuck with Jerry for a name?" I laughed. "Way to go."

"My real name is Geraldo, but my teachers kept pronouncing it wrong, so I became Jerry. Tell me where you live, princess."

"What are your parents' names?" I asked.

"Carlos and Rosa, but my mother passed last year." He looked a little pained as he said it and I instantly felt bad, but not bad enough to tell him where I lived yet.

"I'm sorry about your mom," I said sincerely.

"Thank you. She was a beautiful woman, inside and out."

I didn't think he wanted to dwell on that topic, so I didn't.

"You don't want to know anything about me?" I asked.

"What do you want to tell me about yourself?"

"Oh," I said, not knowing where to start. "Technically I am an only child, but my best friend's family pretty much adopted me, and there are five of them. Freddy, Charlotte, Lucy, Emmet, and Emmy." It felt awkward talking about Emmet as if he was a brother, because he so was not, but I didn't see any point in going into that with Jerry.

"Why did you spend so much time with them?" Jerry looked at me curiously.

"Because my mother wasn't much of a mother," I said, unable to meet his eyes. "She did try to make up for it before she died."

"And did she?"

I had never thought about whether or not she had adequately made up for it, but she was dead, and that was punishment enough.

"Yes," I answered finally.

Jerry halted, and I stumbled because he had stopped so abruptly. He steadied me easily with a hand on my waist, but he didn't remove it even after I was clearly okay to stand on my own. He stepped in close to me, so close that I could feel his breath on my face. My own breath hitched, and I wanted to look away from those killer eyes, but I couldn't.

"Are you going to tell me where you live, Donya, or should I kiss you here on the street?"

"I'm not really down for the insta-love thing," I said in a voice that didn't match the dazed look on my face.

"No one said anything about love, princess. It's just a kiss."

"If it's just a kiss then you can just kiss someone else, couldn't you?"

"But I want to kiss you," he said in a purposely pouty voice that somehow sounded sexy.

"I'll tell you what, Jerry," I said, putting a hand on the lapel of his coat. "I'll take a cab home, alone. You can call me tomorrow and ask me out on a proper date. You can ask me for a kiss if the date goes well."

He groaned. "I can honestly say that you're the first woman to turn me down so adamantly."

"Well, there are some things you have to work for in this world," I said, stepping away from him. I stepped to the curb and waved for a taxi. "And I am one of them."

With perfect timing, a cab pulled up to the curb.

"I don't have your number," Jerry said, chuckling.

"Guess you'll have to work for that too," I said and climbed into the back of the taxi.

Most men would have been furious, or at least irritated, but when I looked back at Jerry standing on the sidewalk, I only saw his dimpled grin.

~~*

Later that night after I changed into some warm clothes, I sat on the bed with my laptop and navigated to MySpace. I wasn't really into the site, but a lot of my friends had a page that I could follow, and there was a surprisingly decent amount of people that followed me. I never really had much to say or post though. I mostly went on there to stalk Emmet.

Lately, he had been posting pictures of himself and a woman named Cassandra, Casey for short. There was nothing particularly damning about the photographs. There were some pictures of them at the beach, often standing side by side, wearing sunglasses and smiling at the camera with the sea behind them. There were more of them wearing hiking gear in some hilly region I guessed not to be Florida since I had never seen anything but flatness during my visits there. In a few, they were being silly and made ridiculous faces. The one I hated the most was of the one with his arm across her shoulders and her arm around his waist. Friends posed like that all of the time, but something in their smiles just seemed...intimate.

I shut the laptop and twisted my hands in my lap. Whenever I spoke to Emmet, he never spoke about Casey, and it wasn't that he had to, but the fact that he didn't made me believe he didn't want me to know about her. He thought me to be lacking in the internet skills. He knew that I had an assistant that mostly ran my page, and I typically had nothing to do with it, so of course he wouldn't expect me to find him on the website or to scroll through everything he posted since it was made public.

I opened the laptop again and looked at his page. In the short minutes that I had sat pondering, he had posted again. My chest tingled just knowing that he was awake and moving around down there in Florida, probably getting ready for bed. I smiled a little as I leaned in to read what he had just posted, but my smile quickly faded. He had posted another picture of him and Casey. Again, it wasn't damning in any way on its own, even if he was embracing her. It was the words that accompanied the photo that had me biting my fist to keep from sobbing.

"Sometimes you have to let go of the past to embrace your future."

I could have been misunderstanding what he meant, but I knew it as sure as I knew that I was sitting on that bed within four walls that the past he was speaking of was me, and the future was *her*.

Ironically, the closer I got to stepping away from my career over the years, the lower the odds became that Emmet and I would end up back together. The tether was ever present and like a live wire whenever we were near each other, but away from me, Emmet carried on with his life, to the fullest. However, I still carried hope in my heart. I didn't get involved with any other guy because I didn't think it would be fair to them. I didn't think I could love anyone else, but it was possible for Emmet to love someone else, apparently.

I closed the laptop and put it carelessly on the floor before turning out my light and curling up under my blankets, *refusing* to cry myself to sleep.

~~*

At nearly one in the morning, my cell phone rang next to me on the bed. I shot up in bed when I heard the noise and stared down at it in confusion for a moment before comprehending that I was supposed to answer it. Then my heart began to race, because only a few people had my number and none of them would call me in the middle of the night unless someone were terribly sick, dying, or dead.

I fumbled with the phone without checking the caller ID display and answered.

"Hello?"

"Good morning," Jerry said. "Would you mind calling your security and telling him to let me come up?"

"Of course I mind," I snapped. "It's almost one in the morning."

I put a hand over my speeding heart.

"I know what time it is. Now be a good girl and call down to the desk. Even though I've proven to them that I am a famous athlete, they still won't let me past the lobby."

"Maybe they don't follow hockey," I guessed.

"Damn adorable," he said. "Come on, princess. It's getting lonely down here. I might have to cuddle up to Bill and Ward here, and I'm guessing by the way they're eyeing me, they would not appreciate it."

"How did you get my number? How did you find out where I live?" I questioned.

"My publicist called your publicist and told her that you and I had gone out to dinner together, but I accidentally left your phone number on a napkin in the diner. Then your publicist called your assistant and I only had to show her my dimples and talk about our shoot a little today and she was very forthcoming."

I scowled. I didn't use Eileen to pick up my dry cleaning, to do my food shopping, or to do any dirty work. She had to keep my schedule straight, screen my calls and take messages. It wasn't a lot. All I asked for in return—*demanded* in return—was for her to be discrete. In fact, she had to sign a confidentiality agreement when I hired her. Telling Jerry my phone number *and* my address were grounds for firing and a lawsuit.

"She's fired," I growled.

"Don't fire her," Jerry said soothingly. "She believed that she was doing you a favor."

"Then she should be fired for stupidity."

"Call security, princess. They're eyeing me like they're going to throw me out."

"Why are you calling me at one in the morning?" I asked, ignoring his observations.

"Last night you said I could call you tomorrow. It's tomorrow."

"I meant during the hours when I am awake."

"You're awake now," he said and then purred, "Come on, princess. Let down your figurative hair so I can climb up."

I shivered slightly and smiled, because that was kind of sweet. And stupid.

"You're hard to get rid of," I said. "I'll see you in a few minutes, but you're not staying long."

I ended the call before he could object and then called down to security to give Jerry permission to come upstairs. A few minutes later, I was leaning in my doorway watching him stride towards me. He had changed into a pair of jeans and I could see a gray sweater peeping through the top of his jacket. He had on a knit cap to keep his head warm and a pair of leather gloves. He looked really good and I looked at him appreciatively.

"Do you always stalk women?" I asked him when he stopped a couple of feet away from me.

"I never have to," he said solemnly. "None of them are as hard to get as you."

"I guess they fall into your lap," I said dryly.

"Sometimes," he shrugged.

"You know if you're trying to win me over, you're failing miserably. You may as well pull your tail between your legs and go home now."

"I'm not going home because you're about to invite me in," he said and rocked back on his heels.

"No, I'm not," I scoffed. "I'm sending you away."

"If you were going to send me away," he said as he leaned in close to me. He put an arm above my head on the door frame. His body almost touched mine. "You would have done it before I got up here," he concluded.

"You're standing in my personal space," I tried to say it like I was irritated, but it came out breathy.

"I know," he smirked and then looked me up and down.

"So, step the hell back before I fuck you up," I whispered as I looked into his eyes.

"Oh, you're a tough girl."

"When I have to be."

"Well, tough girl, I have news for you. You're already fucking me up in ways I've never been fucked up. I only just met you not even twenty-four hours ago and I can't stop thinking about you. It's like you crawled under my skin and nailed yourself to my body, because I can't shake you."

"Sounds painful," I managed to say and swallowed hard.

"You have no idea. Can I kiss you?"

I looked at his lips and licked my own. "No," I whispered.

"You're going to change your mind," he said, running a finger down my cheek and over the curve of my neck. "You're going to let me inside first, and then you're going to let me kiss your fucking adorable mouth."

"You think so?" I breathed. I was seriously feeling warm in the chilly hallway.

"I know so," he whispered in my ear.

His lips grazed across my cheek but stopped at the corner of my mouth. Bravely, I turned my head so that my lips grazed his, making him gasp.

"Work for it," I whispered against his mouth.

Before he understood what was happening, I had slipped back into my apartment and closed and locked the door.

"Call me tomorrow," I called.

"It is tomorrow!" he called back in frustration.

"Well, you fucked up by coming by so early. So now you'll call me *tomorrow*, and if you call me before nine a.m. tomorrow morning, I won't answer."

I heard him groan and it sounded like he dropped his forehead to the door. He muttered something in what I presumed to be Spanish and I even found that rather sexy.

"Will I get to kiss you tomorrow?" he asked, sounding hopeful.

"We'll see," I said. "Goodnight, *Geraldo*."

He let out another groan and then said, "Goodnight, princess."

Jerry was well behaved and didn't call me until nine the next morning. I agreed to go out with him that afternoon to Rockefeller Center to go ice-skating and then dinner afterward. I didn't let him into my apartment and I didn't let him kiss me on that first date, or our second, third, and fourth dates. He was comically frustrated, especially since our dates were so spread out due to our schedules, but he never tried to push his way into my apartment or force me into the kiss. For our fifth date, I invited him to my apartment for dinner. While I was in the middle of cooking and chatting, Jerry very quietly and very politely asked me if he could kiss me.

"Okay," I had whispered.

"Yeah?" he asked, eyes open wide.

"Yeah," I said with a smile.

Jerry held my face carefully in his hands and pressed his plump lips to mine. He was very gentle and very sweet as his lips moved slowly against mine. When his tongue sought entry, I opened immediately and sighed as his tongue made contact with my own. Slowly, he stroked the inside of my mouth with his moist tongue. I wrapped my arms around his neck and he wrapped his around my waist and pulled my body flush with his.

He kissed me until it was clear that something was burning on the stove. He hastily released me, reached over to the stove, moved the offending pot to a cool burner and turned the stove off. Before I could object, he had pressed me up against the counter and his tongue was slipping into my mouth again.

Chapter Forty-Five

Emmet shook Jerry's hand and smiled and said how it was nice to meet him and even went as far as saying he was a fan. If I weren't able to see past the surface of Emmet's words and demeanor, I would have believed he was genuinely happy to make Jerry's acquaintance, but I *could* see past the surface. I was the only one who could. I had insight that no one else in the universe had. I could *feel* his seething hatred of Jerry and his pain and resentment towards me.

After seeing a small article about Jerry and me in one of the gossip magazines, Emmet had called me and asked me if Jerry and I were together. I didn't think he had any right to ask, but at the time, I was honestly able to say that we weren't serious yet, and then a couple of weeks later I brought him home to meet the parents. If I had known Emmet was going to be there, I wouldn't have gone.

Spring training started in two days and Jerry was leaving Louisiana the next afternoon for Clearwater. It was a last minute decision of mine, to ask him to meet the family before he headed to training. He was reluctant in the beginning, because he usually didn't enter into long-term relationships, let alone meet the family of the woman he was seeing. We still had not labeled our relationship after several weeks. I had the feeling he was waiting to see how I handled his busy schedule, but I was interested in seeing how he handled mine.

After dinner that night, Fred engaged Jerry in a conversation about fishing. Apparently Jerry loved to fish too.

"I know a great spot to fish at this time of night," Fred had said as an offering.

"Sure, why not," Jerry agreed easily.

"Don't get eaten by a gator," I warned him.

"I promise you, princess, if it is me or the gator, I'll walk through that door with some hot gator skin accessories for you to model for me." He kissed the corner of my mouth tenderly and then followed Fred out of the room.

"I like him," Sam said slyly as she collected dishes from the table.

"Me too," I said with a smile.

"I was starting to believe you turned into a lesbian," she said. "If you were a lesbian, that would be okay, but I have to admit that I'm much happier knowing you can have sex with a penis and give me grand babies. I was worried you were going to dry up so bad your hymen would have grown back."

"I'd rather not discuss my hymen or dick with you, Sam," I said. I dared a glance at Emmet, wishing Sam would shut up. She had no idea that she was antagonizing a beast in her son.

"I'm just saying," she said with a shrug. "When you cut your hair a couple of years ago, I thought that was it. I thought you were going to start dating girls and wearing plaid."

"My hair looked *great*, and short hair and plaid does not a lesbian make. And for the record, I wouldn't be caught dead in plaid."

"Well, it don't matter, I guess," she said, shrugging. "You have Jerry now. I'm sure *he'll* end your dry spell."

Sam left the room, leaving me alone at the table with a fury ridden Emmet. A moment later, she turned the kitchen radio on to some oldies station. The music was loud. Elvis Presley was singing "Hound Dog." It was a personal favorite of Sam's. I imagined her absently singing along to the song in her frilly apron as she cleaned up.

Emmet made no effort to disguise his emotions once we were alone. The cord between us was hot with his anger, making my chest burn. His eyes were blazing emerald orbs that scorched me through and through. When he spoke, his words were dipped in venom.

"So, you're Jerry Vasquez's groupie of the month," he said tacitly. "There is a whole league of women like you, following him around with doting eyes, accepting his fancy gifts and laughing at his pompous humor… spreading their legs. By the time the season starts he will have moved on to the next brainless, pretty girl. So, you should suck up as much time as you can get with him." He held up his glass of water, as if toasting to that.

I was shocked into silence. I don't think I had ever been so hurt by anything Emmet had ever said to me. I didn't think it was possible for him to hurt me more with his words. I was wrong.

"You've lowered your standards and now you're spoiled goods," Emmet said with a shrug. Then he laughed, a hard, humorless, nasty laugh. "You're as good as his whore."

My water glass was flying across the table before I even realized I had picked it up. Emmet ducked gracefully from the blow of the glass, but water had splashed on his face and clothes. The glass shattered on the floor behind him.

The Supremes were singing on the radio in the kitchen now, and covered the sound of the shattering glass with "You Can't Hurry Love." Emmet's looked at the glass on the floor, and then his eyes narrowed on mine. I could barely see him through the tears that had formed in my eyes.

I got up from the table and started for the door.

"Go ahead and run away," Emmet called after me. "You've always been particularly good at that. I'll bet Jerry doesn't chase you. You're so easily replaceable, why bother."

I continued out the door, hurried past the kitchen before Sam could see my tears, hurried through the living room and out the front door so that Fred and Jerry wouldn't see me as they were leaving.

I dashed out into the cool twilight and halted. I didn't know where to go. I didn't even know what I was doing outside. I was only aware of the pain and anger I felt and my desire to get away from Emmet. It was equal to my desire to run to Emmet, and I swallowed a frustrated scream at the absurdity of it all.

I felt him closing in on me, but I didn't know where to go, so I just stood there and waited.

"Why did you bring him here?" Emmet asked a couple of feet behind me.

"Had I known you were going to be here, we wouldn't have come," I snapped over my shoulder. Then I spun around to face him. My attention was momentarily drawn to Fred's truck driving away down the road.

"Can you feel him leaving?" Emmet asked with a quiet harshness. "Do you feel connected to him? Or is your connection simply physical."

"I didn't act like an ass when you brought Laura here," I said to him as I wiped angrily at my tears. I was especially angry at myself for crying.

"You were the one who couldn't be bothered to make the time for a boyfriend," Emmet snapped, taking a step closer to me. "I was within my right to be with her and to bring her here. I wasn't the one who threw us away. That was you. Besides, you had become notorious for saying you were going to be someplace and then not show up. I didn't think you would make the time to come down here when you could be somewhere inflating your ego for a few dollars."

I sucked in a breath and balled my fists at my sides. "So, did you expect me to save myself for you all of these years? Is that what you thought, Emmet? That I would be this tragic girl, pining after the very person she pushed away, and unable to be with anyone else?"

"It would have been what you deserved," he said icily.

He may as well had lain me down in the grass and stomped on my chest, because that was how much it hurt. I stared at him through my tears like he was a stranger. I had no idea who this Emmet was.

"I'm sorry to disappoint you," I said with as much steel as I could gather in my tone. "I did pine for you, and it was tragic, but I didn't save myself for you. After that weekend you brought home that idiot woman, I went back to New Jersey and *fucked* Benjamin Munn that very night."

I must have been losing my mind, because when I saw the hard lines in Emmet's face grow harder and his eyes widen and felt the pain it caused him, I smiled through my tears and continued.

"I fucked him twice that night, and when he was able to produce proof that he was clean a couple of weeks later, I fucked him raw and sucked his dick."

I blinked and Emmet was on me. He meant to grab my shoulders, but surprised by his sudden movement and the absolute hatred I felt coming from him, I had tried to bolt, but I tripped over my own feet and his and fell backward. Emmet fell with me, landing on me hard and knocking the wind out of me. His face was in mine, nose to nose as he gripped my shoulders and shook me violently. Nat King Cole's voice was faint from inside the house, but I could still hear him singing "When I Fall in Love."

"I loved you!" Emmet shouted. "I was ready to give up my whole fucking life for you and you fucking denied me! But you spread your legs for Benny like a common slut! You didn't have time for me—me! The one who was always willing to give up anything for you and now you're with this fucker? What is he going to ever give up for you! He'll never give up *anything* for you!"

"Get the fuck off of me!" I yelled and thrashed to try to throw him off of me. My arms were pinned down by the weight of his body and he was not budging even though I was trying my hardest.

"But you'll give something up for him, won't you?" Emmet snarled. Roughly, he pushed a hand between us and shoved his hand up my skirt until his hand was pressed against my sex.

"Emmet!" I screeched. "Stop it!"

He removed his hand, but he did not get off of me.

"Why did you bring him here?" Emmet demanded again.

"Get off of me," I said firmly even though my voice was thick with tears. "Go back to Florida and go 'embrace your future' with Casey."

He paused and stared down at me as if he just remembered that Casey even existed.

"You didn't think I knew?" I almost laughed. "You really do think I'm brainless. Get the fuck off of me. Now!"

Reluctantly, Emmet finally got off of me and got to his feet. He stared down at me as I lay there trying to catch my breath as I blinked up at the sky. In the last several minutes, night had fallen over us.

After a minute, I pushed myself off of the ground, ignoring the bruises I felt forming on my back and the aching in my head from when it hit the ground. I knew I had dirt and grass in my hair and on my clothes and my legs and arms, but I didn't care. I was completely devastated by the things that had transpired since the moment Sam left me alone with Emmet. My heart was shattered and a large part of me was dying, and my god did it hurt. All of the pain I had felt in the past was overshadowed. This pain eclipsed all.

I felt Emmet's sorrow, his regret, and a bit of concern, but I mostly felt his anger and pain. It had not diminished much, and by the way he was breathing heavily and glaring at me, it wasn't going to fade anytime soon.

There were no words left to say. If Emmet had taken me into his arms and asked me to leave Jerry for him, I would have given in. I would have finished up the jobs I already had scheduled and I would have given Emmet my everything. But Emmet didn't do that. Emmet had become a monster, and until I experienced it for myself, I would have never believed it. My Emmet was gone.

I started to walk around him to go into the house, but I must have hurt my knee when I fell, because it hurt like a bitch, but I didn't stop walking. I went inside and managed to avoid Sam. In a state of shock, I moved about my room, getting clothes and toiletries before making my way to the bathroom. On my way, I heard Sam bitching about the shattered glass and Emmet snapping at her. I turned on the shower as hot as I could stand it, stripped, and got inside.

Not until I was under the heated spray did my shock begin to wear off. I stuffed my fist into my mouth to quiet my cries of disbelief and agony. I bit down so hard that blood seeped slowly out of my knuckles. I knew I'd never be okay again.

I felt Emmet leave, and I hated how the stretching of the twisted, rotting cord felt in my chest.

When I finally came out of the shower a half hour later, I took off the bracelet that had been with me all of those years. I went into Emmy's room and dug an envelope out of the small desk in there. I hastily addressed the envelope to Emmet's home address and dropped the bracelet inside. I dug around until I found some old stamps and though I probably over did it, I smacked all of them on there.

I put on some clothes and flip flops, ignored Sam's line of questioning, took the keys to my rental and took off at a high speed down the dirt road. I sped into town to the small post office there. Leaving the engine running, I got out and walked up to the blue mailbox for outgoing mail. Without any hesitation, I dropped the envelope in the box.

I couldn't sever that fucking cord, but that was as close as I was going to get to doing so.

I got back into the car and started back to the house, banishing any more fantasies about a life with Emmet Grayne.

Chapter Forty-Six

I sat at the little kitchen table with my knees pulled up to my chest, sipping a cup of hot tea and peering at Jerry over the rim of the mug. His skin was a toasty brown from hours and days spent in the sun playing baseball. His hair was cut short, but when he let it grow out a little bit during spring training, the waves were silky smooth to the touch. He had the body of an elite athlete, strong, muscular legs, tight, rippling abdomen, firm pectorals and powerful arms.

I liked his body, especially when it was on mine, but that wasn't my favorite thing about Jerry's appearance. My favorite thing was his long eyelashes. They were abnormally long and thick, making his gray eyes irresistible when he really wanted to use them on me.

"I feel you staring at me," Jerry said. He was reading the newspaper, but his eyes had shifted to me when he spoke.

"I'm staring at your pretty eyelashes," I said with a smile.

The paper dropped to the table and he looked at me incredulously. "Did you just call me pretty, princess?"

"No, I called your eyelashes pretty."

"Do they make my eyes pretty, too?" he asked in a girlish manner and batted his eyes.

I giggled and said, "Your eyes are pretty all on their own."

"Well, that's a relief," he said, getting to his feet. He leaned down and kissed both of my eyes. "Your eyelashes are pretty too."

He carried his empty plate and mug into the kitchen and put them in the sink. I put my tea down and unfolded myself from the chair so that I could give him a proper goodbye.

"I'll see you in two days," Jerry said, putting his hands on my hips.

I shook my head. "No, you will see me in ten days."

"Ten? I have a double header in Oakland and then I'll be home."

"I am leaving for Japan late tomorrow morning and then I'm going to India and won't be home until next Sunday. Did you forget?"

"I did," he said, frowning. "Then I guess it will be twelve days before I see you because—"

"You have a game next Sunday in Houston," I finished his sentence and nodded.

"For someone who still doesn't know what an RBI is, you know my schedule pretty well," he said with a grin.

"You would think that after dating you for so long that I would know what an RBI is, but…" I shrugged. "I still don't follow much lacrosse."

"It's a good thing you're adorable," he said and kissed a corner of my mouth. His smile faded, however, until it had turned upside down.

"Why are you frowning?" I asked as I poked gently at his mouth.

"When we first met I told you that I didn't get serious with women because they couldn't handle my schedule," he said quietly.

"Yes, I remember."

"You have handled our scheduling conflicts like a champ."

"So have you," I said, putting my hands on his chest.

He took one of my hands into his and held it against his chest over his heart. His expression was one of utmost seriousness.

"I don't want any more scheduling conflicts," he said gruffly. "I now understand how those women must have felt, if they felt even half for me that I feel for you. I always thought that I would be okay with things the way they have been these past eight months, but I'm not okay anymore." He pulled my body flush against his. "I love you."

I sucked in a breath. That was the first time he had said it. It had always been implied in his actions and words but never said outright. He had tried to be aloof and pretend that he wasn't as attached to me as he really was, but I knew that he was. I had kept quiet about it and played along. I didn't want to push or be pushed into something we weren't ready for.

I loved him too, though my love for him would never be like my love for Emmet. The two were in two different dimensions. I couldn't even begin to compare one with the other, but I left Emmet out of my feelings for Jerry, because that just was not fair to Jerry or me.

"I know," I finally breathed with a smirk.

He laughed softly. "That wasn't what I was expecting to hear."

"I don't know what you were expecting," I said nonchalantly.

"Oh, I think you know, and you better say it to me before I walk out that door."

"Or what?" I challenged.

"I'll ask Sam to be here when you get back."

"No need to be cruel," I admonished. "Fine. You win. I love you. There. Are you happy now?"

"Say it like you mean it," he commanded softly.

"I love you," I said slowly.

"I know." He kissed me, long and sweet and then left.

On my way to Japan the next day, since I had nothing else to do during the long flight, I thought about Jerry and me and wondered what was next for us. I wasn't even sure what I wanted to happen. He said he didn't want any more schedule conflicts, but I wasn't sure what that meant. I truly doubted he was going to quit playing baseball, but did he expect me to quit modeling?

My belief many years ago that my career would fizzle out by the time I was twenty-six or so was wrong. I was going to be twenty-eight in a few days and amazingly, work was practically falling into my lap. I still got booked for incredible shows and I was still very much in demand. I had staying power. While that made me feel very good about myself, as I got older, I decidedly wanted more out of life. I was growing anxious for a life that didn't have me on an airplane every other week. I was ready to settle down, but I didn't want to make my decision based on what Jerry wanted. I had to do what I wanted to do because I wanted to do it, not because he thought I should do it.

My shoot in Japan had gone very well and the photographer was one of my favorites, but I had overheard a couple of people discussing a model who was only a little older than me. Suzie had been very successful when she was younger, but at twenty-nine, she was barely touched in the industry. Something about her stopped appealing to the powers that be. The common reason

I tended to hear from others was that she was just too old, but there were models older than her still working their magic.

However, the more I thought about it, the more I realized that was the problem. Suzie lost her magic. She grew tired and weary and frustrated, and instead of bowing out before her career consumed her, she hung in. The very things that had made her amazing at what she did diminished because her heart wasn't in it. Instead of retiring with the respect of the industry, they figuratively kicked her into the gutter. I didn't know if it bothered Suzie, but I thought if that happened to me, it would bother me. I had worked hard over the years, and made colossal sacrifices. I would be damned if I was going to go out like that.

I had several credits under my belt from taking online college courses over the years. I only had about a year and a half left of schooling, but I would have to physically go to classes. Once I finished, I could start a whole new career if I wanted to. I had plenty of money to support myself while I completed my education. I could leave the business before I lost my own magic, and make my years of work and sacrifices *mean* something. I wasn't sure where Jerry would fit in with my changes, but one thing was for sure, our schedule conflicts would be at a minimum.

I called Emmy before I even left the beach where the shoot was, so that I could talk to her about it. I hadn't spoken to her in a couple of weeks other than some text messages. The first thing she did was wish me a happy birthday. I had forgotten about my birthday by the time I landed in Japan. It was ironic that I was considering making such a drastic change on the day that I had forgotten was my birthday.

I told Emmy about Suzie and told her I thought I was ready to wrap it up.

"I want to quit while I'm still good at what I do," I told her. "I don't want to be a washed up has been."

"You lead such a fabulous life though," Emmy said. I could hear the trace of doubt in her voice.

"I lead a lonely life," I admitted.

Traveling alone all of those years was beginning to take its toll, and even though Jerry and I saw each other as much as possible, we spent more time apart than together. Since Emmy left college and started working in the real world, she didn't travel with me much, so most of the time I was completely alone.

"I want to have a somewhat normal life. I want a family, a permanent home and a minivan."

I didn't know where that came from. Of course someday I wanted to have children, and definitely a permanent home, but a minivan? That was over the top. That was definitely going to shock Emmy.

Emmy gasped, as expected. "Now you're going too far. A minivan? Unbelievable."

"I knew that would hit you hard," I laughed.

By the time I hung up with my best friend, my mind was made up. I was going to quit modeling. I was going to stop taking on more work and finish up my commitments and start a new era of my life. I was happy about my decision, but part of me was sad that I wouldn't be starting that new era with Emmet.

It was a milestone in my life that he had been longing for, but he would never reap the benefits of it. We hadn't spoken to or seen each other since that terrible night in Louisiana. I wondered what would happen if I told him I was quitting. Thinking about it was bringing me down when I should have been excited, so I hastily pushed it out of my head as best as I could.

I was considering calling Jerry to tell him my decision as I let myself into my hotel suite. I had no idea what his intentions were. For all I knew, he was going to break up with me because we were too serious.

I crossed the threshold and halted. My eyes widened, and my jaw dropped.

There were brightly colored flowers everywhere in my small suite—on the floor, on the table, on the bureau, on the desk, on the window sill, and on the night stands. On the bed lay an enormous bouquet of roses with a card resting against it. I slowly began to cross the room towards the bed, but couldn't stop gaping at the bright, multicolored flowers in every direction I looked. Where had they come from? How the hell did they get them in there? I felt like I had just stepped out of Auntie Em's and Uncle Henry's tornado-thrown house and into Oz.

I picked up the bouquet of roses and brought them to my nose and inhaled. I had smiled at the smell before I plucked the envelope off of the bed. I sat down on the edge of the bed, opened it and pulled out a folded note. The words were typed, but I had no doubt that if Jerry could have sent a handwritten note to the other side of the world in a day, he would have.

Donya, I hope you have a beautiful day today, but if you didn't I hope these flowers have cheered you up. I can't wait to see you again. I am counting down the days, the hours, the minutes, and seconds. When you come back, there is something I want to ask you regarding our future together. I love you always.
Jerry

I clutched the note to my chest like a giddy school girl and squealed. I looked around at all of the flowers, grinning like the biggest fool. So much for wondering what Jerry's intentions were. I think I figured them out just fine.

~~*

I was feeling rather melancholy as I looked at the diamond on my left ring finger. The ring Jerry slipped on my finger when he proposed when I returned from Japan was beautiful. He spared no expense buying it. It was huge, and I was sure that when I turned my hand the right way in the sunlight, it blinded anyone within a half mile radius. I wasn't one for flashy jewelry, but I knew that Jerry was thinking with his heart when he bought it and gave it to me, so I didn't mind wearing it.

I was happy, for the most part. I felt like my life was pulling together as it should, but sometimes when I caught a glimpse of the ring on my finger, I was reminded of the ring that Emmet had given me when I was practically still a kid. I had been happy then too, and I couldn't have imagined a life without him. Now I had someone else's ring on that finger and I was moving forward in a life that had nothing to do with Emmet. In fact, I was moving forward rather quickly, because I was only about twenty-four hours away from marrying Jerry Vasquez.

Spring training was starting in less than two weeks. Once that started, Jerry wouldn't have time for a wedding. I had suggested that we wait another year and get married after the season ended, but Jerry was insistent. He said that besides his career, he had never wanted something more. He wanted to start the season with me as his wife.

I had felt panicked about getting married so quickly. We got engaged in mid-October and our wedding date was set for mid-January. I hid my panic and gently tried to dissuade Jerry from the January wedding. I reminded him that I was still working, that it would take several months before things settled down for me, but by early November, the decision was made and we were planning our nuptials.

The day after our wedding I had to fly to Paris for an appearance at an event that I could not get out of. I then had to go to London and then Madrid. By the time I would get back to the states, Jerry would be in spring training. For quite some time, we would still have a scheduling issue, but I chose not to bring it up. Surely he had to know that too.

I wasn't sure if I was doing the right thing. Was I marrying Jerry because I really loved him and wanted a life with him? Or was I marrying him because I didn't have Emmet? Worse yet, was I marrying him to spite Emmet?

I asked myself all of those questions and more, and the best answer I could come up with was: Yes, I loved Jerry and I wanted a life with him, but maybe a tiny, rebellious part of me was marrying him to spite Emmet as well. I wanted to prove to him that it didn't matter what the hell kind of sick cord connected us, I could live without him. That's what I told myself, and I had to believe it was true to move forward.

The wedding was taking place at the house in Louisiana. It was Jerry's idea. The weather was warmer than it would be up north, and the grounds at the house were extensive, and the beautiful lake view was a bonus. I agreed with him, but I felt a little bit like I was betraying Emmet by having the wedding figuratively and literally in his own backyard. I wasn't sure if he was coming or not. I didn't personally invite him, but Emmy, who had no idea that we weren't speaking sent him an invitation.

I didn't tell Emmy about our fight. I didn't tell anyone. I had a feeling Sam knew more than she let on, but she never brought it up other than to yell at me for breaking a glass and not cleaning it up. It was easy to hide the fact that Emmet and I weren't talking, because he lived in Florida and I lived up north. I traveled a lot and when I wasn't traveling, I was with Jerry.

Everyone assumed that we were communicating, but I never confirmed or denied it and I guess Emmet didn't either.

After the wedding rehearsal, we all made our way to the rehearsal dinner. It was at a country club that Sam and Fred belonged to not too far away. It was an upscale place with exquisite food and a great atmosphere. What I really liked about it was that on Friday nights they had dancing. After a delicious meal where there were a few speeches, some funny and some tearful, I convinced my soon-to-be husband to take me to the main dining room for some dancing.

The night was going well. Almost all of us were dancing, including Sam and Fred. I was passed around from partner to partner, every male wanted a chance to dance with the bride. It was while I was dancing with Fred Jr. that I felt it. It was as if a rubber band had been snapped and now it was quickly retracting.

When a rubber band snaps back, if your fingers are in the way, the rubber stings. My whole damn body was in the way. The initial sting started in my chest and quickly radiated throughout my entire body, affecting my throat, my lungs, and my heart.

My throat felt like it was closing up, it became a chore to force air in and out of my lungs, and my heart pounded at my chest cavity without mercy. I peered over Freddy's shoulder. Through all of the others on the dance floor, I met the piercing green eyes of the man who was walking across the dance floor with a purpose.

I looked around frantically, hoping I would find a means of escape, but it was already too late.

"I'm cutting in," Emmet said to Freddy without ever taking his eyes off of me.

"Nice of you to show up," his brother snorted and then released me.

When Emmet stepped towards me, I took an automatic step back, but he wasn't going to let me get away. He put his hand on my waist and roughly pulled me closer to him. So not to cause a scene, I relented and put my hand on his shoulder and my other hand in his.

For a long time, Emmet didn't speak. He simply stared at me, completely oblivious to the room full of people surrounding us. I put on my supermodel personality and painted on a small smile. I looked away from him and let my eyes travel casually around the room. When I saw Jerry dancing with Emmy, I pleaded with him with my eyes to rescue me, but he didn't see the plea and went on dancing.

"Don't do this," Emmet said in a low voice.

I laughed. I laughed heartily as if I was amused, but I was not at all amused.

"I should have known you didn't come here to wish me well," I said once my laugher died. "After our last meeting, I shouldn't be surprised by anything you do or say."

"I was an asshole, I know," he said hastily. "I was the biggest asshole I have ever been, but don't let that night influence you to make the biggest mistake of your life."

I flinched and my feet stopped moving. Emmet pulled on me hard to make me move again and I did so reluctantly. The small band that played at the club every weekend was playing "Put on Your Sunday Clothes." It was one of my favorite songs from *Hello Dolly*. The song seemed out of place in my current situation. Something mournful would have better suited.

"Don't do this," Emmet said again when I didn't verbally respond to his last comment.

"It's already happening," I said in a tightly controlled voice. "And I want it to happen."

"You don't want it to happen," Emmet said angrily. "You only want to hurt me by marrying him."

"I want to marry him because I love him, Emmet."

"You may love him, but you know love isn't enough, not in your circumstance."

"What circumstance is that?" I challenged him.

"Your heart belongs to me," Emmet whispered. I tried to move away from him, but he held onto me tightly and kept me moving on the dance floor, away from our friends and family, away from Jerry.

"You can put on that supermodel smile and waltz around this damn floor pretending that your life is a fairytale, but it's all a lie and you know it."

"It's not a lie," I began to argue, but Emmet spoke over me.

"It is a lie. You forget that I can see you like no one else." His gaze was intense. I felt like he had stripped away every layer

I had and was peering at me raw, and that he was seeing me better than I saw myself.

But I felt the need to fight him every step of the way, because he had no right to treat me as he did that night and then to show up at my rehearsal dinner for a dance and a chat.

"I don't know why you're here. Where's Casey? Isn't that where you should be? With your 'future'?"

"I know what you're trying to do and it isn't going to work. Casey isn't my future."

"But you said—"

"I know what I said, but that wasn't about me. Casey was having a rough time and I said that for her benefit. The only person I saw in my future was you."

I gave him a doubtful look. "You didn't correct me that night. Your silence was a confirmation."

"Casey is just a friend, Donya. I posted what I posted for her benefit and something that she was going through. It had nothing to do with me and her. I let you believe what you said was true, because aforementioned, I was an asshole and I wanted it to hurt you. If you stopped trying to close yourself off to me, you would have known that without having to ask."

"I'm not trying to close myself off," I objected.

"Yes, you are. I can feel you trying to erect walls and push me out, but you can't push me out, Donya. I am ingrained in you. I am woven into every cell of your body. You cannot eradicate me without losing yourself, too."

I swallowed hard and looked away from him. Everyone else was dancing, laughing, smiling, and enjoying the evening, completely oblivious to the fact that I was suffering, smothering even. Unless I cried out for help, no one would come to my aid, but even if they did, it would make no difference. The only one that could redeem me was the very one making me feel helpless.

"I'm marrying Jerry tomorrow and that's final," I said weakly when I finally looked at him again.

Emmet stopped dancing so abruptly I almost tripped. He didn't release me. He boldly pulled me closer, too close for comfort with my future husband a mere few feet away.

"You may become his on paper tomorrow, but you will always be mine, and I will always be yours. Think heavily on that before you make the biggest mistake of both of our lives."

He kissed my cheek, close to my mouth, tenderly, letting his lips linger too long. Then his breath was warming my ear.

"I love you," he whispered softly.

Then he was gone. He was walking back across the dance floor towards the exit, and he did not look back. I was left standing on the dance floor without a partner while people danced around me, feeling resistance in the cord as it stretched.

Chapter Forty-Seven

I stared at my reflection in the large floor mirror propped against the wall. My Vera Wang dress wasn't custom made because we didn't have time, but Vera herself helped me select it and tailored it to my body.

My makeup was professionally done to a smooth finish by Ginny. My hair was styled by one of the top stylists in the world and topped off with a diamond encrusted tiara, chosen by Jerry, of course. Nothing less for his princess.

I was beautiful. I looked like I just stepped out of a book of fairytales, but my life wasn't a fairytale. For the first time in my life, I wondered if the princes in the fairy tales just looked the part but wasn't what the damsel needed.

I gradually became aware of Sam's fingers touching and plucking and adjusting. I felt as if a monkey was grooming me and it was annoying me. She hadn't stopped talking all day, and I felt like my head was going to explode if I had to listen to her any longer. While she harassed Ginny and the hair stylist, I turned to Emmy and whispered in her ear.

"I really need some quiet time, or I'm going to lose my fucking mind."

Emmy nodded her understanding and then walked across the room to the other three women. She told Sam that she really needed to check on things outside and when Sam was gone she kindly told the other women they could get ready. A moment later it was just Emmy and me.

"You look really stressed out," Emmy said worriedly.

"Honestly, I just need a little bit of time alone," I sighed, and then added for her benefit, "I'll be fine. I'm just tired and cranky."

"Understandable," she said and believed me instantly. Of course she did, because she would trust me to tell her if I was freaking out about marrying Jerry.

Emmy checked the time on her phone. "You still have over an hour left. Take some time and relax. I'll be back in a little while."

"Thank you," I said sincerely and hugged her.

"Cheer up," she smiled after we released each other. "You're getting married to your prince today."

Princess Diana married her prince, too, and look how that turned out, I thought, but I didn't say that to Emmy. I gave her a small smile and watched her walk out of the room.

I picked up my phone and checked it for messages, voice mail—for anything from Emmet. I was disappointed when there was nothing, as there had been all day. I didn't know how speaking to him could have helped at all, but I couldn't help but to hope for it.

I walked over to the window and looked outside. There were heated tents set up on the lawn, one for the ceremony and another for the reception. Even though we were in the warmer climate of Louisiana, the winter months had the potential to get pretty cool.

Many guests had already begun to arrive and were milling around in the yard talking. Just looking at the place where I was going to get married was making me anxious. I turned away from the window, but the room was beginning to feel too small. I felt like the walls were closing in on me. I needed to get out, even if for only a few minutes, out into the fresh air, alone.

I picked up the hem of my dress and slowly pulled the door open. I could hear voices in the house, but they were all downstairs and at the back of the house. As quietly as I could manage in my swishing dress and high heels, I hurried to the stairs that led to the front of the house. I managed to make it down without killing myself but almost immediately ran into a body.

"What are you—" Felix started to ask, but I put my fingers over his lips and shook my head adamantly. He and Ginny had arrived in the wee hours of the morning before any of the media could show up at the end of the driveway.

"I need to get out of here," I mouthed silently.

His eyes widened. He took my fingers off of his mouth and held my hand.

"You're running?" he mouthed back.

"No," I said, shaking my head and then whispered "I just need a break. I'll be back."

He gave me a look that I could only describe as sympathetic. He laced his fingers with mine and led me outside. He made me wait as he fetched the limo that Jerry had hired to take us away after the reception. I wondered why it was there so early, but then I was thankful for the car and its dark windows

Fortunately, there wasn't anyone out front. All of the parking and the activity was at the back and east side of the house. Way down the road the media waited for a glimpse of some celebrity, but they wouldn't know who was in the back of the car.

"Are you going to be okay?" Felix asked as he helped me get into the car.

"Yes, I promise," I said. "I just need some air."

"Okay," he said and leaned in and kissed me on my forehead. "Be careful and call me if you need me."

I nodded and thanked him. He closed the door, and the car began to move.

"Is there somewhere specific you would like to go ma'am, or would you like me to just drive?" the driver asked.

"I'll direct you where to go," I said. "Thank you."

I gave the driver directions and a few minutes later we were turning off of the main road towards the fishing pond. Even before I saw Emmet's car parked there, I felt the cord retracting. When I set out, I honestly didn't expect to see him, but he was probably just as aware of me as I was of him. I decided not to turn away. I had hoped to hear from him all day, and I finally had the opportunity to see him one last time before I changed our lives forever.

"I'm going to get out and go for a walk," I said to the driver, throwing open the door.

"Ma'am?" The driver looked back at me worriedly.

"I'll be fine."

I got out and closed the door before he could make any more objections. I held the hem of my dress and started the short walk through the woods to the pond. As I rounded a curve in the path, I caught site of Emmet, standing by the water and looking in my direction expectantly. The image of him took my breath away. He was dressed casually in a button-down shirt open several buttons at the top and a pair of jeans. The sunlight gleamed off of the water and filtered through the treetops, casting him in a soft glow.

"I used to fantasize about you walking towards me in a dress just like that," Emmet said as I neared. "Except you look more stunning now than you ever could in my fantasies."

He smiled sadly. It was hurting him to see me in my wedding dress, and I wished I had changed before venturing out.

"You know, this is where you proposed to me," I said.

"More specifically right there," Emmet said, pointing to a piece of level, grassy land.

Visions of our lovemaking that day lazily moved across my mind, and I was struck by how long it had been since our bodies had last joined.

"There is so much I wanted with you, Donya," Emmet said, pulling my thoughts back to the present. "I didn't care if we had a big wedding or a small wedding or got married in front of Elvis in Vegas. I just wanted to marry you, to claim you. It didn't matter how."

"Your mother may have had an issue with Elvis," I said with a genuine smile. Sam would have had an epic meltdown if she found out that we got married like that.

"She probably would," Emmet agreed.

His smile was still sad, even though I was standing there in front of him and not back at the house preparing to walk down the aisle. With every passing second that I stood there with Emmet, I wanted less and less to go back to that house and marry Jerry. It wasn't that I loved Jerry any less, but I didn't love Emmet any less either. I had to wonder if when I decided to have the limo driver drive me to the pond, if I wasn't just following my instincts. Maybe I knew Emmet was there all along, waiting for me. Maybe he knew I'd come all along.

Emmet stepped forward, but surprisingly he didn't touch me. Now that he was standing closer to me, I could see that his eyes were moist with unspent tears. Something was wrong—I mean besides the fact that I was supposed to marry Jerry in less than an hour. There was something else very wrong. Emmet wasn't just sad and hurt about my upcoming nuptials, Emmet was frightened.

"I've loved you my entire life," he said weakly before I could speak. "I've never wanted anything more than I want you.

I am not the best man I am capable of being without you," he said with conviction. His last few words were shaky, and his eyes were gathering more moisture.

Alarmed, I put my hand gently on his cheek. "Emmet," I said, feeling his distress. "If you would have just asked the right question last year…" I stopped talking. He was already feeling miserable. I didn't need to poke at the open wound.

"But I didn't ask the right question," he said, and carefully removed my hand. "I said all of the wrong things and that is how we are standing here today in our current predicaments."

"So, ask me now," I said anxiously.

I wrung the hand that had been on his cheek. It literally stung from his quiet rejection, but despite that, in a matter of seconds I had made a decision that would have enormous, harsh consequences.

"Ask me not to marry Jerry," I whispered. "Ask me not to marry him, Emmet."

Something twisted violently inside of him. It was in his face, in the way his hands fisted at his sides, and it was in that damn tether. My breath was wrenched from me in a loud gasp. He wasn't going to ask me. He wasn't going to ask me not to marry Jerry. Something near cataclysmic was about to occur between us, and there was nothing I could do to stop it.

"I can't ask you not to marry Jerry," Emmet said after a long, strained silence. He blinked and a couple of tears escaped his green eyes. I reached out to wipe the tears away and his eyes closed as my hand touched his skin.

"Just. Ask. Me." I pleaded softly.

"Donya," he whispered my name and shook his head. "I don't want you to marry Jerry, and you don't want to marry Jerry," he added knowingly. "But I can't ask you not to marry him right now. It would be selfish and hypocritical. You deserve better than that."

"I don't know what you're talking about!" I cried, throwing my hands up in frustration. "All you have to do is ask, and you can have everything you ever wanted to have with me. Emmet, just *ask me*. Be selfish if you have to, just ask!"

Emmet stared at me contemplatively for a moment. Then he put one hand on my waist, and the other cupped my neck. He looked at me earnestly with his glistening eyes.

"You have to promise me that we will work this out together," he said.

I looked at him in confusion and put my hand on his.

"Work what out?" I asked.

"I have to figure a few things out," he said more to himself than to me. His eyes began to grow hopeful. I should have felt reassured, but there was still something he was not telling me.

"What things?" I questioned.

"I love you," he said as he stared hard into my eyes. "Do you understand?"

"I love you, do you understand?"

New Year's night, many, many moons ago, Emmet had spoken those same words, and they had made me fearful and sad, and now the words carried an ominous threat.

"What aren't you telling me?" I whispered.

"This has no bearing on us, okay?" He spoke quickly now. "This does not have to affect us. We'll work through it."

"Work through what?" I asked wearily.

Emmet was breathing rapidly, his chest rising and falling against mine. He looked like he was building the courage to say something, which scared the hell out of me because Emmet always told me what he needed to say, whether I liked it or not.

Finally, he spoke. And the calamity was epic.

"Casey called me a little while ago. She's pregnant."

Chapter Forty-Eight

I jerked back and away from Emmet, stumbling over the hem of my dress and the uneven ground. I almost fell backward, but Emmet reached out and righted me. I smacked his hands away from me.

"Don't touch me," I said through gritted teeth.

"Donya," he said my name on a sigh as if I was overreacting, when, in fact, I wasn't sure if there was any other reaction except for violence. I was underreacting.

"You said she was just your friend," I yelled. "You come to me the night before my wedding and tell me not to do it because I'm making a big mistake, and all the while you were screwing her! What in your imbecilic mind told you that would be okay to do? You didn't even do me the courtesy of coming to me as a free man!"

"I'm never a free man," Emmet argued. "My heart is always in your hands."

"Oh spare me your starry-eyed bullshit!" I screamed and shoved him back. "This is the second time that your inability to keep your dick in your pants has driven a wedge between us. Why is it so difficult to open a condom and put it on your dick, Emmet? Didn't you learn anything from Stella? It takes less than ten seconds to roll a condom on, even on your big dick! Casey is just as much of an idiot as you are for not insisting on a condom or being on birth control at her age. Then again, maybe she just wanted a baby to trap you with, and it wasn't very hard because you're always more than willing to pull your dick out and jam it into the nearest hole."

I gathered my dress and turned my back on him. He followed close behind me, calling my name.

"I know you hate me right now but—"

I spun around and shouted, "You have no idea how much I hate you right now!"

"I am sorry," Emmet said pleadingly. "You are the only woman I've ever wanted to have kids with."

"That's even worse, Emmet," I admonished. "The fact that you would be so careless with something you wanted to reserve just for me only makes matters worse."

"I know, I know," he said and tried to grab my hand, but I snatched it away. "I am so damn sorry, baby." His voice cracked with emotion. "I know this is a shock—trust me, I only just found out, but we can get through this, Donya. We can get over this and still have a life together."

"There is no getting 'over' this, Emmet," I said sadly. "This isn't something I can just sleep on and feel better about it in the morning. I can't be with you while your baby is growing in some other woman's womb. I can't sit in a waiting room months for now while you're in the delivery room with Casey watching your child's birth. This is *too much*. This is *too far* Emmet, and I can't do this with you."

"Then take the time you need," he said quickly as tears began to spring from his eyes. "Take all of the time you need and when you're ready I'll be waiting for you and hopefully I'll have my shit together."

"You will be waiting a very long time," I said just above a whisper. "It was a mistake for me to allow myself to get sidetracked by you and my feelings for you."

"Donya, please," Emmet said desperately.

"I'm going back to the house, and I'm going to marry Jerry," I said with finality.

"Don't marry him just to hurt me," Emmet pleaded. Tears rolled freely down his cheeks, and I had to look away. I couldn't take seeing him cry. I could barely stand on my own two feet, feeling the desperation and despair inside of him.

"I have to go," I whispered and took a tentative step back.

"No! Donya, don't do this." Emmet dropped to his knees in front of me and grabbed a hold of my hands. "Please don't do this. We can work through this. Baby, please, please, please don't marry him."

I struggled to pull my hands away from his, shaking my head adamantly.

"I can't," I whispered. "I can't do this with you."

I managed to untangle my hands from his, but then he grabbed onto my dress, taking in big handfuls of silk and lace and holding on tightly as he looked up at me, sobbing.

"Please," he begged. "Please, baby, don't do this. Please don't do this. I'll do anything. Whatever you want me to do, I'll do it. Please don't marry him. Donya, don't do this."

"Emmet," I said his name softly. "Let go."

"No," he said, shaking his head. "No, I will *not* let you go until you promise me you will not marry him."

"Let go," I said again and worked to untangle his hands from my dress.

"I'm not fucking letting go!" he screamed. His face was a mess with tears and snot. I had the natural instinct to wipe it all away and kiss his tear stained cheeks, but wiping his face would not wipe away what he'd done, and kissing his cheeks would not make the situation any better.

"Let me go," I said harshly as I tried to remove his hands.

"I will rip your fucking dress off of you if I have to," Emmet snapped tearfully. "I am not letting you go so that you can fucking marry Jerry and forget about everything we've ever had. I'm not letting you go."

"Everything we had is gone," I announced crisply. "It's all gone, Emmet. It's been gone for a long time, and it's time we both face that. Now let me fucking go!" At the risk of tearing my dress, I yanked it as I took a step backward. The fabric began to tear as I struggled to pull my dress out of Emmet's grasp.

"I can't lose you like this," he roared, scrambling to hold on to me.

"You've already lost me," I said icily and then gave one final yank. The sound of the silk and lace tearing was surprisingly loud and was the only other sound I could hear besides Emmet's pleas.

"Please," Emmet whispered, clutching pieces of my dress in his hands.

I picked up the hem of my dress and turned my back on him one last time. I walked away from his weeping that made my knees weak and left ice in the pit of my stomach. He sobbed my name repeatedly, and I struggled not to turn around and run back to him every time he said it.

By the time I cleared the woods, I was running for the limo. The driver was waiting outside the car, and when he saw me coming, he hurriedly opened the door for me. Emmet's voice carried through the trees and over the green field as he cried my name. The driver looked back toward the woods curiously.

"Please, just go," I said and slammed the door shut, and just barely missed crushing his fingers.

I don't remember the drive back to the house. The cognitive part of me was still back in the woods in front of the pond on its knees with Emmet. I could still clearly hear him calling my name and see his tears.

I don't remember getting out of the car or going into the house past Emmy and Sam just before climbing the stairs. I just remember closing the bedroom door, because that was when my cracked façade shattered.

I grabbed the closest piece of clothing, a shirt I had worn earlier, and buried my face in it and screamed. Tears poured out of my eyes, my fingers dug into the soft material of the shirt, and I screamed and screamed like a woman being murdered. In a way, I was being murdered. My heart was being torn from my body against my will.

When the screaming subsided, my body jerked violently as I sobbed. I pulled my face away from the shirt so I could attempt to breathe, but even though I was sucking in big gulps of air, I felt like I was being strangled and no air could move through my windpipe.

I became vaguely aware of the fact that I was sitting on the floor with my dress billowed out around me. I bent myself over in half and clawed at the hardwood floor with my nails as I cried. Several of them broke, and one even tore away and began to bleed, but I didn't feel that pain. I only felt the pain of losing and giving up Emmet.

"Where the hell have..." I heard Sam say behind me, but she didn't finish her thought.

I didn't even bother trying to hide the fact that I was having an emotional breakdown. I couldn't hide my broken pieces lying all over the floor.

There was a knock at the door, and I heard Emmy's voice as the door began to open, but then she objected loudly when Sam stopped her.

"You can't come in here right now," Sam said to Emmy. I had enough sense to put the shirt back to my mouth to help muffle the sounds of my sobbing.

"What do you mean I can't come in right now? It's fifteen minutes until go time, and I am the maid of honor!" It sounded as if she was speaking through a very small crack in the door.

"If you don't mind, I would like a little mother-daughter time with Donya," Sam said impatiently.

Emmy seemed to consider it silently for a moment. "Okay. I get it. I'll be downstairs."

"Thank you, honey," Sam said sincerely and then the door closed, and I heard the distinct sound of it locking. A second later, Sam was stepping around my dress. She stretched out her hands to me. "Come on, sweetie. Get up off of that hard floor."

I stared at her hands for a moment, and then reluctantly put my hands into hers. She helped me up effortlessly and eased me into the chair in front of a vanity. I saw my face and knew I had destroyed the makeup job Ginny had done. Mascara and eyeliner ran down my cheeks, and my lipstick was smeared.

Sam went into the on-suite bathroom and got a wet cloth. Like the true mother she was, she cleaned my face even as I continued to sob softly. In many circumstances, I didn't like having Sam and her big mouth involved in my personal problems, but I trusted her implicitly this time. I knew she would put aside her big personality to take care of me.

"You don't have to do this," she said softly but with conviction as she peered at me in the mirror. "If you want to call this off, all you have to do is say it."

I reached into my purse sitting on the vanity and produced my cigarettes. Sam didn't object or make any comments as I lit up the cigarette and inhaled deeply a few times. It took me a good minute before I was able to speak.

"Casey's pregnant," I said in a dead voice.

Sam's eyes widened, first with surprise, and then narrowed with anger.

"He told me they were only friends," she said, putting a hand on her hip.

"Well, apparently they're the kind of friends that fuck without any form of birth control," I said quietly and took another drag.

"Did he know about Casey's pregnancy last night when he came to the rehearsal dinner to try to stop you from marrying Jerry?" Sam asked dryly.

I looked at her reflection. "You knew about that?"

"Honey, I know you all think that I'm a little dim, but I know my son. I knew when he walked in what he was up to."

"What else do you know?" I asked.

"More than you think I do. Now tell me, did that little jackass know about Casey last night?"

"No," I said, looking down at the makeshift ashtray on the vanity table. "He had just found out when I saw him."

"If she wasn't pregnant, I guess we wouldn't be sitting here right now. I'd be outside making excuses to three hundred guests."

"Yes, you would," I said unapologetically as I snuffed out the cigarette.

"What are you going to do?" Sam asked quietly.

"I'm going to fix my makeup, fix my dress, and marry Jerry," I said, squaring my shoulders.

Sam looked at me with sympathy.

"You do whatever you need to do, but don't marry him just to spite Emmet, honey. Marry him because you know he will be good for you."

"He will be," I said, but I wasn't one hundred percent sure about that.

"Donya," Sam started, and I knew she was about to give me a lecture.

"I am marrying Jerry," I snapped at her. "I let myself get sidetracked, that's all. Now we're getting back on track, okay?"

"I'll get your makeup bag," Sam sighed.

We made quick work of fixing my makeup, clipping my nails until they were all even and cleaning away the blood. We pinned my dress so that the tear was not noticeable, and I thought about those pieces I had left behind with Emmet.

I had thrown one last glance at him just before clearing the trees. He was exactly where I had left him, clutching the fabric and watching me go. I wondered why he didn't stop me from getting into the car, but maybe he knew it wouldn't have made a difference. There wasn't anything that could keep me there with him after his revelation.

I shook the image of Emmet crying on his knees from my head as Sam let Emmy in the room and the pair made finishing touches on adjusting my dress, my hair, or makeup. Emmy chattered on happily, completely unsuspecting of the hell that I had just gone through. We went downstairs and outside and took our places with Fred and the others. Sam kissed my cheek once and dabbed at her eyes. She wasn't crying because it was a happy occasion, she was crying because she knew it was one of the worse days of my life.

The wedding planner went over a few things with us, and then it was time to start. As the procession began, Emmy turned to me, beaming broadly and trying to blink back her tears.

"You look like a princess, D," she said emotionally. "And Jerry is definitely a prince. You have a beautiful fairytale wedding, and you'll have a beautiful fairytale life. I know it."

I no longer believed in fairy tales, wasn't sure if I ever did, but I didn't want to be the one to burst Emmy's happy little storybook bubble.

"Thank you, Emmy," I said softly.

It was her turn to walk inside. I linked my arm into Fred's and clutched at my flowers.

"Are you ready, Kiddo?" he asked. He wasn't smiling as a father of the bride should have been smiling. Picking up on the negativity that was surrounding me, Fred looked at me as if he was waiting for me to say the right word before whisking me away from that tent and the life that I was about to start.

Marrying Jerry wasn't the worse thing in the world. In fact, before I saw Emmet the night before, marrying Jerry seemed like a very fine idea. He was a good man, and he loved and adored me, and that was something to be happy about. Life had not turned out the way I expected, but this…this couldn't be so bad.

"Yes," I said and gave him a genuine, reassuring, but small smile.

He didn't immediately smile back. He looked at me thoughtfully for a moment, but then nodded and gave me a small smile of his own.

The music began and Fred lead me down the aisle to the man I was going to marry, and away from the life and the man I had to leave behind.

Chapter Forty-Nine

Two months after I married Jerry, Emmet married Casey. I wasn't at all surprised. Emmet had his faults, but I knew he wouldn't abandon her, and without me to hold him back, he was able to do the honorable thing to make sure his child was born in wedlock.

Casey sent me an invitation to the wedding, stating that when she didn't see my name on the guest list that I must have been overlooked, because Emmet probably assumed that since I was family that I had an automatic invite. She expressed her excitement at finally meeting me, which led me to wonder how much she knew about Emmet and me, but it didn't matter. I graciously declined the invitation and fortunately with my busy schedule I had a real reason not to go, but I sent a congratulatory card signed as Mr. and Mrs. Jerry Vasquez.

Four months later I received another invitation, this time for Casey's baby shower. I again declined, but sent a gift card for the baby and a gift card for Casey to have a spa day whenever she wanted. Though I was skeptical about her lack of birth control when she got pregnant, it wasn't my problem, and according to Sam and Emmy and Fred, she was a very sweet girl. Besides, all of the fight had left me on my wedding day. I didn't have the energy to be unkind.

While Emmet was having a baby with someone that wasn't me, I was struggling with Jerry's decision about children, as in he didn't want any. I wasn't clueless, of course, we had that conversation about kids before we got married, and he had wanted them then. By the time we were six months into our marriage Jerry had changed his mind.

"I will always love you more than anyone else, even a baby, princess," Jerry had said one night.

That was a very romantic thought, yet also a very disturbing one. I couldn't imagine loving anyone more than my own child, but I had to give him credit because not many people would admit that out loud. I convinced Jerry to think about it for a while, because I eventually wanted children. He said he would think about it, but I couldn't help feeling like he just said that to appease me. When Emmy asked me about kids, I told her we were waiting. I didn't want to admit that I may not have any if Jerry had it his way.

Technically, I had become a New Jersey resident once again after we married, but for the first six or seven months of marriage, I spent a lot of time in New York, and abroad. When I was finally able to settle down in the same apartment Jerry had before we got married, I picked up a full schedule at the local college and became a student and homemaker. Though I was busy with school and supporting Jerry's career, I felt idle. I had been working a heavy schedule since I was sixteen years old. I wasn't used to being home every night and living like a normal person.

Fortunately, we lived close to Emmy, and she helped me get acclimated as much as she could. She worked long hours, sometimes six days a week and the love life that had been nonexistent for her for a few years had sprung to life—a little too much life if you ask me, as my best friend was juggling two men at once.

Luke was her actual boyfriend and Kyle was her boss *and* her lover. It was a very complicated and dangerous love triangle. It was wringing the life out of my poor friend, and it was impossible for her to be happy in that situation. While I didn't judge Emmy for her actions, I wondered how she even found herself in that situation, why she let it go so far. I loved Emmet more than anyone else in the world, my husband included, but I didn't think I would ever be capable of cheating with him, especially on a guy like Luke, who seemed to love Emmy more than what she deserved.

To get Emmy away from her men for a little while, I invited her to join me in Tampa for Jerry's double header one weekend. I was looking forward to spending the time with her and having some fun, and she needed some time away from her situation to clear her head.

Jerry called as I was finishing up my packing for the trip. We still had several hours before Emmy and I had to be at the airport, but I had some errands to run for Jerry before we left.

"Princess," Jerry said in greeting.

"Hi," I said as I struggled to zip my suitcase.

"What are you doing?"

"Trying to close my suitcase."

"Why do you bring so much for one weekend?" he asked with a chuckle.

"I'm a supermodel, only recently retired. I can't look a hot mess."

"Of course. My bad. Wouldn't want you looking a hot mess."

I managed to get the suitcase zippered all of the way and breathed a sigh of relief. I was glad I wouldn't have to pack a third piece of luggage.

"I can't even imagine what the other wives go through when they're packing up their kids too," I said as I settled down on the edge of the bed.

"Well, you don't have to ever imagine it since we're not having any kids," Jerry said easily, as if it had been decided and carved in stone from the beginning.

"You don't really mean that," I said, trying to keep my tone light. "You're just teasing me now."

"Donya, we talked about this last year," he said patiently.

"You said you would think about it."

"I thought about it and I don't want any children, but we don't have to talk about this right now. We can talk later."

"No, we can talk now," I said with irritation. "Jerry, before we got married you were all for having kids. Why did you change your mind?"

If I were an insecure woman, I would have assumed I was the reason, something I was lacking, but I wasn't an insecure woman. It wasn't something I did or didn't do. The problem was Jerry.

He sighed heavily and cursed under his breath. "We don't need to have this conversation right now, Donya. Not over the phone."

"Yes, I think we do," I insisted. "Now tell me why you changed your mind."

Jerry and I didn't argue very often. Our relationship was…sweet and fun. I was content and had no major complaints. His light snoring, crankiness after too little sleep, or inability to hang up his wet towels just didn't seem like good enough reasons to complain. Though I wouldn't say my life was a fairytale-like Emmy believed, it wasn't bad either. I knew we were about to have the biggest disagreement we'd had to date.

"Having children is a heavy, lifelong responsibility, Donya," Jerry said in an exasperated tone. "I like the life we have just the way it is. I don't want to worry about what kind of role model I'm being to my child. I don't want to worry about dirty diapers and runny noses, and kids are time-consuming. My job is time-consuming enough and when I'm not playing I want to be with you and I don't want to share you with a baby."

"You only named all of the bad things about having kids. You didn't mention anything good about having kids."

"Because there will be nothing good about us having kids," Jerry sighed. "And can you imagine what kind of havoc a pregnancy will wreak on your body? I don't ask you for a lot, princess, but it's a given that you maintain your gorgeous figure and continue to look amazing."

I couldn't believe what I was hearing. What he said sounded so damn shallow. Jerry could be self-serving, there was no denial in that, but that was over the top.

"So, I'm just a pretty fucking face, Jerry?" I said loudly. "I'm a trophy wife, is that it?"

"I didn't say that," he said quickly.

"No, you just implied it. You don't want to have children because I may put on some weight and then you won't be able to showcase me on your arm."

"You're blowing this out of proportion."

"No, I think I'm well within proportion," I said, getting to my feet. "You know what, Jerry? I'm feeling a little bloated so I'm not going to be able to make it down there. I wouldn't want to embarrass you with my fat ass and my muffin top."

"Princess," he sighed. "What if I bought you a puppy?"

"Do you really think a puppy will make everything okay?" I asked incredulously.

"Damn it, Donya, I don't know what will make everything okay," Jerry said exasperatingly. "I don't want you upset."

"It's too late for that."

"Because you wouldn't listen to me and let it drop for another time," he said pointedly. "I have to go. We're about to take off. Are you still coming?"

"No," I said stubbornly.

"Okay, fine," he snapped, and then gritted out, "I love you."

A beeping noise sounded in my ear indicating that Jerry had ended the call. I immediately called Emmy to cancel the current plans. It worked out better for her anyway, because she was going to go to Luke's and confess that she was cheating. I thought she was going to be in for some shit and I told her as much. Suddenly, even my big problem seemed small in comparison to what was about to go down with my friend.

After the phone call, I sat there a little while longer trying to decide what to do with my weekend. I couldn't sit in the apartment and dwell on the argument I had with Jerry.

"Or, I can, and eat anything I want and get nice and plump for his return," I said aloud to no one.

That plan sat well with me. I could go out and skip Jerry's errands and go to the store instead and buy all of the movies I'd ever wanted to see. I'd load my cart up with all of the junk food I had been disciplined about over the years. I'd make root beer floats and popcorn with too much butter and pour Reese's Pieces into the bowl. I would eat ice cream from the carton and dip chocolate covered pretzels into the cold treat.

In the morning, I'd hop the bridge and go to Federal Donuts in Philly and load up on fresh and hot donuts that melt in the mouth, and if I got there at just the right time, I could get chicken too and I'd get it in every variety they had. I would go by the Water Ice Factory and get a gallon of my favorite flavors of water ice and eat it until I got brain freeze and then start again. By the time Jerry got home in a few days, he would have to roll me around in a wheelbarrow.

Nothing was going to make up for not having kids, and that wasn't the end of that fight, but my pigging out idea brought a satisfied smile to my face. I stood up, raring to go, but my cell phone rang. I answered it without looking, thinking it was Emmy.

"Did you handle your shit that fast?" I asked as I walked out of my room.

"Umm? Depends on what shit we're talking about," an unfamiliar voice said with a soft southern accent.

"Oh," I said, coming to a halt. Confused, I said, "Sorry, who is this?"

There was a gentle laugh that reminded me of the princesses in the fairytales Emmy was always comparing to my life.

"Hi, Donya. This is Casey."

The hallway tilted and it took me a moment to realize it was because I had tilted. I was slumped against the wall at an angle as I gawked at the air in front of me.

"I'm sorry to just call you like this. I know you're busy with school and your husband, but I lost your address. We're throwing a big anniversary party for Fred and Yasmine and Lucy put me in charge of invitations."

"Oh, yeah it's been twenty years already," I said, trying to sound unaffected by the sound of Casey's voice. Even after the other two invitations and the Christmas card that was rumored to have a cute family picture on it that I didn't have the nerve to open, I didn't expect to hear from her.

"Yep. That's a long time these days," she said distractedly. It sounded like she was doing something in her kitchen. I heard water running and what sounded like dishes clattering together. "And they're very happy together. Fred really dotes on Yasmine."

"Yes," I agreed. I only saw Fred maybe once a year, but he did seem to adore his wife.

"Did you get my Christmas card?" Casey asked. "I'm not sure if you got it. A couple of them got lost in the mail."

"Honestly, I don't remember," I lied. "Jerry and I were traveling and the mail piled up." That part wasn't a lie, not really. We went to the Dominican Republic to see Jerry's family and then went to Aspen for a week.

"Oh, right," she said as if remembering. "Emmet said ya'll went away. How was it?"

How did Emmet know that I went anywhere? I hadn't spoken to or seen Emmet since my wedding day.

"It was nice," I said. "Relaxing for Jerry."

"He has a double in Tampa this weekend, right? I'm not a Philly fan, but he's a good player. You must be very proud."

"I am," I said honestly.

I heard a small voice in the background and it made my heart stop. That had to be Owen, Casey's and Emmet's little boy.

Casey spoke to her son for a moment and then apologized to me.

"It's okay," I said softly. I tried to swallow back the pain before speaking again. "Is he walking yet?"

"Owen started walking at eight months and has not slowed down since," Casey said in an exasperated, but loving voice.

I listened to her talk about all of Owen's milestones and illnesses and his likes and dislikes for twenty minutes. Every moment was killing me, and when she mentioned Emmet's name, it cut me that much deeper, but I didn't have the heart to stop her. She really was a nice girl and I felt bad for assuming the worse of her. Her soft southern accent was as sweet as her personality and it was no wonder that Emmet cared about her.

When Owen started to get cranky and demand Casey's full attention, she quickly jotted down my address and told me how good it was to finally have an opportunity to speak to me. I wondered how much she knew about Emmet and me, but if she knew anything at all, she was willing to overlook it. Either that or it was a keep your enemies close kind of thing, but I strongly doubted that. She was too nice.

After the phone call had ended, I lost my desire to make myself fat. I collapsed on the couch instead and threw an arm over my eyes as I tried to process how I was feeling about Casey's attempt at friendship. It could have been worse. She could have been out for my blood. Then again, that could be her MO, to lure me with her super sweetness and then attack me while my defenses were down.

My phone rang again. I didn't look again before answering it, because who could be a more shocking person to call me than the previous caller? Well, there will always be someone to trump the person before...

"Hello," I said tiredly.

"You didn't even look before you answered or you wouldn't have answered," Emmet said.

My heart stirred in my chest at the sound of his voice. It took me a moment before I was able to speak.

"Yeah, I didn't look and I wouldn't have answered," I said honestly.

"I'm sorry," he said softly. "I didn't know she was going to call you."

"It's okay. I was about to do something terrible and the phone call thwarted that."

"What were you about to do?" he asked. He sounded concerned and it sent waves of emotion rippling through my chest.

"I was about to go to the store and buy every bad movie I've ever wanted to see and fill my cart with junk food. I was going to order pizza or Chinese and in the morning I was going to go to Federal Donuts."

It was quiet for a moment. I thought maybe he had hung up and I didn't hear the beep, but then he spoke in a very grave tone.

"You need an intervention."

I actually laughed a little. "Your wife intervened," I pointed out.

"I'm still sorry about that," he said sincerely.

"It's not a big deal," I lied.

"You're lying," he said softly.

"It was a shock," I admitted, holding a palm to my forehead.

"Obviously, you're not even going to Federal Donuts in the morning."

"Maybe not that much of a shock," I said hastily.

"I thought you were going to be in Tampa this weekend."

"Are you stalking me? You seem to know a lot about what I'm doing."

"Did you think I would just let you disappear into obscurity?" he asked, but before I could respond, he continued speaking. "My mom told me you were going to Jerry's games."

"Oh," I said. "Of course she did. Well, I'm not going."

"Why not?"

"Because he made me angry."

"About what?"

I bit my lip and stared up at the ceiling. Did I really want to tell Emmet about my personal problems with Jerry? I often thought about him telling me that Jerry would never give anything up for me, and I didn't want to confirm that for him. I didn't want him to be right about that.

"I'd rather not rehash it with you. Are you working?"

"Yeah," he said with a sigh.

"Don't like it?"

"What's to like about this place," he muttered.

"Should have stayed with the family business," I sang out softly.

We talked only about the law office Emmet was working for over the next half hour. During that time, I was able to forget about my pain and my heart beat normally and I was able to breathe. I got comfortable on the couch and had even closed my eyes as we spoke, but when that conversation died down and we fell into silence, my rapid heartbeat returned and I suddenly felt like there was someone sitting on my chest.

"I thought you would never speak to me again," Emmet said quietly, breaking the silence.

"We share a family," I said. "We would have spoken eventually."

"I guess so," he said doubtfully. "How long will it be before I speak to you again?"

"I don't know," I said weakly.

"I can't go without talking to you again, Donya. I know we are literally living separate lives, but we are not separate. You know that, don't you?"

How could I ever possibly forget it? I loved my husband and we shared a wonderful life, most of the time, but I wasn't connected to him. I wasn't bound to him in the way that I was bound to Emmet. That tether will be there forever.

"I do know that," I whispered. "And that's why I can't be your friend."

His sigh was so sad that it brought tears to my eyes.

"You still hate me," he said in a small voice.

"No, no," I said hurriedly. "I don't hate you, Emmet."

"Then say it," he quietly commanded.

I was struck mute for a moment. I thought about Emmy and her predicament. I didn't think I was capable of cheating, but I forgot about the strong pull Emmet had on me. Good decision making was imperative, even when in a cloud of emotion.

"I love you, Emmet," I said hoarsely. "But we need to return to our lives now. You have your sweet wife at home and I have Jerry."

He exhaled, like he had been holding his breath waiting for me to say those three words.

"I love you, too," he said sadly. "Will I see you at the anniversary party?"

"I don't know," I answered honestly.

"Okay." He was reluctant to hang up and I knew how that felt because I could have listened to his voice all day. As much distress as it brought me, it soothed a part of me that no one else could access, not even me.

"Bye, Emmet," I said, fighting back tears.

"Bye, Donya."

I wanted to lay there and feel miserable and zone in on that bereft feeling I felt, but that would be no good for me and no good for my marriage. I rolled off of the couch and hurried into my bedroom. I quickly put my shoes on and adjusted my hair before grabbing all of my luggage. I struggled my way to my car and threw everything into the trunk.

A little under two hours later I was boarding my flight to Tampa. I felt like I had crossed a line that had been drawn in the dirt the moment I said, "I Do." Regardless of how I felt about Emmet, I needed to stay on the right side of that line. I had to keep my senses about me, and to do that, I needed to be with my husband.

A few days after we returned from Tampa, Jerry came home from practice with a gift for me…a gift that whined and let out little puppy barks, wearing a nametag that said Dusky. I gave him a sideward glance that said, "You've got to be kidding me," even as I hugged and kissed the black lab.

Jerry gestured to something attached the bow that was tied around the puppy's collar. It was a rolled up piece of paper, like a miniature scroll. Balancing the dog in one arm, I unraveled the piece of paper and read aloud.

"Dusky is the first addition to our family. We will make the second addition together." I grinned and blinked back tears. "Jerry. Does this mean…"

"Yes, but," he put his finger up in warning. "I can't promise you when I'll be ready, or if I'll ever truly be ready, but someday we will try to have a baby, okay? But we have to talk about it first. No turkey basters and poking holes in the condoms."

I threw my free arm around his neck and kissed him. No, we weren't connected, but we were happy, and I wouldn't jeopardize that, ever. I hoped down in Pensacola, Emmet had found his happiness with his family, too.

Chapter Fifty

A year and a half later, Jerry stared at me, not comprehending what I had just told him.

"What do you mean you're pregnant?" he asked, his eyes narrowed in confusion.

"What kind of question is that?" I asked, irritated by his reaction. "I can't make the statement 'I'm pregnant' any clearer than that."

"But you're on birth control," he argued.

"Remember when I switched prescriptions because the first one was making me break out?"

"Not really."

Of course, he didn't remember. It didn't directly apply to him.

"Well, I switched birth control pills and there was a small window of time when we had to be careful."

"I pulled out," he said and gave me a suspicious look that I didn't appreciate.

"Did you learn anything in Sex Ed? Pulling out is not an effective form of birth control, Jerry."

He looked around the room as his mind began to truly process what was happening. When he met my eyes again, his eyes were a bit chilly.

"We agreed to discuss this first," he said.

I stared at him incredulously.

"I am sorry if my egg and your sperm didn't sit us down over coffee and discuss the situation before they joined," I said.

"I'm not ready for this," Jerry said, holding up his hands as if he was out of the equation. Like that was enough for him to step back and make it all my problem.

"Obviously," I snapped. "I wish I could take full responsibility, but last I checked it takes one male and one female to make a human baby, so you better get your shit together."

I started to walk out of the room, but Jerry blocked my path and put his hands on my shoulders.

"You're not hearing me, princess," he said in a hard tone. "I am not. Ready. For this. We have to take care of this."

My rage and violent need to protect myself and my unborn child was immediate. I shoved him away from me and then with a cry of pure resentment, I balled my hand into a fist and connected it to his mouth. Jerry stumbled back, stunned. He touched his lip and when he saw the blood on his fingers, his eyes widened.

"I'm sorry," he said as he stared at me in disbelief. "I'm sorry. I didn't mean that. I panicked."

He moved toward me, but I backed away from him.

"Don't touch me," I warned icily.

"Princess," he said softly and held out his hand.

"Get out," I said and pointed to the door.

"You're kicking me out?" he asked. He looked at the door and then at me.

"Get out!" I screamed.

Dusky stood at my side, barking and growling at Jerry, as if to say, "Didn't you hear Mommy? Get the hell out!"

He looked at me for a moment longer and then cursed in his native language as he stormed over to the closet by the door. He took out his coat but didn't put it on. He grabbed his keys and opened the door. Cold winter air blew in and made me shiver. Jerry gave me one last look as if he expected me to change my mind, but I remained silent. He shook his head and muttered something I couldn't hear before walking out, closing the door behind him.

I held my breath for a few seconds until I heard the distinct sound of his Camaro starting.

"Fuck!" I exploded and shook my hand. I examined it visually first, noting that it was already swelling and turning odd colors. I was able to open it and close it and flex my fingers, but not without a good dose of pain.

I went into the kitchen and took an icepack out of the freezer. I wrapped it in a dishtowel and sat down on the couch while my hand iced. Dusky was entirely too big to sit on my lap, but he lay across my lap anyway.

I leaned back and tilted my head up towards the ceiling as I tried hopelessly to blink back my tears. I understood Jerry's initial shocked reaction, I had expected that. I even thought it was possible that he would not immediately be happy about the situation, because he had been so adamant about not having a child before we planned to do so together, but I did not expect his cruel proclamation that we had to 'take care of this'.

What other women did with their bodies was their legal right and I didn't judge, but terminating a pregnancy was not something that I was capable of doing and Jerry had to have known that. Even if he didn't know it, he should have been ready and willing to sit down and have a discussion about our options instead of insisting on only one.

I wanted to call Emmy and tell her about the pregnancy and vent about how Jerry reacted, but I couldn't, because my best friend had her own troubles, and I believed they were far bigger than mine.

The love triangle she had been in disintegrated when Luke, who had reached his tipping point, broke up with her and moved away to Chicago to be with his family and to get away from Emmy. It was about three months later that Emmy learned that she was pregnant. In my opinion, it was questionable who the father was, but Emmy seemed adamant that it was Luke, but she did not tell him. She carried on with her reckless relationship with her boss, Kyle, for another few months, but then something happened around the very beginning of the year. It was still unclear what exactly had transpired, but it had changed her—*irrevocably* changed her. Emmy was *broken* and I had no idea who or what gave the killing blow. One day, without even telling me, she picked up and left the state and went down to Louisiana.

I later found out that Kyle was in rehab for some unknown addiction, and when she caught wind that he was going to get out, she begged me to take her far away. I took her to the only place I could think of, I took her to Helene and Marcus in France. She stayed with them in their country cottage until she was probably way too pregnant to fly overseas, but she made the trip home nevertheless and gave birth to Lucas, a beautiful, blonde haired baby boy in Louisiana.

When Lucas was five months old, he and Emmy flew to Chicago where she broke the news to Luke and told him he was a father. A week later she moved in with him. They weren't together as a couple, but Luke wanted an equal share in his son's life, and he was owed much more than that.

Whenever I spoke to Emmy, she was only a shell of the woman I used to know. I always pretended that she didn't sound like a walking dead woman. After each phone call, I would be on the verge of tears. I had no idea what had killed her spirit or how to help her, but calling her was out of the question. I didn't want to burden her with my problems. A small part of me wondered if she even had the wherewithal to care.

I still couldn't believe that Jerry suggested I terminate the pregnancy. With that reoccurring thought, Emmet's words bounced around in my skull.

"He'll never give up anything for you."

Those words stung me now. Jerry expected me to give up something I had always wanted while he gave up nothing. In fact, since we got married, he had given up nothing. I wanted to quit modeling, so I couldn't hold him accountable for that, but my whole life orbited around his. I took good care of him. I cooked, I cleaned, and I threw myself into his career. I did all of the charity events that the team wives did. I went to every home game, even when I was in school and working hard on getting my degree. The one away game a month he required soon became three or more, because he wanted me there. The media always commented on what a devoted wife I was and Jerry liked how that made him look.

I didn't have a job, because being Jerry Vasquez's wife was my job. My degree sat useless in a drawer. Even though going to any of my family's gatherings could be awkward, what with my ex-fiancé and his new wife and baby, I would have liked to have had the option, and I lost that option when I married Jerry. Every holiday or special occasion was spent with his family here in the States if it was within baseball season, but during the winter holidays, we traveled to the Dominican Republic.

My social life was nearly nonexistent because I spent so much time just being Jerry's wife. Mayson was the only friend I really had since Emmy left and I didn't get to see her often.

I didn't mind being selfless for Jerry. I felt useful and my husband loved and adored me, but after his selfish suggestion, I suddenly felt…used and unappreciated, and I was having a difficult time with the fact that Jerry had never given up a damn thing for me, just as Emmet had predicted.

Emmet wouldn't have asked me to give up my baby, I realized. As far as I knew he didn't expect Casey to do that either, even though he clearly wanted me and not her. In fact, he gave up a great deal to do the right thing by her and Owen. Emmet had made some poor choices over the years, but I knew he would always try to make the right decision for Owen, and I supposed even for Casey.

I had an unexpected yearning for Emmet. How different my life would have been had I married him instead of Jerry. Dealing with Casey's pregnancy had seemed impossible back then, but I wondered if the pros would have outweighed the cons of that situation. I would have Emmet, who loved me unconditionally and wanted kids as much as I did. He would have appreciated me and he wouldn't have cared if I got fat and got stretch marks from a pregnancy.

Sighing, I decided I needed to push those thoughts out of my head, because what-ifs didn't mean anything. I had to work with the reality that I had created for myself and hope for the best.

Chapter Fifty-One

I almost backed out. My fingers were poised over my phone, ready to dial Emmy and tell her I couldn't make it. I would feign sickness, exhaustion, or Braxton Hicks. If I had to, I would troll the internet and find some way to put myself into labor.

It was that thought that made me put my phone down and give myself a mental slap.

"Really, Donya? You'd risk your baby's life?" I asked myself aloud as my hand automatically rubbed my round belly. "I'm sorry," I told my baby girl. "I didn't mean it. It's just that I'm nervous about seeing Emmet again and meeting his wife and kid."

She kicked me for my stupidity.

It was Lucas's first birthday, and Luke and Emmy were throwing a big party at Luke's sister's house. I was due to give birth in a little more than a month, and my doctor had advised against traveling, but I had not seen Emmy and Lucas since they moved to Chicago, and if I didn't see them this time, it would be several more months before I would have the opportunity.

Late in the winter, Emmet, Casey, and Owen also moved to Chicago. Luke offered Emmet a position in his law firm and Emmet took it. When Emmy told me that Emmet was considering it, I knew he would take it, because he still had the same job he had told me he hated. I wasn't sure how I felt about him living closer to Emmy. It increased the odds of me running into him whenever I visited his sister, but then again, I probably wouldn't visit very often anyway, at least not for the first year of my baby's life.

Emmet and his family were going to be at the party. It was going to be the first time we saw each other since the day I married Jerry and left Emmet crying for me in front of the pond.

I could already feel him, I felt him the moment the plane landed. With my sensitive, hormonal emotions in place, I didn't know how I was going to handle being in the same space with him. I didn't know how I was going to react to Casey in person.

How was I going to react to Owen? He was an innocent three-year-old boy. Could I possibly resent a three-year-old?

My cell phone rang, dislodging my thoughts about Owen and his parents. It was Sam calling to tell me she and Fred were ready to go. I grabbed my purse and checked my hair in the mirror, being careful not to look at my wide body, and then left to meet Sam and Fred in the lobby.

Fred typically drove slow enough to drive anyone crazy, but the ride into the burbs felt as if he had kicked it up to warp 8, because before I could really prepare myself, we had arrived at Lorraine's house. The pull of the tether was instantaneous. I walked behind the old folks towards the house knowing I wouldn't be able to stop myself if I tried. Emmet was calling to me, and even after all of the insanity we had been through, my body and heart still answered his call. I was equally relieved and terrified.

There were a few people hanging out in the front yard smoking. I looked at them with envy, because I could have really used a cigarette, but under no circumstance is a pregnant, smoking woman either attractive or acceptable.

You're being ridiculous, I told myself. You have been in the public eye for over sixteen years and have done some terrifying stunts, and you can't handle this? You got this! He's just a guy…

Even though the last part was a lie, Emmet wasn't just a guy, the rest was true. A good portion of the civilized world saw me topless in my last movie appearance and I have modeled in transparent lingerie on more than one occasion. I met the leaders of three countries and one prince, and I have done terrifying thrill chasing activities such as skydiving, zip lining, and hell, some of my fellow models were terrifying individuals. I could handle this.

I squared my shoulders as I followed the parents into the house and put on a smile that could light up the moon. I was barely through the door when a little boy with dark hair threw himself into Samantha's arms. I knew who it was before she could even say his name. His longish hair fell into his eyes just like his father's tended to do, and his green eyes were bright with joy and mischief.

"Owen, say hello to Aunty Donya," Sam said after she kissed him to within an inch of his life and after he transferred his little body to Fred's arms to escape the deluge of kisses.

"Hi," he said and waved a little hand.

"Hi, Owen," I said and put my hand to my throat to massage away the lump. With the exception of the shape of his mouth, he looked just like Emmet. I did eventually see pictures of him, but nothing prepared me for how much he looked like his father.

"What's her name?" he asked his grandfather.

"Don-ya," Fred said slowly.

"Donnie?" His forehead creased, just like Emmet's did when he was trying to understand something.

"Close enough," I managed.

"Donnie, it's almost my birthday, but now Lucas has his birthday."

"Yes, and how old are you?" I asked.

"Thrfree. Lucas is this many." He held up a single finger.

"That's right," I said and couldn't resist the urge to brush his hair out of his eyes. That action made Owen stretch out his arms to me expectantly. I looked at him with confusion until Fred straightened it out for me.

"No, Aunt Donya can't hold you right now, pal," Fred said.

"Oh," I said, understanding. I stretched out my arms for him. "It's okay. I can hold him."

"You really shouldn't," Sam warned, but Owen had already wrapped his little arms around my neck.

Fred reluctantly let him go and then he and Sam let out collective sighs.

"I'm pregnant, not enfeebled," I said to them.

I turned away from their disapproving murmurs as a woman identifying herself as Lena, Luke's oldest sister introduced herself. I liked her instantly. She was very talkative but didn't mince any words. She asked me a few questions about my pregnancy that left me blushing until Emmy rescued me.

"Why are you carrying that kid?" Emmy asked and playfully pinched her nephew's cheek.

I looked into Owen's face and he smiled at me and I think I fell in love a little. It was not something I expected to feel. Of all of the things that I expected, I did not expect to love him at first sight, especially since he was the reason Emmet and I weren't together.

No, I chastised myself. *You and Emmet are the reasons you and Emmet aren't together.*

"He's a cool kid," I said with a shrug.

"You look really good," Emmy said, looking me up and down. "It sickens me that you still look like a supermodel and you're about to have a baby. And you're wearing heels! I would have fallen on my face!"

"Are you kidding me? I'm as wide as the state of Illinois and by the end of the night my ankles will be swollen and I'll be waddling back to my hotel suite."

Emmy looked doubtful. "Whatever. You look fantastic. Isn't Aunty Donya pretty, Owen?"

He nodded and then stroked my hair. "I wike your hair."

"I wike your hair, too," I told him. "But Aunty Em looks hot."

"Don't tell him that!" She admonished, but looked pleased by my words.

I offered to put Owen down to play with the other ten thousand kids running around the house, but he refused and held on tighter. I followed Emmy into the kitchen. There were about a dozen people in there, but the second I walked in, I met Emmet's eyes from across the room.

My heart leaped and jumped in my chest, but I managed to keep my smiling face in place, though I knew Emmet knew my emotions regardless of the mask I wore. He and Luke, who was holding Lucas, were talking to a couple of men I didn't know. I smiled in their general direction. Luke waved as he continued to speak, but Emmet scowled. He was irritated, I could feel that clearly, but irritated at what? Was he irritated that I showed up?

I didn't have time to think about it, because I was suddenly surrounded by family members and friends I had not seen in a long time. We were all chatting when Emmet pushed his way into the circle and held his hands out for Owen. Surprised and mildly irritated myself by his behavior, I turned aside to keep him away from his own son. I was getting pissed because after all of the time it had been since we last saw one another and after all of the shit that transpired between us, I expected a better greeting than an irritated scowl.

"You shouldn't be holding him," Emmet snapped. "He's too heavy."

"He's fine," I snapped back.

"Donya, you're what, eight months pregnant? And wearing those ridiculous high hooker heels? You shouldn't be holding him."

"My shoes are not ridiculous! These are Manolo Blahniks, custom made for my feet!"

"Dude, what's your problem?" Mayson said. "She knows what she's doing."

"I carried baskets of your dirty ass laundry heavier than Owen when I was that pregnant," someone said from behind me. I instantly knew it was Casey, and that was confirmed when she stepped up beside me with her hands on her hips as she glared at her husband.

I glanced at her heart shaped face, cute button nose, and hazel eyes and instantly resented her presence. I didn't dislike her, but there was no doubt that I resented her.

"It's okay," I said, giving in. I handed Owen to his mother instead of his father, but she immediately put him down.

"Go play instead of hitching rides with pretty women, lady killer," she said and sent him on his way.

"He's a cute kid," I told her. I had to say something or else I would have stood there and scowled at her like Emmet had been doing to me moments before. His scowl was gone, but he was uneasy as he watched the exchange between his wife and me.

"Yes, but he uses his looks on easy prey like you to get what he wants," she said, smiling. "He would have had you stealing cookies in a matter of minutes." She hugged me. I was a little startled, but I awkwardly hugged her back. "It's so good to finally meet you in person."

"You, too," I half lied.

Fortunately, I didn't have to talk to her long. Luke came up to me with Lucas, and he hugged me as if we were old friends. I hugged and kissed and tickled Lucas and wished him a Happy Birthday. Luke put his hand on my swollen belly without asking, which usually bothered me, but I was okay with it that time. He looked awed and sad at the same time, because he had missed that stage of Lucas's budding life.

"Your husband must be excited," he said quietly when only he and Emmet remained with me in the corner of the kitchen.

The truth was Jerry was not excited at all. Jerry was the opposite of excited. Every time he looked at my rounded belly, it was with indifference or irritation. It was always one of the two and never anything in between. He never touched the basketball size bump, unless by accident, and even then he withdrew his hand as if I had tried to eat it.

He stopped having sex with me the day I started to show. He made up lame excuses, but I knew it was because of the pregnancy. He went to one doctor's appointment with me in the beginning, most likely just to confirm that I was indeed pregnant, and never went to another. When I told him we were having a baby girl, he only shrugged.

"He's too busy to really think about it," I said and forced a small smile.

Emmet's face had been relaxed since his wife and the other women had gone away, but after I said that, I knew he knew there was more to it. He frowned as he looked at me.

"Well, congratulations and good luck," Luke said and gave my belly one last touch before walking away.

"You should probably sit down," Emmet said, eying me carefully.

"I'm fine," I said quickly.

He sighed and met my eyes. I wanted to look away, because I knew he could see into me with those eyes, but I held his gaze.

"Can you please sit down?" he asked softly. "For me."

I hesitated a moment and then silently nodded.

"We can sit outside," he said, gesturing to the sliding doors that led into the backyard. There were several people outside, a lot of kids, and a couple of men stood around a grill drinking and barbecuing burgers and hotdogs and steaks. Emmet put his hand on the small of my back and led me across the yard to a seating area that was away from the rest of the party.

"I'll be right back," he said after he made me sit. He disappeared back into the house for a few minutes and then reappeared carrying a bottle of water and a plate of fruit and cheeses. He set them down on the table in front of me and even went as far as to open the bottle of water for me.

My hormones suddenly turned on me. I turned my head away from him as I started to cry. Why the hell was I crying? It was just fruit and cheese.

No, it was Emmet looking out for me as Emmet always did. Even with so much time, space, and heartache between us, he still wanted to take care of me.

I only cried for about fifteen seconds before my hormones jumped back to the land of the normal. I turned back, but focused my eyes on the plate of food and ignored Emmet's heavy gaze.

"So, this is really happening," he said with resignation.

"What is really happening?" I asked quietly as I pushed a grape around with my fork.

"You're having a baby and she isn't mine."

His hands fisted on the table not far from my plate.

"Yeah, well, welcome to my world," I said a little harsher than I meant to.

"How much more am I going to be punished for what happened?" He asked earnestly.

"Here's a piece of interesting news, Emmet," I said as I looked at him again. "I did not get pregnant to hurt you."

He sighed, but fell into silence as he stared at my belly. After several seconds, he scooted to the end of his chair until his knees touched mine, and to my surprise, he placed his hand on my unborn baby. I gasped softly and my body trembled slightly. Seeing Emmet's hand on my pregnant belly stirred a pot of emotions inside of me that had me blinking back more tears.

"I really wish things were different," Emmet said, just above a whisper. "I wish you were carrying my baby, Donya. I love Owen and I would never wish him away, but I wish we had made different decisions and then this baby would have been ours, together."

I was thankful that my back was to the men at the grill and most others in the yard, because tears streamed down my cheeks and I couldn't stop them.

"But even though she isn't mine, she is a part of you, and I know I'll love her," Emmet said. His eyes were moist. He managed to keep the tears at bay, but he seemed to be unable to take his hand away.

I raised my hand off of the table and then hesitantly covered his hand with my own. In that exact instant, the baby moved and we watched as our hands were pushed upward by her movement. It was almost as if she knew what kind of love was there in those two hands and she was reaching for it, because my belly rose again and again.

"This is how it was supposed to be," Emmet whispered as his eyes met mine.

"There you are," Casey's voice infiltrated our moment and I hastily pulled my hand away and wiped away my tears. Emmet only reluctantly pulled his hand away as his wife approached. She stopped beside Emmet and made a sympathetic sound. "Oh, God. Pregnancy hormones?"

I forced myself to laugh lightly and wiped my eyes again. "Yeah, I mean who would have thought that cheese could make a girl cry?"

"Tell me about it. I cried about everything, too."

I didn't want to hear about Casey's pregnancy. Seeing Owen was different, but hearing about those months would bother me. Fortunately, she didn't continue, but what happened next bothered me just as much if not more. Casey pushed Emmet's hair off of his forehead and out of his eyes.

"I hate when your hair gets this long," she murmured.

I loved when his hair was longish like that. I loved the way it fell across his forehead and how random strands fell into his eyes. How could she hate that?

Emmet pulled away from Casey's touch. A hurt expression crossed her face, but she quickly covered it with a chuckle and let her hand drop to her side.

I didn't know what to make of that. Maybe they had a fight earlier in the day and Emmet wasn't over it. Even though I could normally sense Emmet's emotions, I couldn't get a read on what he was feeling for Casey, and after some thought, I realized I didn't want to know.

I stood up abruptly.

"I'm sorry," I said to them. "I need to go find Emmy. God only knows when I'll see her again after today."

"Right, of course," Casey said, smiling. It could have been my imagination, but her smile looked a little tight and I had to wonder how much she saw happen between Emmet and me.

Later that evening I sat at the kitchen table watching Emmy and Luke. When Emmy first moved in with Luke, things were tense and she was clearly unhappy. I was under the impression that Luke didn't like her very much for all of the things she had done, but in a matter of months, their relationship had improved dramatically. They weren't romantically involved, but their relationship was more than just raising a son together. It appeared that they were friends, and maybe more, judging by the way Luke looked at her when she wasn't paying attention. Maybe there was some hope for them.

I wished that I had the same confidence about my own circumstances.

I don't think that Jerry ever truly meant his promise that we would eventually have kids. He probably would have said anything to keep me placated and on his arm. If he ever wanted kids in the future, he would have gotten over his initial shock and he would have been excited about our baby. Instead, he avoided me as if I had a communicable, deadly disease. I was already having some regrets by the time I entered my last trimester. However, after the way Emmet lovingly caressed the baby bump that was in no way his, my regrets were threatening to drown me, right there in the middle of Lucas's party, in front of a dozen other people, my soul mate, and his wife.

~~*

Rosa Andrea Vasquez slept peacefully in my arms, oblivious to my tears that fell on the soft blanket she was swaddled in.

It was just us, just she and I. Jerry did not show up to watch his daughter's birth or to even support her mother. I knew he wasn't happy about becoming a father, but I honestly believed he would have put that aside for this.

When I called him on my way to the hospital, he was getting ready for a home game. He could have easily gotten out of it, but he didn't even try. He behaved as if my labor and subsequent childbearing were somehow inconveniencing him. The game had been over for hours, but still Jerry did not show.

I couldn't stop thinking about Emmet, our hands on my belly and his obvious love for a baby that he had no part in creating. I wanted Jerry there because he was my husband and Rosa's father, but my need for Emmet while I sat there in that hospital bed holding my daughter was emotionally and mentally crippling.

He was the man I should have been having a baby with, just as he said. It was meant to be that way. I went against our nature. I was not meant to be sitting in a hospital room alone with my hours-old baby. I had no one to blame but myself. I had no right to hold Emmet accountable for impregnating Casey while I was planning a wedding with Jerry. Even as hurt and angry as I had been, I should have canceled the wedding. The price of my folly was more than I could pay.

My tears fell in a deluge now, and my body trembled violently with my sobbing. The nurse walked in, took one look at me and instantly took Rosa from my arms.

"I'll take her down to the nursery," she said gently. She took my baby away despite my tearful objections.

Then I was entirely desolate and decidedly inconsolable.

Jerry arrived early the next morning, just in time to pretend to be the happy new father in front of Sam and Fred, who flew in late the night before. I didn't play into his false excitement over Rosa. I didn't do much of anything. I sat quietly, always with tears brimming, as Sam, Fred, Jerry, and later Jerry's sisters made a fuss over Rosa. I couldn't pull off Supermodel Donya and pretend to care, because she was sitting in a corner crying hysterically.

The doctors tried to diagnose me with postpartum depression and feed me drugs, but I was very blunt with them.

"My husband was never interested in my pregnancy and didn't bother to show up for our daughter's birth. He's pretending to be happy now because people are watching him, but he doesn't want her. He doesn't want children. Last month I saw the man I should have married and he showed more interest in my pregnancy and my baby than my husband has shown in nine months. There aren't enough drugs in the universe to fix this."

After I had convinced him that I did not have any violent feelings towards my baby, he backed off and signed my release papers.

I refused to wallow in my self-pity after Rosa and I went home. I couldn't fix the past and what I lost with Emmet, but I could fix my current situation or move on. My first night home from the hospital, I stayed up late waiting for Jerry to come home from his game. The door had barely closed behind him when I started to speak.

"You have a choice," I said quietly, but firmly as I sat in the dimly lit living room in an armchair.

He stood there, unsure of what to say or do. It was the first time in months that I stayed up to wait for him after a game. We had been living two separate lives. We only slept in the same bed out of habit, not because he wanted to feel my warm body wrapped around his in the night. I had learned early in my pregnancy not to touch him. The rejection hurt too much to repeat.

"What are you talking about?" he finally asked, with a tired sigh. He dropped down on the couch and waited patiently.

"It's after midnight, it's a new day," I said. "What we couldn't or refused to fix yesterday, we can fix today. Today you can choose to be the husband I married; funny, sweet, loving, and caring. You can choose to be the father you are more than capable of being and love your daughter. It doesn't matter if you didn't want a child before I got pregnant, you have one now. You can do those things or Rosa and I can leave and we will get divorced. I can raise her with or without you and I can live with or without you. I love you, but I don't need you, Jerry."

Jerry looked at me for a long time before dropping his gaze to the floor. He was silent for so long I thought for sure had made his decision. I started to get up, but his voice stopped me.

"I haven't been good to you and I haven't been good to the baby," he said.

"Her name is Rosa," I said sharply.

"Rosa," he weighed her name on his lips. He finally looked at me then. "I love you and, believe it or not, I love Rosa. I can't tell you that I'm going to become Husband of the Year or Super Dad, but I will… try. I don't want a divorce, Donya."

I should have asked for explanations—why didn't he want a divorce, why would he only try and not do, and if he still loved me and if he loved Rosa, why had he been so cold and distant for so long? But I didn't ask. I took his word at face value.

"Okay," I said after a moment. "Thank you."

I stood up and started towards the bedroom, but Jerry's hand on my shoulder stopped me. He moved in front of me and put his arms around me. Automatically, I reciprocated and put my arms around him, too. He held me close and whispered in my ear.

"You're still my princess," he said. "I'll try to make you happy again."

I didn't answer. I just let him hold me, but I knew deep down that only one person could ever make me truly happy, but I didn't have him. So I'd have to make do.

PART THREE
Tied

Chapter Fifty-Two

I watched with apprehension as Emmy transformed from a smiling, glowing, happy woman into a monster, shouting and snarling. Seconds later she burst into tears.

"Why can't everyone just do what I want them to do?" she asked no one in particular. Luke pulled her into his arms, and she mumbled some other indiscernible words that were muffled because her face was in his shirt.

"I said I would do it," I said, still staring in shock at her shaking back. "I just thought that maybe that was something you would want to handle yourself."

For the rest of my life, I will swear that Emmy's head twisted around on her neck like some demonized fictional character, and her eyes were orbs of fire. I'll stand by that statement for the rest of my life. "Obviously I can't handle it myself," she snapped at me in a raspy voice that was foreign to her vocal cords.

I put a hand on my hip. I flew into Chicago earlier that day, alone, with a baby, so that I could be of some assistance to her and Luke. There was a snow storm due the day I was supposed to fly back home, which meant I would most likely be stuck in the tundra of Chicago for no less than a week. I could have stayed the hell home and sent a congratulatory card. I was just about to put her in her place when a strong arm closed over my shoulder and gently pulled me back away from Emmy.

"We'll do what you asked us to do," Emmet said soothingly. "We'll go to the venue and talk to the caterers, choose your new linens and make sure everything is in order there."

Emmy had pressed her face against Luke's chest once again, so her next words were muffled and barely understandable.

"And you'll pay the bakery for the cake?"

I wanted to ask her what exactly she would be doing, but Emmet quieted me with a light squeeze of his hand. I looked at him with a scowl, but he shook his head. When Emmet didn't immediately answer, Emmy looked at him and screeched "And you'll pay the bakery for the cake!"

"Yes, you miserable beast," I snapped before Emmet could stop me.

That quick, she changed. She smiled tearfully and threw herself on me.

"I'm so glad you're here. I love you so much."

I rolled my eyes and patted her back. She released me and stood on her toes to kiss Emmet's cheek. She probably would have hugged him to death as well if he had not been holding Rosa in one arm. He had been holding her since he walked into the house soon after my arrival. His face lit up when he laid his eyes on her, and he hadn't stopped telling her what a beautiful baby she was.

"Thanks, guys," Luke said with a sigh.

"No problem," Emmet said. He nodded towards the family room. "You think Diana will mind having an extra kid to watch?"

I looked at him and offered Rosa my finger, which she gratefully took and pushed into her mouth. "No, that's okay. She can come with us."

"It's like six degrees outside and raining," Emmet said, looking at me.

I had only ever left Rosa alone with Sam, Fred, and Mayson. Luke's young cousin Diana or Diane or whatever, seemed like a nice girl, and Emmy, Emmet, and Lena swore by her, but I was nervous about leaving Rosa behind.

"She'll be fine," Emmet said softly.

"Diane is awesome with kids," Luke said.

"Are you guys going to leave soon? The day is only so long." Emmy was starting to turn sour again. I had never seen so many mood swings within such a small space of time.

I looked back to Emmet, and he squeezed my arm reassuringly.

"Okay," I conceded.

A few minutes later I was leaving Rosa behind with a virtual stranger, but she seemed happy enough. Lucas was entertaining her, making faces and making her laugh hysterically as she sat on Diana's lap. Emmy would be home all day, so I took some solace in that.

"Your sister is a bridezilla," I said to Emmet as he opened the passenger door for me.

"To the nth power," he said with a laugh.

He closed my door and walked around to the driver's side. He opened the door, quickly closed the umbrella and got inside. I rubbed my hands together as I waited for the heat to kick on and wondered if the heat ever really came on high enough to defeat the frigid air outside. Emmy was lucky that I loved her because there was nothing else in the world that would ever bring me back to Chicago in the dead of winter.

Emmy's relationship with Luke had changed dramatically since she and Lucas first moved in with him. Hell, it had changed dramatically since Lucas's party. Several months later, they were pregnant and getting married, and Emmet and I were put into wedding serfdom by an apparently insane Emmy.

Her pregnancy hormones could make any man think twice about wanting to knock up his significant other, but Luke was patient with her, and clearly adored everything about her, even her demonic mood swings. I was truly happy for them. Despite Emmy's sordid past, she would make a good wife, and Luke was the champion Emmy needed to battle her many demons.

She was lucky. She was marrying her champion. My champion was married to someone else.

"I don't think I could ever get used to this ridiculously cold weather," I said, rubbing my hands in front of the vent as if it was a campfire. A cold, unlit campfire, because the air blowing out of the thing did nothing for me.

"Give me your hands," Emmet said, holding out his gloved hands.

I looked over at him, feeling unsure, a bit uncomfortable, and a little thrilled. Hesitantly, I put my hands together and pushed them toward him. He enclosed my hands with his and began to rub vigorously. I looked at our hands and was reminded of a night of skateboarding and having cold hands.

I met Emmet's eyes, wondering if he remembered it too, and I could tell by the intensity in his eyes that he did remember. Without taking his eyes away from mine, he brought our hands to his lips and blew warm air onto my hands. I shivered slightly, but it wasn't from the cold.

"Better?" he asked quietly a moment later. He gave my hands one last rub down and then released me.

"Thank you," I managed to say as I turned to face forward in my seat. I was startled to find that the windows had quickly fogged up. The things that could signify made me blush and made my stomach flutter. "Let's get going before bridezilla comes storming out here and destroys the city."

Our first stop was the venue. By the time we arrived there, Emmy had already called to add to our list of things to do. We went inside and spoke to the event host and confirmed the final count of guests, discussed how the room for the ceremony should be set up, and then had to correct the way the reception hall was set up. Due to a mishap on the venue's part, we also had to choose different linens for the reception. We nailed down some other necessary details and after an hour we headed back out into the cold to run a couple of other errands that Emmy had given us.

For a little while, I forgot that it was the first time in years that Emmet and I had spent any extensive time together. After those initial first few minutes in the car, our conversation came easily. We cracked jokes and Emmet talked about work. We talked about our kids, but we did not talk about our spouses. It seemed to be a mutual understanding that Casey and Jerry were off limits.

After we had paid for Emmy's and Luke's wedding cake, we each got a couple of pastries to go. As Emmet paid for it, I bit into my gourmet cupcake and moaned happily as the sweet buttercream hit my tongue. Emmet looked over at me, amused.

"You're worse than Owen," he said.

"What are you talking about?" I asked, even though my mouth was full of cake.

He looked me in the eyes, reached out and gently swiped his finger across the corner of my mouth. When he pulled his finger away, I saw a decent amount of frosting on his finger. I started to laugh at myself, but then Emmet put the finger in his mouth and slowly sucked the frosting off. There was nothing innocent in the move. It was sensual and made me feel hot under my layers of fabric.

While I stood there stunned, Emmet took a hold of my wrist and brought the cupcake to his mouth. He took a bite, from the same spot that my teeth and mouth had been on moments before, and I was reminded of an ice-cream cone on the boardwalk when I was just a kid. He licked the frosting away from his lips. If that wasn't enough to make Donya, Sex Goddess and Lover stir in her deep, long slumber, Emmet very quietly said, "You have frosting on your lips," and then licked his lips again. He looked at my mouth as if he wanted to take a bite out of it.

"You are a beautiful couple," the old man said jovially from behind the counter.

Startled by our one-man audience, his words, Emmet's actions, and my inaction, I dropped the cupcake on the floor. It landed with a soft plopping sound.

"Oh, shit," I said and bent over to pick it up.

That hot, confusing moment ended there and the rest of our time together that afternoon was quiet as each of us tended to our own thoughts.

~~*

Later that evening, Emmet drove Rosa and me back to our hotel. I knew he would make sure that we were safely in our room before taking off, but to my surprise, he had taken his coat off, like he was going to stay awhile.

For an hour, he played with Rosa, showering her with the kind of love she had never received from Jerry. Emmet was truly taken with my daughter. When he gazed at her, it was with love, sadness, and remorse. He didn't have to say what I already knew. She should have been his all along.

I once questioned whether or not I was capable of cheating on my husband. I didn't judge Emmy for her place in a wicked love triangle, but I didn't think that could ever be me. However, after Rosa was asleep, and as Emmet's fingers grazed over my cheek, my jaw and down my neck, I realized that could be anyone, *especially* me.

"You're more beautiful every time I see you," he whispered as his lips just barely touched the skin under my ear.

He didn't kiss me, but he wanted to. It would only take one small move from either of us to make it happen. I could move only a quarter of an inch in his direction, and his mouth would be on my skin. One of his hands held my hip firmly. I was inches from feeling his hardness against me, but we both resisted the urge to move forward.

I curled my fingers in the fabric of his shirt and deeply inhaled his scent. I wanted to rub my body all over his, capture that scent in my pores and make it a permanent part of me.

"I love you," Emmet breathed on my neck. "Do you still love me?"

"You don't even have to ask," I whispered.

"I want to hear you say it."

"I love you."

He sighed heavily with relief and his hand squeezed my hip as he resisted the urge to pull me closer.

"You should go," I said, even as my fingers curled tighter in his shirt.

"I should," he agreed, but made no move to do so.

Tears suddenly stung my eyes. I inhaled a shuddering breath and simultaneously released Emmet's shirt and took a large step back away from him. My body's natural instinct was to go back to its home, but I resisted and wrapped my arms around myself for some comfort that didn't quite hit the mark.

Emmet looked disappointed but resigned. He knew just as well as I did that we had crossed a line. We poked at it with our toes in the car earlier, and then stood squarely on the thing in the bakery, and before either of us could get our bearings, we had crossed it and had stood on dangerous territory.

"Thank you for bringing us back," I said to him.

"You don't have to thank me. I'll do anything for either of you."

"We're not your responsibility," I whispered.

Emmet stared at me for a long time. He was hurting, and I was hurting, and we were both feeling rather guilty. I rubbed my chest to try to alleviate some of the pressure.

"I will always have a responsibility to you," he finally said. "And now to Rosa, too."

He didn't wait for me to respond. He picked his coat up off of the couch and headed to the door. He pulled it open and turned around to look at me.

"I'll see you tomorrow," he said.

I nodded as I continued to rub my chest. He didn't want to leave. It was clear in the way he hesitated at the door, the way he looked at me, and the way he felt. I didn't want him to leave either, but I knew he had to. Just when I thought that I would ask him to stay, he turned and left. I collapsed onto the couch and began to mentally and emotionally redraw the line.

Chapter Fifty-Three

Early the next morning when I was still trying to see straight, one of the hotel employees knocked on the door and handed me a small manila envelope.

"What is this?" I sleepily asked her.

"It was just dropped off for you at the front desk," she said pleasantly. "The gentleman said you lost it, and he was returning it and didn't want to disturb you."

"What gentleman? And what is it?" I searched my mind, trying to recall if there was something I was missing.

"I don't know ma'am," the woman said apologetically.

She walked away, and I let the door close. I weighed the envelope in my hand for a moment as I tried to guess what could be in it. Finally, with a yawn and a shrug, I turned it over and proceeded to open it. I tipped it to expel the contents and gasped when it landed in my hand. It was the charm bracelet I had mailed to Emmet years ago after our biggest fight ever.

"Oh my god," I whispered as I stared at the bracelet.

I thought for sure that Emmet had gotten rid of it long ago. Why did he hold on to it for so long?

I looked inside the envelope and discovered a folded piece of paper. I pulled it out and unfolded it, careful not to drop the bracelet.

"This is yours, always, as is my soul."

I dropped the note and envelope on the couch and eyed the bracelet in the palm of my hand. It was shiny and looked brand new. The heart and the kiss were polished and the diamonds twinkled in the light. As I examined the bracelet, I discovered yet another charm. It was a flower, covered in pink diamonds. At the center of the flower was the letter R, created with Rosa's birthstones. It was incredible and the most beautiful piece of jewelry I owned. A hand went to my mouth as I attempted to stifle the sudden sob that tried to push through my lips.

"Emmet," I whispered.

Rosa started to stir in the other room. I brought the bracelet to my lips and then put it on my wrist. It wasn't until it was securely latched that I realized how naked my wrist had been all of that time. I dropped my arm and felt the familiar cool metal slide into place and went to get the baby.

~~*

Emmy didn't want a bachelorette party if she couldn't drink. Instead, I treated her, Mayson, Tabitha, Lorraine, Lena, and Casey to a day at the spa. All of the men were forced to babysit their own kids, but Emmet had volunteered to watch Rosa because Jerry wasn't due in until the morning of the wedding.

I couldn't stop the smile that appeared on my face when I saw him that morning at Emmy's. My hands and wrists were covered to block out the cold air, but I mouthed a thank you to him, and he understood that I received and was wearing the bracelet. Casey appeared at his side as he took Rosa from my arms.

"She really likes you," she commented as she watched Rosa put a slobbery hand on Emmet's cheek. I froze, waiting for him to freak out as Jerry did whenever Rosa got any bodily fluids on him, but he didn't.

"I really like her," he answered with a big smile as he began to pull the zipper down on Rosa's snowsuit, and I relaxed again.

"I see that," Casey said lightly, but there was some tension around her eyes. She turned to me and said, "Are you sure I can't help you with the spa bill?"

I smiled at her. It was a genuine smile, but I still resented her.

"No, it's not a problem," I said.

"Mrs. Scrooge McDuck over here," Emmet said with a grin as he tossed Rosa's outerwear onto the couch.

"What?" I asked with a serious expression. "Doesn't everyone have a room full of gold to swim in?"

Emmet chuckled, which made me smile. He said, "I'm sure you have enough money by now to buy a small country."

"How do you know I didn't?" I laughed.

"Do all of your residents have to abide by the no white after Labor Day rule? Do you literally have Fashion Police?"

"The Labor Day thing is just a myth," I said with an air of superiority. "And if any of my deputies were here, they'd arrest you for that garish sweater you're wearing."

"I...bought him this sweater," Casey cut in softly. I had forgotten she was even standing there, and now that I looked at her, she looked like she knew that we had forgotten she was standing there.

"Oh," I said and looked at her apologetically. "I want to lie to you and tell you I didn't mean it but..." I shrugged helplessly.

"Miss Fashionista would explode into a million shreds of polyester before she'd lie to someone about their fashion mistakes," Emmet said to Casey without taking his eyes off of me.

"Really, Emmet," I said with a huff. "Polyester?"

We both laughed, and I loved how it felt to laugh with Emmet again. We had some laughs the day before, but this time it felt more...free, and real. Whatever pieces of our binding that were frayed had begun to mend. They always did, and always would.

"Well, I can't compete with a supermodel," Casey said with a tight smile as she crossed her arms. I felt like she was saying more than what she was actually saying, like I had to read between the lines to understand her meaning.

"I can't compete with a wife," I smiled tightly also. "So, buy all of the sweaters you want. Excuse me, I'm going to check on Emmy."

I leaned in and kissed Rosa's cheek and hurried from the room.

~~*

"This spa visit is going to cost more than I make in a year," Mayson said as we checked our coats.

She tapped a boot on the marble floor and spun in a small circle taking in the high ceilings, the beautiful art and the tropical looking plants that helped bring ambiance to the place.

"Depends on which job you're talking about," I said as I handed over my coat. "The one at Sterling Corp or your night job on the street corners of Camden?"

"Oh, you would know all about that because I service your husband every night, sweetheart," she retorted.

"That explains the crabs."

"You two are disturbing," Emmy said, even as she shook her head and laughed.

"Come on preggo, let's get those eyebrows tweezed," I said with my hand on her shoulder.

Her mouth flew open, and her fingers flew to her brows. Before she could say anything, Casey cried out, "Oh my god!" Her claw closed around my forearm, and she held my hand to her face.

"Where did you get this?" she asked in a high voice, and there was no doubt her tone was rather accusatory. "I've seen this bracelet before," she added sharply before meeting my eyes. Her eyes were full of questions and accusations.

"Probably," Emmy said, eyeing Casey with one eyebrow up. "She's had it since she was what…seventeen? Eighteen?" Emmy asked me.

"Sixteen," I answered quickly and swallowed and tried to pull out of her grasp, but Casey held tight. Her eyes narrowed.

"I saw this," she said slowly, but forcefully. "But not on your arm, not on anyone's arm."

"Casey," I said her name quietly. "If you don't let go of my arm…" I trailed off, but my tone and my death stare was enough to make her release me and murmur an apology.

"Emmet gave Donya and me almost the same bracelet when we were kids," Emmy said to Casey. "I lost mine, but Donya has always had hers. You probably saw it in pictures or something."

I could tell by her expression that she didn't quite believe that, but she nodded anyway. "Yeah, I guess so," she said. "Sorry, Donya."

"No problem," I said, forcing a smile. "You just really need a good day at the spa. I'll make sure you get the full package."

She forced a smile, too, and the rest of the girls that had watched the whole thing moved on. Casey followed after them, leaving Emmy and me to bring up the rear. Emmy looked at me with her mouth in a flat line and her eyebrow raised slightly.

"What?" I whispered to her, irritated by her look.

"I haven't seen that bracelet on your wrist in a few years," she whispered back. "What the hell was that about?"

I looked away from her and said nothing.

Soon we were all wrapped in fluffy towels and wearing comfortable slippers. The other girls went to sit in a steam room while Emmy and I sat down so that some hunky guy could rub her feet. She couldn't go into the steam rooms or hot tub or get a traditional massage, but, fortunately, the place I chose catered to pregnant women. Having her feet rubbed by a gorgeous, muscular man was one of the perks she got for being knocked up.

"Spill it," Emmy said after her massage therapist found a rhythm she enjoyed.

"Spill what?" I asked dumbly.

"Where did the bracelet disappear to in the first place and why are you wearing it now?"

I could have given her some bullshit response, but that wouldn't have been fair. We had been hiding enough secrets from each other over the years.

"The year before Jerry and I got married I took him to Louisiana to meet the parents. I didn't know Emmet was going to be there. Long story short, when Fred took Jerry out for some night fishing, Emmet started this huge fight with me, and after he had taken off, I put the bracelet in an envelope and mailed it to him."

Emmy's mouth was hanging open. "But...you and Emmet hadn't been together for a long time when you met Jerry. Right? Or is there a whole chunk of shit you failed to tell me again?"

"Don't do that," I said, sighing.

"Don't do what?"

"Don't try to make me feel guilty for not telling you every nuance of my life. Some things are just private and between Emmet and me, just like there are some things that are private and only meant to be between you and Luke."

"There are no private things between you and Jerry?" she asked dryly.

"There's plenty," I snorted.

"Okay, I want to know about the bracelet. I'm not absolving you from the rest of it, but I want to know about the bracelet."

"This morning one of the girls from the front desk at my hotel brought me a little manila envelope that was left there for me. When I opened it up, it was the bracelet."

Emmy's eyes narrowed. "You're leaving a lot of shit out," she snapped. "What happened to make him give that back to you today of all days?" She gasped. "Did you guys do something while you were out yesterday?"

"No we didn't 'do something,'" I said, irritated. After a sigh, I recounted what happened in the car, the bakery, and reluctantly, I told her what happened after Rosa went to sleep in my hotel room.

"Oh my god," Emmy said in a whisper, and then snapped, "But you're still not telling me shit!"

"Someday, eventually, I will tell you everything. I just don't want that day to be today."

Emmy sighed and relaxed a little in her seat. "Fine, okay. So, do you think Casey saw the bracelet in Emmet's possessions?"

"Probably," I admitted. "And now she's freaking out because she knows it wasn't meant for her."

"It's like that part in *Love Actually* when Alan Rickman bought the bracelet for the slutty office chick and Emma Thompson's character thought it was for her, but then she never got it."

"Umm, yeah, kinda," I answered slowly.

"Can you imagine how she feels?"

"Emma Thompson?"

"No, asshole. Casey. She's probably seen it over and over again and maybe she expected him to add more charms or something before giving it to her and then one day she finds it on *your* arm, the ex-fiancé."

"I don't think she knows that we were once engaged."

"Oh, she knows," Emmy nodded. "She's mentioned it to me before. Why wouldn't she know? She's his wife, and it's not like you're some random girl. You're family. She was bound to find out. You really didn't think she knew?"

I mutely shook my head.

"She's not stupid you know," Emmy said and looked at me as if I was the stupid one. "I don't know what is happening between you and Emmet. For that matter, I don't even know what is happening between you and your husband these days either, but whatever it is, keep the drama away from my wedding day or I will cut you."

Her expression softened, and she reached for me. I put my hand in hers and suddenly felt like I was going to bawl.

"Don't go down that road, Donya," Emmy whispered, shaking her head softly as her eyes burned imploringly into mine. "Take it from me. You do not want to go there. It will tear everyone around you apart. Do whatever you have to do to end this before it can really get started."

I shook my head as I blinked back tears. "But we didn't..."

"Cheating isn't always physical, D. An affair of the heart is so much worse than a physical one. When you're ready to talk about what's going on between you and Jerry, I will listen, but in the meantime, you need to let Emmet go."

Casey and Mayson stepped into the room, and the conversation halted, but Emmy gave my hand a squeeze and gave me an encouraging, yet sympathetic smile. I excused myself, found the restroom and locked myself inside to cry.

Chapter Fifty-Four

Emmy's and Luke's wedding was incredible. My own wedding was much larger and grander, but their quaint wedding was more personable. Their vows were built on the purest, real love while mine was built on false pretenses. There was no comparison; Emmy had the better wedding.

After the bride and groom were announced at the reception and were seated at their table at the front of the room, I went to find my seat and cursed when I realized the seating arrangements. Jerry, Rosa and I were at a table with Mayson and her mom, Tabitha and Emmet, Casey, and Owen. The only open seat was between Jerry and Owen. At least it was Owen and not his father, who I had been actively avoiding since I left the spa the night before.

When I had picked up Rosa after our spa day, I kept conversation to a minimum and averted my eyes. I knew that he knew that I was pulling away from him, but with Casey right there, he didn't challenge it. It was easier to avoid him while getting myself and Emmy ready for the wedding, but sitting two seats away from him at the reception was going to be harder to accomplish.

The second my ass hit the chair, Jerry passed Rosa to me. I was so accustomed to the handoff that I didn't think anything of it until I felt Emmet watching us. I dared a quick glance and found him looking at Jerry and me with his brow furrowed. Then he looked at Rosa, and his expression softened some before he turned his attention to Mayson after she asked him a question. I sat quietly looking around the room while Jerry sat quietly on his phone.

Soon dinner was being served, but I pushed my plate away so I could feed Rosa first. She liked to feel included and eat when everyone else was eating, or she squealed like a banshee. Again I felt Emmet watching me, but I avoided meeting his gaze. Even after I finished feeding Rosa, I didn't eat, because I would spend more time taking food out of her grabby little hands.

Jerry was chatting with a couple of Luke's friends at another table, talking about the upcoming baseball season. When he finished his dinner, he and the other men all got up and went to the bar.

Emmet suddenly stood up and walked around Owen. Without a word, he took Rosa from my arms. His expression was dark.

"Eat your dinner," he said quietly. He found a smile for his son and reached out his hand. "Come on, buddy. Let's go look at the fishies."

Before taking the kids to the large aquarium at the back of the room, Emmet cast me a brief look that was heavy with his past words. *"He'll never give up anything for you."*

I pulled my plate closer, picked up my fork but only pushed the food around on my plate.

"Where is your bracelet?" Casey leaned toward me and asked quietly.

I looked at my naked wrist. "It just didn't seem like a good idea to wear it," I answered honestly. I grabbed my purse and pushed away from the table. "Excuse me."

I went outside and joined a couple of other guests in the front of the building for an after dinner smoke. I was smoking more and more since I had Rosa. At home, the moment she went down for a nap, I would grab a cigarette and stand at a window in the kitchen and light one up. At night after she was in bed, I would take the baby monitor out onto the back deck with me and smoke and drink a whole bottle of wine. There was no one else there to give a damn how much I smoked or drank.

When I went back inside, Emmy and Luke were just making their way to the floor for their wedding dance. I scanned the room in search of my daughter and was relieved to see Fred had her and not Emmet.

I stood between Fred Jr. and Charlotte at the edge of the dance floor and watched the couple dancing as close as Emmy's pregnant belly allowed them to get. She looked more at peace with herself and the world than I had ever seen, and anyone looking at the way Luke was looking at his new wife could see that the man was deeply in love. Had I looked that way when I married Jerry? Did I look at Jerry as if he was my one and only and I would need no one else ever again? Did he look at me as if he would happily drown inside of me?

The song ended, and I clapped obligingly. When Freddy asked me to dance, I almost said no. I wanted to sit in a corner somewhere and think about my life, what was wrong with it and how to fix it, but it wasn't the time or place. It was my best friend's wedding day, and she deserved every bit of happiness I could conjure and share with her.

"Sure, big brother," I said to Freddy and gave him my hand.

I immersed myself into the festivities, dancing, eating too much cake, laughing and chatting while actively avoiding Emmet. I allowed myself to enjoy myself for Emmy's sake, and maybe for my own, too.

~~*

Sleep did not come for me that night. I lay in bed beside Jerry, staring up at the dark ceiling as the minutes and hours ticked by. I was unable to shake the images of the night from my mind. Harsh words that played like a broken record. The night had been going so well, and then Emmet and I were over that line again…

I had danced with Luke, and we had a candid conversation.

"I just want you to always be conscious of your actions, Luke," I had told him. "It's very easy to find yourself standing on the wrong side of the line without ever meaning to cross it."

I had made a mad dash off of the dance floor soon after that. I needed to get out of the building, away from Emmet and his wife, and Jerry. I had followed a stone path to the back of the building, away from the other smokers, away from the wedding celebration. I should have known that Emmet would follow me. It didn't take long for him to come up behind me. I didn't have to turn around to know it was him.

One of his strong arms encircled my waist. He plucked the cigarette I had just lit from my lips and tossed it away. He wrapped his other arm around me, and I shamelessly let my head fall back on his shoulder. He pressed his cheek against me, and there we stood, just like that, for several minutes as the sun sunk below the horizon and full darkness fell.

Emmet kissed the side of my head, and his arms tightened around me. His mouth moved close to my neck, and I knew he wanted to kiss me there. I wanted him to kiss me there, and I hated myself for it. I turned in his arms to face him.

"Emmet." His name passed through my lips in a breathy whisper. My palms were flat against his chest as if to keep some distance between us, but he had already pulled me close again.

One arm released me and then my eyes closed when his fingers lightly touched my cheek. He traced a slow swirling pattern to my lips where he paused for a moment before I felt his fingers move across my bottom lip. I opened my eyes and looked into his green eyes. My right hand slid into his coat, across his hard chest and stopped above his heart. His fingers moved languidly down my neck, under my coat, and across my collarbone. He traced a line over the naked swell of my right breast and across my chest until he reached my heart. He flattened his hand over my heart.

"Do you still feel me?" he whispered.

"Always," I whispered back.

"You are a part of me," Emmet said.

"You're a part of me, too."

His hand moved to my neck, and he slowly angled his lips to line up with mine. I felt his breath on my mouth, but I didn't pull away. My lips parted slightly to give him the access we both wanted, needed and had been deprived of for too long.

"Emmet!" Fred's voice was like a whip, snapping into us and forcing us to release each other and take quick steps back from each other.

I stumbled in my hastiness and Emmet reached out to steady me as Fred approached like a deadly storm about to put lightning bolts in our asses.

"Dad, I—" Emmet started, but Fred held up a hand to silence him.

"There are not enough excuses in the world to explain away what you were about to do out here," Fred growled. He got into Emmet's face and said, "Your wife and son are inside looking for you and you are out here with someone else's wife!"

"Dad, I wasn't—" Emmet stammered.

"You weren't what?" Fred demanded. "You weren't about to push your tongue against her tonsils?"

Fred Grayne is a man of impressive size. He was a Marine in his younger years, before Emmy and Emmet were born. Though he was in his early seventies, he had not gone soft. He still had a thick, muscular body and strong hands that could crack a skull. His temper didn't flare often, but when it did, it scared even his grown sons. Emmet's body tensed at Fred's proximity and his hands were balled into fists at his sides as if he was prepared to fight, even though Fred had never given him reason to feel like he had to defend himself. I couldn't blame him. I had never seen Fred so angry before.

"Your mother and I tried to warn both of you," Fred said, glaring at us. "We warned you that Donya's career and your schooling would push you apart, and you both were so damn headstrong and thought you knew it all."

"That was a long time ago," I objected softly and then winced when he glared daggers at me.

"And your inability to use your head then is having a calamitous affect now," he growled. "You two had plenty of opportunities to fix your relationship. Emmet, when you graduated from law school, it was your bonehead decision to move hundreds of miles away."

"That's bullshit," Emmet argued. "You and Freddy wanted me down there to help out!"

"I wanted you to help out temporarily!" Fred roared. "I didn't tell you to stay there and start your career! You could have sat for the New York and Connecticut bars. I know Donya was still traveling and busy, but her main residence was in New York. You could have made it work then, but you chose to stay in Florida."

Emmet looked away from his father with his brow furrowed.

"I maybe pushed him away," I said in a small voice.

"Real men fight for what they want!" he snapped at me. "And you…"

"Leave her alone," Emmet demanded.

Fred ignored him and said, "As soon as you knew you were going to retire from modeling, you should have gone to him. Instead, you married someone you didn't want."

"I loved Jerry," I said defensively.

"That may be, but he wasn't the one you wanted. I walked you down the aisle, Donya," Fred said harshly. "I felt your hand shaking on my arm. I heard your anxious breaths and saw your tight, fake supermodel smile meant to appease anyone looking at you."

Emmet looked at me now with questions on his tongue, but he remained quiet.

"I had just found out Casey was pregnant," I said helplessly. I was startled to feel tears on my cheeks. I wiped them away and said, "I would have canceled the whole thing. I begged him to ask me not to marry Jerry, but he couldn't because he had just found out he knocked Casey up."

"He shouldn't have had to ask you not to marry Jerry!" Fred shouted.

"I begged you not to marry him," Emmet said angrily. "I was on my knees begging you not to marry him!"

I shrunk back from the angry, yelling men and choked on a sob. Having both of them bitterly angry with me was too much.

"But she did," Fred said, looking at his son. "And you married Casey, and that should have been the end of it. You both made your decisions, as poor as they may be, and now you have to deal with it. If you're not happy in your marriage, fix it or get out, but *this*..." He pointed at the ground between us as he looked back and forth at us. "This is unacceptable behavior. You are *married* with *children*. Casey is a good woman and does not deserve this from you," he said to Emmet. He looked at me and said, "I don't know what is going on between you and Jerry, but don't cheapen yourself this way."

Emmet's chest rose and fell rapidly as he stared at the ground again. There were too many emotions churning inside of him for me to get a fix. Suddenly he turned his back on us and took several quick steps forward. He halted for a moment and his hands flexed at his sides. He started to look back over his shoulder, but snapped his head forward and stormed down the sidewalk.

The tether contorted and quivered and groaned in protest. I put both hands on my chest in an attempt to keep my heart from bursting from my ribcage and splattering red on the white snow.

Fred put his hands firmly on my shoulders.

"When you were still practically a little girl, you asked me how you would know if you were doing the right thing," he said earnestly. "What did I say to you?"

"That I'd know when I was doing it," I said as tears continued to pour from my eyes.

"Does this feel like the right thing, Kiddo?" he asked in a harsh whisper.

I shook my head and then a loud, keening sob broke free. Fred held me tightly and rubbed my back.

"Kiddo, I'm not telling you to ignore what your heart wants, but this isn't the way to do it. You are my sensible child, and I expect you to be sensible. Do you understand?"

I nodded my compliance.

Fred stepped back and pulled a handkerchief out of the inside of his tux jacket. He wiped away my tears, and like I was a little kid again, he even wiped my nose.

"Let's get you back inside so you can get my beautiful granddaughter to bed," he said with a heavy sigh. He offered me his arm, and I took it, much like I did when he walked me down the aisle.

By the time we made it back inside, Emmet and his family were gone.

Jerry stirred next to me, bringing my mind back to the hotel room hours later, and the man beside me. I rolled on my side to look at his dark profile. There was a time when I couldn't get enough of looking at his handsome face and long eyelashes and touching his strong body. I couldn't remember the last time I paid it any mind.

His reaction to Rosa was unacceptable, but maybe I didn't help matters any. Jerry relished his time with me before I got pregnant. He soaked up every minute, even if he knew I was in the stands watching him play. Maybe if I gave him more of myself, he would soften again and maybe whatever it was that emotionally blocked him from his daughter would start to fall away.

When I stripped away my clothing and straddled my husband that night, I knew my reasons were selfish. I wanted to feel better. I wanted to push away the pain in my chest, but I thought it could be a start, too. Maybe things could change, and I could be happy with Jerry again.

I shut off my brain and allowed my body to succumb to a physical pleasure that only proved to farther scar me emotionally.

Chapter Fifty-Five

I had just fallen asleep when Rosa's cries came through on the baby monitor. I waited to see if Jerry would go to her this time, but he rolled over, nudged me in the side, and told me Rosa was crying.

Sighing, I rolled out of bed and stumbled to the nursery. My baby stood in her crib, nose running, cheeks flushed, and tears were dampening her cheeks. She had been sick for days, we both had, and even though we had gone to the doctor when she first got sick, there seemed to be no improvement. She had been asleep for a couple of hours, but then I couldn't fall asleep because I had been coughing. I was pretty sure I had bronchitis, but I hadn't had time to take myself to my doctor.

"Hey, pretty baby," I said to her as I reached for her. When my hands made contact with her body, I felt the heat of her skin through her pajamas. I quickly picked her up and put my hand on her forehead. She was burning up.

I rushed over to her dresser and grabbed the thermometer. I took her temperature and my heart dropped. 103.3 was entirely too hot for anyone, but especially someone Rosa's size. I raced into my bedroom.

"Jerry," I called his name as I looked around for a pair of shoes or slippers to put on. "Jerry!"

He rolled over, grumbling, and pushed up on his elbows.

"I need you to get up and take us to the ER," I said hurriedly as I struggled to push my feet into a pair of sneakers. "Get up!" I cried before racing out of the room with a crying Rosa.

I took her back into the nursery and gently put her down on the changing table so I could change her diaper. Dusky sat at my feet, looking up at Rosa and whining with worried eyes for a moment before wandering back out of the room.

"And get a couple of her juice cups from the fridge, please!" I called out to Jerry through the open door. "And maybe grab a few snacks incase she's feeling better enough to eat later."

I quickly stripped her out of the diaper only to realize I had no wipes. They were across the room on top of her dresser. Jerry appeared in the doorway then. I didn't pay much attention to his facial expression, but I probably should have.

"Give me those wipes, will you?" I asked, with my hand extended, but my face turned back to Rosa.

I heard him pick up the box of wipes and a second later I felt something hard slam into my side. I looked up just in time to see the sippy cup soaring through the air. I gasped and turned my body to block Rosa, and the cup slammed into my back. I looked over my shoulder in absolute shock as the second cup flew through the air and slammed into my upper arm. Jerry wasn't a pitcher for the team, but he had a very strong throwing arm. I knew whatever he threw at me would leave a bruise. And he wasn't finished…

He snatched up the small pink lamp off of the dresser and threw that to the floor, but the heavy book of fairytales, he threw at me. The dog stood outside of the room barking at Jerry as I watched with wide, disbelieving eyes as he began to wordlessly trash the nursery.

Pictures were pulled from the walls and thrown to the floor. The baby monitor was hurled into my back. Toys and stuffed animals were thrown at me and to the floor. When he began to stomp toward us with nostrils flaring and fists closed tight at his sides, I scooped Rosa up and tried to move away. He shoved me out of his way, sending me crashing into the crib and I nearly lost my footing as I struggled not to drop my screaming baby. I had just enough time to turn away from him as baby powder, diapers, lotions, and other baby items were thrown at me. Powder floated through the air after he threw a larger bottle against the wall in front of me and it busted open. Dusky was still barking, but he was not an aggressive dog. He didn't enter the room to avenge Rosa and me.

"I am fucking tired," Jerry said evenly behind me. I heard him trudge through the mess and walk out of the room past our whining first addition to our family. A couple of seconds later our bedroom door slammed shut.

I was stunned, absolutely bewildered, and hysteria was building inside of me, but I had to ignore it. I couldn't think about what just happened because Rosa needed a doctor. Breaking down was not an option. Not an option.

With trembling limbs, I put Rosa back on the changing table and quickly put her in a diaper. I zipped up her pajamas and put her in the crib, the only safe place in the room, so I could quickly pack her a bag. I stuffed it with clothes, diapers, wipes, and her now empty cups. I was vaguely aware that my shirt was damp from the juice, but I didn't care. I threw the bag over my shoulder, grabbed Rosa and carefully navigated out of the room. I hurriedly put her in her coat even though I worried that it would make her hotter. I didn't bother to grab anything for myself to put on; there was no time. I picked up my purse and then raced out of the door to get my baby to the hospital.

~~*

For a year, I tried to save my marriage and convince my husband to love his child. I changed up my hair and lost a few pounds. I stopped wearing sweatpants and beat up clothes around the house, and I made sure my hair and makeup were done every day. I hired a babysitter so Jerry and I could go out alone and we had at least one mandatory date night a month. I started attending his home games again, and I went to one away game a month like I used to do. Sometimes I would bring Rosa to the home games, but mostly she stayed with the sitter.

It seemed to be working for us as a couple. Jerry was nicer, downright sweet sometimes, and he started calling me princess again, but he was still distant from Rosa. He held her, he talked to her, and he helped out with her, but it was clear that his heart wasn't in it. He rarely even smiled at her, even when she grinned up at him and looked at him adoringly. By the end of the year, I realized that he was never going to be close to her. I tried not to let that affect us as a couple, but the more I thought about it, the more I realized that his relationship with Rosa was a part of us, and if that wasn't strong, neither were we. His complete meltdown in the nursery was solid proof of that.

I sat in the hospital next to Rosa's little body in the big bed as the nurse adjusted the IV embedded in her little arm. I was still in a state of shock and barely functional. My head was cloudy, and except for what I felt for the baby, I was otherwise numb.

Rosa was expected to be okay. Her lungs were clear, and she tested negative for the flu. It was a bad viral bug, for which there was no cure, but they were treating her symptoms. When the nurse asked me if I would like to get looked at myself, I declined. It would take me away from my baby, and I wasn't leaving her room for anything.

As the sun began to rise outside, I knew I had to make a decision. I couldn't go back home. I didn't have my cell phone to call anyone, and I wasn't sure who to call. I couldn't remember if Emmy and Luke were back from their vacation yet. Fred had a heart attack only a month after the wedding. I didn't want to stress him out by going down to Louisiana, so I immediately ruled that out. Mayson had her own problems, and my other friends weren't people I'd let into this aspect of my life.

When the sun was up fully, I asked the nurse to find a phone number for me. When she returned a little while later, I took my credit card out of my purse and dialed the number. Rosa and I were not going back home. Ever.

~~*

I handed the cab driver a hundred dollar bill.

"Wait here. If we go inside, you can leave and keep the change, but if we can't get inside, I will pay you another hundred to drive us back to the city to a hotel."

He nodded his acceptance and wished me luck.

I climbed out of the car with Rosa in my arms and my purse and diaper bag on my shoulders. It was snowing pretty hard. It had just started when the plane I chartered landed. The talkative cab driver said they were expecting almost a foot of snow on top of the half a foot that was already on the ground.

I walked up the driveway, noting that it was empty of cars. It was a little disheartening, but I thought maybe they could be in the three car garage. I went up the two steps and opened the storm door. My hand was poised to press the button for the doorbell when I felt him, stirring around inside, beyond the door.

I hesitated and thought about turning away, but where would I go? To a hotel maybe, but my body was failing me, and I needed help with Rosa, and besides, it was already too late. If I could feel him, surely he could feel me. I pushed the button.

I heard muffled voices and seconds later the door opened, and Emmy stood there looking at me with a stupefied expression. The sight of her made relief rush through my body and suddenly the weight of the past sixteen hours slammed down on me.

"Shit," Emmy cried, rushing forward to catch Rosa and me. "Luke!"

My world was darkening, but I felt Emmy take Rosa from my arms and I heard her panicked voice, and then I heard his voice, yelling.

"What did he do to her?" Emmet demanded. "What did he do to her?"

Rosa started to cry as I was lifted into strong arms, but it wasn't Emmet. Luke's voice was close to me as he called my name, but I could barely hear him over Emmet's shouts. Rosa continued to cry, frightened by the hysteria in the room, and then Kaitlyn and Lucas joined in until there was a chorus of small crying children.

"Emmet calm down!" Emmy yelled. "You're scaring the kids."

"Donya, open your eyes," Luke said calmly after lying me on a couch.

"Tired," I murmured as I tried to force my eyes open. I started to cough uncontrollably and Luke lifted me into a sitting position and rubbed my back.

"What's wrong with her?" Emmet demanded.

"She's burning up," Luke said. "You should probably call an ambulance."

I opened my heavy eyes to slits after my fit of coughing passed. Luke was right beside me, supporting me. Emmy was standing in the middle of the room holding Kaitlyn with a phone to her ear and looking at me anxiously. Emmet stood behind her, holding Rosa, trying to comfort her, but unable to shake the panic that gripped him as he looked at me.

"I'm just tired," I whispered and only then did I realize how dry my lips and mouth were.

"I think you're more than tired," Luke said. "What happened?"

"I think I need a divorce lawyer," I said. I smiled and weakly lifted a hand to touch his face. I don't know why I smiled. It wasn't funny.

And then I went to sleep.

Chapter Fifty-Six

"This isn't my sock," Luke announced, holding up a pink, frilly sock. He was standing in the hallway dressed in a suit with one shoe on and one shoe off.

"Oh, that's Rosa's," I said and snatched it from his hand. "Thanks." I patted his chest and continued to my temporary bedroom.

"What are you doing?" I heard Emmy ask.

"I can't find my blue sock!"

"So put on another sock."

"Do you know what kind of a field day Vivian will have with me if she sees me wearing two different socks? I want my blue sock. It matches this suit."

I shook my head and closed the door. Vivian was Luke's arch enemy, a barracuda of a lawyer that made grown men quake in their shoes—according to Emmet and Luke anyway, but it was she that Luke asked to represent me in my divorce.

I liked her instantly, though her personality was a bit intimidating, even to me. She played dirty, without being illegal—I think. Before Jerry could even oppose anything I was asking for, Vivian sent his lawyers pictures of the bruises on my body from all of the shit he had thrown at me, and pictures of the wrecked room.

Luke and Emmet had acted quickly. They contacted Mayson who had a spare key to the townhouse I shared with Jerry. While he was out of the house for his daily trip to the gym, which he did not deviate from even after abusing his wife and child, Mayson went in and took pictures of the still wrecked room. He hadn't even bothered to clean it up two days after I disappeared from his life. She grabbed my dog Dusky, my cell phone, my bracelet and a few other small things and took off before Jerry could return.

Jerry got to keep the house, but he had no visitation rights with Rosa, not that he even tried. And he was giving up half of his money. That was his offer, not a request of ours. Emmy wondered if it was because he felt guilty for being a lousy dad and husband, but the rest of us surmised that he didn't want those pictures to hit the media.

I had been at Emmy's and Luke's for nearly two months. I never went back to New Jersey. Mayson said I pulled an Emmy, but that wasn't quite true. When Emmy left New Jersey, she was a broken individual, brutally scarred, and only a whisper of the person she had been. She had closed herself off from her friends and family and burrowed deep into a psychological dark hole. I wasn't burrowing any fucking where.

My first twenty-four hours in Chicago was spent in the hospital, getting pumped full of IV fluids for dehydration and pneumonia. I gave myself that day and the following day to cry and feel miserable, and that was it. I had a baby to take care of, and I had myself to take care of too.

I had neglected to take care of me during my marriage with Jerry, because as Emmet had predicted, he gave up nothing for me. I had allowed myself to look at my life through a frosted glass and did not see things clearly until that damn wipe box slammed into my side. I once thought Jerry was a great man, and maybe he was, but he wasn't the man for me. Sometimes I got sad, because I had some good memories with him, but the sadness always passed, because I doubted he was sitting around thinking about me with sadness.

"Here's your sock, little girl," I said, tossing Rosa's pink sock on the bed. She and Lucas were sitting on my bed in their pajamas watching cartoons.

"Mam?" she asked, picking up the sock.

"Rosa?"

"Fee?"

"Yes, it is for your feet," I said, smiling.

I sat in a chair in the corner of the room and started folding the basket of laundry I just carried upstairs. Emmet walked through the open door a moment later, and Rosa's arms instantly shot up. He dropped his old Ghurka briefcase I had given him many years ago on the floor. I had been surprised to find that he still used it and even more surprised to see him using the pen.

Emmet scooped Rosa into his arms and kissed her all over her face, making her giggle.

"Have a good day, baby girl," he said to her.

"Mehmet," she said his name as she put her little hands on his cheeks. "Buh byes."

"Yes, buh byes." He kissed her once more and set her back on the bed. He put his hand out for a high-five from Lucas. Lucas gave it to him and then they did a fist bump. "Take care of the lady folk, little man."

Lucas already lost interest and was watching television again. Unless he needed food from the lady folk, he could care less.

"Have a good day," Emmet said to me, his manner more subdued.

"Thank you," I said softly. "You too."

He hung out near the door, watching me for a moment longer. "Okay. Bye."

"Bye," I said and watched him leave.

Luke came in next to hug the kids, but he didn't linger and have an awkward moment with me. He kissed the top of my head like he would a kid sister and then plucked me in the arm before racing out of the room.

So, there had been many changes...

When I showed up at my best friend's door two months ago, I had no idea that Emmet and Casey had separated two months before that and that he was staying with his sister until he could figure out what he wanted to do. I almost moved out after I recovered from pneumonia, but Emmy begged me to stay, and Emmet offered to move out instead, but then I felt bad making him move out when he and Emmy were finally getting to know each other again. We all said we would have to think about what would be the best thing to do, but that was nearly two months ago, and nothing had changed.

Those first several days were awkward and stressful. Emmet was still fuming about the condition I arrived in. Several times Luke and Emmy had to talk him out of getting on a plane and flying to New Jersey to, "kill that motherfucking pansy bat swinging asshole."

The incident hit a little too close to home for Emmy and her past, and she was noticeably quiet for a few days, but soon we all fell into a routine. Emmet immediately became attached to Rosa again after we arrived. Even if he had Owen with him, Emmet took care of Rosa like his own. Every weekend morning, or any day he had off, he would let me sleep in and take Rosa downstairs for breakfast. He made time for her every day after work, and he even took her with him on errands sometimes. He loved her, and Owen loved her, and she loved them.

Emmet and I were polite to each other, but other than dealing with Rosa and Owen, we kept our distance. Before I showed up, we hadn't spoken since that night he walked away from Fred and me at Emmy's wedding. I didn't know why he and Casey split up. He didn't volunteer the information, and I didn't ask him. I did ask Emmy, and she wasn't sure either, but I'm sure it looked suspicious to anyone else that both of our marriages dissolved within a couple of months of each other and then we were both living under the same roof.

Emmet spared Casey the shock of finding me there when she dropped off Owen by talking to her beforehand. She didn't have much to say when she came by, but she too was polite. Everyone was so damn polite.

I was getting restless in the Kessler camp. I loved being around Emmy all of the time, but I was beginning to feel like I was cramping her and Luke. It was awkward to walk into the kitchen and find them in a moment together, or to overhear an argument or disagreement. It was especially uncomfortable to hear them banging like bunnies in their bedroom at all hours of the day. They never encouraged me to move on or seemed to care that I was there, but *I* cared. Two months was long enough to take advantage of my friends' hospitality.

So, that morning after I wrangled Lucas and Rosa downstairs for breakfast, I used Emmy's laptop to start searching for somewhere else to live. I didn't even know what I was going to do for a living yet. I had some ideas, but nothing solid.

I had been seated for a few minutes when the doorbell rang. Emmy was upstairs bathing Kaitlyn, so I got up to answer it.

"Hey, no throwing cereal," I warned Lucas as his arm raised to throw a Cheerio. He gave me a heart melting grin and dropped his arm.

I peeked out of the little window by the door before opening it and cursed under my breath. I had forgotten that Casey was dropping Owen off. That was another thing that had become routine. Casey dropped Owen off on specified days of the week whether Emmet was present or not. Emmet would keep Owen for a few days and then take him back to his mother. He called him every day that he wasn't with him and would sometimes go and pick him up even if it wasn't his day to have him. Casey and Emmet seemed to agree upon all things that had to do with Owen.

"Hey, Case," I said, opening the door to let them in. "Hi, Owen." I ruffled his hair that was so much like his father's.

"Nonan, come eat ceewreal," Lucas called from the kitchen.

"Wowo!" Rosa called.

"Go on in the kitchen," I told Owen, and he gladly took off to go be with his friends.

I fully expected Casey to turn and leave as she always did. Emmy and I always offered her a cup of coffee or to come in and sit for a few minutes, but she always declined. I think it was hard for her to be with Emmet's family since she wasn't with Emmet anymore. She seemed uncomfortable with the idea every time it was presented to her, even though the Grayne's went out of their way to try to make her feel like she was still part of the family.

When she didn't immediately hightail it out the door, I again offered her a cup of coffee.

"No, thanks," she said, shaking her head. "But I wanted to know if you could give something to Emmet for me."

She reached into her purse and produced a large manila envelope. I had a feeling what was inside, and I didn't think I should be the one to hand it to him.

"Maybe you should give it to him," I suggested when she tried to hand it to me.

"I…" she paused and licked her lips nervously. Her smile was just as nervous. "I don't want to see his face when this lands in his hands. I don't want to see the relief that he's sure to feel."

I shook my head and still refused to take the envelope. "Casey, I'm sure this is hard for him, too."

"Yeah, but not for the same reasons," she whispered. "He feels guilty, but trust me," she sighed heavily. "The contents of this envelope are a gift to him."

Whatever resentment I had for Casey had passed the night of Emmy's wedding, but I suddenly felt guilty for resenting her in the first place. I had no doubt that when Emmet proposed to her she really believed that he was marrying her because he loved her above anyone else and wanted to spend the rest of his life with her. When there were any signs or symptoms to the contrary, she must have chosen the same frosted glasses I did for my marriage. I wondered what it took for her to take off her frosted glasses.

"Please, you give it to him."

I accepted the heavy envelope in my hands even though I still felt unsure about being the one to deliver it to him.

"You know, Emmet and I aren't exactly..." I shrugged. "We don't talk really. We live under the same roof, and we share in taking care of all of the kids, but...we don't chit chat or hang out or anything else."

"Well, maybe you should," Casey said solemnly. "Have to start somewhere, right?"

I looked at her. Was she suggesting that Emmet and I get together?

"I didn't know that he was in love with you when I married him," she said suddenly in a rush of words. "I know people think that I trapped him, but I didn't. Emmet was my friend, maybe even my best friend. I had a hard life when I was younger, and he helped me become a better person. I got pregnant after only one night of unexpected sex. I would have been okay with raising Owen as a single mom, and I should have said no when he proposed, but I loved him, and I thought he would eventually love me, too, but he never did. I mean, not like he obviously loves you.

"For a long time I couldn't quite put my finger on what was wrong with our marriage. Emmet was kind to me, he provided for me, and he's an excellent dad, but there was something empty about our marriage, and I didn't know what it was. Even after I figured out that you two were engaged before, I still didn't think that you had anything to do with my marital problems because you guys hadn't been together in a long time. But..." She paused and looked at the floor for a moment.

"Lucas's party was the first indication of his feelings for you. Then that morning before we went to the spa, the banter between the two of you came easily, and there was never banter between me and Emmet. Not like that. And then later the bracelet..."

I felt like shit for what she had gone through, and I was a little mad with Emmet for putting her through it. I felt guilty for the many times we crossed over that line while Casey was waiting for him to show some interest in her.

"I tried to change for him," she said, looking out of the storm door absently. "I lost weight, I changed my hair and started wearing makeup. I started wearing designer clothes and getting my nails done and getting waxed." She looked at me. "I was trying to be enough like you to matter, but it didn't work. And it was on a day when I was seriously thinking of surgically altering my body that I woke up. The problem wasn't me. I was fine. I was more than fine. The problem was that we should have never married in the first place. When he came home from work that day, I had a bag packed for him and a couple of boxes of items I knew meant a lot to him, and I told him I was done. I told him that I deserved a husband who could give me no less than one-hundred percent; that I deserved a husband who loved me like a wife and not a buddy. I promised him that I wouldn't keep him from Owen. I told him I loved him and then I told him to leave. And you know what? He didn't argue. He teared up and apologized for taking away years of my life that I could have been with someone who loved me the way I deserved to be loved. He hugged me for a long time..." She stared sadly into that point of time for a moment before her eyes found mine again. "And then he left."

"I'm sorry," I whispered to her sincerely. "I don't even know what to say."

"Look, Donya," she said in a strong voice. She straightened her shoulders and looked at me intently. "You and Emmet obviously have something that most people in the world only read about in books or see in the movies. I'm hurt, but I'll be okay and I'll move on. I still love him, and I want him to be happy, and you're the only one who can make that happen. I'm sorry your husband turned out to be an asshole, but I don't think it's a coincidence that both of our marriages fell apart around the same time. I think you and Emmet were meant to be, and those papers are the first step in making that happen. Don't waste it."

She pushed open the storm door, gave me a weak smile, and then hurried across the lawn to her car.

~~*

I didn't want to give Emmet the papers in front of the entire family. I waited until Emmy and Luke were cuddled up on the couch watching a movie, and all of the kids were asleep. I was glad that Owen was sleeping in Lucas's room as I knocked lightly on his door. I knew he was awake because I could not only hear him moving around in there but, of course, I could sense it.

"Come in," he said after a moment of hesitation. He probably wondered why I was coming to him since I only came to him if it involved Owen or Rosa, and Rosa was drooling in sleepy land on my bed.

I opened the door and stepped inside. Emmet sat on one side of his bed with a law book in his hands, a highlighter and small sticky notes. I tried not to notice the curved muscle of his upper arm that stretched the tee shirt he had on, or how his hair looked sexy and mussed like he had been repeatedly running his hands through it.

"You know, you graduated law school years ago," I teased, hoping that he totally missed the vibe I had been putting out.

"Unfortunately I lack the brain capacity to retain every law known to man," he said with a smile. "What brings you to my door late at night?"

"Am I disturbing you?"

"You never disturb me, Donya," he said softly. I resisted the urge to smile like an idiot and stepped farther into the room.

"This is for you," I said, holding up the envelope. "It's from Casey. She wanted me to give it to you."

His eyes zeroed in on the envelope and then he nodded solemnly. "How was she?" He asked after some hesitation.

I gave a small shrug. I didn't want to tell him what we discussed, so I said, "Okay."

He gave me a suspicious look. Of course, he knew I wasn't telling him the whole story, but he didn't push. He reached out his hand for the envelope, but a gust of wind swept in through a window that was open a few inches, and one of his papers blew to the floor at my feet.

"I got it," I said and tossed the envelope on the bed, making another few papers float to the floor.

"You know you're not helping, right?" Emmet teased as I crouched to pick up the papers.

"I know, I'm sorry," I said. "But why do you have the window…" I trailed off as my fingers touched the corner of a canvas sticking out from under the bed. Absently, I slapped the papers on the bed but didn't take my eyes off of that familiar object. My fingers closed around the edges of the canvas, and I slowly pulled it out. I held it up and examined it.

"Shit," I said and felt the need to sit. I sat on the edge of the bed, holding the painting I had done nearly twenty years ago for Valentine's Day. That night I had fought with Emmet in the parking lot and the following morning his lips and his hands had pleased me and made up for upsetting me the night before.

"Have you always had this?" I asked Emmet without taking my eyes off of the macabre art.

"Yes," he answered quietly. "It was in Louisiana in storage for a long time, but I brought it back home with me the last time I went down."

I looked over my shoulder at him. "Why did you keep it?"

"It is an incredible piece of work," he said with a shrug. "And you made it. That's reason enough."

I looked away from him and focused again on the painting. "I was so angry and hurt when I painted this, ramped up on my teenage hormones, totally pissed off with myself for loving you," I reminisced. Then I turned back to him. "If it is so incredible and meaningful for you, why is it on the floor under your bed?"

"I don't have anywhere to put it right now," he said, looking guilty.

I looked around the room and saw the perfect spot. I got up and put the canvas on top of a chest of drawers and leaned it back against the wall.

"There," I said with my hands on my hips.

"I approve," Emmet said.

I looked at him smugly as I walked back over to the bed. "I wasn't waiting for your approval. What else do you have under this bed?"

I dropped to my knees and lifted the bed skirt. It was hard to see, so I flattened my body on the floor to get a better look.

"Are you seriously looking under my bed?" Emmet asked disbelievingly. Seconds later, his face appeared at the other side, upside down. "What if I don't want you looking under my bed?"

"I wasn't looking for your permission either," I said and reached for a small box.

Emmet groaned as I pulled the box out. I sat up and leaned back against the bed and crossed my legs.

"I don't want you to open the box," Emmet warned as he stretched out across the bed on his papers to try to take it from me.

"What do you have to hide, Grayne?" I teased.

"Donya," his tone was serious, but I felt compelled to open the box. I couldn't help it. Something in that box was calling to me.

I took the lid off and just stared for a long time. Emmet was very still behind me.

The first thing I discovered inside of the box was the scraps from my wedding dress that Emmet had torn off while he was on his knees begging me not to marry Jerry. The two jars I had given him when he went away to college were wrapped carefully in cloth, but I didn't need to pull the cloth away to know what they were. I carefully took the jars out of the box and set them on the floor beside me and put the pieces of my dress on top of them. There were dozens and dozens of magazine clippings of me in one pose or another, and there were photographs of me when I was a little kid, as a teenager, and more of that day in Emmet's hotel room just before I gave him my virginity. There was even a picture of me in my maid of honor dress from Emmy's wedding.

We were both silent as I looked through some of the clippings and photographs. I didn't look through all of them, but I did look through a great deal. I was about to put back what I had taken out when something else at the bottom of the box peeking out from under a picture caught my eye. I reached for it, a small red velvet sack. I probed at it with my fingers before opening it. I did know what was in it, but I still pulled it open. I had to see them.

Carefully, I spilled the platinum engagement ring and its matching wedding band into the palm of my hand. They were so beautiful. I remembered how perfect the engagement ring had looked on my hand and how it felt when he had first slipped it on my slender finger.

"Wow," I said, swallowing hard as I put the rings back into the sack. I proceeded to carefully put everything else back into the box. "You keep everything."

Emmet said nothing, though I sensed his sadness. He sat back up as I pushed the box back under the bed. I was about to speed walk myself back to my room so I could think when two more objects under the bed in the shadows caught my eye. I gasped and eagerly reached for both and rolled them out.

"You kept my old board!" I said excitedly as I got to my feet, holding two skateboards. "And you kept yours!"

Before he could respond, I tossed his board onto the bed and ran out of the room excitedly. I was glad I didn't pull my sneakers off yet as I hurried down the front stairs and pulled open the front door. I ran outside to the driveway. I put the board down, put one foot on it and wondered if I could still do it or if I would bust my ass. But then I didn't care. I pushed off and easily coasted down the driveway and into the street. I laughed when I saw Emmet come out of the house carrying his board.

"Race you to the end of the street," I said to him before he could even mount his board, and then I took off.

"You little cheater," he called out behind me.

Soon my hair was blowing slightly in the cool spring air and the feelings of surrender, peace and clarity that I used to get while boarding came back to me. Emmet caught up to me, but he didn't try to pass me as we neared the end of the block. We rode in a comfortable, but exhilarating silence and continued to the next block and the next after that. We finally stopped when we reached the main road. We stood on our boards, facing each other, slightly out of breath because we were *old*. I grinned at him, and he grinned back.

"We should get back," Emmet said after a minute of us just grinning at each other like fools. "We are parents now."

"Oh god," I slapped a palm to my forehead. "I'm such a bad mom. I can't believe I just left her there like that." I got off of my board and picked it up and tucked it under my arm and started to walk back.

Emmet did the same, but said, "You're not a bad mom. Emmy and Luke are there, and you knew that when you went outside."

"Yeah, but Emmy doesn't like black babies," I said and giggled to myself at an inside joke that had come to be during a heartbreaking experience I shared with Emmy.

"What?" Emmet looked at me like I was crazy.

"Nothing," I said. "I still shouldn't have just run out like that."

"Well, we won't do it again," Emmet said and then took my hand.

We walked hand in hand back to the house, talking quietly about nothing serious, like about the box that was clearly all about me, or his divorce, or mine. We did not talk about our hands linked together and the tether that hummed contently between us.

Chapter Fifty-Seven

I tapped on Emmet's door and walked in without waiting for an answer. He was just out of the shower and pulling a t-shirt on. I watched as the shirt was pulled down over his taut abdomen and felt disappointed that he covered it up.

"Can I help you?" Emmet asked, snapping my attention to his face. He smiled smugly, well aware of what I was looking at.

"Uh…right. Yes," I said shaking my head to clear it. "Yes, you can. I am taking Rosa and Owen for a walk. Would you like to come?"

"I would love to come," he said in a low voice that made my whole body tingle.

"Okay, great, I'll be downstairs," I said in a rush and hurried out of his room and back downstairs to the kids.

It had been a few weeks since Emmet and I skateboarded off into the night like a couple of teenagers. Our days of politely avoiding one another were over. The conversation came easily for us and there was no more awkwardness. We started texting each other during the day while he was working and there were nights when we would sit up talking until our voices were hoarse and one or both of us couldn't keep our eyes open anymore. We would always retreat to our own bedrooms rather than fall asleep together. He held my hand a lot, though. We also did a lot together. We went out to dinner, lunch, or went to the grocery store together, and sometimes we just took the kids to the park.

On this particular day, my walk had a purpose, though he didn't know that yet. I guided him and the kids around the corner and to the next street. When we got to a big yellow house with a SOLD sticker stamped over a For Sale sign, I stopped on the sidewalk in front of it.

"What do you think?" I asked Emmet.

"What do you mean?" he asked me as he picked Rosa up into his arms.

With my fingers lazily moving through Owen's hair, I asked, "Do you like it?"

He looked away from me and back at the house. "Yeah, it's nice. Why?"

"I bought it."

"You buyed a house?" Owen asked incredulously.

Emmet looked at Owen and then at me. "Yeah. You buyed a house?"

I smiled and shook my head at the father and son. "Yes, I *bought* a house—this house," I said pointing to it.

"You sneaky little brat," Emmet said, staring at me disbelievingly.

"Let's go inside and look around," I said and took Owen's hand.

A minute later we were walking into the spacious foyer and stepping onto a beautiful hardwood floor. Emmet put Rosa down and she and Owen took off to go explore.

"Whoa! You buyed a big house, Donnie!" Owen shouted from the living room.

Rosa tried to shout the same thing, but it came out in baby babble as she tried to keep up with Owen. I showed Emmet the kitchen with its marble counters and view of Emmy's back yard which was right up against mine. I showed him the large laundry room and the mudroom off of that and we even looked inside the large garage.

The large dining room was promising for hosting the family dinners I had gotten accustomed to doing with Luke's family, since they assimilated Rosa and me into the family almost instantly. There was a full bathroom, a formal living room and a family room, and an office.

We took the kids upstairs and explored the five bedrooms and two and a half baths up there. The master bedroom had a skylight and the on suite bathroom had a large garden tub and a separate shower stall. The kids went in and out of closets, opened and closed doors, and ran back and forth between the bedrooms.

"Rosa this is your room," Owen said and pointed to the floor. "Stay there and I'll go to my room."

He started to walk away and Rosa began to follow.

"No, stay here," Owen said patiently, gesturing with his little hands. He walked to one side of the room through a door that led to a joint bathroom shared with a bedroom the same size as the one we were standing in.

"Now I'm in my room," he shouted to Rosa from the other room.

"Wowo?" she called.

"You can come to my room, Rosa, but it's a boy's room. So, you can't always come in here."

Rosa ran off in her little toddler run to go be with Owen.

Emmet and I stood by the door laughing. As we followed the kids through the house for a while longer, I asked Emmet again what he thought.

"It's great," he said, smiling sadly at me.

"Why are you unhappy?" I asked, crossing my arms.

"I'm not unhappy," he sighed.

I punched his arm and made him stop to look at me. "Hello? It's me you're talking to. I know how you're feeling without even trying."

A long time ago, I may have put my hand over his heart and told him that we were connected, but I didn't do it. I crossed my arms again and fisted my hands.

He stood with his feet apart, one arm folded and his hand on his chin as he watched the kids. He looked so damn sexy in his basic green t-shirt and a pair of jeans.

"You're going to move out of Emmy's," he said finally.

"I'm moving literally a yard away," I pointed out.

"I know, but you're moving on already and I'm…I don't know…stagnant. At first I stayed because I didn't know what to do. Then I was getting to know my sister again." He looked at me suddenly. "I threw her away, Donya. I didn't want to look at her and be reminded of you, but I was wrong. She's still my sister—my little sister—and I don't know what happened to her while I was avoiding her all of these years, but I know I wasn't there to protect her like I should have been. I feel like I have a lot to make up to her."

"You do have a lot to make up to her," I said quietly and then reached out to put a hand on his arm. "But you don't have to live with her to do that. You have to get on with your life. It's not like you don't have the money to do it."

"You're right," he said after a moment. "But it's still a little embarrassing that after all you went through with Jerry you're picking yourself up and going full steam ahead while I'm living with my kid sister."

"I give myself very little time to mourn the things I've lost," I said quietly.

"Really," he said, looking at me curiously. "Does that apply to all things?"

I knew what he was asking me. He wanted to know if that applied to him as well. Of course, it didn't.

"All things but one," I said softly. "There are some things, or people, that will always stay with me, but even if I'm dying inside, the only way I know how to survive is to keep going."

I walked away from him then, because all that we had lost over the years suddenly slammed into my chest without warning and it wasn't something I was prepared to deal with at that moment.

"Okay, kids, let's go get some lunch," I said to Rosa and Owen.

"Can we have McDonalds?" Owen asked me as he put his little hand in mine.

"I think McDonalds sounds great."

I locked up my new home and took Owen's hand again. Emmet lifted Rosa into his arms and took my free hand and we walked back to Emmy's linked together.

~~*

My divorce was finalized the week after I showed Emmet the house. The media had all kinds of wrong ideas about what broke up our marriage, but I tried not to pay it any mind, especially when they suggested that I cheated on Jerry with Emmet.

I made a quick trip out to New Jersey a couple weeks later to get the rest of my belongings that Jerry had packed up and put in storage, and to say goodbye to my Dusky that Mayson had claimed for herself. I hired movers to take my things back to Illinois and had dinner with Mayson and Tabitha before catching a flight back to my new home.

I was exhausted as I entered my house in the early morning hours. It still smelled of fresh paint and…newness.

Emmet and Owen had helped us pick out the furniture and every day after work Emmet came over to help me put away my new purchases or set up a room. I even gave Owen his own room, the very one he picked out for himself, because he felt more and more like my own child and I wanted him to have his own space when he was with me.

I went upstairs and stopped first in Owen's room to check on him, only to find his bed empty. I checked Rosa's room next and her bed was also empty. I swallowed back any panic that had begun to rise and opened my bedroom door. I sighed with relief and then smiled at the scene before me.

Emmet was sleeping in the middle of the bed with both kids curled up on either side of him. Tangled was playing on the television. I carefully removed the remote from Emmet's hand and turned the TV off. I had just resigned myself to sleeping in Owen's bed or the couch when Emmet's eyes fluttered open.

"Hey," he said, smiling sleepily up at me.

"Hey," I said, smiling back.

"You're back."

"Yeah, I just got in."

"You look tired," he said with a yawn.

"Exhausted," I said moving away from the bed. "I'm going to go sleep in Owen's bed. I have always wanted to sleep under Batman sheets."

He grinned and said, "I thought you were going to say that you've always wanted to sleep under Batman."

I grinned too and said, "Well, it depends on which Batman we're talking about. Michael Keaton isn't my type and I hated Clooney as Batman."

"So, that leaves Adam West, Val Kilmer, and Christian Bale."

"Okay, so I wouldn't mind sleeping under Christian Bale," I said with a wicked smile.

Emmet chuckled softly. "Are you trying to make me jealous?"

"How can I make you jealous of someone that is so far removed from us in this little Chicago suburb?" I asked, laughing.

"Bullshit. I have proof that you personally know Christian Bale," he said.

"So?" I shrugged. "Christian Bale don't got nothing on you, honey," I said sweetly. "Goodnight."

I waved my fingers and started to walk out of the room, but Emmet called my name as loudly as he dared.

"What now?" I asked, yawning. "I swear to you that I didn't sleep with Christian Bale."

"I'm not sure if I really want to know who you've slept with besides the three of us that I am aware of."

"Well, there's the whole list right there," I said, throwing my hand up.

Emmet stared at me for several seconds as he tried to ascertain whether or not I was being truthful.

"You can read me like a book, Emmet," I said and actually felt myself blushing. "You know I'm telling you the truth. Don't look so surprised about it."

"I'm not surprised, I mean I am, but it's just...why?"

"Why what?" I asked impatiently.

"Why didn't you sleep with anyone else? I mean it's not that I wanted you to, but you have been around some of the most attractive men in the world and I'm sure some of them probably wanted to take you to bed."

I kicked at Rosa's shoe that was on the floor and didn't meet his eyes when I spoke. "It's hard to have an orgasm while trying to imagine that the guy I'm with is someone else. So, I didn't bother trying."

Emmet was quiet for a long time, but I knew he understood my meaning. Even though Jerry was a decent lover, my mind often drifted to Emmet. While some women could pretend and orgasm that way, I couldn't.

"Anyway," I breathed out as I again began to turn away. "Goodnight."

"Wait, Donya, that's not why I called you back in here. I'm sorry."

"What did you want?" I asked, daring to look into his face again.

"I just wanted you to lay down with us," he said gently and beckoned me with his hand. When I only stood there looking at him and the kids, he smiled and said, "Just sleep."

"Just sleep," he had said a long time ago with his bed between us.

After another moment of indecision, I kicked off my shoes and climbed into the king size bed next to Rosa.

"Thank you," he whispered and tucked a loose tendril behind my ear. He began to stroke my hair and it put me at ease. Soon my eyes closed and I began to drift off, but then a thought occurred to me.

"Emmet," I murmured.

"Hmm?" he responded sleepily.

"Remember what we wanted a long time ago? In New York, in your hotel room?"

He was silent for so long, I didn't think he remembered, but then he spoke. "I've never forgotten," he whispered.

"If you want me again, all you have to do is ask, or demand, or just take." Emmet had teased so long ago.

"I will always want you," I had answered. *"But that isn't why I'm looking at you. I'm just trying to imagine us ten years from now. Will it be like this you think?"*

"Maybe with a kid sitting in bed with us?" Emmet had said, looking at me with gleaming green eyes.

"Maybe two kids?" I had smiled.

"We have our two kids," Emmet said in the present. "But part of the equation has eluded us."

That made us both sad, and the sleep that had been ready to take me moments before didn't return for a long time.

~~*

I woke up cocooned in Emmet's strong arms, my head against his chest, my arms and legs wrapped securely around him. I was more comfortable than I had been in years. It felt so damn good and he smelled so damn good and…

I pushed Emmet's arms off of me and sat up in a panic.

"Where are the kids?"

Emmet bolted up and was on his feet and hurrying out of the room before I could even make it off of the bed. As I stepped out of the bedroom, he was coming out of Rosa's room.

"They're downstairs I think," he said and took the stairs two at a time.

I followed after him, but only taking the stairs one at a time because falling on my face would help nothing and no one. By the time I got to the landing, Emmet was calling out that they were fine. I went into the kitchen and was relieved to see the two kids sitting at the table eating cereal. There was cereal all over the table, though, three different types. Amazingly there was very little milk spilled.

Emmet had the trashcan and was swiping cereal off of the table into it.

"Rosa was hungry," Owen said conversationally.

"Mam?" Rosa said, looking at me.

"Rosa," I said, rubbing the sleep out of my eyes. I started to sweep the cereal into piles with my hand.

"Wowo imme eerial."

I sighed and looked at the mess. "I see that."

"Owen, next time wake us up, okay? You could have hurt yourself getting the cereal down," Emmet said distractedly as he cleaned up.

"Okay, Dad."

"Dad?" Rosa said.

And Emmet...bless his absent-minded soul...Emmet said, "What," as he used paper towels to soak up the milk.

Rosa repeated what she had told me about the cereal and Emmet nodded and said, "Yes, baby girl."

I stood there in shock, staring at him as he absently cleaned up the mess. He realized I was staring at him and looked at me with his brow furrowed.

"What?"

"Nothing," I said quickly and went back to helping him clean up.

"It's not nothing," he said.

"I need to get the broom. Do I have a broom?" I asked no one and hurried from the room to search for a broom.

After the cereal was all cleaned up and the kids were cleaned up, Emmet asked me if I wanted breakfast as he opened the fridge.

"I made my sister breakfast," Owen said as he and Rosa colored at the table.

This time, I didn't allow my shock to show. I busied myself washing their cereal bowls and spoons, but I knew Emmet was frozen at the fridge behind me.

"I could go for some eggs and bacon," I said casually. I looked at the clock on the stove and thought better of it. "Actually, I have to go soon."

"Go where?"

"Remember? I told you I have a meeting with a few people about my business idea?"

"The business idea you still haven't told me about," he said sourly. "On a Saturday though?"

"Yes, on a Saturday," I said and turned around to face him. "I can take Rosa to Emmy's if you have something you have to do or somewhere to go."

"She can stay here with us," Emmet said, looking at me with uncertainty.

"Why are you looking at me like that?" I asked in a voice higher than I meant it to be. It had been a long morning already and I just woke up. I woke up in Emmet's arms and then Rosa called him Dad and then Owen called Rosa his sister. It was too damn much for one morning.

"Because you're behaving strangely and you are pretending you didn't just hear that."

I laughed. "Yeah I heard that and something else, too, but you were too distracted to hear it."

His eyes narrowed in confusion. "Hear what?"

"It doesn't matter," I said, waving a hand. "I have to shower and get ready to go."

I started to leave the room, but Emmet caught up to me and put a strong arm around my waist and pulled my back against his front. It was the closest contact we'd had while conscious since the night of Emmy's wedding.

"What didn't I hear? And what is this business meeting about?" His lips moved against my ear as he spoke in a low, sexy, dangerous voice. I stifled a moan, because it would have been all kinds of obscene in front of the children.

"Dad?" Rosa said again. I felt Emmet stiffen. When he didn't answer, Rosa said it again. "Dad?"

"Dad, Rosa is calling you," Owen said, sounding annoyed that his father hadn't answered his 'sister.'

Emmet released me and together we turned to look at Rosa.

"Rosa..." Emmet said her name carefully.

She pointed to the picture she was coloring and giggled as if she had just shown him something hilarious.

"Yes, that's funny," he said to her and offered her a big smile. Then he turned to me without the smile.

"Hey, don't look at me," I said, holding my hands up and backing up. "Why don't you ask her 'brother' about that?"

I turned and hurried from the room. I ran up the stairs—two at a time—went into my room, closed the door, and asked the room "What the fuck is happening here!"

No one answered.

Chapter Fifty-Eight

It was late in the afternoon when I got home. When I opened the door, a savory smell wafted into the foyer and made my stomach growl with anticipation. I opened the hall closet and hung up the garment bags I came in with and then walked down the hall and into the kitchen. Rosa and Owen were sitting at the table again, coloring, just as they had been when I left hours before. Emmet was at the stove stirring something in a pot. How domesticated my life suddenly was.

Emmet looked very comfortable in my kitchen. Honestly, he looked like he belonged in my house. He didn't look like he should leave it any more than I should.

I had been thinking about him all day, even when I should have been focused on business. I thought about our late night skate, how exhilarating it was, and how much I felt like the young girl that Emmet kissed while she was standing on her skateboard. I thought about our shopping excursions while trying to find furniture for the house. I chose nothing without his input, so when I saw him sitting at the table or lounging on the couch or even in my bed, it looked like he was at home. I thought about all of the items he had in that box under his bed and the painting that was now hanging in my bedroom, and of course, I thought about his relationship with Rosa.

"Even though she isn't mine, she is a part of you, and I know I'll love her."

He loved her as if she had been his all along, and maybe she had. If I had been his all along, wouldn't any extension of me also be his?

I thought about that night of Jorge's party when Emmet had been kneeled down in front of me with his hand on my cheek while my hand was in his hair. I thought about that first kiss in the empty parking lot where we used to board, and that morning in his bed after the night we fought in the rain. I thought about our breakup on the boardwalk and our subsequent reconciliation in Louisiana, and the heartless words I uttered at the end of that summer that separated us for several months.

I remembered how his hands felt on me the night of Felix's party when he refused to leave my side. I could hear our bodies moving together and our moans and smell the arousal during our first time making love. I never forgot how when I needed Emmet the most, he had flown all the way across the country to be with me. I could feel the dirt and grass pressed against my back at our pond after he proposed and I joyfully accepted.

Other memories flooded my mind—our time split between New York and Cambridge, the big fight we had when I accepted a job in Paris instead of going away on vacation with Emmet and the makeup in Felix's French penthouse with the perfect view of the Eiffel Tower. The heart-shattering breakup that I thought had been for Emmet's own good when, in hindsight, it was out of selfishness on my part. The New Year's love making with the crowd celebrating below us. Our big fight the night he met Jerry, and the horrible scene at our pond a year later.

So many memories. So much wasted time. I was tired of wasting time. I was tired of being without the only person I ever truly wanted, the only person in the world that I couldn't get away from no matter how far I went, because we were bound together by a force bigger than us.

"Hey," Emmet snapped his fingers in my face, shaking me out of my deep reverie. "You okay?"

"Yes," I said, shaking my head lightly.

He looked at me skeptically. "What's going on in your head?"

"A lot," I said truthfully.

"Okay," he said. He looked at me for a moment and then went back to the stove.

After dinner, Casey came to pick up Owen. Rosa cried for ten minutes after he left and it was Emmet who finally soothed her and made her smile again. She was still calling him Dad, and neither of us did anything to stop her. Every time the word left her lips, I sensed his heart swell and cry out at the same time. He was conflicted, because he really, truly loved her like a daughter, but he wasn't in a position to make it official.

Once she was asleep for the night, Emmet and I settled on the couch in the family room and he again asked me about my business meeting.

"Oh, it's best if I show you," I said and got to my feet.

"Show me what?"

"You'll see," I said over my shoulder as I walked out of the room and down the hall. I took out one of the garment bags and went back to the family room. "Can you stand up and hold this while I unzip?"

He gave me a questioning look but got up and held the hanger at the top of the bag while I unzipped it. I carefully removed the bag and then took the hanger from him. I held it up to my body and nervously and quietly said, "Ta-da."

Emmet looked over the long black strapless gown with the pink silk sash just below the bust line, and the small glimpse of the pink petticoat underneath the full skirt. Wrapped neatly around the hanger was a long, thin decorative scarf in the same pink color as the sash, to be wrapped neatly around the neck and to hang down the open back of the dress.

"You're going back into modeling?" Emmet asked, frowning.

"Not exactly…" I said slowly. "I designed this dress."

His eyes widened and his mouth dropped open. "You did?"

"Don't look so surprised," I said, frowning.

"No," he said holding up a hand and looking apologetic. "Baby, that's not what I mean. I'm never surprised by your many talents. I just can't believe that I didn't know that you had an interest in design."

The stupid half smile that appeared on my face was because he called me baby.

"I started sketching out designs years ago," I said softly. "It was something of a stress reliever at first, but over the years I started doing it more seriously. I still didn't think much of it until more recently."

"I'm really proud and happy for you," Emmet said sincerely, but I could see the 'but' on his face. "But won't you have to do a lot of traveling? Maybe not as much as you did as a model, but you will have to travel often, right?"

He looked disappointed by the idea of me having to go anywhere.

"Well, I will have to do some traveling for what I am going to do, yes—at least at first," I said and gestured for the garment bag. As we began to carefully recover the dress, I continued telling him my plans. "I am going to open a boutique in the heart of Chicago," I said. "Later, I hope to expand to New York, L.A. and maybe a couple of other places, but we are starting here in Chicago."

"We?" Emmet asked as he zipped up the bag.

"Felix is going into business with me," I said triumphantly.

He raised an eyebrow and crossed his arms. "Felix is a designer now, too?"

"No, not exactly," I said. Emmet followed me as I walked back down the hall to put the dress away. "Felix is more or less going to be a public figure. He'll handle most of the public relations end of the business, and for every movie premiere or award show or talk show—anywhere that he is scheduled to be in public, he will wear the brand, and so will I."

After I had closed the closet door, Emmet asked me, "So, how much traveling will you be doing? How often will you be away?"

"Maybe three times a year, four at the most," I answered and then quietly added "Nothing like before."

He studied my face for a moment and then nodded.

"I'm proud of you," he said softly. "I know everything will work out well for you."

"I hope that applies to more than just business," I whispered.

I was standing against the closed closet door and he was standing only a foot away from me. We stared at each other, and I waited for him to step towards me, to put his hand on my hip and maybe one on my cheek. I bit my bottom lip as I looked at his lips and tried to recall the taste of his mouth and my mouth began to water when my taste buds remembered.

"I better go," he said hoarsely, to my surprise, and took a step back from me.

"Oh," I said, disappointed, and followed him down the hall and into the kitchen. Since my back yard was right up against Emmy's, Luke cut an opening in the privacy fence that separated the properties for easy access between our homes. It made more sense than walking around the block.

Emmet opened the sliding glass door that led to my deck and stepped out into the cool spring night. It had begun to rain since I arrived home. It came down steadily, but at the moment Emmet was protected by the awning that covered a large portion of the deck.

"Thank you for taking care of Rosa," I said. "Thank you for everything."

I couldn't believe he was just going to leave. Couldn't he feel what I felt? Didn't he know I wanted him to stay?

"Don't thank me for that," he said, shaking his head and looking at me sternly. "I love her. I'll always take care of her," he paused and hesitantly added, "And you."

"I'll take care of you. Always," he'd said when we were just kids.

"Goodnight, Donya," Emmet said, but didn't move.

I reached out and wrapped my arms around his torso for an embrace. I needed to feel his body against mine, if even only for a moment.

Reluctantly, his arms caged me against him. I could feel his heart beating against my chest and I wanted to put my hand there, but I was afraid and I don't know why. Emmet turned his head slightly and his nose grazed across my jugular, making me sigh and tilt my head more to allow him easier access. When I felt his lips gently press against the racing pulse, I had the strong desire to pull his head closer and demand he kiss me there, but I resisted. Why was I so scared?

Suddenly, Emmet pulled away from me and took several steps back until he was standing in the rain. His chest heaved and he stared at me with darkened eyes.

"Goodnight, Donya," he said again. He turned away, jogged down the steps and hurried his way across the two yards.

I stood in the open door, watching him go, feeling him go, feeling that tether stretch uncomfortably. Why did I let him go? Why do I always let him go? My life was incomplete without him and I always let him go.

I watched as he slid open Emmy's sliding door and stepped inside. He turned around slowly and looked back at me. I knew he was looking at me, because I could feel it. I could feel him, the conflict within him, the fear, the lust, the love, the want, the need, and more fear. It was everything I was feeling, too.

"Come back," I whispered. "Come back. Come back. Come back." I chanted the words over and over as we watched each other, in the dark, through the rain and across the span of the two yards.

When Emmet turned away, my body slumped and the pressure in my chest climbed up into my throat until I was trying to swallow around a large lump.

"I will not cry," I whispered breathlessly, as I went back inside and closed and locked the door and drew the blinds.

I started turning out lights as I slowly made my way through the house. I planned on crawling into my bed and resting my head on the pillow Emmet had used so that I could inhale him all night.

A terrifying thought struck me as I stood in the hallway near the stairs. What if Emmet didn't react to me because he could no longer feel me? What if the tether was deadened on his end? What if I had denied him one time too many and it irrevocably damaged the cord that bound us together?

Worse yet, what if we were no longer bound together? What if everything I thought I felt for him was all in my head, an illusion my mind created to mirror my own emotions?

I turned around and faced the dark kitchen and the dark glass behind the closed blinds that led into the dark night.

"Come back," I said with panic rising inside of me. "Come back. Come back. Come back. Come back."

If he didn't come, I would know. I would know that I ruined us and we were irretrievable.

After what felt like several minutes of chanting for Emmet to come back, I stopped suddenly when I knew he wasn't coming. I didn't trust myself to try to feel him out because I was becoming more and more convinced that he couldn't feel me at all and vice versa.

I sunk to my knees and buried my face in my hands as an onslaught of tears poured from my eyes. It hurt so fucking much, more than any other pain I'd ever experienced with Emmet. I didn't know how I was going to live through this one. I didn't think I'd ever really recover and I would become my mother, sad, depressed, broken, and a shell of someone I couldn't even remember and completely unable to take care of my child. History would repeat itself. Emmy and Luke would care for Rosa like their own. Owen would treat her like a sister until they were older and he'd fall in love with her, and if she followed in my footsteps and her grandmother's footsteps, she would eventually lose him, too. Forever.

"Get up," I whispered vehemently to myself. "You are not going to sit here and die. Get up." I rose to my feet. I looked at the sliding door as if I could see through it, the rain, the night, and Emmy's walls and find Emmet wherever he was.

I refused to become my mother. I refused to give Rosa that kind of life.

I am Donya Elisabeth Stewart, also known as Sensible Donya and Donya Sex Goddess & Lover. I am a successful supermodel, actress, and soon to be entrepreneur and I will be a super success at that, too. I am Rosa's mother, Emmy's sister and best friend, and daughter to Fred and Samantha Grayne. I am Emmet Grayne's destiny and he his mine. Destiny is inescapable.

"You can't escape," I said aloud.

I marched through the kitchen to the sliding door. I wouldn't leave my own yard with Rosa sleeping in the house behind me, but if I had to stand at that fence and shout Emmet's name all night I would. The second I got my hands on him, I would drag him back at any costs. If I had to hit him in the head with a shovel and tie his unconscious body to the bed, I would.

I turned the back yard light on and boldly marched outside into the steady rain and down the deck steps. I glanced to my right where a shovel leaned up against the deck, left there by the previous owners. On a whim, I grabbed it and started across the yard. I was half way to the opening in the fence when I felt him. Instantly I knew that the line was never broken, and thought about how stupid I was to believe that it was. It was unbreakable.

Emmet walked through the fence opening and I thought it was strange that I hadn't seen him come out of Emmy's house.

"I didn't see you come out," I said when he reached me.

"I was standing out here for a few minutes," he said and eyed the shovel. His eyebrow rose. "Are you out here to bury bodies?"

"No," I said, standing up straighter. "It's for you."

He crossed his arms and looked amused. "Really."

"Yes. If you refuse to come back with me, I plan to hit you in the head with it and knock you out. Then I'll drag your body into our home, up the stairs and tie you to our bed."

He was trying not to smile when he said, "That's a lot of heavy work."

I shrugged. "Well, I'm sure after I hit you with the shovel, adrenaline will kick in and I will have superhuman strength."

"So, you are going to get your prize by any means necessary," Emmet said.

"Yes. We supermodels are highly motivated individuals. Why were you outside in the rain?" I asked. The fact that we were both now standing in the rain was not lost on me.

Emmet unfolded his arms and put his hands on the shovel. I held it tightly for a few seconds, afraid he would take the shovel and leave, but after I had realized how ridiculous I was being, I released my hold on it. He gave me another amused look and tossed the shovel aside.

"Why were you outside?" I asked again when he settled his eyes on me.

"You called me."

I gasped and said, "Wh-what?"

His big, damp hand connected with the skin over my heart. "You called me," he said again, in a softer tone.

Whatever power that made my crying cease minutes before was gone. A loud sob tore through me and before it could even fade, Emmet had pulled me into his arms. I held onto him fiercely and sobbed uncontrollably. He released me but cupped my face in his hands and bent slightly to look me in the eyes.

"I heard you, baby," he said as his voice cracked. "I heard you."

He kissed me while lifting me off of the ground. I wrapped my legs and arms around him and met his tongue stroke for stroke as I continued to cry. The rain cascaded down our bodies and mingled with tears.

"I'll never leave you again," Emmet promised with his lips resting against mine.

"Don't let go," I sobbed.

"I'll never let go," he said and nipped at my bottom lip. "I promise I will never let go."

"I am ingrained in you. I am woven into every cell of your body. You cannot eradicate me without losing yourself, too."

"Stay," I whispered tearfully.

"You have me, baby," Emmet said in a choked voice. "Forever."

Chapter Fifty-Nine

Shivering and with my teeth clattering together, I stood in the middle of the bedroom with my arms up over my head. Emmet pulled off my damp shirt and threw it on top of his own damp shirt that lay in a heap a couple of feet away. The rain had made my pale pink bra transparent. He looked down at my damp breasts and traced his fingers over the hard nipples that pressed against the wet fabric. I sucked in a breath and my back arched automatically.

"You were perfect before," he said. "But you're even more perfect now."

I had gained a whole cup size when I was pregnant with Rosa. By the way Emmet palmed my breasts and squeezed and kneaded them in his hands, I knew he appreciated the change. He kissed me slowly and methodically as his fingers began to unhook the front clasps of my bra. Once my breasts were sprung free, Emmet again palmed them. My nipples hardened even more against his hands. As he continued to slowly explore my mouth with his tongue, he pulled the hard buds between his fingers and squeezed gently. I moaned and clenched my thighs together as the heady sensation shot from my nipples straight to my core.

"I've missed touching you," Emmet whispered against my lips when he broke the kiss. "I've missed my hands on your body."

His thumbs flicked over my nipples and then his hands began to travel down my body. He caressed my belly with his fingertips. He tilted his head to gain access to my neck and grazed my skin with his nose as he inhaled my scent.

"I miss tasting your skin," he murmured. I sighed as his tongue slid over the sensitive area below my ear. He leisurely dragged his tongue down my neck to my shoulder where his teeth slowly sunk into the flesh there.

"Emmet," I moaned and lightly scratched my nails down his arms.

He continued with his kissing and tasting, down my chest, between my breasts, and down my stomach. His tongue dipped into my navel before continuing down to the skin just above the waistline of my pants. On his knees now, he began to slowly unbutton my capris. He looked up at me as he did and I pushed a hand into his wet hair. He began to pull the soaked material and my panties down over my hips. A moment later the wet clothing was tossed aside and I was naked before him.

Emmet traced his fingers across the top of my mound.

"Do you miss me touching you, Donya?" he asked huskily as he gazed at my sex.

"Yes," I breathed.

"I miss your reactions to my touches," he said and then gently swiped his finger over my clit.

I moaned and my legs tried to close automatically. Emmet grinned up at me, fully aware of the effect he had on me.

He got to his feet and pulled my nude body against his and kissed me deeply. His erection was prominent through his jeans and he pressed it against my sex. I moaned into his mouth and rocked my hips against the rough denim, already desperate for a release. He indulged me, put both hands on my ass and ground into me as he groaned into my mouth and his fingers dug into my flesh. The friction against my clit was making me weak in the knees, and again my legs tried to close as the sensations built to be nearly unbearable. Emmet's hands moved down to my upper thighs and he easily lifted me off of the floor and my legs wrapped around him. He held me tightly and continued to grind into me and there was no escape for me. I attempted to tear my lips away from his as my orgasm took over, but Emmet refused to release me from the kiss and I was forced to cry out into his mouth. He gently bit down on my tongue as I rocked against his clothed cock and my legs trembled around him. Before the orgasm fully subsided, he carried me over to the bed we picked out together. He broke the kiss after lying me down.

"I need to taste you," he said and quickly moved down my body. "I miss how you taste after you've just come," he growled.

His tongue dipped inside of me and we both groaned. He licked and sucked at me as if he was trying to draw out every drop of moisture. When he seemed satisfied, he climbed back up my body and kissed me again. I tasted myself on his lips. I suckled on his tongue, enjoying the taste of me and his mouth mixed together.

I reached between us and began to unbuckle his belt. He lifted his hips a little to give me better access. Once his jeans were undone, I pushed them halfway down his ass and eagerly reached inside of his boxers for his silky erection, making him hiss and thrust gently in my hand.

"I miss touching you, too," I said and nipped at his chin. "I miss everything about you," I added in a whisper as my thumb glided over the head of his shaft, making him groan.

I stroked him from base to tip as his tongue moved in my mouth at the same rhythm. My free hand was on his ass, lightly scratching the muscle with my nails. I really did miss touching him and listening to his deep moans when my small hand attempted to wrap around his thick manhood. I missed the weight of his cock in my hands, in my mouth, and inside of me.

Emmet broke the kiss and reluctantly broke free of my grasp. He stood up and quickly removed his jeans and boxers before returning to his position on top of me. His hard cock rested on my sensitive sex as he took my mouth again. When he ground against me, I moaned and pushed my hips up to increase the friction.

My hands roamed up and down and across his back, his perfect ass, his strong arms, and his hard chest. I felt like I would waste away if I stopped touching him. His body was meant to be touched by me and only me, and my body was meant to be touched by him and only him. It is why his skin heated under every caress and why my own skin felt super charged with an electric current wherever his skin met mine.

Emmet once again pulled away from my lips. It seemed to be getting harder and harder for him to do each time. He gazed into my eyes as he positioned the head of his engorged penis at my entrance.

"I love you," he whispered as he pushed in a little.

"I love you," I moaned.

"You were always meant to be mine," he said as he pushed in another couple of inches. "You were born to be mine and I was born to be yours. No one will ever be able to change that."

My nails dug into his shoulders and I cried out when he gave one hard thrust and buried himself inside of me. Emmet's cock was perfect for me, made just for me. It filled me just right. Even the pain that accompanied the invasion was just right, just perfect, and added to my pleasure.

He groaned and dropped his forehead to mine.

"You feel so fucking perfect," he breathed. He tried to speak again, but as he began to move inside of me, he became speechless.

No other physical gratification in the world felt as good as it did when Emmet's body collided with mine. Our groans and moans, the skin against skin sounds our bodies made and the very slight sound of Emmet sliding into my drenched sex all created an exquisite melody that went on and on. The smell of my arousal and our love making perfumed the air and excited our senses. Emmet's thrusts became more forceful and deeper, as if he was losing himself in me. I was losing myself with him inside of me, so I understood the loss of control he was feeling.

Abruptly, Emmet rolled over on his back, taking me with him and impaling me on his organ. His hands gripped my hips and he held me tightly as he continued to thrust inside of me. The new position allowed me to take him impossibly deeper and to rub against that hard to reach spot inside of me.

"Emmet," I cried out as the head of his cock repeatedly hit that wondrous spot. "I can't…I'm going to…"

In response, Emmet thrust harder. My head fell back and my whole body turned into a raw nerve as my orgasm began to consume me. When Emmet's thumb pressed on my clit, I tried to knock his hand away, but he was relentless, rubbing in fast, hard circles as he continued to hold my hip with one hand and drive his cock inside of me.

My mouth opened, but only gasps and small sounds of a struggle escaped because I was choked by my delectation. When sound finally left my mouth, it was sob, a scream, and a moan. Emmet released my hip and reached up and rolled a nipple between his fingers. Without any control over my body, I rocked on his cock as my orgasm took me higher than I have ever been before. His rigid penis deep inside of me, his thumb on my clit, his fingers rolling my nipples and his heated, loving gaze was so good that it hurt. I collapsed on Emmet, trembling, breathless and with fat tears falling from my eyes. He wrapped his arms around me and kissed my face as he continued to gently push his erection inside of me.

After a few gentle moments, Emmet pushed himself up into a sitting position. I wrapped my legs around him and draped my arms over his shoulders and locked my hands behind his neck.

"You are so beautiful," he whispered as he pushed several strands of hair out of my eyes.

We moved slowly now. I nibbled gently on Emmet's ear lobe and kissed his neck. I loved the taste of his skin and his soft gasps when my teeth bit into his flesh.

"Are you on birth control?" he asked softly as I suckled on his neck.

"Mmmhmm," I answered and moaned as I felt his cock twitch inside of me.

"The pill?"

I licked the place where I just marked him and said, "Yes."

Gently, but firmly, he grabbed a handful of my hair and pulled my head back so that we were face to face.

"I want you off of it," he demanded. "Don't take anymore. Throw the pack away. Do you understand?"

Did I understand? Yes. Emmet wanted a baby. With me.

I nodded and gave him a small smile. Satisfied with my response, Emmet rolled us over again and then kissed me briefly.

"You are going to be my wife," he said as he began to push and pull his hard rod inside of me again. He groaned and licked his lips before speaking again.

"And we are going to make a baby," I breathed.

Emmet's eyes closed briefly, as if my words brought him just as much pleasure as my body.

"Yes," he breathed. "Yes."

He wrapped his arms around me and kissed me deeply as he began to thrust madly. I held onto him as he drove his cock hard and deep inside of me and his pelvis rubbed against my clit. Emmet was moaning loudly into my mouth as his rhythm increased. After a minute or so he released my mouth to murmur incoherent words in my neck.

"I want to feel you come inside of me," I panted in his ear.

"Donya," he groaned. His body began to shudder and with another loud groan, Emmet began to come. When the first burst of hot semen was released, my legs closed around him and I tried to pull him in deeper. His cock jerked violently as more of the warm cream filled me. When it finally stopped, Emmet's weakened body slackened against mine.

Debilitated and exhausted, my hand leisurely stroked his hair as I struggled to keep my eyes open. We lay like that for a long time, until our breathing regulated and our hearts resumed a normal cadence.

"Are you okay?" Emmet asked. I didn't open my eyes, but I felt him turn his head to face me.

"I'm more okay than I've been in a very long time," I said tiredly.

"Good. Me, too." He left a light kiss on my lips and then got up.

I opened my eyes and watched as his naked ass walked into the bathroom. When I heard the shower start up a moment later, I pushed myself out of bed and went to join him.

"Well, hello, sexy," he smiled when I stepped into the stall with him.

"Hi," I said, wrapping my arms around his wet body. I rested my head on his shoulder as he smoothed my hair.

"This feels like a dream," Emmet said after a while.

"Wake up, baby," I said and pinched his arm. "This is real."

"You're really going to marry me?" he asked quietly. I didn't miss how his body stilled when he asked the question.

"Yes," I said and squeezed him tighter. He relaxed, but not completely.

"And you are going to give me more children?" he questioned.

"Yes," I said and kissed his shoulder. "I promise. I'll give you anything you want, Emmet. I love you."

He held me closer and breathed a deep sigh of relief. "I love you so much, Donya."

"I'm sorry I wasted so many years," I said, feeling pressure building in my chest. "We should have been together a long time ago. I was so selfish. I—" I was silenced when Emmet pulled out of my embrace and put his finger to my lips.

"Don't," he said softly as he looked me in the eyes intently. "We were both at fault, okay? We can't change what happened back then. We're together now and that's what matters. Besides," he smiled. "We have two beautiful kids, and neither of us would ever erase that."

I nodded silently.

"I love you, Donya," he said and kissed my nose. "I'll never get tired of saying that or hearing it. I love you."

"I love you," I said, caressing his cheek with the back of my hand.

Emmet gave me a smile that lit up every dark corner that existed within me. He leaned in to kiss me and my lips parted for his kiss. My body molded with his. My heart and his heart beat together as one.

Chapter Sixty

Six weeks later, I stood in front of a full-length mirror, gazing contently at my reflection. The strapless, pale pink, ruched tulle, empire waist wedding gown I designed was elegant yet simple. I wore the charm bracelet on my wrist, my engagement ring on my left ring finger, and a pair of small diamond and white gold studs in my ears. I skipped the obnoxious tiara and let my curled hair fall loosely over my shoulders and I pinned a pink orchid on one side of my head. I did my own makeup, light, simple, and fresh.

Sam fussed over every tiny detail—my dress, my hair, my jewelry and shoes, and makeup, but I wasn't annoyed. I didn't feel the need to get away. The term about wild horses dragging me away couldn't hold truer than it did on this day. In a matter of minutes, I was going to marry Emmet Grayne, and it would take forces greater than the universe to stop us.

"We were meant to be together. The force holding us together is bigger than us; it's bigger than the entire universe."

"How do you feel?" Emmy asked me as she stood beside me looking into the looking glass.

"Perfect," I said and met her eyes.

Perfect was an understatement. Even with Rosa in my life, I hadn't felt whole. A part of me was always with Emmet, and deep down I knew that I could never be complete without being joined to him. I imagined that once our vows were read and we became one, that the universe would celebrate with shootings stars and grand cosmic happenings in the skies above. Sparks would erupt from our bodies as we held each other and sealed our nuptials with a kiss.

"I'm sorry," Emmy spoke softly to my reflection.

"For what?" I turned and looked at the real Emmy next to me. I was alarmed to find her eyes welling with tears. "What is it?" I asked, taking her hands into mine.

"Sweetie, what's wrong?" Sam asked and wiped away one of the tears that had begun to trickle down her daughter's face.

"I see it now, what you and Emmet mean to each other," Emmy said, sniffling. "There is this…power…that radiates from the two of you when you're together. It's dazzling and blindingly beautiful, and I'm responsible for keeping you apart for all of these years."

"Emmy, no," I said softly and wiped her tears with my thumbs. Now I was starting to tear up. "That was us, not you."

"I made so many derogatory comments when we were kids that you felt that you couldn't be out in the open about your feelings for him. Damn, Donya…all of those times I brought up all of Emmet's conquests…" she laughed humorlessly. "I'm not even sure how many of those were true. And don't forget the doozy. It was me who convinced you that your life and career was more important than your relationship with Emmet. You could have been together all of this time and been spared all of the heartache and pain you guys have had."

Sam sniffed and wiped away her own tears and looked at me guiltily. "I saw there was something between the two of you when you were very young and it didn't fit in with what I wanted for you both, so I'm just as responsible for keeping ya'll apart."

"You two are so stupid," I laughed and cried at the same time. I took their hands into mine and then they held hands, forming a tight triangular formation. "If anyone is to blame, it's me. Emmet wasn't afraid of you and Fred," I told Sam. I looked at Emmy and said, "And he sure as hell didn't care what his kid sister thought about the situation, but I did. I didn't want to upset anyone and I didn't want to have to fight with anyone. When I made the decision to follow my career, Emmy, that was all me. That conversation with you just made it happen sooner rather than later. Stop blaming yourselves. Besides," I said with a small shrug. "We have Rosa and Owen and I wouldn't change that for anything."

They each nodded and smiled at that.

"Now stop this damn crying," I demanded as I pulled them in for a group hug. I held onto my true sister and mother for a few moments. I was so thankful for each of them. I wasn't sure how my life would have turned out if I never met Emmy and if Sam and Fred never took me in.

"Okay, we're running out of time," I said, pulling away. "I can't be late to my own wedding."

We fixed our ruined makeup and made some small final adjustments to my hair and dress. Emmy handed me my simple bouquet of pale pink and white orchids. Her bouquet was similar but smaller. Her maid of honor dress perfectly accented my gown, because I had designed it of course. It was a white, strapless dress with an empire waistline like mine, but an A-line skirt that fell just above her knees. The sash tied around the high waistline just under the bodice was the same pale pink as my dress. Sam had a pink and white orchid pinned to her white dress, and yes, you guessed it. That was also designed by yours truly. I designed the garments for the entire wedding party, long before I knew I would be using any of it in my own wedding.

"I wish your mama was here to see this," Sam said sadly as she stood back to admire me.

"Me, too," I said quietly. "She's missed a lot."

"She would have been proud, and happy for ya, honey, I know it," Sam said. "I know she had her problems, but we all do."

I nodded and we let the conversation drop, because I didn't want to be sad on my wedding day.

With only about ten minutes left until the ceremony was to begin, there was a light knock on the door.

"Who is it?" Sam demanded with a hand on her hip. She refused to let anyone see me before the start of the ceremony.

"Father of the Bride," Fred called from the other side. "And flower girl extraordinaire."

I smiled and turned around just as Sam opened the door for Fred and Rosa.

"I'll wait for you outside," Sam told her husband. I felt like I should look away when he took his wife's face into his hands and kissed her tenderly.

"Ick. Gross," Emmy murmured beside me, but when I looked at her, she was smiling warmly at the pair. "I'll see you in a few minutes," she said and followed her mom out of the room.

I adjusted the pink and white flowers in Rosa's hair as I smiled down at her. She looked tired and I hoped that she would be able to make it through the ceremony without having a meltdown.

"I've never seen you look as beautiful as you do now, Kiddo," Fred said, blinking rapidly.

"Oh, no, not you, too," I said, putting a hand on his arm. "Why are you about to cry? You didn't cry...last time."

With the tears threatening to spill out of his eyes, his words came out strained, like he was trying not to break down. "Last time I knew it wasn't right," he nodded solemnly. "I knew that you loved him, but your heart wasn't really in it, because your heart was with Emmet."

I was blinking back tears again. "Why didn't you stop me?" I whispered as I stroked Rosa's hair. If he had stopped me, I wouldn't have her, but I had to know why he let me make such a monumental mistake.

"It couldn't be me to stop you," he said, shaking his head and looking at me knowingly. "You know that. You wouldn't have listened. The only person that could have stopped you was Emmet."

I couldn't even deny it. Sam had tried to talk some sense into me also, and I blew her off. I was determined to do what I wanted to do, even though I knew it wasn't the best thing to do. So headstrong, so stupid.

"And now?" I asked weakly.

Fred smiled lovingly. "Now this feels right. You and Emmet belong together. I've never seen two people more right for each other."

I smiled and kissed Fred's cheek. "Thank you, Dad."

I had never seen a grin as big as the grin that appeared on Fred's face with that one small term that I uttered. He kissed both of my cheeks and then took Rosa's hand.

"Come on, Mini Kiddo," he said to her. "You have flowers to throw around."

"Bye bye," Rosa said, waving to me.

"Bye bye," I waved back and watched until the door closed.

I was completely alone in the dressing room, but Emmet was there. Emmet was always there. I closed my eyes and felt his presence swarming around me, enveloping me in his warmth and love. I knew he stood at the alter feeling me, too.

As I stood there in the quiet room, I reflected on my life. How different it could have been if I had not befriended the sassy girl that sat at my table in Kindergarten. Who would have cared for me in the way that the Graynes cared for me? Who would have been a friend through thick and thin, blood, sweat, and tears as Emmy had been for me? What path in life would I have chosen if I was left to my own devices entirely, without my mom and dad present? I shuddered to even consider it. The possibilities and sad stories that could have been are endless. What if I never had the opportunity to meet Emmet in the way that I met him? I knew without a shadow of a doubt that we were born for each other, but how would we have found each other if we had lived different lives?

The what-ifs, I realized as I opened my eyes, didn't count. The real things that have already happened and that could happen in the future were all that mattered. My present state mattered. I did befriend that sassy girl in Kindergarten. Her family did care for me as one of their own, and Emmy was more than my loyal friend, she was my sister. My path in life got bumpy at times, but all in all, I had a very good run, despite who my biological parents were. I had enough sad stories in my reality; I didn't need to think about the ones that never happened. I did meet Emmet. We did find each other, and that was what truly mattered in the end.

I took one last look in the mirror and grinned. It was time for me to fulfill my destiny.

~~*

As the small orchestra played a beautiful instrumental rendition of Christina Perri's "A Thousand Years", I walked the stone pathway covered in the pink and white rose petals that Rosa had thrown to the ground. Though I could feel Emmet, I couldn't immediately see him. As I followed the stonework, the curved path straightened out and I saw him, standing at the altar in his tuxedo and pink bowtie. The hundred or so people that were standing on either side of the aisle faded into the background. Even Helene snapping pictures in front of me faded and I was barely aware of her presence. The only person I saw was Emmet.

I wanted to run down the aisle, but I managed to walk in the slow cadence we had practiced. I did not need Fred to give me away. Walking down the aisle alone was symbolic. I did not need to be given to Emmet, because I was already his. I had always been his, and he had always been mine. I didn't understand it as a child, but then I knew that on that very day I first met him in the family's backyard on the swings and he taught me how to propel myself, how to fly, I had claimed him and he had claimed me.

When I finally reached him, I barely registered Emmy taking my bouquet from my hand. Emmet took my hand into his as he smiled lovingly at me and led me the last few steps to the Justice of the Peace that performed the ceremony. I couldn't take my eyes away from his brilliant emerald eyes. I barely paid any attention to the words the J.O.P. said until he announced that it was time for us to read our vows.

I sucked in a deep, excited breath. I had no idea what Emmet was going to say to me. We wrote our own vows and agreed not to share them until the ceremony.

"Donya," he started as his thumbs caressed my knuckles. "Some men are born to do great, extraordinary things. I am one of those men, because I was born to love you, and aside from the love we have for our children, there is nothing else in the universe that is greater or more extraordinary than loving you. You are the only person who can complete me. You are the only home my heart knows. I have always belonged to you and you have always belonged to me, and I will never again let you go. We are tied together and there is no power great enough to sever that tie. I promise to love you, to cherish you, protect and honor you until my last breath on this earth."

Emmet released my hands to wipe my tears away.

"I love you," he whispered to me, but thanks to the mic that was attached to his jacket, everyone heard it. There was a chorus of "awws" and a lot of sniffling and a few giggles.

I wanted to break the rules and kiss him and feel his embrace, but I stood my ground. I was so overwhelmed by his powerful words that it took me a minute to get myself together to read my own vows.

I put my hands in his again, and with my tears still flowing, I recited the vows I had written for him.

"Emmet, I was born into this world bound to you. You are the only person in the world that can make me feel whole. You are the other half of me. You are the core of my existence and the essential life force that keeps my heart beating day after day, year after year. It is impossible to live without you. You are my destiny, and there is no force powerful enough to change that. I promise to be brave and selfless. I promise to honor and respect you, and to love you wholeheartedly, with my whole soul, and my entire being until the end of time."

Emmet's eyes glistened, and judging by the way they dropped to my mouth, I knew he was resisting kissing me too.

Moments later, the platinum diamond wedding band that matched my engagement ring was poised at the tip of my finger.

"Do you Emmet Matthew Grayne take Donya Elisabeth Stewart to be your lawfully wedded wife, to love and to cherish, through sickness and in health, until you fall asleep in death?"

Clear and loud and with passion, Emmet announced, "I do."

I laughed, feeling drunk and giddy with excitement as Emmet slid the ring onto my finger. I held my hand up to our guests and wiggled it, eliciting soft laughter and a cat call from Felix.

Emmy handed me Emmet's platinum ring that matched my set.

"Do you Donya Elisabeth Stewart take Emmet Matthew Grayne to be your lawfully wedded husband, to love and to cherish, through sickness and in health, until you fall asleep in death?"

"Yes!" I nearly shouted, getting more laughter from the crowd. I slid the ring onto Emmet's finger and bounced excitedly a few times.

"Now the bride and groom would like to do something a little different," the J.O.P said as Luke handed Emmet two thick cords of white rope. "Emmet and Donya would like to literally tie the knot, symbolizing their love for each other and the connection they share."

We each took an end of each rope and began to entwine them.

"Each of these ropes are a representation of your pasts and the lives you lived apart. The ropes entwined into one represent your present as your two lives also become one."

Once the two ropes were entwined into one, we began to tie it into a knot.

"The completed knot will be symbolic of your future and the strong marriage you will have."

With some laughter, a little frustration, and some goof ups, the knot was tied. Even the process of tying the knot was symbolic because our roads to that moment were laden with laughter, frustration, and goof ups.

"Emmet and Donya have now tied the knot," the J.O.P. announced. "When the ends of the knot are pulled, the knot will become strong and no matter how frayed or short the ends get, the knot is forever. Emmet and Donya, please pull on the ends of your knot."

We pulled, and the knot became strong. I grinned at Emmet and he grinned at me.

"I now," the J.O.P. said with liveliness. "Pronounce you man and wife. Emmet, you may kiss your bride."

We didn't let go of that rope, even when Emmet dipped me with one arm and kissed me with his sweet, soft lips until I was dizzy.

Chapter Sixty-One

"Owen, your mom is going to be here in a few minutes. Put the controller down and get ready to go," I told him for the third time. I gave Emmet an evil glare that he could feel even though his attention was on the video game he and Owen were playing.

"Okay, buddy," Emmet said, putting his controller down. "Listen to your mom."

"Okay," Owen sighed, and reluctantly put the controller down. He tore himself away from the television only after Emmet used the remote to turn it off. "Sorry," Owen said as he passed by me to go upstairs.

"It's okay. I don't know if your mom is going to feel like hanging around. I like you to be ready when she gets here."

"Okay," Owen said as he went up the stairs.

I turned back to my husband of two years. "You are a bad influence."

"Yeah, but I'm cute," Emmet said and planted a kiss on my cheek.

"The jury is still out on that one," I teased.

"Hey, little guy," he smiled at the toddler in my arms.

Emmet Junior was born almost exactly nine months after our wedding day. I was pretty sure that we created him on our wedding night.

Emmet took EJ from my arms. "We'll go get Rosa," he said and then kissed me properly, which should have been illegal in front of our kids. Emmet's 'proper' kisses were the kind of kisses that made me want to throw him down on any surface and let Donya SGL out to play.

We walked into the kitchen together. I went back to the stove to work on dinner and father and son went out the back door to walk to Emmy's to get Rosa.

This was my life on the weekends. Emmet and I didn't work, unless it was absolutely necessary. Owen was usually with us for at least half of the weekend and Rosa and Emmy's daughter Kaitlyn usually played either at our house or Emmy's. We were always back and forth between the two houses, especially during warmer weather. We were totally cliché, too, borrowing eggs, sticks of butter, and cups of milk while in the middle of making a meal or dessert. There were family barbecues and parties, and every other month Emmet and I hosted Sunday dinners for our extended Chicago family and friends. We were completely domesticated, at least on the weekends. The weekdays were another monster...

Three days before my wedding, I did a photo shoot with *Vogue* in my wedding gown. Helene and I also gave them photographs of the wedding and the wedding party. When the small article accompanied by several photos of my gown and the wedding party wearing clothes I designed appeared in the magazine, my phone began to ring and didn't stop. Before I opened my boutique, I threw together a show to introduce the fashion world to my label Emmya. By the time the boutique opened, the clothes I had featured in the show and even my wedding gown were in demand. I thought I would have enough time to feel the business out and get acclimated, but Felix and I hit the ground running and haven't looked back.

We hired a few reliable, responsible and knowledgeable staff members to run the boutique and I did the administrative work at home. We also hired someone to oversee the seamstresses that brought my designs to life and another person to do the bulk of the necessary traveling work, especially since we just opened another location in New York and needed someone to keep an eye on things there.

With Emmy's help, I worked from home at first, but the business grew too large too fast. I had to set up shop in an office building near the boutique, and within a year, Emmy helped me to hire a strong, but small staff to run Emmya.

I continued to work from home as much as possible, but there was still a couple of days a week that I had to show up to the office. So, I had to hire a nanny to keep an eye on the kids while I worked. I was always in a meeting of some kind or dealing with a situation, and of course I had to have time to continue to create my designs.

Emmet was working hard, too. Luke's law firm had grown significantly, thanks to hard work and a few high profile cases. Emmet was now a partner in the firm that occupied a whole corner building. While he had fewer cases than he did when he was just an associate, the few cases he did have were huge.

He would try to be home by six every night, but sometimes it wasn't feasible. With our crazy schedules, it was difficult at times to get any time together until after all of the kids were in bed, and by then we were exhausted. So, we made Fridays our early days. He comes home by three and I end my business for the day by two, and, with the exception of a few circumstances, every weekend is work free.

Despite our busy schedules, we are happy. We have a beautiful family, great friends, and we are together. The boutique and the firm can burn to the ground, and we will still be happy.

The doorbell rang a few minutes after Emmet and EJ left. I wiped my hands on an apron—a pretty, frilly, June Cleaver kind of apron given to me by Sam as a wedding gift—and went to the front door.

"Hey, Casey," I said, as I opened the door for her.

"Hi." She smiled as she came inside. "Oh my god what are you cooking?"

"Spaghetti and meatballs," I said as I led the way into the kitchen. "You want to stay for dinner?"

"Oh, that's tempting." She lifted a lid and peeked into the pot of meatballs. "But we're going to my brother-in-law's for dinner."

"I'll put some in a container. You can eat it for your midnight snack." I smiled as I reached for a container.

"Yeah, you know how much we love those," she said, rubbing her round belly.

After Emmet and Casey had split up, she started spending time with her single neighbor, a widower and father of two. Only months after Emmet and I married, Casey married Tyrone. I really liked Tyrone. He was a good father to his children and to Owen. He worked hard in construction, and he doted on Casey, something she had been missing in her last marriage.

I know it's strange to an outsider, but Casey, Tyrone, and his kids became an extension of our family. Casey and Emmet were friends before they got pregnant and got married, and now their friendship is renewed. It wasn't unusual for their family to end up in our back yard or Emmy's for a barbecue or party, and last year they even flew to Louisiana for the big Thanksgiving celebration. Now Casey and Tyrone are expecting their first child together, and both Emmet and I are happy for them, Emmet especially. He was glad that she was able to find someone who truly wanted and loved her.

Casey and Owen left and a few minutes after that Emmet, EJ and Rosa came home. As he helped me get dinner on the table, I knew that he had something on his mind. Besides the fact that I could feel his pensive state, there were telltale signs. He was quiet and distracted. Rosa had to ask him the same question three times. I wasn't worried, because I knew he would tell me what was on his mind when he was ready, and I was very right about that.

After the kids were in bed that night, we settled down on the couch in the living room to catch up on our weekly shows that were on DVR. It was our Saturday night ritual. I made popcorn with too much movie theater style butter and Emmet dumped a handful of Reese's Pieces into the bowl. We drank root beer floats or milkshakes, or whatever either of us felt like making. Emmet had the remote in his hand, but didn't turn the television on. He looked over at me and I knew he was ready to talk.

I put the bowl of popcorn on the floor and turned my body towards his. "What's on your mind?" I asked, running my fingers through his hair.

"Emmy told me about Fashion Week," he said, getting right to the point.

I sighed. "What about it?"

"Why aren't you going to do it? I thought you would love to show your label on the same runways you used to walk."

I shook my head and shrugged a shoulder as I tried to find the right words. "Doing the weeks as a model and doing the weeks as a designer are entirely different. There is an enormous amount of prep work, months and months ahead. I'm already busy, and doing even just one show can consume a tremendous amount of my time."

"So, you don't want to do the extra work?" he asked.

"I don't mind the work," I said with another shrug. "I just…I don't want to be responsible for driving a wedge between us again because of my job."

Emmet took my hand, and smoothed my hair back off of my face. "Do you want to do it, Donya?" he asked softly.

I looked down at our hands. There was no hiding how I felt, because he would know anyway.

"I do, but it's not necessary."

His fingers lifted my chin until I was looking into his eyes. "I want you to do it."

My eyes widened. "What? No," I shook my head and waved a hand. "You don't really mean that. Really, baby, you don't have to say that just to try to appease me. I don't need to go."

"Donya, most of the girls you used to work with have melted away into obscurity. They didn't have staying power. If you wanted to, you could probably still get booked for shows now, because you're that good. You not only survived the industry, but you evolved within the industry. While other 'older' models are selling furniture with their name or doing infomercials on late night television, you have *Vogue* and *Elle* and other publications paying close attention to what you'll be hanging in your boutiques next. I want you to do this. If I have to take more time off of work to accommodate you, I'll do it. You are the most talented person I know and if you want to do this, I want you to do it, too."

"Emmet," I sighed. "You wanted me to model a long time ago, and then you regretted it. I don't want to relive our past. I promised you that I would be selfless, and if that means not doing Fashion Week, I'm okay with that."

Emmet gave me a look of frustration and without a word he got off of the couch and walked out of the room. I watched him go up the stairs and wondered what the hell he was doing. Less than a minute later, he jogged down the stairs and came back into the family room carrying our unity knot. He stood in front of me and held it out to me, but I didn't immediately take it. I looked up at him in confusion.

"This knot was once two ropes entwined into one. The two separate ropes represented our past lives, and despite our connection, our lives were still separate. Together you and I entwined those two ropes into one rope, thus entwining our two separate lives into one life that we share in the present. Together again, we tied that one rope into a knot. This knot represents our future. *Together* if we each pull on end of the rope, the knot strengthens. Pull your end of the damn rope, Donya."

I looked at the rope again and then reached out and pulled my end.

"You are going to go to Fashion Week and you are going to kick some fashion ass, and whether I am there with you or here at home, I will be pulling on my end and you will be pulling on yours. The ends may fray or burn or break, but the knot will remain strong. We will remain strong."

He dropped to his knees before me and gently took the rope from my hands and laid it on the floor beside him.

"You will never have to question whether or not I am pulling on my end, Donya," he said softly. He put his hand over my heart. "You'll feel me right there with you."

I kissed my husband, my other half, the soul on the other end of the line that has always been there. The movie and junk food were forgotten.

Epilogue

I am walking down the runway with an armful of flowers as spectators cheer and applaud in a standing ovation. I feel an elation I have never felt before while in the spotlight. I blow a kiss to Emmet and wave to Emmy and other family and friends who have come to see my first appearance in New York's Fashion Week. As I walk back to the line of models that are clapping, I gesture to them, not wanting the audience to dismiss their hard work. I turn and do a curtsy and blow more kisses and wave once more before heading backstage.

There is a chorus of congratulations, innumerable hugs, handshakes, and photographs. I thank all of the models for their work, but don't delay them because many of them have other shows to get to. There are two in particular I really liked working with and I have my assistant speak to them about a campaign, but I won't make any final decisions on them without discussing it with Felix first.

Felix is still my best friend after Emmy. He is still gorgeous, a little cocky, and a lot of flirty. I don't know how is wife Ginny puts up with him, especially since their little boys are beginning to follow in their father's footsteps. I love him, though, enormous ego and all, and I often think about how different my life would be if we never met all of those years ago during a photo shoot. I am thankful for his friendship and for always looking out for me. He approaches me now and embraces me, lifts me off of the floor and swings me around in a circle.

"Put her down before you hurt her," Ginny demands and smacks his arm. She is seven months pregnant and glowing. I think some of the glow is definitely from her pregnancy, but I think Felix is responsible, too. She tries to be tough about his antics, but there is always a trace of an amused and adoring smile under her serious tone.

Owen and Rosa squeeze through the crowd of admirers to hug me. Owen looks more and more like his father every day, right down to the hair that falls into his eyes. Rosa looks a lot like me, and she is a spoiled rotten daddy's girl. She has Emmet in her pocket and they both know it.

I look around for the nanny and spot her across the room, sitting on a chair with EJ sleeping in her arms. His dark blonde curls peek out from beneath a knitted blanket.

As I am talking with Felix and a few other people, Emmy approaches. I turn to her and accept her fierce embrace. She releases me, we hold hands and I admire the new bracelet on her wrist that Emmet bought for her. He couldn't find the same one he had bought for her so many years ago, but the new one was close. Emmy had cried for a good two hours after Emmet gave it to her.

"It was perfect," she says of the show, and smiles warmly.

Emmy is the organizational genie of Emmya. She was just helping out before, but I hired her on permanently after I decided to do Fashion Week. She makes sure that all administrative aspects of the business run smoothly. She catches problems before they can occur, but if they at first escape our notice, she handles it and conquers it like a beast.

I kind of stole her from Kessler, Keane & Grayne, and Associates. It was Emmy that had put the law firm on the path of success soon after she moved to Chicago. Luke gives me a hard time at every opportunity he gets about taking away his administrative diva, and I love to rub it in his face.

"I'm not a fashion expert," Luke says to me now, slinking an arm around his wife's waist. "But I think you're very talented."

"I'm glad you think so. Now maybe you will stop crying about me taking Emmy from you," I tease.

"Don't count on it," he grins. He puts a hand over his wife's baby bump and kisses the side of her head. Emmy, like Ginny, is also seven months pregnant. She is also glowing, and I know that Luke has just as much to do with her healthy glow as her pregnancy.

I look over Luke's shoulder and smile at Sam and Fred as they make their way over to us. Sam hugs me so hard that I find it difficult to breathe.

"It was wonderful," she says, wiping at her eyes. "And your hair looks...well, it isn't bad."

"I'll take that as a compliment," I say, rolling my eyes before turning to Fred.

He holds me for a long time, and tells me how proud he is of me. I don't know why, but when Fred tells me he is proud of me, it carries a heavier weight than it does when it is coming from Sam or even Emmy.

"Thank you for always being there for me," I whisper to him.

"I love you, Kiddo," he says and kisses my cheek tenderly.

"Grampy, what about me?" Rosa asks, poking her lip out as Fred releases me.

He moves to pick her up, but a warning glare from Sam and me stops him. He shouldn't be picking up five-year-olds if he expects to keep his heart in decent shape. Instead, he settles for kneeling down and embracing her.

"I love you, too, Mini Kiddo," he says.

"Don't kiss me," Owen says, holding up a hand.

I laugh and then listen to Sam as she sends regards from the rest of the family. They couldn't all make the trip to New York, though she and Fred brought three of the teenage granddaughters with them. I hug my nieces and I tell them I have every intention of upholding my promise of taking them shopping tomorrow.

I am vaguely aware of Helene snapping pictures of me. She is no longer a freelance photographer, but works for Emmya. I don't like to keep her and Marcus away from home for long periods, but every few months or as needed, she and her husband travel to whatever location I need them in—usually the Chicago headquarters—and we work, and dine, and enjoy each other's company. I'll never forget her kindness the day I met her when my heart was aching over Emmet.

I feel that familiar tug in my chest and know without looking that my sweetheart has walked into the room, but I look anyway. I always will look. I meet his eyes through the chaos and hold his gaze as he moves purposely towards me. He's carrying a groggy looking EJ in his arms.

"It was perfect," Emmet says and kisses me sweetly on the lips.

I admit my trepidation was great after Emmet convinced me to do Fashion Week. Every night that I had to work late I went home full of anxiety as I worried about Emmet's reaction. I had a difficult time focusing whenever I had to go away for a day or two for business, because I couldn't help thinking that the distance and time away from home was eventually going to be too much for our marriage and family, but Emmet's reaction was always the same. He missed me, he hated being without me, but he always spoke encouragingly. He always gave me his full support, and eventually my nervousness faded.

"I couldn't have done this without you," I say to him.

"You can thank me later, Mrs. Grayne," he says in a whisper that sends tingling sensations throughout my body.

"Oh, I plan to, Mr. Grayne," I answer with a wink. I put my arms out for EJ, but Emmet sets him down on his feet instead. He ignores me entirely and runs to his big brother, his hero. Owen ruffles his little brother's hair affectionately. I smile at the brothers, but I give Emmet a look.

He shrugs and says, "He's getting too big for us to be carrying him around anyway."

I don't point out that he was just carrying him and that he still picks Rosa up from time to time, and she's three years older than EJ.

I know his motivation for setting EJ free, and as much as I want to scold him for it, I can't. He is taking care of me, as he always does.

Emmet takes my hand and we rejoin our family and friends.

~~*

After the show, we all went out to dinner. Afterward, Emmet and I set the nanny free for the night and then we piled into our bed with the kids in our suite to watch movies. Rosa and Emmet Junior fell asleep halfway into the second movie and Owen went to bed when it ended.

"It's been a long day," I say quietly around a yawn.

"Are you feeling okay?" Emmet asks as he reaches over the two sleeping little bodies to push my hair off of my forehead.

"Just tired."

"I want you to relax tomorrow, okay?"

"I promised the girls I'd take them shopping."

"Let Mom do it," he says, giving me a firm look. "I want you off of your feet for the day."

I am too tired to argue. "I'll make it up to them another time."

Emmet smiles with satisfaction. He reaches for me and rests his hand on my belly. Apparently, pregnancy is contagious and I caught it from my friends, because I am four months pregnant.

"Is this everything you hoped it would be?" I ask him after a few minutes.

"What?"

"Our life, our family, all of it," I say.

"It is more than I could have ever hoped for," Emmet says with a fascinated gleam in his green eyes. "I knew we would make each other happy, but I never imagined that we could be this happy. I never imagined that our life would be this perfect."

"It's not perfect all of the time," I say, thinking about some of the arguments we've had over the years, and some of the unexpected speed bumps.

The biggest one we had was when the ink was still wet on our marriage license...

Jerry had called me out of the blue only weeks after Emmet and I married. He was in town for a doubleheader and got permission from his coach to take off for the morning to meet me for breakfast if I was willing. I refused the breakfast, especially since Emmet was in federal court and I couldn't discuss it with him first. I did agree to meet him at the Buckingham Fountain in Grant Park. I didn't need the media sniffing out this very public meeting, but I refused to be alone with him.

"You look really good, princess," Jerry said when he found me at the fountain.

"Don't call me that," I had snapped at him. I stood before him with my arms crossed and all of my defenses up. "What do you want, Jerry? What do you have to say that you couldn't say over the phone?"

He sighed and hung his head for a moment. He then pushed his sunglasses back on his head so I could see his eyes, but I kept my sunglasses in place. "I'm sorry, Donya. I'm sorry for what I did to you and Rosa, especially on that last night."

"It's been months, Jerry," I said angrily. "*Months*! You never even checked to make sure your daughter was okay. We left and you didn't care, so why do you care now?"

"I've always cared," he said with another sigh.

"If you're just going to stand there and spew bullshit than this is a waste of my time," I said and began to turn away.

"I want a second chance with Rosa," he said quickly before I could take more than a couple of steps.

I froze for a moment and then spun around to face him. I was astounded that he had the nerve to even say that. To me!

"I've been in therapy," he said softly and looked away, embarrassed. "I don't have a reasonable explanation for my behavior right now, but I do know that I've missed out on a lot and I want to get to know my daughter."

I shook my head, both in disbelief and to deny him. "No. No way, Jerry. I don't care how much therapy you've had. I have no reason to believe that you won't physically and emotionally hurt her. You've done enough of that."

"But I'm her father," he argued quietly.

"No, Jerry," I said. "You are a sperm donor. I just married her father. A matter of fact..." I opened my purse and produced a manila envelope and passed it to him. "Consider yourself served. My lawyer was going to do this before your game tonight."

"What is this?" he asked, eyeing the envelope skeptically.

"I want you to sever your parental rights," I said. I actually felt a little bad for handing him the paperwork right after he just asked to see Rosa. "Look, Jerry," I sighed. "I really appreciate your apology, but for once in Rosa's life be fair to her. Let her go. Emmet loves her like his own and he's the only real father she's had in her life. If you love her at all, you will sign those papers and let her go."

He suddenly looked so sad that I had to look away. When Emmet and I decided to go through with this so that he could officially adopt Rosa, it was easy because I had not thought I would have to lay my eyes on Jerry again. I never thought I'd have to see his face when he received the news. Furthermore, I never thought that he would care.

"Can I think about it?" he asked after a moment.

"You have some time," I said, shrugging my shoulder. "But there isn't much to think about," I added softly.

I had nothing else to say, and I didn't want to listen to any more of his apologies or to see his sad and confused face anymore. So, I gave him a final look and then walked away.

Meeting Jerry had sparked an enormous argument between Emmet and me. He didn't like that I went to meet him by myself. I had argued that I was perfectly safe, but Emmet said that my saying so didn't make him feel any better. He said that he would never forget how I passed out on Emmy's front doorstep sick and weak. He said he'd never be able to shake the images of my frail and bruised body from his mind. I understood at once, and I stopped arguing and apologized repeatedly. Emmet forgave me, but he was angry for days afterward.

Several weeks later Vivian called me to tell me that Jerry had signed the papers, but a judge still had to approve it. Jerry had all of those weeks to contact me, to put up a fight for his daughter, and prove that he was a changed man, but he didn't do any of that. I knew he wouldn't, but I felt rejected on Rosa's behalf anyway.

It was more weeks after that when we found out that Jerry's rights had been severed. Emmet immediately began the paperwork to adopt Rosa, and now she is Rosa Grayne.

I look at Emmet now in the present and say, "We've had some issues."

"We've had our issues," he agrees. "But we get through them, and it's the fact that we do get through them that adds to the perfection of what we have."

I put my hand on top of his hand that is on my belly. I smiled sleepily at him and let my eyes close. I have never felt as content and happy as I do now. I always knew that Emmet would make me happy, but like him, my mind could not even imagine this level of happiness.

I used to mourn the time that was lost in our years apart, but then I learned a valuable lesson. Destiny can be tricky. The road to your destination is not always a straight shot. Sometimes the road splits off into different directions and you have to choose. It's hard to say whether or not your choice was a bad choice or not, because maybe the other path was just as bumpy, or just as rewarding, and the fact is that you can never know for sure. You can sit around for years wondering, "What if I had gone the other way," and you will never have a true answer.

On our mutual journey to our destination, the road sometimes crowded with other people or maybe parts of the road crumbled away. We often had to travel uphill, and we often had to travel in a sad and solitary country. There were very often obstacles to climb over, go around, or destroy.

It doesn't matter what the road looked like or how many times it branched off, all roads led to the same destination. It doesn't matter how we got here. We were destined to be here and we would have arrived no matter what route we took, and even if our respective roads did not always parallel, we were always able to find each other. That line between us was always present, linking us to each other on every level no matter where we were. That connection will *always* be present.

We will always be *tethered*.

The End

Also by L.D. Davis

Accidentally on Purpose

Worthy of Redemption

Worth the Fight

Girl Code

Friction

Pieces of Rhys

Coming Soon

Things Remembered

Printed in Great Britain
by Amazon